SOUL DRINKERS
ANNIHILATION

Chapter War

When the planet of Vanqualis comes under attack from orks, the Soul Drinkers answer, Chapter Master Sarpedon seeing a chance to prove their loyalty. But factions within the Chapter are moving against the brave leader, eager to forge a different destiny, one that will lead them further down the path towards Chaos.

Hellforged

The Space Marines of the disgraced Soul Drinkers Chapter attempt to elude their pursuers in a desolate area of space, but soon find themselves in the midst of a new war. Sarpedon and his battle-brothers must fight for their lives against a deadly new enemy – the ancient and unstoppable necrons.

Phalanx

Phalanx, the great star fort of the Imperial Fists, is playing host to Space Marines from half a dozen Chapters, alongside inquisitors, Sisters of Battle and agents of the Adeptus Mechanicus. They have come together to witness the end of a Space Marine Chapter, as the once-noble Soul Drinkers, now Chaos-tainted renegades and heretics, are put on trial for their crimes against the Imperium.

A WARHAMMER 40,000 OMNIBUS

SOUL DRINKERS
ANNIHILATION

Ben Counter

BLACK LIBRARY

A Black Library Publication

Chapter War copyright © 2007 Games Workshop Ltd.
Hellforged copyright © 2009 Games Workshop Ltd.
Phalanx copyright © 2012 Games Workshop Ltd.
All rights reserved.

This omnibus edition published in Great Britain in 2013 by
The Black Library,
Games Workshop Ltd.,
Willow Road,
Nottingham, NG7 2WS, UK.

10 9 8 7 6 5 4 3 2 1

Cover illustration by Imaginary Friends Studio.

A CIP record for this book is available from the British Library.

UK ISBN 13: 978 1 84970 312 3
US ISBN 13: 978 1 84970 313 0

See the Black Library on the internet at

www.blacklibrary.com

Find out more about Games Workshop
and the world of Warhammer 40,000 at

www.games-workshop.com

Printed and bound by CPI Group (UK) Ltd, Croydon, CR0 4YY

It is the 41st millennium. For more than a hundred centuries the Emperor has sat immobile on the Golden Throne of Earth. He is the master of mankind by the will of the gods, and master of a million worlds by the might of his inexhaustible armies. He is a rotting carcass writhing invisibly with power from the Dark Age of Technology. He is the Carrion Lord of the Imperium for whom a thousand souls are sacrificed every day, so that he may never truly die.

Yet even in his deathless state, the Emperor continues his eternal vigilance. Mighty battlefleets cross the daemon-infested miasma of the warp, the only route between distant stars, their way lit by the Astronomican, the psychic manifestation of the Emperor's will. Vast armies give battle in His name on uncounted worlds. Greatest amongst his soldiers are the Adeptus Astartes, the Space Marines, bio-engineered super-warriors. Their comrades in arms are legion: the Imperial Guard and countless Planetary Defence Forces, the ever-vigilant Inquisition and the tech-priests of the Adeptus Mechanicus to name only a few. But for all their multitudes, they are barely enough to hold off the ever-present threat from aliens, heretics, mutants - and worse.

To be a man in such times is to be one amongst untold billions. It is to live in the cruellest and most bloody regime imaginable. These are the tales of those times. Forget the power of technology and science, for so much has been forgotten, never to be re-learned. Forget the promise of progress and understanding, for in the grim dark future there is only war. There is no peace amongst the stars, only an eternity of carnage and slaughter, and the laughter of thirsting gods.

CONTENTS

AUTHOR'S INTRODUCTION

Warning: If you haven't read the novels in this omnibus, then this introduction contains spoilers. Continue at your own risk.

If I learned one thing during the first three Soul Drinkers books, it was that Sarpedon and his Chapter couldn't go on forever. It had become more and more obvious that their place in the galaxy was untenable, their enemies too numerous and their friends too suspect.

The first reason for all this was the sheer practicality of numbers. With every book, more of the Soul Drinkers died and, with their attempts at recruiting having resulted in the disastrous events of *Chapter War*, their numbers were strictly finite. The second, and perhaps more important, reason was that in the 41st millennium, nothing can last forever. This is a huge and uncaring galaxy in which even the brightest lights glimmer for just a short while before the overwhelming darkness snuffs them out. The Soul Drinkers fought for freedom and honour, and while those are noble goals, they don't have a place in the heart of the Warhammer 40,000 universe. The cruel truth at the heart of the setting is that while the Imperium and the galaxy as a whole is an oppressive, grim and gruesome place, it has to be, otherwise the Imperium would fall and the human race would become extinct. From this cosmic irony stem all the core conflicts of the setting, and there was no way the Soul Drinkers could avoid it, no matter how hard they might fight.

Their downfall had to be more than simple attrition. All the truest enemies come from within, especially in Warhammer, and so the fall had to start there. I had earmarked the Chaplain, Iktinos, as the agent of the plot that would destroy the Soul Drinkers. He was at once both

Sarpedon's most steadfast ally and, as a Chaplain who had to stand spiritually apart from the rest of the Chapter, in a unique position to be manipulated into bringing Sarpedon down. I needed a principal villain, the architect of all this, and since the Soul Drinkers had already faced off against aliens, daemons and agents of a vengeful Imperium, this had to be something different. In the first couple of books I had created the legacy of Daenyathos, a philosopher-warrior who had created the Soul Drinkers way of war, and suddenly it occurred to me that perhaps this figure, this icon of genius from the Chapter's history, might still be around, manipulating the Chapter for his own ends.

This plot lay in the background for two or three books. After all, the Soul Drinkers had enough on their plate. But things accelerated in *Hell-forged*, as Iktinos's treachery became more open and the Soul Drinkers were taken into custody by the Imperial Fists. It was no accident that the Imperial Fists were used for this. Not only were they fellow inheritors of Rogal Dorn, and so very much brothers (for all the good and bad that entails) to the Soul Drinkers, they were also one of the most storied and popular Chapters in Warhammer 40,000. In particular their number included Captain Lysander, who had been a prominent character in the background for years and could finally step out into prose. Their titanic space station, the *Phalanx*, was also begging to form the setting for a novel. Another part of the plot was the novella *Daenyathos*, which described Daenyathos himself, very much with a view to explaining why he might become a villain and what he wanted to do to the galaxy, and foreshadowed his re-emergence in the final novel, *Phalanx*.

There was never any doubt that it would all have to come down to Sarpedon and Daenyathos, one on one. It is a truth of the 41st millennium that fate will eventually put every soldier toe-to-toe with his greatest enemy, and that the two will then duel it out for the fate of both their souls.

Ben Counter
October 2012

CHAPTER WAR

'What is the greatest failure against which we must guard?'
'The failure to die when death would serve the Emperor's purpose.'

– Daenyathos, *Catechisms Martial*

CHAPTER ONE

'Present arms!' yelled Lord Globus Falken, and thousands of troops drew up their autoguns to salute the Aristarchical Pavilion. Magnificent in white bearskins and jackets of midnight blue and silver brocade, the Warders of the Vanqualian Republic trooped in perfect formation across the grand Processional Quarter with the banners of their ancient regiments flying alongside the topmost spires of Palatium. They were by far the mightiest fighting force in the Scaephan sector, the primary defenders of the Obsidian system and the proud sons of Vanqualis, and they looked the part. Their officers were resplendent in the heraldry of the Falken family from which they all hailed, and even the casings of their artillery and the hulls of their tanks shone in brass and blue.

'Sloppy this year,' said Count Luchosin Falken, whose uniform was so ornate it looked like his ample frame was swathed in hundreds of clashing flags. In a way it was, for he had to symbolise all the regiments of the Warders. The sun beat down hard on Palatium. The Aristarchical Pavilion, tented in silks and with several valet-servitors trundling around serving drinks, was one of the few places in the Processional Quarter that was not sweltering. Even so, Count Luchosin sweated gently where he sat.

'Globus has got them digging trenches and mucking out the horses,' said Lady Akania Falken-Kaal, standing idly beside Count Luchosin. Lady Akania looked rather more rakish than most of the men, sporting an athlete's frame under her cavalrywoman's uniform and an eye patch thanks to a hunting accident in her youth. 'No damn respect.'

Lord Sovelin Falken, sweating under his bearskin and the heavy crimson sash of the Vanqualian Artillery, looked out across the sea of marching men and their forest of raised autoguns. To him it was still astonishing, a wondrous and powerful statement of Vanqualis's stability and traditions. Far away from the jungles that surrounded Palatium and covered the continent of Nevermourn, there were towering hives with billions of citizens who lived and died beneath their churning factories. Were it not for the rule of the Falken family, and the traditions such as the Trooping of the Warding Standard, the whole of Vanqualis would be like that. Nevermourn, a continent of magnificent natural beauty, was a miracle. It was far more fashionable to denounce it as dull and crude, but it filled Lord Sovelin's heart with pride.

'Globus wants them ready to fight,' said Lord Sovelin. 'I don't think there's anything wrong with that.'

Lady Akania cocked her one visible eyebrow. 'Fight? This is not an army for fighting, Sovelin! This is an army for reminding those vermin in the cities who is in charge. If it weren't for that the citizens might realise there are more of them than there are of us. The Falkens rule Vanqualis by magnificence, Sovelin, not by the gun! Killing them in the streets is fine for the rest of the Imperium but we do things differently. Do you not agree it is better this way?'

'Of course, Lady Akania,' said Sovelin. Lady Akania was an aunt of his a couple of times removed, though he was not much younger, and he was fairly sure she had seniority over him. Most of the family members on the Pavilion were higher up the ladder than Sovelin, which was probably why he had been palmed off on the artillery.

'Fight!' snorted Lord Luchosin with derision. 'What's there to fight?'

A sharp volley of gunshots rippled across the assembled troops, tens of thousands of autoguns loosed off to salute the sons and daughters of the Falken family. With perfect timing the regimental bands opened up and blared the ancient songs of war and rulership, the rhythm punctuated by volleys of disciplined gunfire. It echoed around the white stone spires of Palatium and the immense jungle trees that crowded up around the city walls, around the regimental banners and the gilded eagles atop the minarets of the Temple of Imperator Ascendant.

'No respect,' spat Lady Akania. She turned and walked off briskly, waving away a regimental underling who tried to get her attention. He was carrying a field vox-unit.

'Not now,' said Lord Globus. 'It's not the time.'

'My lord,' said the officer. 'It is a communication from Fleet Admiral Thalak.'

'Thalak has no idea what we are doing here!' growled Lord Globus. 'The man's a peasant. He can wait.'

Sovelin waved over the officer. The man was sweating and it wasn't just from the heat. He wore the uniform of the Mechanised Cavalry.

'It's the emergency channel, my lord,' said the officer.

'Give it to me,' said Sovelin. He took the vox handset and put it to his ear, wincing at the harsh screech of feedback.

'...the love of the Throne!' shouted a voice, barely distinguishable from the howl of static. 'The *Starstrider* is down! They've hit the docks! They're killing us up here! They're killing us!'

'Killing us, you hear?'

Fleet Admiral Thalak was thrown off his feet as the *Sanctis Chirosian* rocked again, as if it were afloat in an endless sea and great waves were battering against it. Thalak's head cracked against the deck and the vox handset kicked out of his hand and clattered away.

Hot blood sprayed over him. He coughed, covering his face, trying to wipe it out of his eyes with the sleeve of his black Naval greatcoat. The sound was tremendous, metal screaming – and men screaming, too, screams cut short as steel pounded against steel.

Thalak rolled onto his front and got to his knees. The blood was from Petty Officer van Staelem, who had been impaled through the abdomen by a great shard of metal. Her body was split open and she shuddered as she died, blood running down her chin.

Thalak had to fight to remember where he was. This place, with its dark wood panelling and friezes of silver cherubim, was the Cartographers' Hall where the navigation officers pored over huge map tables or immense orreries suspended from the ceiling alongside the chandeliers. Now half the hall was caved in, huge jagged blades of twisted metal pushing through from the industrial guts of the ship. Lights flared as a display of planets and stars fell free of its mountings and crashed to the floor, enormous metal globes crushing fleeing crewmen as they ran, sections of the silver hoops cutting ratings in half. Greyish liquid sprayed in from a torn fuel line and caught light, flame flowing around the wrecked metal and devouring the injured crewmen crawling away from the destruction.

Thalak spat out a mouthful of van Staelem's blood and ran, stumbling as the deck tilted again. It felt as if some huge hand had grabbed the *Sanctis Chirosian* and was dismembering it, crushing it here and tearing it apart there.

He ran towards the communications helm that budded off from one end of the Cartographers' Hall. A ringed planet rolled by, its thin silver rings slicing through the floor like a blade as it rolled, cutting Senior Navigation Officer Rorkren in two. Fragments of burning star charts fell in flurries. The ship tilted alarmingly again and the mass of twisted metal forced its way in further, crewmen scrabbling away from it and screaming as it crushed them against the far wall.

'Admiral!' yelled someone from the communications helm. Thalak looked up and saw an arm reaching down to drag him into the helm. The helm was set into a large spherical room with its walls covered in monitors, its officers slumped in grav-couches with their faces covered by the heavy interface units through which they communicated with the other ships of Battlefleet Scaephan. Several of the monitors had blown out, like blinded eyes, and the others showed images from throughout the battlefleet's moorings around the orbital station Ollanius XIV.

The young woman officer's face was streaked with blood and oil. She was a junior officer, probably from the communications support crew whose duties involved making sure the officers were tended to during the months they were wired into the *Sanctis Chirosian*. 'Admiral, what is happening? Who is attacking us?'

'I don't know,' said Thalak, breaking his own rule of never revealing any ignorance or weakness to his crew. 'Someone who was waiting for us. It's not just us, they're going for the whole system.'

'You've heard from Vanqualis?'

'I don't need to,' replied Thalak bleakly. 'It's the Trooping of the Warding Standard. The whole damn army's in Palatium. That's what the attackers were waiting for.'

The officer pushed a strand of bloody hair back from her face and looked up at one of the monitors. It was showing a great chunk of burning wreckage drifting above the pitted metal surface of Ollanius XIV, venting streams of burning fuel and air. 'The *Skystrider* is down,' she said.

'I know,' replied Thalak. The *Skystrider* was a grand cruiser, the largest and most powerful ship in Battlefleet Scaephan. Without it, the battlefleet's power to oppose an invasion was cut in half. 'The *Defence of Phantis*, too. They've hurt us. But we're not down yet.'

As if in reply, the *Sanctis Chirosian* was wrenched over savagely. The ship's gravity suddenly shifted and snapped into reverse, the floor becoming the ceiling. Thalak grabbed onto the doorframe as he fell, stomach lurching as the din grew. Massive map tables heavy as boulders crashed into the chandeliers of the Cartographers' Hall, and bodies broke against the decorative bosses of the ceiling.

The communications officer fell past him and smashed into the monitors on the ceiling of the communications helm, her body spasming as electric current ran through her and spat sparks from her fingers. The smell of cooking blood turned Thalak's stomach one final time and he vomited, heaving up his guts as he clung grimly to the doorway. He heard a grisly snap above him and a pair of booted feet hung beside him. The comms officers, hard-wired into the ship's systems, had fallen down but they were still attached by the interface units clamped around their heads and their necks had snapped. Like a scene from a mass execution, they all hung silent and dead in a ring above Thalak.

A new sound, louder and even more appalling, battered against Thalak's ears. It was a rhythmic scream of metal through metal. Something was biting through the ship, crunching through decks and bulkheads.

Thalak looked through at the Cartographers' Hall and somewhere in his battered mind it all made perfect sense. He was in hell. The Imperial creed had many hells, although some priests argued they were all one and the same, but one of them definitely looked like this. Bodies impaled on shards of metal. Corpses guttering in the flames, some of them still alive and writhing. Great wet streaks of blood sprayed up the walls. Lights flickering, screams cut off, the boom of escaping air shuddering through the ship. Thalak had served his Emperor, but it had not been enough, and now he was in hell.

As if to prove him right, the ruined side of the Cartographers' Hall was forced open like a great metal mouth with teeth of jagged steel. Bodies slid into it as it howled, metal against metal screeching. Guttural voices yelled from inside and dark shapes clambered out, misshapen, hulking forms.

Thalak snarled and clambered back into the burning ruin of the Cartographers' Hall. He took his laspistol from its holster – it was a good gun, and it had been his uncle's before Thalak had followed him into the Imperial Navy.

There were more of them. Dozens. A hundred. Dark and monstrous, swarming into his ship.

'For the Emperor!' yelled Thalak, and fired. The crimson las-blasts streaked past gnarled dark green skin and flickered in tiny, furious red eyes. Gunfire opened up in response, heavy-calibre fire sprayed at random, splintering the panelling behind Thalak. Thalak dived to the floor, rolled and came up firing, forcing himself to ignore the pain.

He was terrified. The fear inside him was like a chunk of ice where his heart should be, freezing his mind. But the rest of him kept fighting, because some part of him told him that was what an officer did.

A fist slammed into him and he was driven into the floor. The shattered remains of a chandelier cut into him. A brutal face with tiny violent eyes above a huge mouth filled with filthy tusks roared down at him and a kick crunched into his ribs. One of the creatures stamped down on his hand and the laspistol was gone.

Greenskins. Orks. Animals, killers, the oldest enemy that mankind had among the stars. They were on Thalak's ship, and they were killing him.

An ork bellowed and the creatures bearing down on Thalak parted for one of their number, easily twice the height of a man and hugely muscled. Its face was so deeply scarred it was barely a face at all but in the midst of the ugliness, there was a glimmer of intelligence and malice in its eyes far more terrifying than a hundred ignorant killers.

There was no part of Thalak now that felt anything other than terror. The greenskin leader reached down and gripped Thalak by his shoulder. Its other arm was artificial, a bionic so crude it looked like it could have been powered by steam. Metal claws fixed around Thalak's elbow and tore his arm off at the shoulder; white horror flooded through him and his body reeled with the shock.

The greenskin held Thalak up into the air. For a moment he could see the ocean of orks flooding into the *Sanctis Chirosian*, butchering injured crewmen where they lay, blazing away with crude deafening guns at those few still on their feet. The orks seemed completely at home amid the destruction and death. They were a natural part of this hell.

Thalak was held high and shaken like a standard to rally the orks. The leader roared and the orks roared with him, cheering the death of the ship and the mutilation of the fleet's commander. Then Thalak was thrown back down and a dozen feet stamped down on him, shattering his bones and battering against his head. Finally the *Sanctis Chirosian* was gone, and there was only blackness.

It was just after the Warding Standard was unfurled that the attack came.

The first blast hit the Processional Quarter square on, throwing broken bodies and severed limbs into the air, a hundred men blown to bits in a split second and dozens more sliced apart by shards of shrapnel. The Warding Standard itself, stitched together from a dozen regimental banners and festooned with battle honours and campaign ribbons, fell tattered and bloody to the ground, draping itself over the chunks of uniformed meat that remained of the honour guard regiment escorting it.

The second blast hit the Aristarchical Pavilion. Lord Globus was vaporised. Lady Akania was beheaded by a shard of missile casing and tumbled down onto the square. Counts and barons were shredded. Lords and ladies were thrown broken against the front of the Herald's Chapel and the Lord Magister's Basilica.

It was an orbital artillery strike. Guns high up in orbit above Vanqualis threw explosive shells down at Palatium. It came utterly without warning, because with Battlefleet Scaephan stationed in the system nothing could possibly have got through to threaten Vanqualis. And yet it had, because now enemy spaceships were spitting fire and death down at the jewel of Nevermourn.

In the moments that followed, the Warders of the Vanqualian Republic reacted to the shock. Guns were hurriedly loaded, officers yelled for battle order, and cavalry tried to control their starting horses. The gates leading from the vast parade grounds of the Processional Quarter were jammed as thousands of troops tried to get out and take cover among the lofty civic buildings of Palatium. In the panic, few of them took heed of the shadow now cast over the parade ground, or of the dark spot that appeared in the air and got larger and larger.

The third blast was not a missile or bomb. It was the impact of a huge dark slab of rock, pitted like an asteroid, that slammed into the centre of the parade ground so hard it drove a deep crater into the ground. The front of the Herald's Chapel collapsed and the roof of the Lawkeeper's Chamber fell in. Spires fell with the impact, buildings spilling their floors out into the parade ground.

Through the choking dust, the survivors could see hundreds of bodies and scores of groaning wounded. They helped their brother soldiers, dragging them towards the scrum at the processional gates. Cries went up for regimental medics, only a few of whom had been permitted to carry their bulky, inelegant medi-packs on procession. Men screamed, shorn of limbs or with their abdomens split open by shrapnel. Some tried to claw their way out from beneath the dead. Others bit back the pain and waited to die, knowing no one would come to save them. Many looked to the scions of House Falken to deliver them, but House Falken's proud sons and daughters were mostly dead in the burning wreckage of the pavilion.

The dust began to settle. The outline of the rock itself could be seen. It wasn't just a rock – its underside had been heavily plated with slabs of metal to help it survive the impact and it was studded with crude engines that had directed its fall. A gunshot rang out, and a screaming man fell silent.

Shapes emerged from the deep pits in the rock. At first they were just more bodies, the inhabitants who had died in the impact being kicked out to make way. Then a terrible cry went up from inside, a deep animalistic war-bellow echoed by hundreds of bestial voices.

As one, the attackers charged out of the rock. They surged forward with their guns blazing, raking through the bodies, great rusted blades dispatching the wounded as their hulking shapes lurched through the near-darkness.

Some of the soldiers turned and readied their autoguns, bayonets fixed. The attackers crashed into them and the Wardens of the Vanqualian Republic saw their enemy for the first time – huge, brutal, green-skinned with murderous red eyes, maddened with battle. Orks, someone yelled – aliens, foul xenos come to defile Nevermourn and the world of Vanqualis.

The battle at the gates was short and bloody. Blades fell on uniformed flesh. Autoguns chattered in response but the orks had the numbers and the momentum, and hundreds of troopers fell. More were crushed as the retreat forced its way through the gates and out into the civic districts of Vanqualis, the orks hacking into the backs of the troopers as they turned to run.

The resistance in the Processional Quarter collapsed, but the orks did not stop. As more rocks slammed into Palatium and disgorged their alien passengers, the orks surged forwards into the streets of the city.

Sovelin could hear Palatium dying. From his position by the Malcadorean Gate he could see huge columns of dust and flame spewing from all across the city as more asteroids smashed into it, and more bombs streaked down from above. The sky was almost dark, only a blood-red tinge across the horizon remaining of the daylight, and Sovelin could see silver specks hanging high above in orbit. Spaceships, he realised – and it wasn't Battlefleet Scaephan. The battlefleet was gone. Vanqualis was alone.

'You!' he yelled at an artillery crew trying to manhandle their bulky mortar carriage towards the gate. 'Unlimber the damn thing and carry it!'

Hundreds of troopers swarmed around Sovelin, all from his regiment, the Vanqualian Rearguard Artillery. He had got them off the parade ground as soon as their part in the Trooping of the Warding Standard had been done with. He had known that something was wrong, and he had known that no one would listen to him. They would not put the army on alert; certainly not break up the Trooping, on the word of someone like Sovelin who was barely senior enough to be spared the marching. So he had got his artillery out of the Processional Quarter and had been taking them to man the walls, just in case, when the first bombs had hit.

The sound was horrible. From far across the city he could hear more explosions mixed with screams. People were in the streets now – the Terran Avenue was lined with the homes of functionaries and house servants, and they knew that something terrible was happening to their city. Another rock streaked down from above and slammed home, the closest yet to the Malcadorean Gate, kicking up a plume of wreckage. Chunks of stone and red roof tiles scattered across the street. More and more civilians filled the streets, emerging from their homes or running from the areas of the city already under attack.

'Get up on the wall!' shouted Sovelin to his men. 'Protect these people!' The soldiers began to turn their artillery pieces to face the street and ready their guns, sheltering behind the monuments that flanked the Malcadorean Gate – a great stone serpent, the heraldic symbol of the Falken family, and an eagle representing the Imperium to which Vanqualis paid fealty.

Sovelin heard the orks and knew then what the forces of Vanqualis were facing. There was nothing else that could explain the war cries and the shrieks of raw terror that moved in front of them like a bow wave. Panic filled every face Sovelin could see as gunfire stuttered from the alleyways and windows smashed.

Closer. Sovelin could hear their grunting alien tongue and the screams of people who fell beneath their blades. Closer still and a building along the avenue collapsed, its front spewing rubble and shattered furniture into the street. Dark green forms scrabbled over it, blazing gunfire. More of them, thick like a green tide, flooded down the street.

People were pouring from their homes, running and screaming. They were heading for the Malcadorean Gate, beyond which was the jungle and the hope of safety. Perhaps they could make it to the coast, and from there reach the cities of Herograve.

But they would not make it. Not unless the guns of Sovelin's artillery made a stand, and bought them time with their lives.

'What do we do, sir?' said Captain Laesc, who had his laspistol and sword drawn as he crouched down by the closest autocannon mount.

Sovelin couldn't answer for a moment. Thousands of people were now crowding the street and the orks were surging forwards. Sovelin could see the crude totems, festooned with severed hands and heads that the orks carried ahead of them, the gleaming bone of their tusks, the savage glee in their eyes as they cut down the civilians who straggled behind.

'We run,' said Sovelin. 'Run! All of you! Now! Go!'

The Vanqualian Rearguard Artillery broke cover and ran, Sovelin at the heart of them, hauling their autocannon and mortars with them as they headed between the monuments of the Malcadorean Gate and out into the deep green mass of Nevermourn's jungles.

As Sovelin's troops broke and ran a great cry went up from the fleeing civilians of Palatium. They were the men and women who served the Falken family, for Palatium was not a city like the towering hives elsewhere on the planet but a place that had been built as the seat of the Falken family's reign. Its civilians had given their lives to House Falken and now the army, led by scions of that same family, was fleeing before them.

Many gave up and died beneath orkish blades, trampled by the booted feet of the xenos. Others scrambled over one another and trampled fellow citizens, even friends and loved ones, in the scrum to escape. Those who made it to the Malcadorean Gate were crushed against the huge stone pillars of the gate itself or the podiums on which the statues were mounted. The serpent and the eagle looked down sternly on the carnage and panic.

Then the orks overran the gate and the butchery began in earnest. Thousands died in a few moments and the orks plunged into the

crowds and emerged again covered in gore, exhausting the magazines
of their crude guns and laying into their prey with swords and cleavers.

Survivors streamed from the Malcadorean Gate, a fraction of those
who had fled the orks. The screams followed them and many of them,
like Admiral Thalak, were sure that they had indeed already died to an
orkish bullet and were now simply fleeing further into hell.

The hugest and greatest ork to ever emerge from the war-worlds of the
Garon Nebula strode towards the pulpit of the Temple of Imperator
Ascendant. The temple was a riot of howling orks, ripping down the
tapestries that depicted the founders of House Falken taking their first
steps on the shores of Herograve or forging through the jungles of Nevermourn. The greenskins blew the faces off statues with their guns and
smashed the bronze plaques that showed scenes from the lives of Imperial saints. They smeared blood on the pale stone walls, blood from the
temple's clergy now being dismembered by the small slave-creatures
who followed the orks everywhere. Dung and gore were heaped on
the temple's altar and the image of the Emperor now lacked a face, the
intricate altarpiece scarred with gunfire.

One cleric was still alive and the slave-creatures were toying with him,
kicking a gun away from his outstretched hand as he reached for it to
take his own life. Again and again he reached haplessly for the skittering
gun, and each time the lean, scurrying creatures howled with laughter.
They looked up as the great ork's shadow fell over them and their faces
fell, cruel red eyes widening in fear above their sharp wicked little faces,
and they scrambled out of his way to hide between the dark wood of
the temple's pews.

The other orks bellowed their triumph as their warlord walked
among them. The warlord was bigger than any of them, twice as tall as
most, its great gnarled head thrust brutally from between his shoulders
and its huge jaw scowling around the forest of broken tusks. Its skin was
as dark and gnarled as the bark on an ancient tree, and its eyes, even
sunk deep into its bestial skull, burned with an intelligence and drive
the other orks lacked.

The warlord only had one normal arm, with which he batted the
closest slave-creature out of the way. His other arm was a contraption
of metal and steam that spurted hot gouts of vapour as he moved, and
ended in a great three-fingered claw large enough to rip the turret off
a tank. The machinery encasing his ribcage and his spine was a rusted
ladder of metal chunks that hissed black lubricant as he moved. Thick
green cords of muscle had grown around his mechanical parts, loosening and contracting as he moved. To have survived the replacement of
half his torso with such crude replacements suggested a level of tough-
ness abnormal even for an ork.

The warlord roared, but not with the triumph and gloating bravado of the other orks. The orks fell silent, even the burliest of them shuddering at the warlord's displeasure. The warlord glowered at the greenskins and his eyes fell on one of them, who was slashing up one of the temple's tapestries with the rusted, bloody blade of his cleaver.

The warlord darted forward with speed far too great for something of his size, and seized the vandalising ork with his natural hand. His fingers closed around the ork's muscular throat and lifted the creature off the ground. The warlord shifted the ork to his mechanical hand and threw it across the temple. Its body slammed into the far wall leaving a crumbling dent in the stone, and slumped to the floor unconscious.

The warlord turned back to the slashed tapestry, pulling it off the wall closer to his face as he examined it. It showed the earliest Warders, the troops of Vanqualis who first protected the shores of Herograve as the planet's cities were settled under the banners of House Falken. The soldiers were capturing a ridge, their stylised uniforms bright and their autoguns held high. The bodies of orks, cut up into pieces, were piled beneath their feet. The artist had shown them as weak and skinny, pathetic creatures barely worthy of Vanqualian bayonets.

The warlord yanked the tapestry off the wall and held it high, so the assembled orks could see the slain orks trampled by human feet. He yelled at them, spitting the hateful syllables of the orkish tongue.

The Vanqualians had won this planet from the orks. This planet belonged to the orks. This world, like so many of the worlds across which the warlord had strode, was green – and it would be green again. But these humans, the same humans now being slaughtered in the streets of Palatium, had once crushed the orks just as surely as the orks were crushing them. They were resilient and resourceful. They were driven. They believed in things that made them perform extraordinary tasks. To underestimate them, to treat them as blade-fodder and playthings, was a way to ensure the same defeat that had befallen the first orks to claim Vanqualis as their own.

If the orks in the temple understood this, any sign of it was hidden under the fear the warlord's smouldering anger instilled in them. The warlord threw down the tapestry and spat on it. He noticed the only surviving cleric hiding behind the pew beside him. The man was elderly, his creased, terrified face smeared with blood and dirt, his fingers bloody and his dove-grey priestly robes tattered. Near him lay the gun he had been trying to grab off the slave-creatures.

The warlord bent down and picked up the gun. He crushed it in the fingers of his mechanical arm, and threw it back down at the cleric's feet. The cleric looked down at it, then stared up at the warlord, terrified tears filling his eyes.

As the warlord stomped towards the pulpit the slave-creatures fell upon the cleric and the temple filled with noise again, the cleric screaming, his robes and his flesh tearing, the slave-creatures cackling as they slicked themselves with his blood. The orks took the racket as a signal to continue destroying the icons of the human enemy and gunfire roared again, blasting censer globes from the ceiling and blowing holes in the pews.

The warlord ignored them. Perhaps once, he had been the same, a simple and brutal creature with nothing but the love of war burning inside him. But the warlord was not like that now. Even the cleric, in the last horror-filled moments of his life, had realised that. He was not an ork, for an ork was a simple thing. An ork was not driven by convictions that equalled those of his most zealous human opponent. An ork did not live by cunning as well as strength, the lust for supremacy as well as the desire for violence and carnage. The warlord did.

He stomped to the top of the pulpit, which overlooked the main nave of the temple. Instead of facing the rows of pews as the temple's preachers had done, the warlord looked the other way, past the ruined altarpiece and through the smashed window that still had fragments of stained glass clinging to its frame.

Palatium stretched out before him. It was a small city, built as a place for the planet's human leaders to rule from instead of a centre of population and industry. Even so, the speed with which the orks had overrun it was impressive. Tiny green figures cavorted on distant rooftops, tearing down the banners of House Falken, hurling masonry and roof tiles into the streets below. Buildings burned, and through the palls of black smoke descended huge ponderous craft, daubed with the crude glyphs of the many ork clans united under the warlord.

Many such craft were already disgorging thousands more orks to fuel the invasion of Vanqualis. Some of the orks were specialists in the warlord's army, sought out and won from their own warlords in fighting pit duels or all-out battles. There were orkish veterans in massive suits of powered armour, heavy and brutal as walking tanks. A squad of expert infiltrators, faces smeared black with camouflage, moved with silence and economy unbecoming of the more raucous ork warriors – these were the scouts and assassins whose natural habitat was a jungle war zone. Masked slavers with barbed whips lashed forwards squabbling crowds of slave creatures, who would be herded in front of the warlord's main force to absorb bullets and set off mines. Other ships were lowering down rickety, temperamental war machines and tanks, with slaves scrabbling all over them to tighten screws and oil joints.

The humans who had slain the first orks to inhabit Vanqualis doubtless had no idea that orks could muster such soldiers. They assumed that the greenskins were nothing more than a horde of animals, all alike in their crudeness and brutality. For the most part they were right, but then for the most part the orks did not have leaders like the warlord to marshal them into a fighting force as deadly as anything the humans could field.

The warlord looked beyond the city, to the jungles. Beyond those jungles was the sea, and beyond that the coast of Herograve, the polluted rocky wasteland with its teeming cities and billions of humans. Weak, cowardly, doomed humans, for whom the cleaver or the bullet was too honest an end. Nevertheless, that was how they would die, because Vanqualis belonged to the orks and no greater desire burned behind the warlord's eyes than to see it in the hands of the greenskins again.

For a long time, the countess was silent. The only sound was the hiss of the air recyclers pumping stale, cold, dry air into the pinnacle chamber. Her small, frail frame swamped by the sweeping pearl-studded gown, her hollow-cheeked face framed by the tiara of diamond spines, the countess seemed to sink deeper into the juvenat throne.

The chamberlain waited politely. He was a small and officious man who had lived a lifetime of service and delivered his share of bad news to the sons and daughters of the Falken family, but never had the news been this bad. He kept his composure and cast his eyes to the floor, awaiting the countess's reply.

Countess Ismenissa Falken took a deep breath that rattled through her aged body. 'When did this happen?'

'But less than an hour, my lady.'

'And of my husband?'

The chamberlain had evidently expected this question. 'Nothing is known of him. With the grace of the Emperor it may be that he still lives...'

'Spare me not, chamberlain,' said the countess, cutting him off. 'Is my husband dead?'

The chamberlain swallowed. 'Lord Globus was on the Aristarchical Pavilion, my lady, and it was thought destroyed in the first attack.'

'Then he is dead.'

'Very probably, my lady.'

'I see. Are there any of the family left?'

'We do not know. Many citizens have escaped Palatium but with little order. Perhaps there are some scions among them. I fear I have little to tell you that is certain.'

'It is certain that the greenskins have returned,' said Countess Ismenissa. 'And it is certain that our world is invaded. It is also certain that we cannot stand alone.'

The countess stood up. From the black slabs of metal that made up the juvenat throne snaked several thick cables that fitted into the rear of the jewel-studded bodice of her dress. Several children, dressed in the same crimson coattails as the chamberlain, stepped out from the shadows behind the juvenat throne, some holding the hem of her long skirts off the floor, others gathering the cables as they slid from the throne so they did not become tangled as the countess walked regally towards one of the tall arched windows that ringed the chamber.

The shadows behind the throne could not hide their blue-grey skin and hollow black eyes, nor the way they walked hunched or on all fours like animals. The wives of House Falken dutifully produced many children, not all of whom survived their childhood, and it was from those lost sons and daughters that the countess's hem-bearers were created. The servitor technology leased to House Falken by the Adeptus Mechanicus was complex and flawed, so the half-living children fell well short of the cherubic ideal.

The chamber was at the pinnacle of one of Herograve's hives and from it could be seen the vast slope of the city, studded with lights against the night's darkness, sweeping down towards the polluted plains that surrounded the city. In the far distance could be seen another mountain of scattered lights, smudged through the polluted air – a neighbouring city, one of the several that studded the continent of Herograve. Billions of Vanqualians lived within those cities, and in a few hours they would start to learn that their ruling class was all but destroyed and aliens had invaded Nevermourn.

In the sky above, just visible through the layers of smoke from the hive factories, were the tiny specks of light reflected from the undersides of the orbital defence network. Thousands of turbolasers and missiles speckled the sky above Herograve's cities, protecting them from bombardment. Vanqualis did not have the resources to protect its entire orbit in such a way, and so had chosen to spare its cities from enemy bombardment. That was the reason that orks were not raining down on the hive cities, but that would be little comfort to the survivors of Palatium who had seen their loved ones butchered in the streets on distant Nevermourn.

'We must ask for help,' said Countess Ismenissa. 'With the Warders broken and House Falken decimated, we are alone. We are isolated here, far from the worlds of Imperial dominion, but it is only the Imperium that can help us. Now is not the time to be proud. We will beg if we must.' The countess looked away from the window at the chamberlain. 'Summon the astropath and bring him here. He must be ready to transmit immediately.'

'Of course, my lady,' said the chamberlain. 'Should I take steps to inform the populace?'

'Of the invasion?' The countess waved a hand. 'Yes. Give it to the Lay Parliament. Have them debate it. It will give them something to do.'

The chamberlain did not scurry off to his duties, as the countess expected.

'Yes?' she said.

'There remains one further matter. With Lord Globus... gone, you are the only representative of House Falken in a position to assume leadership. You are the ruler of Vanqualis, my lady.'

The countess sighed. She had never looked older than she did in that moment, framed against the blackness of her city, swamped by her finery. 'Very well. I am sure there is a ceremony for it somewhere. Have the archivists dig it out.'

'It shall be done.' The chamberlain bowed briskly and hurried out to his duties.

The countess was well over two hundred years old, thanks to the efforts of the house physicians and the constant attentions of the juvenat throne. In all that time it had never been this bad. She had lived through the Hive Scorcid revolt, the scandals of her uncle Baron Malifiss Falken, and the schism forced by the emergence of the now-defunct Cult of the Terran Resurgence. She had seen upheavals and unexpected deaths, conflicts with the governors of the Scaephan sector and crises where the hive cities were starved of food or water. But never anything as bad as this. She was an old woman, and she felt every year.

And now, for the first time in its history, Vanqualis would have to beg for help from the Imperium, that distant power to whom House Falken had paid the tithes of its cities' riches in return for sovereignty over their world. The orks had their foothold on Nevermourn now, and there was no doubt where they would head next. With Nevermourn infested Herograve would follow, with its cities and its teeming billions.

The countess walked to an ornate bookshelf, which held several large volumes. Her dear Globus had always been more concerned with military than planetary matters and the countess had felt it prudent to become familiar with the history and geography of her world, in case she had to take a more active part in the governing of Vanqualis. Now, the entire responsibility for that government fell on her.

Countess Ismenissa took a heavy book from an upper shelf, the children crawling like obedient pets to carry her skirts around her. The book was an atlas, presented to her by one of the hive universities in return for some state function she had performed half a century ago. One of the children turned a handle that reeled her cables back in as she returned to the throne. She sat down, feeling the juvenat liquids flowing through her veins again, holding back the effects of ageing on her bones and organs. She laid the book open on her lap as the children took their positions behind the throne again, and began to read.

Maps of Nevermourn flickered past her eyes. At that very moment, refugees and greenskin filth alike were streaming through those valleys and hills, fighting, killing, making for the shore and then Herograve beyond them. There would be a war, long or short depending on how the countess led her people in the following days, and perhaps at the end of it all Vanqualis would still stand and House Falken would still rule. But the centuries had taught Countess Ismenissa to be pragmatic, and she knew in her heart that Vanqualis and all those billions of citizens would probably not survive.

'Against whom will the battle at the end of time be fought?'
  'Know only that it will not be against enemies from without.'

– Daenyathos, *Catechisms Martial*

CHAPTER TWO

Deep in the heart of the hulk, so far from the massive churning warp engines and the tramping of power-armoured feet it might have been deep underground on some forbidden planet, lay the sanctum. Its original purpose was uncertain – presumably it had been a part of a spaceship at one time, because the hulk was an amalgamation of space-craft welded together into strange and ugly shapes by the forces of the warp. But it was stone, not metal, and its elegant, simple temple was not built in a cargo hangar or a ship's bridge, but in a dark half-flooded cave dripping with stalactites. The temple was partially submerged, the roof of a long covered processional leading up to it now forming a tiled walkway just breaking the surface. Dim lights glowed under the water, glow-globes that had been lit when the cave had been discovered and had probably been lit for hundreds or thousands of years, patiently waiting for its worshippers to return.

Chaplain Iktinos walked along the path, the lower edges of his purple and black Space Marine power armour lit strangely by the light from below. He wore a grim skull-faced helmet, its eyepieces black and expressionless, and an eagle-topped mace, his crozius arcanum, hung at his waist. Iktinos, like any Space Marine, was huge, not much shy of three metres tall in his armour, but even so it was with humility and reverence that he passed over the threshold into the temple itself.

The sanctum within the temple was also half underwater, the lights below the surface casting strange shifting lights along the ceiling. The altar, along with slabs of carved stone that had fallen from the above, broke the surface and Iktinos used them to reach the large slab of fallen ceiling in the centre of the temple. Beside it a statue reared up from the water – it had the upper body of human woman and the head and lower body of a snake, and had its arms raised crookedly towards the ceiling. It was from a cult or religion that had probably been forgotten for centuries. Iktinos ignored its broken, accusing gaze as he kneeled down by the collection of monitoring equipment piled incongruously on the platform.

This place was Iktinos's sanctum, as sacred to him as it had been to whichever worshippers gathered there before their ship had been lost in the warp and become a part of the space hulk *Brokenback*. Iktinos removed his helmet to reveal a smooth, unmarked face with larger, more expressive eyes than deserved to belong beneath the sinister grimace of the skull. Shaven-headed and with light brown skin, Iktinos's real face had just as much presence as the Chaplain's skull. It was rare for Iktinos to take off his helmet, as it was a badge of office, an indicator that he was a man apart from the rest of the Soul Drinkers Chapter. Here, in his sanctum, it was safe for him to do so.

Iktinos checked one of the monitor screens. A single green blip jumped across it. He pulled a long spool of parchment with various readouts scrawled on it from the base of the monitor and cast his eyes over its information, evidently satisfied. Then he walked to the edge of the platform and reached down into the water.

A Space Marine's strength was awesome. Iktinos planted one foot on the stone and hauled a large rectangular slab of stone from the water. With a bang that echoed off the rocks of the cave beyond the slab slammed onto the platform, splintering the marble beneath. On the upper surface of the slab was carved the image of a stern-faced, bearded man dressed in ornate, archaic armour, such as might be found on the noble warriors of feral worlds. He had a crown on his brow and his hands were clasped over his chest holding the pommel of a double-headed axe. All around him were carved letters from a language that Iktinos did not recognise, one that had probably been forgotten as long as the temple's snake-headed god. The slab was a stone coffin for a long-dead king, and the image was carved on its lid.

Iktinos opened some metal clasps, evidently late additions, holding the lid closed, and hauled the lid off the coffin. The muffled screaming began instantly.

Inside the coffin was a wretched, skinny, filthy figure. Its robes were black with dirt and it had a bag over its head with tubes and wires snaking from it, wires that were ultimately connected to the monitors beside Iktinos. The figure reached up and groped blindly at the air in front of it, the skin on its hands pallid and sagging from the damp, wrinkled and rotting. The stench was awful.

Iktinos pulled the bag off the figure's head. The face of the man underneath was swollen and white, splitting along the seams of his features. A wide tube ran down his throat and another up his nose. His eyes were wide and blind, pure white without iris or pupil.

Iktinos pulled the tube from the man's throat and the man could scream properly now, howling sobs of desperation and fear. For several long minutes, the man could only scream. Then there was not enough left in him to scream any more.

'Please...' gasped Astropath Minoris Croivas Vel Scannien, voice hoarse and feeble. 'Please... oh, my Emperor, stop... just... just let it end...'

Iktinos looked down at him, his face as expressionless as the skull-masked helmet at his feet. 'Stop?'

'The nightmares. Let me out. Or... let me die. Please.'

'You begged us for this.'

'I didn't know!' The words came out as a sob, like that of a child. 'How would I know?'

'You begged us to take you,' continued Iktinos. 'You said you would do anything to get away from Dushan, from the Multiplaeion.' He held out his hands to indicate the coffin. 'This is what you are doing.'

Croivas Vel Scannien put his hands over his face and sobbed. There was barely anything else left in him, no words, not even terror or hatred now. There had been a man inside Croivas Vel Scannien once, but he was almost completely gone.

'Why?' he said, voice just a whisper. 'What do you want?'

'You know what I want.'

'Throne of Earth, what... what do you want me to tell you?'

'All of it.'

Croivas took his hands down from his eyes. 'You know I can't do that. I've told you, why won't you listen? It's... every one of us does it differently. It has to be directed at you, you have to know the codes... With me it's dreams, and at the best of times...'

'You said you were the best,' replied Iktinos, interrupting him. 'You said you could do it when I took you away from Dushan. It was why I took you at all.'

'You really... you really think I wanted this?'

'I don't care what you want. You mean nothing. Which is why you will do as I tell you.'

Dushan had been a world of mutilations. Deep scars across its continents, great ravines splitting its cities apart. Volcanic and tortured. Herds of slaves mined the perfect, flawless gems, forged in the fury of the planet's mantle, for use in precision equipment like cogitators and spaceship sensors. Those slaves had revolted and murdered the Imperial classes – classes that included Croivas Vel Scannien, an astropath, the planet's link to the Imperium at large. The Soul Drinkers had arrived there to draw recruits from the rioting slaves and in doing so they had been approached by Croivas, who wanted to go with them too. It was to the Chaplain, the spiritual leader of the Chapter, that Croivas had gone with his offer. The Chaplain had accepted. The rest of the Chapter had never known.

Since then Croivas had been Iktinos's prisoner. He had been in the coffin for longer than he could remember and his mind was broken. Croivas began to beg, offering Iktinos things he could not possibly deliver or claiming he had a loved one, a woman, back on Dushan who might still be alive. Iktinos calmly explained that there was nothing Croivas possessed that Iktinos could want, and that even if there was a woman she would be buried in the mass graves of the mine pits where the Imperials had been thrown by Dushan's slaves.

Then Croivas began threatening Iktinos, and so desperate was he that some of his threats even sounded realistic. He would strip Iktinos's soul away from his body, drive him mad, wipe his memory so he turned into a drooling infant. Tell the rest of the Chapter what Iktinos was doing. But Iktinos knew that, as powerful a psyker as the astropath was, he would have long ago enacted his threats had he really been able to pull them off.

Eventually, after almost an hour of ranting which left Croivas raw-throated and exhausted, the astropath gave in to Iktinos and sank back down into the nightmares. Astropaths sent and received psychic messages, the only means of sending information across the Imperium's immense interstellar distances, and every one had a different method of doing so. Croivas did so through dreams, receiving the complex symbolic messages while asleep and rebuilding them according to astropathic codes when awake. It was while he had slept in the coffin, sealed underwater, that fragments of communications from across the Imperium had flickered through his mind.

Cadia was at war. It was the lynchpin of Imperial defences around the Eye of Terror but now its commander Ursurkar Creed had demanded assistance from all who could render it to fight off the hordes of traitors and abominations spewing from the Eye. Dramatic news, to be sure, but Iktinos demanded that Croivas move on.

Aliens, of a type never encountered before by the Imperium, had carved out an empire for themselves on the southern fringe, among worlds evacuated or wracked by the century's wars against the tyranids. To Iktinos, such things were irrelevant. The millions of citizens begging for deliverance meant nothing. Less than nothing – they were a distraction. Or would have been, to someone without Iktinos's superhuman dedication.

Skeletal mechanical creatures were slowly infesting a cluster of stars close to the galactic core in the Ultima Segmentum. An entire empire had seceded from the heartland of the Imperium, along the western spiral arm of the galaxy, and the call had gone out for the upstarts to be crushed. Religious schisms had plunged the planets near holy Gathalamor into war, and the diocese of Gathalamor itself was begging for assistance in keeping the conflict from its sacred shores.

No use. None of it. Iktinos pressed Croivas harder, but Croivas was falling apart. His lips were bloody from the effort of speaking and the cacophony of symbols forcing their way through his mind was driving him insane. Iktinos did not care, and demanded that Croivas continue.

Daemons summoned to the streets of a world isolated by warp storms. Greenskins flooding through the jungles of a planet deep in the Segmentum Tempestus. Mutants rioting, burning the crops of agri-worlds and threatening hive planets with starvation. Fleets of xenos pirates preying on pilgrim ships, devouring the very souls of their captives. Alien gods demanding worshippers, plagues of insanity and heresy, a hundred thousand wars burning across a million worlds...

'Stop,' said Iktinos.

Croivas gasped and coughed up a clot of blood. His lips still worked, mind festering with the symbols that had bombarded him as he lay in the cold stone coffin.

'Go back. The greenskins.'

'The... the great beast,' gasped Croivas. 'Came without warning. Shattered them. Without help they'll die.'

'Where? What about the black stone?'

'The... symbol. The code. Black stone. Onyx. And... glass.'

'Volcanic glass,' said Iktinos. 'Obsidian.'

'Yes.'

'What else?'

'Now this land is ours, we shall never mourn again,' said Croivas. It sounded like a quotation from somewhere, not Croivas's own words.

'What else?'

'The world. A grave for heroes. Van... Vanqualis. A stone serpent rules. Pride.'

'And the beast?'

'Thousands of greenskins raining down from the sky. Too many to count. Destroyed their armies in a heartbeat. And their fleet is... gone.'

'Is it an exaggeration?' Iktinos's voice was not lacking in emotion now. There was steel in it, an implicit threat so powerful he could have been holding a knife to Croivas's throat.

'No. No, they will die without help.'

'Will they get it?'

'They are far away from anyone. Perhaps there was an answer.'

Iktinos stood back from the coffin. He glanced down at the monitors – Croivas's heart would not take much more.

'I expect more,' he said. 'You told us you were the best.'

'Then let me go,' gasped Croivas.

In reply, Iktinos picked up the tube he had taken from Croivas's throat and forced it back into the man's mouth. Croivas reached up to fend off Iktinos but Iktinos simply grabbed his flabby claw of a hand and crushed its softened bones in his fist. Croivas's scream was strangled and weak. His remaining hand flapped against the lid of the coffin as Iktinos forced it over him again and the shadow fell back over Croivas Vel Scannien's blinded eyes.

Croivas's whimpering was barely audible as Iktinos put his shoulder to the side of the coffin and pushed it back into the water.

Iktinos glanced back down at the readouts, made a few adjustments to the air mix and sustenance regimens, and then walked back out of the sanctum and towards the cave entrance. As he did so he pulled his helmet back on and his face was replaced with the grimacing Chaplain's skull.

Iktinos had served well and never given up where even stout-hearted Space Marines, even fellow Chaplains, had chosen to discard the sacred word and turn their back on the traditions of their order's foundation. Now Iktinos would be rewarded – not with riches or peace, but with the chance to play a part in the greatest work all mankind had ever known. Space Marines, and the Soul Drinkers in particular, were immensely proud, but Iktinos had gone beyond that and it was not pride that swelled his heart as he went to do his duty among his fellow Soul Drinkers.

It was the knowledge that when he was done, nothing in this galaxy – in this universe – would remain unchanged.

Chapter Master Sarpedon of the Soul Drinkers took to the centre of the auditorium, watched by the hundreds of fellow Soul Drinkers. He was a horrendous sight. From the waist up he was a Space Marine, a psychic Librarian, with his purple power armour worked into a high collar containing the protective aegis circuit and the golden chalice symbol of the Chapter worked into every surface. He was an old man by most human standards and his shaven head was scarred by war and sunken-eyed with the things he had seen. From the waist down, however, he was a monster – eight arachnid legs, tipped in long talons, jutted from his waist where human legs should be. One of his front legs was bionic, the original having been ripped off what felt like a lifetime ago.

'Brothers of the Chapter,' he began, his voice carrying throughout the auditorium. 'We have come so far it is difficult to imagine what we once were. And I am glad, because it shows how far we have left that time behind. Some of you, of course, have never known the Chapter other than as it is now. And I am glad of that, too, because it shows that in spite of everything the galaxy has thrown at us we can still recruit others to our cause. We have never given up, and we never will. The new initiates, and those who have now earned their armour, are proof of that.'

Sarpedon looked around at the assembled Soul Drinkers. There were faces he had known for a long time, back into the earliest days of his service in the Chapter before he had led it away from the tyranny of the Imperium. Others were new, recruited by the Chapter in the days since the schism.

The auditorium had once been a xenobiology lecture theatre on an explorator ship that had become lost in the warp. Large dusty jars containing the preserved bodies of strange alien creatures were mounted on the walls, and Sarpedon himself spoke from on top of a large dissection slab with restraints still hanging from it.

'We have been apart for some time,' continued Sarpedon. 'Captains, make your reports. Karraidin?'

Captain Karraidin was one of the most grizzled, relentless warriors Sarpedon had ever met. A relic of the old Chapter, he wore one of the Soul Drinkers' few suits of Terminator armour and had a face that looked like it had been chewed up and spat out again. He stood with the whirr of both his massive armour's servos, and the bionic, which had replaced his leg after he lost it in the battle on Stratix Luminae. 'Lord Sarpedon,' said Karraidin in his deep gravel voice. 'Many of the novices have earned their full armour in the Suleithan Campaign. They intervened in the eldar insurgency and killed many of the xenos pirates. They have done us all proud.'

'What are your recommendations?'

'That Sergeant Eumenes be given a full command,' replied Karraidin.

Sarpedon spotted Eumenes himself among the Soul Drinkers – he knew Eumenes as a scout, one of the new recruits of the Chapter, but now he wore a full set of power armour and he seemed perfectly at home among its massive ceramite plates.

'Sniper Raek has distinguished himself in scouting and infiltration duties,' continued Karraidin. 'I recommend that he remain a scout and take command of other novice forces. Given our current situation I believe the Chapter would benefit from veteran scouts like Raek.' The slim-faced, quietly spoken Raek was the best shot in the Chapter – as good, some said, as the late Captain Dreo.

'Then it shall be so,' said Sarpedon. 'And of the latest recruits?'

'The harvest has been bountiful again,' said Karraidin with relish. 'They are born soldiers, every one of them.'

The Soul Drinkers recruited new members from among the oppressed and rebellious people of the Imperium and turned them into Space Marines as the old Chapter had done, but without such extensive hypno-doctrination – Sarpedon wanted to ensure their minds were as free as the Chapter itself. For the last several months Karraidin's novices had been earning their place in the Chapter, intervening to fight the Emperor's enemies around the scattered worlds of the largely desolate Segmentum Tempestus.

'Then we are winning our greatest victory,' said Sarpedon. 'The forces that deceived once wanted us broken and desperate, whittled down one by one, reliant on those forces to keep us from sliding into the abyss. We have clawed our way out and built ourselves a future. Some of our best have been lost to win this victory, and I have no doubt there are those who will still try to stop us. As long as we take new novices who believe in our cause, and those novices earn their armour fighting the Emperor's foes, our enemies will never win.

'But those enemies never tire. Ever since Gravenhold we have had to rebuild ourselves and now I believe we are ready to fight as a Chapter again. The Eye of Terror has opened and Abaddon has returned, it is said. More and more of the Imperium's military are diverted to countering the tyranid fleets. The underbelly is exposed and the Imperium is too corrupt to defend itself. We are sworn to do the Emperor's work, and that work is being neglected in the galaxy's hidden and isolated places.'

'Such as the Obsidian system,' said a voice from among the assembled Soul Drinkers. It was that of Iktinos, the Chaplain, distinguished by his black-painted armour and the pale grimacing skull that fronted his helmet. He was surrounded by his 'flock', the Soul Drinkers who had lost their sergeants and gone to Iktinos for leadership. They accompanied him in battle and often led the other battle-brothers in prayers and war-rites.

'Chaplain?' said Sarpedon. 'Explain.'

'The *Brokenback* picks up many signals from across the galaxy,' said Iktinos. 'We are far from the Imperial heartland but nevertheless there is chatter, transmitted from ship to ship. I have been sifting through it to find some indication of the Emperor's work remaining undone.'

'And I take it you have found somewhere?'

'I have, Lord Sarpedon. The Obsidian system, in the Scaephan Sector, to the galactic south of the Veiled Region. The planet Vanqualis has been invaded by the greenskin scourge. The people there have begged for assistance from the Imperium but as you well know, the Imperial wheel is slow to turn and the orks will surely devastate their world.'

'So there is the Emperor's work to be done?' asked Sarpedon.

'They are people of an independent spirit,' said Iktinos. 'They have resisted the Imperial yoke and remained true to their own traditions. They have survived for a long time alone, and we may find adherents to our cause there. Certainly there are many billions of Emperor-fearing citizens who will perish without help.'

'We are not a charity,' said Librarian Tyrendian sharply. Tyrendian was a lean and handsome man, seemingly too unscarred and assured to have seen as many battles as he had. Like Sarpedon he was a powerful psyker – unlike Sarpedon his power manifested as devastating bolts of lightning, like psychic artillery, hurled at the enemy. When Tyrendian spoke his mind it was with a self-important confidence that won him few friends in the Chapter. 'There are countless worlds suffering.'

'This one,' said Iktinos, 'we can help.'

'We should be at the Eye,' continued Tyrendian. 'Chaos has played its hand.'

'The whole Inquisition is at the Eye,' retorted another voice, that of Captain Luko, the Chapter's most experienced assault captain. 'We might as well hand ourselves over to our enemies.'

'It is also the case,' said Iktinos, 'that our Chapter is not rich in resources. We are lacking in fuel and ordnance. The *Brokenback* cannot go on forever, and neither can we. The Obsidian system has a refinery world, Tyrancos, from which we can take what we please. Tyrendian is correct, we are not a charity, but we can both help secure our future and help an Emperor-fearing world survive without being ground down by the Imperial yoke.'

'And it's better,' said Luko, 'than sitting on our haunches here waiting for battle to come to us.' Luko was known throughout the Chapter for the relish with which he approached battle, as if he had been born into it, and Sarpedon could see many of the Soul Drinkers agreed with him.

'Lygris?' said Sarpedon, looking at the Chapter's lead Techmarine.

'The Chaplain is correct,' said Techmarine Lygris. Lygris's armour was the traditional rust-red and a servo-arm mounted on his armour's back-pack reached over his shoulder. 'Without significant re-supply soon we will have to reconsider using the *Brokenback* as a base of operations. We would have to find ourselves another fleet.'

'Then I believe the Obsidian system may be our next destination,' said Sarpedon. 'Iktinos, assist me in finding out whatever we can about Vanqualis and its predicament. Lygris, prepare the warp route. We must be ready for…'

'Let them rot,' said yet another voice from among the Soul Drinkers.

It was Eumenes who had spoken, the sergeant who had recently earned his full armour. He pushed his way to the front, close to the anatomy stage at the centre of the auditorium. He was a brilliant soldier and looked it, sharp intelligent eyes constantly darting, face as resolute as it was youthful.

'Scout Eumenes,' said Sarpedon. 'I take it you disagree?'

Eumenes grimaced as if the idea being discussed left a bad taste in his mouth. 'The people of Vanqualis are no better than any of the rest of the Imperium. They will be as corrupt as the rest of them. You say you have turned your back on the Imperium, Sarpedon, but you keep dragging us back into its wars.'

'On the Imperium,' said Sarpedon darkly. 'Not the Emperor.'

'The people *are* the Imperium! These vermin, these murderers, they are steeped in the corruption we are fighting against! If we have to bring the whole damned thing down, if we have to set worlds like Vanqualis aflame, then that is what we do! The Imperium is the breeding ground for Chaos! The Emperor looks upon this galaxy and weeps because none of us have the courage to change it.'

'Then what,' said Iktinos darkly, 'would you have us do?'

Eumenes looked around the assembled Soul Drinkers. 'The underbelly is exposed. You said so yourselves. We strike while we can. Break it down. The Adepta, the bastions of tyranny. Ophelia VII or Gathalamor. Imagine if we struck at Holy Terra itself, blotted out the Astronomican! This tyranny would collapse around us! We could help rebuild the human race from the ashes! That would be the Emperor's work.'

'Eumenes, this is madness!' shouted Sarpedon. 'If the Imperium fell the human race would follow. Destroying it is not the way to deliver its people.'

'If what I say is madness, Sarpedon, then a great many of us are infected with that same madness. Do not think I am alone. And we could do it, Sarpedon! Think about it. The Imperium has been on the brink for thousands of years. We are the best soldiers in the galaxy, and we know what the Imperial vermin fear. We could bring it all down, if we only made the choice!'

'Enough!' Sarpedon rose to his full height, which on his arachnoid legs put him a clear head above the tallest Space Marine. 'This is insubordination, and it will cease. I am your Chapter Master!'

'I have no master!' Eumenes's eyes were alight with anger. 'Not you. Not the Imperium. No one. You cling to the ways of the old Chapter so dearly you are no more than a tyrant yourself.'

No one spoke. Sarpedon had fought the Chapter before – he had led the Chapter war when he had overthrown Gorgoleon and taken control of the Soul Drinkers, he had battled adherents to the old Chapter's ways and even faced one of his own, Sergeant Tellos, who had become corrupted by the dark forces against which the Chapter fought. But a conflict like this had never come into the open so brazenly.

'I see,' said Sarpedon carefully, 'that the Chapter does not unite behind me and cast down the rebel.' He cast his eyes over the assembled Soul Drinkers, reading their expressions – anger and offence, yes, but also apprehension and perhaps some admiration for Eumenes's boldness.

'Then you cannot ignore me,' said Eumenes. 'As I said, I am not alone.' The young Soul Drinker smiled and stepped forward into the centre of the auditorium, face to face with Sarpedon himself. 'They used to say that the Emperor would give strength to the arm of His champion. That Rogal Dorn would counsel victory to the just. Do you believe He will lend you strength, Sarpedon, if we settle this in the old way?'

The old way. An honour-duel. One of the Soul Drinkers' oldest traditions, as old as the Imperial Fists Legion, the Legion of the legendary primarch Rogal Dorn, from the ranks of which the Soul Drinkers had been founded almost ten thousand years before.

'First blood,' said Sarpedon, with a steely snarl on his face. 'I would not grant you anything so noble as death.'

In the heart of the *Brokenback* lay the dark cathedrals, the baffling catacombs and ornate sacrificial altars that once adorned the *Herald of Desolation*. Nothing was known of the *Herald* except that it had at some time in the distant past been lost in the warp and become a part of the ancient space hulk, and that its captain or creator must have been insane. Hidden cells and torture chambers, steel tanks scarred with acid stains, tombs among the catacombs with restraints built into the stone coffins – the purpose of the *Herald of Desolation* was lost amid the hidden signs of madness and suffering, smothered by the dark, ornate magnificence that blossomed in the heart of the *Brokenback*.

The dome that soared over Sarpedon's head was crowded with statues, locked in a painful, writhing tableau of contortion and violence. Below the sky of stone agony was a thigh-deep pool of water broken by oversized figures that had been sculpted to look as if they had fallen down from above, and reached up towards the figures of the dome as if desperate to return. The dome was vast; easily the size of the Chapel of Dorn in which the last honour-duel among the Soul Drinkers had taken place.

The Soul Drinkers, stood observing around the edge of the circular pool, seemed distant and dwarfed by the strange majesty of the place. In the centre, Sarpedon and Eumenes stood, armoured but unarmed. This was their fight, and theirs alone – when it was done the results would affect the whole Chapter, but for now it was a matter between them.

'Why have you brought us here, Eumenes?' said Sarpedon. 'You could have come to me earlier. There was no need to bring the whole Chapter into this.'

'It's not just me, Sarpedon.' When Eumenes spoke there always seemed to be a mocking note in his voice, as if he couldn't help but scorn those around him. 'There are dozens of us. And you can't hold out forever.'

'Are you just here to threaten me, Eumenes, or to decide this?'

Eumenes smiled. 'No witchcraft, Sarpedon.'

'No witchcraft.'

Eumenes darted forwards. Sarpedon ducked back and raised his front legs to fend off Eumenes but Eumenes was quick, far quicker than Sarpedon anticipated. Eumenes drove a palm into Sarpedon's stomach and though the impact was absorbed by his armour Sarpedon tumbled backwards, talons skittering through the water to keep him upright. Eumenes jumped, span, and drove a foot down onto Sarpedon's bionic front leg. Sparks flew as the leg bent awkwardly and Sarpedon, off-balance again, dropped into the water and rolled away as Eumenes slammed a fist into the floor where his face had been. Stone splintered under his gauntlet.

Eumenes had learned to fight twice. Once, among the brutalised outcasts amongst whom he had grown up – and again with the Soul Drinkers, under the tutelage of Karraidin. He was dirty as well as quick, brutal as well as efficient. And he really wanted to kill Sarpedon. Sarpedon could see that in his every movement.

Eumenes followed up but Sarpedon was on his feet, backed up against a huge broken stone arm that had fallen from above. Eumenes struck and parried but Sarpedon met him, giving ground as Eumenes tried to find a way through his defence. Sarpedon's front bionic leg dragged sparking in the water as he skirted around the fallen arm, watching Eumenes's every flinch and feint.

'What do you want, Eumenes?' he said. 'Why are we here? Really?'

Eumenes ducked under Sarpedon's remaining front leg and darted in close, spinning and aiming an elbow at Sarpedon's head. Sarpedon grabbed him and turned him around, using the strength of Eumenes's blow to fling the young Soul Drinker over his shoulder. Eumenes smacked into an oversized sculpture of a contorted figure, his armoured body smashing its stone head into hundreds of splinters. Eumenes slid down into the water on his knees but he leapt up immediately. His face had been cut up by the impact and blood ran down it as he snarled and charged again.

This time Sarpedon reared up, bringing his talons down on Eumenes and driving him down so he sprawled in the water. Eumenes struggled under Sarpedon's weight as Sarpedon reached down to grab him.

A stone shard, sharp as a knife, stabbed up from the water. Sarpedon barely ducked to the side in time as Eumenes tried to stab him in the throat. Eumenes swept his legs around and knocked Sarpedon's talons out from under him, and now Sarpedon toppled into the water.

Suddenly he was face to face with Eumenes. Eumenes had the knife at his throat, Sarpedon gripping his wrist to keep the weapon from breaking his skin. He was looking right into the youth's eyes and what he saw there was not the emotion of a Space Marine. Eumenes might have been implanted with the organs that turned a man into a Space

Marine, and he might be wearing the power armour so emblematic of the Astartes warriors – but Eumenes was not a Space Marine. Not in the way that the old Chapter understood it. Sarpedon had not understood what he was doing when he began the harvest anew and made Eumenes into the man fighting him now.

Eumenes tried to force the point home but Sarpedon was stronger and the stone blade was slowly pushed away. Sarpedon held up his free hand, which had a dark smear of blood on one finger. Blood from the cuts down Eumenes's face.

'First blood,' said Sarpedon. He held up his hand so the watching Soul Drinkers could see. 'First blood!' he yelled, signifying the end of the fight.

For a few moments Sarpedon saw nothing in Eumenes's eyes but the desire to kill. The honour-duel was forgotten and Sarpedon was not a fellow Soul Drinker to Eumenes – he was an enemy, something to be destroyed. Eumenes really believed in his own cause, Sarpedon realised. To him, Sarpedon was as foul an enemy as the daemons that preyed on mankind.

Eumenes's grip relaxed and the stone shard fell into the water. Gauntleted hands took Eumenes's shoulders and pulled him back away from Sarpedon. The hate in Eumenes's face was gone, replaced with something like triumph, as if Eumenes believed he had somehow proven himself right.

'Take him to the brig,' said Sarpedon, pushing himself up out of the water with his seven remaining legs. 'Post a guard.'

Apothecary Pallas hurried up and shook his head at the ragged state of Sarpedon's bionic. 'This will take some fixing,' he said.

'Be grateful it's the same one,' replied Sarpedon. Had Eumenes shattered one of his mutated legs and not the bionic, Eumenes would have won the duel to first blood. It had been that close. Sarpedon might be stronger, but Eumenes's ruthlessness had almost brought him out of the duel as the victor.

'Your orders, Lord Sarpedon?' said Techmarine Lygris.

Sarpedon looked up at Lygris. Like Pallas, Luko and others, he was one of Sarpedon's oldest and most trusted of friends, veterans of the Chapter War who had been with him through everything the Chapter had suffered. He realised then that such old friends were becoming rarer, and the Chapter would have to rely on its new recruits.

'Take us to the Obsidian system,' said Sarpedon. 'Find out everything we have on it. And make the Chapter ready for war.'

'But what of the masses of humanity, the Emperor's flock?'
  'Pay them no heed, for their greater number is already damned.'

  – Daenyathos, *Catechisms Martial*

CHAPTER THREE

'Down! Everyone down!'

General Varr had barely yelled the words before the first shots slammed home, bursting among the soaring trunks and branches of the Wraithspire Palace, filling the air with shards of burning wood.

The men of the 901st scrambled for cover. The grounds of the palace were magnificent, the riotous jungles of Nevermourn manicured into stands of flowers and ornamental lakes, but in that moment they became just another battlefield. Varr dived into the cover of the massive tree trunk beside him as debris rained down, dark sheets of shrapnel shredding the palace lawns and more ordnance exploding among the branches.

Varr saw one man cut in two, the halves of his body flopping into an ornamental pond in a burst of pink foam. Another stumbled by with one arm missing, clutching at the bleeding stump as another trooper dragged him into cover behind a cluster of statues. Varr tried to see where the fire was coming from. The enemy must have artillery beyond the tree line that formed the border of the palace gardens – dull orange flashes between the trees were followed by great dark explosions in the gardens. Varr couldn't see the enemy, only hear the reports of their guns and feel the thunder of the shells ripping into the gardens.

'Report!' yelled Varr into the vox-unit's handset, struggling to hear his own words over the bombardment.

'Hundreds of 'em!' came the yelled reply, broken up by static. 'Kullek's seen 'em on the ridge! All of them, full frontal assault!' Kullek's positions were further forward, closer to the tree line, and he formed the first line of defence.

Varr handed the vox-unit back to the trooper beside him. He turned to Lieutenant Fulgorin who stood with his back to the tree trunk. 'Fulgorin, they're charging. Get the men ready to receive the enemy.'

'They'll be caught in the bombardment...' began Fulgorin.

'Of course they will!' snapped Varr. 'Why do you think they sent us here?'

Fulgorin hesitated for a moment. He was an aristocrat, someone used to being respected, and he made a natural officer. But he still believed that the men of the 901st were human beings in the eyes of the Imperium.

'The greenskins'll kill us quicker than the damn bombs. Get to it!'

'Yes, sir!' Fulgorin ran across the palace grounds, yelling at the men to ready for the charge. If Fulgorin had ever been an Imperial Guard officer then he was an old-fashioned one who led from the front, taking his place among his men with his lasgun and bayonet. Troopers of the 901st braved the falling artillery to set up firepoints among the raised plant beds and splashed through ornamental ponds to take up firing positions on the banks. Thousands of men, thousands of guns, the drab green of their fatigues almost lost among the greenery. On the far side of the battlefield were the Warders, a small contingent of artillery that had escaped the first ork attack on Palatium. They were commanded by a noble-born officer that Varr had only spoken to over the vox – Lord Sovelin Falken, his name was, and Varr had little doubt that he would prove to be every bit as outclassed in battle as the officers who had been slaughtered in Palatium's streets. Varr could see the Warders' deep blue uniforms and colourful sashes from where he stood, and pick out the brass and silver of their gun mountings. They would not last long, he thought, but the 901st needed all the manpower they could get.

In front of the 901st and the Warders, the tree line of Nevermourn's jungle rose like a dark green curtain thirty metres high, its deep shadows giving way to the soaring fronds of the canopy like a roof spread over the world. It seethed with life, and as General Varr watched a torrent of creatures streamed from between its roots and branches, a dark cloud of birds, lizards and insects driven from the jungle.

The jungle knew what was storming through it to take the Wraithspire Palace.

The Wraithspire Palace, which the troops were defending, speared up from those jungles like a hand reaching for Vanqualis's turquoise sky. Wrought from the mightiest of the jungle's greatwood trees, enormously enlarged and moulded by some forgotten bioscientific technique, the Wraithspire Palace was the most spectacular man-made sight on Nevermourn. Its state rooms and audience chambers, nested like the chambers of a seashell, were hollowed from the living wood, and from the enormous spread of branches that ringed the palace like a collar hung chapels and private landing pads like ornate baubles. The Wraithspire Palace was a symbol of human mastery over the jungles and, had the greenskins not struck during the Trooping of the Warding Standard, many of House Falken's senior aristocrats would have been sheltering amid the palace's finery at that moment.

Shells burst against the side of the Wraithspire Palace, sending slabs of burning bark and shorn branches tumbling lethally into the palace grounds. Varr drew his own laspistol and took up position alongside his command squad as another man died within earshot, his screams mingling with the explosions overhead and the orders barking back and forth. The fallen trooper had been impaled by a falling branch and squirmed like a pinned insect, gore spurting.

Varr looked away. Once, a very long time ago, it had been hard to watch the deaths of his men. It still was, in a way, but he had come to understand that dying in the Emperor's service was a victory of sorts for the men of the 901st, and given the scale of the ork forces it might well be the only victory they could win.

Varr turned to his vox-operator, Mekrin. Mekrin's face was covered in knife-shaped black tattoos that doubled as urban camouflage and ganger markings. The first rule of the 901st was that you never asked what the other guy did to get sent here, but in Mekrin's case it was obvious.

'Where's Lieutenant Kullek?' Varr asked Mekrin.

'By the lake, sir,' replied Mekrin, the vox-set handset held tight to his ear. 'The one with the bridge. Says he's gonna race the men to a hundred greenskin ears.'

'Here,' said Varr, taking the handset. 'Kullek!' he yelled into it as more ordnance burst in the grounds, throwing clouds of dirt and tumbling bodies into the air.

'I can smell 'em, sir!' came the roar from Kullek. Varr peered through the falling earth and saw Kullek's mob, the Butchers, crowded around the shores of an ornamental lake with a bridge leading across it. He could even pick out Kullek himself, a bear-like man with a shaven head who seemed completely at home surrounded by a mob of murderers who aspired to match the depths of his brutality. Kullek's crime was no secret – he was a multiple murderer, a taker of skulls, a predator. He loved war.

'Pull your men back into the line, Kullek! We draw them in and catch them in a crossfire! Get firepoints to your flanks and bring your centre level with Trox's position!'

'Smell 'em, sir!' continued Kullek, as if he hadn't heard the general at all. 'Like... like livin' gone bad, like all them murders stood up and come to life! Gonna be a good one, lads! Gonna taste like all our old days at once!'

Varr could hear the Butchers roaring in agreement. There had been a time when Varr would have made a point of rooting out men like Kullek and having them executed before their savagery infected the rest of the regiment. But that was a different time, a different regiment, and now Kullek was one of the forces that held the 901st together.

Gunfire spattered from the tree line. 'Hold!' yelled Varr, hoping Kullek would pass the order on to his men and keep them from running off into the jungle. 'Kullek, get your men back, form a line and...'

A tremendous sound boomed from the jungle, a monstrous trumpeting accompanied by the crash of splintering trees. Varr saw the shadow of it first, a great blackness seething from the heart of the jungle. Then it burst out into the open air, mighty greatwood trees crushed before it, a horde of howling greenskins charging around its feet.

It was immense, maybe fifteen metres high, covered in shaggy matted hair. It was a four-legged creature with enormous tusks and a vast maw so crammed with teeth it couldn't close it. Violent red eyes flared with pain and anger, for on a platform precariously lashed to its back were scores of smaller greenskins goading it forward with spears. Its front legs ended in huge shovelling claws that lashed around it as it reared up, carving gouges from the ground and throwing orks aside.

Varr saw Kullek's Butchers break from cover and open fire, crimson las-blasts criss-crossing the zone of the destruction in front of the beast. Orks were pouring out of the jungle now, guns blazing, visibility cut by the volume of gunfire and shrapnel.

'Heavy weapons!' ordered Varr. 'Every big gun on the beast! Get Lord Falken's men to hit it with the artillery!'

Mekrin began to relay the order to the 901st's officers, and to Lord Falken on the far flank. The other troopers of Varr's command squad hunkered down with their guns up, ready to defend the general from the advancing orks – Shenshao with his plasma gun ready, even the medic Morn with his laspistol drawn. Varr himself drew his sword – not the power sword he had once wielded as a Guard commander, or even a chainsword, but a simple infantryman's blade he carried to distinguish himself in battle.

Gunfire sprayed up at the monster as the greenskins goaded it into the palace gardens, flowerbeds and stands of manicured trees disappearing beneath its claws. A missile streaked into it and blew a boulder-sized chunk of flesh from its shoulder, igniting the matted hair, but the damage was superficial and it would only make the beast angrier. It lowered its head and drove its lower jaw along the ground, churning up turf and soil, and wrenched its head back up flipping two or three troopers into its maw.

Varr's heart was pounding. He had no idea that anything like the orkish behemoth existed on Nevermourn. He hadn't been expecting it, and any plan he had for the defence of the Wraithspire Palace was falling apart in his mind. But he had reached his previous rank by being able to read a battle and react to its ebb and flow. He tried to do that now, even as Shenshao fired a plasma blast towards the indistinct forms of the greenskins rampaging through the 901st's forward line.

'Mekrin, get to Trox,' ordered Varr.

Mekrin fiddled with the various dials and switches on the vox-readout and passed the handset to Varr.

Trox, inevitably, was praying. '…from the Throne on high, for He who watches us in our wretchedness, for Him do we seek redemption in the blood of His foes…'

'Trox!' shouted Varr into the handset. 'Fall back to the palace gates!'

'The xenos are amongst us, general!' came the reply, Trox's throaty preacher's voice quavering with fervour. 'The Great Beast looks upon us and hungers!'

'Fall back and give them the centre, that's an order!'

Varr's guts were knotted. He had known that this would be a hard fight, one they might not win. The beast was one thing, but the sheer number of the orks was the real deciding factor – hundreds were already among the 901st, duelling in point-blank firefights or leaping among the troops, cleavers rising and falling. He could see men dying amid the carnage and clouds of fire and debris, here one with his torso blown apart by ork gunfire, there a man dismembered and held high by his orkish killer like a gory standard for the other aliens to rally around. Falken's flank was embattled, too, the artillery firing sporadic bursts of mortar shots over the battlefield as the loaders fended orks off the gun with bayonets and autogun fire.

Then, Varr saw the ork warlord amid the chaos. The warlord was substantially larger than any other greenskin – Varr understood that orks tended to grow larger and stronger as they achieved battlefield successes and that the biggest of them were invariably the leaders, creating a cycle that resulted in truly immense killing machines leading the orkish hordes. But the warlord wasn't a hollering, battle-lusting killer like the other orks now rampaging through the palace grounds – he moved with grim determination, stalking through his own lines, observing the flow of the battle in much the same way as Varr himself was doing. The warlord had a crude mechanical arm and had the tiny, sharp-faced creatures – gretchin, some of the Guard called them, or grots – scampering around his feet, but it was the warlord's glowering presence that struck Varr. This was not just a horde that wanted to kill and destroy. The warlord wanted something more than simple destruction.

The 901st were falling back. Varr could actually hear Trox preaching, bellowing the praises of the Emperor even as his grenade launcher punched glittering bursts of shrapnel through the charging orks. The men were scrambling back over the cratered, scarred mess the palace grounds had become, keeping up lasgun fire with the battleground discipline that Varr had tried so hard to instil in them.

The waves of greenskins were blunted by the storms of fire but they kept pressing, the gargantuan creature ripping its way through the orna-mental lake and crunching through its bridge as the orks forced the 901st back towards the doors of the Wraithspire Palace.

It wouldn't work. Varr could see it, even as he gave the order for the flanks to push up and surround the orks, catch them in a crossfire at the palace threshold. There were too many orks, and they were filling the palace grounds like water filling a chalice, fighting through one another to get to grips with the 901st. The huge shaggy beast was out of control now, rampaging through the 901st towards Lord Falken's artillery. Varr had little regard for Falken, who after all was a part of the planetary defence force that had so spectacularly failed to blunt the invasion of Palatium – but even so the idea of the behemoth trampling its way through the Warders turned Varr's blood cold.

Varr's thoughts were broken in a rush of movement and noise. His flank surged forwards and the orks turned to face them, roaring with appreciation that the 901st was giving them a proper battle. Lasgun stocks shattered under ork cleavers. Las-blasts bored through gnarled green flesh. Heads were struck from bodies, torsos were blown open by bursts of gunfire, corpses were trampled underfoot. The 901st roared as they charged but the orks drowned them out with discordant battle-cries.

Through the devastation a massive dark shape loomed towards Varr. Varr shot it through the eye with his laspistol but another one followed it, bringing an ugly serrated blade down at him. Varr caught it on his own sword but his blade shattered under the ork's assault and Varr was on his back, rolling under what seemed to be a tonne of writhing orkish muscle. He jammed the broken blade into the back of the ork's head and felt it spasm as it died. Varr rolled the stinking body off him in time to be almost blinded by a plasma blast fired by Shenshao into the face of an ork following up to kill Varr on the ground.

The ork's charred body toppled into the mud and Morn grabbed Varr's collar, dragging him free as las-fire sprayed over their position, fending off the charging greenskins.

'Anythin' need fixin'?' asked Morn.

Morn's grin showed a mouth full of missing or blackened teeth, and the man's skin was so lined it looked like it was covered in knife scars. His thinning hair was straggly and grey, and Varr once again marvelled that Morn was alive at all, let alone a medic.

'Not yet,' gasped Varr and got to his feet, snapping shots off at the hulking orks looming through the thickening smoke and showers of falling debris. The troopers of the 901st were crowded more densely around Varr's position beside the main trunk of the palace, and Varr knew that many of them were meeting their redemption there in bursts of gunfire or welters of blood, or suffocated down in the mud under bodies and trampling feet.

An ork flamethrower incinerated a trooper standing just a few metres away, sending him tumbling to the floor, spreading guttering flame along the churned turf. Blood sprayed over Varr as another man was carved open by an ork cleaver, and across the battlefield the behemoth trumpeted as it threw a dozen Vanqualian Warders into the air with a toss of its immense head.

They were all going to die there. A new clarity came over Varr's mind and the carnage seemed to slow down around him. This was his punishment. He had been sent to Nevermourn to die. It really was that simple.

A roar of engines streaked overhead. Varr just saw twisting contrails rippling through the air above him, coiled through with leaves torn from the branches of the Wraithspire Palace. A split second later the explosions kicked in, chains of deafening impacts that sent enormous columns of pulverised earth and broken greenskin bodies high into the air.

Lieutenant Fulgorin tumbled into cover beside Varr. His face was streaked with blood

'What in the hells was that?' he asked breathlessly.

'Thunderhawks,' said Varr, unable to keep the note of wonderment out of his voice.

The canyon-like street of the hive was crowded with people, silent in their mourning, thousands of pale faces turned up in pleading towards the countess as she passed. Palace guards carried her aloft on a palanquin, her attendant children skulking along beneath the platform carrying the various elements of the juvenat equipment, which invigorated her ancient body when she was forced to travel outside the security of her pinnacle chambers. The children had the customary strange, feral look in their eyes and they hissed at the crowds, snapping at the ankles of the palace guards carrying their mistress as if jealous of them.

Countess Ismenissa could see the tears in the eyes of the citizens watching her pass by, and with a faint nod of her head gave silent approval for their vigil. All over the city they were out in the streets, clogging all the hive's thoroughfares in their billions, silently praying for deliverance. This was the way of Vanqualis's commoners – stoicism and acceptance, their sorrow always silent, their fate always accepted. Tragedy was kept within.

'They're killing us!' cried a solitary man's voice from the crowds. 'What are you going to do? What will save us?' The voice was silenced as the crowd rippled around the protestor and he was cut short in a mercifully brief flurry of punches and kicks.

The palace guards shoved the crowds aside and carried the countess through the sea of longing faces into the entrance hall of the Basilica Praector. The basilica, like much of the hive, was built in the style favoured by Vanqualis's founders – pious and industrious, solid dark steel girders and mesh floors embellished with columns and devotional plaques. The whole city spoke of labour and prayer, the two activities that should make up the whole of a commoner's existence.

The senior archivist hurried from among the towering data-stacks that filled the Basilica's main dome. His long, aged face bobbed above the data-slate that had replaced his hands, constantly spooling out a stream of printed parchment. He bowed as best he could, his nib-tipped fingers scribbling information down as he spoke.

'Countess,' he said hurriedly. 'I had not thought, with the current situation... I had not believed that you would be here... that is, to attend personally...'

'This is a matter I must see to myself,' replied the countess. The children scuttled to their places behind her as she stepped down off the palanquin, the palace guards in their brocade and finery shouldering their riot shields. 'When our very world is at stake, one can trust only oneself.'

'Of course,' replied the archivist. Behind him a gaggle of other archivists, some of them even more aged and bent with their hands and faces replaced with writing or sorting devices, hurried around the data-stacks. Above them, the black-clad soldiers of the Archive Regiment walked the tops of the stacks, their carbines ready to defend the precious historical information. With war and chaos looming, every institution on Herograve was on high alert.

'You will wish to see the document,' continued the archivist.

'I will,' said the countess.

The archivist led the countess between the stacks, the children scurrying behind carrying the long trailing hem of her dress and the juvenat units connected to her by cables through the back of her bodice. The archivist did his best to hide his revulsion at the dead children shambling and crawling along, but the countess was the only person who had ever really got used to their presence.

The data-stacks were crammed with thin black sheets of crystal, the medium on which the commoner authorities of Herograve's cities recorded their histories and decisions. House Falken, however, used the more reliable and traditional method of illuminated tomes, created by house retainers whose lives were spent recording the words and needs of Vanqualis's nobles. These tomes were contained deep within the refrigerated heart of the basilica, where the cold created a layer of freezing vapour underfoot and the shelves glowered with endless lines of heavy books, some of them many hundreds of years old.

The book that Countess Ismenissa sought was in a void-safe in a small clearing among the stacks, held aloft by a pair of winged steel cherubs.

'The safe is gene-locked, countess,' explained the archivist. 'I cannot open it. Such a thing would be above my station.'

A look of mild distaste came over the countess's face. She disliked any activity that might damage or violate the physical form she had kept in good repair for so many centuries. Nevertheless, these were extreme times. She ran a finger over the reader on the top of the safe, wincing as the tiny laser pulse drew a drop of blood from her finger. The micro-cogitator inside whirred for a moment, trying to unravel the countess's genetic code from the jumble of age-reversing drugs in her system.

The void-safe slid open and the countess took out the slim, steel-bound book inside. The cover was engraved with the twin symbols of the serpent and the griffon, emblems of House Falken and of those who owed House Falken a debt.

'This document is one of our most precious house relics,' said the archivist. 'Though some are older, none of them are of such importance to…'

The countess silenced him with a look, before opening the cover. Pages of flexible crystal covered in shining, flowing script slid past her as she turned them. They spoke of honour, of oaths so crucial they were sacred, binding the authors to the soil of Vanqualis and the soul of House Falken. They were powerful words, and in the darkness on the edge of the Imperium it was rare indeed to find honour held so deeply.

The final page bore two signatures. One was that of Heradane Falken, a mighty noble lord from decades past who reigned when Nevermourn was still largely untamed and Herograve's cities were just scrapes in the dirt, struggling to find a foothold on Vanqualis. The other was that of a man named Orlando Furioso, his mark embellished with the symbols of the eagle and the griffon.

'I had never looked upon it till now,' said the countess quietly. 'I wonder now if I really believed it was true.'

'It is in order?' asked the archivist.

'Of course it is,' snapped the countess. 'The house's retainers spent years crafting every word. And honour of this strength allows no failure. I had to see it for myself before I could really understand the debt I was to call in.'

'Then, countess, what is your decision?'

The countess paused for a moment, running her age-dried fingers over the signatures. 'Bring forth the astropath,' she said.

The palace guards muscled forwards a lean man in shackles, his face dominated by the yawning hollow sockets where his eyes had once been. Symbols were incised into the pale skin of his cheeks and shaven scalp and they glowed faintly, as if power smouldered within the man. His hands and feet were shackled and he wore black robes marked in crimson.

The countess despised witches, as did all Vanqualis's Emperor-fearing folk. But an astropath, though psychic, was the only communication with the Imperium at large. The dead eyes of the countess's children followed the astropath as he approached. The countess stroked the head of the nearest child as if comforting it in the presence of the hated witch.

'I must have a second message sent,' said the countess. 'It must be received, and quickly, but the symbols given are very precise and the receiving astropath must be powerful indeed. I expect it to be received and acted on with all haste, so inaccuracies will not be accepted. Understood?'

'Understood,' said the astropath, shivering in the cold. 'But you are as aware as I am that our art cannot be precise. The call for help I sent out two months ago was only received by a few, and only the 901st Legion was close enough to act. To reach a specific recipient, in addition, requires a great deal of power and skill, and the most precise symbolic discipline on both ends. Our isolation here means that...'

'It means you must do better,' snapped the countess. 'You have one purpose here, and that is to connect us to the Imperium outside. I had expected our call for help to bring forth the Imperial Guard and Navy, not the smattering of criminals that were sent in their stead. Now you have a chance to redeem yourself for that failure. This message will get through. Vanqualis will accept nothing less.'

'Of course, my lady,' said the astropath grimly.

'The message,' said the countess, 'is that Vanqualis is doomed by the orkish scourge and the Imperium has sent us nothing but a gaggle of criminals to defend us. House Falken of Vanqualis is therefore compelled to call in an ancient and grave honour debt. I do not take this step lightly, but I take it in the name of House Falken and all the peoples of Vanqualis. Without help, we shall all surely perish and the unholy xenos will have dragged another world from the Emperor's light.'

'It shall be done, countess,' said the astropath. 'To whom is this message to be sent?'

The countess held the document in front of the astropath and he ran his fingers over it, his psychic near-sense reading the script on its crystal pages. They told him of the exact details of the debt, and the people who owed it.

His mouth hung open. Had he still possessed eyes, they would have been wide in wonderment, and not a little fear.

'Can it be done?'

'It can, countess,' gulped the astropath. 'It is a strenuous task to communicate so urgently across the gulf of the immaterium, but as you say, their own astropaths will surely be of the highest quality.'

'Then again, I will accept no failure,' said the countess. She snapped the document shut and put it back in the void-safe. 'Now that the decision has been made, I must return to the people. They must see their countess unafraid.' The palace guard brought forth her palanquin and she was conveyed back through the basilica to where the huge crowds held their endless vigil, expressing their fears and hopes with the silence appropriate to the commoner.

The astropath knelt on the floor of the basilica, visualising the images that formed the coded message to be received and decoded by another of his kind far across the interstellar gulf.

The debt had been called in. There would be no going back now. If Vanqualis survived, it would be because honour had overcome the brutality of the xenos. It was a slim thread on which to hang the hopes of a world, but when the Imperium was so distant and the enemy was so close, it was all Vanqualis had.

'What of the times when the enemy is stronger, in body or in numbers?'

'No xenos is more cunning than humanity. No traitor has the courage of the pious.'

– Daenyathos, *Catechisms Martial*

CHAPTER FOUR

The Thunderhawks roared over in another pass. Heavy bolter fire was stuttering down, kicking up crescent sprays of dark ork blood. Varr could see the Thunderhawk gunships banking, their nose-mounted heavy bolters boring streaks of fire down into the orks as their engines kept them hovering above the battlefield. They were painted dark purple and he caught a symbol on the tailplane of one – a golden chalice. Varr wasn't familiar with the Chapter, but he had served in Imperial armies long enough to know what the gunships' appearance meant.

Space Marines. The Adeptus Astartes.

Following the long space voyage after receiving Vanqualis's distress call, the 901st had been on Nevermourn for two weeks, and Varr had always known that if the full force of the ork horde ever hit them the 901st would fall and Vanqualis would be lost. Now, for the first time, it looked like Vanqualis might be worth fighting for after all.

One gunship swooped low, behind the mass of orks crowded in front of the palace gates. The Thunderhawk's side doors slid open and bolter fire chattered out. One Space Marine leaned out, bare-headed, and pointed down at a space in the throng with his lightning claw. The Thunderhawk tipped almost onto its side and maybe twenty Space Marines dropped out, bolt pistols blazing and chainswords raised up ready to strike.

'Astartes!' shouted one of the 901st's soldiers. 'Tears of the Throne! They've sent in the Astartes!'

The effect on the soldiers was instant. Even these impious criminals had heard of the Space Marines, either as figures of the Emperor's wrath in preachers' sermons or as whispered soldierly legends. They said a Space Marine could do anything – rip a man apart with his bare hands, live forever, take on the most horrible aliens and win. Some didn't believe they really existed, but treated them as a symbol of the power the Emperor instilled in His citizens. Others spoke of them as the soldiers who fought the battles that really mattered, far away from the pits of war where the Penal Legions were sent to die.

Now they were here, fighting alongside the 901st.

For a moment Varr could only watch them, the gunships firing streams of explosive death into the orks as their payloads of huge, armoured Space Marines made ready to drop into the fray. Then the officer in him took over again.

'All fronts advance!' he yelled. He held his broken sword high, standing clear of cover so as many men could see him as possible. 'Charge!'

'Who are they?' asked Sarpedon over the vox, trying to block out the roar of the Thunderhawk's engine. Through the open door beside him swung the view of the battlefield – the handsome grounds in the shadow of the Wraithspire Palace, now seething with a mass of orks and the thin cordon of soldiers trying to contain them.

'Not the Guard exactly,' replied Lygris, his voice transmitted from the *Brokenback* in orbit over Nevermourn. 'There are a couple of troop transports in deep system space, staying out of the way. Looks like the Penal Legions. The Chapter archive won't have any records.'

'I'm not surprised,' said Sarpedon. Penal Legions rarely lasted long enough to amass a regimental history – they were sent into the teeth of vicious conflicts and were considered fortunate if they existed in any form afterwards. 'This is the Imperial response?'

'Looks like all of it,' said Lygris. 'There isn't much in the way of military build-up here. Vanqualis is lucky to have what has turned up.'

Sarpedon looked down at the motley collection of killers and criminals, united only by their mud-spattered dark green uniforms and their collective failure to serve the Imperium.

'They're here to die,' said Sarpedon, more to himself than to Lygris. 'This is their punishment.'

'Engaging!' came Luko's voice over the vox, against a backdrop of clashing blades and gunfire.

Soul Drinkers units were making landfall among the orks, taking the greenskins by surprise. Sarpedon could see the shockwaves rippling through the mass of orks as they turned to face the threat suddenly boring through them.

'Take us down!' Sarpedon shouted and the gunship banked low, fire stuttering down from its nose and door mountings. Sarpedon glanced back into the passenger compartment – Squads Salk and Graevus were unhooking themselves from their grav-restraints, bolters ready. Sergeant Salk was rapidly earning the status of a veteran among Sarpedon's most trusted officers, and Graevus led his assault squad with a quiet authority that contrasted with the brutality and skill with which he wielded his power axe. Graevus was also one of the more obviously mutated members of the Chapter – one of his hands was grotesquely huge and taloned, a fleshy vice that let him wield the bulky power axe one-handed as lightly as a fencer's sword.

Sarpedon could see the off-white glint of orkish tusks amid the gnarled green flesh, even the hateful red eyes and spatters of human blood on their blades. He could smell the stink of ork sweat and blood.

'Go!' he shouted. He had his force staff gripped in both hands as he pushed himself out of the Thunderhawk on his mutated legs, the mass of orks sweeping up towards him. Salk and Graevus followed, bolters chattering even as they fell.

Sarpedon took the fury inside him built up over a lifetime of battles, first the wrath at the Imperium's foes, then his rage at the Imperium itself that had betrayed and tried to destroy his Chapter. He took it all, concentrated it until it was white-hot, and let it flood out of his mind, around the spiralling aegis circuit of his armour, and out into the reality around him.

Sarpedon was the most powerful psyker the Soul Drinkers Chapter had ever fielded. He had no finesse, no fine control, but he made up for that in raw power.

His hate flooded out of him, and a great many orks learned for the first time what fear really was.

General Glaivan Varr had never fought in a battle like the one the 901st fought for the Wraithspire Palace, and he was grateful for it. He had seen many terrible, soul-scarring things, especially at the Eye of Terror where he had held his last command as a free Guard officer. But none of them could quite compare to the vast, dark figures that strode over the battlefield, more imposing than even the Wraithspire Palace itself. Their bodies were made of shadow and their eyes burned with purple flames. Fire leapt between them, as if a hellish reality were layered over the battlefield, somewhere populated with figures crafted from pure fear. Their hunched shapes and violent eyes, and the splintered maws which opened up in their faces, gave them the looks of malevolent orkish gods, come down to punish the greenskins.

Varr had witnessed enough psykers using their powers on the battlefield, and yet the spectacle had still struck fear into him on a primal level. The effect on the orks was astonishing. A terrible wailing went up from the orks, something Varr had never heard before. He saw green-skins running, and volleys of gunfire cutting them down.

'They've got the greenskins scared!' shouted Varr as loud as he could. All around him the men of the 901st were pressing forward, and Varr was well aware that he was one of the few factors keeping them going. 'Put them to the blade! Put them to the gun! Show them why the Emperor sent you here!'

The battle was a blur. Varr was aware of the fighting around him, of hot ork blood spraying up his arm, of a rusted combat knife in his hand in place of his discarded sword hilt. Part of him registered the flame-thrower-wielding ork who fell, its face blasted open by Varr's pistol, and Varr's command squad falling on it to finish it off. Another part saw the arcs of fire streaking from the centre of the battle where the Space Marines were laying waste to the ork centre, and how the orks weren't charging towards the 901st's troops now – they were fleeing into them, throwing themselves into firefields and bayonet lines to get away from the Astartes assault.

But most of Varr simply marvelled. He couldn't direct the battle any more – he had set it in motion and done everything he could to direct the men well, but now it would unfold on its own. There had been a time when Varr could manage every unit and every manoeuvre of his regiments, when he was leading seasoned and disciplined men who treated his words as that of the Emperor. But the 901st were not those men, and Varr's role now was to fight with them and lend what he could to the battle with pistol and knife.

The huge shaggy monster that had so nearly broken Lord Falken's artillery was rampaging through its own lines now, driven mad with the psychic fear looming over the battlefield. Even the monster was overshadowed by the huge dark shapes, and in terror it had thrown off the gretchin goading it and was trampling orks beneath its huge front claws. The Thunderhawks were hovering over the battlefield and firing streams of fire into it, blasting one side raw and bloody, and Varr could glimpse broken bones jutting up through the mass of gory muscle.

The beast fell, and what resolve was left in the ork push fell apart. The 901st surged forwards over the ground that the centre had given up and Varr saw Kullek, somehow still alive, he and his butchers taking on the orks at their own game of close-quarters murder.

'Trox, Kullek, take the centre forward! The whole line will advance to the tree line! Fulgorin, hold the rear!' Varr wasn't sure who had shouted the order until he realised that it was him.

'A thousand, give or take,' said Mekrin matter-of-factly. 'Another five hundred will be dead before we move out.'

Varr looked out across the lines of Imperial dead. Fifteen hundred sinners had done the Emperor's work for the first time in their lives, by dying. That left about five thousand in the 901st and Vanqualian Warder artillery. If the line had not held, there would have been far fewer left to carry on the fight.

Varr turned to Lord Sovelin Falken, who shared the makeshift command post in a reception chamber just off the entrance hall of the Wraithspire Palace. The place was spectacular, the living wood trained into decorative swirls and staircases spiralling up through the trunk, but its majesty was dulled by the drab-uniformed penal troopers using it to regroup and treat their wounded.

'Your men took a mauling,' said Varr.

'I cannot deny that,' said Sovelin. He was a young man, slightly too pasty to look like a real soldier. He was always moving, too, his eyes darting and his hands wringing.

'Half your planet's inhabitable land is covered in jungle and your men weren't trained to fight in it.'

Falken looked as if he might bristle at that, but his pride had taken enough of a battering at Palatium to let him swallow it for the moment. 'The Warders were founded to defend the cities of Herograve and put down uprisings by its commoners. Nevermourn was our haven. There was no need to defend it.'

'A haven? It's the underbelly, Falken! Herograve's covered by orbital defences, enough to put off any invader. But the jungles have nothing, and once the greenskins reach the coast it is just a short hop across the sea and they'll be in your cities. Nevermourn was begging to be invaded–'

'Do you think I don't know that, Varr?' snapped Falken. 'This planet has been alone for centuries. The only outsiders we ever saw were Administratum collectors come to take away our tithes. Is it any surprise we ended up blind to the outside?' Some of Falken's surviving artillerymen were tending their own wounded in the palace entrance hall, their blue uniforms spattered with mud and blood, their brocade and uniform brasses dull. 'I saw Palatium die. I know what our failures were.'

Varr didn't need to ask Falken to elaborate. He had seen more planets fall to ignorance and complacency than to the brilliance of an enemy commander. 'How many Warder regiments got out of Palatium?' he asked.

Falken shrugged. 'Mine. Apart from that, some civilians who might make it to the coast.'

'That's it?'

'The greenskins knew just when to hit us.'

'And the Space Marines knew just when to hit them,' said Varr. 'The Space Marines are the best soldiers in this galaxy. This world isn't lost yet.'

'My world is,' said Falken, and Varr could see in the nobleman's face that he considered the responsibility for the fall of Palatium to fall on his own shoulders. 'I have men wounded, I should see to them.'

Falken headed off to where his Warder artillerymen were patching up their wounds. The 901st and the Warders were not mixing, which was understandable since in every sense they came from very different worlds. Elsewhere Varr could see Brother Trox preaching to a group of men whom he had adopted as disciples. Trox was deeply religious and had been some kind of a preacher before he had been condemned. As ever the exact nature of his crime was a secret but the rumours tended towards something to do with women. Trox had a haunted look in his hollow eyes as if he was certain the Emperor's wrath would fall upon him at any moment, and his followers gradually ended up the same, fatalistic and grim, not caring much if they lived through the next battle.

For a moment Varr wondered if these men were really alive at all in the eyes of the Emperor, or if they were just marching through drawn-out deaths to make their existence worthwhile. They included Varr himself, of course – maybe he was already dead, and he had simply not found an appropriately reverent way to die yet.

'General!' called someone behind him. Varr turned to see the Space Marine walking in through the palace's grand doors and into the command post. None of Varr's command squad or officers dared to challenge the new arrival – the Space Marine's incongruous size and the heraldry of his power armour gave him an air of power that simply brushed men away from him. It was the Astartes that Varr had seen leaping from the Thunderhawk, still wearing his lightning claws blackened with scorched orkish blood. His helmet was still off – his hair was shaven into a single dark strip down the middle of his scalp and instead of the stern granite face Varr expected of the Emperor's finest, he had a wide face that broke easily into a triumphant grin. 'Captain Luko of the Soul Drinkers. We sent those greenskin vermin packing, did we not?'

Varr returned Luko's greeting with a slightly bitter smile of his own. 'I don't know how much we had to do with it. I am not afraid to admit that we were lost until your battle-brothers waded in.'

'Commander Sarpedon sent me,' continued Luko. 'The gunships have taken a pass over the tree line. It looks like the orks have retreated into the jungle and are regrouping.'

'So they'll be back.'

'That they will.'

'We've blunted them, though, and that's more than they expected. I suggest we take the chance to fall back in good order. Give them the palace and find another point to defend. The orks will be heading for the coast so we make them pay for every step they take.'

'Sarpedon agrees.' Luko indicated the battlefield outside the palace doors. The grounds of the Wraithspire Palace were heaped with green-skin dead. 'There can only be so many of them, eh?'

Varr had imagined that Space Marines would all be grim, devout warrior-monks but Luko had something like savage joy in him. Maybe Luko actually enjoyed what happened on the battlefield – Varr couldn't imagine anyone actually looking forward to battle, but then Space Marines were said to be the perfect soldiers.

'There are always more,' said Varr. 'That's how the greenskins fight. Always more of them. The Guardsmen used to say they grew out of the ground, just to spite us.'

'Then we'll kill them faster than they can grow them,' replied Luko. 'How long before you can move out?'

Varr glanced back at his men. 'If we take all the wounded, an hour. I can't speak for Lord Falken's men, but they'll just have to keep up.'

'What are your numbers like?'

'In total, just under five thousand men plus some armour. The jungle won't make supply any easier but I can keep them going for long enough.'

'That's five thousand more soldiers than the orks were expecting,' said Luko. 'The 901st fought well today, general. These are some tough men you have here.'

'We are scum, captain.'

'That's what I said. And the ork might never retreat for long, but he can be killed. As you said, we draw them in, kill them off, and by the time we reach the coast there won't be enough left to hit Herograve.'

'I wish I shared your confidence, captain. The truth is that my men have been condemned to death and the 901st was sent here to die. We weren't selected to defend Vanqualis because of our skills in battle, that's for sure – we were the only unit close enough to the Obsidian system when Vanqualis sent out the distress call. I knew two weeks ago that this was not a particularly winnable campaign. With your Chapter here that has changed, but my men are still here on Vanqualis as a punishment.'

Luko stepped closer and Varr felt dwarfed by the size and presence of the Space Marine. 'No. You were sent here to save this planet. If you think these men can serve their Emperor by dying, think how much better they can serve Him by surviving.'

'All respect,' said Varr, 'you do not know what it means to be declared beyond the Emperor's light. Many of these men are looking for death.'

'Then you will command them to survive,' replied Luko. 'And do not presume to know what the Soul Drinkers have gone through.'

Varr was not in the habit of backing down, but somewhere inside him he knew that Luko could be right. There was more than just pun-ishment facing him and his men. Perhaps there was some redemption on Vanqualis for the men of the 901st Penal Legion. Not the nebulous, abstract thing the preachers spoke about – actual, honest-to-Throne redemption that washed away your past. 'Then we'll be with you,' said Varr.

'If,' said Luko slyly, 'you can keep up.'

'Is that a challenge, captain?'

'Only if you accept it.'

'Then we have a deal. The 901st will put the Space Marines to shame.'

'And the Space Marines will show the 901st how to fight.' Luko held out his gauntleted hand. Varr shook it, acutely aware that Luko had to take care not to crush the man's hand.

'We move out in an hour,' confirmed Luko. 'I hope the greenskins enjoy their new palace. Your men made sure they paid enough for it.'

Luko walked off back towards where the Soul Drinkers were mustered, among the smouldering craters and heaped dead of the palace grounds where they were watching for the orks to return.

'One thing,' said Varr.

'General?'

'The witchcraft.'

Luko grunted a laugh. 'Commander Sarpedon is a powerful psyker, General Varr. He takes what he thinks the enemy will fear and throws it out there, a hundred metres high. Usually works, too.'

'My men are a superstitious lot. They'll say psykers are bad luck.'

'Bad luck it is,' replied Luko, turning again to leave. 'For the orks.'

The humans had thrown the orks back into the jungle and slain the huge monster that the horde had driven before it. Death and destruction had come with the humans, and worse things besides – gods. The gods of the greenskins, suddenly angry at the orks. They had loomed over the battlefield, dark and terrible, but instead of roaring their approval at the bloodshed they had spat down wordless curses and refused to crush the weakling humans.

The orks skulked through the jungle, thousands of creatures lurking in the dense undergrowth among the mud and vermin. Word passed rapidly about what they had seen, their gods turned against them, the humans breaking the charge of the unbeatable horde. Anger and fear were like a disease, spreading from ork to ork in an instant. Guns flared in the darkness. Blades flicked into the shadows and came out wet with blood. That fear and anger turned an ork against its fellow greenskin, started brawls, started wars, and enough orkish worlds had burned because the orks turned on themselves.

Crude, brutal voices were raised, barking the base insults that made up the bulk of the ork language. One mighty ork, a scarred warrior with one eye missing and dozens of kill-trophies hanging from rings stuck through its skin, bellowed its rage through the jungle. Other voices were raised, now emboldened. Bones were broken and scores settled. Dissatisfaction rippled out and for a moment it felt like the horde would surely fracture.

A mechanical hand closed around the mighty ork's head. He had not seen the massive shadow looming behind him, silent and glowering. The rusted, bloodstained steel claw closed around its skull, the thick bone fracturing. Its remaining eye popped out and its teeth shattered, spilling from its mouth before its head crunched flat and the claw let go. The ringleader slid down into the mud. Insects, smelling blood and brains, scrabbled over its ruined skull.

The warlord stepped out into the open. Las-burns, like charred craters in his skin, still smouldered. Silver glinted where a bayonet had broken off unnoticed in his shoulder. His mechanical parts were slathered in greasy mud and gore, steaming with the heat of the engines built into his chest.

He reached down into the mud and picked up the veteran's body, its head a twisted mess. The warlord shook the body like a rag doll and threw it down again, stamping on it and shattering its ribs in an insult so crude even the most blunt-minded ork could not fail to get the message.

The warlord was in charge. His goal was the goal of the horde, and of every ork there. He was a creature of vision, a creature of drive and willpower that none of them possessed. Without him, the orks would never have left the Garon Nebula, and would still be squabbling over meaningless feuds waiting for a warrior to rise and lead them onto something greater. Without him, they would be nothing. Only the warlord understood how to make the orks more than mere animals, only he knew how to take away what the humans loved and inflict that which they feared.

He barked his anger at the orks, who fell prostrate before him or scrabbled out of sight. The slaves who followed him melted away into the undergrowth, tiny beady eyes watching him with fear, for they knew he was willing to kill again and again if that was what he had to do to make his will known. The warlord might be more than an animal, more than an ork, but that did not mean he had ever shown anything like mercy or leniency. He was more ruthless than the most bloodthirsty of his orks, for his killing was driven by more than just the joy of battle and the desire to be strong.

The gods had not come to the battlefield to taunt the orks. It was a trick! It was a lie spun by the humans! For that was what humans did, they won by lies and trickery, baser than the cruellest slave-creature. The ork gods were watching them, and they had not come down to lend them strength because the orks did not deserve it. They had fallen upon

Palatium when its defenders were unawares, and then been thrown back by the unexpected arrival of the humans' armoured elites. They had done nothing to deserve the presence of the gods, for good or ill. They were nothing yet, and only when they had proven their worth in the burning cities of Vanqualis would the gods even deign to spit upon them.

The warlord ceased his ranting. How many of the orks understood what drove him? Very few. Perhaps none of them. But as long as they fought for him, it did not matter.

He strode through the undergrowth, kicking slaves out from underneath his feet. He could see, through the trees, the battlefield in front of the enormous palace the orks had tried to capture. The orks rarely bothered with burying their dead so the warlord paid no mind to the heaps of ork bodies piled up around the ruined palace gardens. What made him growl and glower were the armoured forms among the carnage, the human elites, who had snatched a victory away from him. They had struck from above like lightning, and destroyed the victory that the warlord had all but grasped. The false gods aside, they had used strength and skill to defeat the orks, and that was what offended the warlord the most. These armoured warriors had not tricked him or led his army astray – they had simply been too strong for his orks. It was that simple. None of the horde would ever admit it, but it was true. These purple-armoured humans, much taller and far braver than any other human he had fought, had beaten the warlord in a straight fight.

From the depths of the jungle, the low booms of distant explosions shook the canopy overhead. More roks and crude ork spacecraft were making landfall, depositing thousands more orks into the jungles. The warlord had brought many tribes with him, far more than had participated in the strike on Palatium. The destruction of the city had been about timing, throwing the forward elements of his horde at the humans when their guard was down. The conquest of the jungle, and the destruction of this planet's cities, would be about numbers, willpower and strength. That was the battle he had forged his horde to win. He had been on the planet for more than sixty days and nights, and it was only the force of his will that had kept the horde together while the main bulk of it was deposited in the jungle.

When the whole horde came to grips with the humans, even the armoured warriors and their witchcraft would not save them. Then, the whole of Vanqualis would burn.

'How must we honour our fallen?'
    'With every bullet and every blade, with every moment of victory and pain.'

– Daenyathos, *Catechisms Martial*

CHAPTER FIVE

The ork ship tumbled in a bright fiery arc towards Vanqualis, far more graceful in destruction than it had ever been in life. The guns that bristled from the twisted prow of the *Brokenback* threw a further volley of lance fire and ordnance shells into the ork wreck and it came apart, spilling ribbons of burning fuel and vented gases as it dissolved into thousands of chunks of flaming wreckage.

'Not enough,' said Lygris to himself. The sight through the great bridge viewscreen was astonishing but there were plenty more ork craft in the invasion fleet and the *Brokenback*, formidable as it was, simply couldn't destroy them all. In any case their real damage had been done – they had disgorged smaller landers, and even hollowed-out asteroids, to bring hordes of greenskins down to the planet's surface.

The bridge of the *Brokenback* was dark, so Lygris could concentrate on the image from the viewscreen. Lygris knew the ship so well he could control most of its systems from the command pulpit that faced the screen. Everything was lined in the screen's harsh light, dense shadows were cast every time another explosion burst amid the wreckage of the ork ship. Lights winked on the data-lecterns dotted around the bridge and in the cogitators and data-engines under the grille of the deck.

'How goes the battle, Techmarine?' came the voice of Chaplain Iktinos.

Lygris was surprised that the skull-faced Chaplain had remained on the *Brokenback* – Iktinos had elected to lead the reserve force of a hundred or so Soul Drinkers, who would be sent down to Vanqualis in case the main force could not react to a threat in time. 'Good. But not well enough.' Lygris waved a hand dismissively at the image of the ork ship breaking up. 'There are many more like this and most of them have already served their purpose. The jungle is too dense for us support the battle on the ground. We're just cleaning up here, the real war is on Vanqualis.'

'And the rest of the Obsidian system?'

'The orks only seem to care about Vanqualis itself.' Lygris pressed a few keys on the command pulpit's instrument array, and called up a diagram of the Obsidian system on the main screen.

The closest planet to its sun was Proxiphan, a dead, scorched ball of rock, then the boiling firestorm of the gas giant Infernis Magna. A great gulf of space separated Infernis Magna from Vanqualis itself, the only planet in the system with a significant population. Beyond Vanqualis was Voiderhome, a small rocky world that saw exploration from the early colonists of Vanqualis before they discovered there was nothing on Voiderhome but suffocation and cold. The final planet in the Obsidian system was Tyrancos, another gas giant, orbited by a few refineries and processing plants built in an attempt to draw some wealth from the titanic blue-green mass of the planet. Beyond Tyrancos there was just Ollanius XIV, the monitoring station that had seen the Battlefleet Scaephan annihilated at dock by the first ork attacks.

'What is here that the greenskins want?' wondered Iktinos aloud.

'What do they ever want? Conquest and battle.'

'And there isn't anything to conquer in the system other than Vanqualis?'

'It appears so.'

'Then this system would seem a strange choice of destination. There is only one planet's worth of slaughter here for the orks.'

'Perhaps,' said Lygris. 'But then greenskins aren't known for strategy. Maybe the Obsidian system was the first place they came to.'

Lygris's vox chimed. 'Bridge here,' he said.

'Techmarine Lygris, we're picking up a communication,' came the reply. It was one of the Chapter's scouts, manning the comms helm towards the hulk's prow.

'From Vanqualis?'

'No, sir. Tyrancos.'

Lygris glanced back up at the diagram of the Obsidian system. Tyrancos was just a footnote to the Obsidian system – its refineries were abandoned and it had a population of zero. 'Who is it from?'

'I can't tell. But it's powerful. Looks Astartes.'

'Send it through to the bridge.'

Screens lit up on the pulpit's array in front of Lygris.

'Anything?' asked Iktinos.

'It's us. It's the Soul Drinkers.' Lygris fiddled with a few controls and a blip appeared on the screen, showing a point in orbit around Tyrancos. 'There. It's a Chapter code.'

'We have no men on Tyrancos.'

'I know. And it's an old signal, too. From the days of the old Chapter, before Sarpedon took over. A lot of our sensors were salvaged when we scuttled the old fleet, which is why the *Brokenback* can decode them.'

'The old Chapter? That makes little sense, Lygris.'

'But it's there.'

'Perhaps Commander Sarpedon is not telling us the whole truth about why we have come to the Obsidian system.'

Lygris turned to Iktinos, his face stern. 'No, Chaplain. We know everything he knows. This is something else.' He looked back at the monitor. 'It's a distress signal, standard. Probably automated. I'd suggest investigating it, but...'

'I shall go.'

'You, Chaplain? You might be needed here.'

'It may be that contact with the old Chapter, in whatever form it takes, could be hazardous to the Soul Drinkers, particularly to the newer recruits who never knew the days before Sarpedon led us away from the Imperium. As Chaplain, it is my duty to become aware of such moral threats and eliminate them where I can. I should go.'

'I see. Take one of the Thunderhawks, then. And I suggest you not go alone.'

'Of course. I shall speak to the men, and lead the rites. Then I shall be gone.'

As Iktinos left the dark sphere of the bridge, Lygris brought up the image of Tyrancos on the viewscreen. It was a gas giant, no more or less remarkable than millions of such worlds in the galaxy. A few decrepit refineries, on platforms or refitted asteroids orbiting the unforgiving gas giant, were all that suggested that anyone had been anywhere near it. And yet, the old Chapter had been to Tyrancos in some capacity. Lygris had fought alongside the old Chapter for many decades before Sarpedon took over the Soul Drinkers and he had certainly not heard of any involvement in the Obsidian system.

As Iktinos had said, it made little sense. But it was also less pressing than the battle for Vanqualis. The targeting array had locked onto another ork ship, larger this time, a bloated construction of flaring engines and melded asteroids typical of orkish technology so crude it was a wonder the greenskins managed space travel at all. Lygris put thoughts of the old Chapter out of his mind and sent the *Brokenback* towards the target, ordnance chambers reloading and lance batteries recharging, ready to bring a taste of the Emperor's wrath to the greenskins.

'The jungle loves war,' General Varr said.

'You believe so?' said Luko.

'I know it. The men who fight in wars want them to end, but war itself wants to continue. The jungle helps keep wars alive. It doesn't give you battlefields where you can settle things with a single conflict. It keeps us killing each other one at a time, never winning or losing decisively, always being dragged deeper in.'

Squad Luko stood watch around the edges of a clearing formed by a fallen greatwood tree, which Varr had chosen as a temporary command post while the whole of the 901st and the remaining Warders caught up with him. The dark purple of the Soul Drinkers' armour melded with the shadows that flooded the bases of the vast gnarled trees. Captain Luko himself stood by a portable communications unit, its viewscreen folded out. General Varr sat beside him on a fallen tree trunk. Darkness was all around as were the sounds of the jungle, the whistling of birds high up in the canopy and the creaking of the trees. Kullek, the bear-like man who had somehow contrived to survive the battle for the Wraithspire Palace, stood toying with a serrated combat knife beside a pale and weak-looking Lieutenant Fulgorin. Fulgorin's left arm and shoulder were heavily bandaged, and the fear in his eyes probably came from the fact that the jungle was a very bad place to pick up any kind of wound. Nevermourn's legions of insects loved the smell of blood.

'Sometimes you don't have a choice,' said Luko.

'Well, someone did,' replied Varr. 'The greenskins chose the jungle. They love war, and the jungle helps them wage it. Any officer worth his stripes will avoid the jungle at all costs if he can, especially if he's up against greenskins.'

'Maybe so, general,' said Luko. 'A Space Marine would take this jungle and make it into his weapon.'

'Can the Soul Drinkers do that with Nevermourn?'

'Watch us.' Luko smiled as only he could, as if battle and bloodshed were a hearty joke to him. 'Commander,' he said into his vox.

The communications unit flickered into life, its screen now showing Sarpedon's gnarled face. The high collar of his Aegis suit was obvious – what was not clear were his horrible mutations. Luko knew that Sarpedon had to be wary of the reaction his mutations would gain from other Imperial soldiers. If nothing else, they would suggest that the Soul Drinkers were renegades, a fact that could turn Emperor-fearing troops (and even the assorted scum of the 901st) against them.

'General Varr,' began Sarpedon. 'It was good to know you survived the Wraithspire Palace.'

'I appreciate that, commander,' replied Varr, 'but that survival will not mean a great deal if we let the orks surround us. They're bringing more into the jungles and we won't be able to stop them so bluntly a second time.'

'Very true,' said Sarpedon. 'So we take the fight to them.'

'Are you... are you sure that can be done?' It was Lieutenant Fulgorin who had spoken. Fulgorin had probably never seen a Space Marine in the flesh before, and Luko was no doubt as intimidating to him as the greenskins.

'Anything,' said Sarpedon with a look like steel, 'can be done.'

'What do you suggest?' said Varr, ignoring Fulgorin.

'My scouts have gone ahead of us and identified high ground, the only such ground for many miles around. The ork army is large and unruly and they need a relatively defensible place to regroup. The heights is it. They'll head there and capture it, and use it as the base for their push on the coast.'

'Bit brainy for orks,' said Kullek, who seemed to show no qualms about speaking out of turn in front of the Space Marines. But then, Kullek was crazy.

'These are different,' said Varr. 'They had the intelligence to fall on Palatium when it was at its most vulnerable. And they have a leader who seems to know what he is doing.'

'We know where they are going,' continued Sarpedon. 'So we trap them. To get such a large body of men to the heights, they will need to negotiate a long valley, half filled with swamp.'

'Kullek,' said Varr. Kullek took a battered, blood-stained tactical map out of his filthy fatigues. Varr took it and spread it out as best he could on the fallen trunk beside him. 'Here,' he said, indicating the long, narrow depression which swept up towards a cluster of hills. 'The Serpentspine Valley. If we position our troops along the head of the valley below the heights we can trap the greenskins.' The valley was just one feature in a vast swathe of jungle, broken here and there by ruins or outcrops, but mostly unbroken canopy and marsh. At the top edge of the map the jungle met the seas in a rugged coastline broken by sandy beaches that would have been a vision of paradise in peacetime, but which were now set to be the scene of a bloody endgame in the defence of Herograve. 'We can keep them pinned, but not for long.'

'You won't have to,' said Sarpedon. 'We'll bombard them into the dirt.'

'With what? My ships are just troop transports and they're orbiting Voiderhome to keep out of the sights of the ork ships. Falken's artillery could do some damage but it won't nearly be enough.'

'With our fleet,' said Sarpedon. 'With the orks hidden by the jungle there isn't much the big guns can do. But when they're pinned down in the valley, we can carpet them with ordnance.'

'You mean...'

'Wipe them out,' said Luko with relish. 'Kill them all. That's how we'll beat the jungle.'

Varr was silent for a moment. The boldness of the plan was the opposite of the way war was normally conducted in such an environment. 'We'll lose a lot of men,' said Varr. He glanced up at the huge armoured forms guarding the clearing. 'Well, I will.'

'You'll lose them anyway,' said Sarpedon. 'This jungle will take them.'

'I know. But it means that we won't get many shots at this.'

'In the Adeptus Astartes, we are accustomed to only needing one.'

'Then it will be done,' said Varr. 'I'll have the men make for the valley as soon as the stragglers are in. I'll have to get them moving at the double if we're to keep ahead of the greenskins.'

'Good. We will regroup below the hills and form the line,' said Sarpedon. 'I'll have men towards the rear of our lines in case the greenskins try to slow us down. I shall have my men move out immediately.'

Varr folded the map back up and Mekrin picked his way through the mud and undergrowth to pack away the comm-unit. Varr motioned for him to stop.

'Commander Sarpedon,' said Varr. 'I fought through the Eye of Terror with the Kar Duniash Heavy Lancers and never saw a single Space Marine. For every one of you there might be a million of us. Why are the Soul Drinkers here?' Varr looked into the comm-unit's screen – even on screen, few normal men were able to look Sarpedon in the eye.

'Because no one else can do it,' said Sarpedon. 'I'll see you at the Serpentspine Valley, general.'

The ship was a great temple to honour and to fallen comrades, the pale marble of the walls and floor inscribed with thousands of names, and times and places of death. Braziers lit every corridor and shrine, so no fallen battle-brother's name ever fell into shadow. The high ceilings and wide spaces made the spacecraft more like a place of reflection, quiet and sombre, and in every great gallery and mustering chamber a huge ever-burning fire hung in the air like a caged sun. It was said that every single fallen brother had his name inscribed somewhere on the *Cerulean Claw*, thousands of battles remembered in the endless march of names. Many names had been added in the recent past, for the Chapter and the *Claw* had settled a grudge that had stood for many hundreds of years, and paid in the blood of their brethren to do so.

Chief Librarian Mercaeno of the Howling Griffons knelt to examine one such name, newly cut into the floor of the Manse of Furioso. It was a captain of the Fourth Company, who had fallen to the daemon Periclitor in the final bloody struggles. So many had fallen to the daemon's blade, so many had their minds shattered by its evil.

But not Mercaeno. Mercaeno had survived, because it had been Mercaeno who killed Periclitor.

'How many were lost?' came a voice that was not that of a Space Marine.

A man stood on the smooth tiles that wound their way between the inscribed marble slabs of the floor, forming a path so that no Howling Griffon would have to tread on the names of his fallen brothers. He had the face of a scholar or an academic, his thinning brown hair swept back and speckled with grey, his eyes hollow enough to suggest his recent past had seen trauma, too. He wore a long dark flakweave coat over black clothing. He did not wear the stylised 'I' to show his affiliation, but the fact that he spoke to Mercaeno as an equal was enough to demonstrate his rank.

'It is of no concern.'

'I think it is.'

'To you,' said Mercaeno. 'The destruction of Periclitor was one of the most sacred tasks of this Chapter's recent history. Many old vengeances were made good. Many new ones were born. These matters do not go beyond the Chapter. Our oaths are our own to uphold.'

'I understand you killed Periclitor, Mercaeno.'

Mercaeno fixed the man with a withering stare. Mercaeno had immense presence, his long, leathery face dark with the years, his eyes black like flint, all surrounded by his massive power armour in the gold and deep red of the Chapter. Oaths, some of them unfulfilled since the day he first took up a bolter for his Chapter, were inscribed into the armour, endless lines of obligations and honour-debts that tied Mercaeno into the Howling Griffons. But in spite all this, the inquisitor did not flinch. 'Why are you here, Thaddeus?'

'I like to know a little about my hosts.'

'You are not a guest. Were you not an inquisitor you would never have been permitted to set foot on the *Claw*.'

'But I am,' replied Thaddeus. 'And as an inquisitor, I'm inquisitive. For instance, I'm glad you're heading with all speed towards the Obsidian system, but I'm still curious as to why. Inquisitive, you see.'

Mercaeno couldn't tell if Thaddeus was trying to be amusing. Very little amused Mercaeno, who after all had seen more death, destruction and dishonour than most men could comprehend. 'We permitted you to journey with us, inquisitor. That is more than the Howling Griffons would grant anyone else.'

'We're close,' said Thaddeus. 'It won't be long before we're in the Scaephan sector.'

'We will not drop out of warp until we are in-system,' said Mercaeno.

'Within the Obsidian system?' Thaddeus cocked an eyebrow. 'It'll be infested with ork ships.'

'The greenskin has nothing that can compare to a Space Marine strike cruiser,' replied Mercaeno bluntly. 'We shall appear among them and scatter them. We do not give our enemies the luxury of seeing us coming. You have much to learn about the Astartes way of war.'

'You'd be surprised what I know,' said Thaddeus.

Mercaeno was about to round on Thaddeus, but seemed to think better of it. Instead, he walked a little way across the manse to where one wall was dominated by a carved mural of a Howling Griffons commander, magnificent with the spiked arc of an iron halo around his head and an axe with blades like the wings of a hawk.

'Inquisitor, do you know who this man was?'

'He was more than a man,' said Thaddeus. 'That's Orlando Furioso.'

'Chapter Master Furioso, indeed. What do you know of his death?'

'I do not…'

'No, you do not. Inquisitor or not, we keep our histories to ourselves. Chapter Master Furioso died by the hand of Periclitor, whose name you will no longer speak in the presence of my brethren. We were gathering to celebrate the fifth millennium since our Chapter was founded from Guilliman's sons. Traitors ambushed us. Renegade Astartes. Their leader was named Periclitor. Chapter Master Furioso threw them back from his flagship but it was crippled and crashed onto Arios Quintus. There Periclitor's traitors fell upon the Howling Griffons and butchered them. Periclitor mounted Chapter Master Furioso's body on the prow of a Thunderhawk and set it adrift, so that we would happen upon it when we came to search for our brethren. An oath of vengeance was sworn by the Chapter, to be borne by every battle-brother that followed until it was made right. That was more than three thousand years ago, inquisitor, but to a Howling Griffon Furioso's murder was as raw a wound as if it had been committed yesterday.'

'So you killed Per… the traitor,' said Thaddeus.

'No,' said Mercaeno. 'We fought as the sons of Guilliman and of the Emperor. We quelled rebellion and battled aliens. We threw daemons back into the warp. We took on a hundred oaths, a thousand, and every one of them burned as bright as the oath of vengeance against Periclitor. Some of them still stand, and every one of them is a shame that I cannot articulate. Came the time that Periclitor rose again, this time at the Eye of Terror, and in the millennia that had intervened he had committed countless atrocities and become elevated to a daemon. The Howling Griffons hunted him across the Eye, from daemon world to dead space, and when we finally came to battle his army it was only the raw wound of Furioso's death that kept us fighting until we were victorious. Periclitor, a prince of daemons, a champion of the foul gods, did not comprehend the determination of a Howling Griffon to fulfil the oaths he has sworn. Chapter Master Furioso did not die three thousand years ago. He died the moment Periclitor fell and he was avenged. Only then could we grieve for our lost brother. Do you understand now, inquisitor, what manner of men you are dealing with?'

'I do, Lord Librarian. And I have my oaths, too. I have sworn them only to myself and to the Emperor, but I must still pursue them.'

'This is the way of the Inquisition, then?'

Thaddeus gave a bleak smile. 'No, it certainly is not. But it is my way.'

'Very well,' said Mercaeno. 'I have settled some of your curiosity. I have questions of my own. What interest does the Inquisition have in the Obsidian system?'

'None,' replied Thaddeus. 'The Inquisition does not exist. Only inquisitors do, each one doing the Emperor's work in his own way.'

'Then what interest does Inquisitor Thaddeus have there?'

Thaddeus paused, looking up at the face of Chapter Master Orlando Furioso. 'I failed to do my duty a long time ago,' he said.

'You seek redemption, then?' said Mercaeno.

'You could say that. Unfinished business, if you like. Any more than that, Lord Librarian, is for Inquisitorial ears only.'

'So be it, inquisitor.'

'I take it that your mission to Vanqualis is a matter of honour, too?'

Mercaeno gestured towards the image of the Chapter Master. 'Lord Furioso himself gave his word. Were it not kept, all we have done to avenge him would be for naught. Deliverance must come to Vanqualis and it must be the Howling Griffons who bring it. You understand now why I must take so many of my Chapter to fulfil this obligation.'

Inquisitor Thaddeus looked around the Manse of Furioso, the place dedicated to the fallen Chapter Master. Several squads of Howling Griffons were in the huge room, paying their respects at shrines to fallen heroes or gathered overlooking the inscribed names of their brethren, performing rites to cleanse the soul and prepare them for the battles to come. Mercaeno's force consisted of more than three hundred Howling Griffons, a major force by Astartes standards, and the fact that the rest of the Chapter was still fighting in the battles around the Eye of Terror suggested the importance of Furioso's oath to Vanqualis.

'We are all here because we believe,' said Thaddeus. 'And because we cannot back down. It's what the Imperium is built on.'

'Quite so, inquisitor. Now, if you are satisfied, we shall shortly arrive in the Obsidian system and I must attend to the Rites of Detestation. There will be a great deal there that we must be prepared to hate.'

Mercaeno left Inquisitor Thaddeus in the Manse of Furioso. If the inquisitor still did not understand the depths of the Howling Griffons' determination, then he would once they fell upon the greenskins and showed them how the Griffons kept their promises.

'How must the alien be met on the battlefield?'
'The alien fears our purity and nobility. He must therefore be met with the most pure and noble hatred.'
– Daenyathos, *Catechisms Martial*

CHAPTER SIX

'What is this place?' said Raek, advancing warily through the harsh stripes of shadow that lay across the asteroid's surface. His sniper rifle was shouldered and he held his bolt pistol in front of his face, ready to snap shots at anything that moved.

'Nowhere,' replied Chaplain Iktinos.

Behind Iktinos was the colossal boiling disc of Tyrancos, a swirling blue-green mass so immense it almost overwhelmed the void around it. The shadows were cast by the Obsidian system's sun, a hard painful diamond hanging in space, undimmed by an atmosphere. Raek and Iktinos were on one of the many asteroids orbiting Tyrancos, on which refineries had been built to create useful fuels out of the gases piped up from Tyrancos itself. The asteroid rolled out before them, small enough for the horizon to curve round as if distorted, its surface broken by thousands of intake spines and bulky cylindrical refining units. Nearby was an enormous ragged hole as if something immense had taken a bite out of the asteroid, exposing torn layers of stone and metal underneath.

'Why would the old Chapter have come here?'

'Perhaps they did not. It is our task to find out.'

Raek lowered his pistol and knelt down, one hand on the red-black rock of the asteroid. Raek was a natural scout, attuned to his surroundings. Even through the faceplate of the voidsuit worn over his scout armour, he could taste the environment. If there were enemies waiting, hiding, Raek would know where. He would know which paths the bullets from their guns would take. He knew how to move unseen, even when the star Obsidian was bathing the asteroid in diamond-hard light.

'The place has gravity,' said Raek. 'At least two-thirds Terran standard. So something here still works. But no one's been here for a long time.'

Iktinos looked closer at the nearest intake spine. The asteroid had been fitted with the spines to draw in gases from Tyrancos's upper atmosphere, which could then be refined into fuel or materials. The spine was corroded – not rusted, but crumbling and pitted from the stark solar radiation and the biting of particle winds whipping up from Tyrancos.

'There may still be fuel,' said Iktinos. 'The *Brokenback* can re-supply here.'

'Maybe,' said Raek, 'but I don't like the look of that.' He nodded towards the hole that bit down deep into the horizon. 'It's not a meteor or a weapon impact. Looks like it was dug.'

'Then let us be certain,' said Iktinos, and walked away from the Thunderhawk docked behind him.

The hole was bitten deep down into the asteroid's crust, thrown into pitch-black shadow by the harsh light. The guts of the refinery had been sliced through, melted machinery sagging from between layers of scorched rock.

A suspended walkway of stone slabs led down into the interior of the asteroid, not suspended by wires or supports, but hanging there in space.

'Anti-grav,' said Raek. 'Someone built this. They hollowed it out and built something inside.'

Raek kept his pistol ready to come up and fire as he took the first step onto the walkway. It stayed firm beneath his feet. Chaplain Iktinos followed just behind, his augmented sight picking out the ragged mess of the crater giving way to polished, smooth stone beyond the threshold of the interior.

'Throne above,' said Raek quietly. He had seen what was mounted above the threshold, like a signpost warning against delving into the heart of the asteroid.

It was pitted with corrosion, but still unmistakeable. It was a golden chalice, marking the entrance to the asteroid. The symbol of the Soul Drinkers.

'Chaplain?'

'We move on, sergeant.'

Raek continued into the shadows. Around him opened a spectacular sight. The whole asteroid had been hollowed out and filled with an astonishingly complex mass of floating columns and arches, as if a hundred temples had been broken up and haphazardly reconstructed inside the asteroid. The blocks constantly tumbled and moved around the asteroid's centre point, at which, half-glimpsed, floated a building of gold and obsidian like a tomb. The asteroid's gravity suddenly reversed as Raek crossed the threshold and the inside of the hollowed-out asteroid became the floor, Raek now looking up at the tomb floating high above him through concentric floors of shifting architecture.

The chalice was everywhere. The Imperial aquila, too, the two side by side emblematic of the old Soul Drinkers, before Sarpedon renounced the Imperium and made his Chapter renegades. Carved faces tumbled by, perhaps the images of past Soul Drinkers, while friezes of battle scenes could have been lost campaigns from the Chapter's past.

'What do you know of this?' asked Raek.

'I checked the Chapter archive before we left the *Brokenback*,' replied the Chaplain. 'There was no mention of Tyrancos, or of anything like this.'

'That's not what I asked,' said Raek.

Iktinos turned to Raek, the rictus of his helmet's faceplate falling on the sergeant.

Raek was shaken. He was good at hiding it, but he was surrounded by the unknown. 'Chaplain,' he continued. 'Why did Sarpedon bring us here? We are your battle-brothers, even if we did not all fight through the Chapter War as you did. We deserve to know.'

Before Iktinos could answer, movement flickered in the floating temple. Amid the ponderous shifting of the temple's architecture, it was as bright as day to a Space Marine's enhanced vision. Raek's pistol was holstered instantly and the sniper rifle was in his hands, his raw instincts turning to the weapon with which he was most comfortable.

Lights danced. Silver gleamed. Dead greyish flesh corded between slabs of armour decorated in gilt and flaking purple. Glowing red eye lenses flickered into life as blades and gun barrels unfolded from bodies. They were everywhere.

'Gun-servitors,' said Raek as more shapes unfastened themselves from layers of architecture, like blocky metal locusts on thrumming anti-grav motors. Beams of reddish light swept through the temple, seeking out movement and body heat. 'Someone wanted to keep us out.'

'No,' said Iktinos. 'Someone wanted us to be worthy.'

The first shots spattered down, rapid storms of laser spattering between the slabs orbiting above the two Soul Drinkers. Raek threw himself to one side. Iktinos drew his crozius and plasma pistol.

'So the old Chapter has not done with us yet,' he said calmly, as Raek opened fire.

The warlord bellowed and the horde surged on. The beasts of the jungle swarmed before them, even mighty predators panicked by the war-cries of the orks and the tramping of feet. The horde had swollen with the arrivals from orbit and they boasted crude war machines, tracks churning through the undergrowth. Walking machines, with massive guns for arms and armoured bodies like great metal barrels, stomped through the mud with insane gun-happy orks at the controls. Snarling attack beasts, their bodies no more than fang-filled maws and a stomach, strained at the leash as their handlers whipped them forwards. And thousands upon thousands of orks tramped forwards, firing into the air or waving their cleavers with joy at the impending bloodshed.

Some of them had replaced their teeth with chunks of gold, or covered their bodies in war paint. Others wore skull masks, or carried the biggest, flashiest custom guns they could afford, or wore the body parts of their enemies as trophies. They were showing their affiliation to their clans, but in truth, there were no clans in the jungle. The warlord had welded them into one army – while back on their homeworlds in the Garon Nebula they would have been murdering each other over a look, under the warlord they were one horde, united in war. Only in battle did the orks put aside their weaknesses, and become what they were born to be.

The warlord, for the first time on Nevermourn, allowed their spirit of battle-lust to infect him. He hollered as he marched alongside them, snapping his enormous mechanical claw and letting the billows of steam hiss violently from the vents in his torso. He was a greenskin like them, a born killer, sent by the orkish gods to conquer the galaxy and exterminate everything that stood in their way.

The horde poured into the valley like a flood. The valley was choked with trees and the rotten remains of dead plants and animals that had tumbled down from above, waist-deep in the swamp in places, tree roots reaching overhead like arched doorways and venomous serpents writhing through the blackness. But the orks surged forwards, too powerful a force to be slowed down by the jungle. Fighting machines dragged down trees that had stood for centuries and tank tracks ground through the mire. Orks fell, sucked down by the mud or devoured by lurking predators. But they were a drop in the green ocean.

The warlord was at their head, storming towards the heights. Once they had the hills, the horde could group up and be strengthened, ready for the final bloody push on the coast. The orks were too set on murder and destruction to realise the relative subtlety of such strategies, but the warlord did. That was why the greenskins would raze the cities of Herograve, and why Vanqualis would be theirs.

An ork fell, a hole bored through his torso by a long-las shot. Snipers' targeting beams flickered through the dense foliage. Another shot coughed through the leaves and blew the side off an ork's head.

They were here. The humans. This time, not even the armoured warriors and their false gods would save them from the orks. The warlord bellowed like the hate-fuelled beast he was, and the orks charged into battle.

'Cold and fast, Soul Drinkers!' yelled Luko as the horde roared up from the green-black depths of the jungle. He could smell them, rotting meat and gunsmoke, old blood and choking exhaust.

Graevus was beside Luko, the power field around his axe crackling as he weighted it in his grotesquely deformed hand. Luko's own power claws leapt into life, spilling arcs of blue-white power off the ends of the blades. 'Don't get lost down there, Luko,' said Graevus. 'Just draw them up here, in and out. You don't have to kill them all yourself.'

Luko grinned savagely. 'Don't tempt me, Graevus. I might have to wipe these xenos out just to teach you a lesson.'

Then the time for talk was over. With a scream of escaping steam and the crunch of gears, a lurching machine of metal three times the height of a man tore out through the trees. One arm spat gunfire through the jungle, sending the Astartes of Squad Graevus and Squad Luko throwing themselves to the sloping ground of the valley. On its other hand was mounted a screeching circular saw, slicing through a tree trunk as it slashed towards the nearest Soul Drinker and sending the trunk crashing down through the canopy.

'Cover!' yelled Graevus as torn wood and gunfire rained down. 'Leave it for the guns! Take the greenskins!' Graevus's assault squad re-gathered their wits in a moment and suddenly they were a tide of armoured bodies and roaring chainswords, diving down the valley slope towards the dark tide of orks scrambling towards them. With a crunch of blade on flesh Graevus's men slammed into the orks and dark greenskin blood sprayed up from the carnage.

'Open fire!' cried Luko, but he didn't need to. Already the bolters of his tactical squad were blowing charred holes in the side of the war machine. The machine's metallic foot stamped down and crushed the leg of Brother Zalras – Luko dragged his battle-brother away but the act only grabbed the machine's attention. As it turned towards him Luko saw the glyphs stencilled onto the machine's cylindrical hull, stylised ork skulls and fist symbols, kill-markings and clan glyphs. Teeth and rotting, severed hands hung from leather thongs looped across its chassis. The blade carved down at Luko and he barely threw Zalras aside before it bit deep into the ground.

The difference between a Space Marine and a normal man was far more profound than just a suit of armour and physical size. The true difference, the one that made a man a Space Marine, was that a Space Marine was never ruled by fear. Fear clouded the judgement of normal men and made them do insane things – showing their back to the enemy, trying to hide, lashing around at enemies who weren't there. A

Space Marine's mind was not so clouded. He knew what fear was, but when it sparked in him it never caught light. He mastered his fear and pushed it down, banishing it from his mind and never letting it take control. He knew that he was safest not running away from the enemy but toe to toe with it, face to face, where his strength and wargear counted for the most. So Luko ducked under the war machine's gun barrel and raked down at its leg mounting with his power claw. His arm jarred as the blades met metal but he forced them further down, the power field rupturing metal like a normal weapon tore flesh.

The machine lurched, gears inside it grinding angrily. Luko was barely able to throw himself aside as the saw blade scythed up at him again, carving a slice out of his shoulder pad. He rolled through the mud, exposed roots crunching beneath him, instinctively skidding into the cover of a massive thick tree trunk. Gunfire from the machine tore into the trunk, shredding wood and pulp, chewing through the tree's girth.

Squad Graevus tore through the branches and foliage above, their chainswords spraying ork blood as they churned, the flaring exhausts of their jump packs carrying them away from the orks surging forward to avenge their dead. Graevus himself twisted in mid-air and dropped down behind the war machine, carving a deep gouge out of the back of its armour with his power axe.

Luko rolled out of cover and lunged at the machine, punching his claws so deep into the machine's chassis that he felt muscle and bone giving way inside. The machine screamed, steam gouting from its churning engines.

Luko reached up and dug one claw into the machine, pulling himself up to the top of its body. He slammed his other claw into the metal and pulled, the power field flaring as it shattered the machine's hull. Every scrap of strength went into wrenching the top of the hull off and in a shower of sparks it came free.

The machine toppled over, fire and sparks spraying from its ruptured engines. Luko tumbled to the ground, as did the machine's pilot, a soot-blackened ork, torso torn open, violent red eyes gleaming above an insane grin. In its hand was a bundle of explosive sticks tied together with a detonator at the top. The ork ripped the pin out of the detonator and began to cackle at Luko.

Graevus hit the ground behind the ork and grabbed it with his free hand. His jump pack gunned into life and he soared up towards the canopy above, crazed ork in his hand. With tremendous strength he hurled the insane greenskin towards the ragged line of orks charging up the slope, following Graevus's assault squad. The ork slammed into his fellow greenskins and exploded, blowing apart a dozen aliens, throwing sundered limbs and spinning shards of wood through the jungle.

The war machine was down. Luko picked himself up as the gunfire stuttered from Luko's squad, even Brother Zalras propping himself up against a torn tree stump to snap bolter fire into the green mass seething into the bloody gap left by the explosion. Orks were falling but more were clambering over the top of them, eyes bright with hatred and the lust for revenge.

Luko glanced at Graevus. His battle-brother was sprayed from head to toe in ork blood. While Luko was fighting the war machine, Graevus's squad had been butchering orks down the valley slope, knowing their skill and the range of their jump packs would let them hit the ork line hard and pull back before they were surrounded.

'Didn't have to kill them all,' said Luko with a grin. It was his way of thanking Graevus for saving his life.

'Think we got their attention,' said Graevus.

'Pull them back,' said Luko. 'Squad! Suppression fire and fall back!'

The Soul Drinkers moved back through the forest, keeping volleys of fire thudding down through the trees. For every ork that fell two or three more scrambled over its body and stormed forwards. Luko led the squad back up the valley slope to the top of the ridge, thinning out the orks' front ranks, breaking up their charge, and even as the greenskins bellowed their hate the momentum was flooding out of them. They were slogging through their own dead, the front runners isolated enough for Luko's men to pick them off with bolter shots.

'Now!' yelled Luko. 'Volley fire!'

Squad Luko dropped to the ground. Graevus's men leapt up into the air on their jump pack exhausts, arcing back towards the ridge.

'Redemption!' yelled a voice belonging to a man Luko had heard named as Trox, the Penal Legion officer in charge of the flank force. 'Seek it now in the eyes of the xenos! Tear it from his bloodied hand!'

Lasgun fire opened up in a crimson storm. Three hundred troopers of the 901st, stationed at the top of the valley slope, fired as one. Lasers scoured bark from trees and leaves from branches. The orks in the front rank were shredded, bodies riddled with scorching holes, limbs sheared from bodies. Fire stuttered back up from them but the determination to charge up the slope had left their fire scattered and ineffective. A couple of Penal Legion troopers fell, but they meant nothing.

Luko's men continued to fire from prone, bolters punching great gory holes in the orks as laser fire streaked over their heads and they writhed back towards the ridge, still firing. A few of the 901st's shots fell short but Space Marine power armour was among the best in the galaxy and lasguns, appallingly deadly against exposed flesh, could do little more than scorch the paint from the Soul Drinkers.

'Scourge this stain from the Emperor's sight!' yelled Trox, his fanatical ranting a constant background to the gunfire. Silvery bursts of shrapnel exploded among the orks from his grenade launcher. A heavy bolter thudded shots into the orks and gradually the horde was masked by smoke and shrapnel, a veil of superheated earth and vaporised blood. Shapes loomed through the smog, a particularly large and violent ork leading a party of tough veteran greenskins towards the 901st's line. As Luko's Soul Drinkers took their place alongside the Penal Legion troopers, Graevus's squad charged forward to blunt the ork attack. Their leader's axe flashed down and the ork leader fell, carved nearly in two.

'Luko here!' shouted Luko into the vox. 'The flank's holding! We're drawing them off and keeping them pinned!'

'Well done, captain,' replied Sarpedon over the vox. 'Hold the line and let it bend if you have to. The main force will hit us soon.'

Black water, like sweat, beaded on the walls of the brig. The *Brokenback* had plenty of places to hold prisoners – almost every one of its component ships had a brig, and some of the craft were entirely given over to cells and torture chambers. Some of them were bafflingly alien, while others were grimly prosaic in the manacles hanging from their walls and the channels cut into their decks to drain away the blood. The brig currently used by the Soul Drinkers on the *Brokenback* was more down-to-earth, part of a gigantic prison hulk sectioned off and reinforced, its bleak corroded steel corridors protected by sentry guns. Bones, decayed almost to grey sludge, still lay in the furthest corners, for the prison ship had evidently been full of inmates when the warp claimed it. Now, however, only one living thing was locked up there.

Brother Theylanos's last thoughts were of those final moments, when the otherworldly madness of the warp had rolled down these corridors like poisonous mist. The *Brokenback* brimmed with such stories, horrors implied by the strange dark corners of the hulk, and the screams of those chained prisoners still seemed to echo through the mass of blackened steel.

It was a dangerous thing to imagine. Too much thinking about such matters could be dangerous. It corroded the mind. In a sense, the whole of the *Brokenback* was a moral threat – without the Soul Drinkers' strength of will, it could have rotted their sense of duty and destroyed them. But they were strong enough. The screams of men long dead did not eat away at them as it would normal soldiers. The Soul Drinkers were better than that.

As the point of the knife slid in between the corded muscles of his throat, Theylanos thought for a terrible weak moment that the warp had come to the prison ship again, that silvery fingers of insanity were reaching from beyond realspace to drag him down.

Then the blade passed through his spine and wrenched up into the base of his brain, and the last image in his mind was the screaming faces of the prisoners welcoming him as one of their own.

* * *

Scout Nisryus pulled the blade free of Theylanos's neck and let the body slide to the ground. Nisryus was pallid and seemingly far too thin-faced to be a Space Marine, and his eyes wouldn't stay still, constantly focusing on things no one else could see.

Scout Tydeus crouched down and checked the wide wound on the Soul Drinker's throat. Blood was already crusting around the wound. 'He's gone,' said Tydeus with customary shortness. 'Is there anyone else?'

'Not that I can feel,' said Nisryus. The Space Marine had precognitive powers and one day, perhaps, he would be able to tell the future, an exceptionally rare talent – and very dangerous in every respect. Nisryus's studies with the Chapter's other Librarians had been slow as his power was unusual and risky to use, but he could still see eddies of time and space that let him react quicker than the laws of physics allowed. 'If there is, they won't find us for a while.'

'Move up and let's do this,' said Tydeus. 'Scamander?'

Lexicanist Scamander was watching the corridor behind them, in case more Soul Drinkers detailed to guard the brig were about to happen upon the scouts. Though he wore the power armour of a full Space Marine, Scamander was very much one of Tydeus's men. Scamander was psychic, too, but while Nisryus's power was subtle and complex, Scamander's was very simple. He was a pyrokinetic, the results of his power showing in the scorched skin around his eyes and the sides of his face. His eyes had turned dark red and smoke constantly coiled from the joints of his armour. 'We're clear,' he said. 'Stand aside.'

Scamander moved up to a cell door set into the wall of the corridor. The door was a massive slab of age-blackened steel solid enough to have held firm for thousands of years. Scamander put one hand against it, the gauntlet blistered and blackened. The metal under Scamander's hand hissed and began to glow cherry-red. His face hardened and faint flames licked from his eyes – the armour down his other side was becoming frosted, crystals of ice forming where water dripped on it from the ceiling. The heat created by Scamander had to be drawn from somewhere and he took it from his own body, so that his flesh and armour became deathly cold as the metal softened and parted beneath his touch.

Within the cell, a single prisoner sat on the bench that protruded from one wall. He stood up as the metal came apart under Scamander's hand. The dim light from the corridor fell on his face – it was Eumenes, stripped of his armour and locked up on Sarpedon's orders.

'Is it done?' said Eumenes from within the cell as the door came apart.

Scamander stood back, breathing heavily, the flames around his eyes replaced with a coat of hoary frost. Tydeus stepped forwards. 'Not yet, sergeant.'

Eumenes's face darkened. 'Where is Raek?'

'Called away to investigate a distress signal from Tyrancos. He went with the Chaplain.'

Eumenes suddenly smiled darkly. 'That will save us a task, then. With Iktinos on board we would have trouble. Have you had to kill anyone?'

'One,' replied Tydeus.

'Then they'll miss him soon,' said Eumenes. 'We have to move fast. And get in contact with the surface, too. What news from there?'

'The greenskins are pressing home. Won't be long before Sarpedon gives the order.'

'Then we'll have to be finished here before it does.' Eumenes nodded at Scamander. 'Good to see you, scout. How are things in the Librarium?'

'Lexicanist now,' said Scamander, still catching his breath. 'Tyrendian has big plans for me.'

'So do I,' said Eumenes. 'Nisryus, are we still clear?'

'We get out of the prison ship just fine,' said Nisryus, the flickering, restless look in his eyes showing he was reading invisible psychic currents around them. 'I can't see further than that.'

'I can,' said Eumenes, clambering through the ragged, smouldering hole torn through the door by Scamander's power. 'I know exactly how this is going to end. Send the word to the others, it begins now. Nisryus, take point, and Scamander stay with me. We hit the bridge first.'

The warlord's horde poured through the Serpentspine Valley, crashing into the foothills of the heights beyond like a wave. The 901st were positioned along the side of the valley, herding the greenskins towards the cliffs at the head of the valley where the first foothills of the heights rose over the dense green canopy.

The Soul Drinkers and the tougher elements of the 901st drew off parts of the horde in diversionary attacks. Luko and Graevus drew hundreds of orks up into a savage crossfire, while on the other side of the valley Salk held an outcrop of lichen-covered rock that anchored the 901st's line. Countless greenskins died, but there were many, many thousands more rampaging towards the cliffs. The 901st's line bent but did not break and the Soul Drinkers held firm, but they were fighting secondary battles that only stacked the odds. When the orks hit the cliffs, the real battle began.

'Open fire, Lygris!' yelled Sarpedon, throwing another ork off the cliff.

'Yes, commander,' replied Lygris from orbit. 'The guns are hot. Fire's coming in a few minutes.'

Sarpedon stabbed with his force staff, discharging its build-up of psychic power into the chest of an ork rearing up at him.

Sarpedon's Soul Drinkers were holding the first foothills of the heights, the long dense green mass of the Serpentspine Valley rolling out before them. The whole valley seethed with greenskins and it was funnelling their advance towards the cliffs held by Sarpedon's line. Orks were clambering up the vine-covered cliffs and Sarpedon was throwing them back down. Soul Drinkers around him were emptying bolter magazines down over the lichen-covered rocks, blasting wet ragged holes in the orks who tried to scramble up them.

It was a short climb and the orks were tenacious, and every time one tumbled down into the canopy the greenskin behind it got a little further towards the cliff top. Fire was hammering back up at the Soul Drinkers, too, thousands of guns pointed upwards firing wildly, turning their air hot and metallic with flame and shrapnel.

'They've broken through!' cried Karraidin, the Master of Novices, who commanded a crowd of scouts and newly inducted Soul Drinkers guarding against the orks forcing through the 901st's line and around the cliffs. 'Hold them off! Hold them! For Dorn and the Emperor, earn that damned chalice on your shoulder!'

'They'll get to the artillery,' voxed Sarpedon as he knocked another ork down off the cliff-top. They were in chainsword range now and the Soul Drinkers were fighting the greenskins hand-to-hand at the top of the cliff. 'Keep them off the Vanqualians, we need every gun we can get.'

Sarpedon stabbed down with one leg, pinning an ork's hand to the rock with his front talon before spearing its head with his staff. Another clambered over the dead ork's body and three rapid shots from another Soul Drinker, one of Karraidin's novices, blasted it off the cliff to send it tumbling back down through the canopy.

Sarpedon was about to thank the young Space Marine when a terrific roar rose up from below the cliff, huge and monstrous. A sudden surge pushed the Soul Drinkers back from the cliff, orks throwing themselves on the Space Marines' guns and chainswords to force them back. Sarpedon lashed around him but was forced onto his back legs and had to scuttle back from the edge to keep himself from being isolated. Orks were all around him, hulking veterans with twisted faces almost hidden amongst scar tissue, all power and violence.

Behind them rose a true monster. It was huge, huger by far than any other ork on Nevermourn – bigger than any ork Sarpedon had ever seen. Its body was half mechanical and its eyes were so full of hate that Sarpedon knew instinctively it was not just a near-animal like all the other greenskins. It was old, the years etched onto it in scar tissue, and its sheer power was made obvious as it threw orks aside and stormed towards Sarpedon.

But Sarpedon was a monster too. He braced his many legs against the rock beneath him and squared himself, holding the head of his staff towards the warlord like the point of a spear. The warlord bellowed like a bull, lowered a shoulder and charged, and Sarpedon stood firm.

The warlord's mechanical fist slammed down with a sound like a meteor strike. Sarpedon barely stepped aside but his force staff hit home, the eagle-winged tip forced deep into the warlord's chest with the weight of its own charge.

Sarpedon's staff was carved from very rare psychoactive wood, and it served to conduct the massive reserved of psychic power he could call upon. When he focused his mind and drove the staff home, the discharge of power would rip the target apart and blast its soul from its body. Sarpedon focused like that now, driving every drop of power from the depths of his mind into a white-hot spike driven towards the warlord's burning bestial soul.

But the warlord's willpower was stronger than anything Sarpedon had ever felt and his power splintered against its soul. The ork wrenched the staff from its chest and closed its mechanical claw around Sarpedon's upper body. The Space Marine forced an arm inside and held the claw open as steam sprayed from the pistons trying to close the claw around him. Sarpedon was exceptionally strong, but the warlord was nothing but muscle and rage, and for an awful moment he knew the claw would shatter his bones and crush him to death.

A piston blew and a great gout of smoke and flame sprayed from the elbow joint of the ork's arm. The pressure was suddenly off and Sarpedon fought back, trying to force the claw open to escape. The warlord roared and hurled Sarpedon with all its awesome strength. The Soul Drinker crashed through branches and tree trunks, tumbling as he fell, fighting to keep a grip on his force staff.

Sarpedon rolled as he landed, flipping rapidly upright on his agile legs. He could hear the warlord charging towards him. He was deep into the jungle that covered the foothills of the heights now, and close behind him was the Vanqualian artillery. He couldn't take another step back; he had to stand and fight. The ork was one of the few things Sarpedon had fought that was physically stronger than him, and toe to toe he might fail. He turned on the Hell.

The warlord was almost upon him, crunching through the trees. Sarpedon had tasted its willpower, and knew it would not be frightened by the parlour tricks that had shaken the greenskins at the Wraithspire Palace. It had to fear something. Everything did. Somewhere in this galaxy was something that the warlord feared, something that would distract it long enough for Sarpedon to get onto the front feet and beat it.

It wanted Vanqualis. It wanted this world. But if this world was gone, it would have failed. That was what it feared – failure. It was probably the only thing that Sarpedon himself feared, too.

The Hell tore out from Sarpedon, rippling through the trees, and to his psychic eye the jungle was blasted away, stripped down to the bare blackened earth. He tore the sun from the sky and the life from the earth. For him and the warlord, Vanqualis was a barren, worthless place, only unforgiving stars in the sky and torn, dead land stretching in all directions. The Hell showed Vanqualis as a meaningless prize, a place where thousands of greenskins had died for nothing, a pathetic memorial of failure to the warlord's horde.

The warlord was upon him. For a moment the giant ork faltered, the Hell showing him a terrible truth about the futility of his greenskins' crusade. That was all Sarpedon needed. He squared his back legs and dived forward, and he and the warlord crashed together with a sound like thunder.

'What is the greatest sin?'
'The greatest of them is treachery, for it is a sin against the very soul.'

– Daenyathos, *Catechisms Martial*

CHAPTER SEVEN

Lord Sovelin Falken ground his face into the mud, ears ringing from the explosions. He writhed through the muck under the closest mortar carriage as the ground shuddered under the explosions, and for a moment everything was blackness and deafening white noise.

He pushed himself onto one knee to see what was happening. Most of the Vanqualian Warders had also taken cover from the fire that had burst down through the ragged canopy and exploded among the artillery pieces. Men lay dead, one beheaded by shrapnel, another with both arms torn off lying face-down in the undergrowth. Another was still alive, just, the lower half of his body a foul gory mush. His face was bone-white and his eyes were open in fear as the life leached out of him into the mud.

Dark shapes were lurching through the trees along one side of the clearing. Several of them were lugging huge guns, barrels still glowing hot in the darkness. The orks had got their artillery out of the valley and had shelled Sovelin's own artillery positions, which meant that they were about to charge and butcher the Vanqualian Warders so they could no longer fire on the main ork horde below.

'Form up!' yelled Sovelin. 'On me! Form the line!' He could barely hear his own voice through the ringing but soon men were scrabbling towards him, their uniforms covered in mud and their faces pallid with fear.

He was in charge. That fact hit him. If he didn't lead these men, they would die.

Somewhere amid the chaos Sovelin gave the order to fire. The firefight was brutal, ork gunfire rattling off the gun carriages, autoguns replying. The orks were trying to set their heavy weapons up for another barrage but most of them were shot down as they did so. Others drew cleavers and charged, running across the clearing to be cut down. One made it to the line and suddenly Sovelin was fighting the alien itself – a foul thing with half a face, the rest of it blackened grinning skull. Sovelin's autogun stock shattered as he brought it up to block the ork's cleaver and the alien barged him to the ground. It hacked down at him with its cleaver and Sovelin couldn't roll out of the way fast enough – the cleaver missed his head but the ork's huge weight was on him, crushing him. Panicking, Sovelin wrenched his laspistol from its holster and unloaded it at point-blank range into the greenskin's abdomen. The creature spasmed on top of him, grunting its foul breath into his face, and for a moment Sovelin was sure it would chew his face off with that huge scarred maw.

Then the ork slumped down and breathed out a long death rattle. Hands reached down to haul it off Sovelin – two of the Vanqualians dragged it away and Sovelin saw the huge wounds he had blown in its stomach. He had probably severed its spine. Sovelin had never killed anything, certainly not up close, before.

'We need…' said Sovelin, catching his breath, 'we need to group up. Like a firing squad. We can out-shoot them but we have to keep them away.'

But they were all around. Hundreds of them. Thousands. The orks had broken through somewhere and they were attacking the artillery. Sovelin was going to die, and all his men with him.

A deep bass note in the back of Sovelin's mind suddenly rose to a roar and the world changed. Another image was laid over the jungle – a bleak, endless wasteland, a tortured and lifeless world with black void for a sky. Sovelin couldn't focus, and both the Vanqualians and the orks reacted the same. The firing stopped and men took cover, holding their heads as the strange images pounded at them.

It was witchcraft. The Space Marine psyker who had terrorised the orks at the Wraithspire Palace was here. That meant the Space Marines were here, too, and that the Vanqualian artillery might be saved.

Sovelin stood up and tried to find another gun so he could carry on leading the Vanqualians. His mind wouldn't focus – he could barely grasp the gun that lay at his feet and the world was swinging around him as if he was dizzy or drunk.

A monster crashed through the trees, wrestling with a Space Marine. It was an ork, bigger than Sovelin had believed possible, half its body a smoking mechanical horror. But no matter how huge and foul the alien, Sovelin realised with a lurch in his stomach that the Space Marine was worse.

The Space Marine was a mutant. The lower half of his body was a horrendous parody of nature, with eight articulated legs like those of a spider or a scorpion. He moved with speed and viciousness alien to a human. Strike by strike, step by step, the mutant battered the ork back into the forest. The other orks advancing on the artillery let out a terrible howl as they witnessed their leader being matched, and even bested, by the mutant.

But the orks were the last thing on Sovelin's mind now. Horrifyingly, he saw the truth. The mutant. The witchcraft. The sudden appearance on Vanqualis. And for the first time, he saw clearly the chalice symbol these 'Soul Drinkers' wore on their shoulder pads. It all made perfect sense. An awful cold horror filled Sovelin more profound even than the fear of death the orks had brought with them.

And Sovelin was the only one who knew.

'You!' shouted Sovelin, pointing to the nearest Vanqualian. 'Get me the field vox! Now!'

'Sir?'

'We have to warn Herograve,' said Sovelin. 'The Black Chalice have returned.'

Techmarine Lygris realised there was something wrong when he saw the guns.

The scouts had surrounded him on the bridge. There must have been thirty of them and Lygris instinctively knew that Eumenes, who stood in the centre of them with his arms folded in an attitude of complete confidence, was in charge. They had their bolters aimed at Lygris and he was covered from every angle.

Lygris turned from the viewscreen, which was showing the target area in the Snakespine Valley for the *Brokenback*'s guns. 'Eumenes. What is the meaning of this?'

'We're taking the ship, Lygris,' replied Eumenes smoothly.

Lygris was tough, and he had fought in plenty of actions under Sarpedon and with the old Chapter before that. But there were too many Soul Drinkers with Eumenes, scouts and full Space Marines, among them some veterans whose experience rivalled Lygris's. Eumenes himself was an exceptional soldier. 'Why?'

'You know why, Lygris,' sneered Eumenes. 'It's over. We're taking this Chapter from Sarpedon. We should be bringing down the Imperium instead of losing our brothers down on Vanqualis for a world the Emperor doesn't care about.'

'This is treachery,' said Lygris, his voice hard.

'I know,' replied Eumenes steadily. 'That's why we're not doing you the insult of asking you to join us. Just step down from the pulpit and let us take the ship, and you will live.'

Lygris walked down the short flight of steps onto the bridge deck. As he moved, he thumbed a control stud on the instrument array, praying silently that none of Eumenes's men saw him. 'You know I can't give you the bridge, Eumenes.'

'And you know I have to give you the choice.' Eumenes cocked the action of his bolter. 'Shall we do this?'

Lygris rapidly scanned the faces of Eumenes's Soul Drinkers. He recognised Scamander and Nisryus, two new psychic recruits who were supposed to be the future of the Chapter Librarium. He saw a few more experienced battle-brothers, but most of Eumenes's men were from the recent intake of recruits. Then Lygris's hearts skipped a beat when he saw the white armour trim of an Apothecary,

'Pallas,' he said, unable to keep the shock out of his voice. 'What are you doing?'

Apothecary Pallas had been there from the start. He had fought on the Star Fort, when the Adeptus Mechanicus had stolen the Soulspear from the Soul Drinkers and started the terrible cycle of events that led to the Chapter War and the break with the Imperium. It had been Pallas who had diagnosed the rampant mutations threatening to destroy the Chapter, and who had helped save the Chapter and make the recruiting of new Astartes possible. Pallas was as fundamental to the Soul Drinkers as any of them, and yet here he was standing alongside a traitor.

Lygris tore his mind away from Pallas. Beneath the deck, amid the cogitators and electronics, a red warning light blinked and he could just hear the thrumming of heated metal buckling.

'You won't understand, Lygris...' said Pallas.

'This is betrayal, Pallas! Of all of us!'

'I don't believe, Lygris! I don't believe in Sarpedon, not after what happened to Tellos. We're falling apart and Sarpedon can't see it. It's either this or watch the Soul Drinkers die out. Eumenes has a lot of us on his side, Lygris, a lot, and if it comes down to it he's going to win. This is the only way.'

'No,' said Lygris dangerously. 'There is always another way.'

'Enough,' said Eumenes. 'Kill him.'

Lygris had no more warning than those two words before bolter fire stuttered towards him. He threw himself behind the command pulpit, the bolter rounds slamming into the delicate machinery, showering him with sparks.

Heated metal below the grille of the deck flared cherry-red, and the only warning was a screech as the outer casing of one of the cogitators fractured and superheated air sheared out.

The last control Lygris had activated on the command pulpit had dumped enormous amount of information, all the input from all the *Brokenback*'s sensors, into one cogitator beneath the deck. The volume of information had overloaded the equipment to the extent that its physical shell shattered, and a moment later an explosion of flame and razor-sharp data-crystal shards burst up from below the deck.

Eumenes's men took cover. Lygris jumped out from behind the pulpit and sprinted for the glowing hole now torn in the deck. Gunfire ripped around him, shots smacking into the pulpit and thudding into the viewscreen. Lygris tumbled through the tangle of smouldering equipment, turned end over end, until he felt the solid floor of the bridge sphere beneath him. He felt in the near-darkness and found an opening where one of the floor's panels had been removed to allow thick cables to snake through into the cogitators. Lygris grabbed a handful and pulled them free, opening up enough room for him to clamber into the network of conduits and tunnels beneath the bridge.

'Hold fire!' Lygris heard Eumenes yelling. 'You'll hit the equipment! You'll blind us!' The voice got quieter as Lygris pulled himself further down, and finally fell down into a wider tunnel.

Beneath the bridge was a long, winding tunnel of steel, bored through the mass of the *Brokenback* like the lair of a vast worm. Lygris had used it to lay cables from sensors and engine clusters all over the hulk, and he was the only person in the Soul Drinkers who had any idea where its various branches led. Lygris ran, head down, into the darkness, as the last few bolter shots rang dully through the metal.

Eumenes had betrayed the Soul Drinkers. Pallas too, and Throne knew how many others, were with him. And now they had the *Brokenback*. Lygris was the only one who could take it back off them, but he couldn't do it alone, and for the time being alone was exactly what he was. So he kept running, seeking the darkness in the heart of the hulk.

Eumenes knelt down to peer into the smouldering hole in the deck, through the equipment below the bridge, where Lygris had escaped.

'Don't bother,' said Pallas behind him. 'Lygris knows this hulk like the inside of his helmet. He can run forever.'

'But he won't,' said Eumenes. 'We've betrayed him. And you're with us – he's known you since long before Sarpedon ever led us astray. That's the worst kind of treachery there is. He won't just hide out as long as he thinks there's something he can do to hurt us.'

Pallas's expression was impossible to read behind the faceplate of his white helmet. 'Maybe,' he said. 'But he won't be easy to find. Certainly not by blundering after him.'

'I know you'd like your old friend to escape this,' said Eumenes. 'But he had his chance and didn't take it. He dies, Apothecary.'

Pallas didn't speak for a moment. 'Very well,' he said.

'And you know him best. Take a squad and find him. And Nisryus, go with him. Lygris can't hide from you.'

'Not from a precog,' said Nisryus, as if to himself. 'Not when I can see him first.'

Pallas left the bridge, the young psyker Nisryus behind him. Eumenes turned back to the rest of the bridge. The command pulpit was bleeding sparks and smoke was still coiling from the hole torn in the deck. 'Tydeus, do we have any ordnance control?'

Tydeus was crouched by one of the bridge helms. 'Just,' he said. 'We can aim the guns from here. It's not perfect, but...'

'It doesn't have to be,' replied Eumenes sharply. 'Target the heights. Then open fire.'

Sovelin crouched against the bole of a huge greatwood tree as he tried to pick out a voice from the static spooling from the vox-unit's handset. His artillery still held the clearing behind him. Sporadic gunfire was still spattering from the jungle and Sovelin's Vanqualians had formed a firing line among the artillery pieces, and when Sovelin had finished raising the warning he would join them to hold the hill. Sovelin should have felt proud that they were showing such discipline in the face of the enemy, taking the fight to the orks instead of abandoning the guns and running. But there was no room left amid the horror for anything like pride.

The Black Chalice. The very thought of it turned his gut. He had heard the stories as a child, everyone on Vanqualis had, and he had thought they were some kind of allegory – a personification of evil and corruption. But the Black Chalice was real, and its bearers were here, on Vanqualis, just a gunshot away.

'...palace of the countess,' said an officious voice, transmitted from the distant cities of Herograve. 'Unless you have an appointment, I am afraid...'

'No!' shouted Sovelin. 'No! I am Lord Sovelin Falken! I am commanding the Vanqualian Artillery in Nevermourn! Listen, the countess is my... she's my great aunt. Yes, great aunt. I spent summers at her retreat on the shores of Lake Felandin. She never thought I'd make it in the Warders. Ask her.'

'Sir, I...'

'Listen, damn you! There are orks everywhere and I might never be able to repeat this!'

'Very well,' said the voice, evidently trying to regain its composure. 'I shall be sure the correct members of the countess's household are informed.'

Sovelin gulped, and told the countess's chamberlain of the Black Chalice.

He was almost finished when a column of red-white fire lanced down from the sky and incinerated his artillery.

The handset still in his hand, scalding air battering against him, Sovelin Falken watched open-mouthed in horror as a pillar of coruscating laser blasted his Vanqualian Warders into dust and melted the mortar and autocannon pieces into sprays of white-hot liquid metal. Pulses of laser blew a deep crater in the ground and ignited the leaves of the trees ringing the clearing. The skin on Sovelin's face blistered in the heat and he was barely able to drag himself behind the tree, tongues of flame licking past him.

'It's started!' Sovelin couldn't hear his own voice and he was sure the link had gone down, but he had to try, he had to tell them. 'They have a fleet up there! They're killing us!'

The betrayal had begun. The Bearers of the Black Chalice had manipulated Vanqualis's defenders into position, and now they would wipe them out. Sovelin curled into a ball amid the storm of fire, and prayed to the Emperor that he would survive long enough to seek revenge.

Sarpedon shoulder-charged the warlord with every last drop of his strength, slamming into the beast's chest. Step by step he had forced it back, ground his way through the fight keeping the greenskin on its back foot, striking hard and fast without giving it a moment's respite. They had fought through the dense trees that swathed the hill, past the clearing where the Vanqualians were holding out, and back into the open ground that ran along the top of the cliff.

The warlord met Sarpedon's charge like an immovable wall of flesh and steel. It was wreathed in smoke, flame bursting from the joints of its metal-caged arm and chest as the mechanics of its repaired body burned hotter to keep it matching Sarpedon. Sarpedon and the warlord were face-to-face now, their conflict boiled down to a test of strength. The warlord's muscles writhed beneath its green-black skin and its eyes were narrowed to hateful red slits, its claw pressing against Sarpedon's chest while the creature's natural hand tried to dig its claws into Sarpedon's throat.

Sarpedon's ears were ringing with white noise as he poured everything into forcing the warlord back. He could smell the blood hissing against the red-hot mechanical plates of the warlord's body, and hear the huge bestial heart thudding in the ork's chest.

Sarpedon looked into the warlord's eyes. There was something horribly human there, something that echoed Sarpedon's own hatred of this alien who had come to Vanqualis to burn and destroy. The thought that there was something human about the creature's hatred filled Sarpedon with a sudden flood of rage and disgust.

With that final burst of raw anger, Sarpedon barged the ork off the cliff's edge. The warlord bellowed as it fell, reaching up with its mechanical claw. But it was too late – the claw closed on thin air and the warlord fell back down towards the canopy below. Its flailing knocked other orks off the cliff and everywhere there rose a terrible ork-ish cry of rage and sorrow as they saw their leader bested.

Pride swelled in Sarpedon's hearts. He had beaten the best the orks could throw at him. The defence of Vanqualis looked a little closer now, and the greenskins looked weak for the first time.

As if in reply to that thought, a lance of fire bored down through the sky behind him. Sarpedon turned in time to see the flash as the Vanqualian artillery was vaporised and flame rippled through the treetops. The shockwave almost knocked Sarpedon off the edge of the cliff and the nearby Soul Drinkers, who had been holding the cliff edge as Sarpedon battled the warlord, dived to the ground to take cover. The laser pulsed and rings of flame washed off the impact site, shredding the surrounded trees into flurries of burning leaves. Sarpedon held his ground, keeping an arm in front of his face to keep his skin from being scorched by the flame-hot wind tearing through the jungle.

'Lygris!' voxed Sarpedon as soon as he could hear himself think. 'What in the hells was that?'

There was no reply from orbit. 'Lygris? Was that from our guns? Lygris, come in!'

'Sarpedon!' yelled a familiar voice. It was Karraidin, his huge Termi-nator-armoured form crashing through the trees towards Sarpedon. 'Lord Sarpedon, it's…'

His voice was cut short by a volley of gunfire that slammed into the back of his enormous Terminator armour. Karraidin turned and fired back into the trees behind him with his storm bolter, rattling off a fear-some spray of fire. The replying fire didn't let up, and more and more shots smacked into Karraidin's armour, slamming deep scars into the ceramite plates, thudding into the thick armour encasing his torso.

'Captain!' yelled Sarpedon, sliding behind a boulder for cover.

'It's treachery, Sarpedon,' grimaced Karraidin. Sarpedon saw there was blood on his lips. 'They've got the ship. We're next.'

'Who?'

A bright flash of plasma burst from the trees and hit Karraidin square in the abdomen. The superheated liquid plasma ate through his abdominal plate and pushed Karraidin backwards, his armoured boots digging into the rock beneath him. But Karraidin did not fall – with awesome strength he held his ground, and when the flare of the plasma blast died down there was a great crater melted in the armour cover-ing his stomach. Amid the metallic stink of vaporised metal, Sarpedon could smell cooked flesh.

'Us,' said Karraidin, reloading his storm bolter.

Treachery, realised Sarpedon, betrayal from among the Soul Drinkers.

With a sickening lurch in his stomach, he realised that could be the one enemy that he couldn't defeat.

Fire battered into Karraidin, so heavy it tore chunks out of his shoulder pad and greave. Karraidin took a step forward, defying the enemies firing at him, the captain's form almost lost amid the explosive impacts that tore into him. Sarpedon could not help him now – if he left cover he would be shredded too. He could only watch as Karraidin carried on firing even as burning loops of entrails began to hang from the massive plasma wound in his stomach.

Slowly, agonisingly, Karraidin's steps faltered and he sank to one knee. He yelled wordlessly as he fired, and he was still firing as his white-hot storm bolter misfired and exploded in his hand.

'Fall back!' ordered Sarpedon to the rest of the Soul Drinkers holding the cliff-top. 'On me! Fall back!' He backed away from Karraidin, trying to keep cover between himself and the enemies firing on Karraidin. A few stray shots hit the rocks around Sarpedon, but it was Karraidin they were after.

Sarpedon had to watch as Karraidin literally fell apart before his eyes. Fire tore through one shoulder pad and Karraidin's arm came apart. Sparks flew as his bionic leg was shattered and buckled beneath him. The ammunition left in his storm bolter burst and took his other arm with it. He was still bellowing his defiance as he toppled backwards, the massive blocky form of his Terminator armour falling as slowly as one of the greatwood trees that rose around him.

As he fell back, Sarpedon could see shapes moving in the tree line. Space Marines, scouts and full battle-brothers in power armour, the barrels of their bolters glowing with the heat of sustained fire as they skulked forwards to finish off Karraidin. He was still breathing, gasping curses and threats, as the purple-armoured forms closed in on him. Sarpedon was too far away by now to see the old captain's final moments, but he could hear the point-blank bolter shots into ceramite and he knew that Karraidin was finally dead.

Sarpedon reached the tree line, and saw the Soul Drinkers he was leading closing around him. They were following him back, away from the cliffs. The traitors were following them and fire was falling on them now, zipping between the trees.

'Luko,' voxed Sarpedon. 'How's your position?'

'Quiet here,' replied Luko. 'The greenskins got tired of dying and joined to push on the heights.'

'Then be prepared to defend it. We're falling back to your position.'

'Falling back, commander? What happened?'

'We have been betrayed. Make ready, Luko, there is more at stake than greenskin blood now.' Sarpedon switched channels as he moved with his fellow Soul Drinkers towards the side of the valley held by

Luko. One Soul Drinker, Brother Farlumir, fell, his leg blasted open by a bolter shot. A volley of shots chewed through him as he struggled on the ground. A neat kill, fast and sure. A Space Marine's kill.

'All Soul Drinkers!' ordered Sarpedon over the vox. 'All loyal sons of Rogal Dorn! Fall back to Captain Luko's position! General retreat, and watch your backs!'

Acknowledgement runes flickered. Questions, too, flashing over the vox – why were they falling back? What had fired on the heights? Several officers did not reply at all – perhaps they, like Karraidin, had already been executed, or perhaps they were in league with the betrayers.

Sarpedon led his men into the trees and the dark green shadows closed around them. Everywhere there was chaos – gunfire from the orks and the troopers of the 901st as the greenskins scaled the cliffs again unopposed, the chanting of the aliens as their warlord readied them for another attack, bolter fire spattering through the trees as brother turned on brother in the darkness.

Betrayal. Sarpedon could barely believe it. Yet he had heard Karraidin die and known his fellow Soul Drinkers had fired the shots that killed him. And the *Brokenback* had fired on the Soul Drinkers' own lines. It had to be true. And that meant that Sarpedon had failed, because the traitors had laid the groundwork for this rebellion behind his back.

'I just had to kill Brother Gerontos,' voxed Luko. 'He was one of our new recruits. He tried to shoot Graevus in the back.'

'Then I failed,' said Sarpedon. 'I was supposed to teach them. I didn't teach them well enough. This is my doing.'

Eumenes was a natural fit for the *Brokenback*'s bridge. He looked like he had been born to direct the unfolding battle on Vanqualis. The stern industrial feel of the armoured sphere, and the finery of the battle honours hung from the curved ceiling, gave him trappings of power that suited his air of absolute confidence.

'Is it done?' said Eumenes into the vox-unit mounted on the command pulpit.

'Yes,' came the reply, transmitted from the surface of Vanqualis.

'Scout-Sergeant, seeing him fall is not enough. Karraidin is the toughest son of a grox I have ever met.'

'He's dead,' replied Scout-Sergeant Hecular. Hecular had been brought into the Soul Drinkers at the same time as Eumenes, but unlike Eumenes he had remained with the scouts. 'I turned his body over myself. There isn't much left.'

'Good.' There was satisfaction in Eumenes's voice. 'Karraidin was the bane of our lives. We couldn't cock a bolter without him telling how Sarpedon was leading us towards the promised land. Killing Karraidin was the first step in taking back the Chapter.'

'Then what's the next?' said Hecular. There was gunfire in the background of the transmission, and howls of static from the interference caused by the lance strike on the heights.

'Killing Sarpedon,' said Eumenes.

'Hah! I'll leave that one to you, Eumenes.'

'That's the plan. For now, get your men back, Hecular. The next strike is incoming and you're not important enough to hold fire for.'

Hecular signed off and Eumenes glanced up again at the screen showing the head of the Snakespine Valley. A huge crater smouldered on the crown of the lowest foothill – many men had died there, destroyed in the blink of an eye, and all Eumenes had done was give an order.

Eumenes had never claimed to be driven by a need for power, but it could not be denied that he had ended so many lives with nothing more than a word. Many, many more would die, of course. And it would take more than a simple order to kill Sarpedon.

'What news is there from the rest of our units?' said Eumenes.

'It's good,' replied Tydeus, who was manning another of the lecterns at the back of the bridge. Lygris had done his job well, and almost all the important systems on the hulk could be accessed from the bridge of the *Brokenback*. 'The Soul Drinkers are falling back towards the eastern ridge. Hecular drove them off the cliffs.'

'And the eastern ridge?'

'Salk's holding out there,' said Tydeus, with a smile. 'But our big gun's got the rest of it locked down. The penal troopers didn't stand a chance.'

'Then that's our strongpoint. Our brothers can gather there then strike out for the forest. We'll send down the Thunderhawks to pick them up once they're in a defensible position.'

'The 901st haven't broken down yet,' said Tydeus. 'There's a chance they could regroup and make things hard for us.'

'I don't think that will be a problem,' said Eumenes coldly. He flicked an activation stud and the whole of the *Brokenback* shook as the power coils of its laser batteries brimmed with power again.

The pict-screen in front of him flared again as a massive pulse of laser smashed down into the ground. This time the strike hit the cliffs themselves, boring through the rock and blasting shards of stone like meteors in every direction. A huge pall of smoke billowed up from the strike, and there could be no doubt that hundreds of greenskins as well as any Soul Drinkers and soldiers nearby had been killed instantly.

The cliffs collapsed, a massive drift of shattered stone flooding like water down over the canopy and into the valley. For several long moments there was stillness save the billows of smoke dissipating over the valley.

Then there was movement, tiny at first, from the high viewpoint looking like ants crawling over the long tongue of spoil that now reached into the valley. Orks, first hundreds then thousands of them. The collapse of the cliffs had created a slope leading up to the foothills, the perfect route for the greenskin horde to take the heights for which so many orks had already died. The army seethed forwards, covering the slope in dark green bodies, the thousands of orks bottled up in the valley suddenly free to charge forwards and raise hell among the soldiers who had kept them penned in.

'The 901st are dead,' said Eumenes as the orks poured up the slope into the heights. 'So is this planet.'

Most men would have thought twice about approaching a cordon of Space Marines, standing guard around an Astartes command post. But General Varr, spattered in mud and blood, walked straight towards the ring of Soul Drinkers standing guard in the dense jungle beyond the western ridge of the valley.

A gauntleted hand gripped his shoulder. The Soul Drinker looked down at Varr, the general's muddied face reflected in the eyepieces of the Space Marine's helmet.

'Halt,' said the Soul Drinker.

Varr was about to remonstrate with the man when a familiar, weary voice came from the clearing beyond. 'Let him go, Brother Kallidas.' It was Sarpedon's voice, but it didn't sound as confident or fearless as when Varr had spoken with him while planning the Serpentspine Valley operation.

The hand left Varr's shoulder and the general proceeded more carefully through the dense bank of trees ahead and emerged into a dank clearing, drenched in the permanent rain of water running off the almost solid canopy overhead. Several Soul Drinkers were on guard, ready to shoot – bolters swept over Varr before it was confirmed he wasn't an enemy. In the centre of the clearing stood Sarpedon.

Varr stopped dead. He had witnessed mutations on corrupted traitor soldiers before, and even sometimes hidden among his own men – tentacles for hands, extra eyes, vestigial tails, scaled skin and much stranger things besides. But he had never seen a mutation as spectacular as Sarpedon's arachnoid lower half, his eight legs of jointed exoskeleton packed with dark muscle.

'Throne above,' said Varr. It was all he could think to say, as if his ability to speak had been all but struck from him. It wasn't disgust that he felt, or even fear. It was a cold, disbelieving shock, for the combination of Space Marine and mutant monster was so utterly incongruous that for a moment Varr didn't properly register what his eyes were telling him. But the moment passed and Sarpedon the mutant was still stood in front of Varr

'General Varr,' said Sarpedon. 'You see now why I spoke to you through Captain Luko. I can never predict what a man's reaction will be when he sees me.'

'You know why I came here,' said Varr, swallowing back his shock. 'Your Space Marines deserted my lines and your fleet destroyed the Vanqualian artillery. Now the greenskins have run rampant. I have a thousand men dead at the very least, and half the survivors scattered around the valley. If I can regroup them I'll be fortunate to have half an army left. I want answers, commander.'

'Our Chapter has been betrayed,' said Sarpedon. 'Someone is usurping my command. One of our own. The Soul Drinkers are in revolt. The traitors have seized our ship and are trying to destroy us on the ground. Does that answer your questions, general?'

Varr looked at a loss. 'Betrayed? You are Space Marines! Do you mean to say the Emperor's finest have mutinied? You were… you were an inspiration! I saw the looks in my men's eyes when they realised the Angels of Death were on their side. They thought we could really save this planet. But no, Vanqualis will fall and my men will all be lost because you're no better than the scum I command. Hells, you're worse – my men are killers and thieves but at least they're all on the same damned side!'

Sarpedon reared up, and at his full height he was almost twice as tall as Varr. 'Do not presume, general, to know what manner of men we are.'

'There are those who worship you,' said Varr. He had gathered his wits now after witnessing Sarpedon's appearance, and the pride still left in him refused to be cowed by Sarpedon's presence. 'Do you know that? You are the Emperor's will! You are supposed to be the defenders of this Imperium!'

'No,' said Sarpedon gravely. 'Not us.'

Varr paused. 'You're not Imperial.'

'Not for a long time,' said Sarpedon. He indicated his mutated legs. 'The Imperium would hardly tolerate the likes of us defending it, do you not agree?'

'Then… what are you?'

Sarpedon settled down again, his legs folding down beneath him so he was just the height of a normal Astartes. 'That, general, is a more complex question than you realise.'

'You're renegades.'

'That's the short version, yes. We rejected the Imperium. Now we do the Emperor's own work, not the will of the Lords of Terra. Dark powers tried to corrupt us to their own will, but we broke away from them for they are the Emperor's enemies. That struggle resulted in the mutations you see.' Sarpedon looked Varr in the eye. 'The

Inquisition has killed men for knowing less than I have told you. The concept of the Emperor's finest going rogue is a dangerous piece of knowledge.'

'I have seen many things,' said Varr. 'This is not the strangest of them.'

Sarpedon allowed himself a smile. 'And you are a renegade yourself,' he said. 'Of sorts.'

'The Inquisition took exception to the bravery of my men,' said Varr bitterly. 'The Kar Duniash Heavy Lancers. Elites, armoured cavalry. An honour to command. We were stationed near the Agrippina system and we fought... I don't know what we fought. I can't describe them. Daemons, I suppose.'

'In the days before we split from the Imperium,' said Sarpedon, 'we saw it often. When the Imperial Guard fought against the servants of the Dark Powers, the Imperium would decide that they might have seen too much.'

'They wanted them dead,' continued Varr. 'Executed. The Inquisition ordered me to lead them into the middle of the desert where they would be bombed from orbit. They would be wiped out because they had not broken and fled like everyone else, they had fought and gone face to face with the Great Enemy. So I led my men into the mountains instead, into the caves, where the bombs wouldn't find them.'

'And for that, you were condemned. That sounds like the Inquisition I know.'

'Hah! More than just that, commander. The Inquisition had to send a regiment of stormtroopers down to that world to kill us. We gave them a hell of a fight. Months, it took them, up there in the mountains, to kill us all. It cost them a good few lives to take me alive. That's what sent me to the Penal Legions. That's why they didn't just shoot me on the spot. I humiliated them, so they wanted to humiliate me in return.'

'And did they succeed, general?'

Varr waved a dismissive hand. 'That,' he said bleakly, 'is for the Emperor to decide. In any case, even if you do the Emperor's work as you say you do, that does not change the fact that half your Astartes seem to have different ideas. And my men are still trapped on this world surrounded by orks.'

'I am afraid I cannot give you the answers you want to hear,' said Sarpedon. 'My Chapter is at war. I cannot fight my own brothers and save Vanqualis at the same time, nor can I help the 901st. I have no wish to see you and your men die here. But you have to fight this battle yourselves. Soon my men will move out to hunt down the traitors and fight them before they can get off-world, and it may be that very little of this Chapter survives. If there was another way to do this, Varr, I would take it, but you and your men are on your own.'

Varr shook his head as he turned to leave the clearing, to rejoin the men of the 901st and try to fight their way out of Nevermourn. 'We always were,' he said.

'How can we know when the battle is won?'
'Know only this. There is but a single battle, and it will never be won.'

– Daenyathos, *Catechisms Martial*

CHAPTER EIGHT

Laser fire rang around Raek's head as he ducked down behind a stone pew. The pew jutted absurdly from a chunk of chapel wall that orbited the gilded obsidian sarcophagus in the centre of the asteroid's bizarre temple. He was about halfway up, clinging on as the architecture shifted and laser fire lanced through the air towards him. The gun-servitors were old, and that meant they were good – they were fast and accurate, their targeting cogitators far more agile than those of the lumbering tech-constructs Raek had fought on the *Brokenback*'s training decks.

Raek leaned out a fraction and brought his rifle's barrel up swiftly, instantly drawing a bead on the servitor firing at him. The red of its metallic eye blinked as it registered Raek as a target, an instant before the sniper rifle's bullet sliced neatly through one of the servitor's anti-grav units. The servitors' shells were armoured but the anti-grav units were not and the machine tumbled down towards the curving polished floor below.

'Iktinos!' shouted Raek.

'Almost there,' came Iktinos's calm reply. He was somewhere above Raek, climbing through the precarious shifting layers of the temple as the gun-servitors flitted around him.

An icon flickered against Raek's retina. It was an incoming vox – and not one that Raek could ignore.

'Sergeant,' said Eumenes, the superiority and determination in his voice obvious even through the background noise.

'Eumenes,' said Raek. 'We're under fire here.'

'It's started,' said Eumenes. 'The rebellion is in the open now.'

'Then you need me to…'

'Yes. And bring me back something the Chaplain can't live without. Iktinos will be difficult to kill. Don't leave it to chance.'

'Chance, Eumenes? I don't believe I'm familiar with that concept.'

'And make it quick. I need to get the *Brokenback* out of this system as soon as I can.'

'It will be done. Raek out.'

Raek flicked the vox-link shut. Eumenes had been correct, of course – the first Space Marines had been created by the Emperor to be difficult to kill, and Iktinos was tougher than most. But no matter how superhuman, Iktinos would go down just like everyone else with one of Raek's bullets through his eye.

Raek's thoughts were broken as every muscle in his body tensed on instinct. He had been born with his senses hard-wired to throw him into maximum alertness at the slightest stimulus, like a hair trigger in his mind.

It was the silence. The gunfire had stopped.

The gun-servitors hung in the air, the red target-lights extinguished. The spindly barrels of their lasguns hung limp below them like the folded legs of hovering insects. Slowly, they floated back towards the metallic pods set into the chunks of floating architecture.

Raek scanned carefully, rifle high. The servitor pods hissed closed and there was silence again, roaring in his ears.

'Chaplain?' he called out. 'What happened to the defences?'

'I shut them down,' said Iktinos from above. 'We are safe, novice.'

Raek stood up, keeping the rifle high. Iktinos, he thought, was anything but safe.

The Chaplain was somewhere above him. Raek climbed, keeping his footing on the marble and granite, his gun held in the crook of one arm so he could bring it up and fire in an instant. He reached up and pulled himself onto the next chunk of architecture as it drifted past above him – it was a section of an arch, almost upside-down so it was like Raek was now sitting on a crooked crescent moon of stone.

He could see Iktinos, on a lip of obsidian jutting from the entrance to the tomb around which the rest of the shattered temple orbited. Raek brought up the rifle and against any other target he would have sent a shot right through the spine or the back of the head. But Iktinos wore artificer power armour, and only a shot through one of the critical weak spots – the eyepiece, the tiny spot over the throat, the joint under the arm where a shot from the right angle would pierce both hearts – would produce the guaranteed kill Raek needed. Iktinos walked into the tomb, and Raek's chance was gone.

Raek was a patient man. He could wait for days, for weeks, before taking a shot. The only thing he really remembered from his childhood was the baking heat of the desert sun as he lay on the hot sands for days, the scope of his hunting rifle scanning the horizon for that one shot. He had been the best hunter on that planet even before the Imperial Guard had arrived to take away the many mutants of his tribe, and his family and friends, and he had learned the kill-spots that would take down a guardsman. He had learned quickly how even a disciplined soldier will take risks to save his fellow trooper when that trooper has a bullet in the gut or a shot through the knee. And he learned to recognise when only a headshot would do.

They had never found Raek. Even when his people were gone, the adolescent Raek had survived to kill again. They had sent whole squads, whole platoons after him, and they had never got him. It had been Iktinos who had heard the tales of the invisible killer, and gone out into the desert to find him. The fact that Iktinos was now his target meant nothing at all to Raek, no more than the Guardsmen whom Raek had murdered from kilometres away over the sand dunes.

Raek jumped lightly up onto the next level of the floating, shattered temple, close enough to see a little way into the tomb. A faint pale bluish glow came from inside. The cut obsidian of the walls was gilded with symbols of the old Chapter – the chalice of the Soul Drinkers, stylised images of Space Marines more like hieroglyphics telling a story than portraits of Astartes. Gilded letters ringed the images, but Raek didn't recognise the language.

Raek made it to the threshold of the tomb. He pulled himself onto the ledge outside the doorway and gravity suddenly shifted. While the gravity in the rest of the temple had pulled towards the inside surface of the great spherical chamber, it now pulled Raek to the floor of the tomb, as if the tomb were a normal building on solid ground on any other world.

The tomb was big, bigger than it had looked from the temple entrance. Space seemed to flow strangely in the asteroid. Raek's enhanced vision struggled to pierce the veil of darkness inside. Raek pulled the hood of the voidsuit back from his face – there was a breathable atmosphere in the tomb, and he didn't want anything between his target and the naked eye.

'Chaplain?' he said, hoping to gauge Iktinos's location from the reply. But there was none.

Beyond the tomb's threshold, the darkness lifted. Inside the tomb was even larger, the ceiling high above Raek, the cavernous space criss-crossed with walkways and ladders. It was a library, and thousands upon thousands of books must have been stacked on the miles of shelves and cases, made of gold and black glass, that covered every surface. Soaring pillars were encrusted with shelves groaning with scrolls, and overhead hung huge smouldering censers that bathed everything in a deep amber glow.

At the far end was a golden chalice, five metres high and flanked by the images of two Space Marines, rendered in gilt against the obsidian wall. There were gun-servitors, too, standing mute guard over the library, hovering over bookcases or high up near the gilded ribs of the vaulted ceiling.

Iktinos had known how to shut them down. The library was defended by extensive security systems, but Iktinos had simply walked in. He had known all along what was in the asteroid.

Raek had thought that he was the traitor here. But perhaps Iktinos had betrayed them all.

Raek's rifle played between the bookcases and pillars, seeking out Iktinos on the high walkways and among the shadows that pooled around the ground level. The air here was dry and cold, no doubt to preserve the books, some of which looked very old indeed. But there was no movement save the slow, pendulous swaying of the censers overhead, and the corresponding shadows that flowed across the floor like the waves of a black sea.

'Novice,' came Iktinos's voice behind Raek. 'Do you now understand what it means to be a Soul Drinker?'

Raek froze, every nerve wound up tight. Iktinos had got behind him. That was impossible. No one had ever managed such a thing before, not against Raek. The place must have addled his senses somehow, dulled his mind or deceived him.

'We are the inheritors of a tradition as old as the Imperium, novice,' continued Iktinos, his voice so calm and level it was almost hypnotic. 'This Chapter is more than an army. It is the instrument of the Emperor, His hand lain upon the Imperium. In blindness we have gone for so long, but now we are free, the final stages can begin.'

Raek could feel Iktinos behind him, standing close among the shadows by the threshold. He could leap back and drive the stock of his rifle into Iktinos's throat, or whirl around and hope he was quick enough to fire before Iktinos got out of the way. Against a normal human opponent there would have been no question, but Iktinos had a Space Marine's reflexes and a lifetime of battle experience.

For the first time Raek cursed himself silently. He should have seen this coming, he should have accounted for Iktinos being one step ahead. He should have just been better.

'But the details elude you, novice. You do not know what all this means. You do not know the future. This revelation is all you will ever know. The Chapter's destiny will be written without you.'

Raek dropped to the floor, bringing his rifle round to blast Iktinos in the midriff. His senses slowed time down and the library swung around him ponderously. Iktinos's black-armoured form came into view, his bone-white grinning mask, the venom-green glint of his eyepieces.

Iktinos was faster. He caught Raek around the throat and tore away his rifle barrel. Raek tried to pry his captor's gauntleted hand away as his air was cut off.

'If you understood,' intoned Iktinos as Raek struggled, 'you would beg me to be a part of it. But you never will.'

Iktinos dropped Raek and the rifle. Raek hit the ground hard and lunged for his gun. Quicker than thought, Iktinos had his crozius in his hand. The power field flared, edging the obsidian and gold of the tomb in harsh blue-white. The crozius fell in an arc – again, time slowed down, so Raek had to watch it as it followed its, deep, pure crescent through the air towards his head.

The crozius cracked into the side of Raek's skull and took his head clean off. The head thudded wetly into the side of one of the bookcases and the body slumped to the black stone floor, pumping blood out into the darkness, one hand a few centimetres from his rifle.

Iktinos looked down at the novice's body. There had been a rebellion, of course – it had been prophesied that another Chapter War could occur, and pose a threat to the grand plan. In some ways it was a shame that a novice had to die – the novices were a foundation of the next phase in the Chapter's history. But Iktinos had to survive. He was the last of the Chaplains, and everything depended on him.

Iktinos looked up at the library, the weight of the knowledge held inside like a stone slab on Iktinos's soul. Some men, had they known what knowledge was contained there, would have broken down and wept when they imagined what appalling devastation would be wreaked if it ever became known by the Imperium at large. But nothing caused Iktinos fear. He had faith. That rarest of commodities – true, pure, absolute faith.

Iktinos walked to the closest bookcase and took a book down from its upper shelf. The chalice embossed on its cover told him everything he needed to know. He opened it and began to read, and the blessed truth flowed through him like blood.

The Hall of Commanders was dominated by monumental sculptures of the Howling Griffons' great past – commanders and Chapter Masters who had orchestrated the Chapter's most glorious campaigns. They loomed over the circular hall, jewelled eyes focused on the huge tactical holomat like a round table in the centre of the room. The images of these legendary commanders were there to remind the assembled officers of the Howling Griffons to show humility, that there was always something the Chapter's fallen heroes had to teach them.

'A trap,' said Mercaeno, 'is the only way.'

Mercaeno stood over the holomat, which was showing a three-dimensional map of Nevermourn, along with the short stretch of sea and the coast of Herograve. The hives were glittering jewels of projected light, and it was obvious from their size how many billions of people would die if the orkish tide reached Herograve.

'The greenskins landings are confirmed here,' continued Mercaeno. Indicators appeared all over the map, angry red blips that signified where ork asteroids had come down in Nevermourn's jungles. 'The first landings were at Palatium. The planetary defence force was destroyed and the orks are opposed only by a Penal Legion. It is unlikely the troops will do anything more than slow the orks.'

'Jungle is their ground,' said Captain Darion, of the Ninth Company. His red and gold armour was studded with gemstones, each one signifying a notable kill. 'War has to be up close. Greenskins love it.'

'That is why,' said Mercaeno, 'we give them Nevermourn.'

A murmur went around the Hall of Commanders. A dozen or so officers were gathered there, resplendent in the heraldry of the Howling Griffons, each one proudly displaying kill markings or inscribed oaths on his armour. Mercaeno commanded the whole force, along with the veterans of the First Company. Darion had the Ninth, a company heavy in assault units – Darion himself was a formidable assault captain with hundreds of kills to his name. Captain Borganor led the Tenth Company, which had until recently consisted of newer recruits and scouts. The bloody battlefields that had led the Chapter to Periclitor had seen most of those young Astartes attain the rank of full Space Marine, and the Tenth was now as battle-hardened as any other company in the Chapter.

'Give it to the alien?' said Borganor, a leathery and allegedly unkillable veteran whose body was loaded with bionics to replace the many body parts he had lost.

'Orks are simple creatures, captain,' said Mercaeno. 'Their strategies can easily be predicted. They will surge towards the coast and assemble there to strike against the shore of Herograve.' The holomat showed a stretch of coastline. 'This is where they will land. The crossing is easiest here. With the Warders gone the orks will have no reason to think it will be defended by anything more than a handful of civilian militiamen.'

'But it will be defended by us,' said Captain Darion.

'Exactly. The greenskins will be at their most vulnerable when landing. We will meet them there and gun them down. The surf will be choked with their dead and the scourge will be thrown back into the sea. A drawn-out, purposeless conflict in the jungles will be dispensed with and the enemy will be destroyed with one stroke. This is the way of Roboute Guilliman, and the word of the Codex Astartes.'

'There is risk,' said Captain Borganor. 'We will only have one chance. The greenskins do not have enough tactical acumen for anything other than a single massed invasion of Herograve. If we do not stop them there…'

'We *will* stop them,' said Mercaeno. 'This Chapter swore an oath. It will be kept.'

'The orks will take a far greater risk with the invasion,' said Darion. 'It is they who will be punished for it.'

'Then I agree,' said Borganor. 'This is the way of Guilliman.'

'No,' said a voice from the back of the Hall of Commanders. 'It is not. Guilliman never gave ground to the enemy. He never threw away the lives of Imperial citizens.'

The eyes of the officers turned to Inquisitor Thaddeus. In spite of his rank, Thaddeus was still just a man, and as such he was dwarfed by the Astartes around him.

'You talk out of turn,' said Mercaeno sharply. 'Guilliman would sacrifice a billion lives if it would save a billion and one. You know that as well as I do.'

'Exactly, Lord Librarian,' said Thaddeus, approaching the holomat. 'Sacrifice. Tens of thousands of refugees from Palatium and elsewhere on Nevermourn are making their way to the coast. If we hold back, they will never make it. These are Imperial citizens, those same citizens of Vanqualis you swore your oath to defend. This Chapter should be down there in the jungles now, ensuring their safety.'

'Your tone,' said Darion dangerously, 'suggests we are lacking in courage. Inquisitor, you should know by now that such a thing is ill-advised in the company of Astartes.' Darion's hand strayed towards the sword at his hip.

Mercaeno raised a calming hand. 'Darion, there is no need for offence. The inquisitor here does not understand honour as we do. To him, honour consists of succeeding in his mission no matter who must break their oaths or fail in their duty, so long as this exalted agent of the Inquisition succeeds.'

Thaddeus didn't return Darion's offended glare. 'Lord Librarian, the fact remains that if the orks gather strength in Nevermourn they might never be defeated. Every hour more land in the jungles of–'

'I command three companies of the finest army this Imperium has ever fielded!' barked Mercaeno. 'No greenskin vermin can threaten our victory! You know as well as I do that fighting on Nevermourn is a waste of battle-brothers' lives. No man worthy of the Inquisition would be so foolish. Why are you here, Thaddeus? You care nothing for Vanqualis or its people. What do you seek on Nevermourn?'

Thaddeus was silent for a long moment, the officers of the Howling Griffons staring at him accusingly.

'That,' said Thaddeus at length, 'is for the Inquisition to know.'

Borganor banged a fist on the edge of the holomat table. 'Enough of this!' he sneered. 'The inquisitor is privileged even to be here. The trap will be laid.'

'Yes,' said Mercaeno. 'The trap will be laid and the greenskin will die. Inquisitor Thaddeus, it is clear to me that your mission here does not coincide with ours. Your authority has little foundation here. You are very far away from your colleagues and among us you are just a man. I had hoped that we had come to understand one another, but it seems that you cannot change. Be grateful that I have not yet ejected you from the fleet.'

'Take your leave, inquisitor,' said Captain Darion darkly. 'My tolerance has its limits.'

Thaddeus looked around the room, at the dark eyes looking back. 'Very well,' he said. 'This battle is yours to command, Lord Librarian.' Thaddeus turned and walked out of the Hall of Commanders.

Mercaeno and his captains looked back to the holomat, and plotted out the details of the trap that would end tens of thousands of greenskin lives in the name of the Emperor.

Vanqualis's moon was a sinister green eye with a great dark crater as a pupil, glaring down at Nevermourn. Its thin greenish light barely penetrated the jungle canopy and dappled the mud-spattered dark purple armour of the Soul Drinkers squad as it advanced through the murk.

'Damn this filth,' said Sergeant Salk bleakly. 'This place will never clean off.'

Among the roots and mud around him, the rest of his squad slowly, quietly advanced to the top of the small ridge, their armoured feet sinking knee-deep into the near-liquid mud. 'We'll have to leave some scars of our own, then,' said Brother Karrick, Squad Salk's heavy bolter gunner. Karrick sported a bionic arm, strong enough to let him carry the bulky heavy bolter with ease. 'To make it even.'

'Visual,' said Brother Treskaen, lying on the slope of the ridge so he could see beyond. Salk scrabbled up beside him and followed his gaze.

In the centre of a large clearing in the jungle ahead of Squad Salk stood a fortress. The fortress was very old, probably dating to the time of the earliest colonies on Nevermourn when House Falken was only just beginning to carve out its safe havens in what had been then an unexplored jungle paradise. It was a crumbling edifice of reinforced rockcrete, rusted bands poking through the pitted surface like ribs, its blocky cylindrical base surmounted by ugly, brutish battlements. Varr and Sarpedon had not expected the fortress to mean much to the orks, who weren't in the habit of capturing strongpoints or holding ground. But it wasn't orks that Squad Salk were stalking.

'Is there movement?' asked Salk.

'None yet,' said Treskaen, sighting along his bolter.

'Wait,' said Karrick, sliding into the mud beside them. 'There. South-west. Light.'

Salk could see it. It was the laser sight in a sniper rifle, typically used by the best shots among the Chapter's scouts. It was playing along the foliage that crowded up against the side of the fortress, and as Salk followed the thin crimson line he could see the scout crouched down, almost in pitch darkness, among the brutal battlements.

'It's them,' said Treskaen. He spat into the mud to the side of him. 'Traitors.'

'They're dug in,' said Karrick. 'Look at that place.'

'There will be a way in,' replied Salk. 'There always is, unless Dorn himself designed it.'

'If we had the *Brokenback* we could burn them out,' said Treskaen, with hate running deep in his voice. 'Burn them all. Let them rot in the mud.'

'These are our brothers,' said Karrick.'

'*Were* our brothers,' hissed Treskaen. 'Now they're no better than the xenos filth we came here to kill.'

'I know,' said Karrick defensively. 'But it wasn't long ago we fought alongside them.'

'It wasn't long ago, brother, that we fought for the Imperium.'

'They are both traitors and brothers,' said Salk as he watched the scout move along the battlements, keeping a careful watch on the jungle around the fortress. 'Somewhere along the line we made this happen. One of us made a decision that led to this, and the rest of us accepted it.'

'You mean Sarpedon?' said Karrick.

'This is no one man's responsibility,' replied Salk.

'Tell that to the betrayers,' said Treskaen, little of the venom gone from his voice. 'Sarpedon's the one they want. Karraidin was a warning. The first chance they get they'll kill him.'

'No,' said Karrick. 'First chance they get they'll make it off this planet and strand us here. Maybe take a few pot shots with the *Brokenback* before they disappear.'

'Then we shall not give them the chance.' Salk flicked onto the command vox-channel. 'Salk here. I've got a squad to the fortress perimeter.'

'Any sign of them?' came Sarpedon's voice.

'The traitors are holding it. It's in bad repair but it's still solid enough.'

'Make a circuit if you can,' said Sarpedon. 'We need to know entrances and exits. But don't be seen.'

Salk looked back towards the squad fortress, its dark grey mass picked out in sallow green by the glaring eye of Vanqualis's moon. 'They'll know we are coming, commander.'

'I know,' said Sarpedon, something like resignation in his voice. 'But this is how it has to be done. I'll have the rest of the men move up towards your position and make ready for an assault. They could be gone by morning.'

'Understood. And commander?'

'Sergeant?'

'Do we know who is leading them? Who instigated all this?'

'I have some guesses, sergeant, as do you. When I see the answer with my own eyes, then I will be sure enough to tell it as the truth.'

'Should we have seen it coming?'

Sarpedon paused before replying, a moment too long. 'We gain nothing from looking for failures in our past. Our duty now is to put it right.'

'Understood,' said Salk. 'I'll take my squad around to get the layout of the place.'

'Good work, brother,' said Sarpedon. 'We will be with you soon. Be ready to fight at dawn.'

'What is it that makes us Astartes?'
  'Our augmentations and battlegear are as nothing compared to the mastering of our own fears. It is this that places us above the human race.'

– Daenyathos, *Catechisms Martial*

CHAPTER NINE

That night, the stars that shone down on Herograve shone down on blood. The city reeked of fear, and in countless places that fear blossomed into death. One of the great squares, where the hive city's grand avenues intersected, saw such a blossoming, and Vanqualis's ice-green moon stared impassively as men and women died in fear.

The people were piled up in the square, clambering over one another. At the walls and in the corners they formed huge quivering mounds of human forms, writhing through limbs and bodies to reach higher up the smooth unforgiving walls. They thronged the avenue behind, shoving forward, and even from the balcony high above their screams could be heard. But they kept coming, streaming from their homes, climbing over the bodies of their fellow citizens to scale the walls of the square into which the packed avenue emptied. At the top of the walls were spiked battlements with firing slits manned by House Falken's family retainers, who watched bemusedly as thousands upon thousands of citizens died in the crush below.

'Why do they do this?' asked Countess Ismenissa.

'It is said that a cardinal has arrived from off-world,' said the countess's chamberlain, stood beside her on the balcony. 'And that he will bless all who file past his throne with the Emperor's beneficence. He is supposed to be beyond that wall, in the vault of the Temple of the Imperial Soul.'

'And is this true?'

'No, my lady, it is not,' replied the chamberlain. 'It is not known whence this rumour came.'

The countess sighed, and shook her head. 'Send a detachment of house troops,' she said, 'with gas grenades and water cannon. Disperse the crowds in the street and start clearing the square.'

'Yes, my lady.'

'And keep telling them to stay in their homes. Some of them may listen.' Countess Ismenissa waved a hand at the square below the balcony, where many men and women were dying beneath heaps of their fellow commoners. 'I must take my court from this tower. I do not dare imagine the stench come morning.'

'It shall all be done. With your leave, my lady.'

'To your duties, chamberlain.'

The chamberlain left the balcony, walking through the grand windows, which stood open onto the astonishing view of the hive, marred by the tragedy unfolding below. It was not the first such occurrence among the cities of Herograve. Word had got out about a shipment of food and weapons for the house enclave in Hive Scendalean, and the riotous looting of the convoy had turned into an all-out battle in the streets. It was still smouldering among the soaring, age-blackened hab-towers that rose from Hive Scendalean like nails driven into the city.

An apocalyptic cult had proclaimed the orks to be a scourge sent by the Emperor to punish the sinners of Vanqualis, and had set off bombs and committed massacres in Hive Lastrantus and the Ashcoast Colonies to kill as many citizens as possible and spare them the terrors of the greenskins' wrath. In every hive commoners were being seized by an insane desperation, and were killing themselves and their families to end the horror. Random killings and lootings were spreading faster than any disease. The orks had ended countless lives among the people of Herograve, and not one greenskin had even set foot on the continent yet.

Countess Ismenissa turned away from the grim sight below and walked from the balcony into her state rooms. They were lavish, with deep carpets and expensive drapings everywhere, gilded and hardwood furniture, and many of the tapestries in the style for which House Falken was famed. Though the rooms were fully furnished and had an imposing four-poster bed, they were purely for receiving diplomats and other family members – Countess Ismenissa lived day to day in the far humbler rooms on the level below. A couple of the countess's children stared down at the carnage below, though their dead minds could not understand the suffering unfolding down in the square.

A House Falken retainer, in the emerald green and deep orange silk uniform of a herald, was waiting for her inside the room. The countess had planned to spend some time reviewing the situations in each of Herograve's major cities, and she had not expected to be interrupted.

'What do you want?' she asked sharply. The countess realised with a start that she had not slept for some time, and her temper was frayed.

'My countess, Lord Sovelin has contacted your court. He said his was a matter of the gravest urgency.'

'Sovelin? I do not recall the name.'

'He left instructions that you be told about the summers on Lake Felandin, should you not remember him.'

'Sovelin. Yes... yes, one of Althelassa's brood. Slated for the Warders, though that skinny sickly boy could never have held a gun, I thought. He's alive, you say?'

'As of an hour and a half ago, my lady,' said the herald. He was young, and obviously did not relish his task of passing on what was sounding more and more like bad news. The countess's children hissed at him quietly from behind their mistress's skirts.

The countess held out her hand expectantly. 'Then let us see what he has to say.'

The herald handed her a folded parchment on which Lord Sovelin Falken's message had been transcribed. The countess's eyes flickered over the fragmented message transcribed from Sovelin's own words, which in many places had been unintelligible thanks to the gunfire and explosions in the background.

The mention of the Black Chalice made her hands tighten around the parchment, and her face become even paler and more skeletal as if her skin was translucent and her face was the skull beneath.

'The Black Chalice,' she said to herself. She heard the children flinch behind her.

'They are here?' said the herald, shocked into speaking out of turn.

Under other circumstances the countess would have had the herald chastised, but this time she could not blame him. Every child of Herograve was taught of the Black Chalice – fairytale monsters from the planet's blackest past, monsters from beyond reality of whom the vilest of heretics and cultists were but mere shadows. Preachers used the Bearers of the Black Chalice as allegories for evil and corruption, and mothers told their children fanciful stories of how all evil on Vanqualis flowed from it. The countess knew, and most commoners suspected, that the Chalice had its foundation in reality, some horrendous trauma that had wounded Vanqualis so deeply that the stories of the Black Chalice and its bearers had never ceased to be told.

'Open up a link with the *Cerulean Claw*,' said the countess. 'It should be close enough to forgo the need for an astropath. This is no longer just about the greenskins, the Dark Powers have their eyes on our world and our allies must be warned. Go!'

The herald hurried out of the state rooms. The countess was left alone with Sovelin's message in her hands. Who would have thought that Sovelin, that pasty wretch banished to the artillery, would have a part to play in the return of the Black Chalice? The Emperor's will could be obscure sometimes.

The screams from the square below were getting louder, mixed in with gunfire and the engines of riot control vehicles. The countess closed the grand windows to shut out the sound, as she contemplated how to tell Chief Librarian Mercaeno of the Howling Griffons that his Astartes would be going to battle with something far worse than the greenskins.

Dawn broke through the jungle, tinting everything a dark green as Vanqualis's sun forced its rays through the canopy. The greenish light turned the purple armour of the Soul Drinkers black as they gathered in a broad crescent echoing the curve of the fortress's southern wall.

'In position,' came Salk's vox. Salk held the western end of the Soul Drinkers' line.

'Ready here,' voxed Captain Graevus, whose assault unit anchored the eastern point of the line.

'Good. You two are the ends of the line. If the traitors counterattack and get round you, they will surround and crush us.'

'If they get past me then I'm dead,' said Graevus. He didn't speak with bravado – it was a simple statement of fact.

'Soul Drinkers,' said Sarpedon over the all-squads vox channel. He could see his Astartes all around him, beetle-black in the breaking dawn light, crouched down deep among the undergrowth and looping roots, huddled in the cover of the massive gnarled tree trunks. 'Every battle we have fought has brought us a new test. Nevermourn has led us to the sternest test yet. The enemy are our brothers, yet they are also traitors who must be defeated. Let there be no doubt – our objective is to kill them, those Space Marines alongside whom we have all fought many times. Some of you were there for the first Chapter War. All of you have heard tell of the depths we had to reach to come through it. This battle will be no less terrible. Nevertheless, a Space Marine must know neither fear nor doubt in the midst of battle. Know the traitors are telling themselves exactly the same thing. The next time we are together in peace, we shall be celebrating our victory and mourning those who had to die. This is the way of Rogal Dorn and of the Emperor. Cold and fast, Soul Drinkers, and move out.'

As one, the line moved forwards towards the great dark shape of the fortress. Over the years the fort had sunk into the waterlogged soil and it was surrounded by a mass of sucking mud, thick and deep enough that anyone weaker than a Space Marine would have been dragged down and trapped there. Sarpedon's talons cut through the morass as he moved forwards shoulder to shoulder with the men he could still call battle-brothers. It was dark in the shadow of the fortress, its glowering battlements only edged by the sun's first rays, but the sharp, enhanced eyes of the traitors' scouts would surely spot Sarpedon's Soul Drinkers advancing and start the battle well before they got to the walls.

The southern side of the fortress had a wide, pitted rockcrete causeway leading to an enormous gate of age-stained plasteel. This was the Soul Drinkers' objective, and it would surely be the place most heavily defended by the traitors. If Sarpedon wanted to get inside and deal with the traitors face to face, he would have to fight a battle they had prepared, throwing his men at the gates to force the traitors to face him.

It was ugly. No sane general would have accepted it. But Sarpedon was not a general of the Imperial Guard, who had to cope with the weaknesses and indiscipline of their men. He was a Space Marine, and so were those under his command. Tactical insanity, the willingness to fight battles that no commander of lesser men would contemplate, was the weapon of choice for the Space Marines.

With bleak inevitability, the first streaks of gunfire thudded down through the overhanging foliage into the mass of mud and rotting vegetation through which the Soul Drinkers were advancing. Sniper fire whistled down into the mud. A Soul Drinker stumbled and fell, and was dragged forwards – alive or dead – by one of his squadmates so he was not left behind by the advance. Movement up on the battlements showed the traitors were preparing, gathering for the sacred moment when the enemy came within bolter range.

Sarpedon had been there many times. That range was etched into the consciousness of every Space Marine – the place where war turned from big guns and artillery to cut and thrust, single shots, volleys of fire and diving for cover.

More fire. Another battle-brother fell. A missile streaked down from the battlements and threw a black claw of mud into the air. Bolter range hovered closer, and the Soul Drinkers were sighting down their bolters ready to open up. Sarpedon's psychic powers did not allow him to receive telepathic messages or read minds, but even his latent power picked up the tension, the wound-up intensity that replaced human fear in a Space Marine's mind. He could feel it from the traitors, too, vibrating through the jungle, and he knew then that these were his brothers, fighting because they believed as completely as he did.

The advancing Soul Drinkers crossed bolter range. 'Charge!' ordered

Sarpedon, and his voice was drowned out by a curtain of burning shrapnel as hundreds of bolters opened up as one.

Brothers fell. A body tumbled from the battlements. The noise was appalling. More and more traitors were joining their brothers on the walls.

'Demolition teams forward!' ordered Sarpedon over the vox. Several squads ran onwards through the mud as the rest of the Soul Drinkers covered them, hunkering down behind shattered tree stumps or knots of rock-hard roots.

But the fire was too heavy. The traitors had won too many of the Soul Drinkers over to their side. The demolition teams were pinned down, and more of Sarpedon's battle-brothers were dying with every moment. Brother Phokris died, his helmet blown wide open even as he pressed the firing stud on his missile launcher. Brother Wrackath fell to the ground by Sarpedon's side, his leg sheared off by heavy bolter fire. Sarpedon himself folded his legs beneath him to crouch down behind the trunk of a massive fallen tree, mud spraying all over him as bolter rounds smacked into the ground.

The closest demolition team, led by Sergeant Salk, was prone in the mud, surviving only thanks to the slope of the low rise ahead of them. They couldn't advance. None of them could. The ruined jungle around the fortress was becoming a no-man's land, and the traitors' fire was too heavy for the Soul Drinkers to make it across.

Against any other foe, the Soul Drinkers would have stormed the place, cold and fast, just as their Philosopher-Soldier Daenyathos had described in his *Catechisms Martial*. Against human rebels or alien scum, they would have braved the fire and relied on the shock of their assault to carry the day. But not against fellow Space Marines. No more dangerous opponents existed in the galaxy.

Through the gunfire, Sarpedon could hear a scream of engines from overhead. He glanced up and saw a flare of engines through the canopy, bright against the darkened dawn sky.

With no further warning, the Thunderhawk gunship plunged down through the canopy, its nose-mounted guns instantly opening up and raking the battlements of the fortress with fire. A side door opened and a figure leaned out – black-armoured with a faceplate of pale bone. Iktinos.

Iktinos leapt out of the gunship, trusting in his battlegear to protect him from the long fall. As he hurled himself out of the door the gunship's engines flared and the Thunderhawk hurtled towards the battlements.

Traitors dived for cover among the huge rockrete slabs of the battlements. Some of them were too late. The Thunderhawk slammed into the battlements, the back of its armoured body breaking against the

fortress, and skidded along the top of the wall. Ammunition cooked off
inside the shattered craft and its fuel load followed, erupting in a great
orange-black bloom.

'Forward!' yelled Sarpedon, as the fire from the battlements faltered.

The Soul Drinkers line advanced, the demolition teams breaking
cover and running. Sarpedon could hear war cries going up from
his battle-brothers. He followed them, feeling the aegis circuit of his
armour pulsing as he drew on the great well of psychic power inside
him.

Fear. That was Sarpedon's weapon. He delved into the lower reaches
of his mind to dredge up that which caused him an emotion most
resembling the fear that normal men were cursed with.

The primarch Rogal Dorn strode over the battlements, the golden
yellow of his armour burning with hatred at the traitors. Great gilded
eagles, vast and terrifying, loomed down from the canopy. From the
burning wreckage of the Thunderhawk strode the heroes of the Soul
Drinkers, those who had died to make the Chapter free – and among
them was Daenyathos, the Philosopher-Soldier who had written out
the Soul Drinkers' way of war thousands of years before.

The traitors, like all the Soul Drinkers, had trained with the Hell to
help steel their souls against the hallucinations Sarpedon could conjure
– and even without that experience, as Space Marines they were difficult
men to shake. Sarpedon forced the Hell higher, casting wrathful flames
into the eyes of the Chapter's dead and making Dorn tower over the
fortress, his rage like lightning tearing down through the jungle.

Salk's demolition team threw themselves against the base of the wall
beside the gate, where the overhang of the battlements shielded them
from the guns of the traitors. Sarpedon spotted Salk attaching a large
metallic device to the side of the gate. Other teams were making it to
the wall, too, while some were still pinned down by fire from the traitors who had stayed at their posts.

Iktinos strode through the mud and carnage, bolter shots flying
around him. He was battered and covered in mud, but the presence the
Chaplain brought with him was undiminished.

'Chaplain!' said Sarpedon, as he ducked behind a bullet-scarred rock
to concentrate on the Hell. 'It is good to see you alive. I feared the traitors would do for you.'

'Not for want of trying, commander,' replied Iktinos. 'They sent one
of their scouts to kill me. They were not successful.'

'Do you know who is in charge?'

'I have my suspicions.'

'And they are?'

'Eumenes.'

Eumenes. Of course. Eumenes was brilliant – brave, decisive, intelligent and ruthless. The scouts would be on his side, which was why so many of the Chapter's new recruits had joined the rebellion. And Eumenes was persuasive. He had been an officer of the future. Sarpedon had even imagined Eumenes leading the Chapter when Sarpedon himself was gone.

If Sarpedon failed here, that was exactly what would happen. Eumenes would command the Soul Drinkers into a future of treachery.

'Ready,' voxed Salk.

'Ready here!' echoed Sergeant Dargalis, who had taken his assault squad through the storm of fire to the other side of the gate.

Sarpedon checked the status of the other forward squads. Some were not in position, still pinned down. Others didn't respond at all. It would have to be enough.

'Do it!' ordered Sarpedon.

Twin explosions ripped through the wall either side of the fortress gate. The ground shook, felling trees weakened by shredding gunfire. Thunderheads of dust and vaporised mud roared forwards. Chunks of rockcrete fell as thick as rain, and even a Space Marine's eyesight could not penetrate the solid mass of dust and smoke that rippled from the gate.

'Forward!' ordered Sarpedon. With Iktinos beside him, and the rest of his Soul Drinkers half glimpsed through the sudden hot gloom, Sarpedon scuttled over the fallen tree and towards the shattered gates. The gunfire was quiet – the bolter exchanges from the flanks of the Soul Drinkers' lines might as well have been on a different world. The din of battle was gone for a brief moment as the smoke and dust clung to no-man's land.

On the battlements, the traitors would be recovering rapidly from the detonation of the demolition charges. They would be getting back to their posts, checking their bolter loads, ready to massacre the loyal Soul Drinkers emerging from the gloom. The Hell would be dying down, Rogal Dorn's titanic figure turning distant and the glowering heroes of the Chapter's past just dim ghosts against reality.

Sarpedon had trained them too well. Any other enemy would crumble. Not the traitor Soul Drinkers.

Sarpedon could see the wall now, dark against the filmy grey of the clearing dust. The gate had fallen completely, massive slabs of corroded metal lying twisted on the shattered rockrete causeway. The battlements over the gates had crumbled, forming a great drift of rubble choking the gates. Armoured forms were moving over the top of the rubble, taking cover ready for battle.

Sarpedon recognised the high collar of an aegis circuit and the double-handed force sword in the hands of one traitor on top of the rubble slope. It was a Librarian, one of Sarpedon's fellow psykers among the

Soul Drinkers, and a man who had seen everything that Sarpedon had, from his earliest battles at Quixian Obscura to the Chapter War and everything beyond.

Sarpedon strode into the open. 'Gresk!' he yelled.

Librarian Gresk looked down at Sarpedon, and held up a hand to halt the fire of his fellow traitors ready to attack from the ruined battlements. 'Commander!' called back Gresk. 'Though you cannot call me a brother, we are still Soul Drinkers. We still have a duty to one another. I have no wish to see you die here. You can still turn back and there will be no battle here.'

'You know I cannot do that, Gresk,' said Sarpedon. Around him, the Soul Drinkers were taking up positions at the end of the rubble slope, sighting down their bolters over slabs of rockrete and the lips of impact craters on the causeway. 'This ends here, either way. But you are correct, you have a duty. A duty to tell me why.'

'This had been happening for a long time, Sarpedon,' said Gresk. In the eerie pause in the battle, his voice carried as clear as thunder. 'Even since we discovered what we were, since the death of Abraxes. Look at where you have led us. We are on this Emperor-forsaken place, fighting for an Imperium you claim to despise. Our own brothers were nearly our downfall on Gravenhold. We barely survived Abraxes's curse, and the Inquisition nearly did for us on Stratix Luminae. Your rule is leading us towards destruction. We cannot survive with you in charge any more. Just as you usurped Gorgoleon, we are usurping you in charge.'

'"We?" You mean Eumenes,' said Sarpedon.

'Eumenes organised the scouts right under your nose. After Gravenhold he had the loyalty of all the new recruits. He is brilliant, Sarpedon, and he leads as if he was born to it. He has beaten you for the soul of your own Chapter. Those of us who have sided with him are simply joining the winning side.'

All around the two Librarians, the tension was being ramped up again. One gesture, one word, and both sides would be consumed by the kind of murderous short-range slaughter at which Space Marines excelled. Sarpedon could see fingers tightening around triggers and thumbs ready to activate the exhausts of jump packs. That was all it would take – one word. Gresk was a master of the Quickening, a psychic power that enhanced the metabolism of his allies so they moved with incredible speed and grace. In such a battle, the power could turn the tide.

'I thought you must be dead,' said Sarpedon. 'Because I could not imagine you joining this rabble. You still have a chance to abandon this madness before the killing begins.'

'You do not understand, Sarpedon,' replied Gresk, and there was genuine sadness in his voice. 'I have no wish to see you die, but Eumenes wants your blood. My task here was to hold you in place. To keep you at the walls, to give you ground as long as I slowed you down long enough. There will be no more battle. Turn back. Do you understand?'

Sarpedon realised why they were there. The canopy of the jungle petered out just before the fortress walls – the Soul Drinkers were open to the grey-green dawn sky.

'The *Brokenback*,' said Iktinos beside him.

'Fall back! All units!' ordered Sarpedon. 'Retreat!'

The Soul Drinkers were not used to the order to retreat. No Space Marine ever took it lightly. But Sarpedon was still their Chapter Master, and they broke cover to fall back into the chewed-up battlefield of mud and fallen trees. Sarpedon himself scuttled backwards, watching Gresk turn back from the battle and walk back into the body of the fortress.

The first lance strike hammered down, shearing deep into the ground where Sarpedon had stood. Superheated air slammed into Sarpedon like a wall and he barely kept his footing as the ground shuddered and split. Another strike, bright as a second sun, hit home and Sarpedon saw a body flying, half-chewed away by the immense power of the laser bolt.

The bombardment was ripping down all around them, awesome in its power. Had the Soul Drinkers been advancing on the gates, they would have been annihilated completely. Many of them still died, torn apart by the columns of laser that burst into being in front of the fortress gates.

'Chaplain!' shouted Sarpedon over the din. 'This battle is over! Regroup with the men in the jungle!'

'Yes, commander,' replied Iktinos. He was an icon of the Chapter, more so perhaps than even Sarpedon himself, and if the Soul Drinkers would follow anyone now, it was him.

As Sarpedon ran through the destruction, lit by the strobing pulse of the lasers firing down from the *Brokenback* in orbit, he realised that the thought of another man, such as Iktinos, leading the Chapter was more and more acceptable to him. Gresk was correct – Sarpedon had led the Soul Drinkers almost to destruction. He had seen them all but torn apart, and all because he believed he knew what path the Chapter should take. If he was wrong, if the traitors were justified, then Sarpedon did not deserve to rule the Soul Drinkers.

'For Guilliman, son of the Emperor! For the Founding Father!'

Mercaeno's voice was echoed by the hundreds of Howling Griffons gathered in the vast Battlecry Cloister, the spectacular vaulted temple of war that served the *Cerulean Claw* as a mustering deck. The floor was tiled with trophies – scraps of xenos armour, fragments of shattered traitorous skulls, alien bodies crushed like specimens on a slide, stamped flat beneath millennia of Howling Griffons' boots.

'For the oath and the word! For the honour that men fear! Howling Griffons, what say you to the oath sworn by your brothers long dead?'

'Honour them!' cried the men, ranked up by company and squad, their officer out in front of them leading them. And in front of them all was Mercaeno, voice as proud and rousing as a preacher's.

'Even though it may cost your life?' bellowed Mercaeno, challenging as much as encouraging. The wordless roar of approval that came back at him was answer enough.

'Though your soul be rent and your bodies broken? Shall you honour this oath, Howling Griffons, inheritors of Guilliman?'

The roar again, louder, more insistent. The fervour of the Howling Griffons to honour the Chapter's ancient oaths bordered on mania. The fire inside them flashed in their eyes. It was only the merciless discipline of the Adeptus Astartes that kept them from rioting, from expressing that power within them in random violence.

'Then make your oaths, Howling Griffons.'

Captain Darion stood out in front of the assembled Howling Griffons, his power sword held high so all could see him. At his side trundled a scribe-servitor, its hunched form carrying a long spool of parchment and twin electroquills quivering on armatures extending from its eyes sockets. It would take down the oaths made by the battle-brothers of the Howling Griffons as they made them to Captain Darion, as was the tradition among the Howling Griffons. Their oaths were sacred, and to return to the Chapter without having fulfilled them brought great shame. Howling Griffons had stayed away from their Chapter for years, even decades, seeking ways to fulfil oaths they had made before battle. Some of them were still out there in the galaxy, questing until they settled their matter of honour, or until they died.

'What is the meaning of this?' came the harried-sounding voice of Inquisitor Thaddeus as he ran across the trophy-laden floor of the Battle-cry Cloister. He was still pulling on his long flakweave coat.

Mercaeno turned to the inquisitor and stepped in front of him, so he was kept away from the oath rites that were specific to the Chapter.

'No doubt you will rejoice,' said Mercaeno, although there was no congratulations in his voice. 'We are landing on Nevermourn.'

'What changed?' said Thaddeus.

'The oath we swore to Vanqualis was to do more than simply defend it. An ancient enemy has returned, perhaps in league with the green-skins, perhaps manipulating them. The force must be destroyed.'

'Who?'

Mercaeno shook his head. 'That, inquisitor, is not even for your ears.'

'Wait, Lord Librarian,' said Thaddeus. 'There may be forces at work here that you do not understand.'

'Your words grow tiresome, inquisitor. Whatever your mission here it cannot compare to the fulfilment of our oath to Vanqualis. It is one of the most ancient of…'

'You seek the Grail of Damnation,' said Thaddeus.

Mercaeno was silent for a moment. Behind him the Howling Griffons crowded around Captain Darion, swearing they would take an enemy's head or avenge a lost battle-brother, or be the first man to set foot on the ground of Vanqualis.

'Or whatever you call it,' said Thaddeus. 'There are many names, but they all mean the same thing. Please, Lord Librarian, you cannot just–'

'You know nothing of the Black Chalice!' roared Mercaeno. 'Whatever devilry you intend on Vanqualis, you shall not interfere in our mission!'

'I know a great deal about the Black Chalice, Lord Librarian, more than any man alive. And I cannot allow you to take your men into a battle you do not understand.'

'Allow? You do not allow us anything, inquisitor! You have no authority here, Inquisitorial seal or not! The Black Chalice is an evil that has blighted Vanqualis in ages past and vowed to return. Now that time has come, and it must be destroyed. Not studied, not contained, not negotiated with – destroyed, utterly and forever, with honest gunfire and chainblade.'

Thaddeus's eyes were wide with horror. 'You do not understand what you are fighting, Lord Librarian.'

'Then that is where you and I differ, inquisitor. I do not have to understand my enemy. I must merely destroy. Stay out of our way, Thaddeus, lest you become that enemy.'

Mercaeno turned back to his men, hearing the oaths that they would defeat a bearer of the Black Chalice in single combat, or that they would walk upon the shores of Herograve and proclaim to its people that they were at last free.

'This is your last chance, Lord Librarian,' said Thaddeus.

Mercaeno glanced back at him, a hand on the force axe at his belt. 'You wish us to let the Black Chalice live, Thaddeus. I have battle-brothers here who would kill you on the spot for voicing such a thought. Should I call them forth, or would you rather face me here?'

For a moment Thaddeus looked like he would draw a weapon from beneath the flakweave panels of his coat, and accept Mercaeno's challenge. The oaths of the Howling Griffons faded out and the only two men in the cloister were the inquisitor and the Librarian, ready to settle their differences in the oldest way.

'Then may your oaths be fulfilled,' said Thaddeus, backing down before Mercaeno as all men did. 'And may the Howling Griffons find victory.'

Mercaeno did not reply, instead joining the rest of his Astartes and making his own oaths to be recorded and fulfilled as was the Chapter's way.

Mercaeno swore that Vanqualis would be saved.

And that the Black Chalice would be finally shattered forever.

'How can we tell our friends from our enemies?'
  'It is said that all but our battle-brothers will become our enemies in the end.'

– Daenyathos, *Catechisms Martial*

CHAPTER TEN

'I thought you were dead, brother!' said Sarpedon, with a joy in his voice that had not been there since the catastrophe at the Serpentspine Valley. His voice echoed strangely in the cave, where he had made the Soul Drinkers' temporary command post. He spoke into his vox-unit and the signal was poor, for it had to be transmitted from the *Brokenback* in orbit to the surface.

'It was a close thing, commander,' replied Lygris. 'But by the Emperor's grace I live still.'

'Where are you?'

'In the ruin of the *Abandoned Hope*,' replied Lygris. His voice was severely distorted by the ancient vox equipment he was using and the interference from Vanqualis's atmosphere. 'It's a part of the *Brokenback* that only I have explored. Eumenes and his men are hunting me down but I know this place too well.'

Sarpedon looked around the cave, at the primitive scrawlings on its walls and the skull symbols carved over the entrance. It was hidden in the depths of the jungle, dark, damp and choked with moss and weeds, and had probably not seen sentient life for hundreds of years. 'We're not much better off, Lygris,' said Sarpedon. 'The traitors are led by Gresk down here. They're holding a fortress and the orks are everywhere. It's bedlam on the surface.'

Around the cave, and the natural defences of rocks and trees outside it, the Soul Drinkers were standing guard and tending their wounds,

149

cleaning the jungle filth from their battlegear and performing the personal rites of battle and devotion. They had been beaten, and defeat had its own traditions just like victory – silent, personal rites of shame and atonement, appeals to the Emperor for the chance of redemption, and promises of vengeance. Deeper into the cave were the ruins of a small shrine or perhaps the simple tomb of an ancient ancestor, where Apothecary Karendin was setting broken limbs and transfusing blood.

'Librarian Gresk? Throne preserve us, I never thought Gresk would side against you. Pallas, too.'

For a moment Sarpedon was shocked that Pallas had joined Eumenes's rebellion, but in a way, it made sense. 'Tellos,' said Sarpedon. 'Pallas was the closest thing to a friend Tellos had. And I failed Tellos as much as I failed any of us.'

'I've been keeping a watch on the *Brokenback*'s communications,' continued Lygris. 'Eumenes is making ready to bring the traitors off the surface and onto the ship. Without me it'll be at least two days before he can get the warp engines on-line. Then Eumenes will send the Thunderhawks down to the surface and pick up Gresk and the rest of them.'

'Then we need to be victorious by then,' said Chaplain Iktinos. Iktinos was standing nearby, studying the carvings on the cave wall. They were primitive depictions of warfare, humanoid shapes butchering one another and standing atop piles of skulls. 'For Eumenes would maroon us here, to die amongst the criminals and the xenos.'

'All this means we have the advantage, then,' said Sarpedon.

Iktinos turned from the cave wall. 'How so, commander?'

'We know what Eumenes wants. He wants to get his fellow traitors off Nevermourn. He has to do it before he can escape here. That's how we'll get them out into the open and onto our battlefield.'

'Then you have not yet given in, Sarpedon,' said Iktinos.

'No Soul Drinker has ever given up at anything, Chaplain,' said Sarpedon sharply. 'I have led this Chapter into Nevermourn and I will not rest until I have led it out again. You know me better than to doubt that.'

'Then you do consider yourself responsible for this rebellion,' said Iktinos. It wasn't phrased as a question, more a statement of fact, not quite challenging Sarpedon but coming close.

'Command means responsibility,' replied Sarpedon. 'Wherever this Chapter goes, I have led it there. Whatever obstacles it faces, I have chosen to face them.' Sarpedon's voice was sharp, and for a moment it seemed he would take Iktinos to task for questioning him – but Sarpedon's face softened as he backed down from a confrontation. 'Tellos taught me that,' he said. 'I hope he knew that at the end. I should have watched Tellos more closely, and I should have watched Eumenes, too. And Pallas and Gresk, and everyone else who had joined forces against me. I could have stopped this from happening, so it is my duty to stop it now.'

'Eumenes doubts that you are fit to rule this Chapter,' continued Iktinos, relentlessly. 'With the doubts that so clearly lie within you, can you be sure he is not correct?'

'This is my Chapter,' said Sarpedon. 'I won it from Gorgoleon and led it from corruption. I saved us from Abraxes's curse and the Inquisition, I brought us out of Gravenhold. No one has earned the right to command this Chapter as I have. I have no doubts, Iktinos. There is nothing I will not do to save this Chapter and do the Emperor's work. And to do that, I must see out what I started. I must stay in command.'

For a long moment, the two Space Marines faced one another as if about to strike. Sarpedon was not backing down now, and nothing in Iktinos's grim, skull-faced gaze suggested he would accept he was wrong.

'This is my Chapter, too,' said Iktinos. 'And you are my Chapter Master. I shall fight by your side until the end. And I, too, have no doubts.'

'Commander, Chaplain,' said Lygris over the vox, evidently relieved to have heard any conflict averted. 'The plan.'

'Yes, the plan,' said Sarpedon. 'Lygris, I have two tasks for you. Firstly, I need some images of the fortress and the area around it. Topographical data. Can you do that?'

'Certainly,' said Lygris. 'I can still get into the bridge cogitators remotely, for a short while at least.'

'Secondly, do you have access to the flight decks?'

'The primary decks, yes,' replied Lygris. 'It may not be easy. I'm being hunted down here and the flight decks will be guarded, but there are a few back doors I can use.'

'Good,' said Sarpedon. 'I need you to destroy the Thunderhawks.'

The lower decks of the *Cerulean Claw* were a celebration of the fallen Howling Griffons. The greatest heroes were remembered in places like the Manse of Furioso, but the lower-ranked battle-brothers who had died performing some heroic deed were commemorated in the Remembrance Decks. Memorials to dozens of Howling Griffons stood, crowned with statues of them in the full heraldry of their armour, standing guard over one another in marble or polished granite. They stood in halls remembering the dead of a particular campaign, or of an era in the Howling Griffons' history, and each one was like a weight pinning the past down upon the Chapter.

Inquisitor Thaddeus moved through one of those places now, and it was like a quiet, imposing forest of stone with statues of Space Marines watching him on every side.

Thaddeus had scouted out the layout of the *Cerulean Claw* early on in the voyage, because he knew that he might one day have to steal through it, unseen and probably hunted, looking for a way to escape. He knew that the ship had a secondary shuttle bay and that the complex circuitry in his Inquisitorial seal would probably open it and let him take a shuttle down to Vanqualis. He was an inquisitor, and the best of his kind planned for when everything went wrong.

Thaddeus crept past a statue of a Howling Griffon carrying twin chainblades, the statue's face turned mournfully towards the floor. At the far side of the hall he saw an archway with a blast door leading to the shuttle deck. A few more moments and Thaddeus would be off the *Cerulean Claw*.

'Inquisitor,' said a deep, commanding voice from behind Thaddeus. Thaddeus span around and saw a Space Marine across the tomb chamber. The gold and crimson of his armour marked him out from the forest of stone Space Marines around him. Thaddeus scanned the Space Marine rapidly – he recognised the heraldry and ostentatious oath-texts of Mercaeno's command squad, veterans who acted as his hands and eyes among the Chapter.

'Eyes everywhere,' said Thaddeus. 'Damn Astartes, I swear sometimes you can see through walls.'

'Inquisitor Thaddeus,' said the Howling Griffon, 'Chief Librarian Mercaeno has ordered you confined to your quarters.'

'Does he now? And what's his excuse?'

'He does not trust you.'

Thaddeus smiled bitterly. 'The Lord Librarian is honest, at least. Which one are you?'

'Brother Rhelnon,' replied the Howling Griffon. 'Lord Mercaeno sent my battle-brothers and I to find you, inquisitor. You are being deliberately elusive. I think Mercaeno was right to suspect you.'

Thaddeus moved carefully, keeping the plinth of the closest memorial between him and Rhelnon. 'I bear the authority of the Immortal Emperor of Mankind,' he said, 'and the Adeptus Astartes are subject to that authority whether they like it or not. Worlds could die at my command, Brother Rhelnon. The mighty could be dragged away in chains.'

'None of us dispute the Inquisitorial mandate. But here, you are just a man, and you are alone. Power does not stem from the Inquisitorial seal you carry with you. It comes from this.' Rhelnon patted the barrel of the bolter he held across his chest. 'You are trying to escape, which means you oppose the will of the Howling Griffons. Therefore, you are our enemy. As you are a guest here, Lord Mercaeno has permitted for you to be captured rather than killed. This is not an offer the Howling Griffons regularly make to their enemies.'

'All this because you made a promise you cannot keep,' said Thaddeus. 'Brother, do you even know what the Black Chalice is?'

Rhelnon seemed slightly taken aback by the question – no doubt he had been expecting Thaddeus to either give up or attack, not question Rhelnon back. 'The Black Chalice is a daemon,' he said. 'A thing of the warp, a puppet of the Dark Powers. The Bearers of the Black Chalice are the human vermin who worship it.'

'And they were on Vanqualis a long time ago, and they will one day return,' said Thaddeus. 'No one knows where they went or what happened to them but the Black Chalice is so deeply ingrained on the minds of the people of Vanqualis that it must have been something terrible indeed. Am I right?'

'Inquisitor, your words will do nothing to sway us from our–'

'Brother Rhelnon!' snapped Thaddeus. 'Am I right?'

Rhelnon did not answer. His grip tightened on his bolter and his finger slipped inside the trigger guard.

'They call it the Grail of the Damned,' said Thaddeus, 'halfway across the galaxy in the Scorpanae Cluster. It's the Obsidian Skull on Phylax Minor, where they say it's a drinking cup made from the skull of a daemon and that anyone who drinks from it lives forever. Mercaeno doesn't know what he's dealing with – no one in this galaxy does. The only one who comes close is me.'

'I have my orders, inquisitor,' said Rhelnon.

'I know,' said Thaddeus, a trace of sadness in his voice. 'But what kind of a man would I be if I didn't try to make you understand before?'

'Before what?'

'You know what.'

Rhelnon sighed. 'It can be done without this, inquisitor.'

'Maybe in a perfect galaxy,' said Thaddeus.

Rhelnon moved first. His reflexes were sharper than any man's, even an inquisitor's. Thaddeus dropped to his knees and a short, tight burst of bolter shots zipped over his head and cracked into the stone plinth beside him. Shots burst against the statue above him and a broken chainblade fell, sheared from the hand of the stone Space Marine by the impacts.

'Thaddeus, I will take you in if I can but your death will give me few regrets!' shouted Rhelnon. He snapped off another shot, which nearly took off Thaddeus's foot before he pulled it back behind the statue.

Thaddeus reached into his voluminous flakweave coat and pulled out his gun, a modified autopistol chased in brass and silver. Heavy shots thunked into the chamber as he cocked it.

Thaddeus dived out from behind the plinth, firing as he went. The shots were snapped blind and flew wide. Rhelnon rapidly judged that a mere autopistol would do little against power armour and stepped into the open again, trying to draw a bead on his prey.

Thaddeus flicked a selector stud on the weapon and a single round clicked into the chamber. It was the last of his archeotech rounds, very old, very valuable bullets crammed with circuitry too old to be replicated. Once he had loaded his whole gun with them, back when he had the backing of his fellow inquisitors. But that felt like a long time ago. He had been saving that last bullet for a special occasion, and now that Rhelnon was bearing down on him, Thaddeus decided that the occasion had arrived.

He rolled between two of the memorials and fired. The bullet zipped wide again but then its ancient technology kicked in and it flitted around in a wide arc, arrowing back towards Rhelnon.

Rhelnon threw himself to one side but too late, the bullet smacked into his armour, boring deep inside. He yelled in anger and pain as his right arm was shredded, the bullet ricocheting around inside his armour like an angry trapped insect. His blood spattered up against the stern obsidian Chaplain statue standing over him.

'Traitor!' yelled Rhelnon, opening fire even as he stumbling with the impacts. Bolter shots sprayed in a burning fan. Statues fell, their legs shot out from beneath them, stone heads smashed on the floor. Thaddeus ducked down, the tough flakweave of his coat deflecting shrapnel and knife-sharp shards of obsidian.

Thaddeus had been out in the galaxy for a long time. He had learned never to rely on any weapon he could not carry on him at all times, and never to spare any expense in securing the best. He had known that sooner or later, doing his duty to the Emperor would rely on his ability to survive a close encounter with a hostile Space Marine.

Thaddeus fired more shots, emptying the mundane rounds from his autopistol. Rhelnon was in the open now and shots thudded into his greaves and abdomen, but they did little more than kick sparks from the Howling Griffon's armour.

The pistol's action snapped closed on an empty chamber. Thaddeus dropped the gun and pulled out an ornate hilt from inside his coat. From the hilt extended a shimmering blade, warping the air around it with it strange energy field. He couldn't see Rhelnon now – both men were keeping the memorials between them.

'We should have killed you!' shouted Rhelnon, his voice straining with anger rather than pain. 'Mercaeno should have never let you on board! We should have thrown you out of the damned airlock!'

'If I had told you the truth, you would have done just that,' said Thaddeus as he skulked between the statues, sword in his hand. He could hear Brother Rhelnon moving a few statues away. 'I do what I must. I lie because I serve a greater truth.'

'My Emperor rules from a throne of gold,' replied Rhelnon. 'Your kind sit upon a throne of deceit.'

Both men were trying to distract the other to win the advantage.

Thaddeus listened to Rhelnon's armoured feet on the floor. There were only two statues between him and Rhelnon now.

Thaddeus ran first, headlong between the tombs. Rhelnon's huge armoured form reared up over him, the knife flashing down. Thaddeus had learned his swordcraft from the death cultists who served Lord Inquisitor Goldo, during Thaddeus's apprenticeship as a lowly interrogator. The swift, sharp parry he learned there kept Rhelnon's blade away from his heart and now the Space Marine was in his face – Thaddeus could see the anger in his eyes, smell the hot iron of the blood congealing around his many wounds.

The blade in Thaddeus's hand split into dozens of fluttering shards, like a swarm of lethal butterflies. Rhelnon reared up as monomolecular shards sheared through the ceramite plates of his armour, scored deep red lines across his face and punched right through his back.

Rhelnon roared like a wounded animal, slashing wildly at his foe. Thaddeus rolled away as the sword shards flittered around Rhelnon, opening up dozens of wounds. One by one the force in the shards died and they fell to the floor, the last of them spiralling around Rhelnon until he batted them away. Thaddeus used the time they bought him to roll out from beneath Rhelnon's assault and take cover three tombs away.

He couldn't help but glance up into the face of the statue above him. It was sculpted with the high collar and ornate force sword of a Librarian. For a moment Thaddeus was aware of ancient traditions of the Howling Griffons, and of how he had violated them to the core by lying to Mercaeno about why he had sought passage aboard the *Cerulean Claw*. For an insane moment he wondered if the Howling Griffons buried their dead here, if beneath these memorials were coffins containing the skeletons of those Space Marines, watching him with empty sockets, cursing him for turning on the Howling Griffons in their very own burial place.

Thaddeus chased the thought from his mind. There was no more room for doubt. Rhelnon must have summoned help by now. Thaddeus had to be quick.

'Inquisitor!' yelled Rhelnon. 'You cannot kill me! You are just a man. We are the Emperor's hand. There are three hundred of us on this one ship. You are trapped like a rat. We will try you and kill you, but it will be quick and there will be honour. Down here there is none. You will not be given a second chance.'

'The Emperor's inquisitors do not need second chances,' replied Thaddeus. The words meant nothing – they were just there to fill the hateful void, as if both men were fending off the fact that death would come to one of them in moments.

'I do not know what you want of us,' said Rhelnon, 'or what you seek

by coming to this planet. But it is not the Emperor's work that you do.'
He was moving again, stalking Thaddeus.

This time Thaddeus could hear him flicking the selector of his bolt
gun – he wouldn't try to take on Thaddeus up close again.

The hilt of Thaddeus's sword was reforming, the shards liquefying
and flowing across the floor like quicksilver, but Thaddeus knew the
same trick wouldn't work twice. He had found the sword in the hands
of a xeno-cult on the galaxy's eastern fringe and carried it ever since,
knowing that one day it would make the difference between life and
death. He deactivated the blade and holstered the hilt.

'Die!'

Rhelnon charged, right through the statues. With a terrific sound the
obsidian Howling Griffons shattered beneath him as he leapt between
the tombs, bolter blazing.

Thaddeus did not move. He did not try to roll out of the way or flee
– that would not work.

Light flared around him, almost blinding. The conversion field he
wore could absorb a couple of bolter shots, maybe three or four if
its power coils, hidden in an archeotech amulet beneath Thaddeus's
clothes, held out. The armour field was another relic of the days when
he could still count on the support of his fellow inquisitors, and again,
he had known that one day he would rely on it to keep him alive for a
few seconds longer.

Thaddeus reached inside for the small coin-shaped device clipped
innocuously to his belt. He flicked it out, depressing the charging stud
with his thumb. The grenade hit the statue above Thaddeus, and just
as the conversion field generator shattered with the strain of absorbing
Thaddeus's gunfire, it exploded.

The grenade's detonation tore the statue of the Librarian apart, throwing stone shrapnel into the face of Brother Rhelnon as he bore down
on Thaddeus. Rhelnon's charge never hit home and he fell to the floor
beside Thaddeus, his bolter clattering across the stone tiles.

The light from the conversion field died down, Thaddeus's eyes
adjusting from the glare. He looked down at Rhelnon, who was convulsing and gargling as one hand reached helplessly for the bolter.

The stone force sword from the Librarian statue had impaled Rhelnon
through the chest. Thaddeus knew with one glance that the stone blade
had cut through his lungs and the ruination of his internal organs was
enough to fell even a Space Marine.

Rhelnon was dying. He was covered in blood, dozens of small
wounds all over him. Blood ran from his mouth as his shredded lungs
struggled to breathe.

'For the Emperor, Brother Rhelnon,' said Thaddeus. Then he turned
from the dying Space Marine and headed for the shuttle bay.

There had been a time, as a young interrogator filled with the Emperor's fervour, that Thaddeus would have never accepted the death of a good Imperial servant as a necessary evil. But he was much wiser now.

Deep in the crumbling fortress, all was decay. The faded heraldry of Vanqualis's conquerors, the founders of House Falken, hung on the walls, stained by the rain that dribbled through cracks in their ceiling and pulled apart by the roots and creepers forcing their way up from below. The scouts and Space Marines who had sided with Eumenes stood guard around the chamber, which had been a command centre for the House Falken forces who had originally won the jungles of Nevermourn. Sergeant Hecular stood guarding the doorway – its thick metal blast doors had rusted open, revealing the rotting cavities of crumbling rockrete beyond.

'The scouts on the battlements have the antenna up,' said Hecular.

'I've got a signal,' said Librarian Gresk in the centre of the room. The field vox in front of him was powerful enough for a boosted signal to reach the *Brokenback* even from inside the fortress. 'Bridge? Bridge, come in. This is Librarian Gresk.'

'Eumenes here,' came the voice from the vox. 'I have been watching your progress from orbit, Librarian.'

'Then you'll know we fended off Sarpedon. We can hold the battlements for another day at least before he regroups and tries again, if he dares. We're waiting for pickup now.'

'That was exactly my concern, Librarian.'

'What do you mean, Eumenes? We were victorious.'

'The Soul Drinkers were thrown back into the jungle. That means they are alive. Your orders were clear, Gresk. Keep the Soul Drinkers in place and engage them at the gates so the orbital bombardment would destroy them.'

'I did what I could, Eumenes. Sarpedon retreated before the *Brokenback* could open fire. I gave the signal to fire as soon as I–'

'Sarpedon retreated, Gresk, when he should have pushed on. He could have forced the gates. I saw you two talking, Gresk, breaking cover when both sides should have been fighting for their lives. And I asked myself, why would Sarpedon fall back from his objective, and why should a Soul Drinker loyal to me be parleying with the man he is ordered to kill? I can come to only one conclusion, Gresk.'

Gresk sighed. He was one of the Chapter's real veterans – his psychic prowess might not have been the equal of Sarpedon's own but he made up for that with decades of experience. And yet, he was in a new world now. The old Chapter, and even the Soul Drinkers after Sarpedon's Chapter War, had at least been united in purpose. They had fought as one hand. Now, there was treachery all around him. Eumenes was the expert at treachery – Gresk was the novice now.

'It is enough,' said Gresk, 'that Sarpedon be stranded here. He might never get off this planet and if he ever does we will be long gone.'

'You let him live.'

'I let him live, Eumenes. You might not be familiar with the way this Chapter does things, but there is such a thing as loyalty and it does not die so easily. Those men were my battle-brothers. There is no need to kill them.'

'There is every need!' The anger in Eumenes's voice was clear even from orbit. 'Sarpedon is our enemy! Do you really believe this Chapter will adhere to our cause if we let our enemies live?'

'I am not here because of your cause, Eumenes,' said Gresk. 'I am here because I cannot watch the Soul Drinkers being led into destruction. That is why I took up arms against Sarpedon, for the good of this Chapter. You cannot force me to kill my own brothers, Eumenes. My loyalty to you does not stretch that far.'

'Then you have no loyalty to me at all,' said Eumenes darkly.

'Eumenes, that is not what I–'

'Sarpedon will die. If you cannot accept that, Librarian Gresk, then the future of the Soul Drinkers has no place for you.'

Gresk was about to reply when he heard movement behind him. He glanced round to see Sergeant Hecular standing over him, his scout squad forming a semicircle behind Gresk. They had their bolt pistols drawn.

'Shall we do this, Gresk?' said Hecular.

'I don't–'

'You understand just fine. If you have to take some of us with you, then let's do it. Otherwise, I can keep it simple.'

Gresk was silent for a long moment, looking between the faces of Hecular's scouts. They were new recruits from the worlds the Soul Drinkers had visited, taken from among the Imperium's oppressed and brutalised. And Gresk did not know them at all.

'Very well,' he said. 'If this is what the Emperor's work means to you. Let us waste no more time.'

Hecular brought his gun up to point at Gresk's head, and the scouts did the same. Gresk could probably kill some of them before he fell, but what would be the point? Gresk didn't know which side he was on any more, only that one death was better than many.

He opened his eyes just in time to see Hecular smirk as he pulled the trigger.

Eumenes listened to the volley of gunfire transmitted from the old fortress on Vanqualis. It was impossible to tell whether he gained any satisfaction from the sound of bolter shells smacking into armour and exploding through flesh, or at the clatter as an armoured body fell to the floor.

'It's done,' came Hecular's voice.

'Keep me updated,' said Eumenes, and broke the vox-link. More equipment had been brought onto the bridge and Eumenes was surrounded by thrumming cogitator units and blinking readouts – the only light in the dark sphere of the bridge was from the readouts and pict-screens, so Eumenes's face was edged in hard greens and reds. The viewscreen was dark now, as if Eumenes didn't want any extraneous information distracting him.

The bridge doors slid open and Tydeus walked in. Tydeus had been Eumenes's second in command when Eumenes had led a scout squad in Gravenhold, and he was functioning in the same way now. Eumenes had issued orders that communications with him went through Tydeus. He was a Chapter Master now – he could not be distracted by every little problem that cropped up.

'Tydeus, good,' said Eumenes. 'The situation at the fortress has been dealt with. It is time we left this accursed system. Have the engines readied for the warp. And send the Thunderhawks down to pick up our brethren on the surface.'

'That is why I came here, Eumenes,' said Tydeus, a trace of uncertainty in his voice. 'There is an intruder on the flight decks.'

Crouched down by the hull of the gunship, Techmarine Lygris attached the demolition charge to the ceramite plating just below one of the engines. Lygris knew the structure of a Thunderhawk gunship inside out and he had known exactly where to place the small engineering charge to breach a main fuel line and render the craft useless. More importantly, he had known where on the *Brokenback* an intact engineering deck could be found, which he could raid for the tools and demolition equipment he needed.

With a dull sound of collapsing metal the charge on the next Thunderhawk along the line detonated, sparks and fragments of charred metal spilling onto the floor of the flight deck. The flight deck itself had been some kind of combat arena, with one side inexplicably taken up with a gigantic docking airlock. Rows of seats overlooked the deck, complete with separate boxes for dignitaries and an entrance tunnel that linked to a network of cells and cages beneath the deck that the Soul Drinkers used to contain spare parts and fuel. Just what had happened in that arena before its parent ship had become a part of the hulk was just one of the thousands of mysteries on board the *Brokenback*.

Lygris slid the detonator core into the centre of the circular charge and thumbed its activation switch. A blinking telltale on the detonator told him the charge was armed – another switch would start the timer.

'Lygris,' said a too-familiar voice behind the Techmarine. Lygris span around, bolt pistol in hand, but the person who had spoken was hidden from view behind the Thunderhawk he had just disabled. There were more than a dozen Thunderhawks on the flight deck, some of them survivors of the old Chapter and some of them captured from forge worlds or Imperial battlefields, and their large armoured forms cut off the lines of sight around the flight deck.

Lygris knew the voice straight away, and his hearts sank.

'Lygris, they've got you surrounded. Eumenes's men are on their way. They'll be here in seconds.'

'They're too late,' replied Lygris. 'I'm done here. The traitors are trapped on Vanqualis, just like you meant to trap Sarpedon. It's too late for Eumenes's cronies to kill me now, Pallas.'

Apothecary Pallas stepped out from behind the Thunderhawk. Pallas was a brilliant Apothecary, a skilled scientist and surgeon who had played a major part in saving the Soul Drinkers from the mutations afflicted on them by the daemon prince Abraxes. Without him a part of the Soul Drinkers would die.

'Nisryus is close behind, Lygris,' said Pallas, 'and you cannot hide from him for long. Others are close behind him. Eumenes can flood this place with Soul Drinkers loyal to him.'

'And you expect me to give up?' Lygris's grip on his bolt pistol was tight. Pallas was a man he had trusted absolutely, but now he was an enemy. He hovered, agonisingly, between trying to kill Pallas and treating him as if he were still Lygris's battle-brother.

'No,' said Pallas. He held up his right hand, which was encased in the narthecium gauntlet, containing dozens of tiny needles and other surgical implements for battlefield treatment. A single silver spike emerged from the knuckle of the gauntlet. 'The Emperor's Mercy, Lygris.'

Lygris's voice caught in his throat. The Emperor's Mercy was administered to Space Marines or allies too severely injured to be saved. Its sharp, spring-loaded spike was driven into the back of the skull for a quick and painless death.

'Pallas, you cannot…'

'I do not know what they will do to you, Lygris,' said Pallas, urgency in his voice. 'I know the Librarium were training Nisryus to open up the minds of captives to interrogate them. At the very least they will do everything they can to make you talk. They need to know everything they can about the *Brokenback* and you're the only one who knows. I cannot go back to Sarpedon, not now, but I will do what I must to spare my friend's suffering. I can end it now, Lygris.'

Lygris shook his head. 'No, Pallas. I'm not giving up on my Chapter.'

'Then fight me!' snapped Pallas, but there was more sorrow than anger in his voice. 'If you die, I have spared you. If I die, then…'

'Then you have been spared, too,' said Lygris. 'You no longer have to take responsibility for the choice you have made. You don't have to look your friends in the eye again and tell them you have betrayed them. I won't do that for you, Pallas.'

'Damn it, Lygris,' said Pallas. 'This is the only way! Eumenes won't let either of us go without suffering!'

'You put yourself here, Pallas. You have to find your own way out.'

Pallas roared in frustration and anger, and Lygris was sure he could glimpse tears in the corners of Pallas's eyes as he drew back his narthecium gauntlet and charged. Lygris only dropped to the deck a fraction before the metal spike of the Emperor's Mercy snapped just over his head and embedded itself in the hull of the Thunderhawk.

The servo-arm mounted on the backpack of Lygris's armour reached up and closed on Pallas's head, wrenching him around so his back was to Lygris. Pallas slammed home an elbow into Lygris throat and both men fell to the floor, wrestling on the deck in the shadow of the Thunderhawk.

'Do it!' shouted Pallas as they fought. 'End it now!'

Lygris forced Pallas onto his back and was on top of him. A soldier's instinct brought the barrel of his bolt pistol up to Pallas's face.

Lygris's finger tightened. Pallas was his enemy. But Pallas was his battle-brother too. Those basic distinctions between friend and enemy had broken down. With Pallas bested and ready for execution, Lygris didn't know what to do.

Pallas sensed the moment of indecision. He sneered and threw Lygris off, stabbing down with blades that sprung from his narthecium gauntlet. Lygris rolled out of the way and barely got to his feet, stumbling against the Thunderhawk as he avoided Pallas's blow. Lygris put a hand against the hull below the engine for balance, Pallas's gauntlet dragging sparks from the ceramite.

Pallas kicked out at Lygris's leg and the Techmarine was on the floor again, bolt pistol skidding away from his hand.

'None of us are getting out of this,' said Pallas. 'It's over. The Chapter's over. If you won't spare me that suffering then I'll spare you, brother.' The Emperor's Mercy was primed again ready to strike and, flat on his back and unarmed, Lygris would have few ways to defend himself against a fellow Space Marine.

The explosive charge mounted on the Thunderhawk's hull, which Lygris had armed a moment before, exploded a few centimetres from Pallas's head. The Apothecary was thrown to the ground, sparks and shrapnel flying, smoke billowing from the ruined engine above. The whole Thunderhawk lurched and Pallas sprawled on the deck.

Lygris pulled himself to his feet, grabbing his bolt pistol. He could see that shards of metal had been driven into the side of Pallas's face and neck, and into the armour of his chest and shoulder pad. His face was blackened with soot from the blast and red welts, like fat rubies, were growing where blood was seeping from the cuts and congealing. Pallas stirred very slightly – he was unconscious but not dead. As Lygris had gambled, the blast had knocked him unconscious but was nowhere near powerful enough to fell a Space Marine for good.

Lygris could hear armoured feet clattering against the deck – Nisryus and the other traitor Soul Drinkers had arrived to trap Lygris and kill him. But Lygris knew the flight deck area of the *Brokenback* well, and in a way that no one else did.

Leaving Pallas lying on the deck to be found, Lygris knelt down so his servo-arm could wrench a drainage grille from the floor. Lygris slipped into the shaft below and clattered down into a dark storage chamber, once part of the cells below the arena where gladiators or slaves, or even wild xenos creatures, had been kept before they were herded out for the entertainment of the crowd. Lygris recalled for a moment how he had helped clear out the cells, and remove the age-encrusted skulls where they had built up into ceiling-high piles in the ship's previous life before it became a part of the hulk. He paused to pull the grille back over the opening above him with his servo-arm.

Beside him was a wide, yawning opening that led to an empty fuel tank deeper into the body of the *Brokenback*. Lygris could picture the warren of tunnels and pipes in his head, and he knew that he could hide there for days, weeks, even years if needs be.

'It's never over,' he said to himself, and disappeared again into the darkness.

'Who can we call our allies in the endless battle against corruption?'

'None but ourselves, our own souls and discipline, our own bodies and the weapons in our hands.'

– Daenyathos, *Catechisms Martial*

CHAPTER ELEVEN

The heights over the Serpentspine Valley seethed with activity. The clans had gathered and orkish chanting drowned out the sounds of the jungle – each clan had its own proud traditions, its own war cries and chants, and its own brutal battle-rites from ritual scarring to sacrifices. Here, thousands of greenskins chanted as one around an ancient, wizened shaman who read the future from the entrails of a dead slave. There, a clearing had become a gladiatorial pit, and two orks were settling some overblown feud by trying to tear each other's throats out with bare claws and teeth.

The symbols of dozens of clans were raised over the heights. A clenched fist, a sword through a skull, a stylised gun, daubed in paint and blood on banners hung from the trees. In their natural state those clans would have been at war, intent on slaughtering each other, because that was what orks were born to do. But on Nevermourn, they fought as one. Their old hatred broke out into scuffles and isolated murders, but the instincts for full-scale war were crushed. The orks' hatred was directed outwards, towards the humans who infested this world.

The warlord knew that without him, the orks who made up the horde would break up into dozens of feuding factions and the humans would win. Humans were a bad enemy to fight – which also made them a good enemy, for orks made little distinction between the two concepts. No matter how many humans were killed, there were always more to take their place, shiploads of them brimming with vengeance. Humans were like a weed, like a disease, almost impossible to cleanse from a world. For a greenskin that made them something more than an enemy, for a fight against a favoured enemy was a joyous thing. Orks loved going to war with humans, because defeating the humans meant something.

The warlord would cleanse them from this planet. He would do to Vanqualis what the humans had done to countless ork worlds. It didn't matter what happened after the planet belonged to the orks – what mattered was the victory. The warlord would hurt them. They would remember him. That was the immortality promised by the orkish gods to the greatest of their warriors – the warlord would live on in the fear he planted in human hearts.

The warlord strode through the makeshift camp that had sprung up on the heights. Almost his whole horde was there, thousands upon thousands of orks. By the morning they would be itching for battle. The strange, insanely inspired ork engineers were fixing war machines or making new ones by cutting down trees and cannibalising parts. Ork medics, similarly crazed, were administering crude repairs to wounded orks, replacing limbs and removing damaged organs – the bellowing of their patients was drowned out by the clanking of war machines and the chanting of the greenskins.

The warlord walked right through the camp, barely acknowledging the cheers and raucous salutes as he passed by. He spotted a human soldier nailed up to a tree, being tormented by a pack of orks and slaves. Several others, now dead, hung from branches or lay in sorry bloody heaps in the mud. The humans were still out there in the jungle, and though they had lost many in the previous battles they were still a force on Vanqualis.

As far as the horde was concerned the humans had been sent fleeing like whipped dogs into the jungle and had been utterly defeated, but the warlord knew that they had sent some scouting parties onto the heights to monitor his army, and that there had been plenty of minor gunfights where humans and orks alike had been lost. The human commander must have been an enemy to admire in some small way, for refusing to give up. But the horde was greater by far, and there was no doubt that every soldier who opposed the warlord's will would eventually end up dead in the mud or nailed to a tree trunk being tormented to death by the greenskins. The human soldier died, and the warlord passed by as the slaves dragged the human's body down and began to cut it to pieces in the mud.

At the far side of the heights the trees gave way to provide a view across the jungles, north-west towards the coast. To some more emotional creatures the view would be breathtaking, an awesome rolling vista of the jungle canopy broken by rocky cliffs and the dark snaking ribbons of Nevermourn's rivers. But the warlord cared nothing for such things. The only meaningful feature was his objective – the coast, a dim strip of grey in the far distance just below the horizon. Soon his orks' lust for battle would be too much to contain and they would have to advance, and the warlord would use that momentum to drive them all the way to the coast. He could rely on his engineers, and the abundance of trees, to fashion a way across the ocean.

After that, he would take Herograve. Until now the horde had been given only a taste of battle, frustrating actions against a force that retreated before them and tried to trick them. In the cities of Herograve were millions – billions – of humans, terrified and primed for butchery. The human forces could do nothing to stop them now. In a matter of days the overture would be over, and the real killing would begin.

The warlord turned back to the horde, chanting and scrapping among the trees. None of them really understood what motivated the warlord. They did not understand the almost holy rage inside him, like an addiction that could not be sated until Herograve was drowned in blood. Perhaps, in that final slaughter, they would come to realise that orks existed to kill.

The impact of the drop pod hitting home was heavy enough to shatter a normal man's bones. Chief Librarian Mercaeno didn't skip a syllable as he spoke the last words of the Rites of Detestation.

'...for the Enemy is within, as well as without, and it is within that he shall truly be defeated,' intoned Mercaeno. His command squad bowed their helmeted heads in contemplation of his words. One set of grav-harnesses was empty, for Brother Rhelnon had been killed on the *Cerulean Claw* trying to apprehend the rogue Inquisitor Thaddeus. 'It is only with victory that the Emperor can be praised. It is only with hatred that the victory can be won.'

'Only with hatred,' echoed the command squad in unison, just as the explosive bolts in the hull of the drop pod detonated and burst the pod open.

In a handful of seconds Mercaeno was out of his restraints, force axe in his hand. His command squad, eight Howling Griffons veterans with their armour festooned with oaths and kill-markings, was beside him, bolters and chainswords ready.

The drop pod had come down on target, on the slope of a low rise a short distance from the Serpentspine Valley where the trees were not so dense as to hinder the opening of the drop pods. Many other pods were already down, the Howling Griffons within already deployed and rapidly forming a cordon between the trees that soared overhead.

In an instant, Mercaeno appraised their situation. The jungle

provided lots of cover but it also blinded them, so they could be surrounded in short order without knowing it. Speed was of the essence on
a battlefield such as this, because other, lesser forces would be bogged
down by the terrain.

'Lord Librarian,' said Captain Darion, hurrying across towards Mercaeno's squad. 'The area is secure. No hostiles. The sensor-readings were
correct.'

'Then we must move with all speed before the greenskins get wind of
our arrival and decide to challenge us.'

Darion held up a data-slate on which glowed a topographical map
of the jungle. 'The last readings placed the Space Marine force seven
kilometres from here,' he said, indicating a bright blip on the map.
'If we approach from the east they'll have heavy terrain at their backs,
swamp and river.'

'Are they defending any fortifications?'

'None. It's just jungle.'

'Then they will not remain there for long. It is good that our enemy
calls themselves Space Marines. They fight as we do, so we can read
their every move.'

More drop pods slammed home, kicking up showers of mud. The
sides of the ovoid pods split open and more Howling Griffons emerged
– Captain Borganor pulled himself free of his grav-restraints and began
marshalling the Space Marines of his Tenth Company. Landers, rectangular and much larger than the comet-like drop pods, were making
landfall a short distance away, crushing through the canopy and bringing down the branches of the trees. Birds took flight at the noise and
devastation.

The landers in the jungle did not carry Howling Griffons. They
opened to reveal the armoured hulls of vehicles in the Chapter's livery,
embossed with the heraldic symbol of the rampant griffon that adorned
the shoulder pad of every Howling Griffon. Engines gunned and the
Chapter's tanks were disgorged from the massive landers. Rhino APCs,
Predator tanks, and Mercaeno's command Land Raider rolled out, with
more coming down behind them. The vehicular cargo was fitted with
dozer blades and reinforced front armour to barge through the densest
of Nevermourn's jungle.

'I had thought,' said Captain Darion, 'that there were oaths the Howling Griffons would never fulfil. I thought the Black Chalice must be so
ancient that we would never have the opportunity to face it.'

'Then now you understand a little more about what it means to be
a Howling Griffon,' replied Mercaeno. 'The barriers of possibility that
restrain other men do not apply to us. Every promise we make, we
will keep, though we must fight time itself to do so. We never give up,
Darion. Never, at anything.'

'Of course,' said Captain Darion. 'I assume that tracking down Thaddeus is an oath you have made, too?'

'No,' said Mercaeno. 'When I kill him, it will simply be for vengeance.'

The tanks rolled towards the Howling Griffons' position, and the squads of Space Marines were already clambering into the Rhinos and Land Raiders. Mercaeno's command vehicle, a formidable Land Raider Crusader that bristled with automated boltguns mounted on its side turrets, rolled towards Mercaeno's squad and Sergeant Ossex ordered the squad inside. Mercaeno was last inside, surrounded by the many tactical readouts showing data from the other squads. He read off the readiness runes projected onto one pict-screen – the whole force had deployed and mounted up in a few minutes, with a speed and efficiency that no normal commander could hope for.

The Howling Griffons were the best fighting force that Vanqualis had ever, or would ever, see. And they were there with a mission, inspired by dedication to their duty and by the holy hatred that burned in the heart of every true Space Marine. As the Land Raider roared off at the head of the Howling Griffons' armoured column, there was no doubt in Mercaeno's mind that before his Chapter left Vanqualis the Black Chalice would be shattered at last.

The same scans from the *Cerulean Claw*, that Mercaeno was using to co-ordinate the Howling Griffons' attack, sped past the pict-screens in front of Inquisitor Thaddeus as the shuttle raced low above the canopy. The shuttle's engines stripped leaves from their branches as Thaddeus sped past, trying to keep his heart and hands steady as he approached the battlefield. Somewhere below the solid ceiling of greenery lay thousands of corpses from the battles that had already been fought for Vanqualis, along with thousands more living humans, orks and superhuman Space Marines who would still die no matter what happened. Palls of smoke still rose from the cratered foothills devastated by an orbital strike, and as the shuttle passed over them Thaddeus glimpsed charred bodies and shattered artillery pieces littering the hillside.

Thaddeus had to stay low in case the Howling Griffons had gunships in the air that would shoot him down – even the orks might be a danger if they had aircraft, which was not unknown in spite of the crudeness of their species. But Mercaeno's Space Marines were by far the greatest threat. Thaddeus had made yet another enemy, and they were one of the deadliest yet. There were fellow inquisitors out there in the galaxy who would gladly kill Thaddeus if they got the chance, as well as numerous members of the Ecclesiarchy and half the Adeptus Mechanicus. Few of them, however, could compare to Lord Mercaeno.

The pilot-cogitator did most of the work flying the shuttle, leaving Thaddeus to watch the sensor data from the *Cerulean Claw*. The

Howling Griffons had found their prey, a concentration of Space
Marines breaking across a patch of open ground created by the impact
of an orkish asteroid. The shuttle had access to the data gathered by the
Cerulean Claw in orbit – the crew had shut off the shuttle's access as
soon as they realised it was missing, of course, but Thaddeus still had
some old inquisitor's tricks up his sleeve. The Inquisitorial seal, which
had opened the door to the shuttle bay, also had a code-cracking circuit
that, for a few minutes at least, opened a back door into the shuttle's
cogitator and let him see what the Howling Griffons were seeing. It
wouldn't last for long, but then probably neither would Thaddeus.

The Griffons must have thought they had found the most hateful of
enemies, Chaos Space Marines, renegade Astartes who followed the
Dark Gods of the warp. Mercaeno wouldn't waste much time getting
to grips with them, which meant that Thaddeus had to get there first.

Unfortunately, that also meant he couldn't pick his landing spot. He
would have to come down in the heart of the renegade Space Marine
force, and hope the jungle would forgive him for such a rude entrance.

Thaddeus could see the faint spray of smoke from the still-smouldering
impact site on the target hill. In the earliest stages of the orks' invasion
of Nevermourn, one of the asteroids carrying the first wave of greenskins
had landed off-target, falling at a shallow enough angle to clip the top
of a low hill and blast the trees and foliage off it before impacting at the
foot of the hill and exploding. Thaddeus banked the shuttle and took
over from the pilot-cogitator, gunning the craft's retros so it slowed
dramatically and swooped down into the canopy.

Branches snapped and the shuttle was battered as it crashed down
through the foliage, but Thaddeus knew he wouldn't be taking this ship
off the surface of Vanqualis again. He would be lucky if he ever left the
planet. He had enemies everywhere, and it was quite possible he was
walking right into the hands of one of his oldest.

Thaddeus was gambling his life that Sarpedon wouldn't just kill him
on sight.

'The Onager orbital shuttle,' said Sarpedon, 'is junk. There was a whole
fleet of them on the *Brokenback* that we never used. They've got no
armour and they need a landing strip. We lost all the old Scalptakers
and Hammerblade fighter-bombers a long time ago, and without Lygris
Eumenes has no way to fly the alien craft we found on the *Brokenback*.
With the Thunderhawks disabled, Eumenes has only one choice left.'

'The Onagers,' said Chaplain Iktinos. 'That's how you know the traitors will be here.'

The Soul Drinkers were in position just inside the tree line. Beyond
the tree line, the hilltop was charred and blasted. The taste of charcoal
and smoke was heavy in the air and coils of smoke still wreathed

overhead. Sarpedon's Astartes were in cover among the burned trees, smeared with ash as they moved along the tree line to get the best angles of fire. Their bolters, and the few heavy weapons they still had, could criss-cross the open hilltop into a textbook killing ground.

'This is the only place Eumenes can land,' said Sarpedon. 'The Thunderhawks could have plucked his traitors off the roof of the fortress but the Onagers have to land here. That means the traitors will be here, too, and they'll have to get across open ground under fire to board and get off this planet.'

'My flock will relish it,' said Iktinos. 'Rarely do they have the chance to bring such decisive vengeance to the enemy.'

Iktinos had spoken of 'his flock' before, and the Soul Drinkers who made up his flock were gathered just behind him now, preparing their battle-gear for the coming fight. Iktinos had become the leader of a group of Soul Drinkers whose officers had been killed in the Chapter's various battles, and they were intense in their devotion to Iktinos. Now Iktinos was on Vanqualis they had their leader back, and Iktinos had led them in the rites and prayers they observed so keenly. Slowly, Iktinos's flock had become a unit of shock troopers, almost thirty Soul Drinkers strong, who now cared for nothing but the destruction of their enemies. If Sarpedon had been a stronger Chapter Master and elicited similar devotion from all the Soul Drinkers, the rebellion would never have happened and Vanqualis would be free of the orks.

'Luko here,' came a vox in Sarpedon's ear. 'Company.'

'Where?' Luko was just behind the front line, leading the reserve that would plug any gaps in the line and counter-attack if the traitors got into close assault range.

'Right over you at any second.'

Sarpedon could hear something crashing through the trees. The Soul Drinkers in the line were turning to face the new arrival, bolters sighting through charred tree trunks into the greenery beyond. A great dark shape came down, splintering through the branches, and Sarpedon caught a glimpse of red and gold livery on its hull.

The craft hit the ground, a short distance from the front lines. Its nose carved a deep furrow as it ploughed through the ash, its engines kicking out a wash of exhaust fumes and heat. It was a shuttle, short and stubby, not much more than a one-man craft for transporting dignitaries or officers between craft. Apart from its quartered red and gold colours, any identifying marks had been burned or scratched off. It certainly wouldn't be taking off again.

The shuttle smashed through the burned trees with a terrible sound, disappearing into the ash-black depths of the jungle past the far end of the Soul Drinkers' line.

'Hold!' ordered Sarpedon over the vox. 'Hold fire!'

A few minutes passed. A soft thud from the direction of the shuttle crash was probably a fuel tank exploding. The squads holding the end of the line reported no contacts.

Finally, a figure emerged, limping through the scorched trees. Sarpedon could almost hear fingers tightening on boltgun triggers. The figure was human – not a Space Marine but a normal man, wearing a long battered coat. Memory sparked in Sarpedon's mind. The man's face was older than he remembered, but he definitely knew the man. And it was someone he had been certain he would never see again.

'Hold your fire, Soul Drinkers,' said Sarpedon. 'Guns down.' Sarpedon stood up out of cover and clambered over the fallen trees and burned undergrowth. It took a few minutes for the man to reach Sarpedon and by that time, Sarpedon was certain. The man emerging from the crash site was the same man he had last seen on Stratix Luminae. It had felt like a lifetime ago, a time before the Soul Drinkers began to fracture and turn on themselves.

'Inquisitor Thaddeus,' he said.

'I'm afraid I don't have much time for pleasantries, Commander Sarpedon,' said Thaddeus. 'Although I should say I am grateful to you for not killing me.'

'Don't thank me just yet, Thaddeus,' said Sarpedon. The last time they had met, the two men had united to defeat the mutant overlord Teturact on the frozen tundra of Stratix Luminae. But they had been forced to co-operate in the face of their enemy, and previously Thaddeus had been dedicated to tracking down and destroying the Soul Drinkers. 'I had thought we would never meet again, inquisitor.'

'Your Chapter is certainly elusive,' replied Thaddeus, walking closer. Sarpedon could now definitely see that Thaddeus had aged rapidly. His hair was greying and starting to thin, and he had the slightly haunted, hollow look that Sarpedon had seen in the faces of many veteran Imperial servants. 'It took a lot to track you down to here.'

'Then the Inquisition has not given up looking for us?'

'The Inquisition? I don't know. I have not had friendly contact with a fellow inquisitor for some time, Lord Sarpedon. I am something of an outcast.' Thaddeus smiled, but with little joy. 'Perhaps we have become very similar. I had to anger a lot of superiors to find you on Stratix Luminae and they haven't forgotten it. I'm on my own here. And since the Inquisition ordered all histories of the Soul Drinkers deleted it is very difficult for a man on his own to find you. In truth it was only chance that brought me here at all.'

'Then why did you come here, Thaddeus? On Stratix Luminae we came to a truce and I thought that was the end of it.'

'Lord Sarpedon, surely you have some idea of what the Soul Drinkers mean? A renegade Space Marine Chapter is dangerous enough. The deletion order was carried out because mere knowledge of you could be corruptive. But to have a Chapter who was led astray by its own will instead of something from the warp or some alien power – Lord Sarpedon, there are inquisitors who would refuse to believe such a thing! They would say the very fabric of the Imperium would unravel if a Chapter of Astartes suddenly developed free will! That was the reason I was on my own when I hunted you. My superiors said it was for the good of the Imperium, but I realise now they were just afraid of the very idea of you, in case I found you and the resulting knowledge could not be contained.'

'Then what? You pursued us out of curiosity, Thaddeus? So that you could tell yourself you had found us when other inquisitors would not?'

'Perhaps at first,' said Thaddeus.

'Commander,' said Chaplain Iktinos. 'The scouts on our western flank report movement.'

'The traitors?'

'Most probably. Certainly not greenskins.'

'Then make sure they're watching the skies, too. Have all the men in position. This is the only chance we'll get.'

'Traitors?' said Thaddeus.

'Though I am loath to admit to an outsider,' said Sarpedon, 'some among us believe they should command this Chapter, rather than me.' Sarpedon took Thaddeus's shoulder and led him back from the tree line, into the cover of the burned forest.

'Then I might be too late,' Thaddeus said, with as much sadness as frustration.

'Too late? Explain yourself, inquisitor. And those traitors will be upon us in minutes. Be quick.'

'I could not search for you by normal means, since the Chapter's existence has been purged from Imperial records,' said Thaddeus. His voice was low and urgent now. 'So I had to try something more esoteric. I looked for traces of you left in the mythologies of primitive peoples, who might recall the Soul Drinkers' recent activity away from Imperial censors. And I found something.'

'What?'

'Legends, Commander Sarpedon. Legends of the Soul Drinkers. Ancient, too, thousands of years old.'

'About the old Chapter, then?'

'Perhaps. On an arctic world on the eastern fringes I discovered the legends of the Grail of the Damned, used as the symbol of dark armoured warriors who drank men's souls. I made the connection.'

'I do not know of any wars the old Chapter fought in such a place,' said Sarpedon.

'Neither did I,' said Thaddeus. 'But the Grail of the Damned was not the only reference. I found a Drinker of Souls worshipped by cannibal tribes near the Storm of the Emperor's Wrath. This was across several worlds, Sarpedon, and these people were centuries behind developing space travel. Someone had left those legends there, and left a scar on those worlds so deep they became a religion.'

'Then the old Chapter left an impression on savage worlds,' said Sarpedon. 'This would not be the first time a Chapter has been the foundation of myths among such peoples. I do not understand why that should bring you here.'

'You will, Sarpedon, with just a little thought.'

'Salk here,' voxed Sergeant Salk from the end of the Soul Drinkers' line. 'My men have spotted contrails above us. Looks like Eumenes is sending the landers down.'

'The traitors are almost upon us!' voxed Sarpedon to his whole force. 'Final prayers and be ready for the fight! This time they fight on ground of our choosing, and they will be vulnerable as they flee. They chose to show us no mercy at the fortress. Now we must show the same to them.' Sarpedon could hear the murmured prayers up and down the line, verses from the *Catechisms Martial* and battle-rites older than the Chapter itself.

'Think, Sarpedon,' continued Thaddeus. 'What could bring you and I to this same Emperor-forsaken world?'

The Soul Drinkers were tensed for battle, all of them save Sarpedon himself at their position in the line. But Sarpedon realised the importance in Thaddeus's words.

'Vanqualis has its legends, too,' said Sarpedon.

'The Black Chalice,' said Thaddeus darkly. 'The fountain from which all evil flows. It is said to float in the warp, disgorging the stuff of Chaos. The Bearers of the Black Chalice are giant armoured warriors who wear the chalice as their emblem, and they will one day come down from the sky to claim Vanqualis as their own. Someone connected to the old Chapter came to the Obsidian system a long time ago and did something that left that scar on the minds of the Vanqualian people. I had reached this system to study the legends of the Black Chalice when I realised the Soul Drinkers were here, too. So I came to the surface to warn you.'

'Someone brought us here,' said Sarpedon. 'We have been manipulated.'

'You have an enemy here. I have made many sacrifices to hunt you down, Sarpedon, so I am an enemy, too. But the only thing more dangerous than a renegade Chapter is an enemy who can manipulate them to his will.'

Sarpedon thought rapidly. It was difficult to absorb what Thaddeus was telling him. It could be a trap, a lie typical of the Inquisition – but Thaddeus had let Sarpedon go once before, and there was a sincerity in him that Sarpedon could not ignore. The Soul Drinkers had been brought into a situation that Sarpedon didn't understand, to ground prepared for them by someone in the old Chapter. That idea ignited an old hatred inside Sarpedon, something that had been near the surface ever since the daemon prince Abraxes had offered Sarpedon awesome power in return for a lifetime of servitude.

'No one owns this Chapter,' said Sarpedon darkly. 'We are no one's weapon.'

'I know, said Thaddeus. 'That is why your Chapter has to live.'

The anger flared inside Sarpedon again. The treachery of Eumenes had brought him low, but now he was inflamed again. After all this time, after all these sacrifices made to secure the freedom of the Soul Drinkers, still there was a foe out there who thought he could use the Soul Drinkers for his own ends. Nothing in this galaxy, not the depredations of Chaos or the corruption of the Imperium, not even Eumenes's betrayal, provoked Sarpedon's anger like the knowledge he was being used.

'Vanqualis is lost,' he said. 'When the traitors are dead we will leave this place and hunt down whoever thinks they can bend the Soul Drinkers to their will. We will not rest until it is done.'

'That may not be quite so simple, said Thaddeus. 'I needed help to make it this far, and my hosts were just as interested in the Black Chalice as I was.'

Sarpedon rounded on Thaddeus. 'What do you mean?'

'Contact!' voxed Sergeant Salk from up ahead. 'Armour sighted, incoming!'

'Armour? The traitors have no tanks,' replied Sarpedon on the vox.

'It's not the traitors,' replied Salk.

Sarpedon ran through the charred forest up to the edge of the tree line. On the far side of the clearing he could see dark shapes crashing through the burned trees. The hull of a tank rose up as it ground over the fallen trunks, and Sarpedon caught a flash of red and gold livery. It was a Rhino APC and a Predator battle tank followed it, autocannon turret swivelling towards the Soul Drinkers' position. Sarpedon could see the rampant griffon symbol on the tanks' hulls as more vehicles tore through the ruined forest and roared towards the Soul Drinkers.

'Your hosts, Thaddeus?' said Sarpedon to the inquisitor behind him.

'The Howling Griffons,' replied Thaddeus. 'They believe they are fighting the Bearers of the Black Chalice.'

'Are you armed?'

Thaddeus took his autopistol from beneath his greatcoat. 'Always.'

'Then take your place in the line,' said Sarpedon.

Chaplain Iktinos began intoning the final rites of battle, the final words that shielded a Space Marine's soul against the sins of despair and defeat. As one, the Soul Drinkers readied themselves to face an enemy that Sarpedon knew would not stop until they were all dead.

In spite of the roar of the Land Raider's engine, around Mercaeno it was calm. It was spiritual quiet before the storm, a few short moments of reflection before the killing began.

The axe that had slain Periclitor was heavy in Lord Mercaeno's hand, as if the magnitude of that deed weighed it down. Its head was covered in the scrollwork of the psychic circuit that ran through the weapon, focusing Mercaeno's psychic ability so tightly that he could wrench the very soul from an enemy it struck. The axe had been carried by a long line of Howling Griffons Librarians and like any such Chapter artefact it carried oaths and obligations of its own – admonishment for corruption and laxity, an undertaking to be merciless and intolerant of any failing even among his own battle-brothers, and an overpowering dedication to the utter destruction of the Emperor's foes.

The axe was a symbol of what the Howling Griffons had vowed to do thousands of years ago. It was not enough to defeat the Black Chalice, to hurl them back into the shadows and deny them whatever prize they sought on Vanqualis. No, while any normal soldier would call that a victory, to the Howling Griffons it would be a defeat for which the Chapter would never atone. The Howling Griffons had to destroy the Black Chalice itself, shatter it and cast it to the winds of destruction, and slaughter its bearers to a man. Nothing short of utter destruction was acceptable. The Lord Librarians who had carried the axe before Mercaeno had exemplified that ruthlessness. Mercaeno himself would outdo them.

'Enemy sighted!' came the vox from Techmarine Thol in the lead Predator tank. 'They are Astartes!'

Mercaeno looked up at the pict-screen on which was the transmission from Thol's Predator. Among the grainy darkness of the charred forest he could see purple-black armour like the carapaces of a host of beetles – power armour, Space Marines skulking in the darkness. He could even see the bone and gold chalice on a shoulder pad, emblazoned as if the enemy were proud of their corruption. Mercaeno's disgust was overshadowed only by his anger.

'Then it ends here,' said Mercaeno. Around him his command squad bowed their heads in silent agreement, Brother Rodrigo clutching the First Company's battle standard ready to let it unfurl.

'Howling Griffons,' announced Mercaeno to all his squads. 'The time for prayer and preparation is over. Clear your minds and prepare your souls to receive the wrath of the Emperor. The Black Chalice is before us, overflowing with evil, and we are the Emperor's own fist poised to destroy it! In this hour a thousand years of oaths are fulfilled, a great weight of duty is placed upon us, and it is with fury and hate that we will cast it off! Death to the Black Chalice! Vengeance to the Emperor! Victory to the Howling Griffons!'

Even within the armoured hull of the Land Raider, Mercaeno could hear the rest of his army cheering at his words as three companies of the galaxy's greatest warriors roared out of the forest and towards the Bearers of the Black Chalice.

'What right to we have to pass judgement on a fellow human being?'

'I ask of you, what right have we to presume him innocent?'

– Daenyathos, *Catechisms Martial*

CHAPTER TWELVE

The armoured spearhead of the Howling Griffons crashed into the Soul Drinkers so hard the jungle shook with it. The humid winds of the rainforest turned hot and dry with fire as dozens of vehicle-mounted guns opened up. Autocannon shots from Predator tanks exploded among the charred trees, sending shards of fire-hardened wood flying like steel shrapnel. Lascannon spat fat crimson bursts of shimmering las-fire into the darkness, shearing tree trunks in two and gouging deep glowing furrows in the ground. The spearhead's detachment of Whirlwind support tanks carpeted sections of the Soul Drinkers' line with rockets from their turret-mounted launchers, hammering gaps in the line for the Rhino APCs to streak towards.

The spearhead advanced into the teeth of the Soul Drinkers' firing line. As soon as the spearhead crossed the sacred line of bolter range the air was filled with explosive bolts, rattling in heavy scorching chains that battered against the hulls of the Howling Griffons' tanks. Heavy bolter rounds blew the track off a Predator so it carved a crescent gouge in the earth as it slewed round, more shots hammering against it and blasting the paint off one side.

A missile launcher sent an armour-piercing krak missile streaking into the side of a massive Land Raider and the ammunition for its sponson-mounted heavy bolter detonated, blowing the side off the vehicle and sending the Space Marines inside diving out to escape the burning wreck. The gunfire was so heavy the charred, flat ground was chewed into a pockmarked battlefield in a few moments, and the burned forest the Soul Drinkers held was reduced to a sorry mass of stumps and fallen trees, showered with shrapnel and burning branches.

The sky turned dark with smoke, like a new night falling on Vanqualis lit only by the scarlet of las-fire and the lightning flashes of explosions. Darkness fell, the ruined forest lit from beneath by the blazing of hundreds of boltguns. Men died in that darkness, their deaths picked out frame by frame by the strobing gunfire like images from a pict-viewer. A torso reared back as a heavy bolter shell smacked into a Soul Drinker's chest. A Howling Griffon was crushed as a Rhino was blown onto its side by a missile, spilling passengers from its sundered hull. Bodies slumped over fallen tree trunks or were blasted back through the forest as gunfire blanketed the battlefield.

The first Rhino APC reached the line, its engine gunning violently as its armoured hull rode up over fallen trees and the bodies of Soul Drinkers who had died in the first moments of the battle. The Rhino's top hatch opened and a squad of Howling Griffons vaulted out, blazing with their bolters before they even hit the ground. One or two never left the vehicle, their heads battered into bloodied flowers of torn ceramite by bolter shots, and another clattered to the ground with one arm and shoulder blown off by a plasma gun blast. But suddenly the Howling Griffons were among the line, and the battle was now the close-quarters murder at which Space Marines excelled.

The Soul Drinkers' line bowed and held as more Howling Griffons squads dived into the battle. Captain Luko bellowed and led the Soul Drinkers' reserve into the fray, leaping over their own dead to reach the enemy. Chainblades screamed against ceramite and bolter shells thudded into flesh.

More Howling Griffons were deploying to support the assault, pumping bolter fire into the rest of the Soul Drinkers' line to keep them from helping their battle-brothers. Jump-packed squads arced over the carnage, chainswords falling as they let themselves tumble down into the conflict. Bodies flew as power weapons flared, officers on both sides wading in to lead their men in the slaughter.

Just behind the tip of the Howling Griffons' spearhead, the standard of the First Company was raised, its bullet-holed banner depicting a resplendent griffon rending foul monsters beneath its claws. Lord Mercaeno and his command squad emerged from their Land Raider, the Lord Librarian's mere presence pushing the Howling Griffons forward a step. Mercaeno drew his axe, let the light that poured from it illuminate him as if a shaft of sunlight fell upon him from on high, and then charged.

Further along the line, Sarpedon commanded the Soul Drinkers' defence, ordering his Astartes to hold the line and trust their battle-brothers in the centre to repel the attack. He did not conjure the terrifying hallucinations of the Hell, because he knew that there would be nothing the Howling Griffons were afraid of. Not even the Black Chalice itself, pouring waves of evil and Chaos onto the battlefield, would deter the Howling Griffons from pressing home their attack.

He resisted the urge to plunge into the fight himself because he was needed here, in the line, ensuring the Soul Drinkers were not surrounded by the disciplined, relentless Howling Griffons squads advancing across the charred ground towards them. Iktinos's crozius arcanum, glowing like a beacon, told Sarpedon that the Chaplain was leading the way where the fighting was hardest, and he could even hear snatches of Iktinos's preaching amid the din of battle.

Sarpedon glanced about him, trying to pick out the shape of the battle through the darkness and chaos. He had left Inquisitor Thaddeus behind the front line, and at the periphery of his attention he realised that the inquisitor was now close to the thickest of the fighting, where the shining axe blade of the Howling Griffons' commander now flashed.

'Thaddeus!'

Inquisitor Thaddeus heard his name bellowed through the din. Thaddeus was crouched down beside the bullet-riddled tree stump, autopistol hot in his hand. His muscles froze at the voice, because he knew it was Mercaeno.

Thaddeus glanced past the stump. A dead Howling Griffon lay just beyond him – the backpack had been blasted off and the huge armoured body lay on its front, a gory wet chasm torn into its back. Other bodies lay draped over fallen trees or battered down into the mud. Space Marines battled one another in the thick of the fighting, an astonishing sight – huge figures clashing with appalling strength and speed. And in the midst of them all was the crescent of Mercaeno's axe, rising and falling in the chaos.

Thaddeus drew his alien sword, its blade thrumming with the urge to break up into its component shards and kill. He knew he could not fight in this battle, not when the combatants were Space Marines. A few of the more martially minded and experienced inquisitors were the equal of a Space Marine in combat, and a handful of them were substantially tougher even than an Astartes. But Thaddeus was not one of them. As the Howling Griffons had told him, he was just a man. He also knew that he probably would not have a choice over whether he fought or not.

'Thaddeus!' bellowed Mercaeno's voice. The Howling Griffon burst from the throng, throwing Soul Drinkers aside and battering another to the ground with a sweep of his force axe. Thaddeus froze – even across the ruination he could see the anger creasing Mercaeno's face, the wrath

burning in his eyes. Mercaeno, with a Space Marine's enhanced vision
and a psyker's insight, had picked out the skulking Thaddeus from the
shadows. Thaddeus cursed himself for thinking he could hide.

Most men would have fled. Thaddeus knew that somewhere in the
back of his mind. But most men would not have understood, in the
blind flare of panic, that Mercaeno would have killed him as he ran as
surely as if he just lay down to die. So Thaddeus stepped out of cover
and stood his ground, sword and pistol gripped tightly as the huge form
of Lord Mercaeno bore down on him.

The gunfire was dim and muffled, as if its sound was breaking
through from a different world. The battlefield was blurred and vague,
its fighting Space Marines just shimmers of half-glimpsed movement.
There was nothing on Vanqualis now save Mercaeno and Thaddeus.

Without even willing it, Thaddeus was firing, the autopistol shots
smacking into Mercaeno's breastplate in miniature starbursts.

Mercaeno didn't even notice. It was all Thaddeus could do to throw
himself aside as the axe came down, its glowing blade burning with
psychic fire as it cleaved down through the tree stump behind him.

The force of the impact threw Thaddeus to the ground. He rolled
onto his feet, firing almost blindly at the huge, dark armoured form of
Mercaeno above him.

'You slew my battle-brothers!' yelled Mercaeno. 'You betrayed us!
And you are in league with the Enemy!'

'There is no enemy!' shouted Thaddeus in reply. 'There is no Black
Chalice! All of this is lies!'

'You speak to me of lies? You, whose very soul is deceit!' Mercaeno
slashed at waist-height with his axe and Thaddeus had to drop to one
knee to turn it over his head with his alien blade, the force so strong
it nearly broke Thaddeus's wrist. Mercaeno's form swept over him and
Thaddeus lunged upwards, driving his sword into Mercaeno's body.

The blade hit ceramite just below Mercaeno's arm, and its tip sheared
through his power armour with unnatural ease. Thaddeus willed the
blade into action and as it slid through muscle and bone the blade fragmented, dozens of steel shards flying loose to shred Mercaeno's flesh.
Like great steel insects, they burst from the armour of Mercaeno's chest
and right arm, flitting through the air hungry for blood.

Mercaeno roared. Thaddeus twisted the blade and felt ceramite
fragmenting under it. The pain and destruction wrought by the blade
would have felled anyone, even most Astartes. But Lord Mercaeno's
hand had taken the head of Periclitor, and he had seen every kind of
combat on every type of battlefield. He had suffered worse and been
victorious. What little hope still flared in Thaddeus's mind was extinguished as Mercaeno's left hand grabbed the back of his coat and lifted
him off the ground.

Mercaeno flung Thaddeus with all his strength. Thaddeus flew through the air, his sword and pistol left behind, and charred branches splintered beneath his weight. He hit the ground hard enough to knock the breath out of his lungs and skidded insensible across the ashes.

Thaddeus forced himself to his senses. He had landed beyond the tree line, on open ground. The roaring beside him was the engine of a Rhino APC, one of its tracks blown off and its hatches left open where the Howling Griffons inside had disembarked. He reached inside his coat for one of the many weapons he still carried.

His hand closed around a small metal sphere and he drew it from beneath the folds of his coat. It would have to do.

Mercaeno charged towards him and Thaddeus rolled forwards so he slammed painfully into the Howling Griffon's armoured body. His hand reached up to clamp the magnetic grenade to the back of Mercaeno's armour. If Thaddeus was to die, he could at least help the Soul Drinkers escape destruction and find their true enemy, by killing the Howling Griffons' commander.

Mercaeno's gauntlet closed around Thaddeus's own hand. The Space Marine had seen Thaddeus's ploy coming and reacted with impossible speed. Bones cracked and tendons snapped beneath his grip. Thaddeus was filled with a cold, horrifying pain, echoing through his whole body, and his nervous system lit up with agony.

Mercaeno let go and Thaddeus's ruined hand dropped the grenade. Mercaeno kicked it contemptuously aside and grabbed Thaddeus by the throat. The grenade burst somewhere on the edge of Thaddeus's vision, harmlessly.

'You do not know…' gasped Thaddeus. 'None of you… you have no idea who you are fighting…'

Mercaeno slammed Thaddeus down against the sloping front armour of the Rhino. Thaddeus barely registered the cracking of his ribs, such was the pain from his crushed hand and the desperation running through him.

'By the oaths of justice,' said Mercaeno, ignoring Thaddeus's words, 'you have been judged a traitor to the Howling Griffons and an enemy of the Emperor. There is no punishment fitting your crimes. We pray that the Emperor shall accept death as sufficient.'

'By the authority of the Holy Orders of the Emperor's Inquisition…' gasped Thaddeus, desperately.

Mercaeno sneered and brought his force axe up. The intricate patterns on its surface were lit up with the force of his hate and he brought it crashing down into Thaddeus's body.

The last thing Inquisitor Thaddeus saw was his own blood spraying over Mercaeno's rage-filled face.

* * *

Sarpedon added up the dead. It had become a reflex action, a necessity of command. Acknowledgement runes were dim against his retina and he guessed that thirty or so Soul Drinkers already lay dead amid the furious melee in the centre of the line. The Chapter could not afford to lose a single Soul Drinker, and Sarpedon's stomach tightened as he watched the future of his Chapter dying amid the ruin and mud.

Sarpedon was further along the line from the close-quarters fighting where the Howling Griffons were trying to force their way through. The Soul Drinkers alongside him were keeping up an unending stream of fire at Howling Griffons half-glimpsed through the smoke and swirling ash. Howling Griffon tanks were firing on them, and return bolter fire was getting stronger with every moment as the Howling Griffons advanced their own firebase towards the trees. Soon the whole line would be enveloped in face-to-face slaughter.

Sarpedon had never given into despair before. He had been brought low, he had stared death and the destruction of the Soul Drinkers in the face. But he had never felt the coldness of sheer despair that reached up at him from the scorched ground.

'Luko!' voxed Sarpedon, snapping himself out of feelings that were so unbecoming of a Space Marine. 'Report!'

'They've got numbers and armour!' replied Luko. Sarpedon could hear the sizzle of Luko's power claws and the screaming gunfire all around the Soul Drinkers' captain. Luko was in the heart of the action, trying to plug the gap the Howling Griffons armour had blasted in the line.

'I need your honesty, captain,' said Sarpedon. 'Can we hold this position?'

Luko paused, a little too long. 'No,' he replied. 'Not here. Not against this.'

'Then get them out of there, captain.'

'Yes, commander.'

Another volley of bolter shots whipped around Sarpedon's head, shredding the sorry remains of the burned forest behind him. Sarpedon crouched further, folding his mutant legs under him. If he charged now, he thought, if he led the Soul Drinkers against the advancing Howling Griffons, they would all be destroyed and no one would ever have to know how far Sarpedon had fallen. It would be over, and he would never have to answer to anyone about how his Chapter had been split by treachery, and trapped on an Emperor-forsaken jungle world by the Howling Griffons.

Sarpedon choked the thought down, banishing it from his mind. In spite of everything, he was a Space Marine, and he had a duty to his battle-brothers that a normal soldier could never understand.

'Soul Drinkers!' called Sarpedon over the all-squads vox. 'The line will retreat! Forward squads disengage, line squads cover!' Sarpedon hefted his own bolter, ready to add his own fire to the effort. With every moment more of his battle-brothers were dying, and if this hateful strip of forest could not be held then they were dying for nothing.

The Soul Drinkers turned their bolters on the centre of the line as the forward squads, following the twin icons of Captain Luko and Chaplain Iktinos, disentangled themselves from the furious battle. The Howling Griffons tried to fall on them as they left but Sarpedon led the remaining squads in close, battering back the assaulting Howling Griffons with volleys of bolter fire. The forest around the line's centre was not a forest at all, just a broken wasteland blanketed with a caul of darkness and gunsmoke.

As the Soul Drinkers fell back to the cover of the still-standing forest behind them, Sarpedon could see the Howling Griffons' commander in the centre of the melee. Several Soul Drinkers had been surrounded in the last few moments before the covering fire weighed in and they were being butchered, the commander leading his Space Marines in those final acts of vengeance. The commander's axe rose and fell, cleaving limbs from bodies, and Sarpedon recognised the high collar and force weapon of a Librarian. He could even hear his adversary, roaring in frustration as the Soul Drinkers fell back down the slope of the hill towards the darkness of the valley below, where the jungle was too dense for the Howling Griffons' tanks to follow.

That same determination that Sarpedon himself had fought with time and time again was etched in the blood-spattered face of the Howling Griffons' commander. For a moment Sarpedon wondered if the Howling Griffon would recognise his own qualities in Sarpedon too – but then Sarpedon remembered that to the eyes of any Emperor-fearing soldier he was a hideous mutant, an abomination cursed by the Chaos gods and an enemy of the Imperium.

In storms of gunfire and hatred, the Soul Drinkers fell back before the fury of the Howling Griffons to seek their sanctuary in the jungle's depths.

The false night of battle had dissipated and true night had fallen. Slowly the creatures of Nevermourn's jungles were returning to places where gunfire and chaos had driven them off a few hours before. Sinuous, six-legged lizards wound their way back up tree trunks and flying creatures like winged snakes flitted into their treetop roosts. Beetles with shining emerald-green carapaces dissected the bullet-shredded leaves to rebuild the hives that had been crushed beneath tank tracks or power armoured feet. The night was punctuated by the shrill calls of tiny, brightly coloured birds and the whoops of ape-like creatures as they clambered back towards their territory in the canopy. The larger predators and herbivores that occupied the upper tiers of Nevermourn's ecosystem returned more slowly, nervously avoiding the patch of jungle where the Howling Griffons were encamped.

The Howling Griffons were guarding a knot of deep jungle at the foot of the hill where they had fought the Soul Drinkers. The jungle was dense here, too thick for anyone other than a Space Marine to forge his way through. The ground was sodden and as night fell rain had come with it, sending chutes of water shimmering down through the canopy like miniature waterfalls. Amphibious snakes slid through the standing water underfoot, writhing around the ceramite greaves of the Howling Griffons who held guard.

'Damn this,' said Captain Borganor. His Tenth Company troopers had formed the Howling Griffons' firebase and it was clear that he resented not being in the centre of the line, getting to grips with the enemy. 'They can't even pretend they're Space Marines. True Astartes would stand and fight. Now we've got to follow them through this Emperor-forsaken jungle before we can kill them.'

'They know we would have destroyed them,' said Lord Mercaeno. 'The Bearers of the Black Chalice are no fools. They have evaded justice for thousands of years. They know when they are beaten. And remember how the corrupt will always cling to life, even when death is an inevitability. They stave off their damnation, as if a few more days of freedom will somehow cleanse their lives of sin.'

Borganor and Mercaeno were in a small clearing formed by the hollow, rotted stump of an enormous fallen tree. Water cascaded down one side of the hollow, forming an ankle-deep pool choked with weeds and strange-coloured flowers. Mercaeno was enacting the wargear rites that the Howling Griffons observed, cleansing the taint of the Black Chalice from the holy axe. It had become besmirched with the blood of traitors, which had to be ritually washed away before the weapon was fit to strike through the oaths of the Howling Griffons. On a water-smoothed rock in front of Mercaeno was the axe, and he was slowly, painstakingly lifting off the scorch-dried blood encrusting the delicate patterns of the blade.

Normally the wargear rites would require Mercaeno to remove and purify his armour as well, but Nevermourn was too perilous to allow himself to go so unguarded. Beneath his armour, inscribed into his skin, were endless lines of text, smaller and denser than those on the armour. They were the most powerful oaths, the oldest ones, the promises that had bound him since before he had been fit to pick up a boltgun. Oaths to serve the Emperor, to honour his Chapter, and to guard his soul against the corruption the psyker's gifts could bring. They had been cut deep, so that every time Mercaeno felt pain in battle, he would be reminded of those oaths, and of how they were a physical part of him.

One oath, inscribed in flowing High Gothic across Mercaeno's barrel chest, was newer than the rest. The name of the daemon Periclitor was carved there – and the most recent cut was the line that struck through the daemon prince's name. That oath had been fulfilled. Those oaths, the old ones, remained hidden on Nevermourn. There was no need to display them when they were written across Mercaeno's very soul.

'If we could get the tanks through this terrain we'd have their heads already,' said Borganor bitterly. 'We would be delivering them to House Falken now.'

'The jungle is ours to use as well, captain,' said Mercaeno. He didn't lift his eyes from his task of cleaning Inquisitor Thaddeus's blood from the blade of his axe. 'You are familiar with our surroundings?'

'Of course.'

'Then you will be aware that ahead of the enemy is a swamp.' Mercano gestured at the streams of water falling all around them. 'All the rainfall flows through the jungle to the low ground ahead of them, and they will have to pass through that swamp to get away from us.'

'So we will have to follow them into it,' said Borganor. 'Shamed though I am to say it, it is not a battlefield I relish fighting upon.'

'You forget, captain, that we are not alone here. The enemy may be using this jungle to their advantage, but we have advantages of our own. We have the Emperor, and the blessed variety of His servants.'

Sergeant Ossex of Mercaeno's command squad was at the entrance to the hollow. 'Lord Librarian,' he said. 'We have contacted the general. His command frequency is patched into our vox-net.'

'Good,' said Mercaeno. He saw that Ossex had a new oath recently painted onto one of his vambraces, an oath to avenge the death of Brother Rhelnon. The oath had a name that had been crossed out – that of Inquisitor Thaddeus, who had slain Rhelnon and been slain in turn by Mercaeno. The Howling Griffons had made good on another promise.

'Have they contacted the enemy yet?' asked Borganor.

'Not yet,' said Ossex. 'They do not seem aware of the nature of the enemy they face.'

'Of course not,' said Mercaeno. 'The Bearers of the Black Chalice are too grave a threat to become known to mere soldiers.' Mercaeno flicked through the channels of the Howling Griffons vox-net until he found the channel that had been newly patched in.

'General,' he said. 'This is Lord Mercaeno, commanding officer of the Howling Griffons.'

'General Glaivan Varr of the 901st Penal Legion,' replied a weary voice, rendered grainy through the substandard Imperial Guard vox. 'The Howling Griffons, you say? I had not thought Vanqualis was worthy of one Space Marine army, let alone two.'

'There are no Space Marines on this world save us,' replied Mercaeno sharply.

'Commander Sarpedon would disagree,' said Varr. 'He and his Soul Drinkers.'

'So that is what they call themselves,' spat Mercaeno, the venom clear in his voice.

Varr paused. 'There is something I do not know,' he said carefully.

'More than you can imagine, general. The creatures you know as the Soul Drinkers are traitors to the Emperor.'

'Renegades,' said Varr. 'Hunted by the Imperium. So they told me.'

'Then you should have exterminated them!' snapped Mercaeno.

'We were having something of an ork problem, Lord Mercaeno,' said Varr, tiredness and cynicism weighing his voice down. 'Fighting Space Marines on principle isn't a priority for me and my men.'

'They are no mere renegades, general. These Soul Drinkers are given over to the Ruinous Powers. The Dark Gods of the warp, corruption made flesh. They have come to take this world and give it over in sacrifice to their gods, and they have used the ignorance of you and your men to turn you into tools of wickedness. This is the work of Chaos, general, and you are a part of it, unless you redeem yourself and join us in destroying it.'

For a long time General Varr did not reply, and the only sounds were the trickling of the water and the low, constant calls of the jungle.

'Chaos,' he said.

'Chaos,' replied Mercaeno. 'It is nothing but lies. And believing those lies is the path to corruption. The Enemy has come to Vanqualis, and it is far deadlier than any savage greenskin horde.'

'We fought alongside them,' said Varr. 'We killed thousands of orks…'

'Because they want this world for themselves. The Bearers of the Black Chalice no doubt used the ork invasion to infiltrate Nevermourn. The greenskins be damned, the true enemy has revealed its head and it will be destroyed.'

'Then I take it, Lord Mercaeno, that you are assuming command of the Imperial forces on Vanqualis?'

'That is correct,' said Mercaeno. 'And with our combined forces we will butcher the Bearers of the Black Chalice here and now. What is your position, General Varr?'

'We're encamped on high ground about two kilometres north-west of the head of the Serpentspine Valley,' said Varr. 'We're still receiving stragglers from the battle in the valley. We've got two thousand healthy soldiers here, another five hundred to a thousand holding out in pockets between here and the valley. My scouts tell me the greenskins are moving north from the heights over the valley, which means they're making their push on the coast.'

'We have greater concerns than the orks,' said Mercaeno. 'The betrayers are fleeing from my Howling Griffons through the marshes south of the ruined fortress.'

'I know where you mean,' said Varr. 'I've got it flagged on our maps as dead man's ground. Nothing's getting through there, even the orks would give it a wide berth.'

'And that is where we will destroy the Black Chalice. My men are approaching from the east. You will take the 901st and block the western edge of the marshes. The traitors will be trapped.'

'Abandoning our positions here will give the orks free rein,' said Varr. 'They could get to the coast in three days unopposed.'

'General Varr,' said Mercaeno gravely, 'my Chapter swore to defend Vanqualis a long time ago. When we learned of the greenskins that infested it, I took my Chapter to cleanse these jungles of the xenos. But the Howling Griffons also knew that one day the Black Chalice would return, and until they are destroyed there is room for no other concerns. I despise the xenos as much as you do, Varr – the more so, for I have fought their kind in every corner of the galaxy. But believe me when I say that I would rather every single Vanqualian dies to orkish hands than a lone bearer of the Black Chalice escapes these jungles alive. Do not think to question me, Varr, nor even to guess at what drives us. We will stop at nothing to fulfil the oaths our Chapter has sworn. Nothing.'

'Then my men can be in position in half a day,' said Varr. 'If that is an order.'

'That is an order, general.' Mercaeno closed the vox-link.

'Penal Legions,' said Borganor with some distaste. 'The worst of the worst. Scum not fit to seek the Emperor's redemption.'

'Scum indeed,' said Mercaeno. 'But the greenskins will have weeded out the weaker-willed. Among those men will be the hardest-bitten of killers. And it barely matters if the 901st stand and fight or run like dogs, Borganor. All they need to do is slow the Black Chalice down. As soon as we get to grips with the enemy, the Black Chalice will be destroyed. Whether the 901st survive to fight alongside us is irrelevant.'

'Then they shall serve some purpose in death,' said Borganor. 'Far more than they ever did in life.'

'Have Captain Darion draw in the patrols and make ready to move. As soon as the 901st are in position we will tighten the noose.'

Borganor saluted and left the hollow, leaving Mercaeno to finish his wargear rites.

Finally it would be done and one of the Chapter's oldest oaths would be fulfilled. By the next nightfall another name carved deep into Mercaeno's skin would be struck through, so that every time Mercaeno felt pain he would be reminded of the day the Black Chalice fell.

'How far must we compromise when victory is at stake?'
'The concept of compromise is alien to an Astartes. To die
unrelenting is to be victorious.'

– Daenyathos, *Catechisms Martial*

CHAPTER THiRTEEN

With the twin dramas of the ork advance and the Howling Griffons' pursuit of the Soul Drinkers, a great deal went unnoticed in Nevermourn's jungles. Tiny pockets of Penal Legion troopers held out against scattered bands of orks, both sides cut off from their parent armies, fighting miniature wars for survival. Stragglers were picked off by predators native to the jungle, crushed in the maws of enormous insectoid monsters or dragged down beneath the ground by the articulated tentacles of subterranean beasts. A thousand stories were played out away from Vanqualis's eyes, men and greenskins dying heroic or shameful deaths, prevailing against the planet or falling to one another's blades.

One of those unnoticed dramas saw a number of small, obsolete cargo landers flying down through the last vestiges of the night. They landed clumsily on the cratered open ground on the blasted hill. From the forest around the hilltop emerged the Soul Drinkers loyal to Eumenes, led by Sergeant Hecular. They had watched the conflict between the Howling Griffons and Sarpedon's Soul Drinkers with some amusement, relishing the irony that it was Imperial Space Marines who had seen off their enemy Sarpedon.

Silently, rapidly, the rebel Soul Drinkers embarked on the Onager orbital landers, which trundled around the hilltop and took off again. They rose into the sky as the first tinge of grey-green morning light edged the far horizon, heading for the *Brokenback* so they could finally leave this forsaken planet forever.

* * *

Even Sarpedon's mutated legs made hard work of forcing his way through the foul, sucking swamp around him. It stank, for everything that died in the jungle eventually found its way into the swamp where it lay and rotted, forming a rank sluggish lake of decay and stagnation. The trees that grew there were like skeletal hands reaching desperately up from the swamp, and slime-encrusted roots arced overhead forming archways and tunnels among the filth. The Soul Drinkers had been forging on for several hours, knowing that the Howling Griffons would be matching their every step.

'Commander,' voxed Sergeant Salk from up ahead. Salk's squad included a number of tough field veterans and Sarpedon had found himself using them as forward scouts more and more often. 'We've got contacts up ahead. Half a kilometre from us.'

'Howling Griffons?'

'No. It looks like the 901st.'

'All units, halt,' ordered Sarpedon. The remaining Soul Drinkers, around two hundred Astartes strong, stopped forging on through the filth and held their positions, holding their weapons up out of the stinking water. Sarpedon himself halted and the sounds of the swamp settled around him – chirping insects, the hooting of birds roosting among the blighted trees overhead, and the slow, sluggish grind of the water itself.

'I could make contact, commander,' voxed Salk.

'No, sergeant,' replied Sarpedon. 'We don't know whose side they're on. The Howling Griffons could easily have taken command.' Sarpedon crawled a short distance through the swamp to the thick bole of a tree, which rose on a crown of overhead roots that resembled Sarpedon's own arachnoid legs. Sarpedon clambered up the tree – he could climb as nimbly as an insect, his legs tipped with long talons that dug deep into the bark.

From the vantage point, his enhanced Astartes eyesight piercing the filmy gloom, he could just glimpse the far edge of the swamp where banks of mud rose from the water and the jungle began again. The Penal Legion troopers were well disguised, smeared with mud and wearing improvised camouflage, but they were definitely there standing guard. They crouched down among the undergrowth or kept watch from the forks of trees, scanning the swamps. They were expecting an enemy to come through the swamps towards them, and that enemy could only be the Soul Drinkers.

Between the Soul Drinkers and the 901st's line, several enormous hunks of machinery lay half-submerged in the swamp. A few more were embedded in the far bank, hulks of rusting metal or lumps of scorched rock. They were the remains of the ork asteroid ship that had landed off-target and hit the hill behind them – it must have broken up and scattered itself all over the swamp and the valley beyond. The sight was a sudden reminder that the greenskins had brought the Soul Drinkers to Vanqualis in the first place, but that now the xenos were far from Sarpedon's mind, well down the list of priorities that now began with survival.

'They've been sent to trap us here,' said Sarpedon. 'Poor damned sinners.'

Sarpedon saw movement on the far shore. Chimera troop carriers, rugged APCs used throughout the Imperial Guard, rode up over the tangles of roots on the bank and tipped down into the swamp. Ripples rode through the filthy swamp water ahead of them as they forged forwards.

'They're moving to engage,' said Sarpedon. 'Soul Drinkers! Advance as line!'

Behind Sarpedon, the Soul Drinkers moved forward in a long, forbidding line, each Space Marine an anchor keeping the line taut and relentless. Sarpedon joined them, scuttling down from the tree back into the water. The Chimeras of the 901st were slowing down in the sucking mud and one foundered in the shadow of the orkish wreck. Its top hatch swung open and the men inside vaulted out. The water was chest-high to an unaugmented human and they struggled to keep their footing in the swamp.

One of them shouted. The Soul Drinkers had been spotted. Hundreds of men were in the water now, lasguns ready, a few heavy weapons and plasma guns shouldered ready to fight.

It could be because they are brave, though Sarpedon, that they come forward to fight us. Or it could be that they do not believe they will get off this planet, and they are just looking for a good fight before it is over.

Sarpedon could see the lead Chimera, a command vehicle trailing a cluster of antennae and mounted with vox-casters. The command unit inside were clambering out, and they were just hitting the water when the firing began.

'Advance!' Sarpedon heard – it was Captain Luko, jogging through the swamp, leading a chevron of Soul Drinkers through the spattering of las-fire. The 901st were sending out ranging shots, or perhaps hoping to break up the advance. Space Marine armour was all but proof against isolated las-fire, and it took far more to rattle the Soul Drinkers. As the first bolters rang out, Sarpedon put his head down and ran for the command Chimera.

Almost immediately, the 901st were dying. Dozens of them in those few moments, thrown back against the hulls of their Chimeras or thrown down into the bloodstained filth of the swamp. Sarpedon saw it all as if detached, as if he was watching on a pict-screen far away, the sound of the gunfire around him faint and tinny. These were his allies, the men who had come to Vanqualis to be redeemed, and to fight them was a betrayal. But there was no choice, on either side. The destruction of the 901st was a cruel inevitability, a grim, heartless business to be done quickly and without emotion, like the execution of a battle-brother.

Ahead of Sarpedon, the 901st's command Chimera rocked as a plasma blast bored through its side and flames billowed from the top hatch. The men sheltering around it threw themselves away from the vehicle, stumbling through the murk, their silhouettes hard-edged among the flames.

Sarpedon and General Varr saw one another at the same time. Scorched by the guttering flame enveloping his Chimera, Varr drew his sword – an ornate sabre he had probably taken from a dead Vanqualian artilleryman to replace the blade he had broken at the Wraithspire Palace.

'Fall back!' shouted Varr to the men behind him, without taking his eyes off Sarpedon. 'Give the order! Fall back and hold the shore!'

The command squad's vox-operator hauled his vox-unit through the murk and darkness, relaying the order to the rest of the 901st. Varr didn't follow the rest of his squad as they retreated from the giant armoured forms of the Soul Drinkers.

'Varr!' called Sarpedon.

'Sarpedon,' replied Varr. 'Change in the chain of command. You are the enemy now.'

'I know.'

'If it could end any other way I would take it. I hope you believe that. But my duty is to the Imperium, and on Vanqualis that means Lord Mercaeno.'

'I believe it, Varr. And if it means anything, I would change it, too, if I could.'

Varr dropped back into a guard position, blade held high. 'Make it quick,' he said.

Sarpedon's force staff was in his hand. In a few moments he had crossed the distance between them, and Varr's blade came forward to meet him.

'The Howling Griffons?' said Eumenes.

'The Chapter symbol is the same,' replied Sergeant Hecular. In the dim light of the Soul Drinkers' Chapter archive, Hecular's face looked even more hollow and cruel than usual.

Eumenes swung the pict-screen around on its armature. The Chapter archive still mostly consisted of datastacks that had been salvaged from the old Soul Drinkers fleet before Sarpedon had scuttled it after the first

Chapter War, and was housed in a ship's chapel with mosaics on the floors and faded frescoes on the walls and vaulted ceiling.

The history of the Howling Griffons scrolled by. 'Ultramarines successors,' said Eumenes to himself. 'Guilliman's brood. Guilliman was the primarch who built the whole mess of the Imperium in the first place. I hope Sarpedon kills a few of his sons before they get him.'

'I never paid much attention to Imperial history,' said Hecular.

Eumenes turned to him. 'Then start now,' he said. 'Know the enemy.' He turned back to the Howling Griffons' history. 'The Griffons are just another Chapter of lapdogs. They'll toe whatever line Terra casts out, by the looks of it. We have to be gone by the time they're finished with Sarpedon.'

Eumenes noticed another Soul Drinker approaching – Apothecary Pallas, his face still scorched and raw from his encounter with Techmarine Lygris. Pallas had recovered consciousness a few minutes after Lygris had escaped and torn the flight decks apart looking for him, but the Techmarine had fled. 'The last Onager has landed,' he said. 'All those loyal to us are on board.'

'Good,' said Eumenes. 'And the wounded?'

'There are some,' replied Pallas. 'But the apothecarion can cope as long as I have some of the others to help me.'

'And what of Lygris?'

'Still missing.'

'His escape rankles with you, Pallas,' said Eumenes.

'Of course,' replied Pallas tightly. 'He bested me.'

'You failed me,' said Eumenes. 'I expect more from my officers.'

'I will find him, Eumenes.'

'Eventually, yes, it is inevitable. That is not enough. I want his head, and soon.' Eumenes switched off the pict-screen and spoke over the vox. 'Tydeus? The rest of the Chapter is on board. How long before we can hit the warp?'

'A day at least,' replied Tydeus. The sounds of the engine decks were clear across the vox. Many of the *Brokenback*'s component ships had functional warp engines, which had been connected together so they could move the whole hulk into the warp.

Eumenes's face darkened further. 'A day? Explain yourself.'

'Lygris has been sabotaging the connections between the plasma generators and the warp coils. They can be fixed but it all takes time. It won't stop us, but it will slow us down.'

Eumenes cast a filthy look at Pallas, whose failure had let Lygris stay at large on the *Brokenback*. 'Time is becoming a factor. We will jump into the warp as soon as the engines are ready.'

'Where to?' asked Sergeant Hecular.

'It doesn't matter,' said Eumenes as he closed the vox-link. 'As long as we get away from this damned system. Then we can start planning for the next stage.' Eumenes indicated for Hecular to follow him as he headed back towards the bridge to prepare for the *Brokenback*'s departure.

For a few minutes Apothecary Pallas stayed behind, surrounded by the datastacks, which contained the history of everything he had betrayed. He had turned his back on the old Chapter when he sided with Sarpedon, and now he had turned it on Sarpedon himself. There was no history anywhere now which he could call his own.

Then Pallas, too, left for the apothecarion where the Soul Drinkers injured defending the fortress lay. They had joined Pallas in his betrayal, and now the apothecary's obligations were to help them. They were Pallas's battle-brothers now – Sarpedon, and the Soul Drinkers with him on Vanqualis, were lost to him.

Glaivan Varr's father had taught him to fight. That was why the lesson had stayed. His father had fought in the Locrasian 31st Light Infantry, a very old and distinguished regiment who took their swords as seriously as their guns. The Locrasian fighting style was fluid and rapid, as dangerous as it was elegant. Varr's father was a fair man, but one who knew how harsh the galaxy could be, especially to a son who would follow him into the military. Varr had borne the bruises of a sloppy guard or reckless lunge, and by the time he came of age he could hold his own with the sword against a veteran of the Locrasian Light Infantry.

One day his father left with his regiment to help put down a bloody rebellion, and he had not returned. All that remained of him was a catalogue of parries and thrusts, cuts and finishing blows.

They were all useless. With Sarpedon so huge and lightning-quick, even Varr's father couldn't help him.

Varr fended off the force staff again, his blade now battered and chipped, blunt and barely any use as a weapon. He stumbled and caught the butt of the staff in his back, sprawling forwards, barely able to keep a grip on the sword. He plunged into the water, got his footing and pushed up again. His eyes were full of stinking mud and he didn't know where his enemy was.

His father would have whirled around, brought the blade up in a glittering arc with such poise and confidence that it would have sheared through the guard of his opponent and put the tip at the enemy's throat. Varr did that now, swinging his weight around, all his strength bringing the Vanqualian blade towards his best guess at Sarpedon's location.

The blade shattered. Varr's wrist shattered with it, white, numb pain flooding through his arm. He looked up, the filth running from his eyes, and he saw the sword had shattered on the armour of Sarpedon's forearm.

Varr took a little comfort in the fact that there was a hint of real regret in Sarpedon's face as he drove the force staff through his opponent's chest.

Varr's body slid off the end of Sarpedon's force staff and into the water, foul swamp filth filling the hole torn through the general's chest. Sarpedon watched the body sink down into the blood-slicked water.

'Commander,' said Captain Luko. 'The 901st are falling back.'

'General Varr is dead,' replied Sarpedon.

Luko nodded towards the 901st's positions. 'Then the Penal Legion troops will be leaderless,' he said. 'Give the order and we'll break through them.'

Sarpedon glanced in the same direction. 'There is nothing to gain by that,' he said. 'They weren't put here to stop us, they were put here to slow us down. Even if we got straight through them, they will have achieved that objective. By the time we have broken them the Howling Griffons will be among us.'

'Commander?' said Luko, his face tinged with doubt and concern that rarely troubled a Space Marine. 'Do you mean to fight the Howling Griffons in this swamp?'

'No,' said Sarpedon. 'I have no wish to give Lord Mercaeno what he wants. Tell me, captain, are we still in contact with the *Brokenback*?'

'I don't know,' replied Luko. We haven't had any word from Lygris since–'

'I don't mean Lygris,' snapped Sarpedon. 'I mean Eumenes.'

Eumenes demanded that he be left alone on the bridge with all communications down, so that only he would be party to the negotiations. More and more equipment had been moved onto the bridge so that Eumenes could command the *Brokenback* and his Soul Drinkers alone.

Eumenes took to the command pulpit. It suited him completely.

'Good day, commander,' said Eumenes.

Sarpedon's face dominated the viewscreen. Around him could be seen the twisted trees reaching up from the fouled waters of the swamp. Sarpedon was filthy with the slime of the swamp and the blood of General Varr.

'I want to negotiate,' said Sarpedon.

Eumenes laughed. 'With what? I have the *Brokenback*. The warp engines are primed. In less than an hour we will be gone. What could you possibly offer us that we need?'

'Survival,' said Sarpedon. 'A future.'

'I don't think I am the one whose survival is at stake, Sarpedon.'

'Damn you, Eumenes, don't you even understand what is happening here? I'm not the only enemy you have. The Howling Griffons won't stop until the Soul Drinkers are destroyed. That means your men as well as mine. And even if you escape this system, the Howling Griffons will hunt you down. They outnumber you, Eumenes, and they will destroy you.'

'Let them try.'

'Eumenes, I cannot pretend I do not despise you.' Sarpedon's face was set – he was forcing down the anger inside him. 'You have betrayed me and everything I have fought for. But I cannot allow the Soul Drinkers Chapter to die. All the Soul Drinkers are my battle-brothers, and I will not hand the Howling Griffons a victory they won only because we were divided. Choke down your pride for a second, Eumenes. You know what I am saying is true. As long as we are divided the Howling Griffons will destroy us, one faction at a time.'

Eumenes leaned forwards. 'These are the words of a dying man, Sarpedon. Again, what can you offer me?'

'The Chapter.'

There was nothing to fill the silence that followed Sarpedon's words. Eumenes thought deeply for several long moments, the only movement the blinking of the lights that studded the cogitators and readouts around him.

'The Chapter,' Eumenes repeated. 'The Soul Drinkers.'

'Yours to command,' said Sarpedon. 'I will relinquish my rank as Chapter Master. You will be the new Chapter Master of the Soul Drinkers. You will have everything – the secrets of the *Brokenback*, the battle-brothers who sided with me, everything.'

'They will never fight for me, Sarpedon.'

'They will obey me,' said Sarpedon. 'And I will obey you. '

A long, slow smile spread across Eumenes's youthful face. 'And for this you receive survival. Nothing more. Only survival. Like an animal.'

'Like an animal,' replied Sarpedon. 'If that is what you wish. As long as we can unite to defeat the Howling Griffons, that is what you will have.'

Eumenes's brow knotted in thought. 'I need a way to get you off the planet.'

'Lygris can help you,' said Sarpedon. 'As long as you are quick.'

Eumenes looked the pict-image of Sarpedon in the eye. 'I will hold you to this, Sarpedon. I defeated you once. I will defeat you again.'

'I keep my word,' said Sarpedon gravely. 'There is no limit I will not reach to ensure the survival of the Soul Drinkers. Kill me if it amuses you. Just keep the Chapter alive. If it costs me everything to save the Soul Drinkers, then I accept that.'

'It will,' said Eumenes. 'I accept your offer. We unite to fend off the Howling Griffons. In return I am the Chapter Master of the Soul Drinkers, from this moment on. Defy the terms of this pact, and you and your battle-brothers' lives will be forfeit.'

Sarpedon's shoulders sagged, and for perhaps the first time in his life as a Space Marine he looked truly beaten. 'Broadcast across the ship's vox,' said Sarpedon. 'Lygris will hear. Then we can end this.'

Eumenes rapidly patched Sarpedon's transmission through to the vox-casters mounted throughout the *Brokenback*. 'Done.' Eumenes smirked, no doubt imagining his reign as Chapter Master. 'I will not kill you, Sarpedon. I will bring you low. Everything you believe in will fall apart and you will be alive to see it.'

'I have no doubt that is true, Eumenes. But my word is my word.'

Sarpedon began to speak through the *Brokenback*'s vox-caster, calling on Lygris to report to Eumenes and offer his expertise in calibrating and aiming the *Brokenback*'s precision armaments.

The note of defeat and sorrow in Sarpedon's voice was profound. For a long time Eumenes just stood there at the command pulpit and listened, admiring the ruination he would wreak on the man he had usurped as ruler of the Soul Drinkers.

'What can we learn from the ways of the xenos?'
'We can learn how to hate.'

– Daenyathos, *Catechisms Martial*

CHAPTER FOURTEEN

Lord Mercaeno watched in quiet fury at the bright orange blossoms billowing up over the jungle canopy. He stood on an outcrop of moss-covered rock that rose from the slope near the bottom of the hill, overlooking the swamp-filled valley. The viewpoint overlooked the drab, decaying canopy that stretched over the swamp, dark vegetation like a ragged olive-green blanket draped over the stinking waters. Somewhere in that darkness had been the Howling Griffons' quarry, the Bearers of the Black Chalice and their leader Sarpedon, and the Howling Griffons had come so close to getting to grips with them down in the filth and shadows.

Another explosion tore up from the jungle just in front of the Howling Griffons' positions. It burst up through the canopy on the near edge of the swamp, just where Mercaeno would have been marshalling his forces at that very moment had the bombardment not begun. Time and again the lance strikes and artillery shots hammered down from the sky, stitching a line of smoke and flame along the near edge of the swamp, like a wall of fire that barred the Howling Griffons from advancing any further.

'More deceit,' spat Mercaeno to himself. The ground shook as another explosion rocked the valley, throwing hissing curtains of vaporised swamp water into the air ahead of him. 'More cowardice. The traitors do not have enough honour even to stand and fight.'

'Lord Librarian,' said Captain Darion, who stepped up onto the outcrop behind Mercaeno. 'I've pulled the forward units back. They say we certainly cannot advance until this bombardment is over.'

'I thought as much.'

'And the accuracy is exceptional. An orbital bombardment would normally carpet this valley at random. The Black Chalice must have some very ancient technology at its disposal to fire so close to their own forces with such confidence.'

'Take care, Captain Darion, not to admire the ways of the enemy,' said Mercaeno bitterly. 'Nor to ascribe him a capacity for destruction beyond our own. We are the Emperor's soldiers. This is nothing compared to the strength granted us by our Emperor.' Mercaeno turned away from Captain Darion and switched to the vox-channel of the *Cerulean Claw*. 'This is Lord Mercaeno. Come in, *Cerulean Claw*.'

'*Claw* here,' replied the voice of Flag-Lieutenant Scarlphan.

Scarlphan was not a Space Marine, but part of the Howling Griffons' support structure of unaugmented humans who performed functions like crewing the Chapter's spacecraft, and working in its artificer workshops and apothecarion.

'We are under orbital bombardment. Where is this coming from?'

'The ship's sensors are tracking a very large spacecraft,' replied Scarlphan. 'It's in low orbit. It was hiding on the far side of the planet from us and we have only just found it. It shows considerable speed for its size. It opened fire a few minutes ago.'

'Can we engage?' said Mercaeno.

'It is unlikely the fleet could engage it successfully,' replied Scarlphan. 'Its armaments are considerable and its sheer size would make it impossible to target effectively. There is no saying where its vital points might be.'

'I need everything you have on it,' said Mercaeno. 'Full scans. Risk the *Claw* if you have to get close enough.'

'We have already begun,' said Scarlphan. 'I'm sending it to your slate now, Lord Librarian.'

Mercaeno took a data-slate out from the wargear hanging at the waist of his armour. Its screen lit up, showing a diagram of the enemy ship. It was huge, asymmetrical and ugly. Figures and diagrams flitted by.

'A space hulk,' said Mercaeno.

A space hulk was the result of a number of ships becoming lost in the warp, and clumping together to form an abomination of fused metal, like a bloated parody of a true ship. Every now and again the warp would spit a hulk back out into realspace, usually infested with aliens, renegades, or even the daemons of the warp. It was entirely appropriate that the Bearers of the Black Chalice should travel around in such a craft.

'Life scans?'

'Almost complete,' replied Scarlphan. 'Less than one per cent so far.'

'The damn thing's empty,' said Darion.

It was indeed strange. Space hulks were often infested, either by predators from the warp or mundane xenos, usually mindless vermin that hungrily colonised these floating pits of corruption. The hulk in orbit over Vanqualis was, for want of a better word, clean.

'The Black Chalice do not like sharing their living space,' said Mercaeno. 'And they're alone up there. Captain Darion, how well do you know your *Codex Astartes*?'

Darion looked faintly offended. 'Like my own thoughts,' he said.

'Then you are familiar with the approved tactics for boarding a space hulk?'

'Boarding? Yes, Lord Librarian.'

Mercaeno waved a hand at the swamp valley below, still shuddering with the bombardment. 'The hulk is risking coming into orbit only now. That means the Black Chalice intend to leave Vanqualis and board it so they can escape. That is when they will be vulnerable. And more importantly, we can hit them all at once. All of them, even their spacecraft. We can destroy them for good, so there will be no doubt.'

'There are few actions as dangerous as boarding a hostile craft, Lord Librarian,' said Darion carefully.

'I know of one, captain. Allowing the enemy to escape. Is that far more dangerous than any risk to which we could possibly expose the Howling Griffons? Would it not be corrosive to the very soul of this Chapter to see the enemy gathered before us, and not move to fulfil the oath that requires their destruction? Boarding the hulk is a last resort, but the path of the Space Marine is lined with such choices. Many commanders would let the Black Chalice go, it is true. None of those commanders are here.'

'Of course, Lord Librarian,' said Darion. 'And I agree. But we must go into this fully understanding the risks.'

'And it is my duty to minimise those risks as much as I can,' replied Mercaeno. 'To which end, we shall not be doing it alone.' Mercaeno switched vox-channels. 'General Varr? Come in Varr, this is Lord Mercaeno.'

'Varr's dead,' came the reply. It was a brutish, coarse voice, a world away from General Varr's relatively cultured tone.

'Who is this?' demanded Mercaeno.

'Acting General Kullek,' came the reply. The voice sounded faintly amused at this.

'*Acting* general?' Mercaeno did not bother to hide his incredulity. 'What are you talking about?'

'Varr's dead,' said Kullek. 'Dead man's boots.'

'And you are his second in command?'

'There's no second, not in the Penal Legions. But I'm the one who's giving the orders now, so that makes me in charge. Acting general, like I said.' The man's voice had an ugly, gloating quality to it, as if the death and destruction on Vanqualis was entertaining and participating in it a sport. However, given that the Penal Legions indeed had relatively little command structure, what Kullek said was probably correct. A man could walk far in dead men's boots if he was good at staying alive. It was still abhorrent, of course that Mercaeno should have to relay orders through a man who had doubtless been condemned to the Penal Legions for some horrible sin against the Emperor.

'Very well,' said Mercaeno sternly. 'What contact have you had with the enemy?'

'Still waiting,' replied Kullek. 'The general gave the order to fall back in the first scrap, and then didn't come out himself. The boys are getting restless. Not much fun waiting to get blown up down here. They want to get stuck in.'

'Then they shall have their wish. Your Emperor has need of the 901st. Tell me, acting general, have your men ever fought in a boarding action?'

The air tasted of salt and stone, lashed up by the storm. Even in the green depths of the jungle the warlord could taste that victory. The humans had tried to stop them – they had died beneath the greenskin onslaught, solely to keep them from this point. But they had failed. Armoured killing machines had descended from the skies and tried to fend them off, but these finest warriors of humanity had failed, too. Even the cheap trickery, which had conjured the images of orkish gods to scare the greenskins off Vanqualis, had failed. Only the orks had succeeded.

The warlord normally permitted only his hunters and scouts to venture ahead of the main body of the horde. But now, when victory was so close, he surged through the dense jungle like an ork possessed. His mechanical arm tore up trees at the roots and crushed the trunks of the soaring greatwoods. He kicked through undergrowth that tried to snare his feet as he trampled through it. Steam and smoke billowed from his artificial torso, the fires stoked hot inside him.

He could taste it, the tang of salt and the electric crackle of the storm. The jungle around him shuddered as if afraid, the canopy high above lashed by winds, shredded leaves and broken branches falling like rain. The foliage parted in front of the warlord and he was confronted with the gnarled, iron-hard trunks of a nest of trees. On either side they formed an impenetrable barrier in front of him, blocking his path.

The warlord roared in frustration. A gout of steam spurted from the elbow joint of his huge metal claw as he flexed his artificial muscles angrily. With rage flaring in his eyes he charged into the trees, his metallic fist slamming again and again into the wood. The bark splintered and wood pulped. The warlord jammed his body between two immense trunks and pushed, forcing the trees apart as if they were the ribcage of an enemy. Roots splintered in the ground below and with an awful tearing sound the trunks fell, crashing deafeningly through the canopy down to the ground.

Cold, wet air lashed at him through the gap the warlord had torn in the jungle. He could hear the cries of birds thrown into the air by the commotion of the falling trees. There was grey, swirling sky overhead.

The warlord forged ahead, stamping up the rocky slope in front of him. The temperature dropped and stinging salt-heavy winds battered against him. Finally, after an age confined to the green cage of the jungle, the warlord finally broke through into the open air.

The jungle ended against a high broken ridge of dark stone, like a scar. Beyond that was the sea. The storm brewing overhead had whipped the sea into an expanse of shifting mountains, the cloudy sky reflected in a grim dark grey that merged with the horizon. The waves crashed into the rocks and flung plumes of salt spray over the edge of the jungle, and over the warlord.

This was the objective the greenskins had fought and died for on Vanqualis. The sea. The warlord gazed across the waters towards the horizon where a strip of hazy darkness suggested land. The sea was all that separated Nevermourn and the orks from Herograve, the continent studded with cities full of hateful humans all but begging to be put to death by orkish blades. The warlord could see it – actually see it, for the first time. Herograve, where the greenskins would have their revenge, and where the ork gods would finally have a slaughter worthy of their worship.

The warlord looked down the coast from his vantage point up on the rocks. The jungle hung over the rocky cliffs in many places, turned feeble and brown by the salt spray. Elsewhere spectacular waterfalls plunged down into the sea, their waters swallowed up by the churning white mass that roared around the foot of the cliffs.

A kilometre or two down the coast was a bulge in the coastline where twin spurs of stone, like encircling arms, formed the boundaries of a bay. Within the confines of the bay the waters were less ferocious, and the jungle reached almost to the very edge of a beach of black sand.

For the first time in what might have been a lifetime, a broad, savage smile split the warlord's face. His ancient gnarled face showed joy perhaps unheard of in a creature so driven by hate and rage. The bay was his final objective on Nevermourn. It was the place where, generations ago, the humans had first gained a foothold on the jungle continent. Now all that remained of the human presence here were a few ruined stone buildings and a half-collapsed lighthouse on one of the spurs of the bay, abandoned after the city of Palatium and its spaceport provided a safer way for the humans to arrive on Nevermourn. But now, of course, Palatium burned.

The warlord could already see the orkish boats being built on the shore, sheltered in the bay until the time came for the final charge onto Herograve. The ingenuity and industriousness of the orks knew no limits when the prospect of slaughter and conquest was held in front of them – the horde would work ceaselessly, hewing trees from the jungle and cannibalising engines and weapons from the horde's war machines, until a ramshackle fleet was built to make the short voyage across the sea to Herograve. Many in the horde would be killed during the voyage, blown up by malfunctioning engines or drowned as their vessels sank, but it did not matter. There were always enough orks. And more than enough would arrive on Herograve to make victory inevitable.

It was done. The ork victory would happen. Herograve and its cities would burn. All that remained was for the blood itself to flow.

The other orks of the horde were reaching the edge of the jungle and clambering up the sharp rocks to see the waters spread out before them. They were hooting and cheering, bellowing war-cries towards distant Herograve, jeering at the humans who did not realise just how close their destruction had come. Already the greenskins were in the bay, swarming over the spurs of rock and through the beach-front jungles to secure their base for the voyage. Smoke-belching war machines were driven to the water's edge and slave-creatures whipped and corralled ready to begin the work of building the fleet. Orks worked quickly and paid no heed to safety or sanity – the boats would be built in two or three days, overseen by the insane masters of the horde's war machines.

For a moment the warlord was prepared to stride down to the bay and force the whole horde to congregate before him, so he could crack heads and bellow at them about why they were there. He could tell them of the treachery that had seen the humans take Vanqualis from the orks in the first place, about the orkish gods and how they demanded revenge. He could try to instil in them the same passion and dedication which had brought the horde to Vanqualis and hammered it forward through everything the humans could throw at it.

But they could not understand. Just as some orks possessed freakish abilities for engineering or crude medicine, so the warlord was a born leader, capable of perceiving strategies and truths that passed well over the head of any other ork. They did not know what it meant to pursue a distant dream with a passion, to defy all obstacles in its way, and finally reach the cusp of it. They did not need to know, either – no matter what happened now the orks would cross the sea and destroy Herograve, because they had been born to seek out such slaughter.

Nothing could stop the horde now, not when its momentum had brought it so far already. The warlord himself, even if he had wanted to, could not have saved Herograve from destruction.

The only safe place in the city now was high above it, in the sky yacht owned by a scion of House Falken who now doubtless lay dead in the ruins of Palatium. It was an elegant craft, its broad wings designed to catch currents and send it gliding majestically across the sky. Inside, though small, it was comfortable, and at least it was large enough for Countess Ismenissa to house her chamberlain, a full crew and her hembearers. The yacht was permanently airborne now save for occasional refuelling stops, and the luxurious passenger compartment was bathed in the hum of the trim-jets and whistle of the wind under the wings.

Lord Sovelin Falken knelt before the countess. His shoulders slumped as if a weight had finally been taken off him. Though he had at least made some effort to clean up since he had arrived on the shore of Herograve, he was still unshaven and his uniform was torn and scorched. In any other situation Lord Sovelin Falken would have been a disgrace, unfit to present before the countess.

'My lady,' he said, his voice shaking. 'I bring news from Nevermourn.'

Countess Ismenissa Falken stood over Sovelin. Even in her current surroundings, which were less regal than she was used to, the countess exuded an air of majesty and authority.

'Then you have travelled far,' said the countess. She had changed into her mourning clothes to show her distress at the state of Herograve's cities. Behind her the tormented city, wreathed in its customary smoke, could be seen rolling out through the arched windows surrounding the yacht's passenger compartment. Riots had broken out, and been gradually replaced by pitched battles between angry, frightened civilians and House Falken's household troops. The battles had been bloody, and House Falken had not won them all. The countess's berth on the yacht had been hurriedly arranged to keep her safe from the rampaging crowds. The Countess's magnificent dress was now black trimmed with crimson and her face had been made up with exaggerated darkness around her eyes, to symbolise the sadness of these events.

'From Palatium itself,' continued Sovelin, his eyes still fixed on the floor. 'Through the jungle, where I fought alongside the Imperial Guard until we were betrayed by the Bearers of the Black Chalice. And then to the coast itself, to watch for signs of the greenskins.'

'I did not think you of any note among the members of our House,' said the countess. 'I imagined you would do but little service to your world, and then away from the fires of battle. I certainly did not think you would escape Palatium when men like my husband did not.'

Lord Sovelin wavered, unsure of how to answer. 'No, my lady,' he said.

'But you have survived. Please, what news is it that you bring?'

'I stayed on the coast to watch for them, my lady. The orks. And they came. Through the jungle like a... like a monster, driving even the greatwoods before them. I found a vessel at the old bay, barely seaworthy, and as soon as I saw them I made for Herograve. The greenskins have made it to the coast, a great host of them barely dented by the efforts of the Imperial Guard. They will surely invade Herograve soon. It is but a matter of days, my lady.'

Countess Ismenissa was silent for a long while. She looked down at the city below her, at how some streets were wholly ablaze, forming intricate mazes of flame coiling through the darkness. Her children carried the long strings of mourning beads that trailed from the hem of her black dress, cradling them in tiny dead hands. The portable juvenat units, newer and less efficient than those in her pinnacle chambers, filled the back of the passenger deck and emitted occasional spurts of freezing white vapour.

'Look at me, Sovelin,' she said.

Lord Sovelin looked up at the countess, almost unable to meet her gaze.

'You have journeyed across Nevermourn, and across the sea, and then begged permission to fly a shuttle up to this yacht,' she said, 'just to tell me that we are doomed.'

'No, my lady. Merely to tell you when the greenskins will arrive. If we face them at the coast we could fend them off. It is as they land that they will be most vulnerable.'

'I know this, Sovelin. It has always been the only viable plan for the defence of Herograve. But look!' The countess indicated the city below. Sovelin followed her gaze and saw the flames guttering in the darkness. An explosion toppled a great dark spire and it fell, as slow and powerful as any toppling greatwood, into the mass of the city below.

'The people of Herograve are going mad with fear,' she said. 'Lunatics are walking the streets shouting prophecies and they are believed. The slightest rumour sparks riots. The troops have banished me to this cursed flying contraption because they cannot guarantee my throne chambers will be secure. And the dead are piling up, Sovelin, the dead! Great piles of them, in the streets. The household troops cannot keep order as it is. With the Warders lost at Palatium, we have nowhere near enough men under arms to both keep Herograve's cities from burning, and to fight a battle with the orks at the coast. It cannot be done.'

'Now, my lady, you are the one telling me we are doomed.'

Countess Ismenissa looked at Sovelin sternly. 'Something of the greenskin has rubbed off on you, Sovelin. You forget your tongue. I do not blame you for bringing me this news. You did your duty, after all. But I cannot pretend it spells anything other than disaster for us. And what of the Black Chalice?'

Sovelin sighed. 'I do not know,' he said. 'I fled them.'

'You ran for the coast as soon as you could. You did not stand and fight them.'

'I am just one man, my lady! I knew I could not stand against them. So I concerned myself with the foe we could defeat on our own, with the greenskins.'

The countess did not look impressed by Sovelin's words. 'The Black Chalice will be dealt with,' she said. 'The Howling Griffons answered our plea. They are honour-bound to destroy the chalice and its bearers. The greenskins are another matter.'

'My lady,' said Sovelin, 'if I may beg your leave. At the next refuelling stop, let me off this craft again. I wish to go to the coast and do what I can there to prepare the defences. It is our best chance to defeat the orks. Perhaps a militia can be raised from the cities on the coast. I bear the blood of House Falken and the uniform of the Warders. My presence might make a difference.'

'Make a difference to the battle, Lord Sovelin, or to yourself? To place yourself in the path of the greenskins would be a fine way to absolve yourself from fleeing the challenge of the Black Chalice.'

Sovelin stood, anger and exhaustion getting the better of him. 'I nearly died, my lady!' he snapped. 'Time and time again. I writhed through filth to evade the greenskins, I marched day and night, and I all but drowned to reach Herograve, all to fulfil my duty to my planet and my house! What do you want of me?'

The countess looked down her regal nose at Sovelin, utterly unflustered by his outburst. 'For you to be gone, Lord Sovelin, and for my husband, or one of the other commanders of the Vanqualian Warders, to have survived in your place. That is what I want. Go to the coast and do what you can, if that is where you see your fate. I must stay here and see that my people do not kill themselves before the greenskins ever arrive.'

Lord Sovelin did not answer. He just bowed to his countess, turned and walked out of her makeshift throne room, into the crew compartment from which he could disembark at the next fuel stop.

The countess turned back to the arched window looking down on the city. Far below, the streets of Herograve continued to burn.

The alien craft descended through the canopy of the swamp, its black metal mouthparts slicing through the branches. The light from the bombardment at the swamp's edge cast strange reflections in the liquid darkness of its hull.

Inside the ship, in the cockpit towards its upper surface, was Lygris. He was flying the ship with Eumenes's permission, and with many misgivings. None of the Soul Drinkers could be sure that Eumenes's offer, to let Lygris take them back onto the *Brokenback*, was not some kind of cruel traitorous trick. Only Sarpedon himself had convinced Lygris to take the alien ship from the depths of the hulk and fly it through the range of the *Brokenback*'s guns, down into the swamp.

The Soul Drinkers crouched in the filthy swamp water hurried to take up positions beneath the craft as it descended to chest-height, the alien anti-grav generators around the edge of its dome keeping it eerily aloft without disturbing the water. The first Soul Drinkers clambered up into the ship's belly.

Sarpedon would be the last on. He watched his Soul Drinkers embarking – the alien ship was unarmed and poorly armoured, and the operation had to go quickly and without a hitch lest the 901st or the Howling Griffons had time to aim heavy weapons. Sarpedon hated feeling this vulnerable – it was not the way of the Astartes to place themselves at such risk, but he had no choice.

'I pray, Sarpedon, that this was worth it,' said Captain Luko. Luko's squad were acting as the rearguard, watching for Penal Legion troopers or Howling Griffons who might get close enough to prevent the Soul Drinkers from escaping.

Sarpedon looked at the Soul Drinkers captain next to him. Luko had put on the most warlike face of any of the Soul Drinkers, behaving as if war was something he relished. He had little of that bravado now.

'The Chapter must survive,' said Sarpedon. 'We have made sacrifices before.'

'There is no Chapter any more, Sarpedon. The Chapter died when you killed Gorgoleon. All we have left are the principles for which we fight and when those die, we might as well be another band of renegades killing for no reason. Eumenes does not believe in the same things as you, Sarpedon. If he is in command we will be the Soul Drinkers no longer.'

'If we do not co-operate with Eumenes we will be hunted down and killed on this planet,' said Sarpedon. 'Would you rather die?'

'Yes!' snapped Luko. 'When the alternative is to live a life of dishonour, killing for something I never believed in? Following the man who betrayed me? I would rather die than fight on like that.'

'Then walk away, captain,' said Sarpedon. He indicated the spacecraft into which the Soul Drinkers were climbing. 'These men will probably follow you. Lead them back into the swamp and die down here. If that is what you want, be the one to defy me and die the death you choose.'

Luko couldn't answer straight away. For a long, awful moment he just stared at Sarpedon, trying to gauge whether Sarpedon would really let that happen.

'I do this,' said Luko at last, 'because perhaps it will give me a chance to avenge Karraidin, and our other brothers who died by Eumenes's hand. And because you are still my Chapter Master.'

'Commander, captain,' said Sergeant Salk, trudging through the swamp towards them. 'The men are on board and Lygris is ready to leave. It's time to go.'

The three Soul Drinkers made their way through the swamp to the underbelly of the spacecraft that hovered above them. Sarpedon's Soul Drinkers, almost two hundred of them, were crammed inside the craft, their armoured bodies packed close. One missile fired by the 901st's troopers, one good volley of bolter fire from the Howling Griffons, one misplaced shot from the *Brokenback*, would do for them all. Sarpedon hated the whole situation, the rebellion, this damned planet, which had conspired to make him so vulnerable. It was not just the journey to the *Brokenback* that exposed the Soul Drinkers – it was the fact that for the first time since the death of Gorgoleon they were commanded by someone else, who could order them butchered wholesale if he wanted.

Sarpedon was last onto the ship. The dark liquid metal of the ship's mandibles folded up under him, forming a strangely knurled floor like the carapace of a black beetle. He could feel the eyes of the Soul Drinkers on him – by now they all knew of the deal Sarpedon had made, of how Sarpedon had handed control of the Chapter to Eumenes. He was their battle-brother and their commander and none of them spoke as Luko had done, none of them challenged him. But Sarpedon knew that the accusation in their eyes would be far more stinging than any words.

Iktinos had said nothing. Of all the Soul Drinkers, Sarpedon had expected Chaplain Iktinos to defy him over Eumenes. He had even been prepared to fight Iktinos, to whom the Chapter traditions and the principles they fought for were so important. But Iktinos had quietly accepted the situation and boarded the ship to return to the *Brokenback*, and Sarpedon knew that in no small measure the Chaplain's example was what had convinced many of the Soul Drinkers to accept the deal Sarpedon had made.

'Lygris?' voxed Sarpedon.

'Ready to take off,' replied the Techmarine from the alien ship's cockpit, a cocoon of liquid metal like a quicksilver cyst overhead.

'It's good to hear your voice, Techmarine.'

'It is good to still serve, Sarpedon,' replied Lygris. 'We're ready to take off.'

'Then launch.'

The ship shot up into the sky, the force of the acceleration pressing down on Sarpedon. In a little over an hour they would be back on the *Brokenback*, and Sarpedon had no doubt about the battle he would have to fight there.

First, he would have to face Lord Mercaeno and the Howling Griffons. And then, if any of them survived, he would have to face justice at Eumenes's hands.

'How does a Soul Drinker fight?'
'As cold as the void and as fast as the bullets from his bolter.'

– Daenyathos, *Catechisms Martial*

CHAPTER FIFTEEN

For a few hours, it was quiet. By the standards of the last few days a tense, prophetic silence held sway over Vanqualis.

The greenskins built their ramshackle fleet on the shore of Nevermourn, and the first casualties of ork fire were inflicted on Herograve as orkish catapults flung explosive shells across the sea. They were barely a footnote to the scale of carnage that would erupt as the greenskins made it into the teeming cities.

On Herograve, far more were dying at the hands of Herograve's own citizens and the thinly stretched household troops of the Falken family. A massive riot was sparked by a child's claim to have seen the ghosts of Imperial saints admonishing the people for their sins. The Census-Takers' Offices were stormed by civilians who mistakenly believed that guns and supplies were being stored there. A whole district was set aflame and the household troops, busy keeping looters and rioters off the streets elsewhere in the city, had no choice but to let it burn.

Isolated knots of Penal Legion troopers and Vanqualian Warders struggled through the jungle, some of them fighting bands of orks left behind by the horde's advance. Others drowned in quicksand or were picked off by predators as they trudged exhausted towards the coast.

Tens of thousands died but again, it did not matter. The situation on Vanqualis had long since gone past the point where individual lives mattered. All the sides were waiting, either on the surface or in orbit, for the next stage – the final stage – to begin.

That moment came when ports opened up and down the hull of the *Cerulean Claw* like dozens of hungry mouths. They spat out a stream of silvery darts – assault boats, drill-prowed boarding craft, arrowing straight towards the hideous, misshapen form of the space hulk *Brokenback*.

'Greetings, Sarpedon,' said Eumenes, his voice loaded with superiority. 'It has been too long.'

Eumenes and his men stood ranked up on the arena flight deck. Eumenes had more than two hundred Soul Drinkers pledged to him, including most of the newer recruits and many older veterans, Apothecary Pallas among them. The Thunderhawks on the flight deck were in the midst of repairs, with Lygris's destructive handiwork being undone so Eumenes's Soul Drinkers would be as mobile and swift as before.

Sarpedon and his men were disembarking from the spherical craft onto the flight deck. Lygris clambered down from the craft's cockpit to join the battle-brothers assembling behind Sarpedon, opposite Eumenes and his men.

Sarpedon didn't answer Eumenes. There was nothing he could say. It was obvious who had the upper hand here.

'Your men will garrison the eastern craft,' said Eumenes, 'the engines and the archives. I shall command the west and the prow. That includes the bridge. Neither you nor your men shall be permitted anywhere near the bridge, and my men will shoot on sight if you try to take it. Understood?'

'Understood,' said Sarpedon. He could almost taste the anger within the Soul Drinkers behind him. For a moment he wondered if it would all end there, the Soul Drinkers falling upon one another until none of them survived. Then Chaplain Iktinos walked to Sarpedon's side and saluted Eumenes. Eumenes saluted back, and Sarpedon could feel his Soul Drinkers taking that step back.

'What then?' said Sarpedon. 'If the Howling Griffons are beaten. What becomes of us then?'

'I will have plenty of time to decide that,' said Eumenes. 'Those who accept my authority can stay. The others, I will rule on when we are safely out of this system.'

Captain Luko stepped forward. 'What happened, Eumenes, to turn you into this?'

Sarpedon put a hand on Luko's shoulder, suggesting he should hold back.

Eumenes smiled. 'I remember when you spoke to me in Gravenhold, captain. About how war was something you despised, how all your bravado was just a show and war was a suffering you underwent because you believed in what you were fighting for. Well, I believe, too, and so

I fight. Nothing more. After all, I am a Space Marine. If we do not fight for what we believe, then what are we?'

Sarpedon heard the activation stud of Luko's lightning claws being flicked on, and the faint hum as the power field's coils warmed up. Luko tensed up, and Sarpedon realised he was about to charge.

'Sharks in the void!' came a voice over the vox-casters, transmitted from the bridge of the *Brokenback*. Sarpedon recognised it as belonging to Tydeus, one of Eumenes's scout squad. 'Thirty plus, heading straight for us!'

'How long?' voxed Eumenes.

'Twenty minutes, maybe less.'

'Then the time for talking has passed. Sarpedon, get these men to their posts. The rest of you, battle stations. Bridge, get all defensive weapons online. Make ready to repel boarders!'

From outside, the *Brokenback* was utterly hideous. Its very name came from the painfully twisted nature of its appearance. Dozens of ships were welded together into a single immense craft, in some places grotesquely biological like bulging organs of metal, in others desolate and ruined like stripped-down skeletons of corroded metal. The fused hulls were covered with rust and barnacle-like encrustations, with wings and sensor clusters jutting out at strange angles. Deep scars, as raw as fresh wounds, bled shreds of wreckage, and the hulk's dozens of engines sprayed glowing exhausts in every direction. Weapon turrets swivelled like eyes in sockets all over the hulk's surface.

Towards this monstrosity sped the shoal of Imperial attack boats, huge drills grinding beneath the eagles emblazoned across their prows. More than thirty of them skipped off the uppermost reaches of Vanqualis's atmosphere, undersides glowing, as ranging shots from the *Brokenback*'s weapons spat between them.

The *Brokenback*'s main armaments, the torpedo tubes and orbital barrage guns of its component warships, had too long a minimum range to deal with the relatively tiny attack craft, so power was switched to the defensive turrets. More and more opened up as the assault boats approached and suddenly a hail of fire was streaming from the hulk, thick as rain. Forward shields flared and fell as sprays of laser bolts hit the lead craft. The first one to be destroyed exploded in a blossom of white nuclear flame, the fire snuffed out a moment later in the vacuum leaving a sad tangle of charred wreckage and bodies.

Another fell, and another. But the surviving assault boats streaked on through the fire, passing into the shadow cast over them by the hulk drifting in front of Obsidian's harsh diamond sun.

The first assault boat to hit the *Brokenback* was destroyed, its prow-mounted drills skipping off the encrusted surface and its hull smashing sideways into the hulk. But the next found purchase, its drills boring through the outermost skin of the hull, engines flaring to push it deeper into the ship. Like burrowing ticks the rest of the assault boats forced their way into the hull. For the first time since Sarpedon and his Soul Drinkers had arrived to clear out the xenos that infested it, the *Brokenback* was invaded.

Eumenes led the way through the dark, ancient corridors and gun decks of the *Macharia Victrix*. The old warship was one of the more recognisable parts of the *Brokenback*, the symbols of Imperial allegiance everywhere. Imperial eagles looked through the darkness and prayers written on the bulkhead walls by the crew could still be seen beneath centuries of grime.

'Hecular, take our flank!' ordered Eumenes as his Soul Drinkers reached the primary gun deck of the *Victrix*. Enormous orbital guns, huge and rusted immobile like ancient monuments to war, loomed several storeys high in the semi-darkness. Hecular took his squad and hurried down the gun deck, into the shadows.

'Bridge,' voxed Eumenes. 'Do we have more information on where they're coming through?'

'None,' replied Tydeus from the bridge. 'Only that they're in that sector. Sensor coverage is stretched thin around there.'

'Damnation, Tydeus. What do I…' Eumenes paused. 'Quiet!' he hissed to the Soul Drinkers around him. They stopped stalking along the gun deck, guns up as they scanned the darkness.

Eumenes listened carefully. The sounds of the *Brokenback* were all around – the settling of ancient metal against metal, the thrumming of distant engines, and strange, haunted sounds that echoed around the most ancient parts of the hulk. But beneath it all, there was a faint buzzing, like the sound of an insect.

'Drills,' said Eumenes, indicating the direction of the huge orbital lasers mounted at the far end of the deck. 'That way.'

The Soul Drinkers moved in a disciplined firing line down the gun deck, bolters ready like a firing squad.

Eumenes aimed down the twin barrels of his artificer-crafted storm bolter. He had found the weapon in the Chapter's armoury deep inside the *Brokenback* – presumably it was being kept to reward a Soul Drinker for a promotion to captain or for some great deed of heroism, but Eumenes had taken it for his own now he was in charge of the Chapter. It was a relic of the old Chapter, the barrels nestling between the wings of a gilded eagle. Eumenes enjoyed the irony that he should be wielding an icon of the Imperium.

Eumenes and his Space Marines were level with the first of the truly vast laser cannons, the huge generator chamber slanting upwards towards the high ceiling of the gun deck. It had needed a hundred crewmen to fire it when the *Macharia Victrix* had first gone to war, turning the huge wheels to aim the laser or hosing down the generator chamber to keep it from glowing red-hot and melting with the heat of the las-pulse building within. Now it was silent and corroded, its parts cannibalised and used elsewhere in the *Brokenback*. A sad and crippled relic of a bygone age, just like the Imperium the *Victrix* had once served.

Eumenes could hear something else now. Voices, raised in anger and savage joy. Whooping and cheering. Singing, even. From what Eumenes had learned from the Chapter archives, it didn't sound like the Howling Griffons.

'Get to cover!' ordered Eumenes.

The Soul Drinkers took cover among the enormous machinery of the laser cannon. The voices got louder and an explosion wracked the shadows that clad the very end of the gun deck, throwing plates of corroded metal and a cloud of centuries-old dust into the air. The choking cloud swept over the Soul Drinkers and cut down visibility like a dense fog.

From the darkness, shapes were swarming. It was Eumenes who fired first, storm bolter rounds chattering into the shadows.

From the swirling dust emerged a mass of bodies. With a barrage of foul-mouthed battle cries, two thousand troopers of the 901st Penal Legion charged into Eumenes's Soul Drinkers.

It was a feint. Lord Mercaeno had loaded the entire 901st Penal Legion into the assault boats on the *Cerulean Claw* and sent them to assault the far side of the space hulk. Taking them off Vanqualis in the *Claw*'s Thunderhawks and shuttles was risky enough, given that the jungles were still infested with bands of orks, but any risk was worth it to Mercaeno. The 901st gave the Howling Griffons something that Space Marines could not boast when fighting on their own – an expendable force, a buffer zone of bodies to keep the enemy occupied while the real threat bore down on them.

'They have definitely boarded?' said Mercaeno. He stood on the bridge of the *Cerulean Claw*, which was arranged around an altar to the Howling Griffons' dead. The altar stood on the top of a low-stepped pyramid with the captain's post at the top and the senior crew arranged at their helms around the lower tiers. The pyramid stood in a large circular room, the lower-ranking bridge crew occupying niches set into the walls.

'That is correct,' said Flag-Lieutenant Scarlphan. Scarlphan, being an unaugmented human, was utterly dwarfed by Lord Mercaeno. He had a long and distinguished face and grey hair, and had served the Chapter for a very long time – but it was obvious that no matter how devoted his service, he was always an inferior compared to the Space Marines themselves. 'Some of the boats were shot down but most achieved a breach.'

'Are we tracking any activity on the hulk?'

'The hulk's structure is too complex for detailed scanning. There is small arms fire near the boarding locations.'

'Then the enemy are engaged. The 901st may not last for long and the Soul Drinkers will soon realise the ruse. Bring the *Claw* into her final approach.'

'Yes, Lord Mercaeno,' said Scarlphan. 'Navigation! Ordnance! Final approach vectors, all shields to starboard!'

'Brothers,' voxed Mercaeno to the Howling Griffons squads now quietly observing the pre-battle rites with their officers, gathering on the embarkation deck for the final battle. 'Make ready your souls. The Black Chalice evaded us on Vanqualis and sought to flee from our justice. Now we will corner them like rats on their own space hulk and butcher them. Now they will learn how the Howling Griffons keep their word.'

The Cerulean Claw seemed to move with slow majesty as it rose from the opaque storm clouds of Vanqualis's atmosphere, trailing coils of vapour as it slid into the vacuum. In truth it was travelling with all the speed the ship's crew dared squeeze from the sub-warp engines, but the ship's size made it seem to approach the mass of the *Brokenback* with almost apprehensive slowness.

The *Claw* had allowed its orbit to decay rapidly after releasing the 901st on their assault boats, and slipped into Vanqualis's upper atmosphere like a shark below the waters. Its journey through the storm clouds had been short but dangerous. Mercaeno had judged those risks to be justified if it meant a chance to close distance with the *Brokenback*. The *Cerulean Claw* emerged from Vanqualis's atmosphere directly below the *Brokenback*, twisting gracefully to bring the upper surface of the Howling Griffons ship's hull towards the lower surfaces of the hulk.

The *Brokenback*'s guns had been given enough time to fire on the assault boats in which the 901st had been sent hurtling towards the hulk. But with the distance now so narrow, few of them could draw a bead on the assault torpedoes and gunships that launched from the *Cerulean Claw*, bright in the livery of the Howling Griffons.

The turrets on the *Claw* and the *Brokenback* swapped fire and guns were stripped from the lower hull of the hulk. Mercaeno's orders had been to get the assault ships onto the hulk at all costs, even if that meant risking the *Cerulean Claw* itself. With short-range fire blazing from the *Claw*, the turrets had to split their fire between the huge shape of the *Claw* and the host of glittering assault craft streaking towards it.

The assault craft slammed home into the underside of the *Brokenback*. Las-cutters glittered, spilling showers of crimson energy as they sliced through the outer hull, engines powering them deeper like predators chasing their quarry down a burrow. The *Cerulean Claw* fell away, impacts thudding into its hull as it rolled back down towards the veil of Vanqualis's upper atmosphere. The *Claw*'s job was done now, for the Howling Griffons' strike force had made the perilous journey onto the *Brokenback*, and the second, decisive front had opened up in the final battle against the Black Chalice.

Lygris was the only one who had any real understanding of the *Brokenback*'s layout, and even his knowledge was incomplete. What he knew about the space hulk was summarised in the sketchy data-slate map he was holding. Sarpedon looked over his shoulder at the diagrams of the *Brokenback*'s many component ships, contorted into the strange shapes that filled the hulk. The lights in the gilded, ornate orbital yacht were dim thanks to the power drain feeding the defensive weapons, so the lavish, faded surroundings were edged in the green of the data-slate's screen.

'They're hitting the underside of the ship,' said Lygris. 'That's what the bridge says. They've probably scanned us and want to head for the warp engines.'

'They're going to blow the whole damned hulk up,' said Sarpedon.

'It's what I'd do,' said Lygris. 'If I was in their position. Standard space hulk engagement tactic, straight out of the *Codex Astartes*.'

Sarpedon looked around the yacht. The craft had originally been the lavish private vehicle of some extremely rich or powerful citizen, and its garish, tasteless designs contrasted with the air of decay that surrounded the old place. Sarpedon remembered standing with Lygris and watching the scuttling of the old Chapter's fleet through the observation dome in the ceiling. The yacht was sandwiched between several component ships of the *Brokenback* and formed a crossroads between many of them, making it a logical place to be stationed ready to react to the boarders. Sarpedon's Soul Drinkers were making the final checks of their battle-gear, and several of them were listening quietly to Chaplain Iktinos performing battle-rites.

'What news from Eumenes?' said Sarpedon.

'His men are engaged on the *Macharia Victrix*,' replied Lygris. 'The whole 901st are on board.'

'Divide us and destroy us,' said Sarpedon quietly. 'Mercaeno's sacrificed the 901st to make sure he only has to fight half of us at once. *Codex Astartes* again, but with some imagination behind it. Show me the archive.'

The image on the data-slate shifted. The Chapter archive was in Sarpedon's area of responsibility, within easy distance of a determined boarding force heading for the warp engines.

'They'll have to get through us to get to the engines,' said Lygris. 'But I don't know if we can hold the archive. Not if all of them attack.'

'That's not what I was thinking.'

'Do you have a plan, Sarpedon?'

'Perhaps. Captain Luko!'

Luko looked up from the blades of his lightning claws, which he had been cleaning in a meticulous pre-battle rite. 'Yes, commander? Have you griffon feathers for us to pluck?'

'In time, captain. Your squad will lead the defence of the archive. I want the Howling Griffons held there. While you hold, I will lead the rest of the force and fall back through the old medicae ship to here.' Sarpedon indicated a series of cavernous spaces inside the *Brokenback*, one of the last major features of the ship's twisted landscape before the huge cylindrical forms of the main warp generators.

'The *Herald of Desolation*?' asked Lygris.

'That's right. The Howling Griffons will have to head through it if they are to skirt past Captain Luko at the archives. There we will make our stand.'

'If I may be so bold, commander,' said Luko, 'the *Herald* is far from the most defensible part of the *Brokenback*.'

'It has its advantages, captain. Trust me on this. For your part, the Howling Griffons will send a force to oppose you so you cannot hit the flank of their main force. Fall back and give them the archive, but pin them down in there if you can.'

Luko smiled. He understood this part of Sarpedon's plan at least. 'With pleasure, commander.'

'Then gather your men and to your posts. Chaplain!'

Chaplain Iktinos looked up from his ministrations. 'Yes, commander?'

'I would have you and your flock at my side in the *Herald of Desolation*. We will need you there.'

'Of course. Come, Soul Drinkers. The Chapter needs you.'

Luko saluted as he led his smaller force out of the yacht towards the Chapter archive. The rest followed Sarpedon and Iktinos, their wargear and their souls prepared for the battle. Iktinos's flock followed him like students following a master, taking every cue from the Chaplain. Sarpedon was glad of it, because he was not certain that his authority alone could carry his Soul Drinkers onwards after the pact he had made with Eumenes.

The tension was so obvious and intense it was almost painful. The Soul Drinkers had faced the Howling Griffons once before and they knew the enemy force had superior numbers and equipment. But Sarpedon also knew that he had an ally on the *Brokenback* that Lord Mercaeno could not expect.

He had the *Herald of Desolation*.

* * *

'Die!' yelled Eumenes. 'Die, you vermin!' The storm bolter chattered in his hands and bodies came apart in front of him, chanting, screaming voices all around.

The gunfire echoed deafeningly around the gun deck of the *Macharia Victrix*, bouncing between the corroded metal walls until it became a wall of agonising noise. Eumenes's Soul Drinkers were in the cover of one of the orbital guns, crouching behind machinery or perched up on the body of the gun to get a good firing position. The Penal Legion troopers surged forward again and again, led by frenzied, blood-soaked killers who weren't even afraid of the volleys of bolter fire thundering down at them.

Another surge charged forward. Eumenes fired and another trooper fell to his knees, chest blown wide open, to be trampled beneath the feet of the men behind him. A thousand of them had fallen already, and the way back to the orbital laser was littered with torn bodies – but there were thousands more, the entire 901st, all pouring down the gun deck as if they were fighting for the chance to die beneath the Soul Drinkers' guns. Hundreds of men reached the foot of the gun where Eumenes was positioned, suddenly within arm's reach of him. Eumenes shot the first, blasting his head clean from his shoulders. The chainblade in his other hand stabbed forwards almost of its own accord and skewered another man through the stomach, chewing through his guts and out through his spine. The man's momentum pushed him forward up the blade so he slumped, convulsing on Eumenes, coughing up a gout of hot blood over his armour. Eumenes flicked his wrist and threw the body off, cracking the skull of another trooper with the heavy body of his storm bolter.

The sound of preaching could just be heard between the volleys of gunfire, a voice raised confidently in spite of the gunfire. The words of the Imperial Creed urged the troopers of the 901st to give in to the will of the Emperor, to let the Emperor's fury fill them, to cast aside the false pleasures of long life and happiness in favour of the blessed joy of sacrifice. And incredibly, the men seemed to believe it. They wanted to die so desperately the Soul Drinkers just couldn't kill them quickly enough.

Up on the gun, fire bloomed. Eumenes turned in time to see Brother Scamander, the young Librarian who had once been part of Eumenes's own squad, raise his arms and bring down a rippling torrent of flame that rushed down the side of the gun like a waterfall of fire. The Penal Legion troopers clambering up towards him were smothered in flame. They tried to beat out the flames that suddenly covered them, falling to the deck where they were submerged in the roaring pool of fire forming there. Men ran, on fire, insane with pain – others writhed and screamed where they had fallen, and the smell of cooking flesh mingled with the gunsmoke and ancient dust that filled the air.

Bolter fire swept the 901st's troopers off the gun, throwing broken bodies back down onto the blood-slicked deck. They regrouped behind the next gun, dragging their wounded with them when they could but leaving many of their own mewling and dying on the floor. The preacher's voice was still strident, even now urging them on to attack again. Lasgun fire spat from their positions, ringing off the body of the gun as Eumenes's men snapped opportunistic shots at any head that showed above cover.

Sergeant Hecular slid in beside Eumenes. Eumenes looked up at the Soul Drinkers' positions – a handful of battle-brothers lay on the deck behind the gun, dead or wounded by lucky shots from the 901st.

'Give me an enemy who runs,' said Hecular. 'We could shoot them in the back. But these maniacs just keep charging forwards.'

'They have nothing to lose,' said Eumenes. 'Every one of ours who dies, we lose someone we are hard pressed to replace. But these men are worth nothing and they know it. There are billions more out there to replace them. They came here to die.'

'I don't know if we even have enough ammo left to oblige them,' said Hecular.

'Tydeus!' voxed Eumenes to the bridge of the *Brokenback*. 'What's happening?'

'The Griffons are on board,' came the reply. 'They brought their cruiser in close and boarded on the lower surface, towards Sarpedon's positions.'

'Then the Griffons are heading for the engines,' spat Eumenes. 'And we're here killing off these vermin.'

'What do we do, commander?' asked Hecular.

Eumenes risked a glance over the cover of the gun. Crimson las-bolts spat back at him. 'I'll be damned if I'll let a cheap trick like this get us. Tydeus, how much control do we have over the *Macharia Victrix*?'

'Without Lygris here, not much,' came the reply.

Eumenes looked again towards the 901st's positions. They were massing for another surge. Every time they charged, even if a hundred of them died they won, because Eumenes's men were tied up fighting them instead of getting to grips with the Howling Griffons. One of the 901st was a great bull of a man, a shaven-headed gore-soaked monster who bellowed foul-mouthed orders. The other troopers of the 901st followed his words as if they came from the mouth of the Emperor himself. The 901st wouldn't give up, and they wouldn't take any excuse to slack off attacking.

'Not good enough,' said Eumenes. 'Get more of the *Victrix*'s systems online and tell me when you have them.' He switched to his all-squads channel. 'Soul Drinkers!' he yelled. 'The next time they charge, we'll meet them in the middle! Every man to the fore! Scamander, you're our biggest gun. Give it everything you've got. The rest of you, knives out, chainblades ready. Charge on my order!'

The cry went up, and the 901st made ready to charge again.

'Damn you,' hissed Eumenes as the bellowing giant ordered his men forwards again and the preacher's voice rose once more. 'You vermin. You dogs. Now we're going to have to kill you all.'

Lord Mercaeno was the first of the Howling Griffons to set foot on the hulk. He ducked through the rent torn in the hull by the boarding drills of his assault torpedo and looked around him.

Great dark spaces loomed around him. The high ceiling and vastness of the place suggested it was a cargo bay, perhaps from a civilian ship. The hulk appeared to be made up of many ships welded together by the vagaries of the warp, and the Howling Griffons had reached an unpopulated and ill-defended part of it. Mercaeno waved forward his command squad who advanced out around him, bolters sweeping the vast shadows.

'No sign of them,' voxed Captain Darion, who had emerged through another rent in the wall. More tears were being opened up in the wall as the *Cerulean Claw* drew the hulk in closer and opened up more boarding passages through its outer hull.

'They are near,' said Mercaeno. 'The enemy is no fool. He will be waiting for us.' Mercaeno consulted the portable auspex scanner he held. It had been set to locate an area with great power and heat signatures, which the scanners on the *Claw* had determined were the main generators for the hulk's warp engines. The Howling Griffons had gained a foothold on the hulk a short distance from the generators, but the ground between them and the generators was sure to be held by the most resolute and foul of the Bearers of the Black Chalice.

'Darion, take our left flank. Borganor, our right. The First Company and I shall hold the centre. Howling Griffons, be wary of the enemy's tricks, and advance!'

Three companies of Howling Griffons emerged from the *Cerulean Claw's* boarding units. They moved with the efficiency and confidence born of a lifetime spent studying the ways of the *Codex Astartes* and of their confidence in Lord Mercaeno's leadership. They moved through the cargo areas into the shattered, twisted interior of a half-crushed factory ship, through the ruined cells of a spacebound monastery and the silent autosurgeon theatres of a dust-choked medicae ship. Everywhere there were signs of the hulk's previous lives. Here was a soldier's last words, scratched into the wall above his bunk as a troop ship was dragged into the warp. There were a handful of time-darkened skeletons, huddled together in the store room adjoining a medical unit, deep scratches on their bones suggesting a violent death there as the warp consumed the medical ship and madness reigned.

The hulk was cursed. They all were. Lord Mercaeno directed his squads through the twisted remains of the hulk's ships, certain in the knowledge that such a place could only harbour the servants of the Enemy.

'There's something ahead,' voxed Captain Darion. 'Signs of occupation. Lights. They've cleared an area out. There's a temple or a vault up ahead.'

'I believe we have found them,' said Mercaeno. Ahead of him a series of arches looked onto the dim interior with gilded, sculpted walls and a great observation dome dominating the ceiling. It looked like the inside of a wealthy citizen's private craft. It had turned dark and mouldering with the years, but it had been cleared of wreckage and Mercaeno noticed vox-casters and a communicator handset on the wall, all more recently installed. The observation dome's controls had been replaced and it probably still functioned.

'They were here,' said Mercaeno. 'I can taste them. The psyker's eye never lies, they were here. We are close. Advance, at the double! Guns up! Fire at anything that moves! All of you!' Mercaeno's force axe was in his hands but his greatest weapon lay within his head, honed and tested by the arduous training of the Chapter librarium. Mercaeno's mind was primed to attack, and it was the most powerful weapon the Howling Griffons had.

'It's a library,' came a vox from Darion. 'An archive. There are datastacks everywhere... Movement! We've got contact!'

Mercaeno heard the first flashes of gunfire from Darion's flank. 'Move up, Howling Griffons! Flank the enemy and surround them!' As the centre of the Howling Griffons' line moved rapidly through the decayed finery of the yacht Darion's voice sounded over the vox, ordering his men to advance. More gunfire rattled, fiercer and fiercer.

The yacht's interior gave way to a vast space, brutal and imposing, a mighty span of blackened iron spreading in a ribbed carapace overhead. The far wall gave way to a series of tunnels, grim yawning mouths brimming with darkness. Blocks of age-stained iron stood along the centre of the huge space, from which hung countless shackles and spiked collars. Prisoners had been kept here before they were filed off into the tunnels beyond, and the place stank of old, old fear.

Mercaeno set foot on the floor of the prison, and knew immediately what this place was, and why it felt so fundamentally different, so utterly wrong.

The enemy was indeed no fool. He had chosen his battleground well. But in doing so, he had chosen the one place that Mercaeno himself

would have selected to fight on. It was the last mistake the Bearers of
the Black Chalice would ever make.

'They're here!' yelled Sergeant Ossex of Mercaeno's command squad.
Instantly the line was in battle readiness, scattering for cover among the
manacled blocks or fallen slabs of corroded iron, training their guns on
the shadows clinging to the openings opposite.

Mercaeno saw them. The gloom made the dark purple of their
armour look beetle-black, but there was no mistaking the armoured
shapes of Space Marines or the chalice symbol on their shoulder pads.

'Charge!' yelled Mercaeno, holding his force axe high and letting his
psychic force crackle through it so the blade glowed blue-white like a
beacon for the Howling Griffons to follow. Mercaeno led the charge
himself, and as the first gunfire stuttered across the great space of the
prison the Howling Griffons charged with him.

'For Guilliman! For the Emperor!' Mercaeno was shouting, as he leapt
over a fallen column and drove his axe down at the first of the enemy
he saw.

'What will our fight mean to the galaxy when we are dead?'
'It will mean that the galaxy continues, for without every
drop of Astartes blood it would crumble and fall.'

– Daenyathos, *Catechisms Martial*

CHAPTER SIXTEEN

The Black Ships were legends in the Imperium, dark tales told in hushed voices. Hardened, voidborn, lifelong spaceship crews, told tales in dockyard taverns about how they saw a Black Ship once, sliding from the warp as silent and menacing as a ghost. Starship crews had been telling stories since mankind first invented the warp engine, tall stories of the strange things that might be seen in the loneliest regions of space, and the Black Ships differed from those stories in only one way. The Black Ships were real.

The Imperium asked three duties of its worlds. Firstly, they were to pay the tithes due to the Imperium. Secondly, they must never harbour the enemies of the Imperium. And thirdly, and perhaps most critically, they were to control their psychic population and hand over all their psykers to the agents of the Imperium. This last duty was enforced by the Inquisition, whose operatives monitored the efforts of individual worlds in rounding up their psykers, and to the Adeptus Astra Telepathica, who tested psykers to see which ones were strong enough to be trained up for the use of the Imperium. The rest, those who were too weak to ever resist the perils of the warp – and a few who were too strong to control – were sent to Terra and never seen again.

It was the Black Ships that took them there. Of the countless millions of psykers who had been taken away on a Black Ship, only the slightest fraction ever survived, trained to survive the threat of possession and madness that was the bane of every psyker. The others were held in cells wound about with anti-psychic wards, their spacebound dungeons places of fear and pain. Many of them knew that once they reached their destination, they would never return. Others remained ignorant, often from feral worlds that had barely any understanding of the great empire in the sky, and were driven mad by the terror of the Black Ships. Many tried to mutiny, but the mind-wiped troops of the Inquisition and the psychic interrogators of the Adeptus Astra Telepathica rarely failed to put down such uprisings with brutality extreme even by the standards of the Imperium.

Knowledge of the existence of the Black Ships was proscribed among Imperial citizens. Only senior adepts knew anything but whispered legends about them, and then they rarely had any idea of what went on inside their sleek black hulls, or which planet the Black Ships would visit next. No one, not even the inquisitors who served grim tours of duty on the Black Ships, knew what happened to the hordes of psykers herded off when the ships reached Terra. All they knew was that there were thousands of Black Ships out there, making long, terrible voyages to Terra and back, bringing the vast harvest of psychic humans to the very heart of the Imperium. Each Black Ship was deeply scarred with thousands of years of psychic pain, the agony of fear and the torments of the endless testing. Many inmates died on board the Black Ships and never left, their souls imprinted on the scarred walls. Others poured their hatred and fear into the substance of the Black Ships so that part of them would always survive, echoing through the Black Ships forever.

Every now and again a Black Ship would fail to reach Terra, sometimes attacked by pirates ignorant of the superstitions surrounding the Black Ships, or waylaid by heathen aliens. Sometimes they were simply lost in the warp, even their elaborate wards failing to keep the predators of the warp from homing in on the precious psychic cargo. The psykers on board these ships suffered appalling fates, their very souls torn apart in a feeding frenzy as warp-spawned monsters devoured them alive. Such ships were the scenes of horror that a normal human mind could simply not comprehend.

And one of them was the *Herald of Desolation*.

Sarpedon felt that pain seething along the sweating black steel floor, up the blade-like metal columns and across the dark ribcage of the corroded ceiling high overhead. The *Herald of Desolation* had once been filled with terrified men, women and children, psykers being delivered to Terra, and when the *Herald* had become lost in the warp the insane old ship had brimmed over with fear and pain.

The Howling Griffons were charging across the cloister, guns blazing. Sarpedon's men met them with a barrage of volley fire and men died in those few seconds, Howling Griffons blasted off their feet, Soul

Drinkers falling to the first bursts of fire from their enemies. Sarpedon ducked down behind the fallen slab of ribbed ceiling he was using for cover and looked behind him through the high archway leading to the complex of cell blocks, a baffling dark maze that seemed to defy the rules of geometry and logic.

'Salk! Keep the flank! The rest swing back!' ordered Sarpedon. The firebase on his flank, commanded by Sergeant Salk, was rooted in a spill of fallen iron from the distant ceiling, the metal scarred with the imprints of the psychic wards that had collapsed when the *Herald* plunged helplessly into the warp. Dozens of Soul Drinkers blazed away there as the rest formed up around Sarpedon, sweeping sheets of bolter fire ripping across the cloisters.

Sarpedon could see Lord Mercaeno. He recognised the shard of blue-white light, the blade of his force axe. A corona of power flickered around Mercaeno's head. For a moment Sarpedon could only focus on the leader of the Howling Griffons – finally they were face to face, and Sarpedon knew he would never have another chance to beat them. If this even counted as a chance at all.

The Howling Griffons were upon them, vaulting over the manacle blocks into the midst of the Soul Drinkers. Soul Drinkers lunged forwards to meet them. Sarpedon joined them and suddenly a Howling Griffon was upon him, an officer with a power sword flicking out as quick as a fencer's foil. Sarpedon recognised the marks of a company captain's rank, the kill-markings painted onto the gold and red plates of his armour.

The power sword knifed towards the throat of a Soul Drinker. It clanged off Sarpedon's force staff as he forced himself between the captain and his quarry.

The captain's helmet was off. He was a veteran, with more age inscribed on his leathery face than almost any Space Marine Sarpedon had ever seen and grizzled grey hair clinging to a skull scarred and rebuilt dozens of times.

The captain turned his blade around deftly, forcing Sarpedon's staff away from him as he kneed Sarpedon in the midriff. Sarpedon was forced back onto his hind legs and had to scuttle backwards to keep his front legs being sliced off by the captain's reverse stroke.

'Captain Borganor, Tenth Company,' spat the Howling Griffon. 'A pleasure to kill you.'

Time stopped. Sarpedon forced his consciousness down into the very depths of his mind, the primordial place that boiled over with psychic power. There he could hear the screams of those who had died on the *Herald of Desolation*, and feel the horror in which they had drowned. Using the raw psychic power that Sarpedon possessed, he dragged those echoes, those blighted souls, bleeding from the very fabric of the *Herald*.

This was why Sarpedon had chosen the *Herald of Desolation* to make his stand. The psychic imprint left on it by the Black Ship's inmates amplified Sarpedon's own capabilities. Here, the Hell could rise higher than anywhere else.

The pale, screeching spectres of the dead rose in boiling thunderheads of shadow and pain. White faces loomed, their eyes black wailing pits. Borganor struck around him at the ghosts, face twisted in hatred and disgust. Sarpedon took the chance to dive inside Borganor's guard and drive his force staff forwards like a spear. It slammed into Borganor's chest, Sarpedon's psychic power erupting in a plume of black flame that threw Borganor off his feet. The Howling Griffon slammed into the manacle block behind him.

Borganor tried to raise his sword but Sarpedon stamped down on his wrist with a bionic front leg. Sarpedon swung his staff like a hammer and smacked Borganor's head to one side, opening up a deep gash down the Howling Griffon's face. Spectral hands reached out of the stone towards Borganor, moaning figures looming from the shadows coagulating around Sarpedon.

Borganor yelled in blind fury and tore his hand free, slashing wildly at Sarpedon and the ghosts rising up around him. Sarpedon span on his back legs, drawing in Borganor and pulling him forwards off-balance. Sarpedon caught Borganor's arm as the Howling Griffon fell forward, twisted it around, and snapped the elbow back the wrong way.

Borganor fell to the ground, one arm hanging grotesquely twisted and useless. His power sword clattered to the floor. Sarpedon crouched low on his arachnoid legs, snatching up the sword with his free hand. As Borganor tried to pull himself to his feet Sarpedon cut his left leg out from under him, Borganor's own sword shearing through ceramite and bone. The severed leg clattered to the marble floor in a spray of dark blood.

Gunfire flared all around. More Howling Griffons were pressing forwards, clambering over the cover to get at the Soul Drinkers. Sarpedon stepped back from a spray of gunfire as Howling Griffons saw his mutations and marked him out as a priority target.

'Through the arches!' cried Sarpedon. 'Now! Salk, keep the flank, the rest of you through the arches! Back into the cell blocks!'

Through the smoke and gunfire, Sarpedon could see that Salk's firebase was holding, dozens of Soul Drinkers maintaining their position grimly as the rest gave ground under fire. The Howling Griffons were advancing heedless of the bolter fire sweeping over them. And there were many more of them than the Soul Drinkers could handle here.

Two Howling Griffons were dragging the crippled Borganor back from the front line. 'Witch!' yelled Borganor as the shadows of the Hell died down around Sarpedon. 'Mutant! Kill me, break me, but you can never corrupt this son of the Emperor!'

Sarpedon couldn't deny any of that. He followed the Soul Drinkers back from the cloisters, through the bullet-scarred archways into the closer network of cell blocks. Around him rose a dark, rust-red room, its floor covered with manacles where dozens of people could have been shackled, kneeling, in front of the stern altar to the Emperor that took up one wall. Here psykers had been forced to kneel before their master, the God-Emperor who alone knew what fate lay for them on Terra.

Their cries came unbidden to Sarpedon now, begging for mercy from the warp, or for intervention from an Emperor whose will it was that put them on the Black Ship in the first place. A corridor lined with dismal one-man cells led off in one direction, tasting of pain and anguish. Another gallery that led off had iron frames equipped with restraints along one wall. Madness echoed from that place, minds gradually worn away and broken.

'Fall back and cover!' ordered Sarpedon. 'Draw them in!'

Already the Howling Griffons were following them. There was less space to fight here, the architecture designed to segregate prisoners and confuse escapees with a labyrinth of rooms and corridors. A knot of Soul Drinkers defended the dark-stained mortuary slabs of an autopsy room against Howling Griffons trying to force their way in. An altar became an aiming rest for a Howling Griffon covering his brothers as they charged into a room like a meat locker, with rails and hooks along the ceiling to hang prisoners from. Around Sarpedon several Soul Drinkers were holding the prayer room from the Howling Griffons whose armoured forms could just be seen through the smoke at every doorway.

'Back!' called Sarpedon to the Soul Drinkers around him. He led the way down the restraint-frame gallery to a security point at the far end. The security point was a miniature fortification embedded in the asylum, the only entrances a single door and firing slit windows. Sarpedon had to fold his many legs under him as he entered the room, more Soul Drinkers following him. Slit windows looked out in many directions, each one covering the corridors and rooms beyond. Immediately there were bolters at the windows firing out, forming crossfires through which the Howling Griffons would have to advance.

This place needed no help from Sarpedon to conjure horrors in his mind. Torn souls writhed in pain. Manic prayers, no more than wordless cries of desperation, blared all around him. Through Sarpedon, through the Hell, the lost souls found form, clawing out through the walls and up through the floors. Tormented faces seemed to bulge from the walls. Cracks opened in the floor and blood welled up. Everywhere they came, the dead of the *Herald of Desolation*, finally giving form to their terror.

It was working. The Howling Griffons were broken up by the labyrinth within the *Herald*, and distracted by the horrors assailing them. This was the Soul Drinkers' home ground and they had trained with Sarpedon before so they would not be so gravely affected by the Hell.

The Soul Drinkers could hold out. The plan was working. Incredibly, impossibly, the Griffon's wings were clipped and the *Herald of Desolation* was drawing them into the Hell to be swallowed up by the blazing crossfires of the Soul Drinkers.

In a shower of sparks the door was torn off the security room. Bolters turned to fire on the intruder but the coruscating blade of a force axe hacked left and right and Soul Drinkers fell, bodies sundered, gore pumping through rents in their armour.

The weight of the attacker slammed into Sarpedon before he could bring his force staff up. The rockrete wall behind him gave way under the tremendous force and Sarpedon and the attacker fell through into the room beyond. Sarpedon hit the floor, rolled and just avoided the axe slicing down to cut him in two. He was on his feet, sight obscured by the dust from the collapsed wall.

He was in a large room that had been arrayed as a torture chamber. Rusted, sinister devices of metal frames and blades were arranged down the middle of the room like an assembly line, as if the people tormented in there had gone through an industrial process, cold-blooded and detached. The iron floor had grates to drain away the blood and there were gouge marks on the walls where fingers worn to the bone had clawed hopelessly for escape. The apparitions conjured by Sarpedon's powers were writhing amid the torture devices, broken limbs reaching from between bars, blades slick with black spectral blood.

'Interesting,' said Lord Mercaeno, walking through the ragged hole in the wall through which he had barged Sarpedon, 'that you still believe you can win.' Mercaeno hefted his force axe, ready to strike if Sarpedon gave him the slightest opportunity.

Sarpedon had his force staff held ready, flickers of psychic power sparking off the gilded eagle that formed the head. 'You don't know what we believe, Mercaeno,' he said. 'You don't even understand what you're fighting.'

'And nor shall I, Sarpedon,' said Mercaeno. 'Who would want to understand the corruption of the Black Chalice?'

'There is no Black Chalice.'

'So your ally Thaddeus told me. Just before I killed him.'

The two men circled carefully, looking for an opening to strike. With the screaming of the *Herald*'s ghosts and the torture equipment around them, they could have been fighting a duel in one of the hells of the Imperial Creed, damned men for whom fighting was the only thing left.

'And this,' Mercaeno said, waving a dismissive hand at the faces that writhed in the walls. 'These tricks. These illusions. Did you believe they would stop us, Sarpedon? We, for whom the Emperor's will is our own?'

'Mercaeno, this is your last chance,' said Sarpedon. 'There is no Black Chalice. It was a creation of someone from our Chapter, from the Soul Drinkers, a long time ago. We are renegades now but before that one of our number did something here, in the Obsidian system, which left behind the legend of the Black Chalice. We have both been brought here by lies.'

'The oath we swore is no lie. And your corruption is as plain as could be, mutant. You and your kind die here.'

'Then let it be finished.'

The battle around them was fierce, every asylum ward and charnel house being fought over furiously. But the real battle was in the torture chamber, as Sarpedon and Mercaeno charged for one another.

Sarpedon just had time to see Mercaeno's aegis circuit glowing brightly, light burning up through his armour. Sarpedon could feel Mercaeno's psychic power, hot and sharp like steel in his blood. Then blood roared in his ears and the torture chamber dissolved around him.

Soaring columns of skulls reached up towards a distant ceiling like a sky of bleeding rust. The smell of cooking flesh hung stifling in the air. Blood-filled channels cut into the black marble floor spelled out giant runes that refused to be read. Through pits in the floor could be seen thousands of daemons writhing obscenely far below. Their gibbering and screaming filled the air, a million flavours of madness saturating the place.

Sarpedon fought to stay conscious as his senses were assaulted. He couldn't even look at the abomination in the centre of the enormous temple that had roared obscenely into life around him. Many men would have been broken by insanity in a few moments but Sarpedon held on, desperately forcing the madness from his mind.

Sarpedon looked up. The *Herald of Desolation* was gone. He was standing in the Throne Temple of the daemon prince Periclitor.

Men had died to drive the 901st back.

Eumenes understood something that only true leaders could accept. To gain power, he had to risk lives. If he wanted to command the Soul Drinkers, he had to pay for that power in the blood of those same Soul Drinkers. Most men could not accept risking those lives. But Eumenes was not most men.

It had taken volleys of bolter fire and furious counter-charges to force the 901st back along the gun deck of the *Macharia Victrix*. The 901st still outnumbered Eumenes's Soul Drinkers by perhaps ten to one, even with so many of them forming a long trail of blood and sundered bodies, and every backwards step the 901st took was accompanied by fierce hand-to-hand butchery and the endless exultations of the 901st's preacher.

Eumenes threw the nearest trooper away from him, opening up enough range to blast a great smouldering hole in the man's chest with his storm bolter. He ducked down into the shadow of the last gun on the deck. Ahead of him an archway rose, leading to the next section of the gun deck where titanic orbital lasers rose, huge as buildings in the dusty gloom.

The 901st were reeling, but in a few moments they would regroup around the ferocious bald-headed killer who led them, and they would surge forwards like a pack of starving dogs. They were taking cover behind the archway, keeping up smatterings of fire to keep the Soul Drinkers at bay. Many of them had expended the power packs of their lasguns and fought on with bayonets, and Eumenes could see that more than a few were sporting captured orkish guns, unsubtle massive-calibre weapons perfect for close quarters where accuracy counted for little.

'Scamander!' shouted Eumenes as more Soul Drinkers took cover around the gun. 'Now! Wall of fire, everything you have! Keep them back!'

'Yes, commander!' replied Scamander, standing up clear of the cover of the gun. Las-fire whipped around him, one or two shots pinging off his power armour. The gauntlets of Scamander's armour were scorched and glowing faintly from the fire he had poured through them, while his face and the armour around his neck glistened with fragments of ice and freezing vapour hissed from between his teeth. He drew the heat from inside him, and around him, spidery fingers of frost spiralling across the dull metal of the orbital gun. His hands glowed again, cherry-red then orange, the ceramite of his gauntlets' fingertips beginning to melt and scatter in glowing drops.

A wall of fire, like a shining curtain of flame, sheared up in front of the archway. A couple of Penal Legion troopers, those who hadn't got into the cover of the arch in time, were caught up in it, sent flaming towards the ceiling. One fell to the ground in front of the flames, legs ablaze, and writhed as the fire ate through the muscles of his legs and up into his abdomen.

'Tydeus!' voxed Eumenes through the gunfire. 'Blow the doors! Now!'

For an agonising moment, there was only Scamander's wall of fire holding the 901st back from attacking again. The preacher's voice was raised, crying out that this was the last chance for the Imperium's murderers and scum to claw back a worthwhile life from decades of sin, by dying for their God-Emperor.

Finally the moment was gone. Explosive bolts along the inside of the archway blew, spewing shards of corroded metal. From either side of the arch, twin blast doors were forced across the breadth of the gun deck, carving up centuries of corrosion from the floor, metal shrieking against metal as they cut the gun deck in two.

Scamander gasped, coughed out a spray of frozen saliva, and slumped back down behind the gun. Ice flaked off his armour as he landed, hissing against the white-hot tips of his gauntlets. The wall of fire flickered and died.

The 901st ran forwards. A few of them made it. The preacher was among them, holding his lasgun in the air like a holy icon in the midst of the crush. The doors closed and trapped many of the troopers between their metal jaws – the preacher was one of them, and with his last breaths he tried to spit out a prayer. But only blood came, spattering down his chin as the blast doors crushed him to death. Men died around him, others had limbs crushed and torn off. A few made it all the way through but bolter shots picked them off as they turned to pull their fellow troopers free. The doors boomed shut, shedding bisected bodies as their locking mechanisms slammed home.

The decks were vulnerable, being so close to the hull. The *Macharia Victrix* had been designed to minimise the risk posed by a breach of the hull along the gun decks, with blast doors primed to slam shut and isolate sections of the gun decks. The vacuum created by a hull breach would therefore be contained. Tydeus had managed to isolate the emergency controls on the *Victrix*, and slammed the doors in the face of the 901st.

The doors had thick, age-smoked windows set into them. Eumenes jogged up to them to see the 901st clamouring on the other side of the huge doors. Unshaven, hate-filled faces, mad with frustration.

Eumenes smiled. 'Purge it,' he voxed.

Along the outer hull of the *Macharia Victrix*, open to the merciless emptiness of space, purging valves opened. Another emergency system, in case of fire or contamination. Air boomed from the sealed section of the gun deck in which the 901st were now trapped. It shrieked out in a terrible gale, and even from the other side of the blast doors Eumenes could hear the men shouting out in fear and anger. He heard curses spat at him, even as troopers were lifted off their feet and thrown around the deck by the force of the decompression, battered against the huge dark shapes of the orbital lasers.

A few of the 901st were running for the far end of the gun deck, where their assault boats had bored into the hull. But many were dying even as Eumenes watched – blood running from their eyes, spitting ropes of gore from ruptured lungs, crawling along the deck or being dragged towards the purging vents.

'Tydeus?'

'Commander?'

'It's done. Stand by.'

Sergeant Hecular finished off the last of the 901st on the survivable side of the blast doors. The battle for the *Macharia Victrix*, the Howling Griffons' feint, was done with. 'What next, Eumenes?'

'Next,' replied Eumenes, 'we win my ship back.'

'How do we overcome an enemy who fights with lies?'
'Confront him with the truth of destruction.'
                    – Daenyathos, *Catechisms Martial*

CHAPTER SEVENTEEN

The Throne Temple of Periclitor was hewn from the living rock of a mighty granite crag, the very peak of a vast mountain that was all but drowned in a sea of heaving daemonic flesh. As far as the horizon, the valleys of the mountain range were brimming over with daemons, cavorting and writhing obscenely. Armies of daemons, creatures wrought from the very stuff of Chaos, formed a pulsating layer of wanton corruption that flooded the world like a foul ocean.

The Throne Temple formed a great cavity in the peak of the mountain, surrounded by a web of black granite spurs like the bars of an ornate cage. The throne itself was like a dark parody of the Golden Throne on which the Emperor himself was said to sit – it was hewn from an enormous skull, taken from some vast warp predator, the ivory of its gigantic teeth carved into intricate scenes of violence and debauchery, its eye sockets set with braziers that roared with a baleful multi-coloured fire.

On the throne sat Periclitor. Titanic, winged, with dark grey flesh that oozed droplets of raw power such was the warp-spawned sorcery that fuelled him. His face was a wet maw surrounded by mandibles, dozens of eyes blinking in his hideous head, each one plucked from the socket of a different foe. One of those eyes had once belonged to Chapter Master Orlando Furioso of the Howling Griffons, and all of them rolled in pain even as they gazed out on the temple and the daemonic landscape beyond with an expression that reeked of arrogance and malice.

Once, Periclitor had been a Space Marine of the accursed Traitor Legions, a mortal champion of the Dark Gods. But the blood he shed in the name of Chaos formed a great lake in the warp, and so pleased were the gods that they granted him daemonhood. An enormous cannon, an engorged and twisted boltgun, was leaned against the throne – it dripped with tears from the captive daemons that screamed from inside its ammunition magazine. One shoulder pad remained of Periclitor's power armour, fused with his skin, and it was impossible to tell to which of the Traitor Legions he had once belonged.

Periclitor's many eyes fell on Sarpedon. The Soul Drinker was dwarfed by the daemon prince, and it took all a Space Marine's resolve to keep him from fleeing, or collapsing on the floor in a mad stupor. Sarpedon held his ground, pushing himself up off the floor of the Throne Temple. He reminded himself that as appalling as Periclitor was, Sarpedon himself was hideous, and men had balked in horror just to see him.

'You…' said Sarpedon, barely able to hear his own voice over the gales of gibbering and screaming from the hordes of daemons writhing below the temple. 'You're not… whatever you are.'

Perliclitor's maw opened and the revolting, wet, guttural sound that issued had to be laughter. 'You look upon Periclitor,' it said with a voice like an earthquake. 'Beloved of the warp.'

'No,' said Sarpedon, holding his ground even as Periclitor began to rise from his terrible throne. 'You're not here. I'm not here, it's not real.'

'You, who are as corrupt as the black heart of the warp – you defy me?' Periclitor's voice was as angry as it was amused. 'You wretch! You filth! I am Periclitor, abomination of the Alcmena Nebula, slayer of Furioso! Kneel before your master! Bow down before the warp incarnate!' Periclitor was on his feet now, raw power raining down from his glowing dark skin.

'I defy the warp!' yelled Sarpedon. 'And its gods! They tried to make me one of their own and they failed! They tried to use me, and then to break me, and then to kill me, and my battle-brothers overcame them all!' He took a step forward, even though every nerve of his body was urging him to flee. 'You are no more Periclitor than I am the Black Chalice!'

Periclitor roared, a terrible sound like a black wind of knives. A sword of deepest black, like a shard of the night itself, coalesced in one of his claws and he brought it down towards Sarpedon. Sarpedon dived to one side. The sword carved down behind him into the marble of the temple. A chunk of marble was sliced free and tumbled down into the daemons writhing below.

The swords sliced low this time, like a scythe at waist height. Sarpedon brought up his force staff and met the liquid black blade, the force of it almost throwing him down off his feet. He dug his talons into the stone and held his ground, refusing to give anything, even a backwards step, to the titanic lie in front of him.

He looked up at Periclitor, into his hateful eyes. Periclitor returned his gaze, and in his stolen eyes the faintest trace of frustration flickered. Sarpedon should have been on his knees, begging to serve. But he was fighting back. For a fraction of a second, Periclitor did not know what to do.

Periclitor lashed out in rage. The back of his clawed hand caught Sarpedon in the chest with such force that Sarpedon was flung backwards. He turned head over talon as he flew through a gap in the outer wall of the Throne Temple and out of the mountain peak. The daemon world span around him – the sky with its spiral storms like wounds weeping blood and bile into the clouds, the distant mountains like great gore-encrusted fangs of stone.

Sarpedon plunged onto a sea of daemonic bodies. These were the pure spawn of the warp, hideous malformed creatures of mismatched limbs, mad rolling eyes and drooling mouths that cackled and screeched insanely. Sarpedon lashed about him frantically as the sickly light of the daemon world's sun was shut out by the bodies pressing around him. Daemons came apart under his talons and gauntleted fists but more pushed in, eager to devour this newcomer.

With a roar of defiance, Sarpedon planted his force staff into the rock below him and pushed all his psychic power into its nalwood shaft. With a final effort Sarpedon forced all his power out of the staff in a wave of crackling destruction.

Daemons disintegrated. Lopsided mouths lolled stupidly as the bodies around them were shredded to ash. Sarpedon slammed wave after wave of psychic anger into the sea of bodies around him, blasting a clearing amid the clawing limbs and writhing flesh.

Sarpedon gasped for breath, his psychic power momentarily spent. He was standing in a crater lined with charred, misshapen bodies on the black marble of the mountainside. Sarpedon pulled the staff out of the stone and looked back up at the temple.

'An enemy worthy of the Howling Griffons,' shouted Sarpedon indignantly, 'would never be defeated by a trick like this! You will have to do better than wearing the image of a daemon to have a Soul Drinker begging for mercy!'

Periclitor appeared above Sarpedon, clambering between the curving marble bars of his cage-like temple. The sword was gone and in his hand was an axe – Mercaeno's force axe, blue lightning spilling off its glowing blade.

'You,' said Sarpedon, 'are a lot like me, Mercaeno.'

'Wrong,' said Periclitor. Ghosted over him, much smaller but somehow more imposing, was the image of Lord Mercaeno. When Periclitor spoke, it was with Mercaeno's face. 'You are a crude and brutal weapon. Sarpedon. You are all power and no finesse. The horrors you daub are like the drawings of a child. I forge worlds.'

Sarpedon tried to gather his wits. There was no Periclitor, and there was no Throne Temple or sea of daemons. It was in his head. Lord Mercaeno had put it there. Mercaeno was telling the truth – he had a level of control over his psychic powers that Sarpedon couldn't approach, and he built this entire daemon world in Sarpedon's mind.

'You have failed then, Mercaeno,' said Sarpedon. 'You think I am a servant of the Dark Gods, so you placed this daemon-thing before me in the hope I would kneel before it!'

'All that proves is that your kind have enemies in the warp,' spat Mercaeno. His image was becoming strong and he jumped down from the temple, walking on the writhing daemons beneath him as if they were solid ground. Periclitor was fading out, becoming a pale ghost behind Mercaeno's image. 'For evil despises evil. And that is not why I brought you here. I came to this place, my battle-brothers and I, this nest of foulness in the Eye of Terror itself.' Mercaeno held up his axe. 'This is the weapon that took the head of the daemon Periclitor! For a day and a night we battled him on this peak until only I remained, and yet I did not falter! I fought on, and drew from the Emperor's own strength! And finally I took its head, and I held it up on this mountaintop and watched the daemons fleeing before me. A man would have died in moments. A Space Marine would have fallen to Periclitor. But not a Howling Griffon. I brought you here to show you why.'

Periclitor was gone and only Mercaeno remained. Sarpedon would rather have fought the daemon – he had vanquished daemons before, and he knew that no matter what they would try to deceive and destroy, for that was the reason the Chaos gods created them. But Mercaeno was a different type of enemy.

'Because you made a promise,' said Sarpedon.

Mercaeno smiled. 'Finally, you understand why you must die. We swore to avenge Chapter Master Orlando Furioso. We did not rest until it was done. Not even death could dissuade us. And we also made a promise to defend Vanqualis from the Black Chalice. We will fulfil that oath just as surely.' Mercaeno was close now, within a staff thrust or axe swing, looking down on Sarpedon from the raised bank of daemons – but the daemons weren't really there, and in truth it was the solid deck of the *Herald of Desolation* beneath Mercaeno's feet.

Mercaeno was at home in the *Herald of Desolation*, as Sarpedon was. The psychic force that drenched the place was something Mercaeno, too, could mould, forging it into whole worlds of illusion in the minds of his enemies. But Sarpedon was a psyker, too – Mercaeno himself had said just how powerful he was. Sarpedon didn't have any finesse to his power, but he didn't need it, not now that Mercaeno had done all the hard work of creating a world around them.

'Your fate is sealed, Sarpedon,' Mercaeno was saying. 'Nothing you can do will change that. Fight on if you must.'

'My pleasure,' said Sarpedon, as his mind took hold of the hellish landscape around him and warped it horribly.

The sky fell dark. The daemons melted away and a distant ocean lashed against knife-like rocks of a savage shore. Mercaeno lost his grip on his world and suddenly it was Sarpedon's.

Staff and axe clashed in the darkness, and this time Sarpedon wouldn't be fooled.

It seemed a lifetime ago that the Soul Drinkers had come to the unknown world, a planet of foul, polluted oceans and swarms of pox-ridden insects, to battle the plague daemon Ve'Meth. Dark thunderheads of swarming flies darkened the skies and the churning oceans spat up sea monsters and subterranean horrors. The inhabitants of its scattered, barren islands were cave-dwelling creatures devolved from cannibalistic humans.

On a mighty fortress that rose from an archipelago of black coral, Ve'Meth ruled. Ve'Meth was a disease, a pure vessel of the Plague God's will, and his physical form was a host of diseased bodies that spoke with one voice. Space Marines of the Traitor Legions defended his fortress, bloated and corrupted creatures dedicated to the Plague God Nurgle. Cloven-hoofed, goat-headed men formed his foot soldiers, led by champions whose bodies glowed with the glorious corruptions of Nurgle.

And yet Sarpedon had led the Soul Drinkers here, and the Soul Drinkers had destroyed Ve'Meth.

Mercaeno stumbled in the surf, forced to throw the haft of his axe out to defend from Sarpedon's force staff. He glanced around him, trying to get a sense of his surroundings while Sarpedon bore down on him. He was on a beach, heavy waves thick with filth and scum washing over him, the great fortress overlooking the beach like an enormous pustule of stone. Baleful clouds boiled overhead, thick and foul, and all around was the overpowering stench of decay.

Mercaeno lashed out, battering back Sarpedon's attack and wading through the surf onto the beach itself. He was well beyond fear, but he was still rattled, his psychic power turned against him.

'More sorcery!' he spat.

'You are not the only one,' said Sarpedon, 'who has fought the slaves of the Dark Gods. I slew a daemon here, my battle-brothers and I. We were manipulated and lied to, but all the servants of the warp got out of us was death.' Sarpedon scuttled up out of the surf, psychic power crackling off his staff with the effort of maintaining the illusion of the unknown world. 'I left a part of myself behind on this beach,' said Sarpedon. 'A leg, to be precise.'

Mercaeno sneered. 'You had plenty more, mutant.'

'So I told the Chaos champion who took it,' replied Sarpedon swiftly. 'Before I cut him to pieces where you stand now.'

Mercaeno roared and lunged. Sarpedon caught Mercaeno's axe on his force staff and span, lashing out with the legs down his right side. Mercaeno was swept off his feet, hitting the black sand heavily. Sarpedon cracked the butt of his staff against Mercaeno's head and the Howling Griffon reeled, falling backwards as he tried to get back to his feet. Sarpedon reared up over him but instead of rolling away Mercaeno planted a hand on the ground and kicked up into Sarpedon's stomach, throwing Sarpedon onto his back legs.

Mercaeno was back on his feet, blood running down his face. 'The Emperor knows the truth,' he said grimly. 'And so do I. Do you think you can make me down arms and accept that you are not corrupt?'

'I can't change your mind, Mercaeno. But I can show you the truth, even if you won't believe it.'

'The truth,' said Mercaeno, 'is that to the spawn of the warp will come nothing but death! So spake Roboute Guilliman! So spake the Emperor! And so it shall be!'

Mercaeno charged, a flurry of blows striking so rapidly it was hard to believe he wielded a weapon as huge and murderous as his force axe. Sarpedon was at his limit, bringing the haft of his force staff up like a quarterstaff to defend himself. Bright psychic sparks flashed as each man was forced back in turn, one prevailing over the other before a skilful feint or a blow of raw strength put the other on top. As they fought more memories came unbidden from Sarpedon, monstrous beastmen marching slowly down from the fortress, a hideous silent army come to watch the spectacle of the two Librarians fighting to the death. Torrents of rot flowed down the fortress, waterfalls of putrescence in which danced foul, necrotic daemons of the Plague God. The champion that Sarpedon had killed on the shore was among them, standing silently among the ranks of beastmen watching the battle.

Sarpedon slipped and was rewarded with a deep gouge into one shoulder pad, cutting down to blood and muscle. Mercaeno committed himself to a wild swing, which let Sarpedon crack the eagle-tipped head of the force staff into his face, ripping up a deep slash from temple to jaw.

Even as they two men fought, another battle was taking place. Each one tried to wrest away control of the illusory world and the shore of Ve'Meth's fortress shimmered and warped as they tried to turn it into something else.

With a roar of triumph Sarpedon wrenched control away, psychic power burning in blue flames from his eyes, and suddenly the befouled sky was replaced with the high vault of the Temple of Dorn on the Soul Drinkers' old flagship, the *Glory*. An enormous stained-glass window of Rogal Dorn looked down on them and incense was thick in the air, like a stifling fog. The pews and columns of the temple were smashed, because this was where Sarpedon had fought Chapter Master Gorgoleon for control of the Soul Drinkers. Mercaeno reacted to the shift a moment too late and Sarpedon charged him, slamming a shoulder into Mercaeno's chest and barging him up the steps to the altar below the window. Mercaeno's body smashed into the altar and it splintered behind him, spilling candles and devotional texts everywhere.

Mercaeno grabbed Sarpedon by the collar and waist joint of his armour and lifted the Soul Drinker off him, hauling him into the air and swinging his body around to smash Sarpedon into the ornate pillar beside the altar. The pillar shattered under the force of the impact and collapsed, twenty metres of carved stone toppling like a felled tree onto Sarpedon.

Sarpedon's breath was knocked out of him and suddenly the chapel was gone. He was in a trench now, artillery fire booming all around him, gunfire chattering from all directions. It was night, and the darkness was torn by explosions that sent flashes like lightning bolts high into the sky. The weight on him was not a pillar from the Temple of Dorn, but a heap of bodies – Imperial Guardsmen, torn apart by an artillery blast that had ripped a crater out of the trench behind him. Their blood mingled with the reddish earth, their gore-spattered faces locked in expressions of surprise and panic.

Sarpedon threw the weight off him. He didn't know where he was – this was a world from Mercaeno's memory. He ducked down instinctively as gunfire raked above his head. The trench had been dug for Imperial Guardsmen who were all a good head and shoulders shorter than a Space Marine, and Sarpedon had to crouch down on his haunches to keep his head out of the gunfire.

An engine rumbled and a Rhino APC drove over the trench a short way in front of Sarpedon, las-fire and bullets ringing off its hull. It was painted in the livery of the Howling Griffons, the griffon rampant symbol etched in deep blue over red and gold quarters.

The rear hatch of the Rhino swung down and Lord Mercaeno stepped out, heedless of the gunfire raking all around him. 'Scelus,' he said. 'On the edge of the Eye of Terror. The forces of Chaos spewing from the Eye won it from the Imperium. The Howling Griffons won it back.'

Sarpedon tried to clamber from the trench but a deafening explosion and hot violent darkness thudded into him. The artillery shell blew

Sarpedon clean off his feet and for a moment he was blind and deaf, spitting out the hot red earth, unable to tell which way was up.

It was instinct that forced Sarpedon to keep his guard up. He rolled onto his back, staff braced across his chest, as Mercaeno's axe fell down towards him in an executioner's stroke. The axe cracked into the haft of the staff and Sarpedon pushed all his strength into keeping the thrumming, hot blade away from his face. Scalding rivulets of power dripped off the blade onto Sarpedon's face and the energy flaring off the axe blade was reflected in Mercaeno's eyes, flickering with blue-white flame.

The smoke and dirt rolled away on the hot wind. Sarpedon could see around him now. The trench wound a jagged path through a blasted, barren battlefield. Once it had been a forest but the ground had been chewed up and levelled so much that only isolated clumps of shattered tree stumps remained.

From one horizon rolled an army, a million men, with tanks and Sentinel scout walkers, advancing through withering fire down the slopes of tortured red earth. The Howling Griffons formed the cutting edge, a hard point of power armoured warriors in the heart of the line. Artillery fire thundered everywhere, blowing men and tanks into the air. The opposite side of the battlefield was a vicious snarl of fortifications. Ugly lumpy rockcrete buildings, once bunkers for Imperial troops, were daubed with runes and symbols born of the warp. Tattered banners carried the emblems of the Dark Gods. Bodies were displayed as proudly as heraldry, hands and heads, whole gutted corpses, splayed above firing slits in the bunkers or staked out like scarecrows along the front.

Unceasing gunfire spat from the bunkers, and artillery pieces behind the lines thundered. Chanting carried on the hot wind, the praises of the Chaos gods, the voices of hundreds of thousands of corrupted madmen.

The axe blade was forced closer to Sarpedon's face. 'We won,' snarled Mercaeno. 'We stormed this place and killed them all. That is what you are fighting. That is why you will die, too.'

Mercaeno was strong, but so was Sarpedon. With agonising slowness Sarpedon forced the axe away from him, teeth gritted, every muscle drum-tight.

The battlefield of Scelus shimmered as Mercaeno fought Sarpedon with such an effort that his hold on the illusory world around him slipped. Sarpedon took advantage and wrapped his mind around the world, tearing control of it away from Mercaeno again. Now they were on the hull of the *Brokenback*, the smoke-laden sky gone to be replaced with endless black space scattered with alien stars. In the vacuum, edged by the hard light of the stars, the two Space Marines wrestled. This was where Sarpedon had faced the daemon Abraxes, the servant of the Change God, who had manipulated the Soul Drinkers to the edge of damnation, and been slain for its troubles.

Battlefields came and went, drawn from the memories of both men. An alien world choked in toxic fog and disease, with immense Titan war machines striding through the darkness. The massive battlements of Quixian Obscura, with Soul Drinkers battling the alien eldar high above the ground. An ocean world lashed by nuclear storms, with fleets of ships clashing beneath a sky the colour of blood. Stratix Luminae, where hordes of living dead shambled across the frozen tundra and spaceship wreckage rained from the sky. A multitude of hells, visions of battle from two lifetimes of war, flashing past as each man tried to get the upper hand.

Sarpedon drew deep from the well of psychic power inside him, but he was almost exhausted. Mercaeno's strength matched his own and he knew he had only one chance to turn the tide. He dug his talons into the floor and shifted his body to one side as he let go of his force staff with one hand. Mercaeno's blade hammered down a few centimetres from his face, buried deep in the ground – the ancient stone of a tomb-world where the Howling Griffons must have fought long ago, haunted by skeletal metallic creatures as old as the stars. Titanic ruins rose all around, but Sarpedon ignored his surroundings as he scrabbled to get back on his feet.

Mercaeno had buried the axe in the ground with such force that he had to pause to pull it out. This was the opening Sarpedon needed.

He held his force staff in both hands, and twisted. The nalwood was iron-hard, carved and treated to resist the sternest punishment. But Sarpedon's strength was too much for it. With a thunderclap, the staff broke in two.

All Sarpedon's remaining psychic force flooded out. Like an image painted on glass, the ruins from Mercaeno's memory shattered and fell in great glowing shards. Time seemed to slow down as the senses of both men were assaulted by the collapse of the reality around them. Mercaeno reeled, bellowing in anger and pain as his mind was filled with feedback. Sarpedon stumbled, psychic power flooding out of him undammed.

They were in the domed room of the *Herald of Desolation*, with the ankle-deep water and the curved ceiling covered in carved statues, where Sarpedon had duelled Eumenes before the rebellion. Gunfire thudded dimly nearby as the Howling Griffons and Soul Drinkers continued to battle through the *Herald*'s cell blocks and galleries, but that fighting felt very far away. A hole in the wall and several shattered statues in the water showed where Sarpedon and Mercaeno had fought their way in, pinkish puddles of blood in the water a testament to the fury of their battle. Now for a few seconds they were quiet, the only sound

258   *Ben Counter*

the distant gunfire and the heavy breathing as they tried to pull some strength back into their limbs. The spectres of the Hell were gone from the *Herald* now, because Sarpedon had no energy left to conjure them.

Blood still ran down Mercaeno's face and his breastplate had deep rents torn into it by Sarpedon's talons. Sarpedon's legs bled, the exoskeleton battered and cracked, and blood seeped from one shoulder pad that was cut almost in two.

Mercaeno loped towards Sarpedon, force axe in hand – he looked ready to drop, bleeding and exhausted, animated only by the hatred in his eyes. Sarpedon dropped the broken halves of his force staff and grabbed Mercaeno's axe arm as the Howling Griffon charged onto him with the last of his strength. Sarpedon fell back against the torso of a statue fallen from above, wrestling with Mercaeno now, the men's movements sluggish and heavy. Sarpedon forced Mercaeno's axe away but Mercaeno kneed him hard enough in the midriff to dent the ceramite and knock the air out of his lungs. Sarpedon smashed the heel of his hand into Mercaeno's jaw and threw Mercaeno off him. Mercaeno dropped the axe and reached out to grab Sarpedon's throat, teeth bared and bestial. Sarpedon fended him off as best he could, Mercaeno ducking in and head-butting him hard enough to throw Sarpedon onto his back legs.

The two men traded blows like brawlers, their training and warrior instincts overcome by the exhaustion of their psychic combat. Blood stained the knuckles of their gauntlets and ran down their faces. Sarpedon reared up for one desperate lunge, stabbing his front talons down at Mercaeno, but Mercaeno grabbed a leg and twisted, throwing Sarpedon down onto his back. Mercaeno hauled Sarpedon to his feet and slammed a fist into the side of his head over and over again.

Sarpedon's head rang with a wordless white noise and his vision greyed out, the sinister contorted statues on the domed ceiling seeming to congeal into a landscape of writhing daemons. Sarpedon could hear the voice of the daemon Abraxes, promising him limitless power if he gave his Chapter over to the Dark Gods. He heard the words of the Inquisitorial pronouncement that had excommunicated the Soul Drinkers and damned them in the eyes of the Emperor's servants. He heard laughter, too, laughter from the warp.

Sarpedon lashed out and an elbow caught Mercaeno in the throat. Mercaeno stumbled back and Sarpedon dived forward, hoping to smother him to the ground and punch him until the Howling Griffon stopped moving.

With a roar, Mercaeno slammed an uppercut up into Sarpedon's jaw, Sarpedon's own weight added to Mercaeno's strength. Sarpedon's head snapped back and he spat a long plume of blood from a split lip. His many legs buckled underneath him and he slid into the shallow water, mouth lolling.

Redness tinged everything. The dome seemed as far away as the stars in the void, as did the sound of Mercaeno's footsteps splashing in the water as the Howling Griffon stepped over him.

Sarpedon's head lolled to one side. He couldn't move. Part of him felt almost relieved as he saw Mercaeno stoop painfully to pick up his force axe. Mercaeno's power was spent, too, so the blade no longer glowed with channelled psychic force – but an axe was an axe, and the edge of the blade was so sharp it shone in the pale light reflected by the blood-filmed water.

Mercaeno stood over Sarpedon. He raised the axe like an executioner, eyes fixed on Sarpedon as he wound up to cut off Sarpedon's head and destroy, in his mind, the leader of the Bearers of the Black Chalice.

A blade of purest blackness flickered behind Mercaeno. Recognition flared dimly in Sarpedon's mind.

Mercaeno sensed it, too, and tried to turn around. But he was completely spent, his reactions slow, his limbs too leaden to bring himself round to face the intruder who had crept up behind him.

Eumenes stood behind Lord Mercaeno. In his hands was the Soulspear, the most revered relic of the Chapter, a weapon with twin blades of glowing black vortex. In Eumenes's hands, and compared to Mercaeno's exhausted movements, it flicked as fast as a snake's tongue as Eumenes lunged forwards.

The blade of the Soulspear passed through the back of Mercaeno's head and came out through his mouth. Flesh and blood hissed as the vortex field annihilated the matter it touched. Sarpedon looked up, almost mesmerised, as Eumenes slowly brought the blade up, bit by bit bisecting Lord Mercaeno's head.

Sarpedon searched inside himself for some relief. Mercaeno was dead, the Howling Griffons were leaderless, and Sarpedon was alive. But he could find none. There was no triumph, no joy, nothing good or victorious in the way Eumenes smirked as the life shuddered out of Lord Mercaeno.

There was only horror, a cold horror that filled Sarpedon as he realised that somehow, with Mercaeno dead and his own battle over, he was watching the death of his Chapter.

The blade came free. For a few seconds Mercaeno stood, his eyes rolled back and blank. He took a step back, and the axe dropped from his hand. Blood sprayed suddenly from the dark red line that cut his face in two, and he toppled backwards to land with a crash in the water at Eumenes's feet.

Sarpedon pushed himself onto his front and brought his legs back beneath him. He didn't know if he had the energy left to stand. Eumenes stood watching him, the Soulspear at his side. Eumenes thumbed the gene-locked activation stud on the haft and the twin blades retracted, leaving the short cylinder of the haft, which Eumenes holstered like a pistol at his hip.

'Eumenes,' said Sarpedon. He looked down at Mercaeno's body. His blood felt like it had frozen, but some old proud instinct forbade him from showing the dismay that had swallowed him up. 'Did… is Luko still alive? Have we held the Howling Griffons at the archive?'

'As far as I know,' said Eumenes.

'Then it's over.'

'Maybe. If you were right.'

'I was,' said Sarpedon.

'He would have killed you, Sarpedon.'

'I know.'

'Then you do not deny it?'

'No. He had beaten me. I cannot deny that. You saw it.'

Eumenes smiled. 'Then I saved your life. I am your greatest enemy, Sarpedon. I brought you low when all the gods of the warp couldn't do it. And yet I saved you. You live on because of me. Is that not right?'

Sarpedon looked up at him. Through the blood in his eyes, he could see the look of shameless triumph on Eumenes's face. 'Yes,' he said.

'Yes, *my lord*,' said Eumenes.

'What do our enemies see when they look upon the Astartes?'
  'They see their gods and the heroes of their corrupted myths, gathered before them and heralding the end of their world.'

– Daenyathos, Catechisms Martial

CHAPTER EIGHTEEN

The Brokenback's archive was wreathed in a fog of gunsmoke. Between the bookcases and stacks of data medium lay the battered bodies of Howling Griffons and Soul Drinkers who had fallen during the struggle over the archive, most of them struck down by bolter fire, a few bearing the hideous wounds of chainblades and combat knives.

The guns were silent now. The order to cease fire had been called out by Captain Luko of the Soul Drinkers, and mirrored by Captain Darion of the Howling Griffons.

Darion stepped out into the open first. His gun was in his hand but it was lowered. 'Is this true?' he asked, the question called out to the Soul Drinkers in position at the opposite end of the archive.

Captain Luko stepped out from behind the pillar he had been using for shelter. His armour was pocked with smouldering scars where bolter rounds had hit home. 'Every word,' he said.

Darion looked behind him. Amid the bodies and wreckage was a Howling Griffons Techmarine, dataprobes hooked into one of the black crystal stacks. The Techmarine's eyes flickered as he rapidly scanned the information held in the black crystal data medium.

'Your leader is dead,' said Luko. 'Lord Mercaeno has fallen. Does that leave you in charge?'

'Captain Borganor is wounded,' said Darion. 'So yes.'

'Then it's your decision. You know there is no Black Chalice. Do you fight on?'

'You are still renegades,' said Darion. 'Even assuming the information in this archive is correct. You might not be the Bearers of the Black Chalice but you turned your back on the Imperium. The Inquisition declared you excommunicate traitoris.'

'Maybe so, captain,' replied Luko. 'But there never was a Black Chalice, so the oath to destroy it is void. There is one oath that is not yet fulfilled, and unless I am mistaken about your Chapter, you all take that kind of thing very seriously.'

'Vanqualis,' said Darion.

'Vanqualis and the greenskins. Last time I checked they were about to land on Herograve and kill the people you swore to defend. I'd say that leaves you with a choice to make, captain.'

Darion glanced back at the Techmarine scanning the history of the Soul Drinkers. He only knew sketchy details about what had happened to the Soul Drinkers, but it was enough to suggest that whatever had happened to them the Black Chalice was not involved.

'If this is over, your guns fall silent too.'

'We won't shoot you in the back. We're not so far gone we don't honour a truce.'

'This is no truce,' said Darion bitterly. 'We will find you, renegade. We will bring you to justice.'

'You'll have to get in line,' replied Luko.

Darion cast a final look at Luko, then spoke into his vox-unit. 'Howling Griffons, this is Captain Darion. Lord Mercaeno is lost. Fall back to the boarding units. Repeat, disengage and fall back, all units.'

The Howling Griffons broke cover warily, covering their retreat with their bolt guns as they retreated from the archive back in the direction of the *Cerulean Claw*'s assault torpedoes. Captain Luko watched them go, holding out a hand towards the Soul Drinkers to indicate they should hold their fire.

Slowly, the gunfire from the *Herald of Desolation* began to fall quiet.

Far below, on Vanqualis, thousands upon thousands of greenskins made up the first wave crashing onto the shore of Herograve. There were so many of them that the defenders didn't believe it, and some of them went into fits of fear and madness as they realised for the first time just what kind of threat was setting foot on the soil of their homeland.

The shore was barren and rocky, ill-suited for construction. The coastal settlements, less dense than the multi-layered hive cities further inland, formed a wall of tenement blocks and factorium warehouses to be held by the defenders.

Crouched in tenement windows or among the tarnished metal hulks of industrial equipment, the defenders consisted of House Falken household troops scrounged from the small garrisons trying to keep the peace in Herograve's cities, along with hundreds of militia taken from the coastal districts themselves, armed with anything from ex-Warder autoguns to hunting rifles. They were defending their homeland and in many cases settlements where their families and loved ones lived. Some of them carried weapons and wore body armour that their fathers had handed to them, with a stern warning that one day Vanqualis would have to be defended from enemies fated to return there. Thousands of men and women formed the line that had to hold before the greenskins.

Lord Sovelin Falken had gone to the coast to do his part and earn back some of the honour he had lost in failing to die like a man at Palatium. But he was the only member of House Falken there and he found himself in command without intending anything of the sort. Militia leaders, hard-bitten old men who had often served in the Warders before retirement, saluted him like a general and made their fatalistic reports. The household troops, almost unable to decide anything without noble consent, flocked to Sovelin to ask about the minutiae of their deployment.

Sovelin had done everything he could. He set up his command post in a waste treatment plant, a hideous lump of corroded rockcrete and steel that still pumped industrial effluent out into the sea, but which formed a bastion anchoring the coastal line. He placed the most competent-sounding militia leaders on the ends of the line, and as they left for their posts they had commented about how they had once served under a grandfather or great-uncle of Sovelin's, and how it was an honour to take an order from a Falken once more.

The household troops stayed close, guarding the plant and the areas around it, not because they were necessarily better troops but because Falken didn't want to leave them alone, cut off from the nobles they were sworn to serve, surrounded by militiamen from cities they had only recently been subjugating with brutality.

Lord Sovelin Falken begged the Emperor to show him something else he should do, some detail of the defence that he could see to, so that he could do his duty properly. But the Emperor did not answer, and Sovelin realised he was out of time when the first ork ships appeared among the churning waves. There were hundreds of craft, barely seaworthy, built from the trees of Nevermourn's jungles and crammed with uncountable numbers of greenskins. Their chanting mixed with the crashing of the waves on the rocks into a relentless rhythm of bloodlust and hate. Defenders quailed as they heard it, like a black wind whipping around the battlefield, like a song bellowed down from the orkish gods themselves. For a terrible age, perhaps an hour that felt like days, Sovelin listened to the war-chants getting louder and closer, and he wondered if he would simply turn tail and run at the first sight of a greenskin's hateful, bestial face.

The first ship, an enormous splintering hulk, rode up high on the crest of a wave and crashed onto the cruel rocks before the line. Its hull broke apart, sodden wood tearing with the impact, and the ship disgorged ten thousand screaming greenskin slaves onto the shore.

The battle was already well under way when the warlord set foot on the shore of Herograve. The holy shore that promised so much slaughter, the object of his destructive devotion for so long. Once, this land had belonged to the orks, just like Nevermourn – and like Nevermourn, it now belonged to the orks once more.

Ahead of him the pink blood-laden surf threw a tide of bodies onto the rocks. Slave-creatures littered the shoreline, heaped up where they had fallen in their hundreds. Gunfire streaked from buildings that stood over the shore, tiny dark human figures crouched in windows or on rooftops. The blocky, squat shape of the treatment plant rose in the centre of the battlefield, hundreds of slaves clamouring at its blood-streaked walls. The slave-creatures had served their purpose. They had absorbed the ammunition from the defenders' guns and given them something to shoot at so the real meat of the horde could make it ashore and begin the battle for real.

Thousands upon thousands of orks were storming ashore, charging past the warlord, blades high and guns spraying bullets at the shoreline more in celebration than to kill. They bayed and screamed with joy. Boats made of lashed timbers cut from Nevermourn's jungles crashed into the rocks, orks leaping from their prows – many of the vessels had sunk on the journey and left countless greenskins sinking to the sea floor, but three-quarters of the horde had made it and that was more than enough.

The warlord pointed his huge mechanical claw at the treatment works. It was the anchor of the line, the point where any breakthrough would end the defence of Herograve before it had begun. The orks barely needed the warlord's prompting and they surged past him, clambering over their own fallen, kicking wounded slaves out of the way.

Stray shots from the defenders fell among them, felling a few, and then the humans realised the green tide was powering towards them and concentrated fire thudded into the orks. Autogun shots blasted wet red holes in orkish chests and a few long-las shots from snipers picked off the larger leaders of the horde, tribal chieftains and greenskins who had won renown in the thick of battle. But the horde didn't need leaders now – it just needed a target, and soon the rampart of the dead was high enough for the first orks to make it to the first vent openings of the plant. They threw bundles of explosives into the treatment plant – most died as the ensuing explosions ripped chunks out of the grime-streaked walls but each one had hundreds behind him, fighting among themselves for the honour of being the first into the enemy's den.

Deep within the warlord something new burned. For as long as his orkish mind could remember he had known nothing but hate, and an awful, gnawing lust to bring destruction to his enemies and win vengeance for the orks. But now, there was more, a bright flame that banished a corner of the darkness inside him. Hope. Joy. Pride. At last, at long, long last, victory was his.

A roar of engines overhead wrenched his attention away. He looked up to see a host of gunships, painted in red and gold, swooping down low over the battlefield. Imperial aquilas shone brightly on their prows.

'Fall back and blow the stairways!' ordered Lord Sovelin. 'Blow everything! Hold them back!' He was on an upper floor that covered half the floorspace of the treatment plant, suspended above the enormous treatment tanks that dominated the lower floor. The treatment plant was old and ill-maintained, stained rockcrete walls enclosing a vast floor dominated by treatment vats.

From Sovelin's position he could see the warren of walkways between the vats, held by the household troopers in their emerald greatcoats and peaked caps embroidered with the serpent symbol of House Falken. Many of the troops were holding the windows, pouring autogun fire out at the greenskins clamouring outside the treatment plant. Runners scurried around the plant trying to bring more ammunition to the men at the windows, others dragging the wounded back towards Sovelin's end of the plant where a triage station had sprung up with hollow-eyed medics trying to stem the bleeding. Men were dying there, men were blinded and paralysed. Sovelin's own command post on the mezzanine overlooking the plant was a few sandbags and a field vox.

The sound was the worst. Seeing men mutilated and dying was bad enough, but somehow the chanting of the greenskins chilled even more. Tens of thousands of orkish voices raised as one, a brutal chorus of hatred as deep as an earthquake. It shuddered through the treatment plant as if its walls were parchment-thin.

'Fall back, damn it!' ordered Sovelin over the field vox. 'They'll breach the walls! Get off the ground floor and blow the stairs, keep them penned in!'

The household troops began to abandon the windows and head towards the stairways leading to the gantries and command cradles that spanned the treatment plant. Had the order been given a minute earlier, a lot of them would have made it.

A series of explosions erupted and threw the far end of the treatment plant into a boiling mass of flame and dust. Treatment tanks ruptured and spewed hissing industrial waste, which flashed into white cauls of toxic steam. The building shook and Sovelin fell – he saw one trooper

going over the edge of the platform and another tumbling from the
gantries above. The sound was appalling.

The far wall collapsed. Even with his ears ringing, Sovelin could hear
the chanting of the greenskins as they surged forward, as inevitable as
the tides of the sea they had crossed. They roared with a savage joy as
they poured into the plant. Hundreds of them. Thousands.

Sovelin just stared for a moment as the torrent of greenskin bodies
forcing their way between the treatment tanks. Within a handful of
seconds they were at the stairways. Some household troops brought
fire to bear on them and they fell, but more followed, clambering over
the dead and wounded. A man died under ork gunfire just a few paces
from Sovelin, and another under the blows of a crude cleaver on the
stairway in front of him.

Sovelin thought frantically. How many of the greenskins could the
household troops kill here? How long could they hold the treatment
plant, and buy extra vital minutes for the rest of the line? Not many,
and not long. It wasn't worth the sacrifice of the household troops.

'Fall back!' yelled Sovelin. 'Blow the charges and fall back! All units
retreat!' The trooper next to him relayed the order over the field vox
but he needn't have bothered. The tide of greenskins pouring into the
plant was such that any man with any sense was already running. A
few had formed squads of two or three covering one another's retreat,
but most has simply turned tail as ork gunfire raked through the
building.

Sovelin vaulted over the sandbags, autogun on hand. In front of
him rose a dark green shape, stinking of sweat and blood. He tried to
bring the gun up but a massive force thudded into him and he was on
the floor, feet and fists pummelling him. All around were the wordless
jeers and whooping of the orks, the thud of gunfire and screams of men
dragged down and killed.

All was noise and darkness. Sovelin was carried off his feet, snatches
of the chaotic battlefield flitting by him as he was dragged along on the
green tide. He had fleeting impressions of smoke and screaming, ork
battle-howls, explosions, gunfire and defiant war-cries from the militiamen holding the rest of the line.

He was outside. The greenskins had realised he was an officer of some
kind and they were carrying him aloft like a banner, clawed hands tearing at him as he was hauled along on a sea of charging orks, the open
salt-tinged air tainted by the stink of greenskin sweat.

The shore whirled around him. Gnarled, clawed green hands were
pulling him apart. Pain was everywhere. Sovelin looked up to the
sky, the only thought in his mind now a wordless prayer to the God-
Emperor to make the end quick.

Dashes of darkness moved across the clouded sky. Imperial gunships,

Thunderhawks, in the colours of the Howling Griffons. The faintest spark of hope glimmered through the pain.

Then Lord Sovelin Falken was dragged down into the darkness beneath dozens of greenskin bodies. A blade fell and his arm came off at the shoulder, shocking ice-cold pain hammering through him. His ribs collapsed beneath a hobnailed boot. His skull fractured.

Pain drowned out the hope as Lord Sovelin Falken died.

The warlord saw the treatment plant fall, and the tremendous cry that went up from the orks around him should have filled his heart with triumph as hot and powerful and the fires stoked in his mechanical body. Thousands of greenskins raised their guns to the sky, celebratory fire erupting like fireworks all among the greenskin horde smothering the shoreline.

But the warlord had seen the gunships swooping in. They dived now, looping down for a long pass over the orks, and fire stuttered down from guns mounted on their prows and swinging on mounts from their doors. Explosive rounds stitched long curving lines of bursting blood through the masses of orks. Many of the orks turned their eyes to the sky as those around them fell, blasted open like wet red flowers spraying gore.

The warlord bellowed. He recognised the design of these gunships, blocky and powerful, gunfire streaming off them. In this moment of greatest triumph, the culmination of the crusade he had founded long ago in the Garon Nebula, his nemesis had come to face him. For any other species, the warlord would have been filled with despair, to see his victory jeopardised by the human elites of the kind who had wounded the horde so deeply at the Wraithspire Palace. But an ork did not think like that. For an ork, fighting was an end in itself, and even the driven warlord recognised the best kind of enemy when he saw it.

The armoured elites would make this victory complete, when they lay battered and bloody on the rocks, at the mercy of orkish blades. He could not hoped for a finer enemy to crown this greatest of victories. Steam sprayed from the joints of his mechanical torso and arm as the fires within him raged higher.

The gunships dived low again, coming in for another pass. But they were not just strafing the greenskins now. Doors swung open revealed armoured bodies crammed inside, in a spectacular livery of quartered red and gold. Like orks, they were not cowards. They wanted their enemies to see them. Hatred and respect in equal measure mixed in the warlord's mind, an emotion peculiar to greenskins that meant only they understood war in its purest, joyous form.

The humans jumped. They leapt from their gunships right into the centre of the ork horde, bolters firing even as they fell, chainswords raised to spear down like lightning bolts. Where they landed, a shock-wave ran through the greenskins as if a bomb had hit. Orks were caught unawares and shot through the head or spitted on screeching chainblades, or simply crushed by the weight of the armoured humans crashing down on top of them. The gunships kept firing, spraying fire through the orks who tried to surge towards the human attackers.

Dozens of greenskins died in a few moments. Dozens more followed as the humans found their feet and laid into the orks around them with bolters and blades.

More humans were dropping now, reinforcing the foothold their fellow elites had won. One of them was a leader in highly ornate armour and carrying a glowing sword, a jump pack on his back slowing his descent so he could chatter fire into the orks from his bolt pistol.

There were hundreds of the humans, landing directly in the heart of the army. The whole horde was reeling, orks being trampled underfoot as the horde tried to turn to face this new threat.

The warlord grabbed the nearest ork and threw him out off the way. He stamped towards the battle, his eyes on the human leader as he dropped into the midst of the carnage. No one would stop his horde, not here on enemy ground and now when victory was literally within sight. The human leader was his. All the humans were his to kill, his to rend apart and display as trophies.

Another gunship screeched low overhead, close enough for the downwash of its powerful engines to batter around the warlord like a burning gale. The warlord forged onwards towards the armoured human, crushing fellow orks underfoot in his determination to kill.

War-whoops and screamed prayers filtered down through the din of the gunship's engines. Dark shapes were falling around the warlord. Human shapes, unarmoured this time, unshaven and ragged. The same soldiers who had fought at the Wraithspire Palace – no, not the same, the very toughest of them, the hardest-bitten killers.

The warlord struck all about him. A filthy human who came at him with a bayonet was sliced in two by the warlord's claw. He grabbed another by the head with his normal hand, and crushed the human's skull. He flung the body so hard it smacked another human to the ground. These were no elites – they were ordinary humans, elevated to something more by sheer determination.

The humans were all over him, eager to die, trying to pull him down. The warlord was huge, but the gunship had disgorged many humans right on top of him. The warlord threw them aside, cut them in two, stamped on them and pressed forwards. But they were slowing him down. There were too many to kill all at once. They clung on like biting insects, snapping their bayonet blades off in his gnarled skin and spraying glittering fans of crimson las-fire into him. It wouldn't kill him, it barely even hurt, but he was swamped in fragile human bodies as if these ragged vermin were competing to die first.

The warlord stumbled. A human, big for his kind with a shaven head and an almost orkishly bestial face, rammed a combat knife deep between the warlord's ribs. The warlord wrestled him to the ground, punching. The human rolled to the side and kicked out with a heel so hard he broke a bone in the warlord's face. The warlord screamed. More humans were piling on, jumping on his back as if they were hunters bringing down a great kill.

In front of him the warlord could see the armoured humans. They were fighting atop a heap of dead greenskins. Their leader's armour was dark with orkish blood. The leader saw the warlord and directed the fire of his fellow elites. In a storm of bolter fire the orks between the leader and the warlord were shredded.

The warlord tried to force his way back to his feet to face the human leader. The big human beneath him was still alive, refusing to give in and die. With a roar the warlord picked up the human with his claw and threw him, but he was still on his knees, human hands trying to pull him down.

The human leader activated the jump pack on his back. The twin jets roared with flame but the human did not fly up into the air – he hurtled straight forwards, towards the warlord, glowing sword held out in front of him like the tip of a lance.

The warlord tried to bring his claw down to snatch the armoured human out of the air, but the humans on his back slowed him down a half-second too long. The armoured human crashed into the warlord, the tip of his sword punching through the warlord's metallic torso and slicing through the machinery that churned in his chest. The raging forge that served as his heart was punctured, raw flame spurting from the wound. The sword passed right through him and out through the gnarled flesh of his back.

The warlord reared up, finally throwing the humans off his back. The sword was still stuck through him. The armoured human let go, stepping back in the face of the white fire spurting from the warlord's sundered body. The warlord was bellowing, howling his anger, and it seemed the horde around him shrunk back in shock at seeing their leader wounded.

The armoured human yelled something and scrambled across the blood-slick rocks away from the warlord. The few surviving humans were trying to do the same, fighting to get through the orks still battling around the warlord. The pressure inside the warlord was growing, the unbearable searing heat building up to a crescendo.

The armoured human dived away from the warlord. The warlord stumbled forwards, determined to get to the human and avenge himself. But he was a few moments too late. His armoured torso finally gave way and the fires of the furnace inside him broke free.

In a great searing ball of white flame, the warlord exploded.

The bridge was kept dark, as Eumenes preferred it. On the seating around the edge of the spherical room were assembled the whole remaining Soul Drinkers Chapter. At first glance the gathering looked much the same as the one some time before when Sarpedon had stood before them and explained the Chapter's new destination, but on closer inspection the differences were profound. For one, there were far fewer Soul Drinkers now, as a result of the losses against the orks, in the second Chapter War, and in the stand against the Howling Griffons. Perhaps three hundred remained. There was also an undercurrent, unspoken but powerful, which ran through the assembled Space Marines. Half of them had sided with Eumenes, and the other half had stayed with Sarpedon. There was nothing that could be done to disguise the hatred that boiled just beneath the surface. The battle-brothers seated side by side would kill one another if they had the chance.

The most profound difference was that it was not Sarpedon who addressed the assembled Chapter. It was Eumenes.

'My brothers,' began Eumenes. His armour was now ornate, with chalice symbols on his chestplate and shoulder pad plated in gold, and he carried Lord Mercaeno's axe as a trophy. 'We have gone through the worst of our battles. What we have survived these last few days is the equal of anything the galaxy can throw at us. But we have prevailed. The Soul Drinkers have shed the final shackles that bound them to the past and now I can lead us all on a new path. This is not a path that I have plucked out of nowhere. It began with the death of Gorgoleon and continued with the harvest of new recruits. Finally I can show you that path.'

Young but brilliant, dynamic and convincing, it was easy to see how Eumenes had turned fully half the Chapter to his side before the second Chapter War had begun. Every eye, from the impassive sockets of Chaplain Iktinos's skull-helm to the haunted eyes of Apothecary Pallas, was fixed on Eumenes.

'The Imperium,' said Eumenes, 'is corrupt. It is an evil creation, a breeding ground for everything we hate. And it will be destroyed. It is the Soul Drinkers who will bring it down. We are free from its influences, we are strong and determined, and we have come through such tribulations that the Imperium itself holds no fear for us.

'For too long we have treated the people of the Imperium as if they were victims like us, as if we had some obligation to save them. Now we understand that those same people are the enemy. At best they are weapons, unthinking tools of the Imperium's rulers. At worst they are so utterly corrupt that death for them will be a blessing. Those of you who have sworn to destroy Chaos have also sworn to destroy the Imperium, for it is among the ignorant masses of the Imperium that the seeds of Chaos are sown. We shall burn it all, my battle-brothers. The liars and the butchers, the ignorant and the corrupt, we shall burn them all...'

Eumenes's voice trailed off as he caught movement at the edge of the auditorium. Eyes followed his own to see Sergeant Tydeus stumble onto the upper row of seating. His face was streaked with blood, one eye a red ruin, and panting as if every breath could be his last. With one arm he was supporting Scout Nisryus, the young psychic who had started out as part of Eumenes's scout squad.

'Tydeus!' barked Eumenes. 'What is the meaning of this? You are supposed to be standing guard!'

Tydeus's remaining eye was wide with fear. Fear, in a Space Marine. Tydeus had been taught, like all the Soul Drinkers, to control his fear, to strangle it as it formed in his mind and crush it with duty and discipline. But in Tydeus it had surged to the surface.

'He's... he killed Scamander...'

Eumenes's eyes narrowed. 'You let him loose?'

'He used the Hell...' Tydeus let Nisryus slither to the floor, unconscious. Nisryus's young, pale face was covered in blood.

'You idiot!' yelled Eumenes. 'You broken-minded fools! He is just one man! Can I not trust my battle-brothers to keep a single unarmed man in a cell?' He turned to Sergeant Hecular, who was in the front row of the assembled Soul Drinkers. 'Hecular, get your squad together. Take everyone you need. Hunt him down, leave him no...'

It was pure instinct that cut off Eumenes's words. Slowly, he looked upwards, to the ceiling of the bridge.

Sarpedon clung to the curved ceiling, surrounded by the captured banners and war-trophies, spidery legs splayed out above him. His humanoid upper half hung down and he was watching the proceedings with the faintest amusement in his face.

'You,' said Eumenes, coldly furious. 'You are under arrest. And now you have killed my battle-brothers to escape, your sentence is death!'

Sarpedon dropped with impossible grace, landing on his talons in front of Eumenes.

'I sentenced you to death,' said Sarpedon, 'some time ago.'

'No,' said Eumenes, brandishing Mercaeno's force axe. 'You relinquished command of this Chapter to me and submitted yourself to my authority. That was the deal, Sarpedon. You gave your word! Damn it, Sarpedon, you promised!'

The auditorium was silent now apart from Eumenes's voice, the tension wound up even tighter. Every Soul Drinker there knew how this would end. But none of them could intervene, because they also knew that if this conflict spread to the watching battle-brothers then an all-out battle would break out and would not stop until one side was entirely wiped out. The Soul Drinkers would annihilate themselves. So they just watched intently.

'You betrayed us,' said Sarpedon. 'You had Karraidin killed in front of my eyes. You betrayed every duty you ever had to this Chapter. You betrayed your very Emperor.' He pointed a gauntleted finger at Eumenes. 'You promised first.'

'No! We had a deal! Where is your honour, Sarpedon?'

'When a Soul Drinker speaks of honour, he speaks of the whole Chapter's honour. You say this is your Chapter now, Eumenes, so why do your brothers not gun me down where I stand? If they believe the Soul Drinkers can be traded to you like chattels, why am I still alive?'

Eumenes looked around him. The Soul Drinkers were on their feet now, watching. The tension that had boiled beneath earlier was closer to the surface now, hands on the hilts of combat knives or the grips of bolt pistols. But no one moved.

'If you continue like this, Eumenes, this Chapter will tear itself apart. You know that. You cannot mould Space Marines to your will. You can only lead them as best you can, and pray that they find in you a man worth following. That is what I have learned as your Chapter Master. End this now, and the Chapter War will be over.'

'If you will not obey me,' said Eumenes levelly, 'if my brothers still need a display of my will, then we will settle this the old-fashioned way.'

Eumenes glanced at Hecular, who promptly threw a small dark cylinder towards him. Eumenes caught it deftly in his off-hand and the twin vortex blades of the Soulspear slid out from the haft. With Mercaeno's axe in one hand and the Soulspear in the other, Eumenes squared up to Sarpedon.

'Last chance, Eumenes,' said Sarpedon. 'Every Soul Drinker here knows you will lead us to destroy ourselves. That is why they have let me stand here and challenge you. You lost the soul of this Chapter the moment you began the Chapter War. Do not die for nothing more than pride.'

Eumenes did not reply. Instead he lunged forward, bringing Mercaeno's axe and the Soulspear down in a twin arc to cut Sarpedon apart.

The duel lasted a handful of seconds. The superior reactions and battlefield conditioning of the assembled Soul Drinkers meant they could pick out every movement, every nuance. Fast as it was, it seemed to go on forever.

Sarpedon dropped onto his back legs as Eumenes powered towards him. The twin blades arced past him, close enough for the Soulspear's blade of harnessed vortex to score a furrow down his breastplate. He could feel the whispers of the warp as the weapon passed by him, for the Soulspear's blades were gateways to the warp, caged wounds in realspace. The axe swung in a wide, loping crescent towards Sarpedon's face and it passed just under his chin, whistling as it went.

Eumenes barrelled forward, his full weight bearing down on Sarpedon. But he was off-balance now. Sarpedon shifted his weight, his rear legs forcing him forward to meet Eumenes in a way that only his mutations would allow. The two Space Marines collided.

Sarpedon's front legs were up like the horns of a charging animal. The talons punched into Eumenes's abdomen, the blade of Sarpedon's one bionic leg penetrating Eumenes's armour alongside the chitin and bone of his natural front talon.

Sarpedon pushed himself up by his back legs and lifted Eumenes into the air, his front talons breaking through the back of Eumenes's armour. Eumenes roared in frustration and anger, and Mercaeno's axe fell from his hand as he tried to fight back, wrest himself away from Sarpedon and start the duel anew.

Sarpedon angled his front legs downwards and Eumenes slid off them, clutching at Sarpedon as he fell. Eumenes hit the floor hard, and there was nothing but hatred written across his features. He tried to bring the Soulspear up to defend himself, but gravity and Sarpedon's reactions were faster.

Sarpedon crashed down on Eumenes, his front four legs arrowing downwards with all the force he could muster. Four talons tore through Eumenes's chest, pinning him to the floor, slicing through lungs and hearts, through Eumenes's spine and into the floor of the bridge.

Sarpedon's full weight settled on Eumenes, the talons sinking deep into his chest. Eumenes tried to speak but he could only splutter blood from his lips. One arm flailed upwards, trying to slash with the Soulspear, but Sarpedon grabbed Eumenes's wrist and wrenched his hand back, forcing Eumenes to drop the weapon. The spear's black blades retracted into the haft as it clattered to the floor.

Sarpedon leaned backwards and pulled his talons out of Eumenes's chest. Crimson fountains of blood followed them, Eumenes gasping out his last breaths as the life flowed out of him. The twisted bionic came out last, and by the time Eumenes flopped back to the ground, he was dead.

Sarpedon stood over Eumenes's body. Every one of his battle-brothers, those who had followed him and those who had chosen Eumenes, watched him in silence.

'I have brought us here,' said Sarpedon. 'I chose Eumenes for this Chapter and granted him the armour of a full battle-brother. I failed to see what he was planning and I failed to stop the Chapter War from breaking out. In all these things I have failed you, my brothers. If you will accept my command then I will be your Chapter Master again, not as a spoil won from Eumenes but as a burden of duty as heavy as any I might place on you. If you can no longer trust me to lead you, then I will step down and hand the position of Chapter Master to whoever believes they can lead the Soul Drinkers. No deals, no conflicts, just step forward.'

The bridge was silent. Sarpedon cast his eyes in particular over those who might believe they had earned the right to command the Chapter – Chaplain Iktinos, Luko, Sergeant Hecular – but none of them moved. Sarpedon gave them a long, tense moment to stand up and make their claim. But none of them did.

'Then if you do not accept me as your Chapter Master,' said Sarpedon at last, 'You may leave the *Brokenback*. Take a shuttle and go. There are worlds within a shuttle flight and we will not stop you. The Chapter War has claimed enough of us already. Captain Luko, take the Soul-spear and lock it back up in the armoury. And Chaplain?' Sarpedon indicated the body at his feet. 'Bury my battle-brother.'

From the spire the whole of the city was laid out. In the daylight, fil-tered through the polluted sky, it seemed calmer than at night because the flames were less vivid and the blackouts less obvious. It was an illu-sion. The city still groaned, its billions of people locked in fear.

On the roof of the spire the wind was cold and it whipped the ban-ners that hung around the spiretop, each one bearing a variation on the serpent heraldry of House Falken. The wind brought the taste of smoke with it, from burning buildings and autoguns.

Anchored to the top of the spire was the countess's yacht, its sleek form perching on the edge of the spire as docking-servitors attached fuel hoses to it and changed the air filters. The countess walked slowly down the yacht's embarkation ramp, her children in tow. In the cold wind she felt every one of her many, many years, as if the wind was blowing through her right to her very bones.

The countess looked down at the city. It stretched as far as she could see, merging with the horizon in a smog-choked band of grey. This was her city, and she felt a tinge of the real sorrow implied by her mourn-ing-wear. The people down there were so frightened. They no could no longer rely on House Falken to keep them safe. They did not know when or how the end would come. Countess Ismenissa allowed herself a moment of weakness to feel sorry for them all. Many of them had lost people they loved. The countess had lost her family, who represented the order and tradition that she loved. She had something in common with her people, a rare thing indeed.

The countess's chamberlain emerged from the doorway leading into the spire. The spire itself was a sky-scraping creation of columns and archways, home to one of the city's administrative departments. It was evacuated now because of the possibility of rioting in the streets where it was rooted into the hive, and the countess intended only to stop there as briefly as possible.

'There is news,' said the chamberlain, struggling to make himself heard above the whistling wind. 'From the front.'

'What news?' For the shore of Herograve to be called a 'front' at all suggested that the greenskins had not simply blown past the defences there, as the countess had expected.

'The Howling Griffons have returned to the fray,' said the chamberlain. 'It is said that they have abandoned the pursuit of the Black Chalice.'

'The Howling Griffons?' In spite of herself, the countess felt hope. 'How do we know this?'

'A Captain Darion was in communication with the hive authorities, but only briefly, and he has now returned to battle. Do you know of him?'

'Yes. He was subordinate to Lord Mercaeno.'

'It seems that Lord Mercaeno has fallen, my lady.'

The countess looked at the pitted metal floor of the spiretop. 'Then a great hero of the Imperium has been lost. The Emperor shall weep a tear for him. What of the greenskins?'

'The Howling Griffons fell upon them in force. The ork leader was killed. Orks are a fractious species, much given to conflict among themselves, according to the librarium records. Captain Darion reports that with their leader dead the greenskin force will lose direction. It has yet to break out significantly from the beachhead on the shore. The Howling Griffons are organising the defence. They have with them the troopers of the 901st Penal Legion, though few of them remain. I have taken the liberty of authorising the reinforcement of the defenders there from all hives. Subject to your approval, of course.'

The countess waved a hand. 'Of course. You have it.' She looked the chamberlain in the eye. 'Can we win?'

'Perhaps, my lady.'

The countess sighed. For an instant years of warfare flashed through her mind, the struggle to rebuild House Falken and the terrible wound it would leave on the history of Vanqualis. Even with the Howling Griffons, even victorious, Vanqualis would suffer. But suffering was the nature of the galaxy. The countess had to be strong. She was all her people had.

'Is there any news of Sovelin?' she asked at length.

'His part of the line fell. It is likely that he is dead.'

'I see. And the Black Chalice?'

'Captain Darion was not entirely forthcoming on the matter. It seems that the Bearers of the Black Chalice were never here and that we were somehow mistakenly alerted to their presence. It seems that there has been a great deal of confusion following the invasion.'

The countess shook her head sadly. 'Poor young Sovelin. I feared for him when he was young. He didn't seem Falken material.'

'With Lord Sovelin dead, my lady, it would seem that if any mistake was made regarding the presence of the Black Chalice, it would not…'

'Do you suggest I use Sovelin as a scapegoat for this mistake?' asked the countess.

'Far be it from my station to suggest such a thing,' said the chamberlain, unruffled. 'But given the evident confusion, it behoves us all to ensure that the people and the Lay Parliament are given answers that will satisfy them, until the whole truth can be uncovered.'

The countess looked carefully at her chamberlain. Small, unassuming, his eyes screwed up against the cold wind, he did not seem like much and yet he had served her for a long time and offered her counsel through many crises. With the loss of so many of her peers at Palatium, it was perhaps best that she have someone so shrewd and dedicated to help her in her duties. 'I shall leave such things to you to deal with, chamberlain,' she said. 'I must concern myself with leadership. A new phase of this war is opening up on Herograve and the Vanqualians fighting there will need a figurehead to rally behind. It seems I am the only suitable candidate left.'

'Very well, my lady,' said the chamberlain with a humble nod.

'This war will be a long one. The greenskins might never leave. I only hope I am up to the task.'

'I have faith, my lady.'

'As must we all.' The countess turned to re-enter the yacht and leave the spiretop. 'I shall go to the coast. Even if we throw the orks back into the sea it will be years before we can cleanse the jungles of them, if ever. Perhaps I will not see the end of it, but do what I must for my planet. See to my cities while I am gone, chamberlain. Heal the wounds the orks have already dealt us, now there is hope on Herograve as well as fear.'

'It shall be done, my lady,' said the chamberlain as the countess walked up the ramp back into her yacht.

Years. Decades. The countess knew she would be a fool to think the greenskins were beaten. But if this Captain Darion was fit to take over from Lord Mercaeno, and if the people of Herograve took up arms against the greenskins to re-found the Vanqualian Warders, perhaps Vanqualis might be delivered from destruction after all.

She idly stroked the head of one of House Falken's dear children as the ramp closed behind her and the yacht took off, turning elegantly towards the distant coast.

Many hours after Sarpedon had asserted his position as Chapter Master of the Soul Drinkers, Chaplain Iktinos held funeral rites on the arena flight deck. He jettisoned the body of Eumenes, along with the Soul Drinkers who had fallen on the *Brokenback* against the Howling Griffons, into space. As their coffins spiralled away from the *Brokenback*, Iktinos offered a prayer to Rogal Dorn and the Emperor to accept them into the ranks of humanity. In the battle at the end of time, when mankind finally faced Chaos in the ultimate conflict, the Soul Drinkers would fight side by side with all humanity's honoured dead.

The Chapter was in attendance. Sarpedon said nothing, observing the prayers said for each fallen brother. With the Soulspear locked in the armoury and his force staff broken Sarpedon now carried Mercaeno's axe, and with it saluted the coffins as they were fired off into space. Only those who had chosen to leave the Chapter – mostly scouts, including Hecular's squad – were not there to see Eumenes and the Chapter's other fallen brothers committed to the void.

When the rites were done, Iktinos asked leave to pray for the fallen and meditate on the events of the battle for Vanqualis and the second Chapter War. Sarpedon granted it, and Iktinos left his brothers to their mourning.

Iktinos did not return to his cell, or to the small seminary where he instructed his flock in the spiritual principles by which he guided the Chapter. Instead he headed deep into the *Brokenback*, to the half-flooded sanctum he kept secret from the rest of the Chapter.

The sanctum to a long-forgotten god had lain undisturbed since Iktinos had been there last. He made his way to the altar and read the printouts from the monitoring equipment there. He noted without emotion the point where the irregular scribbles of lifesigns had become straight lines.

Iktinos hauled the stone sarcophagus from the water. Inside lay the bloated, blackened body of Croivas Vel Scannien. The astropath had served his purpose, and Iktinos ignored his corpse. He turned instead to the piles of books and scrolls he had placed there after returning from the library orbiting Tyrancos, before he had descended to Nevermourn to fight alongside Sarpedon. Dozens of books lay stacked up on the altar, along with scroll cases and even a couple of carved tablets.

The Chaplain picked up one of the books. It had lain interred in the temple for thousands of years, its woven crystal pages loaded with such intensity of meaning that Iktinos hesitated slightly before opening it. The script flowing across the first page told him that it had indeed been touched by the hand of his master. It was almost too much for Iktinos to properly comprehend, the weight of that meaning, reaching out across thousands of years to touch his soul.

In the silence of his sanctum, Iktinos read. He learned more of the path along which he was to lead the Soul Drinkers, and the Chapter's ultimate goal.

Sarpedon did not know, of course. He was incidental to the true history of the Soul Drinkers. The Chapter's rejection of the Imperium had been prophesied a long time ago – Sarpedon was just another actor in the great play of the Soul Drinkers, and his part had been written out at the beginning. Iktinos rejoiced inside that he had been a Chaplain when those blessed events had occurred, and that he had been in a position to play his own role in his master's plan.

He read further. The next stage became clear. Iktinos would have to bring the Soul Drinkers to a place his master had prepared for them long ago. It was not far for a warp-capable craft like the *Brokenback* – deep in the Veiled Region, a slice of the galaxy notoriously difficult to navigate, and hence survive. Astropathic messages within the Veil tended to arrive at their destinations distorted, if at all. Iktinos allowed himself a rare smile. It was perfect. The next stage of the plan would be all the more certain if it were enacted within the Veil.

Iktinos memorised the location, and the first tasks he would need to complete once the Chapter arrived there. Iktinos would have to convince Sarpedon to take the Chapter there, of course, but he had needed little prompting to begin the journey to the Obsidian system. Sarpedon's principles and sense of duty made him predictable enough. Iktinos foresaw little difficulty in manipulating him again. Eumenes had been a complication, of course, but he had been dealt with. There would be no such distractions in the future.

Iktinos put the book down. He had much to do. He had to lead his followers in their prayers and counsel the rest of the battle-brothers to heal the rifts that still existed between them. Some, like Apothecary Pallas, would need much guidance before they felt a part of the Chapter again. And, of course, Iktinos would have to work out how to direct Sarpedon towards the Veiled Region.

The will of Iktinos's master would be done, there could be no doubt about that. But first, there was much work to do.

HELLFORGED

'Even when the battlefield gives us every advantage, it is still a part of the universe. And this universe, never forget, despises us.'

– Daenyathos, *Reliquerae Tactica*

CHAPTER ONE

'I swear,' said the rat-like man cowering in the corner. 'I swear I have told you all I know.'

The cell was tiny, just large enough for the prisoner to be shackled against the wall. The prisoner blinked in the sudden light flooding in from the open door, silhouetting the robed figure of Archmagos Voar standing in the doorway. Voar knelt down so he was level with the prisoner.

'I have no reason to believe you,' said Voar.

The prisoner gulped down the recycled air, and sweat ran down his face. The cell was infernally hot, kept sweltering by its proximity to the engines. The man was still shaking, though, his eyes flickering around as if searching for a way out that he had somehow missed in the previous months of his incarceration.

'He told me... He told me he got it from some... some rogue trader, he called himself. Not the real thing, I guess, just some chancer, some salvager. I really don't know anything else.'

'You know,' said Archmagos Voar, 'that it was from the Veiled Region. You know, and you knew when you bought it, that it was forbidden.'

'Of course I did! I told you all that! What more can you want from me? What more is there?'

The man's name was Baradrin Thaal, and once, he had possessed far more money than was necessary. He was the second son of a noble house where a younger sibling, not expected to inherit the responsibilities of the household, was free to waste his family's money on banal sins. One of those sins had been to buy the object that Archmagos Voar of the Adeptus Mechanicus now carried with him. It was Thaal's last and biggest mistake. Men like Thaal had died at the hands of the Mechanicus for tech-heresies far less heinous than his.

Voar took the object out from below his deep crimson robes. It was a mask, roughly humanoid and stylised as if made by some brutalist sculptor. It was not, however, made by a human hand. Any fool could see that. The eyes were triangular slits and the nose was flat, a simple oblong above the grimacing slot of the mouth. The forehead was disfigured by a green gemstone, like a third eye. From the back of the mask hung a nest of wires and probes. It was not meant to be worn – it was meant to be implanted.

'The trader's name was... Devian, I think. Devian something. He got it from some salvager who found it in an archeotech load towed out of the Veiled Region. I don't know any names or anything else. He told me this thing would... That it was the best high xenos tech, better than any nerve-glove or cortical stimm. I just... I just looked for the next thing, you know? Please, I've told you everything I know. Everything. More than you wanted. Let me go. My family needs to know where I am.'

Thaal was crying, his tears mingling with his sweat.

Voar did not feel the heat. His core temperature was well above the human maximum, his sensors told him, but such things had ceased to matter to him now that he had abandoned most of the weaknesses of the flesh. The hand with which he held the xenos artefact was bionic, as were his legs and most of his organs. His face was rebuilt from synthetic flesh, given a cruel, noble caste. His brain was original. That could never be replaced. The rest of him had been almost completely dispensed with.

Voar stood. He glanced behind him. He had not come to Thaal's cell alone. He had hoped that it would not prove necessary to bring Crystavayne along, but Thaal's ignorance could not remain unprobed.

The magos standing behind him, in the doorway of the cell, stepped forwards. He was robed, like Voar, but moved with the stilted clumsiness of a man whose body was still mostly natural. On one of his hands, he wore an elaborate gauntlet with a bundle of blades and knives extending from the palm.

'This man is a magos biologis neuralis,' said Voar to Thaal. 'He can illuminate you as to memories you did not know you had. Though I have given up much of myself to the machine, I have yet to let go of those human weaknesses that compel me to respect the corporal integrity of a fellow human. Therefore, I am reluctant to have him exercise his art upon you.'

'I don't know,' said Thaal, 'what you want me to say. Tell me, and I'll say it. I'll admit to anything. I'll do whatever you say.'

Voar turned to the magos behind him.

'Proceed,' he said.

Magos Biologis Crystavayne knelt over Thaal. The neural gauntlet lit up, the vials on the back of the hand filling with chemicals that formed clear beads at the end of its many needles.

'Please,' said Thaal.

'What dosage do you command, archmagos?' asked Crystavayne. His voice was synthesised and sounded like the buzzing of metallic insects.

'Let him know,' said Voar, 'that he has displeased the Omnissiah.'

'No! Throne, no! I'll admit to anything. I'll sign a confession. Whatever you want, but by the Throne of Earth I do not know!'

The needles of the gauntlet touched Thaal's neck. He was too weak to fight off the magos. He closed his eyes and sobbed.

'Stop,' said Voar.

Crystavayne took the gauntlet away from Thaal's neck. Thaal shook and whimpered, like a scolded animal.

'He is primed,' said Crystavayne. 'His biological readings suggest he is at the point of maximum malleability. If it is to be done, this is an excellent time.'

'He does not know anything more,' continued Voar. 'To your post, magos.'

The magos stood, bowed his head in deference and left the cell.

'I am not an unmerciful man,' said Voar. 'You have transgressed at a time when I am still capable of compassion for a pathetic creature like you.'

'Oh Emperor enthroned,' sobbed Thaal. 'Oh, all His saints...'

'You will never see your family again. You will forever be branded a tech-heretic. That is punishment enough.' Voar held up the xenos mask. 'I have one further question, Baradrin Thaal. Did you ever wear this?'

'No,' said Thaal. 'I dared not. I had to drum up the courage. I was... I was thinking about it on the morning your men came for me.'

'Good,' said Voar. 'Perhaps I will find some use for you on my ship. Until then, your thoughts will be your tormentors.'

Voar stepped out of the cell, placed a bionic hand on the scrutiny plate outside, and the door slid closed on Baradrin Thaal's cell.

Even the magi astrophysicus could not discern quite what had happened to that patch of space to the galactic west of the core. Some speculated that the vacuum had become somehow denser, dragging in matter from all around. Others suggested that some great cosmic event had occurred there, a supernova or the collision of two superdense stars that had started a chain reaction of collapse and rebirth still reverberating through the area. Certainly, it had been a momentous event indeed, because the warp was thick and sluggish there, the beacon of the Astronomican like a night sky's moon reflected in stagnant water.

The place had been known as the Veiled Region since the beginning of recorded Imperial history. It was a place of dense nebulae and new-born stars, buffeted by waves of radiation and discarded stellar matter. Navigation, on the few times it had been tried, was dangerous and haphazard even by the lethal standards of space travel, and settlements within the Veiled Region were prohibited by Imperial law.

The primary danger within the Veiled Region, however, was isolation. Astropathic communications were difficult, and became more so the further a ship went. Eventually, psychic communication was blocked entirely, the warp resembling a sucking mire or endless doldrums where an astropath's mental voice echoed back only silence. Exploring the region, then, was a task rarely attempted and never successful.

Then came Baradrin Thaal and his ill-advised purchase of an alien trinket from a salvager-trader who had never been identified. The artefact was from an alien civilisation that showed signs of great technological advancement. The Mechanicus, having apprehended Thaal and examined the artefact, could not make any sense of its origins, and put Archmagos Voar in charge of finding its source. It was from somewhere in the Veiled Region, Thaal had claimed, and so Voar had assembled a Mechanicus explorator fleet to penetrate the Veiled Region and hunt down the alien hand that had created the mask. His flagship was the *Antithesis*, a fast, tough armed explorer that had forged the first route through the Garon Nebula and circumnavigated the Varlian Anomalies. He had cruisers and escorts drawn from the Martian fleet and regiments of tech-guard with him, because he expected trouble within the Veiled Region.

Stylised and heretical though it was, the mask was of a human face. That meant humans and xenos in the Veiled Region, and with the xenos capable of such technology it was likely the humans were subjects or, even worse, willing allies of the heathen aliens. Human settlements within the Veiled Region were a persistent but unproven rumour, and one of Voar's objectives was to find any human worlds, free them of xenos taint and bring them back into the fold of the Imperium of Man.

The mission was in its second year. The Veil had been penetrated, and light years of steadily thickening nebulae and stellar clouds now lay between the Mechanicus fleet and clear void.

Voar had assembled the officers of his fleet on the bridge of the *Antithesis*. The bridge was a monument to knowledge, a library crammed with thousands of volumes covering millions of subjects, as if the light of that knowledge could illuminate the ship's officers or, by basking in it, they could absorb the collective wisdom and become closer to the Omnissiah.

Like Voar, the fleet's officers were all on the ladder towards the Mechanicus's upper echelons, where a man might lose the vestiges of humanity and become more like the machine. One day they would lose their ability to communicate effectively with humans, their brain functions solely given over to contemplating the greater problems of doing the Omnissiah's work. To earn that exalted status, however, they had to serve.

'Brother magi,' began Voar as he ascended the steps to the altar that crowned the bridge-library. 'Thaal has no more to tell us. Everything we learn from now on, we uncover with our own hands.'

The magi made for a fine officer cadre. They were masters at a variety of disciplines, and, should the mission come to violence, a few of them were capable military leaders. Magos Gladius Hepsebah was a fine weaponsmith and an excellent shot. Her robed form concealed a torso taken up with the power cells for the rotator laser cannon that had replaced her left arm, and one eye was a complicated multi-spectrum targeting array. Magos Metallurgicus Vionel was similarly formidable, although in his case it was his oversized dense metallic skeleton and exposed nerve-fibre bundles, originally intended for industrial purposes, that made him so intimidating in battle.

Others were pure researchers. Magos Biologis Crystavayne, who had threatened Baradrin Thaal with a horribly painful fate, was equipped with enough surgical implements and refrigerated sample containers to make him a walking medical laboratory. The inhuman figure of Magos Xenophysicus Khrul, with his tracked lower body and radiation shielding barely fitting beneath his robes, was invaluable in exploring hostile environments. The fifth magos of the fleet command, Magos Astrophysicus Devwyn, was the most human-looking of the officers, with cranial interface circuits and a pair of verispex mechadendrites his only obvious augmentations.

'It is unlikely,' said Hepsebah, 'that we will receive further human intelligence. Thaal was our best source.'

'Our only source,' said Voar, 'save our own intellects.'

'Then what is to be our course of action?' asked Khrul. His voice was a deep rumble from a vocaliser unit built into his torso.

'We forge on,' said Voar, 'unless the Omnissiah's wisdom can teach us otherwise.'

'The Veiled Region,' said Crystavayne, 'is vast and unmapped. To seek an alien world, even an alien empire, would be beyond a reliable statistical model.'

'I disagree,' said Khrul. 'The Veiled Region has remained unexplored because the resources to penetrate it have yet to be deployed. Thaal's information created the first compelling reason to commit such resources to the region for centuries. We would be in dereliction of our duties towards the Omnissiah if we passed up the chance, not only to locate the source of the artefact, but also to discover what other knowledge lies here. Explorator fleets have barely skimmed the surface of its nebulae since the Great Crusade. There is no telling what we might discover.'

'Devwyn?' said Voar. 'What have you to say on this matter?'

Devwyn kept his eyes on the archmagos, but the glassy artificial eyes on the snake-like mechadendrites fixed to his shoulders wove between his fellow magi. Devwyn, being an observer of the skies, had learned to use his extra senses to keep two eyes on the ground as well.

'The region is a puzzle box to be opened up, Archmagos,' said Devwyn. His voice was natural as his larynx had yet to be augmented or replaced. 'The unknown nature of its contents has dissuaded many, otherwise brave and knowledgeable men, from solving this puzzle. I can think of nothing more worthwhile than working towards gaining an insight into the forces that created this place, and the entities that might dwell herein.'

Voar turned away from his magi. The cogitator units built into his thoracic spine whirred as they augmented his thought processes. It was knowledge the Adeptus Mechanicus sought, and it was knowledge that would guide him.

The command altar of the bridge was on top of a shallow pyramid rising from the labyrinthine library, kilometres of bookshelves winding in a complicated pattern that filled the bridge. Thousands of books and data-slates, loaded with accumulated space-faring wisdom and the philosophy of the Cult Mechanicus, loaded the shelves and stood in piles at every intersection. The ship's navigation crew, tech-priests in their red, cog-toothed robes, stood poring over stellar maps inked on parchment, plotting courses with compasses and quill pens. Dark grottoes among the bookshelf caves hid communications and sensorium helms. The ordnance crew had a room of glass-fronted cases holding rare and sacred tomes of naval battle-lore. They did their bloody work with abaci on large map-tables scattered with markers representing the ship and the area around it. The bridge had few direct readouts of the area around the ship, such as a viewscreen or tactical orrery, because the crew of the *Antithesis* solved most problems through abstract mathematics and geometry rather than through the sensory guesswork that governed lesser craft.

'We forge on,' repeated Voar. 'The Omnissiah's work has yet to be done in this place, and it will be another age before the Veiled Region is penetrated again. Your misgivings have some truth about them, however, and we are to treat the Veiled Region as hostile territory. We have reached the end of the von Carnath Plateau, the only stable route into the region, and soon we will pass beyond the point where our astropaths can communicate with the outside Imperium. Should we encounter trouble, Mars will be ignorant of our plight. Though we go on, we will pray for deliverance from the enemies that surely lie in wait for us. Return to your craft, scholars of Mars, and ensure that their crews are ready for battle.'

The magi bowed and left the bridge, leaving Voar on his pyramid.

Unexplored space: there was so much of it. After ten thousands years questing, only a fraction of the Imperium had been properly explored and catalogued. It was a sacred task that, like humanity's many other battles, would never end, and yet required the dedication of its servants to the exclusion of all else. Space beyond the Von Carnath Plateau was completely unknown, and, for anyone but the Mechanicus with their sacred duties and technology, entering it would be both suicidal and illegal.

Voar looked at the alien mask he still carried. Its obscenity was one of defiled brilliance, of high technology deformed to meet an alien vision. If the principles behind it could be uncovered then one more line of the Omnissiah's eternal work, the book of all knowledge, would be written.

One of the tech-priests was ascending the pyramid. The tech-priest was of sufficiently low rank and limited augmentations that gender was still apparent; it was a woman, with eyes obscured by smoky lenses and her hair tied back to reveal a large information port on her temple.

'Archmagos,' she said.

'Report.'

'We have a contact.'

The Adeptus Mechanicus fleet that flew in a shoal around the *Antithesis* had been assembled on Mars. The *Antithesis* was a cruiser-class vessel, not quite the equal of one of the Imperium's ancient mighty battle-ships, but a swift and well-crewed ship with enough Martian-forged armaments to punch above her weight. Her sister ship, the *Constant*, was slower and less manoeuvrable, but much more heavily gunned, and sported an enormous nova cannon on her prow that could blow an enemy cruiser clean in two. The *Constant* was under the command of Magos Hepsebah who trusted no one but herself to operate the nova cannon. Both craft were in the dark red of the Adeptus Mechanicus, with the half-steel skull of Mars worn as proud heraldry.

Several armed explorator ships of the Asclepian Squadron flew a picket around the two cruisers. They were smaller craft, but they were hardy, built for exploring harsh regions and for resisting the worst excesses of stellar radiation and micrometeorite impacts. They made for capable escort craft, tough enough to weather enemy fire and nimble enough to outfox slower enemies. They had been difficult for Voar to acquire since they had been destined to explore the Imperium's Eastern Fringes. Magos Khrul, his speciality being the same kind of deep-space hostile exploration at which the squadron excelled, was in command.

The light cruiser *Defence of Caelano Minoris* had been fitted out as a laboratory ship, its gun decks stripped out and replaced with medical labs and crucible chambers to research anything the fleet might find. A whole deck was sealed and gene-locked so it could be used for the study of alien artefacts. The *Defence* was the domain of Magos Crystavayne and Magos Devwyn. It usually flew in the wake of the *Ferrous*, an armed factory ship that wallowed obesely through space, dragging an enormous processing and storage section behind it, plumes of plasma fire bursting through the vents down its spine as it turned its cargo of harvested ore and chemicals into fuel for the rest of the fleet. Magos Vionel, the commander of the *Ferrous*, was as much a part of the ship as its chemical tanks and fusion chambers were.

The final element of the fleet, and by far the largest, was the swarm of smaller explorator ships, armed merchantmen, tech-guard transports, cargo containers and single-squadron fighter platforms collectively known as the Fleet Minor. They flew around the larger ships in a silver cloud, serving as flying laboratories, scouts, storage space and fighter response. Should crews be lost on the cruisers, ships of the Fleet Minor could be decommissioned and their crews used to replace the dead. In a naval battle, the Fleet Minor could spoil the aim of enemy ships, outflank hostile formations and distract enemy guns from the real targets. On a mission like the exploration of the Veiled Region, the ships of the Fleet Minor were a mathematical necessity.

The contact picked up by the sensorium dome on the *Antithesis* was some way ahead of the fleet, obscured into a vague shadow by the stellar dust that choked the Veiled Region beyond the Plateau. It was huge, though, far bigger than any ships of the Mechanicus fleet. No ship of the Imperium, even a titanic battleship of the Battlefleet Solar, had ever been built that big.

There were only two possible identities for such a contact. First, it was a craft of alien design built with technology that allowed for immense size. Secondly, it was a space hulk.

'We're being followed,' said Techmarine Lygris, rapidly skimming the reams of statistics spooling out of a bridge cogitator. The rest of the bridge was dominated by several cogitators salvaged from other parts of the space hulk known as the *Brokenback*. They were ill-matched chunks of technology, with exposed circuit boards and banks of valve-switches, constantly clattering and humming. The rest of the bridge looked like it had once been a theatre, with ornate decorative panels fixed to the walls, drilled through to accommodate bundles of cables. It had once been dominated by a viewscreen, which was now blank and blind.

Every sensor and system that still worked on the *Brokenback* was hooked into a web created by Lygris so he always knew what was going on in and around the ship, as well as being able to command it, from the bridge. Lygris had summoned Chapter Master Sarpedon to the bridge shortly before the space hulk exited von Carnath's Plateau and entered unknown space. A couple of other Soul Drinkers were attending to Lygris on the bridge, monitoring the various readouts and sensors, but even the tall armoured shape of a Space Marine looked relatively insignificant compared to the mutant shape of Sarpedon in the ornate armour of the Chapter Librarium.

'Who?' asked Sarpedon.

Lygris glanced down at the data-slate he held, which was wired up to one of the cogitators. 'It's a fleet. A big one. We're too close to the nebula to see much more, but they'll be watching us. They must be taking the Plateau into the region, too.'

Sarpedon, Chapter Master and senior Librarian of the Soul Drinkers Chapter, sat back on the haunches of his eight mutant legs and thought about the predicament.

'I had hoped that, here of all places, we would be alone,' he said. 'As soon as Chaplain Iktinos suggested this place, I knew he was right. The Imperium hasn't tried to explore the Veiled Region for thousands of years. Now there's a fleet on our tail. Can we outrun them?'

'Hard to say,' said Lygris. 'Dropping into the warp here isn't something I'd relish under fire. Just because this hulk's warp-capable doesn't mean I can get all its engines pulling in the same direction without more time to prepare.'

'Can we tell if they're armed?'

'There's at least a couple of cruisers in there. Nothing that big flies into a place like this without being able to handle itself.'

'Set us to battle stations. Get ready to flee as soon as you can. We'll stand and fight until then.'

'As you wish, commander.' Lygris made a few adjustments to the data-slate, and the space hulk's vox-casters blared a warning. The bridge was bathed in deep red light.

Soul Drinkers ran through the corridors past the bridge to their assigned battle stations. There were barely two hundred and fifty Space Marines left in the Chapter, and the last of the Chapter serfs had succumbed to battle or the rigours of space a long time ago. It was a tiny crew for a ship so vast, and Lygris's command of tech-lore was most apparent in the way the space hulk could be commanded at all.

When the Soul Drinkers had first entered the *Brokenback* it was an abomination, an alien-infested amalgamation of dozens of Imperial and xenos ships, lost in the warp to be welded together and spat out again centuries later. The Soul Drinkers had boarded and cleansed it to use as their base of operations. A space hulk was a symbol of the warp's corruption, a harbinger of dread things from beyond real space. It seemed fitting that the outcast Soul Drinkers should have made such a dreaded place their home.

'How's our ordnance?' asked Sarpedon.

'We uncovered a stock of torpedoes on one of the cruiser sections,' said Lygris. 'Very old. High explosive, armour piercing heads. Better than anything the Imperial Navy has. They'll be in the tubes within an hour.'

'Good. I take it you'll remain on the bridge to command. Where do you want me?'

'I had Scout Sergeant Eumenes commanding one of the gun decks,' said Lygris, 'which leaves us one short there.'

'Then I should replace him,' said Sarpedon. 'After all, I'm the one who killed him.'

The relative calm of the Plateau was replaced with the gluey, dust-heavy void of the Veiled Region proper. The enormous vessel being followed by the Mechanicus fleet had dived into the mire, and the fleet had followed, every tech-priest and magos amongst its crews uttering prayers to the machine-spirits of the ships. Normal space died out, and the nebulae of the Veiled Region seemed to crowd around the fleet, reaching out with overlapping fields of lethal radiation, and throwing off flares of half-born stars. The fleet, however, had the advantage of collected millennia of naval lore, and it made good speed through the outer reaches of the Veiled Region. It closed in on the target ship, hundreds of sensorium arrays scouring it to collect a picture of its shape and the energy signatures flickering through it.

All of the information was filtered through to the sensorium grotto, a cave-like appendix to the bridge-library of the *Antithesis*. It was crammed with information that did not take the form of books or dataslates: carved tablets, symbolic statues, and paintings stacked up against one wall. Amongst all this were the sensorium readouts, mostly autoquills spilling out reams of parchment covered in jagged signal lines and pict screens showing streams of numbers. Archmagos Voar peered over the shoulder of one of the tech-priests, watching as the data was compiled into the first image of their quarry.

The forward sensors of the Fleet Minor depicted something so grotesque that they were checked over and over again to make sure they were correct. The enemy ship was a conglomeration of fused spacecraft the size of a city. Every element was deformed and merged with the craft next to it, and its every curve and rupture bore the hallmarks of the warp. It had been born there, in the abyss of the immaterium, from hundreds of ships that had become lost in the warp and gravitated towards this foul lump of tortured metal.

The closest thing to a visual the fleet had was a composite holo-image, fragmented where the sensors had been foxed by the stellar dust.

'It's a space hulk,' said the sensorium tech-priest, 'a big one. The archives put it in the tenth percentile.'

'Signs of life?'

'There's too much interference for any more data.'

Archmagos Voar inspected the grainy image as it revolved above the holo-unit.

'That,' he said, indicating a long stretch of the space hulk's hull, 'is an Imperial craft. And here, this fin towards the stern. An eldar craft, used by their pirates. Xenos.' Voar spat out the last word as if it tasted bad. 'Input all your data to the ordnance decks. Work with them on firing solutions.'

'Yes, archmagos.'

Voar strode through the sensorium grotto, mechanical feet clacking on the stone floor. He emerged into the less stifling gloom of the library. Tech-priests were hurrying between stations, jostling past menials and servitors, carrying stacks of books containing armament equations and tech-liturgies for ministering to the ship's machine-spirit.

'Magos Hepsebah?' said Voar into his internal vox-unit.

'Hepsebah here,' replied the magos aboard the *Constant*.

'You should be receiving firing data from the *Antithesis* and the Fleet Minor. What is your state of readiness?'

'All gun decks are loaded and ready, archmagos,' said Hepsebah. She was still human enough to have a trace of pride in her voice. Hepsebah's calling was weaponry, and few weapons could be more sacred than the mighty guns of a spacecraft. She had seen to it that the *Constant's* gun crews were so well-drilled they could put the proudest Imperial Navy crews to shame.

'And the nova cannon?'

'I am in the process of priming it.'

'Good. You have my permission to break formation and attain high ventral vantage over the target.'

'It will be done, archmagos. What is our plan of engagement?'

'The fleet will pin the enemy down,' said Voar. 'And you will kill it.'

A space hulk was more than a material threat. It was an object of religious hatred for the Mechanicus. There were few tech-heresies as grave as xenos ships being melded with Imperial craft. Those Imperial ships had been sacred once, their machine-spirits ancient things before whom tech-priests knelt and begged for counsel. They were vessels of the Omnissiah's wisdom as well as the Emperor's might, god-machines that represented the human race's greatest achievements in conquering the galaxy. Now they were dead and defiled, inhabited by Throne knew what aliens and blasphemers.

Death was the only punishment.

The Fleet Minor broke out of formation and thrust forwards, thousands of engines flaring like fireflies. Countermeasures were launched, bursting in silver fireworks, throwing sensor-baffling filaments everywhere. The *Antithesis* barged forwards, parting the smaller ships in front of it like an icebreaker, swinging to one side to bring its broadside guns to bear. The rest of the fleet moved around it, the Asclepian Squadron closing in to form a picket around the cruiser.

The fighter squadron carriers, *Sunblade* and *Daggerfall*, platforms shaped like thin cylinders with fighter craft and bombers clustered around them like fruit on the vine, spun through the clouds of chaff to send their squadrons lancing forwards on columns of flame. Electronic warfare ships followed them in towards the enemy, electromagnetic fields crackling between them to form blind spots where the fighters would be safe until they began their attack runs.

The *Constant* rose above it all, protected by its shield of Fleet Minor ships, and blue flames flickered around the barrel of the nova cannon that jutted from its prow.

Sarpedon reached the gun deck. Most of the automated loaders had been reactivated by Lygris's efforts, but plenty of the enormous broadside guns still had to be loaded manually. The Soul Drinkers saluted Sarpedon as he arrived. Sergeant Salk was at the nearest gun, directing his squad to haul the chains, dragging a tank-sized shell into the gun's enormous breech. It was one of a dozen along the steel canyon of an Imperial ship, the *Intolerant*, one of the largest warships in the *Brokenback*'s construction. Sarpedon remembered exploring the place for the first time when the space hulk had first been cleared by the Soul Drinkers. It was amazing that the dead ship's destructive force had been reawakened by Lygris.

'Commander!' called Salk. 'What are we up against?'

'We'll know soon enough. What can I do?'

'Gun eight needs another strong arm.'

Sarpedon glanced down the deck towards gun eight; several Soul Drinkers from Iktinos's command were working it. They were amongst the Soul Drinkers who had lost their officers and chosen to follow the Chapter's Chaplain into battle, forming a flock devoted to Iktinos, who fought with a zeal that bordered on recklessness.

'Then I'll lend them a few limbs of my own,' said Sarpedon. Salk saluted and returned to his gun team. Salk was developing into a very fine officer. He had been new to squad command when the Soul Drinkers had first turned away from the Imperium. Now, he had something new to fight for, and he had become one of Sarpedon's most trusted sergeants. Like the rest of the Chapter, he was learning to strike out on his own.

One of Iktinos's Soul Drinkers was hauling a shell towards gun eight. Sarpedon joined the man, crouched down on his arachnoid haunches and lifted the shell, forcing it the last few metres and into the gun's breech. The other Space Marines slammed the shell home and closed the breech door.

'Ready!' shouted the Soul Drinker crouching at the top of the gun's housing, peering through the targeting reticle that let him see the scene outside the ship. 'Targets! Multiple, small, approaching fast!'

'Lygris,' voxed Sarpedon. 'Who are they?'

'Larger craft supported by smaller,' said Lygris from the bridge. 'They're bringing a lot of interference. Looks Imperial.'

Sarpedon gave this a moment's through. The Imperial Navy would fire on a space hulk if they found one, certainly. Even if they realised there were Space Marines on board, one glimpse of the Chapter's mutations, not least Sarpedon's eight-legged form, would convince them that they were dealing with traitors, and they would redouble their efforts to pound the *Brokenback* to dust.

'Got a good look at one,' continued Lygris. 'It matches one of the marks in the archives, a Sapience-class cruiser. It's the Adeptus Mechanicus, commander.'

'The past is death. But the future is worse still – it is an existence on which order and sanity have yet to be imposed. To fight it, the past is the only weapon we have.'

– Daenyathos, *The Armaments of the Soul*

CHAPTER TWO

The Soul Drinkers and the Adeptus Mechanicus had history.

The Adeptus Mechanicus had sought to recover the pre-Imperial artefact known as the Soulspear, so it could be properly studied. The Soul Drinkers, on the other hand, had wanted it returned to them as it was a relic of their Chapter, and, in particular, of Rogal Dorn, the Chapter's primarch, who had given it to the fledgling Soul Drinkers upon their foundation after the Horus Heresy. The rift thus created had been the first in a series of betrayals that had led the Soul Drinkers to break with Imperial authority, become excommunicated from the human race, and ply a new future as a renegade Space Marine Chapter.

The Inquisition, taking responsibility for hunting down the Soul Drinkers, had ordered the Chapter's name deleted from all Imperial records, so that the danger inherent in the very idea of a renegade Chapter would not imperil the minds of the galaxy's citizens.

The Adeptus Mechanicus did not always follow the dictates of the Inquisition to the letter.

'You are certain of this?' asked Archmagos Voar, looking down at the data-slate in his hand. He was seated on the command throne at the top of the pyramid in the centre of the bridge, surrounded by tactical printouts brought to him by the ordnance and sensorium crew. The tech-priest that had handed him the data-slate was from the

communications crew, who occupied a section of the library dominated
by a monstrous switchboard with thousands of sockets and cables.

'Every piece of data we have is consistent with this conclusion,' said
the tech-priest.

'I see.' Voar put down the data-slate and picked up a book fetched by
a menial from the rare and sacred books section. It was one of the few
copies in existence, since it had been ordered burned by Inquisitorial
deletion squads in the great libraries of the Imperium. No doubt not
one copy remained in the archives of the Inquisition. A golden chalice
was embossed on its cover. It was a military history of the Soul Drinkers
Space Marine Chapter. 'You were right to bring this to my attention. Go
about the Omnissiah's work, brother of Mars.'

The tech-priest bowed and turned away.

'One moment,' said Voar. The tech-priest halted. 'Summon an
astropath.'

The tech-priest hurried down to the pyramid to attend to his orders.

The news he had brought was unexpected, and Voar allowed himself
the luxury of a few moments' thought. The Adeptus Mechanicus had a
long memory; a grudge lasted a lot longer in a bank of data-medium
than it did in a human mind. That memory was not easily erased. The
Mechanicus knew the name of the Soul Drinkers and of the rebel who
led them, Commander Sarpedon. Sarpedon had killed Mechanicus
tech-priests in taking possession of the Soulspear, and had resisted the
best efforts of the Inquisition to bring him and his Chapter to justice.
The Adeptus Mechanicus, in defiance of the deletion order, had collected all the information they could find on the Soul Drinkers. One
such piece of information suggested that the Soul Drinkers were making use of a space hulk named the *Brokenback*, the description of which
had set off an alert in the archive of the *Antithesis*.

'This is Voar,' he voxed to the magi commanding his fleet. 'Target
identified. No prisoners.'

The guns of the *Brokenback* roared, and the seeker shells, relics of an
earlier age of technology, erupted from the enormous broadside guns,
spiralling on columns of fire through the void. Armed with their own
cogitators they sought out targets of opportunity, and drove into the
cloud of smaller ships in the vanguard of the Mechanicus fleet. Blossoms of atomic fire erupted and imploded darkly in the vacuum,
leaving silvery sprays of wreckage.

On the gun deck of the *Intolerant*, Sarpedon watched them on a
grainy pict screen hooked up to the gun's own simple sensors. At this
distance, the enemy cruisers were visible as silver darts illuminated by
light reflected off the surrounding nebulae, and the smaller craft as
sprinkled points of light. Many of them were gone in those first few

moments, homed in on by the seeker shells, and blasted into burning dust.

From Sarpedon's position, perched up on the housing of the gun, he could see right down the gun deck. Twenty guns, most of them automated and the rest operated by the Soul Drinkers, roared in unison. Loading cranes swung into action, and the Soul Drinkers began to reload their guns, their forms in purple power armour scrambling over the gun housings to haul the breech doors open and drag more shells into position. Sarpedon made ready to drop to the deck and lend his enormous strength to the task, when he caught movement on the pict screen: a glittering spray of ships approaching fast, wheeling in formation to approach.

'It's a bombing run!' shouted Sarpedon. 'Get to cover!'

Guided missiles sliced down from the weapon mounts of the approaching bombers. Automated turrets, studding the *Brokenback*'s hull, opened up as they approached, snaring them in a lattice of laser fire. Many were destroyed, sliced in two by the lines of white-hot light, but not before they had released their payloads. Most Imperial Navy craft would have needed to get much closer to strike, but the targeting systems of the Adeptus Mechanicus were superior, and their ordnance streaked into the gun deck of the *Intolerant*.

Sarpedon leapt off the gun mounting. He braced his legs and hit the far wall, his talons finding purchase on the metal. He clung to the wall as the first missile hit home, erupting in white flame at the far end of the gun deck, and shattering the massive structure of a broadside gun. The shock wave hit him, and he clung on as Soul Drinkers were thrown off their feet below him.

The wave of flame was sucked away as the atmosphere shrieked out through the hull breach. Sarpedon's power armour was airtight and could use its own air supply in a vacuum. He still had to hold on, though, as the air ripped past him. Some of the Soul Drinkers below were dragged along by the force of it, grabbing on to loading machinery or grilles in the floor to keep from being pulled through the breach. Silence hammered down as the air was depleted, replaced with the vibrations of the guns, and the space hulk's engines through the metal wall transmitted up Sarpedon's talons.

Sarpedon dropped to the floor and ran for the relative safety of the *Intolerant*'s internal decks. Another missile hit closer, blowing another gun off its mountings and sending the steel tower of the gun barrel somersaulting through the wall. The sounds of destruction boomed through the floor, surreally distant in the vacuum.

The Imperial ship's alarm systems, rigged back to working order by Lygris, were blaring. Sarpedon was in the maintenance decks for the ammunition systems, narrow walkways and corridors slung across steel chasms between the shell hoppers. The loading systems' massive conveyor belts and cranes were clanking along overhead and below, feeding ammunition to the guns that still worked.

'Salk!' shouted Sarpedon into the vox. 'Report! Any casualties?'

'Brother Thoss is down,' replied Sergeant Salk. 'Looks like one of Iktinos's men is dead too.' Over Salk's vox Sarpedon could hear the booming reports of more impacts, scattered with the vibrations from the *Brokenback*'s guns.

'Where are you?'

'Still on the deck. We're regrouping and sounding off.'

'Get out of there.'

'Already on it. We're heading for the cargo decks. We'll put a few hull layers between us and the breach. Salk out.'

Sarpedon switched to Lygris's vox-channel.

'The *Intolerant*'s been hit,' he said.

'I'm tracking the incoming bombers now,' said Lygris. Sarpedon could hear the whirr of cogitators behind his voice. 'They're all over us.'

'Can we take them?'

'Of course. But they're not the danger. They're just spoiling our aim so the cruisers can hit us.'

'How much damage can they do?'

'Ordinarily, a cruiser wouldn't put much of a dent in a hulk this size. But the Mechanicus has plenty of tricks that could hurt.'

Sarpedon knew there were two choices: stand and fight, or flee. The Mechanicus clearly thought they had enough firepower to hurt the *Brokenback*. And the Soul Drinkers would gain nothing from fighting a battle here.

'How long until the warp drives are ready?' asked Sarpedon.

'Another ten minutes.'

'Then get us out of here as soon as you can. The *Intolerant* is being abandoned.'

'Yes, commander. I suggest you and Salk's men go on to damage control. The Mechanicus will get a few free swings at us before we're gone.'

'On my way.'

The *Intolerant* shook as more ordnance hit home. Smaller impacts, like sparks crackling against the hull, were the remains of fighters and bombers scattering against the *Brokenback* after the turrets had done their work.

The Constant drifted up out of formation into a high firing angle. The space hulk's guns, formidable as they were, had been too busy fending off the wasp-like attacks of the Fleet Minor to pay the cruiser any mind until it was too late.

Magos Hepsebah aimed the nova cannon. She had designed it and overseen its fitting to the chassis of the *Constant*, turning it from a vessel of the line into a ship-killer. The barrel was so large it gave the cruiser a lopsided look as if it should topple off balance and tumble through space helplessly, but the cruiser's thrusters kept its enormous mass still as Hepsebah lined up her shot.

No single kill shot could be taken against a space hulk. It was a welded mass of dozens of ships, and any one of them might house the bridge, or the ordnance hangars, or the reactors. Hepsebah's duty was simply to do as much damage as possible.

A burning mass on the side of the space hulk that had once been an Imperial ship was ruined and ablaze. There was little point hitting it again. The swollen rearward quarters of the ship were composed of enormous container ships and beetle-like carapaces of massive alien hulks, which looked like they contained little more than empty space and debris. Hepsebah aimed towards the front of the ship, some way down below the reinforced armour of an ancient warship and a forbidding tangle of silvery alien craft. The ships there were many and densely packed, with more chance of important systems surviving.

Hepsebah ordered the firing chamber menials to drag the two enormous hemispheres of radioactive metal together. Hundreds of men hauled on chains, their muscles burning under their skin in the heat of the firing chamber, their taskmaster barking rhythmic orders to keep the hemispheres swinging. The hemispheres clashed, rang like a great deep bell, and released a massive wave of power funnelled by electromagnetic fields into the accelerator formed by the cannon's barrel. The force of it hit the enormous nova projectile, accelerating it down the barrel at impossible speeds.

The nova cannon fired, and, for a fraction of a second, the *Constant* and the hulk were connected by a bridge of burning light.

Sarpedon arrived at the reactor array of the *Blessed Obedience*, the enormous industrial ship containing many of the plasma reactors that Lygris had got back on-line to make the space hulk warp-capable. The reactor chamber was enormous, close to a kilometre long, criss-crossed with catwalks that gave access to the titanic cylindrical forms of the reactors. The *Blessed Obedience* had carried a dozen such reactors in some previous life as a space-faring refinery, each one powerful enough to fuel a spaceship for decades. Every one of the cylinders contained a vessel full of superheated plasma, locked in a constant reaction that pumped power into the hulk's warp arrays. They were crowned with spider-like arrays of steel struts, supporting the cables and pipes that provided the reactors with fuel and coolant, and drew off their massive outputs of power.

Sarpedon hurried along a gantry between reactors one and two.

Chaplain Iktinos was on a command platform just ahead, along with several of his flock.

'Commander Sarpedon,' voxed Iktinos as he saw Sarpedon approaching. 'I hear on the vox-net that our brothers have fallen.'

'Thoss of Squad Salk, and Renigel of your flock,' said Sarpedon. 'He died when the *Intolerant* was hit. The enemy is going to throw everything he has at us. I am afraid that prayers will have to wait.'

'So it shall be,' said Iktinos.

Sarpedon switched his vox-net to the bridge channel. 'Lygris, I'm at the reactors. It looks like they're holding up well.'

'Stay there,' replied Lygris from the bridge. 'If we lose the *Obedience* then we're done–'

A sound like the death of a world hammered across the reactor chamber. One wall blew in, hurling a hurricane of shredded metal. The nova projectile detonated, and a great gale of fire and shrapnel ripped across the *Obedience*, sending white-hot shards of shrapnel arrowing everywhere.

The shock wave threw Sarpedon off the gantry, slamming him into the wall. His head swam with the force of it. If he hadn't been wearing his helmet he would have been knocked out. Enough of him remained unshaken to remind him that if he fell, he would probably die. Talons lashed out in a reflex, and dug into the wall of the reactor chamber, halting him as he fell.

The reverberations of the explosion bellowed around the chamber. One wall had been completely demolished, beyond it only a glowing labyrinth of torn bulkheads and decking. A gale of fire howled into the maw of the wound as the air was sucked out through the hull breach.

The explosion had sent shards of shrapnel spearing through the vessels of reactors eleven and nine. Reactor eleven collapsed, its upper half too heavy for the shredded foundations. Deep splits opened up as the reactor's crown fell back into the lake of plasma inside, and raw, white burning plasma looped out in great arcs like solar flares, the massive release of pressure sending it lashing in destructive tongues through the roof of the reactor chamber. Gobbets of it bored through walkways and command platforms. A great torrent burst from the lower half of the reactor and flowed in a glowing flood through the tangle of conduits and cabling that obscured the chamber floor.

Sarpedon was aware of another shape falling towards him: a Space Marine. He stuck out an arm and grabbed the falling Soul Drinker by his shoulder pad. The weight almost pulled Sarpedon off the wall, but he held on. He had caught one of Iktinos's flock, the purple paint on his armour bubbling with the heat.

Sarpedon climbed until he was level with the stub of a walkway. Most of it had been ripped away and thrown into the chamber's depths, but enough of it remained to hold the weight of a Space Marine. It joined the wall at a maintenance entrance. Sarpedon hauled the Soul Drinker onto the walkway, and was relieved to see that he was still alive.

Sarpedon looked across the chamber, trying to see more survivors. He spotted a couple of Iktinos's flock clinging to a precarious length of walkway, making their way towards a command post that had survived mostly intact. From there, they could make it up a ladder into the access tunnels above the chamber. Iktinos himself had been thrown onto the top of reactor three, and was making his way towards the crown of pipes and cables connecting it to the ceiling.

'Lygris!' yelled Sarpedon into the vox. The last of the chamber's air was shrieking and superheated, a terrible sound like a gale of fire. 'Lygris, what in the hells was that?'

Lygris's voice barely swam through the static. 'Direct hit! Commander, give me a damage report!'

'Reactors eleven and nine are breached,' replied Sarpedon. 'Eleven's venting plasma. Nine's about to go.'

'Evacuate the area,' replied Lygris.

The last words had barely reached Sarpedon's ears when reactor nine exploded, the pressure inside too much for its failing structure. A pure white starburst of plasma erupted, like a caged supernova, and the structures surrounding reactor nine were obliterated. Bolts of plasma streaked into the nearby reactors, shearing more maintenance walkways from their mountings. The sound, just a vibration transmitted through the wall to which Sarpedon clung, was like the roar of an escaping giant.

The glare died down. Iktinos was crouching from the shock wave of the explosion, still clinging to reactor three.

'Chaplain,' voxed Sarpedon, 'are you hurt?'

'I am not, commander,' replied Iktinos. His voice was distorted almost beyond understanding. 'But there is no way off this reactor.'

'There is for me,' said Sarpedon. 'Hold position. I'm coming for you.'

Sarpedon ran up the wall towards the ceiling. The whole chamber shuddered as the remains of reactor eleven collapsed into the floor. Plasma flooded the lower levels, swallowing up enormous bundles of cables and drowning the lowest walkways. Reactor twelve was sitting in a lake of plasma, and was listing as its foundations were eroded. Below the chamber plasma would be flowing through the rest of the *Obedience*, looking for ways into the ships surrounding it. It would melt its way through a huge area of the *Brokenback*, like a cancer, if it wasn't stopped.

Sarpedon was above reactor three. He could see that a spear of shrapnel had punctured the reactor's side, and plasma was spurting from the wound. The crack was widening, and, every second, the sheet of vented energy grew wider.

Sarpedon ran down a coolant pipe to the top of the reactor. Iktinos was waiting for him.

Iktinos reached up. Sarpedon grabbed the Chaplain's wrist and hauled him off his feet.

Reactor three shuddered and leaned suddenly to one side. Sarpedon glanced up; the conduits were coming away from the ceiling. There would be no way off the reactor in that direction. He spotted a length of walkway hanging from one wall, half-melted away by a bolt of plasma. Sarpedon shifted his grip so that he was dragging Iktinos behind him by the collar of his armour. He crouched down on his back legs and uncoiled, sprinting at full tilt towards the edge of the reactor.

Reactor three split down the middle. Sheets of plasma sprayed out, forming a wall of fire behind Sarpedon as he ran. Metal screamed and heat roared. The metal below Sarpedon's talons became unbearably hot.

Sarpedon reached the edge and jumped with the power of every muscle packed into his arachnid legs. He reached forwards and his hand closed on the handrail of the walkway. The whole structure bent with the weight of the two Space Marines. Iktinos clambered over Sarpedon, pulling himself onto the walkway, before hauling Sarpedon up after him.

'My gratitude, commander,' voxed Iktinos.

Reactor three split completely in two, a torrent of plasma flooding through the lower levels. Sarpedon got to his feet and followed Iktinos towards the doorway where the walkway joined the wall. Another reactor breached as they ran, sinking into the burning mire and splitting open. A wall of radiated heat buffeted them as Iktinos reached the door and hauled it open.

Beyond was a dark, cramped maintenance space, leading to the cargo ship adjoining the *Blessed Obedience*. Sarpedon followed Iktinos through the darkness as the booming vibrations of dying reactors got louder.

'Lygris,' voxed Sarpedon to the bridge, 'we're clear.'

'I'm shutting down the *Obedience*,' replied Lygris. Sarpedon could hear every alarm on the space hulk's bridge blaring at once. 'Make sure you're well clear. That whole area will be lethal.'

'Can you get us out of here?'

'With the reactors down? I can make it into the warp, maybe.'

'Then do it. Whatever hit us will want a kill-shot.'

'Yes, commander,' voxed Lygris. 'I suggest you hold on.'

'Got it,' said Magos Hepsebah with relish. Seated in the targeting observatory of the *Constant*, surrounded by the holo-projections of surrounding stars and spacecraft, she watched another flare of plasma burst from the side of the space hulk. 'Target report!'

Tech-priests' voices from the ship's sensorium filtered back to her through the vox-net.

'Major secondary explosions...'

'Confirm plasma vent. Target reactor breach.'

'Target power levels fluctuating beyond parameters...'

'Arming chamber!' ordered Hepsebah. 'Full recharge! Navigation, line us up for another shot!'

She spun the barrels of the multilaser she carried in place of her left arm. Nothing fired the passions in her like a direct hit: the sum of all her knowledge, brought forth in a single moment of destruction. Such a wonder could only be possible through the Omnissiah's will.

'Magos Hepsebah, excellent damage,' said Voar's voice from the *Antithesis*. 'The Fleet Minor is disengaging. We will coordinate fire and complete the kill.'

'Yes, archmagos,' said Hepsebah. 'The Soul Drinkers, they once did the Mechanicus wrong?'

'Most gravely so,' said Voar.

'Then it will be a pleasure to call in the debt.'

The holo flared red. Indicators around the image of the space hulk showed an enormous power spike.

'Geller fields active!' came an alert from one of the tech-priests in the sensorium.

'They're hitting the warp!' shouted Hepsebah. 'They're insane. That space hulk's bleeding to death. The warp will swallow it alive.'

'It has survived an aeon in the warp,' said Voar. 'Do not presume to know the capabilities of such an enemy.'

'Hit it with everything we have! Now!'

Most of the *Constant's* offensive power was tied up in the nova cannon, but she still sported plenty of medium-range guns and torpedoes. Every one of them fired, spraying massive calibre fire towards the space hulk, even as the enemy ship was surrounded by a shimmering field projected by what power remained in its wounded reactors. Shots tore through the field and impacted against the hull. The *Antithesis* joined in, and a tremendous broadside hammered against the hulk's side, ripping chunks of spacecraft away, and exposing burning metal innards below. Secondary explosions rippled where stored ammunition detonated, and plumes of vented air burst from the impacts.

Space tore. A slash opened up in front of the hulk, so dark it was blacker even than the void. Power boiled within it, a monumental, malicious reflection of the Veiled Region in another dimension. The space hulk sank into it, explosions still studding its gnarled surface as the rip in space swallowed it up.

The holo blinked, and the space hulk was gone.

'We've lost them,' said Hepsebah. She slammed her multilaser against the observatory wall. 'Damn it! We had them! We had them, and we lost them!' She sat back in the observatory command chair, watching the debris cooling and falling off sensor range.

'Even in the Veiled Region, a wounded space hulk cannot pass without leaving a trail,' said Archmagos Voar. 'We have not lost them for long.'

'Once, I saw the xenos as a terrifying threat, the harbingers of our galaxy's destruction. Now I know them for what they are. Vermin, parasites, suckling at the wounds of a galaxy that belongs to humankind.'

– Daenyathos, *War Incarnate*

CHAPTER THREE

'I had thought,' said Sarpedon, 'that no one would find me here.'

The garden of reflection looked like it should have been part of a pleasure yacht, one of the lavishly appointed spacecraft occasionally launched by the fabulously wealthy to demonstrate their superiority to the lesser mortals around them. In fact, it was a part of an Imperial Navy craft, a command ship that had no doubt once served as the nerve centre of a mighty battlefleet. Its captain may have been in command of the most destructive force in the Imperial arsenal – a fleet of battleships that could level cities with their guns – but he still needed somewhere he could be away from the babble of command. The garden's plants were mostly wilted, save for a couple of extremely hardy flowering vines and the artificial trees that flanked the entrance gates. Its raised stone flowerbeds were barren, and the trees that had once formed a secluded pocket of the spacecraft were now just sprays of withered branches. The corroded steel of the walls and ceiling loomed down over the fountain that fed a now-dry pool.

Techmarine Lygris sat down on the stone bench across from Sarpedon. 'There are few places of solace on this ship, commander. I did not have to look very hard to find you.'

'What is our situation?'

'We were able to enter the warp, but we could not stay there for long. We made it to the nebula, though. If the Adeptus Mechanicus is looking for us then they'll have a damned difficult time seeing anything through the dust clouds.'

'Then we're deeper in the Veiled Region?'

'Very deep. This is unexplored space.'

'Well, at least they're as lost as we are. What about the reactors?'

Lygris had suffered facial injuries earlier in his service as a Soul Drinker that had required the reconstruction of his entire face. It had left him with a mask of synthetic flesh, a good approximation of his features, but without the same capacity for expression. Sarpedon had learned that Lygris could be read by his eyes alone. The Techmarine's eyes told him that the news was not good.

'We're down to the dregs of fuel,' said Lygris. 'The last broadsides from the Mechanicus destroyed much of the fuel we took on board at Nevermourn. With the reactors that remain intact and the fuel we have, I can make two more warp jumps. Three would probably kill the reactors entirely. We need more fuel or we will be permanently becalmed.'

'Where can we get it?'

'There are enough working refinery units on board to turn anything from crude oil upwards into fuel. Any civilised world could provide something I could use.'

'Then let us hope we find one.' Sarpedon crouched back on his rear legs, stretching the sinews. The chitin of his spidery limbs was still charred from the plasma fires. His single bionic leg had been warped by the heat and wiring hung from the knee joint.

'You blame yourself,' said Lygris.

'Of course I do,' said Sarpedon. 'Who else is there?'

'The Mechanicus.'

'The Mechanicus wants us dead and they have good reason. They could hardly leave us be when they found us.'

'Then chance, Sarpedon. Fate.'

'No. I am responsible for my Chapter. Gorgoleon and Eumenes challenged me for command, and I killed them both. I cannot take the lives of my battle-brothers to rule this Chapter, and then pretend that I am not at fault when it suffers.'

'The fact that we survive at all is down to you. We could have been wiped out by the old Chapter or the Inquisition years ago.'

'We survive, Lygris? Barely a quarter of our strength remains. I have led us into warzones where we have escaped only at the expense of our dead brothers. Half my brothers disagreed with me so fervently that they rebelled against me and are now dead or fled. This very day, we lost more to the Mechanicus guns. What if we have not survived at all? What if we are in our death throes, wasting away to extinction?'

'If that is what you fear, Sarpedon,' said Lygris levelly, 'then extinction is exactly what will happen.'

'I will not give in, Lygris,' said Sarpedon sharply. 'I will fight until the end of time if that is what I am called upon to do. I would not have decided on this fate if I had been given the choice, but there was never a choice. We could not have fought on as the old Chapter, to pursue our own arrogance at the behest of a corrupt Imperium. When the time came there was no one else to take command, and I will not back down from the role fate has given me. That is why I am responsible for what happens to us, because I have made that choice.'

'Then do not see things to doubt in our situation,' said Lygris. 'The old Chapter sent us technical aspirants to a forge world to study with the tech-priests and learn from them the practices of the Cult Mechanicus. There I learned that a wounded machine, a smouldering wreck, is not a destroyed thing but the potential for a masterpiece. That is how the Mechanicus can make the things they do, for they see everything as a potential vessel of their Omnissiah. We are not destroyed, Sarpedon. We are not lost. There is in our defeat the potential for victory. We just have to make it right.'

'Then that is my duty. To turn this wreck into a victory.'

'If I could tell you how to do that, Sarpedon, then I would.'

'It is enough that you keep the *Brokenback* space-worthy, Lygris. Believe me, if you can do that then we will be halfway there.'

Lygris's vox-unit chirped.

'Graevus here,' came the vox.

'What news, sergeant?' replied Lygris.

'The sensorium has picked something up. There's a planetary system nearby, just within the bounds of the nebula.'

'How far?'

'A short warp jump. We're too far away to see much, but the inner planets are close enough to the star to be survivable.'

'At this point, sergeant, that will have to do.' Lygris looked up at Sarpedon. 'I am needed on the bridge.'

'Go,' said Sarpedon, 'and if you need my permission to risk a jump towards a planet, then you have it.'

'Yes, commander.'

Sarpedon watched Lygris go. The Techmarine had been there from the very beginning, and he had never faltered, not even when Sarpedon had doubted, in the chaos following the break from Imperial authority or the bloody flashpoints at Gravenholm and Stratix Luminae. Even as a student of the Mechanicus ways, Lygris had always been constant in his loyalty to Sarpedon and the new fate of the Chapter.

Sarpedon told himself that he was right. Somewhere in the wreck of the Chapter's situation in the Veiled Region, there was victory. The question was whether Sarpedon had the skill to build it.

The system was bordered by a triumvirate of dead planets, as smooth and lifeless as water-worn pebbles, standing silent guard over the approaches to the star. They were perfectly spaced from one another, surely just a fluke of the system's gravity, but looking as if they had been carefully placed to act as dead sentinels. A pair of gas giants orbited lazily beyond them, and past a band of debris and asteroids lay the inner system where the *Brokenback*'s sensors had strained to pick up an echo of life.

The system's star was swollen and reddish, entering the final stages of its life. In its aged light basked the rocky planets of the inner system, and one of them, a grey ball of heavy cloud broken by equally colourless landscapes, was alive. Sensor waves bounced back off structures that could only be cities or highways.

In high orbit over the planet, space rippled and burst, spilling the necrotic substance of the region's morbid empyrean like gore from an infected wound. The *Brokenback* limped out, still trailing tangles of vented plasma and debris. Its engines flared weakly, as if the hulk was sick. The wound in its hull left by the broadsides and bombing runs against the *Intolerant* still bled.

The hulk settled into orbit over the planet. Through the heavy cloud cover could be glimpsed hints of habitation through the eyepieces and holo-displays of the hulk's various sensors: irrigated fields of greyish crops, and black oceans sprinkled with oil platforms and spindly webs of flood defences. Lygris and the Soul Drinkers assisting him on the bridge interpreted the glimpses of structure and civilisation, and hunted for a city.

Slowly, the clouds swirled and the gaps between them passed over the surface. Eventually, they revealed the edges of a city, a cluttered sprawl of buildings piled up against a natural harbour near the equator. The sensors strained to zoom in and pick out signs of life. The city had all the hallmarks of great antiquity: unplanned and haphazard, cramped tangles of streets giving way to expanses of palaces, and concentric rings of harbour structures radiating out from docks reclaimed from the sea.

Soon afterwards, two of the *Brokenback*'s complement of armoured shuttles was launched.

It was completely silent.

That was the first impression that Sarpedon had of the planet. He had been prepared for hostilities, for indigenous humans or xenos to greet the Soul Drinkers with anti-aircraft fire and ground troops, but nothing had come out to see the shuttles land, not even gaggles of fearful spectators.

Sarpedon stepped off the ramp of his shuttle. The stubby, tough little craft had descended through the planet's clouded atmosphere without receiving or intercepting any communications. There should have been something, anything, to suggest the people down there were talking to one another.

'Still nothing,' voxed Captain Luko. Squad Luko, Squad Graevus, Lygris, Apothecary Pallas and Chaplain Iktinos made up the landing party that Sarpedon had selected. Luko had been the first out of the second shuttle, and his squad had spread into a circle to cover the shuttles' landing position from all angles.

'This place is dead,' said Graevus as his squad deployed behind Sarpedon. Graevus flexed his mutated hand, one of the Chapter's more obvious deformities aside from Sarpedon's own, which gave him the enormous strength with which he wielded his power axe.

'Squad, give me a cordon! All angles!' ordered Luko. His squad spread out and took aim at the buildings lining the area.

The shuttles had landed in a city square. Towering habitation blocks surrounded it, all in white or grey stone with dark grey or black tiles. False columns and carved lintels suggested wealth and age. One edge of the square was taken up with a large domed basilica flanked by equestrian statues; the riders were human, which meant that this was at least a human world. A few tattered merchants' stands were scattered around the square. The roads leading away from the square were empty.

There was not one person in sight. There were no birds in the sky. Even the trees were bare. It was as if the city had been drained of life, of sound and of colour.

Sarpedon let his mind reach out. As a psyker, he had enormous power but little finesse, and he could not read minds or extend his senses like some other Librarians of the Astartes. He was still sensitive enough to notice powerful psykers or the chatter of a million minds packed together, though, and, even to his mind, the city was silent.

Graevus's squad, with their jump packs primed and their chainswords drawn, followed Sarpedon and Lygris as they headed towards the closest habitation block. Like the rest of the buildings, the block was monochrome, reflecting the pale greyish sky.

'Nothing on the auspex scanner,' said Graevus.

Sarpedon opened the front doors. Stale air rolled out, dusty and old. Inside, homes led off from a central hallway, with a staircase spiralling to the upper floors above.

'Looks like post-feudal tech,' said Lygris, 'but not by much. They had electricity. One of the structures we saw from above looked like a space port.'

'This city hasn't been abandoned,' said Sarpedon. 'The buildings aren't ruins. There isn't even any sign of vermin.'

'They could have evacuated the city,' said Graevus, 'when they saw us in orbit. There are plenty of cultures where something like the *Brokenback* would be an omen of the end of the world.'

The nearest home was intact. The people of this world favoured latticed windows and ornate archways, with alcoves everywhere for keepsakes. The table was still laid. Aside from a veneer of dust, the place might have been waiting for its owners to return at any moment.

'Whatever happened here,' voxed Captain Luko from outside, 'they fought it.'

Luko's squad had approached the basilica. By the time Sarpedon had joined them, the squad had flanked the main entrance, a pair of brass doors inscribed with images of soldiers marching. Sarpedon saw that the doors and the stone around them were disfigured with bullet wounds. The statues on either side of the doors were damaged, too, the verdigrised bronze battered by gunfire.

At a signal from Sarpedon, Luko ran at the doors and slammed into them shoulder-first. The doors banged open, and Luko's lightning claws were sheathed in crackling energy as he prepared to fight. His squad stepped in behind him, guns tracking through the basilica's interior.

The interior was a ruin. Once the basilica had been grand, inlaid patterns of black and white marble covering the walls and floor of an auditorium that held court below the central minaret. Wooden benches were in splinters and shafts of pale light fell through tears in the dome.

'No bodies,' said Pallas.

Pallas had been one of the Soul Drinkers that rebelled against Sarpedon at Vanqualis. Pallas had not joined the rebels that had left the Chapter after Sarpedon's defeat of their leader Eumenes. Sarpedon had spoken to him rarely since then; the Apothecary had been key to the survival of the Chapter through controlling their mutations, but he had now withdrawn completely. 'They fought it here, but they were defeated. Then the rest of the city just... gave up.'

'This was somewhere important,' said Iktinos, examining the murals on the nearest wall. They showed stylised humans in debate, or enthroned, or marching in parades through the city's streets. 'An enemy struck here, and when they had finished there was no one left to lead a resistance.'

'And then,' Sarpedon, 'the people were rounded up, and... killed? Taken away?'

'We are assuming,' said Pallas, kneeling to examine the remains of a fallen statue, 'that they aren't still here: either the population, or the people who took them.'

Sarpedon caught a movement out of the corner of his eye. In a fluid reaction, his bolt pistol was in his left hand, and his right was at his back, ready to unsheathe the Axe of Mercaeno he carried strapped to the backpack of his armour.

A tiny black speck clung to the inside surface of the minaret.

'Commander?' said Lygris.

'It's a bird,' said Sarpedon. 'At least there's something alive here.'

The bird flitted down off the minaret. It made a metallic buzzing sound as it swooped down and hovered just above Sarpedon.

It was not a bird. It was an oversized metal insect, held aloft on silver wings, trailing bladed hinged limbs. Tiny red lenses focused on Sarpedon, and its glinting mandibles worked as if in hunger.

The beetle zipped up and disappeared through one of the holes in the minaret.

'Luko!' ordered Sarpedon. 'Get inside and seal the doors.'

'What was that?' asked Pallas.

'I don't know,' said Lygris. 'It looks beyond this world's tech level.'

Captain Luko's squad hauled the doors shut. Two of his Soul Drinkers dragged the remains of auditorium benches over to the doors to barricade them.

Chaplain Iktinos took his crozius off his belt. Like Luko's lightning claws, the crozius was a power weapon, and a blue-white energy field leapt around it. It was a badge of office as well as a weapon, topped with a bladed skull so that Iktinos could swing it like a morning star.

'I can hear them,' he said. 'The voice of the xenos calls us out.'

Sarpedon could hear it, too. A crackling, buzzing sound, deep and resonant, came to them from the grey sky visible through the circular opening in the pinnacle of the minaret. Graevus's squad took up a position in the centre of the basilica around Sarpedon and the officers. Luko's squad held the doors, ready to tear apart anything that came through, with massed bolter fire.

Sarpedon looked up. The beams of sunlight coming through the minaret were cut off.

The minaret collapsed under the weight of tens of thousands of metallic scarabs. They tumbled through the basilica roof in a tremendous metallic avalanche. Sarpedon barely had time to react before they were on him, mandibles chittering as they swarmed over his armour.

Sarpedon yelled, and swung with his axe, shattering a host of the scurrying things. Beside him, Iktinos did the same, clearing the space around him with wide sweeps of his crozius. Pallas fell to the ground, clawing at a scarab trying to bore its way into his face. Lygris dragged him to his feet, tore the creature off him and threw it to the floor. Pallas stamped on it and began blasting at the floor around him. The explosive bolter blasts shattered two or three scarabs each, but there were always more, swarming everywhere to fill the gaps.

'Flamer front!' yelled Luko over the din of the chittering creatures. 'Vorn! Burn them!'

Brother Vorn, who carried Squad Luko's flamer, stepped forwards from the doors, and hosed the area in front of him with liquid flame. The scarabs caught in the flame convulsed as whatever tiny electronics controlling them were melted by the heat. They spiralled up on burning wings like fragments of ash rising from the fire.

'They're everywhere!' shouted Sarpedon. 'Abandon this place! Make for the shuttles!'

Luko turned to the doors his squad had just barricaded, and squared up to barge them open again.

The doors burst inwards. Luko was thrown off his feet beneath the massive sheet of bronze. A creature swept in through the doorway; a solid rectangular body, longer than a Space Marine was tall, hovered impossibly off the ground. Thick, segmented legs curled up underneath it, and a pair of wicked crushing claws projected from its front edge. A head was mounted on the front, little more than a slab of metal covered in lenses and mandibles. Scarabs swarmed all over the creature. It managed to be both completely mechanical, and wholly alien.

Brother Vorn turned in time to see the pincers closing around his head. Instinctively, he blasted a plume of fire up against the creature's underside, sheathing it in billowing flame. The pincers closed, and Vorn's helmet distorted, eyepieces popping out under the pressure. The Soul Drinker was picked up off the floor, and the second pincer closed in, clamping around Vorn's arm and tearing his gun arm away to keep him from firing.

The machine's head opened up like a bladed metal flower. Mandibles jutted out and sliced down into Vorn's face. A proboscis punched out through the back of Vorn's skull, and his head burst open in a shower of blood and meat.

Sarpedon faced the machine. Bolter fire was already hammering against its armoured shell, but it looked like it could take a lot more punishment before going down. An aperture opened on the upper surface of its abdomen, revealing a forge, glowing dark red with heat, another couple of scarabs emerged from it to join the swarm.

'Lygris! Iktinos! Get us another way out! Luko, fall back from the doors!'

Sarpedon ran forwards, crunching a scarab or two under his talons, the Axe of Mercaeno in his hand. The spidery floating creature focused its eye-lenses on him, its optics winking through a layer of Vorn's blood. It dropped the Soul Drinker's body. Flame still clung to it, dripping liquidly from its legs and rippling over its hull.

Astartes from Squad Graevus were following Sarpedon towards the machine, but the scarabs were thick around them, snaring their sword arms and tangling around their feet. Sarpedon was on his own, surrounded by the scarab swarm with the machine bearing down on him.

Sarpedon dropped low, scuttling towards the xenos machine at full tilt. It raised its claws to grab him and tear him apart. Somehow, there was malice in that expressionless face, in the blank lenses and grinding mandibles.

Sarpedon slammed into it just as it began to accelerate at him. Bladed jaws snickered shut just over his head. He powered up off his back legs into its underside, slamming the Axe of Mercaeno into its side. The blade tore through the metal hull and caught there, and Sarpedon grabbed with his other arm and pulled the beast down.

He wrestled it to the ground, forcing it against its anti-gravity motors onto its back underneath him. The legs struck up at him, one catching him hard on the side of the head. Sarpedon's senses reeled and he clung on out of instinct, grabbing a flailing metallic leg and hugging it close to keep it from ripping his head off.

Sarpedon's head stopped spinning. The metal spider beneath him was writhing like a pinned insect, legs kicking out as it tried to right itself. Sarpedon ripped the axe out of its side, and cut to left and right, hacking off one of its legs. He drove his own legs into the ground on either side of its body, anchoring it to the floor of the basilica. The proboscis, like a bladed tongue, snapped up at him, but Sarpedon's reactions outstripped even the machine, and he dodged back out of its reach.

He grabbed the tongue with his free hand and pulled hard. The machine's head was forced back towards its chest. Sarpedon looked for a moment into its eyes, and saw the hatred there, the arrogance of the soulless machine, without anything human behind it.

Sarpedon's stomach churned. The machine's xenos nature was as clear as could be.

With an effort that even Sarpedon didn't know he could make, he twisted the machine's head right around on its mountings. Wires tore and fastenings snapped. He pulled again, and the head came away in its hands.

The metal spider convulsed as its motor functions went haywire. Half-formed scarabs were spat from its hull. It shuddered, its legs curled up over its upturned body, and it was still.

Sarpedon saw a tide of scarabs approaching from across the city square. Thousands of the machines formed a writhing silver-black carpet over the abandoned buildings. More bulky spiders hovered above them, multiple eyes scanning their targets in the basilica.

Sarpedon hauled the remains of the doors shut, and dragged the dead spider machine in front of them as a barricade. He turned to see how the Soul Drinkers were faring behind him. Scarabs still chittered everywhere, but the main swarm had been scattered or destroyed, and the Soul Drinkers were moving down to the far end of the basilica. Squad Graevus was close, rushing to hold the doors alongside Sarpedon. A series of explosions hammered from the rear of the basilica, and

Sarpedon recognised the reports of exploding krak grenades. Lygris had blown a hole in the rear wall of the basilica.

'I would not like to have to wait for you, commander,' voxed Lygris.

Sarpedon made for the new entrance through which Luko was already leading his squad. Pallas was with them, bleeding from the gash on the side of his face.

'Are you hurt?' asked Pallas.

'No,' said Sarpedon. 'You?'

Pallas did not answer. He ducked through the hole, and followed Iktinos and Lygris after the squads.

Beyond the basilica was a river, its banks heavy with grand buildings of government and commerce. There was evidence of a battle here, too, with bullet scars and claw marks on the walls. Sarpedon imagined that the claws had been those of mechanised spiders, closing in on the city's leaders to butcher them and throw the remains to the scarabs. A bridge led across the river, and Squad Luko was already securing it. One of Luko's men carried Vorn's body. It was a dishonour to leave a fallen brother behind, not least because the gene-seed taken from Vorn's body would be used to create the Soul Drinker that would replace him.

'A lander is coming down for us,' said Lygris. 'Fast troop ship. Jackal-class. We don't have many of them left.'

'Where are they coming down?'

'There's an ornamental garden across the river. It's large enough for a landing zone.'

'Then let's move. Soul Drinkers! Cover and run, fast!'

Sarpedon led the way across the bridge, Luko and Graevus using their squads to keep the forward and rear areas covered with bolters and bolt pistols. Beneath them, the river was choked with debris.

Not debris, bodies... hundreds of them. Their clothes were rich, embroidered togas and military uniforms. Sarpedon had seen thousands of bullet wounds in his life, and he did not see a single one on the bodies that bobbed in the filthy water. The dead had been shredded with blades or chewed up by scarab mandibles. Many of them seemed to have been dissolved away as if by acid, layers of their bodies exposed by some force that eroded skin and bone.

'We found the defenders, then,' said Luko bleakly.

The roof of the basilica collapsed, throwing up a cloud of dust and scarabs. The rear wall fell in under the gouging claws of the spiders. Luko's squad opened up with bolter fire, battering one spider back and shattering the face of another. Scarabs poured out from the ruined building, spilling into the river and scuttling along the bridge. One of Luko's squad had picked up Vorn's fallen flamer, and painted the bridge behind the Soul Drinkers with fire, incinerating the scarabs as they approached.

Sarpedon sprinted to the far end of the bridge. Squad Graevus leapt over him on the exhaust blasts of their jump packs to land in the garden beyond. A willow tree stood at the river's edge, leaves trailing in the water, and ornamental hedges cut into the shapes of fanciful animals stood between flowerbeds and mosaic paths. The flowers were all dead.

Sarpedon saw the contrails of the descending lander. It was Imperial, but of an old mark that its forge worlds had forgotten how to produce, with a blunt brutal nose and downturned wings like those of a bird of prey. Hatches opened up in its belly as it descended.

Twin autocannons mounted on the lander's wings opened up and explosions thundered along the bridge behind Squad Luko. Chunks of masonry and shattered scarabs flew. The bridge shuddered, but it was solidly built and would hold.

'We're coming in hot!' said the vox from the Soul Drinker piloting the lander. 'Xenos are converging from everywhere! Make ready for the pass!'

'How's our landing zone, Graevus?' voxed Sarpedon.

'Clear,' came the reply.

'Then get to the gardens and hold, everyone!'

The Soul Drinkers vaulted over the low walls and kicked through the ornamental hedges. From the pall of dust surrounding the bridge emerged a metallic spider, one of its claws replaced with the barrel of a weapon that spat arcs of lightning as it charged up. Squad Luko studded its hull with bolter fire, but it held firm, and fired.

A bolt of green lightning lanced out from the spider's gun, hitting the ground just behind Sarpedon. Soul Drinkers were thrown off their feet, and earth showered down from the impact.

Its second shot went high, streaking through the wing of the lander. The craft stayed airborne, but only just, swinging precariously as air rushed through the hole in its wing.

Graevus didn't wait for the order. He hurtled over Sarpedon, power axe high, ready to strike. The jets of his jump pack cut out and he landed right on top of the spider. His power axe sheared the lightning weapon clean off the spider, and it rounded on him, its remaining fore-limb snapping open ready to slice his head off.

Another of his squad landed beside it, and drove his chainsword into the spider's side, where one of its legs met the hull. The machine flicked a foreleg, throwing the Soul Drinker off in a shower of sparks, but the rest of Graevus's squad was close behind him, and suddenly the machine was surrounded. The Soul Drinkers duelled with the machine, turning its thrashing limbs aside with their chainswords, until Graevus rolled underneath, driving his axe into its underside so hard that the machine's anti-grav units were wrecked and it flopped down on top of him.

Graevus's men hauled the machine to the side of the bridge and pushed it off. They dragged Graevus to his feet, and fell back as the tide of scarabs closed in on them through the dust and rubble.

The lander's engines roared overhead. The craft came in over the gardens and hovered, lowering itself so that the grab-rails around its hatch were within reach of the Soul Drinkers. Pallas and Squad Luko clambered up into the craft, followed by Iktinos and Lygris. Squad Graevus sprinted for the lander, and Sarpedon joined them, leaping up into the belly of the craft as the last of Squad Graevus made it on board.

The ground beneath gave way just as Sarpedon's talons left it. A blast of infernally hot air hammered up at the lander, and it rose up on the swell. Sarpedon's hand closed on the grab-rail. Beneath him, the gardens fell inwards, revealing a great hollow of black earth that swallowed the stands of trees and topiary hedges that remained.

As if from a nest of insects torn open, scarabs swarmed in the unearthed warren. Spider-machines squatted amongst them, birthing new scarabs from their inner forges.

Sergeant Graevus's mutated hand grabbed Sarpedon's wrist, and, with its unnatural strength, hauled him up into the lander's belly. The hatch slammed shut below him.

'Take us back,' said Sarpedon, 'fast!'

The lander tipped up onto its stern and fired its main engines. It rocketed up towards the pallid sky. Sarpedon saw that the pilot was Scamander, the young psyker, who was the only recruit into the Chapter's Librarium since Sarpedon had assumed command.

'What was it?' asked Iktinos. 'What force has taken this world?'

Sarpedon had no answer to give.

The lander tore through the thick cloud cover, leaving the dead city behind.

'The only enemy worth your admiration is one who has accepted the superiority of mankind and knelt before you to be executed. All others are to be despised. Honour means nothing when it is used to oppose the Emperor's will.'
— Daenyathos, *Notes on the Catechisms Martial*

CHAPTER FOUR

Archmagos Voar had seen the readouts on the bridge, but, in truth, he did not believe them. Perhaps that was just what he told himself, and the truth was really that he wanted to see the anomalies with his own eyes. When the last human parts of him had been replaced with the machine, such moments of weakness would not plague him any more.

The observatory on the *Antithesis* filled a dome blistered up from the ship's upper hull. An array of brass-cased telescopes, carefully inscribed with binary prayers of accuracy, and flawlessness, jutted out from the observatory dome. The inside of the dome was frescoed with images of great discoveries, like Magos Land uncovering lost STC fragments and Tech-Priest Gurvann stumbling upon the principles of xenos-specific neurotoxins. It was a place of reflection and inspiration. Magos Voar rarely permitted anyone else to enter it.

Voar murmured a prayer to the telescope's machine-spirit and looked into the eyepiece. The object of the strange readings on the bridge hovered in front of him, glowing darkly in the light reflected from a distant star.

It was a world, but it was not a world. It was rather smaller than Terran standard, but possessed a gravity far higher than its size suggested, a suspicious sign if ever there was one. Its surface was as smooth and polished as an ornamental skull, and it had no polar caps or tectonic canyons, not even meteorite craters, which made no sense given its lack of atmosphere.

The strangest feature of the planet, however, was that it was not alone. Two others orbited the same star, precisely equidistant. They were of the same size and mass. They moved, and even spun on their axes, at the same rate. They could not be a natural phenomenon. Not even millions of years of constant gravity could produce such a solar system.

'Sensorium,' voxed Voar. 'Can we be sure the Soul Drinkers passed this way?'

'We've just picked up a plasma trace,' came the reply from the bridge library. 'The hulk dropped out of the warp in the outer system and headed for the inner worlds. It was still venting plasma, so it wasn't hard to follow.'

'Have we found it?'

'We're searching the inner worlds. If they're in orbit around a planet, they'll take a little longer to find.'

'Good. What do we have on the three outer worlds?'

'Nothing new. The Fleet Minor is sending two scouts on a flyby of the nearest one.'

'That is your second priority after finding the hulk.'

'Yes, archmagos. The first scout is approaching sensor range now.'

Voar held up his left index finger, and a dataprobe emerged from the tip. He inserted it into a socket on the side of the telescope housing and interfaced with the sensors of the *Antithesis*. He felt, for a moment, the fleet around it, the bulky presence of the *Constant* and *Ferrous*, the shape of the *Defence of Caelano Minoris* with its hotspots of energy, and the sensor-heavy shoal of the Fleet Minor. He caught two flitting shapes that had broken off from the fleet and were looping into close orbit around the massive dead presence of the planet. Voar mentally commanded the telescope to focus on the first ship. The telescope whirred around on clockwork gears to focus on the tiny glowing dart.

Voar withdrew the probe and looked back into the eyepiece. The scout ship was fast and agile, its slender body loaded with sensor gear. Its small crew was elite, trained by Magos Khrul in hostile environment operations.

'Khrul here,' came the vox from *Asclepian Gamma*, the ship that Khrul commanded.

'What can you tell me, magos?'

'Mostly metallic crust,' said Khrul. 'No atmosphere.'

'No atmosphere, or minimal?'

'None.'

That was strange. A world of that size should have attracted at least a thin veil of gases around itself. 'Any energy?'

'Nothing geothermal,' replied Khrul. Even across the vox the heavy artificial nature of his voice, piped through his hostile environment chassis, was grating.

'Take them in closer.'

'Yes, archmagos.'

The first craft looped further downwards, the second craft spiralling around it in a double helix dive.

'Wait,' said Khrul, 'I'm syncing the crews' vox.'

'Archmagos! This is Observator Secundus Malian,' said a female voice over the vox. Voar knew that she was nestled in the cramped observatory station of her Veritix-class scout ship, making sense of the masses of data piping in through the craft's sensors, while the pilot crew brought the ship in towards the planet.

'What can you see, observator?' asked Voar.

'It's… It's featureless. Smooth.'

'I can see that.'

'Not just visually. It doesn't even have magnetic poles or a radiation signature. It's totally inert.'

'Then it is not natural.'

'That is not a conclusion for me to draw, archmagos.'

Voar watched the two ships dropping in to skim the surface, so low that their hulls should have been glowing with the heat of re-entry.

'I have a surface feature,' said Malian's voice. A blurry image, judder-ing as the scout craft's cogitator struggled to compensate for its speed, appeared on one of the pict screens in front of Voar. It was a jagged greenish shape.

'Looks like a crystal outcrop. It wasn't there a moment ago.'

'It is reacting to your presence,' said Voar. 'Magos Khrul, withdraw your–'

'Power spike! Something's lit up down there! Systems… Systems down! We're blind!' Alarms sounded as Malian spoke. 'Our pilot's taking–'

Twin emerald-green lances of light punched up through the planet's crust. Malian's voice was cut off mid-syllable, replaced with a howl of static as the scout craft's vox-net was overloaded, and then silence.

Both scout craft had been vaporised in an instant. All that remained of them were puffs of glittering metal dust dissipating over the planet's pale surface.

'What was that?' snapped Voar. 'All ships, battle stations!'

'Massive energy spike,' said Khrul's voice, almost drowned out by the sudden bursts of chatter over the vox. 'It came from beneath the surface. Fleet Minor pulling back…'

A slab of crust the size of an island was thrown off the planet's surface, trailing chunks of broken rock. Beneath it glinted dull silver and metallic green-brown like corroded bronze. From its hiding place

330   *Ben Counter*

emerged a spaceship the size of a cruiser, shaped like a crescent moon, with a towering pyramid amidships studded with green lights. The tips of the crescent housed projector weapons that were already glowing sickly green as they recharged.

'Evasive action, all craft,' ordered Voar. '*Constant*, fire at will!'

The enemy ship was of a design that Voar had never seen. Aliens, thought Voar poisonously. Heathens. Corruptors of the machine.

'More of them,' came a vox from the bridge of the *Antithesis*. 'Three more, at least. One from the closest world, two from the next. There's a huge power spike on the third.'

'I'm lined up for a shot,' said Magos Hepsebah's from the *Constant*.

'Take it,' said Voar.

The nova cannon on the prow of the *Constant* was wreathed in coils of superheated gas as it charged. The emerging xenos ship seemed aware of the threat, rotating rapidly with main engines flaring to push it out of the weapon's path. Chunks of jettisoned surface clattered off it as its bulk shifted sideways, but it was too large for quick or subtle manoeuvres.

The nova cannon fired. The *Constant*'s engines fired to compensate for the immense recoil. The projectile was hurled from the barrel, streaking towards the alien ship on a column of burning light.

The shot slammed into the upper hull of the crescent ship. The energy of the blast flashed so bright the craft was like a second sun, the nova cannon's power discharging in every direction at once.

Every direction save into the craft. When the glare died down, the crescent ship was intact; its upper surface was scorched and studded with fires, but it didn't look like it had suffered any serious damage.

The crescent ship fired, twin lances of green light playing across space.

'What is it firing at?' demanded Voar. 'Navigation, get me reverse targeting solutions and put us on evasive!'

Alerts flared, projected onto the telescope's lens. The discharge of power was enormous. The Imperial Navy didn't have energy weapons that could compare to those opening up on the xenos craft.

'Khrul here!' came a vox from the Asclepian Squadron. Magos Khrul's heavy metallic voice had enough alarm in it to remind Voar that none of them were free of their human weaknesses. 'We're being targeted! Those were sighting shots! I'm putting us on full evasive, all power to the engines!'

The xenos craft fired again.

Asclepian Gamma disappeared in a flash of violent green light.

Over the open vox-channel, Voar heard Magos Khrul dying, and there was just enough time for the magos to scream before the sound was wiped out in a howling gale of static.

Voar's human mind wanted to reel with the suddenness of the attack, to stumble out of the observatory and seek solace, but that part of him would not win out this day. Emotional suppressant circuits fired and logic implants took the strain.

'Break formation!' ordered Voar. 'Navigation, set a rally point. All craft into the warp, full evasive!'

On the bridge, the navigation crew hurriedly set a location nearby to which the fleet could jump through the warp and re-emerge to regroup, hopefully without the xenos following them.

Voar went back to the telescope. The crescent ship was rapid-firing, spitting fat bolts of green energy that detonated among the ships of the Fleet Minor, and sent its tiny burning craft spiralling through the void. Voar tried to ascertain what xenos race might be flying the enemy ship. Eldar ships were sleek, delicate and graceful, with sails that billowed on solar winds. Ork craft were barely space-worthy collections of junk and salvage. Demiurg factory-ships were stocky, brutal, ugly things that seemed too unwieldy even for the vacuum. The ships of Chaos were corrupted or ancient versions of the Navy's ships, of debased but recognisably human design. Voar had seen them all, but the enemy was not among them. This was not an enemy he knew. He was fighting blind and ignorant.

Voar ordered the telescope to focus on the furthest of the three dead planets, where the biggest power spike had been detected. The pale surface was blurry for a few moments as the telescope focused; then its machine-spirit found its length and the planet shimmered into view.

Deep cracks were spidering its surface. Chunks of the crust, like fragments of an eggshell, were flaking away into space. Greenish light pulsed below.

A circular mountain range, like a crown of white stone, was forced up. Its centre formed a deep crater that collapsed, and green light flooded out. It looked like a great green eye had opened up, as if the planet was coming alive to look upon the Mechanicus ships as trespassers.

A huge dark shape forced its way out of the third planet. It too was built of crescents, many of them, arranged around a central spire so that the whole craft resembled an enormous steel claw. It was festooned with guns and lights, and surrounded by smaller craft that flitted around it like insects over a corpse. The central spire flared wide towards the stern and barely contained a raging furnace of emerald and crimson fire, an open reactor that bled power out into space. Streams of that power whipped out of the reactor into long trails looping around the immense craft, and where they touched the ship's weapons they filled up with fire and glowed painfully bright against the void.

It was the size of a battleship. Larger. It was raging with power. It was the most awesome and terrible sight that Voar had ever seen. His logic circuits were at capacity, forcing his mind to contain what he was seeing and not be rendered dumbstruck by it.

'Rally point set!' said a vox from navigation.

'All craft, jump!' ordered Voar.

The Antithesis lurched, its gravity swinging out of kilter as the warp engines accelerated it through the bounds of reality. The *Constant* followed it, Hepsebah reluctantly turning away from its target even as the nova cannon recharged. The orphaned ships of the Asclepian Squadron, then the *Ferrous* and the *Defence*, forced their way through black rents in real space. The Fleet Minor, those spared the fire of the first enemy ship, shifted into the warp behind them. A few stragglers were left behind, thrown out of the wake of the larger ships. The crescent ship closed in greedily, and picked them off one by one with blasts of energy.

The xenos fleet, temporarily free of intruders, gathered on the outskirts of the system. It assembled around the immense mother ship, the smaller craft suckling on the power flooding out of it.

Its drones flitted around the echoes of the rift opened by the Mechanicus fleet's warp engines. There was just a trace there of the interlopers, a scent of the new races, the upstarts who dared trespass upon sacred worlds.

The fleet did not need to hunt them down. The interlopers could not escape. With a thought, the eyes of the Veiled Region began to open.

Pallas carefully prised the chitin of Sarpedon's left rear leg apart and used a pair of forceps to remove the crushed remains of a scarab. He dropped it into a medical waste container on the floor of the sick bay beside him. The sick bay had served the Soul Drinkers as an apothecarion for a long time, and was full of the equipment the Chapter had salvaged from elsewhere in the hulk, or from the fleet they had scuttled when they first broke with the Imperium: autosurgeon units fixed to the ceiling, nutrient tanks, transfusion units, racks of medicines and supplies, and even cutting gear and other basic tools for working on damaged bionics.

Sarpedon winced. His abnormal legs were extremely tough, but pain was pain.

'This will heal,' said Pallas, starting to seal the incision in the tough sheath of chitin with a medical laser. He indicated the mangled scarab in the waste container. 'Unlike that.'

Sarpedon's wounds had not been serious, a minor skull fracture and the usual cuts and impact wounds. As a Space Marine, he would heal them all naturally. Apothecary Pallas, however, was skilled at accelerating the process. Most of the Soul Drinkers that fought at the abandoned city had passed through the apothecarion. Sarpedon was the last.

'I am glad that you remained with us, brother,' said Sarpedon. It was the first time that Sarpedon had discussed the events of the Chapter War with Pallas.

Pallas looked up at him. 'My Chapter is my Chapter. I made a mistake, true, but only a coward would not try to put that right.'

'You had good reasons, Pallas. A mistake it was, but I understand it.'

'You understand treachery?' Pallas looked almost offended by the suggestion.

'I have failed this Chapter many times. I led us to the edge of our destruction. The old Chapter would never have forgiven you, it is certain, but we are not the old Chapter any more and you are still my battle-brother.'

'And I know now that we will continue to die as long as we turn from the Imperium's fold. It is the price we pay for our freedom. When I had to see the dead and wounded from every one of your new dawns, I forgot that. I will not forget it again.'

The laser sizzled against the chitin, and the wound was closed. Sarpedon had removed his armour for the procedure, and the new scar on his leg was just one of many, from the surgical scars from his transformation into a Space Marine to horrible wounds suffered in the First and Second Chapter Wars and everything that had happened in between. Sarpedon had come perilously close to death so many times that his luck was surely due to run out, every close call ticked off in a snarl of scar tissue.

'We all need to remember it,' said Sarpedon. 'To shy away from following the right path because it will cost the lives of my brothers is to let in the doubt that has led many an Astartes to fall. It is a narrow path to walk, between wasting my battle-brothers' lives and backing away when a victory is there to be won.'

Pallas cleaned up the wound.

'It is one that I do not believe I could walk,' he said. 'Which is why I serve as a sawbones and not as a leader.'

'If you did,' said Sarpedon, 'if fate had put you in command instead of me, what would you do?'

Pallas looked up from the wound. 'Fate did not put me in charge, Sarpedon.'

'Imagine it did.'

'Imagination is not a quality becoming to an Astartes.'

Sarpedon's vox chirped.

'Commander,' said Lygris's voice, 'I need you on the bridge.'

'You are clear to go,' said Pallas.

Sarpedon flexed his repaired leg. It hurt, but it was a good pain. He looked down at the scarab Pallas had pulled from his leg.

'Destroy that,' he said.

'Yes, commander. And…'

Sarpedon paused as he went to leave. 'Yes, Apothecary?'

'I would not surrender to the Mechanicus. If I was leading us, I would not let them take us to some forge world for a show trial. I would die first, and my battle-brothers along with me. That is what I imagine.'

'Good,' said Sarpedon, and left.

The Mechanicus fleet had made its warp jump with minimal planning and no preparation, so in interstellar terms it had only travelled a short distance through the Veiled Region.

The first task had been to count the dead: Magos Khrul and the three hundred men on board the *Asclepian Gamma*, several hundred among the Fleet Minor, and the usual handful of casualties among the menials in the engine rooms and arming chamber of the *Constant*.

The *Asclepian Gamma* had been rather more than nine hundred years old, a fine craft built according to principles that were slowly being lost by the shipwrights of the Mechanicus. The squadron was flying one short for the first time in its history. Its machine-spirit had been bright and aggressive, and it made for a tightly run, efficient ship. Now, it was gone forever. A great tragedy had occurred with the loss of that spirit, for such a thing could never be replaced. The second task was to mourn it. Incense candles burned in pools of machine oil, and devotional engines chattered eulogies in machine-code. Tech-priests led the menials in prayers.

The third task was to find out just what had attacked them.

Archmagos Voar pored through yet another volume from the shelves of the *Antithesis's* bridge library. The enemy had been xenos, there was no doubt about that, but that hardly did much to narrow it down. Several thousand alien species had been encountered in hostile circumstances since the Mechanicus records began, and tens of thousands more had been recorded from afar. What was more, creatures native to the Veiled Region were unlikely to be recorded, given the lack of knowledge about the area.

Voar hauled another volume from the shelves and placed it on the reading table in front of him. It described the travels of a rogue trader, whose adventures had seen him skirt the edge of the Veiled Region before he had headed out to the western edge of the galaxy. One of Voar's eyes opened up and a line of green light was projected onto the open page. Two of his fingers split into metal armatures that flicked the pages of the book at blurring speed as the scanner built into his eye swept across the words written there. Pages of High Gothic writing streamed into the logic engine implanted behind his temple and spat parcels of relevant, filtered information into his consciousness.

There were a few encounters with greenskin pirates, a race of sluggish, primitive creatures on a dying world, and a few xenos mercenaries and traders, operating in the lawless barrens of sparsely populated Imperial space, but nothing relevant.

A lectern-servitor trundled around the corner. The servitor had once been a menial, serving on one of the fleet's craft before it had suffered a crippling wound and been turned into a more useful machine. Its spine was bent over and its back made level to serve as a stand for books, while its lengthened arms carried a stack of volumes it had picked out according to the simple logic routines burned into what remained of its brain. The book lying open on its back was an account of a battle fought by the Adepta Sororitas.

The servitor was accompanied by one of the bridge tech-priests. A hundred of them were working on the problem at that moment, searching through the shelves for hints at the identity of the xenos that had nearly shattered the Mechanicus fleet in a single engagement.

'This may be of use,' said the tech-priest.

'Anything else?'

'Not in all the library, archmagos. The semantic engines have finished their work.'

Voar turned his scanner eye to the tome the servitor carried. It was another minor engagement where some pious Imperial servants had stumbled across hostile aliens and fought for their survival. The world was known as Sanctuary 101, and the Sisters of Battle, the military arm of the Adepta Sororitas, had fought valiantly against a tenacious foe.

They had also seen a shape in the sky, awoken by the alien warriors that had stormed the chapel they had defended. It was the last sight many of them had seen.

It was a crescent, hanging black against the sky.

Voar froze his scanner and backed up a few pages. His logic engines sifted through the information again, filtering wider and wider until Voar knew all the pertinent details.

He had it. The Imperium had encountered this foe before, not frequently, and rarely with enough insight to understand it, but at least Voar was no longer fighting completely in the dark.

The Omnissiah had smiled upon Archmagos Voar, because now the enemy had a name.

The *Brokenback* made its third warp jump. There had been little to justify exploring the previous world with its abandoned, machine-infested cities. From orbit around it, however, Lygris had located another nearby solar system just visible to the hulk's sensors through the surrounding nebulae. It was close enough for a civilisation like that of the dead city to have colonised, and, now that the *Brokenback* was in orbit around the new system's fifth planet, it was apparent that Lygris's instinct had been good.

The planet depicted on the bridge holo-projector was a beautiful green pearl, shining in the light of its sun. Endless forests rolled across its surface, from frozen coniferous valleys around its poles to tropical swamps and rainforests around the equator. Instead of oceans, it had thousands of rivers, weaving across its surface.

'The image is good. Very little cloud,' said Lygris. 'It's a long-range scan, but there's plenty of information. Here.'

Lygris fiddled with the data-slate in his hand, and the image zoomed in to show a low-resolution section of the endless forest.

'That,' said Lygris, 'is not natural.'

They saw a structure as straight as a ruler stretching across several kilometres of forest.

'What is it?' asked Sarpedon.

'An aqueduct,' said Lygris. 'Or maybe a raised highway.'

'So there's habitation there?'

'Definitely. Not much, though, certainly not by the standards of the civilisation that settled it. We'd expect to see signs of agriculture, mass forest clearing and cities. Sometimes cultures in the earlier stages of space exploration set aside a world for their ruling classes, a garden world, to be left unspoiled.'

'Human?'

'The scale's right. Otherwise it's impossible to tell.'

'It may be another xenos lair,' said Sarpedon.

'Or,' said Chaplain Iktinos, who had been summoned to the bridge along with Sarpedon, 'it could be a holdout against the aliens. Certainly the previous world was human. If this one is, humans may still be there.'

'Can we make it there?' asked Sarpedon.

'There, yes,' said Lygris. 'Anywhere afterwards? That is debatable. I can force everything out of the reactors and we can probably get a fourth jump out of them provided it isn't too far. Then I fear we will be running on empty.'

'Better to risk what we have,' said Iktinos, 'than to accept the certainty of failure.'

'I agree,' said Sarpedon, 'but I am not going down there expecting anything other than a hostile reception. Full battle order this time. How many Thunderhawks do we have operational?'

'Three,' said Lygris. He had rendered the *Brokenback*'s Thunderhawk gunships inoperable at Vanqualis to help scupper Eumenes's rebellion. In an act of penance, he had begun repairs on them personally.

'I'm taking a company-strength force down there. It's as many battle-brothers as we can spare, but I will not be outnumbered by whatever we find down there. Bring together what you can to carry them.'

'Yes, commander.'

'And Iktinos?'

'Commander?'

'Prepare the men's souls to battle the xenos.'

'It shall be done.'

'Do not forget,' said Lygris carefully, 'that we are not here to fight aliens. We are here to find fuel for the reactors and get out as easily as possible.'

'The enemy had the better of us at the grey city,' replied Sarpedon. 'They will not do it twice.'

Archmagos Voar had cleared out a section of the bridge library. The bookcases around him were papered with pages taken from books, copies of diagrams and key passages, hundreds of them. The whole bridge crew had been sent hunting it all down according to Voar's orders. The incident at Sanctuary 101 had been the key to unlocking it all.

The Omnissiah had given Voar all the clues he needed. As a servant of the Machine-God, Voar had dutifully followed them to their conclusion.

Voar sat at the reading desk surrounded by open books and blinking data-slates. He looked up as the magi entered the sanctum he had created.

It went unspoken that Khrul was not with them, but none of them could ignore his absence.

'Archmagos, why have you called us here?' asked Magos Vionel, whose lumbering body barely fit between the bookcases of the archive.

'My gun crew must be supervised in its re-calibrations,' said Hepsebah as tersely as anyone would dare when addressing an archmagos, 'and we all have repair rites to perform.'

'This is our enemy,' replied Voar. He stood up with a whirr of servos. With a mind impulse signal, a holo-projector hidden among the high shadowy rafters flickered into life. Dim glow-globes died down, and the only light was coming from the holo.

It shone from the wide eyes of a woman. She was young and terrified. Her hair was shorn close, and she wore a shapeless white robe embroidered with golden roses. The image was grainy and jumbled, distorted with artefacts and memory flaws.

'This image,' said Voar, 'is one of the few records we have of this xenos species. It was considered useless by the Adepta Sororitas when they recovered it. They did not have the verispex units that allowed us to enhance it.'

The image shuddered into life. The woman in the image looked nervously up at someone off-screen.

'Take this,' said a strident woman's voice. 'Someone must know.'

The young woman stared dumbly into the lens of the picter. The image shifted forwards as the picter was pushed into her hands.

'I don't know how,' said the younger woman, her voice thin and trembling.

The picter swung, and the other woman came into shot. She wore red armour trimmed with gold: power armour, with bulky shoulder pads inscribed with golden wings and a heavy backpack carrying the armour's power source. In her hands was a boltgun. Even without the old scar splitting her lip and the reconstructed jaw, she would have worn every one of her battles across her face.

'I am Sister Orpheia of the Order of the Gilded Thorn,' she said. 'Seven months ago, ground was broken on a new home for our order. Sanctuary 101.'

The younger woman holding the picter fiddled with the focus and the image jumped again, pulling away from Orpheia. The interior of a half-built cathedral was visible behind the woman. Most of the roof was missing, scaffolding cladding the fluted columns and heaps of construction materials lying everywhere on palettes. The altar was finished, an image of the armoured Emperor enthroned above six Sisters standing guard on a bed of golden roses. Dozens of Sisters knelt before the altar, many of them armoured, others wearing the robes and habits of the non-military Orders.

'Twelve hours ago, the enemy breached our perimeters. It came from below the ground. It was waiting for us. A world consecrated to the Emperor must suffer no xenos to befoul its surface, and we will defend it to the death. These are the duties to which our lives come second.'

A distant explosion sounded, and the holo flickered as the picter was shaken. The young sister gasped. Shards of masonry fell.

'It's a tank!' shouted one of the Sisters standing guard at a window that had been hurriedly fortified with sandbags. 'It's the size of the chapel!'

One of the Sisters before the altar stood up. A cloak trimmed with ermine hung from her shoulders, and her face was studded with golden thorns: a canoness of the Order.

'Sisters Retributor!' she yelled. 'Cleanse it with fire!'

Sister Orpheia shouldered her bolter, and picked up a weapon that had been out of shot at her feet. It was a multi-melta, a twin-barrelled weapon almost as big as Orpheia herself, connected to her backpack by an armoured hose. The metal of its barrels was heavily scorched by years of intense heat. Orpheia patted the gun affectionately.

'This,' she said, 'is the wages of sin.'

Orpheia ran to the barricaded window, and the Sister with the picter followed her. An enormous black shape, a slab of darkness with a halo of green lightning crackling around it, could just be seen through the gaps in the half-built walls. It was still far away, but it already loomed larger than the cathedral. It was enormous.

The Sisters were taking cover. The canoness stood in the centre of the cathedral, defying the enemy to dare take its best shot.

A bolt of green lightning crashed through the wall. Sisters were thrown off their feet. The picter shuddered violently, and the sister holding it fell down, the image shifting wildly as it fell on its side. Another Sister rolled across the floor, wreathed in green fire. The slam of the lightning echoed along with the screams of the wounded.

'Open fire!' someone yelled.

The Sisters Retributor at the window were silhouetted in the fury of the firepower they poured towards the shape. A heavy bolter hammered. Rockets streamed, sending plumes of exhaust shooting back into the cathedral. Orpheia's multi-melta charged for a moment before firing a tremendous beam of red-white heat that seemed to sear reality itself.

The image broke up as gunfire competed with static to create an impenetrable din. It was impossible to make out any coherence among the jumble of images. The Sisters were lit by gunfire. Spindly shapes clambered in through the windows. The Canoness was on the ground, a hand clamped over a wound in her abdomen, yelling orders.

The image was moving. The woman carrying the picter was running through the shadowy, half-built chapel. She emerged outside, into the harsh sun of Sanctuary 101.

'Move it! Fall back!' shouted someone. It was a woman again, another soldier. 'They've taken the cloisters! Get to the mausoleum!'

The image broke up and changed, streaked with static. The holo showed the blood-streaked face of a woman: Sister Orpheia. The picter was on her chest and she was being carried on a stretcher. One side of her face was raw and bloody. It looked like the skin of her face had been stripped away, layer by layer, right down to the bone. Among the Sisters carrying her was the young novice that had taken the images from the chapel. The picter was forgotten as it continued to record from the stretcher where it had been dropped.

More gunfire. Orpheia was being carried in a column of Sisters moving from the cathedral, which was a burning wreck. Dark shapes, like tall buildings looming over the cathedral, were just visible for a handful of frames. Spindly shapes, skeletal and half-seen, clambered through the ruins. It was impossible to make out any more details of the xenos that had come to Sanctuary 101.

Orpheia was turned around, and the view swept over a graveyard covered in eagle-shaped markers commemorating the lost Sisters of the Gilded Thorn, surrounding a grand mausoleum to some heroine of the Order. Sisters were already taking up firing positions among the stones.

Many of them were bloody and wounded, chunks of their armour stripped away.

Green fire fell from the sky, fat searing bolts of it. The Sisters carrying the stretcher dropped it and took cover. Orpheia fell to the ground and the picter rolled off her.

Lying on its side, the picter's image showed a headstone and a stretch of Sanctuary 101's sky. The younger woman slumped against the headstone. Her novice's robes were on fire, flaming green. Her eyes were wide with shock and pain. Her face distorted as layers of robe, and then skin, lifted off the side of her face and shoulder. Red, wet muscle gleamed beneath, and then bone, as she was flayed away by the tongues of green flame. She screamed, the sound lost in static, and rolled onto the ground out of frame.

A dark shape hung in the sky above, like a crescent moon, but black.

The image froze. The glow-globes rose again, and the image became dim.

Voar stepped through the image to address his magi.

'They are known,' he said, 'as necrons.'

'I have walked through valleys of sin and oceans of night. I have looked daemons and traitors in the eyes. I have heard the whispers of dark things that wanted my soul. And I have never once encountered anything that struck the fear into me that a xenos would feel if it ever truly understood the resolve of the human race.'

– Daenyathos, *Battle Prayers XIIIV*

CHAPTER FIVE

From the gunner's position on the Thunderhawk, Sarpedon could see the forests rolling out across the planet's surface, streaking past as the gunship descended. Rivers zipped past, bright silver ribbons in the hot sun. Behind him, two more Thunderhawks banked behind the lead craft, arrowing down into the lower levels of the forest world's atmosphere. Two armoured landers followed in their wake. Between them, they carried more than eighty Soul Drinkers. The firing port of the heavy bolter mount gave Sarpedon an excellent view of the planet as its beauty was revealed beneath him.

Trees, hundreds of metres tall, reached up from the canopy, hanging with enormous brightly coloured fruits. Flocks of birds, like columns of shimmering smoke, swept up from the crevasses and treetops full of nests as the Thunderhawks roared past. Hills tall enough to break the canopy were topped with pastel shocks of flowers.

Sarpedon could see the target in the distance. A pale streak, dead straight, cutting right through the forest. It was the structure Lygris had spotted from orbit. Sarpedon gripped the handles of the heavy bolter mounted in front of him and checked the magazine. The planet was a paradise, but he was working on the assumption that something down there would soon try very hard to kill the Soul Drinkers. Sarpedon was not going to risk getting caught out again. This force was ready to fight.

The Thunderhawk passed over the structure. Sarpedon realised that it was a landing strip, a gash cut into the forest, paved and studded with landing lights. The trees around it had been burned away to keep them from growing back over the strip. The Thunderhawk rounded a hill, and Sarpedon saw that a palace stood at one end of the landing strip.

It had been hidden from the sky by the canopy of trees arching over it, but it was enormous. Several floors of gold and deep red stone were ringed by balconies and raised gardens. Flowering vines draped over balconies like stage curtains. Several grand wings curved around the main body of the palace, dappled with the sunlight falling through the trees, enclosing ornate gardens and artificial pools.

The Thunderhawk made another pass. Sarpedon peered down the sights of the heavy bolter, its bulky body tracking across the palace grounds.

'No targets,' he voxed.

The Thunderhawk swooped around, its exhaust wake stripping the topmost leaves from the canopy, and slowed down as it approached the landing strip. Its nose tilted up as it came down, and its landing gear thudded onto the strip.

'We're down! Clear to deploy!' said the pilot.

Squad Luko jumped from the rear ramp of the gunship as it lowered. Luko was first out, as he always was, already activating the energy field around his lightning claws. Squad Tisiph was next, and Sarpedon followed.

The forest shook with the sound of engines. The second Thunderhawk was coming down. Luko waved his squad into a perimeter, and Tisiph's squad hurried forwards, bolters trained on the forest edge. Tisiph's squad carried several of the Soul Drinkers' heavy weapons, of which the Chapter had very few remaining.

The second Thunderhawk was down. Codicer Scamander and Librarian Tyrendian were with Squads Graevus and Salk.

'Move up for a breach on the building,' said Sarpedon. 'Tisiph, hold here. Luko on point.'

'Yes, commander,' voxed Luko.

Sarpedon watched his force move up towards the palace. Its size was even more apparent from the ground. Beyond it, Sarpedon could see several sub-palaces, shaped like fanciful castles with delicate spires that just pierced the canopy. Between them were stables and servants' quarters, separated by walled gardens and reflecting pools.

Tyrendian moved up past Squad Tisiph. Tyrendian was the Soul Drinkers' only remaining Librarian aside from Sarpedon. With an aquiline face and a unique lack of scars, Tyrendian looked far too handsome to be a Space Marine.

'Who lived here?' he asked.

'Someone rich,' said Sarpedon. The tension in Tyrendian's words was not lost on Sarpedon. He was assuming, as Sarpedon had, that humans

had abandoned the planet. 'Veiled Region's human civilisation probably put this world aside for their leaders.'

'Lucky them,' said Tyrendian.

Scamander was behind them, following Tyrendian. Scamander was
the only one of the Chapter's scouts that had remained with the Soul
Drinkers after the Second Chapter War. He was a pyrokinetic with a lot
of potential, but relatively little control, and Tyrendian had taken him
under his wing to train him up as a full Librarian.

Captain Luko ran up to the main doors, his Soul Drinkers stacking
up behind him. Squad Graevus moved into position on the other side
of the doors.

'No contacts,' voxed Luko. 'The place looks dead.'

'So did the white city,' said Sarpedon.

Behind the spearhead, the other craft were landing. Iktinos had the
third Thunderhawk, and the rest of the Soul Drinkers were jumping
from the armoured landers. Iktinos was directing them to spread out
and advance on a wide front to protect the force about to enter the
palace.

Luko breached the gilded double doors by tearing the hinges off one
side with his lightning claws. The door fell in, and Graevus was over the
threshold, his squad-mates following him into the dark interior.

Tyrendian was in next. His particular psychic power was useful at
close quarters; a well-thrown bolt of lightning could go a long way to
even up a fight. Scamander stuck beside him.

Sarpedon clambered up the outside wall, onto a first floor balcony.
The open windows led into a mezzanine floor overlooking the entrance
hallway, through which the Soul Drinkers were advancing.

The inside of the palace was as lavish as the outside. Gold chandeliers
hung from the ceiling. The walls were red and gold, and the floot was
pale stone. The forest had been brought inside, too, with vines winding
decoratively up the walls and stands of trees in the corners. A raised
pool in the centre of the hallway shone with decorative fish.

'There's nothing here,' voxed Graevus.

Sarpedon headed up the next flight of stairs to the floor above. It was
a feasting chamber, pale and elegant, spilling over with lush tropical
plants.

He could smell it now. It was unmistakeable. Coming from above, it
was a mix of sweet and foetid that would be alien to someone who had
not been around as much death as Sarpedon had.

'Head up,' voxed Sarpedon. He drew the Axe of Mercaeno. They
would not get the drop on him this time, no matter who they were.
'Graevus, Luko, with me.'

Luko and Graevus were on the upper floor in a few moments, moving
up the stairways. Sarpedon followed Graevus, who had his own power

axe ready, with the Astartes of Squad Luko filling the cramped stairway behind him.

The stairway was narrow, and it stank. The air was heavy with death. Unaugmented lungs would have struggled to draw breath. Ahead was a solid wooden door that looked well bolted.

'Go,' said Sarpedon.

Graevus kicked the door open and darted inside. His assault squad followed him in, Sarpedon on their heels.

The room stretched the whole breadth of the palace, high and lofty with tall windows drenching it in dappled light. It had once been an artist's studio, with half-finished sculptures and lumps of cut stone standing everywhere.

Corpses hung from the rafters. There must have been well over a hundred of them. Judging from their clothes, they were the nobles and servants of the palace, ladies in their gowns, footmen in their uniforms and servants in smocks and work clothes. They had been there for some time, and each of them hung above a puddle of corpse liquor, foul and black. Their skin had turned dark and sunken, and their eye sockets seethed with maggots. A few flies, newly hatched, buzzed lazily around their heads.

Sarpedon looked around the room. There were no signs of a struggle. There had been none in the rest of the palace.

'They killed themselves,' said Sarpedon.

'A cult?' asked Luko.

'Maybe,' said Graevus.

'Tisiph here,' came a vox. 'We've got something by the eastern stables. Bodies. Crammed in one of the cellars. Must be fifty of them.'

'Signs of a fight?' asked Sarpedon.

'None,' replied Tisiph, 'and the doors were barred from the inside. Got some gas fuel canisters here. I'm thinking they gassed themselves.'

'Throne of Terra,' swore Graevus. 'What happened here?'

'Whatever was going to happen,' said Sarpedon, 'these people chose death rather than face it.'

'A strange way to kill themselves,' said Luko. 'It's not the quickest or surest way.' Luko climbed onto one of the uncarved stone blocks, and cut down one of the bodies with a flick of his lightning claws. It was the corpse of a footman; the coat he wore had once been bright red, but was now filthy brown. Luko held up the body, showing the ragged dark hole in the back of its skull. 'Bullet wound,' he said. 'This man didn't hang himself.'

'Commander, Iktinos here,' said Iktinos over the vox. 'I have reached the tower to the north of the palace. There is something here that you might wish to see.'

* * *

There were other bodies. Some had hanged themselves in one of the stable buildings. Others appeared to have weighed their clothing down with rocks and drowned themselves in one of the ornamental pools. In the kitchens of the palace was the body of a man, who had taken his own life with vermin poison. A couple even hung from the trees, high up in the canopy. They must have climbed up there to spend the last few moments of their lives among the birds and insects instead of with their fellow humans. Some of them appeared to have hanged themselves, but others had been killed by other means, usually gunshot, before being strung up. Nothing about the palace or the bodies suggested why they might have been hung up after death.

The riches of the palace were in place: art, gold and silver, even spices and other luxuries in the pantries that must have been imported to the planet. What Iktinos had found in the fanciful tower adjoining the palace outstripped them all in value.

It was a map inscribed in gold and inlaid with precious stones the size of a man's fist. It covered one wall of a chapel. The chapel was not dedicated to the Emperor but to a triumvirate of gods; one was depicted as a warrior, another as a woman with silver fire around her hands and another as a crippled man. Statues of them stood behind the chapel's altar, probably carved by the same hand that had once worked in the artist's studio now hung with rotting corpses.

The map was of a stellar empire. The diamonds were stars, rubies and sapphires were planets. Orbits and space lanes were loops of silver. Two worlds were picked out. One of them was surrounded by a halo of green stones, and bore the heraldry of a sword over a leaf.

'This symbol is over the door of the chapel,' said Iktinos. 'It is probably the planet we are on.'

Iktinos stood before the star map with several of his flock standing guard at the windows and doors. The chapel, like the rest of the palace, looked untouched by conflict, save for being abandoned.

'Then this is a human empire,' said Sarpedon, 'and these are its other worlds?'

'Given our route,' said Iktinos, indicating a fat sapphire, 'this is the world upon which we originally landed, the white city.'

'And this?' asked Sarpedon. He pointed to the second planet that had drawn his eye: an enormous ruby, cut with dozens of facets, surrounded by diamonds and fanciful loops of gold and silver. 'The empire's capital?'

'It seems more than likely, commander,' said Iktinos.

'I see. Can we use this to navigate?'

'Provided we can match it up with the stellar bodies around us, certainly. Lygris should be able to model a star map using it.'

'The heart of an empire will have space ports, fuel depots. Even if it is abandoned like this place, we will be able to find what we need.'

Sarpedon's notice was caught by a noise outside. It sounded like the drawing of a blade.

Brother Skoyle of Squad Graevus was alert enough to see the movement, but such was the skill of the infiltrator that it looked like no more than a corpse swaying in the wind.

The body was that of a stablehand dressed in a simple work fatigues and a long leather apron. His face was bloated red and black, his eyes drooping black sacks of ichor and his swollen tongue filling his mouth. He looked like any other body might, strung up from the tree outside the tower and left there to swing for many days.

Beneath those clothes, the skin was slit open and folded over, held together with slivers of metal like steel thread. Its insides had been hollowed out and its chest bulged strangely, the ribs broken and shifted to allow for another pair of arms to fold over another chest, as if the stablehand had become a coffin for another corpse. All this was hidden by the heavy working clothes the corpse was still wearing.

The swaying had been caused by a hand with blades for fingers, slick with rotten blood, forcing its way out of the hollowed corpse and pinging the metal stitches open one by one.

Black gore dripped onto the ground beneath the corpse. Brother Skoyle heard it again and turned to look at its source. He saw the body moving, and this time it was not with the wind.

Skoyle drew his chainsword. The corpse split open, showering him with rotten meat and blood. It unfolded a second figure from inside. Taller than a man, its slender limbs had been folded up inside it like an impossible puzzle, and it was covered in stinking filth.

It was humanoid in shape, but it was not human. It was not anything that had ever been alive. The gore was crusted over the dull metal of its articulated limbs. A thick jointed spine rose from its pelvis to support a wide chest with thick steel ribs, from the centre of which came a faint greenish glow, the thing's power source. Its long arms ended in blades as long as a man's forearm. Its head hung down in front of its chest, a metal parody of a human skull, with a slit in the thin face in place of a mouth and two green crystals set into deep eye sockets. Sheets of torn skin hung over it, as if this stylised skeletal creature was still trying to wear the guise of a man.

It landed a metre away from Brother Skoyle, its unmoving face appearing to leer with anticipation as it darted forwards.

Skoyle's chainsword whirred, and he stabbed it at the creature's chest. The metal teeth skipped off the metal of its shoulder, drawing sparks instead of blood.

The thing was on him. Blades as sharp as needles punctured the shoulder joint of his armour and slit up into his torso. Skoyle yelled and threw it to the ground, stamping down on its leg to pin it in place before driving his chainblade down into its chest.

Green light flashed as its power core ruptured. Bladed hands slashed up at Skoyle, cutting chunks from his armour. The alien creature shuddered and fell still, like a machine with the power shut off.

Graevus ran to help him, followed by the rest of his squad.

'Skoyle! What is it?' shouted Graevus.

'Machine,' gasped Skoyle, gingerly testing his wounded shoulder. Blood was running from the joint, black against his purple armour. 'An ambush machine. It was waiting in the corpse.'

Graevus looked around the tower and the palace. There were corpses everywhere, hanging from trees, lying in foetid pools and huddled in storage. Those were just the ones the Soul Drinkers had seen so far. There could be thousands of them.

'Commander, we've been attacked,' said Graevus. 'It was a machine. It's destroyed, but there could be more. They could be surrounding us.'

'All squads!' ordered Sarpedon. 'Pull in close to the tower! Squad Tisiph, stick with the transports and be ready to cover our retreat!'

The metal creature at Skoyle's feet sprang up. The gash in its chest had been covered over with a surface of gleaming new metal. The light inside it was glowing again.

The thing rammed all its blades up into Skoyle's throat. They punched through the ceramite of his helmet and out through the back of his head. Skoyle convulsed and dropped his chainsword, his arms falling dead at his sides.

Squad Graevus riddled the alien machine with bolt pistol fire. It jerked as the bolts impacted it, blasting off an arm, a leg, battering its head into a lopsided mess. It clattered to the ground, turned hazy, and vanished. Skoyle slumped to the ground where the machine had fallen, but he landed on bare earth. The thing had gone.

The alien machines clambered from the upper tiers of the palace, from the belfry of the tower and the cellars beneath the stables, dozens of them, many still wearing the skins of the corpses in which they had hidden. They had hidden among the bodies strung up in the palace's top floor. When Sarpedon had first seen them, when the Soul Drinkers had wondered what fate must have befallen the inhabitants, the machines had been watching them every step of the way.

Graevus grabbed Skoyle's body and heaved it onto one shoulder. 'Squad! Close guard on the commander!'

Luko's squad ran to the cover of a stable building. They hammered bolter fire up towards the creatures emerging from the palace. Several fell or lost limbs in the first volley, but many more scuttled down the walls and charged towards the Soul Drinkers, moving faster than a man ever could.

Sarpedon could see them emerging from the ground between the Soul Drinkers and the airstrip, hundreds of them, many of them clawing their way out from beneath the soil. These were different, bulkier than the ambushers, and carrying xenos weapons with glowing green barrels instead of bladed fingers.

'Fall back to the tower!' he ordered. 'Get to cover! Defensive positions!'

Soul Drinkers were running ahead of the bloody metallic tide. Sarpedon snapped off a bolter shot and blew the leg off one. Squad Luko's fire cut down several more, throwing shards of gory metal against the palace walls.

When the machines died, they disappeared. They didn't dissolve away or crumble to dust. They just faded away, and were gone.

Sarpedon headed into the tower. Soul Drinkers were gathered around it, sending out disciplined volleys of fire to cover one another. Iktinos's Soul Drinkers were taking up position at the windows and doors of the chapel at the base of the tower.

Sarpedon headed up the stairway that coiled around behind the altar. It wound up towards the tower's upper reaches. He could hear metal claws clacking against the outer wall, and Soul Drinkers yelling as they forced the doors closed under the weight of robotic bodies. The sound of booming metal filled the tower as the star map on the wall was wrenched down and propped up against one window to barricade it. Gunfire stuttered. Chainblades whirred.

The upper floors of the tower were bedchambers and studies, small personal libraries and reception rooms, all understated but lavish. The floor was marble and the walls were covered in elegantly trained vines.

Silver blood-streaked claws reached over a windowsill. Sarpedon reared up out of the window, and split the alien's head in two with his axe before it could crawl in through the window. A balcony beside the window was already crawling with them. Sarpedon jumped through the window and scuttled along the wall, slashing down at them from the wall above. They cut back at him, blades ringing off his armour, but he cut off an arm here, a head there, and sent the machines falling broken back down to the ground.

They formed a seething red-silver carpet, like a swarm of corroded clockwork insects. They were climbing the trees beside the tower, too, to jump from the uppermost branches on to the top of the tower. Sarpedon fired his bolter, blowing holes in a couple of torsos. The other machines, the ones with guns, were in range. When they fired, green flames played across the walls of the tower, and stonework was stripped away as if being dissolved. The alien weapons did not just burn or shatter, they spirited away the matter of the target, boring through it layer by layer.

The enemy scouts wore the skins of the dead, and they had fooled the Soul Drinkers for long enough to stage an ambush. Their warriors possessed weapons employing technology beyond Imperial understanding, and they had killed at least two worlds.

'Tisiph, what is your situation?' voxed Sarpedon.

'Embattled,' came the reply. 'They're coming out of the trees. Machines. Xenos.'

'Can you bring the transports up?'

'Not all of them.'

'What about a Thunderhawk?'

'Yes, commander. I can do that.'

'Then do it.'

'I can't transport the whole force.'

'Then we'll have to use some imagination. Do it.'

'Yes, commander!'

Sarpedon looked down at the horde of xenos assaulting the walls. He could hear chainblades against metal and bolter fire hammering into machine carapaces.

'See, brothers?' shouted Captain Luko, fighting at the doors. 'Metal dies just as fast as flesh!'

'Graevus, get to the upper floors,' voxed Sarpedon. 'To me!'

Sarpedon ducked back into the tower as the window frame was stripped away by the machines' gunfire. The staircase spiralled up further towards the pinnacle of the tower. He scuttled up it to find a trapdoor leading to the roof. He tore it off its mountings and climbed up.

Graevus was following, the armoured boots of his squad hammering on the stairs. Above the gunfire and clash of metal on metal, Sarpedon could hear the engines of Tisiph's Thunderhawk.

'All squads, hold them!' ordered Sarpedon over the vox-net. 'Stand your ground!'

Graevus reached the roof. 'Your orders, commander?'

'Break the siege,' said Sarpedon. 'Follow me.'

The Thunderhawk hovered low over the tower roof. Sarpedon could see Tisiph in the cockpit. Gunfire hammered from the gunship's weapons, battering heavy bolter and autocannon fire down into the xenos. The roof was battered by the hot, chemical-heavy exhaust from the engines.

Tisiph wheeled the hovering gunship so that the rear ramp faced the window and swung down. Graevus led his squad onto the open ramp, holding tight to the overhead railings as exhaust wash screamed around them. Sarpedon jumped on to the lip of the ramp behind them.

The horde was growing. For every machine the Soul Drinkers destroyed, another two seemed to drag themselves up from the earth.

Fallen robots got to their feet again, wounds closed over with liquid metal.

'Luko, Iktinos, you have to take them apart!' voxed Sarpedon, having to yell over the engines. 'Destroy them completely before they repair!'

'A pleasure!' voxed Luko from below. He loved war, and his love for it was infectious. Even as he spoke, his lightning claws flashed at the door and another xenos was reduced to smouldering components.

'Tisiph!' shouted Sarpedon. 'Take us in!'

The Thunderhawk banked away from the window to hover over the centre of the xenos horde. The machines were crowding forwards, clambering over one another to kill.

'Now!' shouted Sarpedon. He jumped off the Thunderhawk's ramp, the Axe of Mercaeno above his head, ready to strike.

Sarpedon hit the ground hard, letting his legs flex under him and take the impact. Graevus's squad followed, bursts from their jump packs slowing their descent. Sarpedon and Squad Graevus landed right in the heart of the machine horde.

The xenos were swarming forwards, competing for the chance to die, forcing their way into the tower. They were not ready for Sarpedon and Graevus to appear right in the heart of them, and attack.

Sarpedon's axe cut one in half, and Graevus's power axe accounted for another. Chainblades thrust out, and bolt pistols hammered. One Soul Drinker landed right on top of an alien, knocking it to the ground, and wrestled with it down in the dirt. Another landed off-keel and fell, machines swarming over him to cut him up with their bladed hands. Graevus beheaded one of the attackers and dragged his battle-brother out from under them.

They were quick and tough, but Sarpedon had the advantage. A Space Marine never gave that up when he had it. Sarpedon speared them on his talons and butchered them with his axe. He threw them aside and trampled them into the ground. Squad Graevus laid into the machines with similar determination, and soon Sarpedon and Graevus had carved out a clearing in the enemy force, surrounded by a rampart of mangled metal bodies. Some of the machines were intact enough to self-repair and clamber back up, but the Space Marines of Squad Graevus carved them back up or blasted their heads off, and few rose a second time.

'Luko! Lead your men out!' ordered Sarpedon as he tore the arm off a machine and split its metal skull in two. 'Crush them between us!'

'You heard him, brothers!' bellowed Luko to his squad. 'Take it to them! To me, my brothers! To me!'

Luko jumped through the doorway, kicking a machine to the ground as he did so. His fellow Soul Drinkers followed, charging from the doorway or vaulting through the windows. A few moments ago the machines would have swarmed around them, cut them off and dragged them down to their deaths, but now they were fighting on two fronts.

Luko laughed as he cut the machines to pieces in front of him.

Sarpedon led the charge the other way, wading through metallic bodies to close with Luko. Together, the two Soul Drinkers forces split the horde in two, and by the time Sarpedon was side by side with Luko hundreds of the machines were wrecked and broken.

Sarpedon cut at the face of a machine lunging towards him. The axe passed right through it as if it was an illusion. The machine faded out and then was gone completely.

The wrecked machines around Sarpedon's feet were dissolving away, too. The survivors and the destroyed were being teleported away.

'Where are they going?' asked Luko.

'Back to their makers?' said Sarpedon. 'To regroup and hit us again?'

It took only a few moments for the machines to disappear. Even the scraps of broken machinery were gone, leaving the Soul Drinkers standing alone on a patch of torn earth.

'Either way,' said Chaplain Iktinos, who had fought his way out behind Luko, 'we cannot stay here.'

'Agreed. Tisiph?'

'Commander?' voxed Sergeant Tisiph.

'Good work, sergeant. Land and cover us for embarkation.'

'Understood.'

The Thunderhawk swooped away towards the landing strip. With the noise of its engines fading, the only sound was the wind through the forest canopy and the pinking of hot bolter muzzles cooling.

'These things must have been waiting for survivors,' said Iktinos, looking up at the hollow bodies hanging from the trees. 'When the enemy came to this world they were not willing to leave a single human alive.'

The din of the battle had come entirely from the Soul Drinkers. Other than the clacking of their claws against armour and stone, the enemy machines had been completely silent. Even when they died, they had not made a sound.

Sarpedon did not know what they were, and he had never seen anything like them before, but he did know what the people of this world, and of the white city, had felt when the xenos machines attacked.

They must have believed that death itself had come for them.

'Death? What is death? It is the natural state of all things. It is life that is the aberration. It is life that should be feared, for it can go by with our work left undone, it can be wasted away on failure and indolence. Death is to be embraced.'
— Daenyathos, *Nineteenth Sphere of Tactical Apotheosis*

CHAPTER SIX

The damage done to the *Ferrous* in the opening exchanges with the alien fleet would have been enough to shred a lesser ship. Some energy bolt or wayward Mechanicus torpedo had blown a hole in the underside of the industrial ship's hull, blowing through and depressurising three decks. The *Ferrous*, however, was so old and lumbering that the destruction was wrought only through abandoned decks, with a couple of redundant systems damaged and the usual handful of menials killed.

The Mechanicus fleet had dropped out of the warp in good order, licking its wounds as hundreds of menials and junior tech-priests mounted running repairs and enacted apologetic rites to placate the traumatised machine-spirits. Among them was a gang of menials that attended to the wound in the underside of the *Ferrous*, which was still bleeding air and debris into the void.

Twenty menials marched through the shadowy, decrepit decks towards the wound. Their skin was almost grey and their faces almost featureless, drooping eyes, tiny black flecks, and mouths, lipless slits that barely ever spoke. Their lives had been spent in space, and they had never seen a blue sky or an ocean, except from orbit.

They pulled on the hoods of their voidsuits as vacuum warnings flickered along the dark corridors, their way lit by chemical lanterns. Walls and decks bowed inwards, crushed by the force of something tearing up through the layers of metal.

The menials were not there to save the decks that had been lost. That

ancient metal had been consigned to the void, to be absorbed back into
the fabric of the universe so it might one day be wrought again into
a work of the Omnissiah. Instead, they were to identify which areas
might be salvaged, and seal them off with sheets of tough flakweave
and rivet guns. Here and there, they sealed a tear in a wall through
which air might yet escape, or a doorway that threatened to give way.
Many places were marked as unsafe, to be cut away like diseased flesh
when the *Ferrous* was next in dock. It was sombre work, for everywhere
hung the necrotic sorrow of the *Ferrous's* machine-spirit.

A section of deck had been torn right through, leaving an enormous
cargo hangar sundered and useless. Hundreds of tonnes of construction materials had fallen out into space. One of the menials, instead of
marching grimly past one of the doorways leading to the condemned
hangar, suffered a spark of initiative and glanced through the frosted
window set into a bulkhead door leading to the hangar.

'What is that?' he asked.

'Keep moving,' said another. The menials had no leader, for they were
so well-versed in their duties that they could be trusted to admonish
one another. 'We still bleed.'

'No. This is not right. Come, look.'

More menials crowded around the doorway. The pane was almost
opaque with ice, but they could still glimpse a great shape of polished
silver and black, like an enormous bullet embedded in the fabric of the
ship.

'It could be unexploded munitions,' said one.

'Or one of the Fleet Minor,' said another.

'Regulations permit us to investigate,' said another.

'Very well.'

'Let us open it up.'

'And see.'

The menials checked the seals and air supplies on their voidsuits
before two of them hauled the wheel-lock open. The thin air in the
corridor whispered out, and silence fell, broken only by their boots
ringing on the deck.

The object had to be a hundred metres long and perhaps twenty wide,
a massive cylinder of black metal inlaid with panels of silver. Its surface
was torn from its entry into the ship, but it was still clear that it was
not of Imperial design. Where was the tarnish of a hundred years lying
in an ammunition hopper, the binary prayers stencilled on the casings?
It had a sheen that suggested materials beyond Imperial construction.
Towards the upper end, the casing broke up into a crown of drill bits,
like a huge snarling mouth that had chewed its way hungrily through
the *Ferrous's* hull.

'What is it?'

'It does not matter what it is.'

'For it is not of the machine. It is an intruder.'

'It must be excised! Let us summon work crews! Cutter units! Let the invader be expelled!'

The menials spread out around the ruins of the hangar to see if there was an obvious way of removing the object. Explosives could dislodge it. A craft of the Fleet Minor could pull it out like a diseased tooth, but that would cause further damage to the *Ferrous*. A less violent solution would be preferable, and would require less mollifying of the machine-spirit.

Vibrations sang through the floor. The side of the great cylinder split open. Inside, lights glimmered, green lights, glowing in silver-chased darkness.

The lights were paired, like eyes, and they narrowed as they focused on the approaching menials.

'We should inform the bridge.'

'We should.'

Emerald lights flared. The menials never got the chance to tell the bridge anything.

Magos Metallurgicus Vionel was touring the industrial base of the *Ferrous*, a series of titanic factory floors and forges running the length of the ship. The purpose of the *Ferrous* was to manufacture replacement parts and refine fuel for a fleet in deep space, allowing the whole fleet to continue operating for long after a conventional force would have needed to return to port due to the attrition of rust. The *Ferrous* was also at risk from the forces of decay, for it was old and the ills of corrosion and weakness had plenty of places to hide among its metalworks and refining halls.

Vionel trudged through the drifts of metal swarf that surrounded the enormous machining floor, raised up on blocks of steel. Thousands of menials laboured there, the hulking machines they served grinding out new components for the factory ship's ailing engines. Vionel's body was a heavily reinforced industrial chassis that clumped loudly up the steps to the machine floor. Overseer Gillard, an older menial, worn into a gnarled lump of a man by years on the factory floor, hurried to greet him.

'Lord magos,' said Gillard. 'Our efficiency targets are well within our sights.'

'But they are not achieved.'

'Regrettably not, lord magos. On a war footing, the energy rationing means that our...'

Vionel held up a huge metal paw to silence the overseer. 'The Omnissiah accepts no excuses. Efficiency is next to godliness. Even in the face of destruction, in the jaws of death, a menial's targets are his sacred duty.' Vionel's vocabulator unit was, like the rest of him, built for ruggedness rather than finesse, and his voice was a relentless monotone grind. 'This is the way of the Machine-God!'

'Blessed be the knowledge He imparts,' said Gillard hurriedly. 'I shall press my menials further, my lord.'

The overseer saluted and returned to the conveyor belt on which the thousands of menials under his command were sorting through heaps of components from the enormous machining unit.

The Mechanicus fleet was in a grave situation. It was pursued by xenos attackers, and its quarry, a space hulk, crewed by Mars knew what renegades and killers, was hostile in its own right. In this rare moment of calm before new orders came from the *Antithesis*, Vionel decided to seek the counsel of a higher power. Vionel let his human mind, one of the few remaining parts of his weak flesh, sink away from his senses, and he felt the mighty ironclad heartbeat of the *Ferrous*.

Magos Vionel, upon taking command of the *Ferrous* decades before, had installed interfaces with the ship's ancient machine-spirit in all of its data vaults and cogitators. The ship's machine-spirit had long been considered a curmudgeonly, silent entity that cared nothing for human beings and kept itself to itself. While many ancient ships manifested sophisticated machine-spirits, not all of them were willing to communicate, and these were generally left alone. Magos Vionel, however, knew that this approach was folly. Instead of assuming that a machine-spirit should become more human to allow for it to interface with its crew, he took it upon himself to become more like the *Ferrous*. He transmitted his personality into the information architecture of the factory ship through the interfaces, and forced his human mind into the shape of the machine-spirit's world.

It tasted of rust and the smoky tang of age. It felt warm and creaking, the heat of the factory ship's massive engines and reserves of power caged in the shell of rust.

In the heart of it was the machine-spirit. Vionel's mind was still too human to make of it anything but a murky storm, billowing purple-black clouds of processing power split by the lightning created by rapid calculations. The storm was contained in a great black vault, like some underground cathedral, Vionel's mind making of the physical restraints of the cogitators and data vaults an arching ceiling, supported by thick iron columns dripping with a constant rain of information.

The machine-spirit did not speak to Vionel directly. He had not yet earned that right. He had to interpret the emotions that whipped on information gales, like some fleshly soothsayer interpreting dreams.

The storm roared up towards him, bellowing wordlessly from a darkness at its heart crammed with pistons and flames. Vionel shrank from it, fearful for a moment that it had become angry with him and would devour his mind.

The machine-spirit was simply in pain. Silver webs were climbing across the surface of its clouds as if something was trying to trap the machine-spirit's functions in a net, restrain them and rob it of its power. Beams of emerald light played across the vault, scorching chunks of iron from the walls, which rusted as they fell.

'What pains us?' asked Vionel, turning his thought into streams of machine code. Their zeroes and ones were almost lost amongst the chaos of the *Ferrous's* pain.

The storm boiled away, sucking itself into a tight knot where the compression turned into glowing heat like the heart of a furnace. Vionel felt his mind struggling to hold on to cohesion in the sudden vacuum of the vault. Then the storm burst anew, lightning crackling across the walls, a hurricane heavy with data battering against Vionel. The sound deafened Vionel's mind, and he fought to hold on to his place in the information structures of the ship. In spite of the burst of energy, the silver web held, shimmering as it stretched around the thunderheads.

Vionel could watch no more. His grip failed, and his mind was shunted back into his body with an impact that made him stumble on his iron-shod feet.

The ship echoed with the machine-spirit's pain. Even the menials could feel it, thrumming through the decks of the *Ferrous* in time with the spirit's screams.

Vionel accessed the ship's vox-net.

'To arms!' he yelled, his metallic voice transmitted all over the ship. 'We are invaded!'

The menials immediately broke out wrenches and shivs, anything they had to hand as a weapon. Overseer Gillard unlocked a weapons cabinet mounted on the side of the machine, and a few menials took shotguns and autopistols from it, simple, ugly weapons, perfect for the sort of close-quarters murder that was typical in a boarding action.

'Bridge!' voxed Vionel. 'Relay to me all reports of intruders. Keep me up to date on damage controls. Tech-guard standby.'

A series of cogitator tones bleeped in response. The *Ferrous* had a complement of tech-guard and trained menials in case of hostile boarders, who were, at that moment, grabbing their flak armour and lasguns and heading through the ill-maintained mazes of the ship's outer decks to meet the sources of the alert.

'Lord magos,' said Gillard, turning from a bank of readouts on the side of the forge. 'What has happened?'

'The ship is compromised,' said Vionel. 'The machine-spirit has given us warning.'

It might not be enough. The ship was huge. There were thousands of ways attackers could get into the vulnerable factory floors or the processing plants in the ship's rear section, or make their way towards the bridge. The tech-guard couldn't hold them all back.

'They saw me,' said Vionel. 'They know I am here. Their target is the machine-spirit.'

The first he saw of them was a flicker of green fire at the edge of his vision, up among the steel rafters of the machining section. A menial working at the forge reared up in sudden pain and shock. A huge chunk, like a round bite mark, had been torn from his back as if by invisible jaws. One arm was gone, too, flayed down to bloody bones.

Vionel's targeting oculars snapped into focus on the enemy.

'Tech-guard, to my position!' he voxed. 'Enemy sighted!'

They were skeletal machines, animated by the green flame flickering in their eye sockets and chests. They had got in through the maintenance access to the section's ceiling, and they were hiding among the rafters. They carried elaborate weapons built around glowing green cores, which had projector units surrounded by haloes of electricity instead of muzzles.

Vionel's mind accessed the images from the recording Voar had found in the bridge archives. Hunched metallic skeletons, robotic, relentless: necron warriors.

Vionel pumped all his auxiliary power into his limbs. They were massively powerful, designed to anchor him to the ground and lift enormous weight, but they were also a lot faster than they looked. Vionel ran up the steps towards the conveyor belt even as blasts ripped chunks out of the floor behind him. Cores of metal were drilled out of the deck and flayed to atoms. The few menials with guns returned fire, and flayer blasts fell among them, shredding limbs and flashing away skulls.

Vionel slammed into a section of the conveyor, heavy with machine components. He clamped his enormous metal hands around the edge and ripped a section away. He spun, his torso rotating freely on its chassis, and hurled the hunk of machinery with all his strength.

The conveyor section hit the girders so hard that several of them fell, hammering into the deck with a tremendous ringing like giant bells. Necrons fell, too, some of them crushed against the ceiling by the impact, others buried by the mass of steelwork collapsing on top of them.

Voar's briefing on the new threat had contained most of the intelligence the Imperium had on what its soldiers called the necrons. They were a machine-race, ancient beyond imagining. Their technology was an obscenity of forbidden principles and xenos heresy. They were a corruption of the Machine-God. It was not much to go on, but it was all

Vionel needed. He was a forger of the Omnissiah's works, a creator, and his duty was to avenge their destruction.

Tech-guard were emerging from entrances beside the forge, in rust-red body armour with mirrored visors, carrying lasguns hooked up to their backpacks.

'Magos!' called the sergeant. 'At your command!'

'Advance!' said Vionel, projecting at maximum volume.

The surviving warriors advanced or got to their feet, their broken bodies re-forming from liquid metal. Others, shattered beyond repair, disappeared from beneath the wreckage. Even torn limbs and fragments of crushed skull vanished.

The tech-guard, a dozen of them in the squad, ran into the cover of the conveyor belt or the lengths of fallen girder. Lasguns spat. The air filled with the smell of burning and ozone.

Blasts from necron weapons hammered against the machinery with a crackling hiss, as if the metal were evaporating. Vionel stomped through the ruined conveyor into cover, but it was rapidly disappearing. Menials died, chunks of their bodies stripped away. Others were still returning fire, and a warrior fell, chest blown open. One of the tech-guard stood clear of the wreckage to send a rapid-fire volley into the necrons, but he fell, too, his body armour and half his torso stripped clean away.

The tech-guard sergeant led the way across the chamber towards the necrons entering the chamber to join those who had attacked from the ceiling. The short-range gunfight blazed, red las-blasts and gouts of green fire exchanged through the wreckage and gloom. Tech-guard fell. The sergeant dived to the floor as the cover around him dissolved.

The first warriors were making it onto the machinery floor. Vionel broke cover and fired, sending a volley of rivets through the body of the first enemy he saw. Steel rivets punched through its face and ribcage and it fell. Vionel's next shot shattered a warrior's weapon, and, in a green flash, the gun's energy discharged, the remains dropping uselessly to the floor.

There must have been fifty necrons, and, every time one fell, another seemed to rise up from the ground. Vionel was not afraid. He had not been afraid since that part of his brain had been burned out and replaced with data storage. The chances of survival were not good, but ultimately, that changed nothing.

Necron warriors clambered over the remains of the conveyor. Vionel knocked the legs out from one and slammed his metal fist down into its body, shattering it so thoroughly that he knew its heathen technology couldn't get it back to its feet. The rivet gun hammered away almost of its own volition, thudding hot metal into the approaching enemy.

The warrior Vionel had disarmed leapt from the conveyor onto his back. Metal hands prised at the cowling of his torso. Vionel tried to throw the creature off, but its hands were inside the plating, reaching for bundles of wires and fragile components, and it wouldn't let go. Vionel stumbled backwards and slammed back into the housing of the machining forge from which the conveyor emerged. The forge was still hammering away, stamping out metal components that spilled out onto the floor with no menials to sort through them. Vionel tried to crush the necron against the side of the machine, but it held on. Bolts of fire burst around him, one shearing deep into his left shoulder and another almost taking his leg off.

Vionel reached up, grabbed the necron around its metal neck and tore it off his back, and threw it into the mouth of the machining forge. The necron scrambled to escape, but it was a fraction too late, and a piston stamped a cog-shaped hole through the centre of its face.

The warriors were still approaching, relentless, their advance slowed by the remaining tech-guard falling back before them and sending las-blasts scoring deep melting furrows across their carapaces. There were more warriors, too, emerging from access points around the machine floor. Vionel knew he could not fight them all, no matter how much satisfaction it might give him every time a xenos abomination was felled by one of the Omnissiah's rivets. He stomped to the side of the forge. He tore a section of panel away and hurled it, the jagged edge slicing the head off an advancing warrior.

'I require reinforcements!' voxed Vionel. 'Armsmen and tech-guard to my location!'

Across the floor, another tech-guard fell, this time in close combat, his lasgun torn from his hands by a necron, who then jabbed the curved bayonet on its gun into the man's gut. The sergeant blew off the alien's arm in response, but only a handful of tech-guard fought back now, scrambling from cover to cover to fall back to Vionel and the forge.

Vionel hammered with his rivet gun and threw chunks of machinery with his other arm. Fire tore into the forge around him. The forge shuddered and broke down, spewing half-formed components. A warrior clambered, grinning onto the machine floor beside him, and Vionel was barely able to swat the barrel of its weapon away before it discharged a bolt of green fire into him at point-blank range. Vionel hauled the warrior into the air, tore its arms off and threw what remained into another necron approaching with its gun levelled at him.

'We are lost!' voxed the tech-guard sergeant.

'We breathe,' said Vionel. 'We think. We reason. We are not lost.'

Three squads of tech-guard burst in through entrances behind the forge. Las-fire fell as thick as rain, the whole chamber glowing red with it. Vionel crouched down as las-blasts ripped over his head, slicing into necron torsos. Vionel lent his rivet gun to the weight of fire, pinning one warrior to the floor, a very unmachine-like relish firing in his brain as he watched the alien squirming like a pinned insect.

Las-fire was not enough to puncture necron armour on its own, but the weight of it was overwhelming. Twenty bolts might bounce off a necron's carapace, leaving a molten red welt, but the twenty-first might hit a vulnerable spot, or melt a little to far and destroy a critical component. Necrons on broken limbs were easy targets, while others were shot through gaps in their carapaces and fell as they advanced. The tech-guard formed up behind Vionel in a firing line, joined by the survivors of the first squad. One of the tech-guard brought a melta gun to bear, and its superheated beam melted through torsos and metallic skulls.

The necrons fell. Vionel held up a paw, and the firing died down. One of the sergeants yelled the order to cease fire.

The bodies were gone, not those of the fallen tech-guard and menials, which lay in pools of gore mixed with the swarf from the forge, but the necrons. They simply disappeared when they collapsed. Vionel advanced slowly, wary of necrons self-repairing to attack him unexpectedly.

One necron lay there, quite dead, but without disappearing. It had juddered along the broken conveyor belt and clattered to the floor.

'Magos,' said Gillard, who had somehow contrived to survive hidden among the machinery surrounding the forge. 'Is it over?'

'No,' said Vionel.

More necrons were emerging from the rusting shadows around the machine floor. The first warriors had been the vanguard, and Vionel could tell that the following waves were deadlier, just with a look. Those on foot were broader-shouldered with solid, stocky spines to support the weight of their larger gauss weapons, and behind them hovered variants of warriors on flying anti-grav chassis. Metallic beetles scurried along the deck in front of the second wave. Green blasts fell among the few remaining menials, powerful enough to strip them down to gnawed skeletons.

Vionel grabbed the fallen necron warrior and slung it over his back where magnetic clamps, which usually fixed stabilising legs and pneumatic lifters to his chassis, held it firm. 'Tech-guard, we cannot hold this place. Fall back to the dorsal saviour pods!'

A few shouted orders saw the tech-guard units covering one another as they moved back out of the chamber, maintaining a spattering of fire to keep the necron guns off them for a few seconds more.

Vionel did not follow them. Instead, he ran at full tilt towards the nearest wall. His enormous weight slammed into it, and he tore straight through the wall, his momentum ripping through the bulkhead into the next section. A section of the ceiling fell in behind him. It would hold off the necrons for the few minutes he needed.

Vionel stopped and let his mind sink down again, the artificial parts of his brain banishing the adrenaline from his system so that he could focus. He entered the ship's information structure again, for the next course of action was not his to decide.

All was pain. Even before Vionel reached past the interface protocols, he could feel it. There was fire, but also terrible cold, as if the chill of the void had bled into the soul of the ship. Vionel's mind conjured metallic walls and corridors to represent the ship's low-level systems, but they were decaying, running like water or blemished with biological stains. Banks of datacrystal, which represented the ship's archives, were rotting, or burning to ash in green flames. Vionel did not panic, for such a useless emotion was no longer part of his augmented mind, but the grotesqueness of it still spoke to the weak human parts of him. This was his ship, a thing of ancient beauty and majesty, and it was sick. That sickness manifested turned Vionel's stomach in a very human way.

Vionel sank deeper. The ship was falling apart inside. Glittering conduits of information streaming from the ship's sensors fractured and broke as the *Ferrous* went blind, chunks of raw data raining down like debris in an earthquake. Vionel guided his mind between them, wary that damage to a tech-priest's mind could prove as fatal as damage to the body.

The roaring, thundering presence of the machine-spirit echoed everywhere. Vionel slipped through the next layer, and its anger hit him like a tidal wave. It was hot and vibrant, a shocking, terrible mass of emotion to come from a machine-spirit that had been so quiet for so long. Vionel had known it previously only as a chained storm, its power the potential energy of its great intellect and knowledge contained in the metal shell of the *Ferrous*. Now it was open and raw, all its centuries of existence powering its fury, and its pain.

Waves of pure agony hammered off it. Vionel forced his mind to conceptualise the machine-spirit as it loomed up from the darkness of the ship's higher systems. The storm clouds were angry red, and they rained blood. Fingers of mercury had wormed their way through the walls of the vaulted chamber. Currents of hot, toxic pain flowed around the storm, lashing at it, and the black lightning of pain arced as the machine-spirit raged.

The liquid metal, like thousands of ropes, reached into a spider's web that strangled the machine-spirit's power. No matter how the storm raged, the silver web tightened, and the storm bled all the more.

'Tell me!' cried Vionel. 'Tell me what I must do!'

A mass of liquid metal welled up, churning like an ocean under the storm. Hands reached up from it, taloned and dripping, and where the lightning struck it the hands grabbed it and dragged it down. Vast reserves of power discharged into that ocean, greedily drained away by the invading force.

The emotion that howled on the gale was not human, but it could not be mistaken. Pain and anger mixed into one, and, in hot desperation, battered against Vionel's mind.

'Please, Lord *Ferrous*! Do not ask that of me!'

There was no reply but the pain. There was no longer enough human left in Vionel to deny it.

The *Ferrous* wanted to die.

Vionel wrenched his mind out of the ship's information systems. He snapped back into his body as it charged and clawed its way down through the outer hull access tunnels towards the lower hull of the ship. The necron warrior fixed to his back was still there, weighing him down with its heresy.

'Vionel to processing!' voxed Vionel.

'Processing here!' came the reply from the overseer. From the sound of explosions and gunfire behind the menial's voice, the necrons had made it into the processing section, too, into the mass of chemical tanks and fractioning towers that the *Ferrous* dragged behind it.

'Open all the catalyst chambers and inundate with fuel!'

'Magos? That will…'

'I know what it will do! You have your orders.'

The menial paused. Menials had not received the higher teachings of the Machine-God, and were unaugmented and weak. A handful of new tech-priests were promoted from their ranks each year, but the great majority of them would only ever be normal, weak humans, ruled by their flesh and their emotions. Sometimes, they could not be trusted to do the work of the Omnissiah. Sometimes concerns like compassion or fear got in the way.

'Yes, magos,' said the menial. 'It will be done!'

'Fight them,' said Vionel, 'unto death.'

'We will.'

Vionel closed the vox-link. With the ship's information systems falling apart, it was up to the menials remaining in the processing section to do the machine-spirit's will. He could only hope that they would overcome the failings of their human minds.

Vionel reached the emergency hatch that led into an array of saviour pods. Each pod could carry half a dozen crewmen, which meant that one was just big enough for Vionel. The tech-guard was already there, in defensive positions ready to fend off the necrons that might burst in at any moment.

'Abandon ship,' ordered Vionel.

As the tech-guard entered the saviour pods, Vionel opened the hatch of the nearest pod and threw the wrecked necron warrior in ahead of him. He was barely able to get his bulk through the hatch. He had to pull out one of the seats and throw it aside, before he could turn to close the hatch behind him.

The *Ferrous* shook. The necrons had found some critical part of the engines, or their assault on the machine-spirit was forcing the ship to tear itself apart. The end was coming for the *Ferrous*, and Vionel mourned it with the part of his brain that could still feel sorrow.

Vionel mentally commanded the saviour pod's charges to fire. The ring of explosives detonated and fired the saviour pod out through its opening in the ship's hull. The pod, and Magos Vionel, spun away from the dying ship, just as tongues of fire began to run up and down its tortured hull.

Archmagos Voar watched the death of the *Ferrous* from the improvised briefing room on the bridge of the *Antithesis*. To him, it was a stream of energy readings spooling across a pict screen, but just as a tech-priest could see meaning in the zeroes and ones of machine-code, so Voar could see the fate of the ship in the jagged lines of the wildly fluctuating power output of the factory ship.

Somehow, even though the Mechanicus had evaded the pursuing ships, the necrons had managed to get at the *Ferrous*.

The *Ferrous*'s processing section exploded. The fleet's fuel reserve went up in one titanic ball of orange flame, as bright, for a split-second, as a sun. Nuclear fires tore the factory ship apart, consuming its entire length and ripping the steel of its hull into atoms.

It was beautiful in its own way. Just as everything had to be forged, so everything had to be destroyed, whether by violence or decay. The *Ferrous* was an ancient craft, however, and, with it, died a spirit that could never be built again.

'Archmagos!' came a crackling vox. Voar struggled to recognise the voice through the distortion, but it was transmitted on his personal vox-net, which meant it was from one of the fleet's magi.

'Vionel?' asked Voar. 'You live?'

'But barely, my archmagos. Necrons boarded us. The machine-spirit bade me destroy it.'

'So that was you.'

'There was no choice. The spirit was corrupted.'

The idea was obscene. A machine-spirit, a fragment of the Omnissiah, violated by alien technology. 'Then you have served Him well,' said Voar.

'I am in a saviour pod and have sustained damage. The area is heavy with debris.'

'I will have the Fleet Minor pick you up,' said Voar, 'and take you to Crystavayne on the *Defence*.'

'It is better that I come to the *Antithesis* as soon as possible, archmagos.'
'Why?'
'Because I have something to show you.'

'Brave men die every day, unremembered. Courage receives no prize, but cowardice and dishonour can buy happiness and renown. The brave amongst us must accept their rewards from within, even in the throes of death.'

– Daenyathos, *Catechisms Martial, addendum secundus*

CHAPTER SEVEN

The Veiled Region became deeper still. The nebula was a bloom of interstellar dust so vast that the solar system could fit into one of its countless whorls. It was lit from within by the fires that burned as the dust clumped together into infant stars. The tides of the nebula heaved slowly, ridges and troughs of dust making for a journey as dangerous as any through the warp.

Micrometeorites, motes of dust from ill-birthed worlds, pattered against the hull of the *Brokenback*. It was heavy going through the nebula, and a smaller, more delicate ship would not have risked it at all. After over twenty-four hours of forging through the nebula, the capital of the fallen empire was in sight, a tiny glimmer orbiting a star that had somehow survived the currents of the nebula long enough to become fat and yellow like Terra's own sun.

The bridge of the *Brokenback* was quiet. Lygris knew better than to take that as an encouraging sign. A hundred warning lights were winking on the various cogitators and readouts, and the reactors could go cold for good at any minute. The ruination of the *Blessed Obedience* was still sparking fires and venting air and fuel, and if Lygris had not disconnected the alarm klaxons the bridge would have been a deafening mass of noise.

'Help us,' said a quiet voice. An unaugmented human ear would have missed it entirely. Lygris strained to hear.

'Help us. You must...'

It was there again, almost hidden by the humming of the cogitators. Lygris worked the control panel of the closest cogitator.

The ship's vox-net was clear, so the voice hadn't come from one of the Soul Drinkers. In any case, the voice had sounded female. Lygris searched through the external comms channels, the spectrum of frequencies across which a signal might be sent to the ship from elsewhere.

He found it. It was weak, only just strong enough to stir the cogitator's vocabulator unit. Lygris amplified it and tried to gauge its origin.

'Help us,' the voice said again. It was accented, but spoke recognisable Low Gothic. 'You must come to our aid. This is Raevenia, last world of the Selaacan Empire, and we are beset by the stars themselves.'

On the bridge a few minutes later, Sarpedon listened again to the whole transmission. It was on a loop, broadcasting constantly, but, with each iteration, the bridge cogitators were closing in on its origin.

'The stars themselves?' he mused. 'What can that mean?'

'Some stellar disaster?' suggested Lygris. Sarpedon and the Techmarine were on the bridge along with Chaplain Iktinos and Librarian Tyrendian.

'Or our xenos friends,' said Tyrendian distastefully.

'We need help urgently,' continued the signal. 'Weaponry and men, to defend our world. Anyone who hears this, join us in our fight, for more worlds, more empires than ours face extinction. Pass us by, and perhaps this doom will fall upon you next. The choice is yours.'

'Is there any indication that the senders of this message still live?' asked Iktinos. 'There's no telling how long it's been looping.

'And where are they?' asked Sarpedon.

'A short jump away.' Lygris examined the screen of the navigation cogitator. 'Still within the nebula.'

'I don't like it,' said Tyrendian. 'We know where their capital is. We're more likely to find survivors there.'

'Assuming,' said Iktinos, 'that this shadow from the stars did not start with the capital and work its way outwards. The message from Raevenia said they were the last survivors.'

'The bodies at the palace had not been dead that long,' said Sarpedon. 'Whatever happened to this empire happened recently. I believe that we must head for Raevenia.'

'Why?' asked Tyrendian.

Sarpedon threw his fellow Librarian a stern look.

'Because they asked for help,' he said. 'Lygris, can we make it?'

'There and no further. The *Brokenback* will be dead in the void after another jump.'

'Then set coordinates and do it. If we can help these people we can ask for fuel and be on our way.'

'And if we cannot?' asked Tyrendian.

Sarpedon did not answer him. Lygris keyed Raevenia's coordinates into the bridge cogitator. The reactors juddered alarmingly as they warmed up to throw the space hulk through the warp a final time.

'We lost good brothers at the palace and the white city,' said Tyrendian. 'How many more will this jaunt cost us?'

'Do you have a better idea, brother?' snapped Sarpedon.

'The commander is correct,' said Iktinos levelly, stepping between the two Librarians. 'Brother Tyrendian, this is our best chance of saving ourselves. Our pursuers are still out there, and are no doubt closing on us. To do nothing is not an option, and the right choice has been made.'

'I feel their deaths as much as you do, brother,' said Sarpedon, 'but this is not a kind galaxy. Sometimes we must die for our brothers, and no one can say who will die and who will survive.'

For a moment, it looked like Tyrendian would argue. Then his face softened almost imperceptibly.

'You are my Chapter Master and I bow to you,' he said. 'Scamander and I must make preparations for the warp.'

'You have my leave,' said Sarpedon. Psykers were more at risk from the occasional influence of the warp during travel. Sarpedon, being unable to receive telepathy, did not suffer much, but Tyrendian's mind was a little more sensitive, and Scamander, of course, was still learning to control his talents.

Tyrendian left the bridge, and Sarpedon turned back to Lygris. 'If we do find an inhabited world, what are our chances?'

'Assuming they are a space-faring people... reasonable, I would guess. That depends on their being friendly.'

'Then we are assuming much,' said Iktinos.

'We always do,' said Sarpedon. 'Any sign of the Mechanicus fleet?'

'I would tell you if there was,' said Lygris. 'The nebula makes it difficult to know either way. We could have lost them or they could be right on our tail.'

'Then they could follow us to Raevenia,' said Sarpedon. 'We need to move quickly.'

'Very well.' Lygris began to key the coordinates into the bridge cogitator.

'What are your thoughts, Chaplain?' asked Sarpedon, turning to Iktinos.

Iktinos wore, as he almost always did, his full regalia of power armour and skull-faced helm. It was the face he showed to his Chapter, so he did not look like one of them but an impassive judge of their souls. 'I believe that we are on the best course.'

'How will the battle-brothers see it?'

'I will see to it that they understand. We are not answering a distress signal, but searching for civilisation to refuel our ship. This is a mission of survival.'

'They all are,' said Sarpedon. 'You have my leave, Chaplain. The Chapter will need to pray for peace in the warp.'

'As shall we both.'

'Say a word for me, too,' said Lygris as he finished punching in the coordinates for Raevenia.

Archmagos Voar had turned his section of the bridge library into a war-room. He had ordered the tech-priests to clear it and bring him everything he needed to appreciate the fleet and its situation: holo-projectors for tactical readouts, a heavy wooden map table with star charts spread out on it still awaiting the first landmarks of the Veiled Region, heaps of books on naval battle-lore, and histories of conflicts with space hulks and alien fleets.

He looked up at the heavy pneumatic footfalls approaching through the library. Magos Vionel emerged into the amber light of the glow-globes.

'Magos,' said Voar, 'I see you have endured close contact with the enemy.'

'Forgive me, archmagos,' said Vionel. Voar was correct. Vionel was effectively naked, although it mattered little given that his body was completely contained within his industrial chassis, with only his half-augmetic face showing. One shoulder was stripped down to the pistons and servos, as if the layers of armour had been peeled away one by one. He was covered in cuts and gouges. He smelled of hot machine oil and torn iron. 'I have come fresh from battle.'

'How badly are you damaged?'

'I require replacement parts. My core functions are largely unaffected.'

'Then what have you to show me so urgently?'

Vionel stomped up to Voar's desk. Voar saw that he had a chunk of wreckage in one fist. Vionel heaved it onto the desk in front of Voar.

'Here,' he said. 'One of them.'

The wreckage was of a robotic humanoid, its limbs hopelessly mangled and its metal skull punched through, robbing it of eyes to go with its lipless mouth.

'A necron?' asked Voar.

'One of their warriors. The basic combat unit.'

Voar stood up and turned over the necron warrior's shattered head.

'There had only been a single exemplar recovered,' said Voar, 'and that was not as complete as this. How did you prevent it from phasing out?'

'I assume it was the damage I caused to it.'

'You were fortunate.'

'The *Ferrous* died under my stewardship. I can see no good fortune in its fate. I hope only that knowledge will flow from my actions.'

'Did the machine-spirit... say anything? Did it have any message before it fell?'

'It could not speak. I believe that destruction was the fate the Omnissiah would grant it. That was all.'

Archmagos Voar knew that sorrow was something that he should feel. He felt its echo. He had grieved before, been sad that some colleague had died, or that he had lost... a friend? He tried to remember the concept of an individual whose importance stemmed from something other than standing within the Mechanicus. It was there, a trace of grief, and he let himself feel that shadow of bereavement for the *Ferrous*. It did not last long.

'I will take this to my laboratory,' said Voar. 'There may be something I can learn from it.'

'What will you have me do?' asked Vionel.

'Take a shuttle to the *Defence*. Crystavayne will repair you.'

'Yes, my archmagos.'

'And Vionel?'

'Yes?'

Voar looked up from the wrecked necron. 'Can we fight them?'

'In numbers? No, archmagos, we cannot.'

'That will be all, magos.'

Vionel bowed, awkward on his squat chassis, and stomped back off the bridge. He limped as he went, one motivator unit in his hip spitting sparks.

Even with most of its face destroyed, the alien machine seemed to leer up at Voar. It was a gangling ruin, studded with rivets from Vionel's gun and mangled by the machining unit, but the malice it contained was undiminished for all that.

'What are you?' asked Voar quietly. 'Where did you come from?' He picked up the head. The plain black circuit boards in its skull glinted through the wound in its face. 'And if you truly are a machine, who built you?'

Voar paused and took the mask from his robes, the mask that Baradrin Thaal had so foolishly bought as a plaything, and which had led the Mechanicus to the Veiled Region in the first place. He held it up to the ruined warrior's face.

It was the same metal, the same dimensions. The mask was not a part of the same machine; it aped a human face, while the necron warrior's head resembled a human skull in only the most stylised coincidental way. It was, however, a relic of the same empire.

'What news is there of the Soul Drinkers?' voxed Voar to the ship's tactical helm.

'We're still tracking them,' replied one of the many tech-priests who were now taking shifts in monitoring the space surrounding the fleet. 'Their last warp jump was off-course from our calculations.'

'Where are they heading?'

'A system towards the nebula centre.'

'Inhabited?'

'It's possible.'

'Follow them.'

'Yes, archmagos.'

Voar sat down at the desk and shut off the vox-links to give him some peace to think.

'What bargain have you made, Astartes?' he said to himself, turning the xenos mask over in his hands. 'What have they offered you? What will you pay?'

Outside the *Antithesis*, the other ships of the Mechanicus fleet were gathering into formation to enter the warp, both to stay ahead of the necron aggressors and close in on the Soul Drinkers.

Whether it cost him his fleet, or even his life, Archmagos Voar would find his answers soon.

Through the dozens of sensors on the *Brokenback*, the planet identified as Raevenia was blue-green, glittering and beautiful. Planets like that got rarer every year in the Imperium, as more were settled by billions of pilgrims and refugees, polluted, stripped bare, or turned into smouldering warzones. Raevenia had rings of stellar ice and dust, and several moons, half-formed captive asteroids, orbiting it.

'The source of the signal,' said Lygris, 'is here.'

The planet was shown on the holo-unit that Lygris had set up on the bridge of the *Brokenback*. The Techmarine indicated a point near the equator, on a large continent that fragmented into dozens of islands along its southern edge. 'It looks like there is a city there. Some pollutants and plenty of structures.' Lygris pointed to a pale spot beside the potential city. 'Given that this civilisation is space-faring, this could be a space port.'

'Is the signal stronger?' asked Sarpedon.

'It was. It cut out about three hours ago.'

'Cut out?'

'Just after we broke warp. I've been trying to raise a response on the same frequency, but there's nothing.'

Sarpedon looked more closely at the holo. 'Is there any sign of conflict down there?

'None yet,' said Lygris. 'That doesn't mean it isn't there. More likely, it's another ghost world and the xenos have seen us coming.'

The two Soul Drinkers were alone on the bridge. Much of the Chapter was preparing to depart for the surface of Raevenia, and the rest were positioned throughout the *Brokenback*, manning the sensorium helms and keeping an uneasy watch over the remaining reactors.

'What do you think of it?' asked Sarpedon.

'This planet? It's definitely inhabited, or at least it was.'

'More than that.'

Lygris thought for a long moment. 'I don't like it.'

'No?'

'It's this whole place, the Veiled Region. It feels like it was… waiting for us. It's drawing us further in so it can kill us off bit by bit, as if it is alive and we are a virus to be killed off. Does that sound sane?'

'Stranger things have been proven to exist in this galaxy,' said Sarpedon, 'but as you say, we aren't going anywhere else. It is Raevenia or nothing.'

'I agree. This is our best chance. I only wish that we had some more appetising choices.'

Sarpedon studied the image of Raevenia some more. Here and there, the forests and plains were stained with dark areas that could be cities, or grey veins that might be roads. North of the possible city was a range of mountains crowned with snow, like white stitches in the planet's surface.

'Whoever is down there,' said Lygris, 'we may have to fight them to take the fuel we need.'

'Then we will fight them,' replied Sarpedon sharply. 'We have done more distasteful things. This is survival.'

'Let us say we do survive. We find a safe berth in the galaxy where we are not hunted. What then?'

'Then,' said Sarpedon, 'we will rule ourselves. That is worth fighting for.'

'Do you think it is possible?'

'Lygris, would I have led you here, would I have led you at all, if it was not? To live free in the Imperium is a fight that might take until the end of time to win, but it is worth fighting. If I believe anything, then I believe that.'

'Freedom?' said Lygris. 'From the Imperium? No one has lived free in this galaxy since the Age of Strife. For my battle-brothers to see it… that is something I would risk my life for.'

'Well said, Techmarine,' said Sarpedon. 'It is the Emperor's work. Had he not been betrayed by the tyrants that followed him then we might not have to fight for it like this. Of course, we won't be fighting for anything if we're stranded here.'

'Very well, commander,' said Lygris. 'I will see to it that the gunships are ready for launch.'

Lygris left Sarpedon to contemplate the unspoilt globe of Raevenia. It seemed too beautiful to harbour anything deadly, too natural and pure to threaten corruption.

A Space Marine never let appearances drop his guard, however. If the fates so willed it, there would be plenty of killing on that planet.

The necron fleet tore the heart out of a star.

It was an old star, fat and red, a lumbering giant that stood as a relic of a time before the clouds of the Veiled Region had gathered. The star darkened, and then collapsed, throwing off outer layers in ripples of radiation millions of miles across. Its remaining substance compacted and heated up, and, for a few final hours, it burned as bright as it had in its youth, spitting violent solar flares and atomic storms in its death throes. Then that energy, too, was sucked out into the void, and the star shrank into a smouldering clump of ashes, burning away the last vestiges of its power.

The star's power fuelled the fleet's alien technologies. The ships hurtled at impossible interstellar speeds, space-time folding through fields of exotic energy, showers of particles that physics determined could not exist streaking across the Veiled Region.

The last echoes of the star's power rippled out as the fleet arrived at its destination. The cold radioactive dust was thrown aside as the necron necropolis ship tore through it, power crackling off its talons. The rest of the fleet shifted into place beside it, the star's stolen power arcing between them and the necropolis ship. Time and space seemed to complain at the violation that had brought the necrons there, shimmering ripples washing out at the speed of light, echoing off the barren worlds around the dead star.

Tombs, sealed before mankind had evolved, split open, and the lords of the host emerged, hot coils of power burning the patina of millennia from their bodies. They raised their staves, and unliving eyes turned on them. Scarabs swarmed everywhere, fixing the systems that time had undone. Information flickered between the command nodes of the host, between the lords and their master, down to the individual warriors. War machines awoke, too, enormous vehicles like hovering monuments to death, fighter craft folded up in their vertical launch decks like colonies of bats.

To the ships of the sentinel fleet would now be added the armies of necron warriors that had already conquered most of the human empire. Neither the defenders of Raevenia, already whittled down by vanguard units, nor the new interlopers would face any point but elimination.

Archmagos Voar had kept the laboratory solely for his own use. Not even the other magi of the fleet had access to this part of the *Antithesis*. Sometimes, solitude was as essential to a tech-priest's studies as his knowledge of the Machine. Sometimes, the things he studied were best kept to his mind, the strongest and best trained, alone.

The laboratory equipment dated back to the building of the *Antithesis*.

Its surfaces were brushed steel glowing faintly over the low light. It was attended by a complement of servitors, silver-plated spidery creations with their once-human components hidden from view.

Archmagos Voar placed the wrecked necron warrior on the dissection slab in the centre of the laboratory. An autosurgeon unit swung into place overhead, and a thin beam of white light fell onto the necron, illuminating it in all the fine detail that Voar's bionic eyes could discern.

A pair of mechadendrites uncoiled from Voar's shoulders. They were thin and delicate, quite unlike the crude articulated cables that lower-ranked tech-priests used as additional limbs. Voar's plucked a medical laser and power scalpel from their rack on the autosurgeon, a miniature field of disruptive energy flickering around the scalpel blade.

Voar had been a commander of the Adeptus Mechanicus forces in the field for a long time, too long, perhaps. The purity of pursuing knowledge in this way, information for its own sake and not as a means to a military end, was like a drug that focused his mind. There was no limit to what a magos could achieve with that focus and the blessing of the Omnissiah upon him. He concentrated on the machine and slowly slit the necron's torso open, heating the alloy with the laser so that it could be slit open by the scalpel.

The vaporised metal did not smell right. It did not glow and deform in the way righteous metal should. Voar had to choke back the sense of disgust. The torso split open, and Voar carefully lifted the two halves apart.

A power core lay beneath, still glowing with unholy radiation with solid black surfaces inscribed with complex patterns in place of wires and circuits. It was nothing at all like the Machine, like the perfection of form as taught by the Omnissiah. Studying it would be taxing on the soul as well as the mind. That was why Voar had to keep it here, in his sealed lab, where it could not infect less well-prepared minds.

'Archmagos,' said a vox from the bridge. It was Magos Hepsebah on board the *Constant*, which was flying in formation ahead of the *Antithesis*.

Voar withdrew the implements from the innards of the dead machine. 'I asked not to be disturbed.'

'They were waiting for us,' said Hepsebah. 'It's all over our scanners.'

'Explain.'

'The xenos. They knew our course before we did. They're here.'

'Anyone outside the fold of the Imperium of Man is an enemy, proven or otherwise, xenos or human. Anyone who lives without the light of Terra walks in darkness.'

– Daenyathos, *The Defence of Xall XIX*

CHAPTER EIGHT

Sarpedon saw the city first as the lead Thunderhawk broke through the cloud cover. It was surrounded by a solid defence wall, with grand gates to the north and south, and the city itself was a great crown of decorative stonework contained within those walls. The towers of palaces and civic buildings reached up from sprawling estates and cramped winding streets. Poorer districts dominated the south, tumbledown tenement blocks built over the foundations of a once-prosperous district, devolving into ramshackle shanties along the south wall and spilling into the woodland beyond the south gate. The lands around it were carpeted with deciduous forests, rolling up towards a line of hills to the far north. A short distance from the city was the structure that Lygris had correctly identified as a space port, several rockcrete landing pads surrounding a control tower, all held within its own set of defensive walls studded with fire-points and watchtowers.

'Commander,' voxed Phol from the Thunderhawk's cockpit. Phol was probably the only Soul Drinker Lygris trusted to fly a Thunderhawk as well as Lygris himself did. 'The Raevenians have come out to greet us. Armed men, several thousand.'

The force had gathered outside the city's south gate. Sarpedon could see them ranked up in regiments, thousands strong, with artillery and cavalry drawn up on the flanks. Banners fluttered in the wind.

'Bring us in, brother,' voxed Sarpedon.

The Soul Drinkers of Squad Luko were strapped into the grav-restraints around Sarpedon. Each one had a pre-battle ritual. Many of them recited passages from the *Catechisms Martial*, the Soul Drinkers' philosophy of war as written by the Chapter's legendary warrior Daenyathos. Others performed wargear rites to prepare the spirits of their weapons and armour, although in truth it was their souls they were preparing.

'Luko,' said Sarpedon, 'we are not going to war. The people down there will decide if our guns and blades are loosed.'

'Is that why you chose my squad to ride along with you?' asked Luko with a smile. 'So you could make sure I stayed my trigger finger?'

'Just make sure your battle-brothers have calm heads on their shoulders,' said Sarpedon.

The Thunderhawk made its final descent, vertical engines grinding as they cushioned the craft into a landing. The trees lining the road leading from the city's south gate shuddered in the choppy gale from the engines. The gunship settled onto the ground.

'Deploy us, Brother Phol,' voxed Sarpedon.

The Thunderhawk's ramp swung down. Sarpedon breathed his first lungfuls of Raevenian air, clean and cool forest air tinged with gun oil and sweat.

The army arrayed outside the gates was huge and magnificent. Its soldiers wore iridescent body armour, gleaming like the carapaces of beetles. They were armed with rifles and machine guns, solid projectile weapons behind Imperial technology, but not by much. The regimental banners were embroidered in silver and gold, and below them stood drummers and trumpeters, and officers resplendent in gold brocade. Behind the army were dozens of artillery pieces manned by gun teams, and a regiment of cavalry armed with sabres as well as rifles.

At the head of the army, standing in the car of a gilded chariot, was a woman in the armour of a soldier and the robes of a monarch. Her black hair was tied back severely, and her strong, handsome face adorned many of the banners flying behind her. Her eyes were a sharp green.

Sarpedon could feel the troops withdraw when they saw him. A Space Marine was monstrous enough, huge compared to a normal man and wearing enough power armour to turn him into a walking tank, but Sarpedon was a literal monster. The spider legs replacing the lower half of his torso were an obscenity that would warrant immediate execution on most Imperial worlds. Any right-thinking, Emperor-fearing citizen would consider Sarpedon an abomination.

Squad Luko emerged from the Thunderhawk behind Sarpedon. The guns of his troops were not aimed at the army in front of them, but in a split second Luko's battle-brothers could be ready to fight.

Sarpedon stood before the woman in the chariot. He was taller than her in her chariot, but even so she seemed able to look down on him with both curiosity and disdain. Sarpedon had seen many humans recoil before him, spitting curses or running in fear. The queen did not.

A soldier hurried forwards. He looked older than the men around him, the polished plates of his armour inscribed with flowing script in gold.

'Her Majesty Queen Dyrmida of Astelok,' he said in accented Low Gothic. Evidently introducing herself was a task beneath the queen. 'Regent-general of Raevenia.'

'Commander Sarpedon of the Soul Drinkers.'

For a moment, there was only the sound of banners flapping in the breeze, and the engines of the Thunderhawk warming down.

'What are you?' asked Queen Dyrmida. Her voice was as strident as the rest of her.

'A Space Marine,' said Sarpedon. 'A warrior from the galaxy beyond, from the Imperium of Man.'

The men in the ranks were jostling nervously. Officers threw angry glances to quiet them down. Even the horses of the cavalry were disturbed by the sight of Sarpedon, straining at their reins.

'The Imperium?' asked the queen. 'What manner of empire is this? One embattled, like our own? Brothers and sisters in this fight?'

'They are no brothers to you, or to me,' replied Sarpedon.

'Then, no empire moves to assist us? In spite of our calls for help, our begging, we see nothing but you and your men? This is the deliverance we abandoned our pride to plead for? How many do you bring with you?'

'Two hundred and fifty,' said Sarpedon.

'Two hundred and fifty! What difference can you make to us? The Undying are upon us. They will care nothing for your presence unless each of your men is worth a thousand of mine.'

'They are,' said Sarpedon levelly.

The silence was broken only by the sound of banners and trees in the wind.

The queen looked past Sarpedon to the Soul Drinkers of Squad Luko behind him, and the landed Thunderhawk beyond. Two more Thunderhawks were circling overhead. Sarpedon couldn't imagine what she must make of the Soul Drinkers with their mutant leader, their massive statures and purple armour, their exotic wargear like Luko's claws and Sarpedon's force axe. The fear was clear in the eyes of her soldiers, for they must have thought they were looking on creatures of legend. The armies of many non-Imperial worlds had crumbled at the sight of Space Marines in the past, civilisations, who thought themselves enlightened and advanced, bowing down to worship the terrifying warriors that dropped into their midst from the sky. Whole worlds had fallen to Imperial tyranny in the past by exactly this method.

Queen Dyrmida was made of sterner stuff. Without her, the army might well have melted away, there and then, without a shot being fired, or they would have attacked the Soul Drinkers at the first sight of Sarpedon. Instead, they followed their queen's lead, and stood firm.

'You are not here to help us,' said the queen. 'If you are as mighty as you claim then you would think my world beneath you. Why are you here?'

Sarpedon settled back onto his back legs. The queen was right. If the *Brokenback* had not been crippled, his Chapter would probably have bypassed Raevenia completely, and ignored their pleas for help. 'We can depart, your majesty, and leave you to these Undying. Or we can give you the chance for survival that you currently lack.'

'My city will soon be under siege by the Undying. If you wish to fight, fight. Otherwise, leave. There is no more to be discussed.' Dyrmida turned to he charioteer. 'To the gates!' she ordered. The chariot wheeled around, and the troops parted as it was driven towards the city.

'All squads,' voxed Sarpedon to the Soul Drinkers in the Thunderhawks overhead. 'Come in to land. Do not open fire on the Raevenians. All weapons silent.'

The troops were falling back, rank by rank, to accompany their queen into the city. Captain Luko held his position behind Sarpedon as the banners receded.

'Perhaps we should have come armed with a diplomat,' said Luko.

Sarpedon turned to him. 'Next time you sharpen your claws, captain, try dulling your wit as well. Take command of the squads as they land and set up a position closer to the walls.'

'Where will you be, commander?'

'In the city,' said Sarpedon.

Lygris reached the bridge just as Brother Feynin was shutting off the alarms. Feynin was one of the Soul Drinkers left on the *Brokenback* while Sarpedon led the rest to Raevenia. Lygris knew that, while they would not say`so, they all wanted to be at Sarpedon's side, fighting whatever battle the planet might throw at them.

'What is it?' asked Lygris.

Feynin looked around from the bridge cogitator. A couple of other Soul Drinkers were on the bridge, examining pict screens or spools of printouts. Warning lights were flashing and the klaxons still echoed through the deck.

'Contacts,' said Feynin. 'In-system.'

'Contacts? From the warp?'

'There's no warp breach. I don't know where they came from.'

Lygris took over Feynin's position at the cogitator. If the bridge viewscreen had been repaired he could have had an overview of Raevenia's

Soul Drinkers: Annihilation389

system in seconds, but had to make do with the streams of figures flickering down the pict screen in front of him. He stopped them and flicked through a few different screens.

'They were hiding in Raevenia's rings,' said Lygris.

'The rings?' asked Feynin.

'They're made of chunks of ice and rock. A ship could easily hide in them.'

'But they'd have to be stone cold to avoid any sensors. If it's the Mechanicus then they–'

'It's not the Mechanicus,' said Lygris, leafing through printouts. 'It's the machines. Here, the energy spikes are well out of any Imperial engine's tolerance. That's alien tech.'

Lygris switched to Sarpedon's vox-channel. 'Commander?'

'Lygris?' said Sarpedon's. 'What news from orbit?'

'The machines are here with us. At least six craft, escort-sized but powerful. They just broke cover from the planet's rings.'

'They're here?'

'In force, commander,' said Lygris.

'Then Raevenia doesn't have long.' Over the vox, Sarpedon's voice was broken up by static. 'What of the *Brokenback*? Can it support us on the ground?'

'I can keep us in a stationary orbit,' replied Lygris, 'but the machine-spirits of the last reactors departed an hour ago. Without fuel we are dead in the void. I can bring few weapons to bear. I fear the *Brokenback* is not much use to you. The best I can do is keep us running cold so the aliens do not register us as a worthwhile target.'

'Very well, Lygris,' said Sarpedon. 'I will get you your fuel, Techmarine, and then we can be on our way. Until then, do the Emperor's work.'

'Do the Emperor's work, commander.'

Sarpedon cut the vox-link.

Lygris looked again at the figures being spewed out by the bridge cogitators. Enormous reserves of power, technology both vastly different and far advanced compared to the Imperial.

Xenos, he thought. One more foe to face before the Soul Drinkers could break out of the chains that still held them. And after then, would there be another foe? Another war to fight?

It did not matter. For a Space Marine, for a Soul Drinker, doing the Emperor's work was its own reward. Lygris turned back to the bridge controls and the task of keeping the space hulk in orbit.

The war room was dominated by a relief map of Astelok. Newly added to the map were the districts of shanties and refugee camps housing the people who had fled to Astelok from the rest of Raevenia, moving before the tide of the Undying. The generals of Dyrmida's armies sat around it, their complements of support officers behind them. Many of them had laid out documents on the tabletop around the map: intelligence reports, maps, plans of attack, statistics.

For all the finery of their uniforms, there was a desperation about them. There was none of the pageantry and self-congratulation of peacetime. These were old soldiers, and they were here to fight a war.

Queen Dyrmida entered the war room. The generals saluted as she took up her place at the map table. She had been disrobed of her armour, and wore simple blue-green fatigues with a sidearm holstered at her hip. Her long dark hair hung loose. She looked as much a soldier as any of the generals.

'Your reports,' she said.

General Heynan cleared his throat. A thin and spiky-looking man with a face as sharp as a hatchet, his uniform bore the embroidered ringed planet that symbolised Astelok's intelligence force.

'The last few reports have come in,' he said. 'None is less than three days old.'

'Do any agents still live elsewhere on Raevenia?' asked Dyrmida.

'It seems unlikely, your majesty. The last information we have is from one of our scouts near Fornow Harbour. He reports the Undying there in great numbers, and war machines converging on the city. Undying scouts were closing on his position when he transmitted. Quite possibly, he fell to them.'

'That puts them within a few days of Astelok,' said the jowly, powerfully built Damask, a general of the army, who had ridden with the cavalry in the wars that had been fought decades ago between Astelok and her fellow city-states of Raevenia. 'With Fornow fallen there won't be anything to stop them forcing one of the mountain passes.'

'What of elsewhere?' asked Dyrmida. 'The Lovinian Principalities? Krassus City?'

'Nothing,' replied Heynan, 'not since the Principalities reported the invaders coming from the sky.'

'I see,' said Dyrmida. 'Then the last of Raevenia's cities have fallen. We are alone. We, the people of this city, are what remains of the Selaacan Empire.'

A few of the less tactful generals exchanged looks.

'Do not pretend,' said Dyrmida, 'that we have not known this all along. When Selaaca fell silent, we knew it could come to this. We know that many worlds have fallen and we cannot assume any others have been spared. Much as it pains us to accept it, much as the death toll must be beyond our understanding, it is the truth. The empire's last stand will fall upon us. The Undying have exterminated all the rest.'

Damask banged a fist on the map table. 'Then we will give these aliens the battle of their lives! The Undying will pay for every brick and cobble of Astelok! I will man the barricades myself and fight them until the last breath! I and my men will–'

'You will give us all glorious deaths, general?' interrupted Dyrmida. 'You accept the loss of Astelok and all who dwell in her?'

Damask did not answer. He glanced around the table for support, but none of his fellow officers spoke up.

'I intend,' said Dyrmida, 'to fight the Undying here, but, unlike General Damask, I do not intend to lose. I am willing to sacrifice Astelok, but not her people. We must evacuate the population to the space port and get them off the planet.'

'No army scout has returned from the Bladeleaf Glades for weeks,' said Heynan. 'That is less than half a days' march away from the road to the space port. We know there are Undying in the Glades, definitely their vanguard, maybe their main force.'

'There is no way,' said General Slake, another veteran of army command with a deep scar across his lips, 'that we can get the people down that road to the space port. Mustering the army to greet the newcomers was risk enough. It would take a day at the very least to move the people to the space port, and the Undying could ambush at any time. Your majesty, it would be a massacre.'

'General Slake's words come belatedly,' said Damask grimly, 'but they are true. Give your people good deaths, your majesty. Do not let them die running.'

Dyrmida rose to her feet.

'We have all left it too late,' she said, 'to do what is right. We were afraid to flee our world, for our fellow Raevenians were standing and fighting, and we would not be the cowards who dared to survive. We feared the ignominy of limping back to our world after the Undying had been fought off, but now that will not happen. The Undying have won, and our world will fall. We have no choice over that, but we can choose whether our sons and daughters, our friends and loved ones, are on Raevenia when it happens. General Damask, I will not believe that any death, while denying the Undying their victory, is a bad death.'

Damask sat back in his chair. Only Heynan had little enough concern for his position to speak up.

'How, your majesty? How will we buy our people enough time to reach the space port?'

'Fight the Undying in the city,' replied Dyrmida. 'Draw them in. Force them to commit their main force to our streets. And keep them fighting long enough to get the people out.'

A few frustrated exhalations were just audible as the generals digested this. Dyrmida, ignoring them, stood and leaned over the map of Astelok.

'Here,' she said. 'As soon as we know which direction the Undying will take, we barricade the streets, and funnel the Undying into the Cemetery Quarter. Force them to fight us in the avenues between estates and basilicas, where their numbers cannot be brought to bear. Collapse buildings if need be. The good deaths you plead for, Damask, will be given to every soldier in the city, and you are welcome to join them at the barricades. The population will make it out while the Undying are tied up in the city.'

'Hear, hear!' said some of the generals, eager to show their loyalty even to the last.

'You expect much of the army,' said Heynan.

'Do you say our men cannot do it?' demanded Slake.

'I am saying their deaths may not be enough!' retorted Heynan. 'No one knows how many the Undying can bring to bear! Two hundred thousand men held the walls of Krassus City, and it fell overnight!'

'Then what would you do, Heynan?' demanded Dyrmida. 'How would you face the Undying?'

The words died in Heynan's throat. Any answer he had, withered away under Queen Dyrmida's gaze.

A commotion sounded at the back of the room. The generals and their officers turned to get a better look. From the dim doorway at the far side of the map room stumbled a soldier, who had been posted there as a guard, clutching his arm. His gun was not in his hand and he lost his balance, scrabbling along the floor.

'I believe,' said a voice from the darkness, 'that the queen's plan is sound.'

Sarpedon emerged from the shadows, the spotlight surrounding the map table catching on the massive plates of his armour and the glossy chitin of his spider legs. The closest generals started out of their chairs, and weapons were drawn, aides pulling out rifles and pistols.

'Stay your weapons!' ordered Dyrmida. She stood up and addressed Sarpedon. 'You! How did you get in here?'

'Your men,' replied Sarpedon calmly, 'showed more enthusiasm than skill in trying to stop me. Fear not, I haven't killed anyone yet.' In one hand he held the rifle he had taken from the guard at the door. He cast it onto the floor. 'My Soul Drinkers, on the other hand, can do things your soldiers cannot.'

'Can you hold the city, Lord Sarpedon?' asked Dyrmida. 'Can you fight the Undying to a standstill, long enough for my people to escape to the spaceport?'

'We can.'

'Then I will ask you again. What do you want from us?'

The two locked stares across the map table for a long moment. The officers had not let their guard down, and a dozen guns were still aimed at Sarpedon.

'Fuel,' said Sarpedon.

'Then you are stranded here,' said Dyrmida, 'and if you fight, you hope we will give it to you.'

'That is correct, your majesty.'

'Then why not simply take it by force?'

'Because,' said Sarpedon, 'we are not invaders. We are not murderers or thieves. We have our honour, too.'

'Good,' said Dyrmida, 'because if you had decided to simply take it, you would have incinerated yourselves trying to get through the defences. When my people are safe in the space port and the first ships are leaving, then we will give you the codes. Is that satisfactory?'

By way of an answer, Sarpedon walked closer to the table to get a better look at the map of Astelok. Having seen the city from orbit, the cemetery hills, spire-topped palaces and southern slums were familiar to him, not as works of architecture or places to live, but as playing pieces in the strategic game that would ensue if the city was invaded.

'A sound plan, your majesty,' said Sarpedon. 'These Undying will have to commit a massive force to break a determined force in the city's centre. Without my Space Marines, it will not work. With them, your people have a chance of deliverance.'

'Then you will fight?' asked General Heynan. 'You will help us?'

Sarpedon looked at him. Heynan shied away from the Space Marine's gaze.

'Both sides will help themselves,' said Sarpedon. 'We have the same objective, to escape this planet. The Undying stand in our way. Fighting them together is the only course that makes sense.'

'Then I have made my decision,' said Dyrmida. 'The Undying will be fought in the city, and held there so that the civilian population can be evacuated. Are there any further objections, my generals?'

A few of the generals exchanged looks. Most of them, however, kept their eyes on the mutant Space Marine that dwarfed them all.

'Good,' said Dyrmida. 'To your duties, men. Your queen has spoken.'

'What is fear? Fear is the absence of duty. Fear is what fills our minds unbidden when our thoughts turn from our obligations to the human race.'

– Daenyathos, *Hammer of the Heretics*

CHAPTER ПIПE

'Perhaps I always knew,' said Queen Dyrmida, 'that it would happen during my reign.'

The entire city was visible from the graveyard upon the hill. Sarpedon saw how it had been built nestling between the hills at first, a fortified town whose walls still existed amid the palaces and monuments at its heart. Astelok had grown large and prosperous since. In the pre-dawn light, the movement of people was obvious, draining like blood through the veins of the city towards the gates to the south.

Queen Dyrmida sat on an old grave slab, some of her retainers and courtiers waiting a short distance away. She had called Sarpedon up here to organise the last few details of the coming battle.

'How could you be sure?' asked Sarpedon.

'Every monarch before me has believed the same thing. We must always be prepared for the death of that for which we are responsible. It is our way.'

'I have seen worlds die,' said Sarpedon. 'Too many people for me to imagine. Not one of them really believed that death would come for them. I do not think you can ever be truly prepared to see such destruction.'

'That, Commander Sarpedon, is because you were not born on Raevenia,' said the queen. 'A man's life does not mean anything if it is not married to a death of equal merit. A hero can be rendered a nothing and buried in a pit outside the walls, if he does not die a hero's death.

A poor and worthless man can be buried up here, amid all its finery, if he dies well enough.'

'And a queen?'

Queen Dyrmida considered this.

'It is unlikely that I will be buried at all,' she said. 'That is a bad death indeed. Only if I am remembered can I expect to be anyone in death.'

'Dying on Raevenia must be an exacting task,' said Sarpedon.

'What of your people? How do they die?'

'In great numbers and ignorance.'

'They sound like bad deaths,' said the queen with a shake of her head.

'They are. That is why the Soul Drinkers no longer fight for the Imperium.'

Dyrmida looked out across the city. Units of Raevenian troops held several crossroads, ready to slow down the advance of the Undying. The Soul Drinkers were concentrated around the centre of the city, where the relatively open spaces of parks and forums would funnel the Undying towards them.

'Your Soul Drinkers will bear the brunt of the battle,' said the queen. 'The majority of my army must secure the route to the space port.'

'Those are the kind of battles we were created to fight, your majesty.'

'You have not returned to your spaceship and abandoned us,' continued Dyrmida. 'You could have done so at any moment. I am not ignorant of that fact.'

'Being becalmed here is not an option for us. If you require us to fight if we are to escape, then we will fight.'

'There is more than that, Soul Drinker. The galaxy has failed us. It has failed you, too, and made you renegades. You claim to fight only for survival, but I think you are trying to prove something, too, even if only to yourself.'

'Do not be so certain, your majesty. We learned what happens when we fight to better the lot of the Imperium, and it did not end well for us.'

A messenger rode up on a horse, carrying a sheaf of reports. 'Your majesty. Dawn breaks and Imnis has sounded the forlorn hope.'

'Very good,' said Dyrmida. 'Commander, to your positions. I must deliver my people.'

Dyrmida was rapidly surrounded by her retainers for the short journey to the south gate, where tens of thousands of people were now thronging. Sarpedon turned towards the north, and the battle for Astelok began.

The northern gates of Astelok were opened just before dawn. They were shod with brass that had withstood sieges before, scarred by cannon and battering rams. They would not withstand this one.

The Queen's Own Cavalry galloped out. Led by General Imnis, they were splendid with banners and mirror-polished armour. Favours streamed from the banner each wore on his back, embroidered with each man's personal heraldry. They were composed of fifty volunteers. Far more had come forward for the duty, but this death was denied to most of them.

Imnis stopped his horse and raised his sabre, bellowing a challenge to the trees and undergrowth covering the hills outside the city.

There only answer was wind and birdsong.

Imnis shouted again, cursing the cowardice of the Undying and promising them dismal, forgotten deaths that would condemn them to nothingness.

He heard nothing in return. Imnis galloped up to the tree line, spitting curses.

A lance of emerald light leapt from the hillside and skinned him alive in a split second. His flesh was pared off him, layer by layer, leaving the front half of his body a wet red mess stripped down to the skeleton. He toppled from his saddle, and his horse, a good chunk of its flank stripped away too, galloped wild in pain.

A shape rose from the trees. It was an Undying warrior, but it was not like the skeletal creatures the Raevenians had witnessed before. Its lower half was a slab of metal thrumming as it kept the warrior aloft. The warrior had one arm, the other, a cannon glittering with emerald fire. It fired again, and this time the beam punched right through the horse of one of the cavalrymen. The horse fell, dead before it hit the ground, and pinned the rider's leg under it.

More of the flying warriors rose above the trees, criss-crossing the clearing in front of the gates with blasts of green energy. Warriors stalked out of the tree line, a silent rank of them matching step as they advanced.

The cavalry charged, those at the front lowering their lances and those behind snapping off rifle shots. A warrior fell, face ruined. After a moment, it stood up again, falling back into step.

The first riders clashed with the warriors. Blue light burst where the power blades of their lances made contact, the energy fields tearing through metal. Automatic fire rattled into the Undying, and cascades of bullet casings rained down around the horses' hooves. An Undying warrior was carried up into the air, impaled on a lance, green fire bleeding from its chest. Others were trampled under hooves. A power sabre lashed out and cut a machine's head from its shoulders.

Green fire flashed. Men and horses fell, stripped to the bone so quickly that their bodies took a moment to start bleeding.

The ground shook. The charge faltered. The trees on the hillside began to fall, toppling as a great bulk forced its way through them.

One of the cavalrymen, in command after Imnis's death, called out for the sons of Raevenia to rejoice and die well.

A hundred Undying stepped in eerily perfect formation from the trees, grinning skulls reflecting the glowing power fields of the cavalry's lances. Bullets rained down into them, but fallen Undying simply stood again, and, those that did not, disappeared, replaced a moment later by another metallic warrior striding into the open.

The ranks of Undying opened fire as one. The cavalry disappeared in a mess of flayed flesh and bone. Horses, stripped in half, screamed out their final breaths as organs spilled out onto the bloody ground. Men died before they hit the ground, insides scooped out, reduced to fluttering scraps of skin and uniform.

Given the circumstances, they had died the best deaths they could hope for. The Raevenians watching from the walls took comfort in that.

Thousands of Undying followed the front ranks out of the trees. More flying warriors flanked them, and glittering scarabs scuttled through the grass around their feet. A great crashing could be heard, and trees fell, scoring a deep line through the forest canopy, as something huge and powerful made its own path towards the northern gate.

Astelok prepared to die well.

'The northern gate just fell,' said Phol's voice over the vox. 'The Undying have massive infantry strength, thousands of them. They have flying support units, too, and something big with them, maybe a siege engine. The cavalry didn't even slow them down.'

Sarpedon glanced up. The Soul Drinkers' Thunderhawks were in the air, among them the one piloted by Brother Phol, acting as the Soul Drinkers' eyes as well as lending fire support.

Sarpedon was stationed with the majority of his Soul Drinkers towards the centre of the city. He was holding an intersection of two of Astelok's grandest streets, lined on each side by mansions and monuments like a canyon of marble. The Soul Drinkers were set up behind makeshift barricades in the street, or in the windows of the buildings. Sarpedon's post was in a semicircular war memorial, inscribed with thousands of names lost in some war between the cities of Raevenia, and crowned with statues of weary soldiers, on the corner of the two streets.

'Tell me when you can see this xenos machine,' voxed Sarpedon, 'and keep me appraised when you have a clear idea of their numbers.'

'Yes, commander. I'll stay over your position. By the hand of Dorn!'

'Trust in your bullets and blades, Brother Phol!' Sarpedon took stock of his command position. Squad Luko had taken up firing positions between the doleful statues, and the rest of the squad crouched in cover nearby, behind makeshift barricades across the street or in the doorways of mansions.

'What do they want with this city?' asked Scamander, who was stationed with Squad Luko where the short-range firepower he kept in his head had the best chance of coming into play. 'What is there on this planet they can't have got enough of?'

'They are machines, Brother Scamander,' said Sarpedon. 'They do not want anything, not as we do. They just conquer.'

Scamander was inexperienced, and he had stained his honour by siding with Eumenes in the Second Chapter War, but he had a quick mind, and he had dedicated his efforts to redeeming himself with the Chapter. His armour carried the gilded insignia of the Chapter Librarium; Scamander was a psyker, and Sarpedon could see his potential as living artillery.

'Targets in the city!' said Phol's voice over the vox. 'The first barricades are falling! The Raevenians are retreating to their second lines. The Undying are pouring in.'

'Lend your guns, Brother Phol, but do not risk the gunship. Soul Drinkers! The enemy is within the gates!'

A pall of smoke was gathering to the north: gun-smoke, burning buildings and the dust of collapsing buildings. Explosions rumbled as booby traps erupted among the abandoned buildings around the gate.

To Sarpedon, the sounds of war were as familiar as his own breathing, but he had never before heard thousands of footsteps, metal against cobbles, stamping through the city in perfect time.

Tens of the thousands of Undying made it through the Raevenian fire from the walls. They streamed through the northern gateway into Astelok. The crossfire that met them was terrific, thousands of Raevenian rifles and machine guns opening up as one. The first ranks of Undying were shredded beyond even their capacity to self-repair, but the Undying did not care about losses. More marched forwards, choking the gate with wreckage. A few moments later, the Undying war machine breached the walls.

It was shaped like a titanic metal-shod beetle, pulling itself along on its belly with thousands of legs that writhed along its sides. Its head was a huge maw, ringed with steel teeth, with power glowing in its throat. Scarabs crawled all over its surface, and behind its long segmented tail it left a deep furrow in the ground as it drove forwards, flanked by the march of the Undying.

The machine's enormous bulk pushed down one of the gatehouses, and tonnes of rubble were sucked into its maw. The useless matter was siphoned off and spewed from vents along its sides as clouds of choking dust.

Men died in its path. The gate district was barren, the forums strewn with half-dissolved bodies and abandoned barricades. A basilica collapsed, detonated to slow the Undying advance with rubble, but the machine just dragged its bulk right through the ruins.

A few Raevenians, who had been wounded or who had run out of ammunition, had been cut off by the rapid Undying advance, and had not been able to give up their last few moments fighting. The Undying turned and herded them towards the giant machine. Some of them threw themselves on the bayonets on the Undying's xenos weapons. Others stumbled ahead of them into the machine's path. They disappeared into the machine's maw, sucked down into its throat.

They were denied the good deaths suffered by hundreds of other defenders. A death in defence of his home, upon the orders of his queen, was a worthwhile goal for a Raevenian's life. There were better, of course, but few men would ever have the chance to even witness them. Plenty of soldiers had asked for the honour of manning the front lines. Plenty of them received their wish in the first few minutes of the battle for Astelok, stripped to the bone by lances of green fire, or chewed into pulp by hordes of scarabs.

Some of them did not die. A man dragged himself along the street, his leg a bloody length of sinew and bone. Another held in the wet heaving mass of his chest, gasping for breath and bracing his gun one-handed for a few more shots. Another curled into a ball to keep the scarabs off his face, howling as their mandibles burrowed through his back.

The machine harvested them too, as the Undying threw them into its throat, or it simply rolled over them as they tried to crawl out of its way. More good deaths went begging.

The dust began to fill the city like fog. The Undying marched through it, into valleys of apartment blocks that had previously been crammed with refugees. Raevenian sharpshooters aimed through the windows, and sniper bullets punched through metal skulls. A flying warrior fell, sheared through the spine, its anti-grav unit cutting out, sending it tumbling into the gutter. More flyers fired their cannon up at the buildings, boring through walls and the men sheltering behind them. Warriors sent fire spattering up, not missing a step as they advanced.

One Raevenian sniper shot down a flying machine, plugging it clean through the head. He fell back into shelter, as return fire from the warriors chewed away at the wall below the window he had used as a vantage point. He was a veteran, his aim honed by sniping birds and stags in Raevenia's forests. The inhuman march of the Undying had not fazed him. He had been raised to kill, and whether it was prize game or alien machines did not make any difference in his mind.

Another soldier ran into the apartment behind him. The place was still scattered with furniture and belongings, the refugees having abandoned anything that could not be carried in a backpack. The soldier was tattered and bloody, wounded by the Undying fire streaking up into the buildings.

'We've got to get out of this building,' said the veteran. 'Keep moving. I'll be right behind you.'

The soldier didn't reply. He slumped against the doorframe. The veteran ran to support him and took the man's weight on his shoulder.

'We'll get you out,' he said to the wounded man. 'You can't die yet. Queen's orders, eh?'

The wounded man turned his head to look at the veteran. His face was a ruin of torn skin. His eyes were lit from behind with green fire. His face split open and bloodstained metal leered through it.

The veteran fought to get out of the machine's grip. Metal claws slid through the dead soldier's skin.

The veteran's scream was lost in the roar of the harvester as it ground through the streets below.

From the window of the southern palace, Queen Dyrmida watched another pall of dust billow up above the city. Another building in the north of Astelok had collapsed.

The Undying weren't just killing her city. They were dismembering it before her eyes.

'We have to go, your majesty,' said Lieutenant Kavins beside her. 'The civilians can't be held here any longer.'

He was right. The refugees cramming the southern half of Astelok were beginning to panic as the Undying approached. Most of them had never seen the Undying, and had built them up as ghosts or daemons from the underworld, inhuman and unstoppable, who inflicted fates worse than death on their victims. Those who had seen the Undying, in the fall of cities and settlements scattered across Raevenia, had terrors of their own, memories of green fire eyes and skeletal killers that never stopped. Religion came quickly to people watching their world being devoured, and plenty of the refugees whispered that the Undying had been sent by the gods to punish Raevenia for her people's impiety.

The southern gate was the largest in the city walls, flanked by memorials to the Raevenians that had died to defend Astelok in ages past. People thronged the thoroughfare in front of it, and soldiers on the battlements had their guns trained on the crowds ready to fire if they turned violent.

'Then we must put trust in our people,' said Dyrmida. 'Open the gates. Make sure the troops keep them from stampeding.'

'Yes, your majesty,' said Kavins. 'The transports are waiting for you. We should get you out of the city as soon as possible.'

'Wait a while,' said Dyrmida. 'I will not flee my city ahead of my people.'

Kavins signalled the soldiers holding the gatehouse, from the palace balcony, and the gates began to grind open. The crowd surged forwards, and soldiers held them back, yelling orders at the crowd. Women and children were weeping, screaming, yelling prayers and spreading rumours of the Undying closing in.

These were the people for whom Queen Dyrmida was responsible. It was a great burden to bear. If she failed them here, they would die, all of them.

The first columns of citizens were moved through the gates. Some were old or infirm, and were left behind. Others bulled their way forward and were clubbed with rifle butts to keep them in line.

The sound was terrible: thousands of voices tinged with panic and desperation. It would take almost nothing to send them boiling over: a stray shot, a glimpse of the Undying, even just a wrong word shouted in fear.

It had to be this way, however. An hour before, the chances of the Undying ambushing a convoy of fleeing refugees were too high. Now, it was less, still high, but low enough to give them hope. That hope had been bought with the lives of Raevenians dead and yet to die, and Dyrmida had no choice but to grasp it and let it play out until the end.

'My people!' she called from the balcony. 'We will be delivered! Trust in me and in our soldiers! Believe, and be calm!'

Eyes fell on her. She recognised the fashions of many other cities amongst those of Astelok. Some of them had been enemies of Astelok in times past. Now, there were no cities. There was just Raevenia.

A tremendous roar went up from the north. Dyrmida saw the spires of the Dawning Palace falling, clouds of white marble dust swallowing the pinnacles where Dyrmida had once held court. The Dawning Palace was close to the centre of the city, and it was one of the most powerful symbols of Astelok's culture, of its past. With the Dawning Palace fallen, the rest of Astelok could not be far behind.

'Fear not!' shouted Dyrmida as panic rippled through the crowds. 'They will not reach us! This I swear!'

Sarpedon saw the first of the towers falling. The palace just ahead was perhaps the grandest in the city, its slender towers of rose-coloured sandstone defining Astelok's skyline. Now one of those towers collapsed across the road ahead, spilling hundreds of tonnes of rubble into the streets. For a moment, some of the palace's finery could be glimpsed: torn tapestries, gilded portrait frames, painted wood furniture. They all disappeared in the churning mass of stone.

'Salk!' yelled Sarpedon into the vox. 'Fall back! Fall back!'

'On it,' replied Salk briskly. Sarpedon could see Salk's tactical squad sprinting across the street as the palace behind them collapsed. One tower fell towards them, fracturing as it piled into the street. Hunks of broken stone slammed into the street a few metres behind Salk's squad, and the Soul Drinkers were swallowed by the tremendous flood of dust erupting from the palace's torn foundations.

'Phol,' voxed Sarpedon. 'Where is their siege engine?'

'Still heading right for you,' replied Phol from the Thunderhawk overhead. 'I'm losing a visual on it. There's too much dust.'

'Soul Drinkers!' yelled Sarpedon. 'Guns up!'

A couple of Raevenian soldiers, fleeing the destruction, ran between the wings of the mansion that made up one part of the crossroads. Their shapes became dim, and then disappeared, as the bank of dust rolled over them.

'Brothers, the siege engine is our target!' ordered Sarpedon. 'If we are to hold the Undying in this city, we must strike at the heart of their attack! Let us see how these xenos fight when their enemies do not flee before their war machine!'

'Nothing like the spirit of improvisation, commander,' said Captain Luko.

'Take the enemy's strength and turn it into their weakness,' replied Sarpedon. 'These were the words of Daenyathos.'

The dust rolled over Sarpedon. The crossroads and the war memorial became a pit of shadow. Even to a Space Marine's enhanced eyes the dust was impenetrable.

'Commander, I've lost you,' voxed Phol from above.

'Keep circling,' said Sarpedon. 'Keep low. Don't give them an easy target. They might still be able to see you.'

'Novitiate!' said Librarian Tyrendian, who was sheltering in the memorial alongside Squad Luko. 'To my side. Prepare!'

'Yes, Librarian,' replied Scamander. 'I am ready.' Scamander's gauntlets were glowing, ruddy in the murk, and Sarpedon could feel the heat coming off them.

Sarpedon heard the tramp of metal feet on stone. The ground groaned with the weight of the war machine. A few voices yelled out, soldiers trying to locate their comrades or crying in pain.

'Coming in on your position,' voxed Salk. 'Hold fire!' Squad Salk emerged from the fog and huddled down in front of the memorial.

Sarpedon looked out over the top of the memorial's wall. He could see a few metres down the street, and then just seething darkness.

Then pinpoints of green fire: Undying warriors, hundreds upon hundreds of them, advancing down the road, between the mansions and across the sculpted gardens.

The war engine bellowed again, throwing out a dark pall of ground-up city that smothered the street in black as if a deeper night was falling. A scream was cut short.

'Soul Drinkers!' voxed Sarpedon. 'We cannot kill all the Undying, but we can hurt them. Our target is the war machine!'

He waited a moment more. He could make out the outlines of the Undying warriors. Their weapons were glowing with pent-up energy as they searched for targets. This window, when the Soul Drinkers could see the Undying but the Undying could not see them, would last only a few moments more.

'Charge!' yelled Sarpedon, and vaulted over the memorial wall.

A lightning bolt leapt over his shoulder and blew a warrior apart right in front of Sarpedon. Sarpedon didn't have to turn to see it had come from the hand of Tyrendian, whose psychic power took a most direct and destructive form. Sarpedon ran into the gap opened up in the Undying ranks, and slammed his axe through the chest of one of them before its electronic brain had reacted.

The Axe of Mercaeno was a force weapon, tuned in to the wielder's psychic power so that he could focus it into the blade and tear the soul right out of an enemy. The Undying had no souls to destroy, so Sarpedon had to rely on pure strength to drive the axe through them. Fortunately, strength was something he had never lacked.

He struck a skull from its shoulders, and stabbed a leg through the abdomen of another Undying, severing its thick steel spine. Squad Luko and Squad Salk were right behind him, blazing at point-blank range with rapid-firing bolters. Soul Drinkers advanced on either side, and Sarpedon heard the roar of jump pack jets as assault squads leapt over the front lines and into the Undying beyond.

The robotic nature of the Undying was not a strength. It was a weakness. They were tough and fearless, but they had no capacity for imagination. They could not react, except to the commands wired into their machine minds. They had come to this battle ready to fight Raevenians, brave but fallible humans who panicked and ran, who faltered when faced with a wall of metal bodies. They had not been ready for the Space Marines.

Sarpedon was at full tilt, slamming into the warriors and bowling them aside. One of the large floating spiders, the same kind he had dispatched at the white city, loomed through the dust, the lenses studding its head swivelling to focus on him. Blasts of bolter and plasma fire hammered into it from Squad Luko, and Luko himself ran beneath the stricken machine and disembowelled it with a slash of his lightning claws. Sarpedon could see the trails of the jump packs, and hear chainswords against metal as the assault squads went into the fray. There was bolter fire, everywhere, criss-crossing in white trails as they ripped through the pall of dust.

The harvester bellowed. Buildings collapsed in its wake.

'Forward!' yelled Sarpedon. 'Take the war engine! Forward!'

The great dark circle of the maw pushed through the dust. It was bigger than Sarpedon had imagined, too big to fit into the grand street, and it ground its way through the buildings on either side to make passage for itself. It was a monstrous vortex of gnashing metal. It was like the eye of death itself.

'Get onto the rooftops!' shouted Sarpedon into the vox. 'Assault squads, jump! The rest, into the buildings and up!'

Undying warriors were converging in front of the harvester to fend off the attackers. Sarpedon scuttled sideways to reach the front of a law court that took up one side of the street. The building was already shuddering as the harvester chewed through the far end. Squad Luko was already entering it, shooting out windows and kicking in the main doors. Sarpedon jumped onto the wall, finding purchase with his talons and running up the vertical surface. Undying warriors, bent and fast wielding claws, like the machines from the forest palace, were following him up the wall or emerging from the windows. One of them wore the skin of a dead Raevenian, making for a horrible bloody parody of a human form. Sarpedon paused to take aim, and blew one of its legs off with a bolter shot. Bolter fire from inside the building threw another off the wall.

Sarpedon reached the roof. Deep cracks were running across the walls and roof of the law court, and the whole building leaned under the advancing weight of the harvester. The first Soul Drinkers were emerging onto the roof.

Sarpedon could see the main bulk of the harvester now. It was immense, like a gigantic beetle with a carapace of bullet-scarred metal. It was bigger even than an Imperial super-heavy tank. Power glowed green beneath its overlapping armour plates.

Techmarine Lygris was on the roof.

'Lygris!' shouted Sarpedon over the din of the collapsing building. 'I need you inside!'

'Very well, commander! Open the door!' replied Lygris.

Sarpedon ran to the edge of the roof and jumped. He landed on the hull of the harvester, just behind the lip of its maw. Lygris followed him. Sarpedon, whose legs and talons held him firm to the hull, held out a hand, and caught Lygris's wrist to drag him up onto the upper surface, which was almost horizontal. The harvester swayed and juddered beneath them. Members of Squad Luko were making the jump, too, or crouching at the edge of the roof to grab an edge of armour plate and clamber their way up. Sarpedon saw that Soul Drinkers were making it onto the machine from the opposite roofs, too, and more were on the rooftops up ahead waiting for their turn to make the jump.

'The carapace is too tough,' said Lygris. 'Can we get a plasma weapon up here to blast through?'

'Allow me,' said Scamander. The Librarian had climbed across from the buildings opposite. Tyrendian was still on the roof behind him, shattering an Undying warrior with a well-aimed lightning bolt. Scamander knelt on the hull and put both his hands on one of the armour plates. His gauntlets glowed, and, as they drew heat from the rest of him, ice crystallised on his backpack and the armour of his legs.

The armour plate glowed as Scamander poured psychic heat into it. The edges and the areas beneath his palms began to run molten. Scamander pulled, and the plate came away, the half-melted metal stretching like sinews. Lygris and Scamander grabbed it, too, and between them they pulled it clear and threw it aside.

The hole Scamander had opened up was big enough for a couple of Soul Drinkers to enter. The cross-section of the hull was riddled with glowing green filaments, humming with the power they channelled around the machine. Sarpedon could see enough room, inside, among the pulsing machinery and power conduits for a Space Marine to move.

Sarpedon led the way in. The Soul Drinkers gathering on the hull followed him, or lined up behind Scamander as he went to work on another armour plate. Many of them covered the machine's hull, sniping at the Undying trying to clamber up at them, or spearing the many scarabs on its back with combat knives.

Sarpedon wiped away the dust that had caked around his eyes. It was cramped inside the harvester, but he could move if he crouched down on his haunches. He pushed between a pair of humming power conduits and saw the chamber opening up before him.

Hundreds of humans, Raevenians, hung from racks on the walls of the cylindrical hull. Their faces were covered by silver masks, like stylised, expressionless faces. A walkway led between the racks of captives. Undying, bigger than the warriors with reinforced spines to take the weight of their enormous cannon, patrolled the interior to fend off boarders.

'Now?' asked Lygris behind him.

'Now we kill it,' said Sarpedon.

'We are born naked and defenceless, save for a shield around our souls that all humans are honour-bound to maintain. That veneer of disgust, that armour of hate, is all that stands between us and the endless death of corruption.'

– Daenyathos, *The Artemesion Campaigns*

CHAPTER TEN

Another ship of the Fleet Minor exploded, a brief nuclear flash sucked
dead by the cold of the void. Glittering debris rained out from the place
where the troop ship had been. Among the debris were the charred
bodies of the tech-guard who had been stationed on the ship.

Asclepian Alpha was trailing ruined hull plates attached by blackened
strings of vented plasma, one side of its hull stripped down to the per-
sonnel decks by the massive ordnance fired at it by one of the necron
cruisers. Half its crew were dead, dissolved away in the blast, or thrown
out into space when the decks decompressed. A skeleton crew and the
escort ship's machine-spirit were all that were keeping it going, and it
shuddered along on a wayward course as if its mind was crumbling,
along with its hull.

The Mechanicus fleet was down three major ships and a few dozen of
the Fleet Minor. The only equipment salvaged from the *Ferrous* was that
contained in Magos Vionel's body, and, without the factory ship, the
Mechanicus fleet lacked the capacity to refine fuel and produce spare
parts in an emergency. With every auxiliary ship that died, the fleet
became a little blinder to the space around it.

Magos Crystavayne, transferred by shuttle from the *Defence of Caelano
Minoris*, entered the bridge of the *Antithesis*. The specimen vials hanging at his waist like a soldier's grenades clinked as he walked, and the
caduceus embroidered on the hem and cuffs of his robes designated his
role as a magos biologis. The command throne at the pinnacle of the

bridge was empty, so Crystavayne reported to the makeshift briefing area where Voar had presented what little intelligence he had on the necrons.

Several tech-priests and senior menials were working in the briefing area, poring over countless tactical maps with compasses and quills, or flicking the stones across abaci to perform long strings of calculations.

'Where is the archmagos?' asked Crystavayne.

One of the tech-priests looked up from his map, on which he had already inscribed a web of arcs and angles. 'The archmagos has retired to his laboratory.'

'His laboratory?' retorted Crystavayne. 'We are at battle stations!'

'Nevertheless, magos, he has left fleet command with the bridge. He has requested the magi assist in maintaining evasive manoeuvres.'

'This is intolerable.' Crystavayne waved an impatient hand, its fingers tipped with syringes and the tip of a retracted bone-saw glinting in his palm. He was about to say more, but he bit back his words. A magos criticising a superior was on shaky ground as it was, and doing so in front of an inferior would certainly result in punishment. 'Then I shall assist him in his laboratory.'

'The archmagos has requested that he remain undisturbed, and has refused in advance any offers of assistance.'

Crystavayne, who was equipped to be the finest laboratory researcher in the fleet, fought down words of frustration again. 'Then what am I to do?'

'You have an enhanced logic centre,' replied the tech-priest. 'We lack computing power. We need your help.'

Crystavayne picked up the map the tech-priest had been working on. The locations and paths of the fleet's ships were plotted out many hours in advance, and notes on possible enemy movements were scrawled in every available space.

'What are the archmagos's orders?' he asked.

'Full evasion,' said the tech-priest.

'Not to attack?'

'No, magos.'

Crystavayne looked at some of the other routes being plotted by the tech-priests and menials. The machine-spirit of the *Antithesis* was working on it, too, as evidenced by the metres of printout being carried by menials.

Crystavayne visualised the position of the Mechanicus fleet, the formations of the remaining Asclepian escorts, the *Defence* and the *Antithesis*, the *Constant* and the swarm of the Fleet Minor.

Then he added the necron ships. They were faster and more agile than their size suggested, but the cruisers moved in a stilted, repetitive pattern, turning on exact axes and in unchanging increments of degrees.

The biggest necron ship was slower and lumbering, with the huge turning sphere required to bring its main weapons to bear. The second part of the necron fleet, the one that had emerged from behind the planet's moon, was faster, capable of sudden manoeuvres beyond any Imperial ship, but they were predictable, and in any mathematical system that predictability could only lead to one conclusion.

Crystavayne drew a long quill from his robes. He grabbed a sheet of parchment and began to draw on it: tiny annotations in machine-code and ruler-straight lines intersected by perfect arcs. The solution was a ballet, something pure and beautiful. The necron fleet was more dangerous than the Mechanicus fleet, but its only objective was to destroy the Mechanicus. That forced it into certain manoeuvres, for it had to bring its weapons to bear. The Mechanicus fleet, meanwhile, had only to survive. That gave it far more options. It also had the Fleet Minor and the Asclepian escorts, which, in terms of cold mathematics, were expendable.

Crystavayne had plotted an impossibly complicated pattern in a few moments, his logic engine covering the parchment in geometric shorthand for a tight helix of movement. The Mechanicus fleet would present its least valuable ships to the enemy guns, and then turn in on itself, diving through its own wake before the necron gunners could respond. Any individual ship's course would appear to be a series or random loops and twists. Taken as a whole, it was breathtaking. It only existed in the data medium of Crystavayne's logic implant and in what remained of his human imagination, but it would work. That was certain. It would buy the Mechanicus more time than any Navy general or xenos pirate could squeeze from the approaching necrons.

'Here,' said Crystavayne. Sweat was running down his face, and, for a moment, he cursed the symptom of human weakness. 'Get this to the fleet captains. Execute immediately.'

The tech-priest looked down at the dense geometry of Crystavayne's plan.

'Right away, magos,' he said, and began barking orders to the other tech-priests and menials to turn the plan into a series of manoeuvres and transmit it to the rest of the fleet.

Crystavayne's pride died down. Emotions were subsiding faster and faster since his last cortical implant. He wondered if he would miss them.

One remained: a faint anger, mixed with frustration, that the fleet's commander had not attended to this crucial matter himself.

'Whatever task takes so much attention, archmagos,' muttered Crystavayne, 'I pray only that the Omnissiah's work is being done.'

Librarian Tyrendian furrowed his brow, and thrust a hand at the Undying advancing along the war engine's main chamber. Caged lightning arced from his fingers. Shards of hot metal and shattered exoskeleton flew. Green crystal shattered, loosing more bolts of light, emerald this time.

Imprisoned bodies fell, torn from the walls by the discharged power. The walkways along the centre of the chamber buckled, spilling the Undying warriors into the machinery below.

Tyrendian leapt from the gantry above onto a remaining walkway. A squad of the Undying stood before him, bracing themselves as they levelled their cannon at him. Tyrendian yelled, and power crackled around him, blazing from his eyes and grounding off his fingers. He hurled lightning like a javelin, blowing the walkway apart. Undying bodies flew. One cracked against the wall, bringing down a few human captives with it. Another was impaled on the twisted guardrail, green sparks spitting from the wound.

An Undying clambered back onto the walkway behind Tyrendian, its ruptured torso self-repairing, green fire blazing in its eyes. With its free hand, it brought its double-barrelled gun up and aimed it at Tyrendian's back.

The Undying bent backwards as its spine glowed dull red, and then bright cherry. The heat spread to its chest and neck, and then to its skull. Enormous heat glowed inside its head, and its skull split down the middle, exposing the circuitry of its xenos mind.

Tyrendian glanced back to see Scamander behind him, his armour caked in ice crystals, and his breath misting white. His gauntlets were glowing hot and hissing.

'Good kill,' said Tyrendian.

Soul Drinkers were leaping down to what remained of the walkways. Sarpedon scuttled along the wall, pausing to examine one of the prisoners. Its face was obscured by the alien mask, and tubes snaked into its veins and under its skin. It was a man, in clothes suggesting it was a farmer or a hunter.

Ahead of the main chamber was a section crammed with machines that sorted out whatever was swallowed by the harvester's maw, and either added it to the prisoner racks with long articulated arms, or threw it into grinders to be spewed from the war engine's vents. There was nothing that way.

The other end of the chamber was the destination of the thick glowing power cables leading from the capacitors beneath the walkways.

'There,' said Lygris as Sarpedon climbed down the wall beside him. 'Lots of power headed that way.'

Tyrendian looked around from the smouldering remains of the final Undying.

'More Undying will be upon us soon,' he said. 'They know we are here.'

'Can you bring this monstrosity down?' Sarpedon asked the Techmarine.

'If there's a cogitator here,' said Lygris, 'I can interface with it and do what damage I can.'

'And if there isn't?'

'I always have faith in explosives, commander.'

'Commander!' said Sergeant Salk's voice over the vox. Salk was up on the hull of the harvester, guarding the makeshift entrances Scamander had opened. 'The Undying are sending their quick ones, the climbers! They're coming in fast!'

'Hold until they're close, and fall back inside,' said Sarpedon. 'You're buying us time.'

'Yes, commander!' Bolter fire drummed away over the vox as Salk's squad levelled another volley at the Undying.

'On me!' cried Sarpedon, and led the Soul Drinkers over the edge of the walkway onto the capacitors filling the lower half of the chamber. They thrummed with power, the note low enough to vibrate the breastplate of fused ribs in Sarpedon's chest. A few chains of bolter fire rattled off as repairing Undying rose up from between the capacitors, and the ruined Undying phased out as they hit the chamber's curved metallic floor.

Tyrendian was just behind Sarpedon.

'You did admirably back there, Librarian,' said Sarpedon.

'My duty done is its own reward,' replied Tyrendian. 'The new boy is proving his worth.'

'I just wish these damnable things had souls,' said Sarpedon. He was the most powerful of the Chapter's Librarians, probably the most powerful the Chapter had ever possessed, but his telepathic assaults were worthless against the alien machines.

'I am grateful,' said Tyrendian, 'that they do not.'

Lygris forced open a hatchway guarding the way into the next chamber, towards the harvester's tail. Thick power conduits curved around him, blinking with emerald pulses of energy. Beyond it, a powerful greyish light shone and the chamber was thrown into extremes of light and shadow.

Lygris, bathed in light, stepped forwards to stand before a huge cube of crystal suspended in a spherical chamber ahead of him. Light crackled off it, but the crystal itself was pure black, as if light could not escape its surface, creating a surreal silhouette in the centre of the glare.

'This is the device that runs the war machine,' said Lygris, 'Its data medium. I can interface with this.'

Sarpedon could see glints of silver behind Lyrgris as the fast-moving Undying skirmishers ran down the walls, leaping between the captives as bolter fire burst around them.

'Firing lines!' called Captain Luko. The Soul Drinkers knelt down in regimented firing lines alongside Sarpedon, ready to pour volley fire into approaching attackers.

'Do it, Lygris,' said Sarpedon, 'and quickly, if you please.'

Lygris placed a hand on the surface of the black crystal. The darkness seemed to seep into him, covering him in shadow. A dataprobe in his palm pierced the crystal, and the Techmarine's body jerked as power and information ricocheted around his mind.

'Keep talking to me, Lygris!' shouted Sarpedon. 'Stay with us!'

Luko yelled an order, and dozens of bolters opened up. Undying on the walls were blown apart. Some fell, phasing out before they hit the ground; others clung grimly to the caged prisoners, ducking down amongst them to self-repair. A terrible rain of body parts fell as the captives were struck by fire. A few whole bodies came loose and clattered down among the machinery.

The prisoners were dead, Sarpedon told himself, or as good as. Even if there was still some life left in their minds, they were better off with that spark extinguished.

Or, at least, he hoped so.

'I'm in!' came a cry from Lygris, strangled as if in fear.

Lygris fell limp as the black crystal pulsed. Tongues of black light licked off it.

'Close order!' shouted Sarpedon above the gunfire. 'Rapid fire!'

Volley after volley of bolter fire poured into the shadows between the capacitors. Undying fell and rose up again, some struck down three or four times before they phased out. Sarpedon snapped shots upwards, shooting down the skirmishing Undying skittering along the walls. One dropped into the midst of the Soul Drinkers, and Tyrendian drew his power sword, spinning into a reverse thrust to drive the blade through the alien's chest. Another, one of its blade-arms blown off, clattered to the ground. Sarpedon reared up over it, and stabbed the talon of his bionic front leg through its skull.

'Lygris!' voxed Sarpedon. 'Talk to me, brother!'

The only sound from Lygris's vox was rapid breathing.

Squad Salk was fighting its way down through the ruined walkways. Salk himself cracked an Undying in the jaw with the butt of his bolter, jabbed the barrel into the alien's midriff, and blew its spine out of its back with a burst of fire. He threw the remains off the walkway, and jumped down after it, the rest of his squad following him.

'Commander!' voxed Salk. 'We cannot stay long. The aliens are converging on us. They're diverting their main force to protect this machine.'

'Then the plan is working,' replied Sarpedon. 'Brother Lygris! We have no time. Whatever you are doing, do it quickly!'

Sarpedon risked a glance back to the chamber. Lygris lay at the foot of the crystal, one hand attached to its surface by the dataprobe. He was convulsing. Blood was running down his chin.

'Brother Lygris! Techmarine, answer me!' There was still no answer. Sparks burst around the dataprobe in Lygris's finger, and power flashed behind his eyelids.

'Damnation!' Sarpedon switched to the vox. 'Salk! Melta-bombs on the capacitors, long fuse! We will bring the fire to them!'

'Yes, commander!' came Salk's reply.

'Captain Luko!' ordered Sarpedon. 'Hold the line!'

'A pleasure!' said Luko, his voice distorted by the hammering of gunfire over the vox.

Sarpedon turned away from the gun-line and ran into the crystal chamber. Lygris was still shuddering. Blood was bubbling between his lips and the skin around his eyes, and the collar of his armour was burning. Sarpedon grabbed Lygris's wrist and yanked the dataprobe out of the crystal.

Lygris gurgled an incoherent cry, blood slopping down the front of his breastplate.

'Apothecary!' voxed Sarpedon. 'Where are you?'

'Still outside,' came the crackling reply from Apothecary Pallas. 'There was no way onto the machine. I'm towards its rear. The Undying are everywhere.'

'We're getting off this machine,' said Sarpedon. 'I need your assistance as soon as we are out. Brother Lygris is wounded.'

'How badly?' asked Pallas.

'He's bitten off his tongue.' Sarpedon hefted Lygris onto his shoulder. 'We have encountered a moral threat. I fear the worst wounds are to his soul.'

'Commander! Melta-bombs set!' came Salk's vox from behind Sarpedon. 'Three minutes before the capacitors go up!'

'Luko! Fall back to me and prepare to breach!'

Scamander scrambled into the crystal chamber. His gauntlets were smoking, and ice flaked off the rest of his armour as he moved.

'Allow me,' he said. He planted his hands against the rear wall of the crystal chamber.

Sarpedon noticed the crystal. The previously flawless surface was mottled and dull, as if some disease had taken control of it and spread milky stains like cataracts across its surface. Whatever Lygris had done, the war machine had suffered.

Luko led the Soul Drinkers into a tight line in front of the entrance to the crystal chamber. Beyond them, more Undying were converging. The Soul Drinkers were dragging a couple of wounded battle-brothers; even power armour was vulnerable to being ripped away by the bursts of green fire raining down from the Undying. Many other Astartes around Luko were missing chunks of armour, cores bored from shoulder pads, or greaves stripped down to bloody flesh.

Wires shorted around Scamander as the rear wall melted.

'Novitiate!' shouted Tyrendian. 'Stay your power! You will kill yourself!'

Scamander stumbled backwards. Tyrendian ran forwards and caught Scamander before he fell, lowering him to the floor.

'Someone take him,' said Tyrendian, the pure white light of a lightning bolt forming in his fist.

One of Squad Luko dragged Scamander onto his shoulder. Tyrendian turned to the half-melted wall, and hurled the bolt right into it. The flash was so powerful that even a Space Marine's augmented eyes were blinded for a split second. When vision returned, the wall was gone, the melted mass blown outwards by the force of the lightning. Through it could be seen the dust-choked gloom of the streets outside.

'Good work, Librarian,' said Sarpedon. 'Soul Drinkers! Fall back and out of this place!'

The Soul Drinkers charged out of the harvester. The Undying were on every side, but if there was one thing that Daenyathos had taught the old Chapter millennia ago, it was how a Soul Drinker could turn retreat into attack. Tyrendian hurled another bolt that blew an Undying off its feet, and Luko led the rest of the Soul Drinkers in opening fire as soon as they were clear of the harvester. The weight of gunfire threw Undying to the ground, and beat the xenos back into the surrounding buildings.

'Thirty seconds, my brothers!' shouted Sergeant Salk.

'Get clear!' ordered Sarpedon. The Soul Drinkers scattered, firing all the time, heading for the cover of half-collapsed buildings along the side of the street.

One side of the Undying harvester swelled up and burst, spewing flame and wreckage. Shards of hot metal whickered around the street, ricocheting off walls. Another explosion blew the tail off, and the blazing cone of segmented metal rocketed past Sarpedon, embedding itself in the building opposite, and bringing the walls down.

Smoke and rubble filled the street. It was denser and blacker than the dust that had heralded the harvester's approach. Everything was darkness and noise, dominated by the ear-splitting howl of the harvester imploding.

Sarpedon looked up from cover. Through the murk, he could make out the burning wreckage of the harvester. The capacitors, with their stores of power, had been breached, and that power had torn the harvester apart.

Apothecary Pallas and the Soul Drinkers who had been caught outside the harvester approached through the rubble.

'Commander,' said Pallas. 'Let me see him.'

Sarpedon hauled Lygris off his shoulder and laid him at Pallas's feet. Pallas's narthecium gauntlet unfolded into a probe that he inserted into a port on the forearm of Lygris's armour.

'I will do what I can,' said Pallas, 'but our brother is in a grave state.'

Sarpedon nodded, glanced down at Lygris, and turned away to look up at the sky just visible through the smoke. 'Brother Phol, what news of the xenos advance?'

The vox crackled with static for a few moments in reply.

'The xenos are diverting towards you,' said Phol's voice. 'Their forces to the west of the city breached the walls to defend the harvester. The civilians are on their way out of the south gate.'

'Then we are successful?'

'So far, commander.'

'Close in and lend us your fire, brother.' Sarpedon switched to the all-squads frequency. 'Soul Drinkers! On me, my brothers! Let us sell these aliens the streets of Astelok at a price they cannot pay!'

Pallas carried Lygris as the Soul Drinkers grouped up. The smoke swirled in the wash from the Thunderhawk's engines, and the gunship's heavy bolters opened up, stitching explosive fire through the Undying. The Soul Drinkers' fire opened up, too, punctuated by Tyrendian's bolts of lightning.

Cold and fast, just as Daenyathos had once written, the Soul Drinkers sent Undying phasing out on every side as they advanced towards Astelok's south gate.

'The legends, the superstitions of your Chapter, are nothing
more than stories to the ears of outsiders. But you know they
are the soul of your Chapter, the collective admonishments
and inspirations of every battle-brother who has gone before
you.'

– Daenyathos, *The Borders of Moral Endurance*

CHAPTER ELEVEN

Queen Dyrmida watched from the walls of the space port. Her retinue of soldiers had known better than to dissuade her from putting herself at risk. She had left the relative safety of the command centre to take to the battlements. It was her duty to watch Astelok die, for she had made the decision to sacrifice it.

A dark pall rose over the city. Most of it was dust from the terrible path the Undying war engine had chewed through Astelok's heart, but there was also smoke and flame, and bursts of green light like lightning. Most of the palaces of the city centre were obscured by the dust, but the few she could see were in ruins, their walls pushed in and their roofs sagging.

'Your majesty?' said Kavins, who had been chosen for the duty of accompanying the queen to the top of the walls. 'The people have asked for you to address them.'

'What can I say to them?' she asked. 'That their homes are destroyed? That the troops that stayed behind are dead? They already know those things. And what of the future? Should I tell them that we will depart for a safe haven that may not exist?'

'I do not know, your majesty,' said Kavins uncertainly.

Dyrmida waved a hand dismissively. 'These are not matters for anyone to concern themselves with save myself. It is my responsibility. Of course I must speak to my people. They must be calmed and reassured. It is the least they deserve from me.'

Astelok's space port was a series of huge rockcrete circles, covered in docking clamps and fuelling rigs, and marked with warning strips corresponding to the landing gear of various types of Selaacan spacecraft. Hangars for equipment and vehicles were dotted around the space port, and a tall multi-spired building contained the command centre, which, in peacetime, saw orbital controllers guiding down trading and passenger craft, welcoming them to Astelok in the name of the queen.

Now the space port was a miserable makeshift city. Maybe three hundred thousand people were making their homes there, sleeping wherever they could or gathering to pray, talk, or simply sit in silence. The soldiers had set up tents everywhere they could, almost covering several of the landing pads, but there were only enough for the children and the infirm, and some of the women. The men gathered together as if they were soldiers, too, mustering in units, ready to defeat the Undying scourge. Perhaps, eventually, they would have to do exactly that.

The ruse, the sacrificing of Astelok, had worked. Dyrmida's plan had been a success, but she could take no triumph from it. The Undying forces had been focused on forcing their way through the city, where the Soul Drinkers were facing them, and so had abandoned the positions outside the city from which they could have ambushed the columns of civilians making for the space port. The population of Astelok had been evacuated, most of them, at least. Some had refused to leave, or were members of the army that volunteered to fight in the defence. No doubt more than a few, who had no loved ones, or had too many and were always assumed to be with someone else, had been left behind to die. But the soldiers had managed the crushes at the southern gate and at the gate of the space port well enough, and the Undying had not descended on the column of civilians before they could find safety. It was what happened next that worried Dyrmida. Once off the planet, there was no telling if another world would be any safer.

'I need a few minutes to myself. Then I will speak to them,' said the queen. 'I will use the space port's vox-casters, or there could be a crush.'

The soldier's eye caught something by Astelok's southern gate, and Dyrmida turned around to follow his gaze. People were emerging from the southern gate. She assumed they were stragglers, survivors of the devastation, who had banded together and found a way out.

She was wrong. They were armoured in purple and armed to the teeth, bloody and battle-filthy, but moving quickly into the trees and undergrowth that dotted the route to the space port.

The Soul Drinkers, they were alive.

'I will give you your voice back, Brother Lygris,' said Pallas. 'It is the smallest honour that can be done.' He leaned over the bed on which

Lygris was laid, and finished soldering the voice box into place, a simple metal case that fitted around Lygris's larynx.

One of the hangars in the space port had been set up as an infirmary. The sickly and decrepit of Astelok had been laid on beds, or on the floor when the beds had run out. The dead were covered in sheets waiting to be carried out. Most of the others were silent, asleep or insensible, or staring at the ceiling waiting for a friend or relative to find them. Every now and again, one of them moaned in pain, or in a nightmare.

Pallas had set up in a corner of the infirmary, screened off by sheets hung from the hangar ceiling. The wounded Soul Drinkers from Astelok were there, tending to their wounds, or lying stripped of their armour, their injuries patched up by Pallas. There were virtually no medical supplies in the space port, and what little the Raevenians had brought with them was inadequate for their own needs, so Pallas could work with only what he carried on him.

Sarpedon stood by Pallas's shoulder. Lygris made for a sorry sight. His right hand and forearm were black with electrical burns, and Pallas had slathered them in antibiotic gel. Lygris had not regained consciousness, not fully, but his eyes were open and unfocused, roving, as if watching something that no one else could see.

'The Raevenians have little augmetic technology,' said Pallas as he soldered flesh to metal around the edge of the voice box. 'I was fortunate that their medics had this device. When I get Brother Lygris back to the *Brokenback* I can give him a far more suitable replacement.'

Lygris coughed, and a little blood trickled from his lips. Pallas had seared closed the stump of Lygris's tongue, but still it bled.

'Brother?' said Sarpedon. 'Can you hear me? Speak to me, brother.'

A metallic braying issued from the voice box, a mechanised cry of anguish.

'He should rest,' said Pallas.

'No,' said Sarpedon. 'He saw the mind of the machine. He looked into the xenos soul.'

'One… One of them…' spluttered Lygris.

'One of them?' asked Sarpedon.

'One soul.' The voice was a mechanical drone, devoid of the pain in Lygris's eyes. He still could not focus, and his eyes darted randomly. 'One mind. There is but one mind among them. The time… the millions of years, the mountains of steel… the lord with the eyes of flame…'

The voice broke down into fractured moans. Lygris convulsed again, and Pallas leaned over him to hold him down.

'Think, brother!' said Sarpedon. 'Tell me what you saw. What do these xenos want? Who leads them? How can they be destroyed?'

'One! One mind! The lord with the eyes of flame!'

Alerts beeped on Pallas's narthecium gauntlet. Pallas jabbed a needle into Lygris's neck, and sedatives flooded his system.

'Give him time,' said Pallas. 'His vital signs are fluctuating. He'll burst a heart without rest.'

Sarpedon sat back on his haunches. 'In my training at the old Chapter's Librarium, we were warned of this. To contact the mind of a xenos is to invite madness. Many good battle-brothers have been lost when a human mind touches that of the alien.'

'It is not right for an Astartes to live on in such a state,' said Pallas. 'I can do no more than tend to his physical wounds. Brother Lygris must fight this madness off himself.'

Sarpedon knew that Lyrgris was strong. All Astartes were. Sarpedon also knew, however, that the Undying were not just creatures with alien mindsets; they were not creatures at all. Lygris had seen what the Selaacans had seen at the white city and the forest world, when their skies went dark and the Undying began to march. He had seen death.

Iktinos was waiting for Sarpedon in the space port's command centre. He was in the observatory, which housed a gigantic telescope that allowed orbital controllers to see spacecraft above Raevenian, and assess any damage they were reporting. It was a grimly industrial place, all greasy metal and shadows, dominated by the telescope, which reached up through the domed roof far above.

A few of Iktinos's flock were with him when Sarpedon entered. They were watching through the telescope's eyepiece or taking readings from the banks of instruments beside it. It was a measure of Iktinos's standing within the Chapter that he had been the Astartes to which those Space Marines had gone to seek leadership, and it spoke of his dedication that he had taken them on as his personal charges.

'Chaplain?' said Sarpedon. 'You asked to see me?'

'The situation has changed,' said Iktinos. 'Most gravely so.'

'Have the Mechanicus tracked us down?'

'More than that. It is best that you observe for yourself.'

The Soul Drinker at the eyepiece made way for Sarpedon, who had to drop down on to the knees of his mutant legs to get level with the eyepiece. He peered through it, and saw the multicoloured mist of the Veiled Region.

Glimmers of light sparkled, darting around like bright fish in a shoal. The telescope focused in on them, and Sarpedon saw that it was a spaceship, shaped like a crescent of dull metal. Slivers of green fire spat from it as it spiralled around a ship of Imperial design.

'Xenos?' said Sarpedon, looking up from the eyepiece.

'So it seems,' replied Iktinos.

'What of the *Brokenback*?'

'It is safe for the time being,' said Iktinos. 'The Mechanicus fleet and the xenos are fighting one another, and it seems they have enough on their minds not to worry about our hulk. That situation will probably not last once the xenos have despatched their enemies.'

'The aliens will win?'

'Oh yes, commander. There is no doubt about that.'

Sarpedon stood back from the telescope. A member of Iktinos's flock took to the eyepiece, making notes on a data-slate. 'Do we know anything about the composition of the xenos fleet?'

'Mostly battleships,' said Iktinos. 'The sensorium crew on the *Brokenback* are assessing their combat potential, but they are far advanced compared to the Imperial ships.'

'I take it, Chaplain, that there is little chance of the Raevenian evacuation making it through the alien fleet?'

'There is none, commander.'

'Then the Raevenians have no chance of deliverance after all. They never did. When their transports leave this space port they will be slain by the Undying fleet as surely as if they had stayed in Astelok and waited to die.' Sarpedon sat down on his back legs, as he usually did when he had thinking to do. 'No matter what we do or how hard we try, Raevenia is dead.'

'Again, commander,' said Iktinos with his customary solemnity, 'there is no doubt.'

'Does there exist in the galaxy, in this universe, a place where enemies do not lie in wait for the Soul Drinkers? Is there anywhere we could look where some enemy does not lurk? If not the Imperium, the mutant. If not the mutant, the alien.'

'Such is the path we have chosen,' said Iktinos.

'That I have chosen. I took on the leadership of this Chapter when I challenged Gorgoleon for it. Everywhere we find ourselves, I have put us there. That is what it means to be Chapter Master.'

'And what will you do?' asked Iktinos. 'Now that we are beset once again. What orders will you give?'

Sarpedon looked up at him. If there had been doubt, it passed in that moment, reflected in the eyepieces of the Chaplain's skull-mask.

'We fight,' said Sarpedon. 'We are Astartes. It is why we were created. We face the enemy and we fight them, and if we fall, we fall. That is the way of Daenyathos. It was the way of the Emperor.'

'Then we will fight the Undying here, on Raevenia?'

'If we flee, the Undying will shoot us down as they will the Raevenians,' said Sarpedon sharply. 'The *Brokenback* is stricken and vulnerable. A man is at his most vulnerable when he flees, for then the enemy can strike unanswered. A Space Marine does not flee. Yes, Iktinos, we shall stand and fight.'

'Then I swear,' said Iktinos, 'that the Chapter's souls will be prepared.'

'I must tell Queen Dyrmida,' said Sarpedon, 'that her people will not escape this world after all.'

'I can do so, if you wish,' said Iktinos.

'It must come from me.' Sarpedon pushed himself back onto his talons. His mutations had made the Raevenians that saw him gasp in disgust, and he knew what they would say when the Undying descended to take the space port and wipe them out. It was the mutant. The monsters. He promised us deliverance, but he delivered us only into the hands of the Undying.

It did not matter what they thought. Nothing mattered now. It was down to duty and dereliction, to failure and victory, and all else was just chaff to be ignored. It was a strange feeling, to know that the universe was pared down to those extremes. A Space Marine was trained, created, even, to make the right choice. It was, perhaps, something of a comfort. Sarpedon did not need to worry about anything except the fighting. The endeavour of battle was all that remained, and, as every follower of the Emperor understood, endeavour was its own reward.

The sound of explosions, muffled by the hull, shuddered the walls of Voar's laboratory. Sample jars jangled on their shelves, and delicate components shifted across the dissection table at which Voar sat. Archmagos Voar regarded the noise with more annoyance than alarm.

The guns of the *Antithesis* were firing, countermeasures probably, sprays of chaff and electromagnetic pulse munitions to throw the xenos sensors off as they targeted the Mechanicus ships. If the xenos used sensors the Imperium understood, of course... if they needed to see the Mechanicus at all.

Voar had laid out the components of the dissected necron warrior on the table. Arcane machines were hooked up to it by electrodes and probes. Winking lights lit the dim laboratory, and the only sounds, aside from the dull thuds of the ship's guns, were the hum of the machines and the clicking of Voar's implements as he worked. The necron's limbs had been broken apart into the many hundreds of struts and servo units that drove them, and lay in neat piles beside the torso. The torso had been carefully carved up, and split open to reveal the circuitry and components clustered around the power unit that still glowed faintly green. The warrior's head had been removed and placed to one side, but it was still connected to the torso by the articulated cable that served it like a spinal cord.

Voar was close. He knew it. The necron's technology was a puzzle, completely unlike anything Imperial or even pre-Imperial that he had ever seen. It had required him to relearn some of the most basic principles of science, of sacred cause and effect. It was unholy, for it breached the basic tenets of the Omnissiah's logic, but it was fascinating. A weaker mind than Voar's could have been seduced by it.

Voar opened up a small unit in the chest beside the power unit. He pared it open to reveal a silvery contact. With precision that a human hand could not match, Voar soldered the end of a wire to the contact. He plugged the other end of the wire into one of the laboratory machines. It was a highly sensitive scanner that could pick out all manner of exotic frequencies and radiation types. It was perhaps three thousand years old, which was how Voar knew it could be relied upon.

Voar carefully watched the readout dials on the machine's brass casing as he cycled through frequencies. The necrons had to be connected to something, some central source of control or power, to account for their abilities and behaviour. When they phased out, they had to go somewhere. Their power units were not generators at all, but capacitors, taking energy from elsewhere and storing it. That power had to come from somewhere.

Someone banged on the laboratory door. Voar looked up, scowling. He had left orders not to be disturbed, even if the *Antithesis* was about to explode. His work was more important than fighting a battle the Mechanicus could not win. It did not matter since the door was sealed with gene-locks that the crew could not access, but any distraction was unwelcome.

The unwelcome guest hammered at the door again. Voar put it out of his mind and continued to search for signals going into or out of the necron. He expected it to be exotic, something the Mechanicus would never normally consider, something as alien as the rest of the heathen creature.

A terrible roar of torn metal filled the lab. The door was ripped clean off its mounts, spilling the remnants of the gene-lock onto the laboratory floor.

Magos Crystavayne and Magos Vionel walked in, Vionel's iron-shod feet stomping on the laboratory floor. The remains of the door were held in Vionel's huge metal paws.

'Archmagos,' said Crystavayne, 'we would speak with you.'

'What logic compels you to defy my orders?' blared Voar.

'Destruction!' bellowed Vionel, throwing the door to the floor. 'The removal of our knowledge from the Omnissiah's work! All we have done, all we ever will do, will be undone at the hands of the alien, and you hide here in the dark!'

'And what do you know of it?' retorted Voar. 'What cares the xenos whether I command or not? What string of logic will bring us victory against a foe that exceeds us in every way?'

'Your duty,' said Crystavayne, 'is to lead us in the pursuit of knowledge, whatever form it may take and whatever obstacle may stand in our way, even to the point of destruction.'

'But that destruction,' said Voar, 'has not reached us. There has been no suggestion to me that we will be die here.'

'We cannot win this battle, archmagos! You said so yourself!'

'The battle, magos, not the war.'

Vionel stomped forwards, and a floodlight emerged from one shoulder cowling, which was still scarred from the necron fire. The acid yellow light glared off the machines and dissected parts on the laboratory table. 'And this will win us that war?'

'The chances are small,' said Voar, 'but they exist. And they exceed any increase in the likelihood of our survival with me at the helm.'

'Where is your sense of duty?' asked Crystavayne. 'Vionel nearly died on the *Ferrous*. Hepsebah is directing the fire of the *Constant* as we speak. Khrul gave his life!'

'Duty,' said Voar, 'is secondary to logic. Understanding that is the difference between my rank and yours.'

Crystavayne emitted a curse in clicking binary.

'You are a disgrace to the Adeptus Mechanicus,' he said.

Voar's hand went to the ornate pistol he wore at his waist beneath his robes. 'If you intend to challenge me for command, magos, then out with it and let us settle this.'

Vionel stepped between Voar and Crystavayne. His rivet gun cycled, lumps of metal thunking into its chambers.

'Archmagos or not,' he said, 'if you abandon us in this battle, we will take over your office. And if you resist, then I shall balance your equation myself.'

One of the machines chirped shrilly. Vionel turned his floodlight on it. A green light was winking in its brass casing.

'It's found the frequency,' said Voar.

'The frequency?' asked Crystavayne.

'The necron warriors are acting on remote orders. They are only semi-autonomous, and the commands must come from elsewhere. They need a signal to give them coordinates so they can teleport out when deactivated, too. My studies have suggested that both functions originate at the same location.'

'Where?' asked Vionel, his rivet gun still trained on Voar.

Voar took the power scalpel and activated the tiny power field around its blade. He fiddled with a couple of the controls on the machine and read off the numbers from its various dials and readouts. Then he moved aside one of the necron's dissected arms and scratched a pair of intersecting lines into the surface of the table. He carved a few figures beside it, frequencies and wavelengths, as he read them off.

'It can be triangulated,' said Voar. 'It's barely perceptible. Either this unit is too damaged to pick it up properly or their technology is far more sensitive than ours. It is a miracle we can hear it at all.'

Vionel's rivet gun dropped.

'Where?' he repeated. 'Where is it coming from?'

Voar took a data-slate and keyed in the coordinates he had just generated.

'Take this to navigation,' he said, 'and find out. I must finish up here.'

For a moment, the two magi did not move. Then Vionel took the data-slate from Voar, and they turned to leave the laboratory.

Voar unplugged the probe from the necron's innards and picked up its skull. He turned it over in his hands, looking into its eyes.

'Let us see how you fight,' he said, 'when you are blind.'

'Often we speak of duty unto death, of defiance to the point of extinction. But what does this mean? What work of ours can change the galaxy, if it ends along with our lives? Works of true devotion, acts of true duty, last far beyond our own lifetimes.'

– Daenyathos, *The Four Pillars of Sacred Hate*

CHAPTER TWELVE

For someone who had just learned that she was going to die, Queen Dyrmida was calm.

She had set up a command centre in the control tower in the middle of the space port, and had ordered the generals and staff to leave while Sarpedon spoke with her. Perhaps she had wanted to make sure the information he gave her was properly controlled, or perhaps she just didn't want to look weak if she received his news with shock. Certainly, she had known from the moment Sarpedon had entered that he brought bad news.

'Why have you told me this?' asked Dyrmida when Sarpedon finished. 'And do not tell me that you are doing the right thing. No one on this planet is doing anything, except what they must do to survive.'

'If we were to flee,' said Sarpedon, 'the Undying fleet would shoot us down. Our ship cannot escape them without fuel. That means that we must fight, and we will have a better chance if the Raevenians fight too.'

'A better chance of what?' Dyrmida's eyes were bright with anger. 'You say, yourself, that there is no chance of getting off Raevenia, and I dare say there is none of defeating the Undying army on the ground. What would you hope to achieve with the lives of my subjects?'

'An Astartes,' said Sarpedon, 'does not kneel for the executioner's bullet. He does not beg for a quick death. Every Soul Drinker will fight on because it is his duty to ensure that his death does not come cheaply to the enemy. And your majesty, I understand something of the Raevenian way of death. Think of the good deaths that would be won at the walls of this space port, lost for monarch and for world. Think of the bad deaths that would be inflicted if the same people tried to flee or surrender. It may not be an easy decision to make, but there is only one decision in the end.'

Queen Dyrmida sighed. Sarpedon realised how much she had aged since the Soul Drinkers had first landed outside Astelok.

'A death means something,' she said, 'only if it is remembered.'

'Then order your people to flee and die, or march out into the Undying's hands. But remember this: the people in that harvester were still alive. They had not long to live, perhaps, but they were prisoners, not trophies. If nothing else, Queen Dyrmida, that is a fate worth fighting to avoid.'

Sarpedon had nothing more to say. Raevenia was going to die, and nothing he did would make any difference to that. He left Dyrmida alone with her thoughts.

'Soul Drinker,' said Dyrmida as Sarpedon left the command centre.

'Your majesty?'

Dyrmida took a data-slate from a pocket in her fatigues and threw it to Sarpedon. 'Were it not for the Soul Drinkers, Raevenia would already have been lost. Those are the codes for the fuel tankers beneath the space port.'

The data-slate in Sarpedon's hand showed strings of numbers and letters in the Raevenian alphabet, recognisably derived from Low Gothic. 'My gratitude, your majesty.'

'If the Undying truly have this planet blockaded then its value is little more than symbolic. But on Raevenia we honour our debts, even in the hour of our destruction. If any of you survive and the chance to escape presents itself, take it, and take whoever survives of my people with you. Then there will be someone to remember all those good deaths.'

'I will need to organise my Astartes,' said Sarpedon. 'The space port has many weak points in a siege. It will need a great deal of fortification and planning to hold it.'

'The army of Astelok will do the same,' said Dyrmida. 'If the Undying have any memory, if they have a history of their damnable species, then the last battle for Raevenia will be a part of it.'

Sergeant Salk was waiting at the entrance to the control centre. The Raevenian ships were being fuelled and prepped for takeoff behind him. They were simple, sturdy ships, unadorned and functional. Each one was large enough to hold several thousand people, and more were being brought up on elevators from the hangars below the landing pads. They were enough to carry almost all the Raevenian survivors, minus the infirm and wounded, who would be left behind. No doubt, thought Sarpedon, those ships would be abandoned and hauled back into their hangars once the news broke of the Undying fleet bearing down on them.

'Sergeant,' said Sarpedon, 'what news?'

'The officers wish to speak with you, commander,' said Salk. Salk, like most of the Soul Drinkers, was still scuffed and scorched from the battle on the harvester, and chunks of his armour had been stripped down to bare ceramite by glancing hits from the Undying guns.

'About what?'

'Tyrendian has a plan,' said Salk.

'For what?'

'For everything.'

The Soul Drinkers were waiting in the makeshift infirmary, where Pallas had tended to the wounded Astartes, and helped the Raevenian medics patch up the few wounded soldiers that had made it out of Astelok.

Tyrendian was waiting in the screened off area, along with Iktinos and Luko. Lygris still lay semi-conscious nearby. Together, they represented the surviving officers of the Soul Drinkers. The sight of them reminded Sarpedon just how many battle-brothers he had lost; the Chapter was barely at quarter-strength.

'Librarian,' said Sarpedon, 'what have you come up with?'

'The Adeptus Mechanicus will be destroyed,' said Tyrendian. 'That is certain.'

'It is,' said Sarpedon. 'No doubt you have seen the situation in orbit yourself.'

'And we will be destroyed shortly afterwards,' continued Tyrendian. The Librarian's manner was reminiscent of many officers from the old Chapter: superior and dismissive, somehow conveying a sense of arrogance no matter what he actually said. Sarpedon had come to understand that beneath that face was a dedicated and intelligent warrior without whom the Chapter would be worse off. 'Along with Raevenia.'

'This is true,' said Sarpedon.

'Then we and the Mechanicus are in a similar position.'

'Meaning?'

'Meaning, we send a delegation,' said Tyrendian. 'We make an alliance with the Mechanicus. Lygris has seen much of the information structure underlying the Undying invasion. The Mechanicus have no doubt sought information on the enemy. If nothing else, we could fight together and buy more of a chance than we have now.'

'You propose an alliance with the Mechanicus?' asked Sarpedon. 'They have gone very far out of their way to kill us.'

'True,' said Tyrendian, 'but they won't, not if the Undying get there first.'

'We have our enmities,' added Luko. 'I hate those red-robed freaks, but they're logical, you have to give them that. If we give them a chance to get out of the Veiled Region with their steel hides intact then they'll take it.'

'And what can we offer them?' asked Sarpedon.

'Lygris can answer that,' said Tyrendian.

'Lygris?' Sarpedon walked to Lygris's bedside and leaned over him. 'Brother? What do you know?'

Lygris's eyes opened a little. 'I saw… inside them. Their system. The… the mind that rules them. The lord… the lord with the burning eyes. Millions of years of hate, all burning through those eyes…' The voice box strained to turn Lygris's slurring into intelligent speech.

'One mind,' said Tyrendian. 'One lord. The Undying are controlled by one intelligence. Lygris saw enough of it in the harvester's data medium to see it. And if we kill it, there will be nothing controlling the Undying.'

'You saw this, Brother Lygris?'

Lucidity sparked in Lygris's eyes. 'Yes, commander. I saw him… it. It watches over everything. It's a spider at the heart of the web. You… you would not believe it. To see it. You would not believe anything could survive in the galaxy but these Undying. We are just… insects. Microbes. Like something on a slide to be… to be ignored, and allowed to wither away. When we have been forgotten in the galaxy there will still be the Undying, and when they rule…'

'Techmarine!' snapped Sarpedon. 'Enough of this heresy! No alien will have this galaxy. It does not matter how long they have waited. Humanity will wipe them out.'

Lygris coughed again, blood running from his lips. 'They… they do not have doubt. They know. They know they will rule.'

Sarpedon glared at Lygris, but Lygris shifted back into a daze.

'The Mechanicus,' said Tyrendian, 'might still be able to find this intelligence and deliver us to it. If anyone in the Veiled Region is capable of inflicting justice upon it, we are. That is the deal we offer them. They find it, we kill it, and the Undying are halted.'

Sarpedon looked between the officers assembled in the infirmary. Tyrendian and Luko had made their case. Pallas, still tending to the wounds of his battle-brothers, had not spoken up, and Lygris was in no position to offer an opinion.

'Iktinos?' asked Sarpedon.

'I have,' said Iktinos, 'misgivings about an alliance with our enemies. Such a path would constitute a moral threat. But my misgivings about remaining on this world to die, when an alternative tactic might remain unexploited, are deeper still.'

'Our options,' said Sarpedon, 'are to stand and fight, and die; to flee and die, or to risk an alliance with the Adeptus Mechanicus. Like Captain Luko, I have little enough love for the Mechanicus, but given the other two options, the decision is clear. Tyrendian, will you head this embassy?'

'I will, commander, if you wish it of me.'

'I do. The Mechanicus may not tolerate a mutant on their ship long enough to hear our offer.'

'I should go, commander,' said Chaplain Iktinos. 'My experience with dealing with those outside the Chapter exceeds yours. It was one of my duties in the old Chapter. Added to which, I am not a mutant.'

'You will remain here,' said Sarpedon, 'to lead the Soul Drinkers at the space port. The focus of the Undying must be kept on Raevenia, or there will be little chance of any other mission succeeding.'

'Then the flock will hold this ground,' said Iktinos. 'If you need a force that will not falter, there is little better choice than my faithful.'

'Tyrendian,' continued Sarpedon, 'Phol will take you. He's our best pilot. Soul Drinkers, to your duties.'

The Librarian and the Chaplain headed out to the landing pad on which the Soul Drinkers had stationed their gunships and transports. Luko and Sarpedon remained in the infirmary.

'It is not like you to keep so quiet, captain,' said Sarpedon.

Luko looked around to see that Pallas was on the other side of the infirmary and Lygris was unconscious. 'I must confess something to you, Sarpedon. Not as an officer to his commander, not even as an Astartes.'

'Speak, Luko.'

Luko paused for a long moment before he spoke, as if the words wanted to stay hidden in his throat. 'When… when I found out that the Undying were ready to invade, and that Raevenia had no chance… I was relieved.'

Sarpedon did not answer. He had never seen Luko vulnerable like this. His infectious ferocity, his love of the fight, was one of the engines that fuelled the Chapter's sudden, shock assault form of warfare. It seemed a different man was wearing Luko's armour and lightning claws.

'I was relieved,' continued Luko, 'because it meant that it would be over.'

'Over?' asked Sarpedon. 'You want to die down here?'

'I want peace,' said Luko. 'Just that. Just peace.'

Sarpedon sat back. Luko sat on one of the infirmary beds.

'Everything I do,' said Luko, 'is a lie. Everything. For… for years now. Since before the Star Fort.'

'You fooled us,' said Sarpedon.

'I know. Forgive me.'

'Luko, there is nothing to forgive,' said Sarpedon. 'You are the best officer I have. Without you leading from the front we would all have been lost many times over. How many Soul Drinkers owe you their lives? What evils would have been perpetrated against the people of this galaxy if you had not lived that lie?'

'But that's it, commander. It was a lie. All of it. Every time I joked about the killing or I acted like I was never happier than in battle, that was a lie. What are we fighting for, if not to find some truth in the galaxy?'

'And so you want to die.'

'If that is the only way it can end, then yes, I want to die.'

'You will not get what you want.' Sarpedon stood up to his full height, and he towered over Luko. 'Not here. Not yet. I promise you, Brother Luko, you will never have peace while I still live.'

'I don't know if I can carry on, commander. I have played an Astartes for so long...'

'You are still Astartes. You still know no fear. Nothing has changed.'

'I cannot go on lying.'

'Then stop. But keep fighting. That is an order. Do you understand?'

'Yes, commander.'

'Good. Stay with your squad. If Iktinos is successful, we may have to move quickly.'

'I understand.'

'And captain?'

'Yes?'

'It will end. Maybe it will be here. Probably, even. But we won't fight forever. Either we'll die out here, and it'll happen soon enough, or we will fight until we carve out a chunk of space for ourselves. Rule it like the Ultramarines rule their own roost. Make of it what the Imperium should be. That's the only way we can continue to exist in this galaxy. If we make it, or if we die trying, then our war of survival will be over. If you trust me, Luko, trust me with that.'

The Defence of *Caelano Minoris* cut a gallant figure as it burned. The Fleet Minor gathered around it like pallbearers as green fire rippled up its hull, forcing its way in through the tears in its hull. Explosions wracked the laboratory ship as the fire cooked off stores of chemicals and fuel. Saviour pods escaped, riding on columns of compressed gas. Some of them barely made it beyond the ship, and were caught in flashes of fire, incinerating whoever was inside.

Two necron cruisers closed in. The efforts of the Fleet Minor, which were deploying every countermeasure they had, had spoiled their aim to the extent that they had to close in to deliver a killing blow. Since the destruction of the *Ferrous*, the Mechanicus fleet had been frustratingly reluctant to hang still in front of the necron guns, and the xenos cruisers eagerly took to the kill. The *Defence* had already lost most of its prow and a good chunk of amidships, its few guns abandoned or stripped away from the hull like proud nails.

The two necron cruisers rotated to bring their main weapons to bear on the ship. Arcs of power flitted between the tips of their crescent-shaped hulls as they charged.

The *Defence* carried several containers of highly volatile chemicals. Usually kept in separate lead-cased chambers, they had been piled up in barrels just behind the plasma vessel of one of the ship's reactors, an experimental power source that provided great efficiency in return for considerable volatility. Magos Devwyn, commanding the *Defence* in Crystavayne's absence, had reasoned that the reactor would explode under enemy fire soon enough anyway.

When the burning prow of the *Defence* was pointed at the closest cruiser, Devwyn gave the order. It was relayed to a team of menials that had volunteered to stay on the ship and command the servitors, who were now set on fire and sent striding into the chemical stockpile.

The chemicals detonated, creating a vortex of exotic particles that obliterated the engine section of the *Defence*. Its stern disappeared in a shining white cloud of vaporised metal.

The reactor went critical, its core bombarded with particles. Its mass was converted instantly into energy. The structure of the *Defence* held just long enough to send the energy mass along the length of the ship as it converted into pure yellow-white light and fire.

The *Defence* fired like an enormous cannon, almost its entire mass, including the volunteer menials and even Magos Devwyn, converted into energy. The bolt of power streaked across the void and speared the necron cruiser at the base of one of its crescent wings. The wing was sheared off, and chain reactions rippled along the remnants of the alien ship, spraying bursts of shrapnel from its hull like steel volcanoes.

The second necron cruiser's engines flared, and it tore itself out of a firing position to avoid the titanic chunks of wreckage spinning out of its dying sister ship. Strange technologies, chunks of glowing green crystal, the bodies of broken necron warriors and sprays of liquid silver poured out of the damaged cruiser's wounds. The lights studding the surface winked out, and the ship drifted dead away from the field of debris marking the site of the *Defence's* sacrifice.

'No knowledge comes without a price,' said Archmagos Voar.

The wreckage that remained of the *Defence* boiled away in a cloud of dimming silver, glittering on the main viewscreen of the observatory.

'And no price,' said Magos Crystavayne, 'is paid without leaving its mark.'

Crystavayne had been in the observatory of the *Antithesis*, following the execution of his navigational commands, when the *Defence of Caelano Minoris* exploded. It had been spectacular, perhaps as beautiful as such destruction could be, but Magos Devwyn had been a fellow walker on the path of knowledge, one without whom the Mechanicus would never have penetrated the Veiled Region. Voar and Crystavayne mourned him in their own ways, in silence, with an internal prayer of machine-code clicking through their logic centres.

'Preparations are almost complete,' said Voar.

'I want to be with the boarding force,' said Crystavayne.

'Then it shall be so.'

'Can we win?'

'That is a more complex question than it first appears,' said Voar. 'It is possible that we will. Should there be, for instance, a form of communications device without which the necron fleet cannot operate, and upon which we stumble, then we shall succeed. Should we capture their ship and are able to operate it, we may flee intact. There are other routes to success, but they are too unlikely to be considered viable. As they are, the chances of success border on the nominal. They are still, however, greater than our chances should we continue to fight as we do now. To answer your question, by the standards generated by a logic engine such as mine, we can succeed, but by the less exact standards of an unaugmented human, we cannot.'

'It does not matter,' said Crystavayne. 'To take the fight to the alien is its own reward.'

The tech-guard troops had been gathered from the fleet's other ships and assembled on the *Antithesis*. The *Antithesis* had few boarding facilities, being limited to a handful of armoured transports and a single complement of boarding torpedoes. It had not been designed as an assault ship, and to launch the attack it would have to get close enough to the necron mother ship, the target most likely to yield some meaningful success, for the mother ship to stand a very good chance of blasting it out of the void. If it got that far, and if the mother ship did not have some heathen technology to defend against boarders, there were no doubt legions of necron warriors on board to fight through.

It was, at least, better than sitting back and waiting to die, but not by much.

Crystavayne took out the neuro-sword he carried scabbarded under his robes. Most tech-priests and magi were armed, and Crystavayne's weapon of choice was a blade of shiny black crystal inlaid with silver circuitry.

'I made this myself,' said Crystavayne, 'to make sure I would never be helpless should the quest for understanding become a battle. It will do me little good against an enemy without a nervous system. What do we have left in the armoury that I could use instead?'

'Here,' said Voar. He took a pistol from a holster on the belt of his robes. It was a miniature melta weapon, its grip moulded around its fuel cell. 'Even without this, I am not poorly armed.'

Crystavayne took the gun. It was an inferno pistol, and was probably the single most valuable weapon on the *Antithesis*, including the ship's guns.

'My gratitude,' said Crystavayne. 'When does the attack begin?'

'In thirty-nine minutes,' said Voar.

'I have one question before we deploy.'

'If the Omnissiah so wills, it shall be answered.'

'After you have attained your rank, archmagos, after you have lost so much of the emotional centres of your brain and replaced them with logic, do you still want revenge?'

'Of course. The desire for vengeance is not an emotion. It is the purest logic of all.'

'Good,' said Crystavayne.

An alert tone chirped in the communicators of both tech-priests. 'Voar here.'

'An approaching craft,' came the reply from the bridge, 'is requesting docking permission. It's Imperial.'

'One of the Fleet Minor?'

'Astartes. A gunship.'

'Astartes?' said Crystavayne. 'The only Astartes out here are the Soul Drinkers.'

'Then logic dictates it is them,' said Voar. 'The two choices we have are to receive them or destroy them.'

'We can achieve the first without ruling out the second.'

'Agreed,' said Voar. 'Bridge, prep a deck to receive them, and do so quickly. They may not survive out here for long.'

Librarian Tyrendian was accompanied by ten Soul Drinkers of Squad Salk. They were met by several squads of tech-guard on the launch deck of the *Antithesis*, and the men looked at the Astartes as if they were facing a particularly volatile and dangerous animal.

Three tech-priests approached across the deck. As Tyrendian descended the embarkation ramp of the Thunderhawk, it was clear that they were senior members of the Mechanicus, heavily augmented, their robes embroidered with symbols of rank. One was an enormous industrial machine, shaped something like a huge metal ape. His head was low between his shoulders, vaguely human with the lower half of his face concealed by a heavy rebreather and vox-unit.

The second was the highest-ranked, although he looked far more

444   Ben Counter

human than the first. He was slender and rather taller than a normal man, with shoulder-mounted manipulator units folded over his back and circuitry woven into the skin of his face.

The third was also shaped like a human, but one of his hands had been replaced with a complex medical gauntlet, hooked up to vials of liquid implanted in his forearm. One of his eyes was a bionic, reminiscent of a microscope, which was probably the function it performed.

The first tech-priest stomped forwards, and a round clacked into the chamber of the gun he had in place of one arm. His armour was pitted and battle-scarred, and he more resembled a machine of war than a tech-priest.

The lead tech-priest stepped in front of the war machine and gave a hand signal that caused the assembled tech-guard troops to lower their lasguns.

'I am Archmagos Voar of the Adeptus Mechanicus,' he said. 'This is my ship, the *Antithesis*.'

'I am Brother Tyrendian of the Soul Drinkers.'

'What is your purpose here?'

'To propose an alliance.'

'To what end?' asked Voar.

'Mutual survival,' said Tyrendian.

'There was little survival on anyone's minds at the Star Fort,' said Voar. 'We know of you, Soul Drinkers. The Inquisition tried to delete you from history, but we have long memories. You are renegades and murderers, and among those who have suffered at your hands are members of the Mechanicus. What promise can there be that you will not betray us? That you are not even working in concert with these xenos?'

'The xenos are the enemy,' said Tyrendian sharply, 'of any human, renegade or not. And they will destroy us as surely as they will destroy you if we cannot find a solution between us. If you wish to die out here, archmagos, without ever having possessed a chance of survival, then reject us.'

Voar paused only for a moment to consider this, but there was little doubt that logic engines in his head were whirring through banks of data.

'What can you offer us?' asked Voar.

'We have information on the xenos machine-spirits. We know of a single intelligence that rules them,' said Tyrendian. 'In addition to which, you will find no better assault troops than two companies of Astartes. What can you offer us?'

'We know where they are,' said the third tech-priest, the medical specialist. The archmagos glanced at him, but said nothing.

'Where?' asked Tyrendian.

'Does it matter?' asked Voar.

'We know who we are fighting,' said Tyrendian. 'You know where it is. Take us there and we can kill it. The Undying operate under the control of a single intelligence, and, if it is slain, we will buy ourselves our only chance at victory.' Tyrendian indicated the tech-guard. 'With these troops you can do nothing against an Undying stronghold. With the Soul Drinkers, you have a force that can break through the Undying and kill it. We just need to get there.'

'The *Antithesis* could do it,' said the third tech-priest. 'It's the fastest ship we have. It can't hold out forever, but we can stay ahead of the xenos fleet for long enough.'

'Do we have a deal?' asked Tyrendian.

Archmagos Voar thought for a longer moment. The tech-guard were tensed ready to raise their guns, and there was no doubt they had orders to execute the Soul Drinkers at a sign from the archmagos.

'Logic dictates,' said Voar, 'that we do.'

Tyrendian walked between the squads of tech-guard and held out a hand. Archmagos Voar shook it.

'In the name of Rogal Dorn,' said Tyrendian, 'this alliance is struck.'

Voar glanced at the huge industrial tech-priest beside him.

'That will no longer be necessary, Magos Vionel,' he said. The tech-priest's gun thudded as it unloaded the rounds back into its ammo hopper.

'Where is our enemy?' asked Tyrendian.

'Here,' said Voar. He took out a data-slate, and one of his manipulators inserted a probe into it. A star map flickered onto the screen. He handed the slate to Tyrendian.

'Selaaca,' said Tyrendian.

'You know of it?' asked Voar.

'It was the capital of the empire the Undying have destroyed. The planet beneath us is Raevenia, where the last survivors of the empire are making their final stand. Part of the fleet you are fighting is the invasion force that will complete the capture of the planet. Once Raevenia is gone, there will be no human force left between the Undying and the Imperium.'

'Then it is unlikely,' said Voar, 'that the completion of their plans in the Veiled Region will have a positive impact on the human race.'

'On that we can agree,' said Tyrendian. 'We must move quickly. Neither of our forces can hold out for much longer. I suggest that we take word back to our commander and return with an assault force. With your leave, archmagos.'

'I concur. I will position the fleet to facilitate a breakout. Primary manoeuvres will begin in two hours.'

'Until then, archmagos,' said Tyrendian. 'Soul Drinkers! Embark!'

Iktinos, Tyrendian and the Soul Drinkers of Iktinos's flock filed back up the ramp into the Thunderhawk, and the ramp swung up to seal them in.

As the sun went down on the space port, the Soul Drinkers loaded the last of the weapons and ammunition back onto their transports. They travelled light, and everything they needed to wage war had been stowed in a matter of minutes. The old Chapter had never fought with many heavy weapons or vehicles. Sarpedon had taught them to fight with hands and teeth if need be, up close in the enemy's face. That was how the philosopher-warrior Daenyathos had written that the Soul Drinkers should fight, and that was how Sarpedon believed an Astartes was at his most effective.

Sarpedon and Iktinos had been joined by Queen Dyrmida. She had informed the people of Raevenia, over the space port's vox-casters, that the Undying would try to take the space port, and they must be fought off before the Raevenians could be delivered from their fate. It had not been completely true, but it was closer to the truth than she had been expecting to tell.

'Chaplain Iktinos will remain on Raevenia with his flock,' said Sarpedon. 'The Undying will be free to attack before we can succeed. You will have to fight hard before this is over.'

'My army is ready,' said Dyrmida. 'I had expected your Astartes to remain until the end of this empire, but if by taking the fight to Selaaca you can strike a blow against the Undying, I am willing to see you leave. Have you taken the fuel you came here for?'

'We will return for it,' said Sarpedon.

'There might be nothing left to return to, commander.'

'My duty,' said Iktinos, 'is to ensure that there will be. We have a defensible position and an enemy operating under a time limit they know nothing about. We will prevail, your majesty.'

'We can hold these walls if you can take down their commander,' said Dyrmida. 'If you man the gates, and if the Undying can be halted from afar, then we can hold.'

'I wish,' said Sarpedon, 'that I could give your world a better chance.'

'Remember the Raevenian way of death, commander. We will all die fighting for our home world, against an inhuman enemy. There are few in our history that can claim a better death than that. Do not fear for our ability to hold this space port, for we fight as soldiers with nothing to lose. Even in death, we shall have victory. When dying is not defeat, we cannot be beaten.' Dyrmida grasped Sarpedon's gauntlet and shook it. 'Best of luck, Commander Sarpedon. When you return, you will find us victorious, whatever happens.'

'For Dorn,' said Iktinos.

'For Dorn, Chaplain,' said Sarpedon.

'Ready for takeoff,' voxed Brother Phol from the cockpit of Sarpedon's Thunderhawk.

'I will speak with you both soon,' said Sarpedon.

'If you do not,' said Dyrmida, 'die well.'

'I'll do my best, your majesty,' said Sarpedon, and scuttled towards the Thunderhawk, which was already obscured by the wash of heat from its warmed-up engines.

'Look into the face of the enemy, and rejoice! For to stand before him, to bask in his fury, is to tell him that you fear him not, and that he is within a sword-thrust of destruction.'
– Daenyathos, Musings Upon Extermination

CHAPTER THiRTEEN

The *Constant* went down fighting. Her full complement of menials and tech-guard went down with her, because they were needed to work the fusion chamber. The nova cannon fired until the end, the final blast barely aimed, in the hope that the projectile would nick a necron ship and send waves of fissile material pulsing through the enemy's corridors and engine rooms.

The necron mother ship took advantage of the *Constant's* sudden lack of mobility. It turned its main gun on the cruiser, even as it absorbed a nova cannon blast that stripped away one of the spurs reaching from its central spire. The mother ship rotated majestically until its gun was in line, and then it fired, a lance of green-white power splitting the *Constant* through her prow and tearing all the way through her stern. For a moment, the Mechanicus cruiser was impaled. Then the force of the mother ship's gun shredded what remained of her interior structure, and boiled away the hull into burning wisps of metallic gas.

The Fleet Minor threw itself as one into the mother ship's path. The necron cruisers rallied around the mother ship and blew the few remaining transport and sensorium craft apart. The mother ship itself sent out a spherical pulse of green flame that tossed the smaller craft around like ships on a storm, ripping guns and instruments from hulls, and splintering the hails of torpedoes the Fleet Minor was firing at it in desperation.

The necron fleet's command routines switched from the harrying of a determined foe to the annihilation of an enemy collapsing under the psychological pressure of battle. Some of the Fleet Minor had fled, disobeying orders to buy themselves a few more hours or minutes of life. Guided munitions and a few broad gun barrages were all that were needed to turn the fleeing ships into sprays of steel dust.

Others defied the most basic tenets of logic to charge into the enemy, sometimes aiming to ram the necron ships in some vulnerable spot. They were even easier to deal with. A few point-blank turret volleys put paid to most of them. The few that got through impacted without causing any significant damage to the hulls of living metal in which the necron ships were clad.

The necron fleet closed in around the mother ship, as if the mother ship was the stem of a vast steel flower and the cruisers were its petals, to concentrate fire on the remnants of the Mechanicus fleet.

Only the *Antithesis* did not succumb to the breakdown the necron fleet detected in the manoeuvres of its sister ships. The cruiser spiralled away from the heart of the battle, releasing every form of countermeasure it had: short-fuse torpedoes, electromagnetic chaff, burning fuel and even heaps of refuse from spent shell casings to the bodies of its dead, to fool the necron guns for a few moments longer. Its main engines kicked in, and it powered away, forcing open a warp rift and diving in. The tactic was dangerous in the extreme; entering the warp in peaceful conditions could be dangerous enough. But the *Antithesis* made it.

The necron mother ship quickly recalculated its response to the change in Mechanicus tactics. The Mechanicus had not given up the fight as the necrons' limited intelligence on human behaviour had suggested. Instead, the *Antithesis* had sacrificed the rest of the fleet to escape.

The mother ship sent its cruisers ahead of it, folding space-time to follow the *Antithesis*. One of them, wounded by a lucky blast from the *Constant*, broke apart as it accelerated, some critical system giving way and causing the cruiser to split in two and implode.

It did not matter. The only two enclaves of human interlopers were on Raevenia, and in the *Antithesis*, and neither had a chance of survival given the resources arrayed against them. As the mother ship joined the pursuit of the *Antithesis*, the necron transport craft began the descent onto Raevenia. They carried with them more than thirty thousand necron warriors and countless war machines, enough to subjugate an entire world.

Their lower hulls began to glow with heat as they plunged through Raevenia's atmosphere.

Queen Dyrmida, standing at a window of the space port's command tower, watched through a pair of magnoculars as the first white streaks of falling spacecraft appeared in the sky over Astelok.

'Sighting fire!' shouted Dyrmida. One of the officers around her spoke an order into the comm-net and the crew of the anti-aircraft guns on the walls swivelled their quad-mounted cannon to aim at the falling craft. Sharp cracks of guns echoed around the space port as they sent tracer rounds up into the afternoon sky.

The reserves of Queen Dyrmida's army were stationed around the command tower ready to act as a reserve to move to any breach of the walls. The queen was in full battle-dress, heavy iridescent carapace armour over quilted flak armour, over her dark red royal robes. She carried a repeating strikelock rifle, a finely crafted weapon with three rotating barrels and a miniature generator in the hilt. She wore the simple battle-crown, a small tiara of steel, which was the regalia of sovereignty when at war.

The population huddled in whatever shelter they could: empty fuel containers beneath the landing pads, spacecraft hangars, equipment sheds and narrow maintenance tunnels. Their fear was as obvious as the sunlight beating down on the space port, or the smell of fuel and gun oil.

Most of the soldiers were on the walls. They did not know from which direction the Undying would strike, so they were stationed all around, erecting sniping positions and makeshift battlements of empty fuel drums and spacecraft parts piled up.

The main gates were the weakest point of the walls. The space port had not been built as a fortress, and the gates would be easier to storm than the walls. That was where Chaplain Iktinos had set up, along with the thirty or so Soul Drinkers he referred to as his 'flock'.

'They're coming down in the city,' said Lieutenant Kavins, who was attending upon his queen. Dyrmida saw that he was right.

'They're joining up with the rest of the harvesting force,' she said.

'Then we know they'll be coming from that direction.'

Dyrmida scanned the sky on the other side of the space port. Bright streaks of vapour were trailing behind craft plummeting towards the woods and hills south of the port.

'I wouldn't be so sure, Kavins,' said Dyrmida.

'Incoming!' came the yell from one of the sharpshooters on the roof of the command tower. Dyrmida followed his outstretched arm. One of the Undying landers, wounded by anti-aircraft fire, was spiralling out of control towards the space port. With a terrible sound like reality tearing, it hammered through the air, and slammed into one of the landing pads in a burst of smoke and shrapnel. The ground shook.

Troops ran from the command tower to snap fire at the shapes they saw moving among the flames and molten metal. A half-melted Undying clambered out of the flames, and its head was blown open by a well-placed round. Another was cut apart as it walked out of the fire, destroyed before it could raise its gun. Metal corpses dissolved away into nothing.

It was first blood, which meant something in Raevenian folklore of war, but in this battle, it meant nothing. There were plenty more where those Undying had come from.

A couple more landing craft were blown out of the sky. They were shaped like inverted pyramids, their lower surfaces studded with engines that glowed white as they slowed the Undying descent. A few of them were larger, massive armoured spheres, tumbling, apparently without any means of slowing them, to impact like falling bombs in the ruins of Astelok.

Dyrmida activated the vox-bead that Iktinos had given her.

'They're making landfall,' she said. 'They're all around us, but the majority will be coming from the direction of the city. Straight towards you.'

'Understood,' said Iktinos from his position by the gates. 'May Dorn's strength be with us.'

'And the Sun Prince's blessing with us,' said Dyrmida.

Silver shapes were already gathering on the walls of Astelok, stranger-shaped enemies among the ranks of metallic warriors. They hovered or drifted, or scuttled down the walls on all fours.

More landing craft slammed into the forests to the south, within sight of the walls. The Undying gathered, and began to march.

The first sight the *Antithesis* had of Selaaca was in information form, picked up by the ship's long-range sensors. The first reaction of the sensorium crew was to wonder what was wrong with their sensors. Repeated scanning showed the same results, however, and eventually they had to go to Archmagos Voar with information they were sure would incense the archmagos with its utter lack of logic.

Selaaca, it seemed, was hollow. Its core had been bored out and vented into titanic clouds of rock dust that orbited the planet in long trails of micrometeorites. And yet it had retained its mass, a fact so impossible that many of the ship's cogitators refused to accept it and spat it out in hails of punch-cards and spools of torn printout. Its interior was a lattice of steel and stranger metals, supporting continent-sized structures that pulsed with as much energy as the system's sun, caged and compressed into exotic radiation that the cogitators didn't recognise. Craft, tiny pinpricks of power, flitted over the surface and through close orbit. There was power everywhere, running through the planet's empty core, scribing glowing lines on the surface, even bleeding out into the toxic remnants of the atmosphere.

The surface was a ruin. The cities of Selaaca had been destroyed, scorched or uprooted, or pounded flat. Here and there, the monuments to the heart of the Selaacan Empire remained: the arms of a harbour wall enclosing a graveyard of sunken battleships; a great fortress in the heart of a desert, walled in by necron defences and left to starve; dozens of villages, untouched but devoid of life as they mouldered away in the hearts of forests.

Enormous wounds cut through the greatest cities. They led into the planet's interior, shattered buildings and shredded layers of history giving way to immense metallic avenues and conduits of power. These wounds were ringed by necron facilities, landing pads and barracks, and sheets of metal, the size of islands, where gleaming necron warriors emerged to march.

Monoliths, immense menhirs of brushed steel, stood at precise intervals between the wounds, anchoring the complex webs of power that flowed across the planet. Swarms of scarabs attended to them, repairing the microscopic damage done by the particles of dust that whipped by on the burning winds that marked the death throes of Selaaca's atmosphere.

Not one living thing was detectable on Selaaca. The absence of life required by the necrons was total. Life, to them, was like death was to humans: an unimaginable aberration, a state where nothing could exist. It had to be banished before any great work could begin. Whatever the plans of the necron empire of Selaaca, of the whole necron race and its gods, it required the obliteration of life. That lesson had never been taught so bluntly as through the dead, torn husk of Selaaca.

Archmagos Voar was absorbing this information when Commander Sarpedon arrived on the bridge.

'I had not been informed,' said Voar, 'that you were a mutant.'

'It's not something that comes up in conversation,' replied Sarpedon. Tech-priests did not generally have a sense of humour, and, given Voar's silence, the archmagos was not an exception. 'It is a complicated story, and one I am not good at telling. It does not affect my ability to lead.'

'Mutation is an abhorrence, commander, but as was made clear in our negotiations we must be willing to overlook a great many sins, given our present situation.'

'What do the xenos have waiting for us down there?'

Voar gave the printout another scan, and waved one of his manipulator units. A servitor, little more than a torso on wheels with a projector unit embedded in the dead skin of its chest, trundled over.

'I forget so easily,' said Voar, 'that not all audiences are equipped with logic circuits. Visual aids are necessary.'

The holo-unit projected a flickering image of Selaaca. Sarpedon tried to take in the implications of the scarred planet with its hollowed-out, metal-filled core visible through tears in the crust, but it just didn't seem to fit into his mind. The necrons – he still wanted to call them the Undying – must have been entombed in Selaaca since long before the humans of the Selaacan Empire had ever set foot there prior to the Great Crusade.

'The spacecraft seem to be transport and industrial ships,' said Voar, 'or the necron equivalents. The surface structures are probably power generator and capacitor facilities. The interior is opaque to our sensors, but a great deal of power is being consumed there.'

'Is there a way in?'

'Here,' said Voar, 'the planet's capital. The site of the largest surface excavation. It is likely that the necron forces first emerged from here after awakening. The signals directing the necron forces emanate from here.'

Sarpedon imagined the necron army marching from a tear in the ground, killing and harvesting as they conquered Selaaca. He could almost see the planet's cities falling, one by one, the blackout of one fuelling the fear in the next.

'What woke them?' he asked.

'Impossible to say. An excavation by the people of Selaaca. Some trigger at a necron outpost, activated by a new colony or off-world exploration. Or, perhaps, just time. Given the materiel being gathered on the surface, it seems they have yet to fully awake. What the Selaacan Empire has witnessed is the first phase of the necrons' refounding of their empire.'

'The first and the last,' said Sarpedon. 'How do we go in?'

'The *Antithesis* is designed for atmospheric flight,' replied Voar. 'I intend to pilot her into the main excavation in the capital city and deploy from there.'

'A crash landing?' asked Sarpedon with a raise of one eyebrow.

'A most precise and calculated landing, commander. There will be no crashing involved. The *Antithesis* is rather more advanced than Imperial Naval standards. Besides, I accept the risk to my ship to fulfil our mission.'

'What forces can you bring?'

'A regiment of tech-guard. Seven hundred and thirty-three men. The tech-priest officer corps of the *Antithesis*, myself and the magi of my fleet.'

'And two hundred Astartes,' said Sarpedon.

'Given the likelihood of our being pursued by the necron fleet,' continued Voar, 'our tactics must emphasise speed over complexity. Once on the ground, we enter the main excavation.'

'And we kill everything we find until either we or they are dead,' finished Sarpedon.

'Quite. Landfall will be in two hours and fourteen minutes. If you have any preparations to make, I suggest you make them, commander, as the necrons most assuredly know we are here.'

* * *

The first Raevenians to die in the last battle for Astelok were pioneers: tough, resourceful men and women recruited into the army of Queen Dyrmida from among the hunters and trappers that lived out in the wilds between city-states. A few of them were caught out by landing craft crashing through the trees almost right on top of them, in the tangled woods lining the road from the city to the space port. Undying warriors clambered out, unfolded their ancient metal limbs and immediately set about killing the pioneers, who tried to flee or hide among the trees.

The Undying guns flayed them to the bone, and left the bleeding, half-fleshed skeletons. Other pioneers were brought down by scarabs that forced their way into their mouths or burrowed through their skin with diamond-hard mandibles. The pioneer units had known before the battle began that they would be vulnerable outside the city walls, and that few of them could be expected to survive. They accepted this fate since they were fighting, not for themselves, but for the people huddled beneath the space port waiting for the Undying to claim them.

The Undying marched relentlessly through the forests, where they had landed to be safe from the Raevenian snipers and heavy weapons on the walls. It was a simple calculation for the guiding intelligence and the officer nodes of the army to make. It had also been made by Queen Dyrmida and her generals.

The traps set by the pioneers erupted just as the Undying units gathered together to march in rank. Dozens of the Undying were blown to pieces by fragmentation bombs made from fuel cells and shrapnel. Canisters of spaceship fuel exploded inside the trunks of trees, sending shards of wood and collapsing tree trunks crashing into the Undying. Some bodies self-repaired, but more phased out.

The officer nodes rapidly recalculated the angles of approach. They moved their advancing units towards the main road into the space port, and a large area of clearer scrub on the opposite side of the space port, where the pioneers would have had a tougher job concealing booby traps.

Hidden pits collapsed, plunging Undying warriors into troughs of battery acid. Pioneers that had begged for a good death on this day manned the guns of vehicles half-buried in the ground, throwing off heaps of branches and camo-netting to blast at point-blank range into the Undying. They died soon enough, torn apart by scarabs or Undying guns, but they wiped out enough Undying to make their deaths good ones indeed.

The Undying force lost relatively few of its number, but the threat was grave enough to force it onto the open ground. Up on the walls, the men of Queen Dyrmida's army manned the guns trained on the target zones, and waited.

* * *

The Soul Drinkers on the muster deck of the *Antithesis* cut a frightening enough sight that even the tech-guard units, many of whom had emotional dampening surgery, looked at them with fear. Twenty squads of ten were ranked up for Sarpedon to inspect, along with Pallas, Captain Luko, Tyrendian and Scamander. Salk and Graevus's squads had the prime places on the ends of the rank, since Sarpedon considered them the senior sergeants of his command. Techmarine Lygris was there too, for he had recovered enough lucidity to demand to be taken on this mission.

The tech-guard were being spoken to by the tech-priests who would lead them. They talked about sacred duty, obedience and sacrifice in the Omnissiah's name, and of the hateful nature of the xenos threat. Sarpedon noticed the magi among them, Vionel, a massive glowering metallic presence patched up with welded-on armour plates, and Hepsebah with extra power packs implanted into her back to fuel her lascannon. Sarpedon had heard speeches like that before, back in the old Chapter where his captain, Caeon, and Chapter Master Gorgoleon would speak to the Soul Drinkers of their position at the top of the human food chain, and of their divine right to herd the rest of the species towards the Emperor's goal.

'Soul Drinkers,' began Sarpedon, 'within the hour, we make landfall at Selaaca, and fight there against a foe with effectively infinite numbers and every reason to kill us. The necrons know we are coming. We have faced them before, and every one of you knows how unwilling they are to die. Make no mistake, battle-brothers, the necrons are the enemy of everything we have fought for. They will turn the Veiled Region into a base from which to treat the human race as cattle to kill or harvest. If we ever had a duty, it is to stop them.

'Chaplain Iktinos is relying on us, as are all the people of Raevenia. They do not deserve the fate the galaxy has placed on them. We have the power to change it. In doing so, we will change our own fate, for we will be changing this galaxy for the better when so many have tried to use us to change it for the worse. Captain Luko?'

Luko stepped out of his squad to join Sarpedon. He looked like he would tear through the ship's hull if it would get him into battle quicker. 'Brothers! We know what we're fighting. Whatever intelligence leads the necrons, that's what we're here to kill. We've seen what these machines can do to good honest flesh, but they're not so dangerous that a couple of companies of Astartes can't turn them into iron filings. The one advantage the enemy has over us is numbers, so we keep moving. We never stop or take a backwards step. Keep charging on, forcing them back, and push on faster than they can wake reinforcements. If you get left behind, you die. Cold and fast, Soul Drinkers, and we'll kill their empire before they finish conquering it.'

'To your stations,' said Sarpedon. 'Final approach!'

The engines of the *Antithesis* screamed as the ship lunged into the toxic atmosphere of Selaaca.

A billion lenses turned upwards. Scarabs paused their work on monoliths and power conduits to look at the glowing streak in the sky. Watchtower constructs, towering robots walking on spindly legs with thoraxes covered in sensors and artificial eyes, tracked it and sent its estimated landing site to the command systems in the planet's interior.

At the centre of those systems, the point at which every node connected, something vast and powerful stirred. It had slept for longer than most biological creatures could imagine. It, too, had been biological once, but that was so long ago that the memory of that time, if it could be said to possess memories in the human sense, was just a slice of information filed away among trillions of other statistics in the crystal-filled planetary core that made up its brain.

It could not move or think for long, only enough for a few key systems to warm up and a handful of milliseconds more to concoct the stream of electrons that made up its orders. The necron empire it ruled was so efficiently constructed that it need give only that single order and its will would be transmitted to every individual necron that could play a part in making it a reality.

Wake them, it said, *all of them.*

And then wake me.

'War is the only place we can be complete. Battle is the only activity at which our excellence can be meaningful. Do not believe that you can be a scholar, or a philosopher, or a leader of men. You are a warrior. When you are not inflicting death, you are not justifying your life.'

— Daenyathos, *Principles of the Astartean Mind*

CHAPTER FOURTEEN

Any other ship would have been committing suicide, sacrificing itself and its crew to smash into the target. It had been done before by Imperial craft whose ordnance was used up and whose gun batteries were dry, or who had suffered such grave damage that the only thing they could still do was move. The necron defences assumed that this was the case, and prepared for little more than surface damage and the loss of a few thousand scarabs and other easily replaced units.

The *Antithesis*'s engines were, however, up to the task of slowing it down even as its prow glowed blue-white with heat. The thin atmosphere provided just enough of a cushion for the ship to slow to a manageable speed under the massive deceleration of its forward-firing engines.

The ship crashed through a net of thread-like metallic filaments, built to keep meteorites from damaging the necron facilities in the capital city. It sheared straight through a sky-bound monorail, spilling containers and their cargoes of ore. The ship levelled out, slowing further, and roaring parallel to the ground. Its enormous prow carved through steel and stone buildings, the hurricane of its exhaust howling through what had once been the teeming streets of Selaaca. Finally, its main engines cut out, and the retro thrusters brought it down, grinding prow-first into the mass of the city.

The destruction was tremendous. Buildings were torn down like paper. The hull of the *Antithesis* split and tore, throwing chunks of metal like titanic shards of shrapnel as the keel hull was stripped away. Broadside guns were torn off and tumbled through ruined streets. The beak of the prow rode up through the remnants of an amphitheatre, scattering chunks of pale stone.

The *Antithesis* shuddered to a halt. Its artificial gravity had been stressed to breaking point to absorb the lethal deceleration that would have turned any living thing inside it to paste. Systems failed and power cells burst, throwing showers of sparks from the tears in the hull. Fires broke out along the stricken ship's length. Fuel poured from a ruptured fuel tank and ignited, blowing out a section of the engine housing in a tremendous tongue of flame.

The *Antithesis* would not fly again, but if the Astartes could do what they claimed, it wouldn't need to.

Luko was first out. Sarpedon couldn't have stopped him if he had wanted to.

'Go! Go!' shouted Luko, and hauled himself up through the exit hatch before it had fully opened.

Toxic air rolled into the *Antithesis*, foiled by the respirators in the helmets of the Soul Drinkers and the gas masks worn by the tech-guard. The Soul Drinkers had mustered in maintenance chambers near the upper hull, where the impact would not cause so much damage, and Luko had taken the first place beneath the hatch that would let them out.

The first impression Sarpedon got of Selaaca was of a sky the colour of night, scattered with stars and obscured by steel-grey wisps of corrupted cloud. He clambered out, his talons anchoring him to the upper hull of the spaceship. The fallen city was metal and stone, edged in silver by the unfiltered light of Selaaca's sun: half a fallen column, a collapsed wall, a statue of some Selaacan noble, standing in a field of rubble.

Metal had spread across the ruins like a stain, deep pools of it, and thick webs of it like the cocoons of metal beasts. Dark steel towers made up a skyline that had once been dominated by monuments and civic buildings, spewing exhaust gases into the air. There was even metal in the sky, orbital installations like spindly new constellations.

The city that had once stood here had been smothered by the webs of steel. Here and there, it fought to the surface as a collapsed wall or a heap of rubble that might have been some great palace or basilica. The impressions of streets still remained, and a skyline of fractured towers. It was losing, however. It would not be long before the scarabs finished spinning their metallic caul, and Selaaca decayed away to nothing. Only the alien would remain.

Was this what the necrons wanted to do to the universe? Smother it in steel, and crush the life out of it?

Then there was gunfire.

Luko caught a blast on the shoulder. He didn't break stride as the blast sliced a chunk out of his shoulder pad, and he dived out of Sarpedon's eye-line, scrambling down the torn hull of the *Antithesis*. His squad followed him, their bolters opening up before they hit the ground.

'Deploy!' yelled Magos Hepsebah, who led the first unit of tech-guard. They were assault specialists with grenade launchers and plasma weapons, looking almost as inhuman as the magi with their gas masks and the heavy ribbed cables connecting their weapons to sensor packs plugged into their spines. The tech-guard emerged from hatches a short way along the hull, Hepsebah in the front rank.

Sarpedon followed the tech-guard down towards the city streets. Graevus, power axe in his mutated hand, was leading the first of the assault squads beside him.

Sarpedon scurried down the hull, and hit the ground running. Emerald blasts streaked around him, boring cores out of the stone and metal of the wreckage surrounding the *Antithesis*.

Behind the ship was an immense valley of ruins, torn by the ship's crash-landing. In front of it was a yawning chasm in the ground, ringed by ruins leaning poised to collapse over the edge. The ground sloped down into the chasm, where the darkness was studded with pulsing green lights. The ruins were infested with necron warriors, their metallic shapes just visible among the destruction. Luko's squad was running for cover among the ruins surrounding the chasm.

'There!' shouted Hepsebah. 'That's the main shaft.'

'Soul Drinkers!' yelled Sarpedon. 'Forward!'

The Soul Drinkers piled out of the *Antithesis*, firing as they ran. Necrons fell, skulls blasted open. More emerged from the ruins as if they had been roosting there, clambering over broken stone to close to firing range. Sarpedon saw Luko jumping a ruined wall and slicing a necron into ribbons with his power claws, as bolter fire cut down another that lurched up at him. Sarpedon followed in Luko's wake, and fired a bolter volley into movement that approached through the darkness.

Streaks of crimson light erupted from Hepsebah's lascannon, the barrels spinning as raw energy pulsed from the power cells mounted on her back. The walls of a nearby building disintegrated, and charred robotic limbs clattered to the ground among the debris.

Sarpedon dived into cover alongside Captain Luko.

'Lots of them out here,' said Luko. 'And there'll be more.'

'Hepsebah!' shouted Sarpedon. 'Think you can keep up?'

'Mock me not, mutant,' replied Hepsebah.

Sarpedon charged on, Luko beside him, leading the Soul Drinkers into the maw. He saw one Soul Drinker falling, leg sheared off by a blast that tore up into his abdomen. Another was being dragged along by his battle-brothers, one arm stripped away to bloody bone. Pallas was supporting another who had lost a part of his leg, blood pumping from the wound in his greave.

Sarpedon reached the edge of the shaft, and his eyes adjusted to its darkness. It curved downwards into the planet's crust, a metal-shod spiral tunnel like the lair of an immense mechanical worm. It was wide enough to act as a thoroughfare for huge vehicles like the necron harvesters. The *Antithesis* could have wedged itself inside if it had stopped a few hundred metres later.

Behind the Soul Drinkers, the tech-guard were covering the rear, sending gouts of plasma pouring into the ruins around the maw. Grenades blew necrons off their feet or brought buildings collapsing around them, and Hepsebah's lascannon arm reaped more wreckage among the necron warriors. The other magi were further back with the rest of the tech-guard, and some of the Mechanicus soldiers were stranded, pinned down by fire and left behind by the speed of the assault.

They would be left there. There was no way the attack could stall to rescue them. If they stopped, they would all die. Many of the tech-guard had simple logic implants, and they would understand. The others would die alone and terrified, cursing the Soul Drinkers. That was the way it had to be.

Up ahead, swarms of scarabs were emerging in shimmering streams from holes in the walls of the metal shaft. Soul Drinkers carrying flamers ran to the fore, spraying a curtain of fire ahead of them. Scarabs ran into the flames and were immolated in the burning fuel, painting streaks of fire across the walls and ceiling as their systems went haywire. Tech-guard units made it to the front, and hosed the walls with their own flamers.

'Lygris,' voxed Sarpedon, 'are you still with us, brother?'

'I can feel it,' replied Lygris, who was towards the rear of the Soul Drinkers formation. 'I can hear its voice.'

'Not for much longer,' said Sarpedon.

The scarabs dispersed, many of them clattering to the floor as husks of smouldering metal. The tech-guard were catching up, and Sarpedon spotted Magos Vionel clutching a dismembered necron corpse in one of his huge industrial paws. Vionel threw the body to one side, and it phased out.

'Forward!' ordered Sarpedon. 'Archmagos, we cannot tarry here.'

'Then we leave the wounded,' said Archmagos Voar over the vox. 'They are commended to the Omnissiah. Tech-guard! Advance!'

Sarpedon led the way down into the dark metallic throat. It curved down beneath the city, its walls threaded with glowing green channels of power. The Soul Drinkers and tech-guard advanced at a run and covered the distance quickly, every man and Astartes well aware of the necrons that would be converging on the city to hunt them down if they hesitated.

Dim light shone from below, and, after a final kink, the throat ended in a circular opening, beyond which was an enormous excavation deep into the earth.

The necrons had not invaded. They had always been there, waiting beneath Selaaca for whatever signal the Selaacans had inadvertently given them to wake up and reclaim their empire. For a moment, Sarpedon could only stare at what they had created.

The necron tomb-city stared back.

'I am minded to pray,' said Chaplain Iktinos, 'for all of us. For our brothers on Selaaca. For the people who face death around us. For ourselves. But also, for our future.'

Iktinos knelt before the gates of the space port. Gunfire was cracking from the walls on either side as the Raevenian snipers in the gatehouses took ranging shots at the Undying warriors advancing in ranks down the road from Astelok.

Iktinos's flock, numbering more than thirty Soul Drinkers, knelt around him. Only Iktinos truly understood the change that had come over them since they had numbered themselves among his followers. They were not just remnants of ravaged units looking for a leader. They were not even spiritually enthusiastic Astartes, who attended to Iktinos as an expression of their faith. They had become something else. In a sense, they were not even Soul Drinkers any more, for they did not follow Sarpedon and his ideals, but Iktinos and his plans. Which, though Sarpedon did not know it, were very, very different.

'It is an honour,' said one of the flock, 'to die for this future.'

'It is a greater honour to live for it,' said Iktinos.

'But to live to see his plan completed,' said another, 'is a blessing too great for me to beg.'

'Do not fear to ask to serve,' said Iktinos. 'Many of you will fall, and you will have done more for mankind than any other in the ten thousand years of misery the Imperium has suffered. Those who live will honour the fallen with every step they take beyond. Cherish the life that fate may grant you, and welcome death! Praise the day that gives us this fight! Praise the death and the dealing of it! Bless every bullet you fire and every wound you take, for it is all part of the same fate. Think not of failure if you die, or of shame if you live. Think only of the future.'

Iktinos took out his crozius and laid it on the rockcrete of the gate road.

'This weapon is an instrument of my will,' he said. 'This will is victory. This victory is to build a future for the human race. If my will is undone, the victory will be lost and the future will die. This is what lies on our shoulders.'

Every battle-brother of Iktinos's flock laid his weapons – bolters, combat knives, flamers, plasma guns – on the ground. They echoed Iktinos's words in an intense murmur. It was not a prayer that could be found in any sacred work of the Soul Drinkers' Chaplains, or in the *Catechisms Martial* of the legendary Daenyathos. It was Iktinos's prayer. This was his fight. His will was being done, and, through him, the will of his master.

Iktinos's prayer was finished, and he looked up at the sky of Raevenia. Undying landing craft were still searing down through the sky, and the dull thuds of the anti-aircraft guns opened up again, spitting red-black clouds of burning flak into the air.

A commotion up on the walls beside the gate reached his ears. Something had alarmed the men up there, and it took a lot to faze men that had seen their home city torn to shreds by the Undying.

Iktinos headed to the gatehouse, a watchtower built into the support on one side of the massive double gates. Makeshift barricades had been piled up in front of the gates, welded with spikes and hooks to snag the Undying as they clambered over. Iktinos wove a path through them and reached the gatehouse door. He ran up the stairs inside, pushing past snipers stationed at windows along the stairway.

Two more snipers were stationed at the top of the watchtower. They started as Iktinos climbed up into their roost. The Space Marine barely fitted into the small room.

'Astartes,' said one of the snipers.

'What have you seen?' asked Iktinos.

The view from the gatehouse was enough to sap most men's wills. Thousands of Undying were trooping along the road, so vast in numbers that they trailed almost to the gates of Astelok. They were in strict formation and in perfect step, all holding their guns at ease, all with the same unmoving grimace on their metal skulls. The air vibrated with the impacts of their metal feet on the dirt. Iktinos quickly calculated there were at least ten thousand in the forward mass, and who knew how many more approaching from other angles or still hidden by the forests. It was an army large enough to subjugate a world, and it had been arrayed against the single space port that still resisted them on Raevenia.

The sniper pointed to the edge of the wood that bordered the road. The woods were still smouldering from the booby traps that had funnelled the Undying towards the gates.

A vehicle was crashing through the trees. At least, a vehicle was the best description that Iktinos could think of. It was a steep pyramid, several storeys high, carried along on a crackling bed of energy that scorched the grass beneath it. A huge green crystal was embedded in its pinnacle, from which arcs of power were playing down the sheer black sides. Around it were the barrels of four energy weapons, dripping with the energy barely contained in their glowing capacitors. One side of the monolith slid open, revealing a liquid black pool suspended impossibly vertical, rippling with energy. Undying warriors marched alongside it like an honour guard. Iktinos could see that these warriors were the elite of the army, bigger and less humanoid with armour plates, not of dull metal, but of deep crimson covered in glyphs picked out in gold. This was the royal guard of whatever called itself the monarch of the Undying.

Another of the huge machines was crunching through the trees on the other side of the road. The dark paths carved through the forests further away suggested there were more still, advancing slowly, but relentlessly.

'What is it?' asked the sniper.

'We will find out soon enough,' said Iktinos. 'What is the range?'

'We've had a few sighting shots. Their front ranks are still past rifle range. The... war engines, whatever they are, will be in range a lot later than that. We know how far the warriors can shoot, but those machines might out-range us.'

'Do not fire upon the Undying in earnest,' said Iktinos, 'until they are three ranks in. You cannot kill them all. Sow confusion instead.'

'Yes, sir,' said the sniper. His voice was shaking, and it was impossible to tell if he was more afraid of the Undying or of Iktinos.

Iktinos examined the approaching Undying more closely. A few of the flying warriors were hovering along the edge of the treeline, many of them with long-barrelled cannon that looked like they had the range to strip the gatehouse away at any moment. The elite, the immortals of the Undying horde, were falling into step alongside the warriors, dwarfing them with their hulking size.

A few among the warriors were taller than those around them, walking fully upright in a grim echo of a man. They carried staffs instead of guns, and their metallic forms were wrought into more elaborate shapes like ornate armour. Their eyes burned brighter with intelligence, and energy crackled around them like emerald haloes.

'Note their leaders,' said Iktinos.

'We... we kill them first, right?' said the sniper.

'If you can,' said Iktinos. But the truth was, he did not think the snipers had much chance of inflicting anything more than nominal losses on the Undying. Killing as many as possible would not win this battle. Raw shock and devastation would be the key. The Soul Drinkers, and the Raevenians before them, had assumed that the Undying were immune to such things, that they had none of the mental weaknesses of men. Iktinos saw that their weaknesses simply had to be exploited.

'There are leaders among them,' voxed Iktinos to his flock. 'Leaders means a chain of command. And a chain means it can be broken. The soulless ones are not immune to the terror and confusion of war; a Space Marine is. That is how we will win, my brothers. The xenos need logic to function, but an Astartes can achieve victories that defy all logic. When they see the certainty of their victory breaking down, they will become as vulnerable as any other enemy.'

Iktinos headed back down the stairs to join his battle-brothers behind the gates.

'Sir,' said the sniper, 'when the Undying get here… where do we go?'

'You stay here,' said Iktinos, 'until you die.' Then he ducked out of the watchtower and left the snipers to their hopeless fight.

A city of tombs stretched so far it disappeared into the horizon, where the metal-clad sky met the ground.

Every tomb was a masterpiece. Crafted from brushed metal, stone and gold, they were the resting places of the necron army's generals, places of worship, monuments to a future without biological life. Some were like temples, their columns surrounding sarcophagi carved with the images of the regal, skeletal things inside. Others were blocks of steel carved deeply with stylised images of conquest and genocide, subjugated xenos and alien eyes picked out in gold. One was an enormous hand of black stone bones, holding a necron form, curled up like an obscene foetus, in its palm. One was a steel skull with its inhabitant just visible in its mouth, wide open as if in mid-scream. There must have been thousands of tombs, arranged in a grid to form avenues between the sepulchres.

Techmarine Lygris pushed to the front of the Soul Drinkers as they formed a gun line at the entrance to the tomb-city.

'Get me to an interface,' he said. 'I can lead us through.'

Sarpedon couldn't see Lygris's face because the Techmarine wore his helmet, but the strength an Astartes carried in his voice was gone. Lygris was a wreck, broken by whatever he had seen when he interfaced with the necron information network. Sarpedon knew that if his old companion were ever to become as he once was, it would not happen on Selaaca.

'Stay back, Lygris. Keep alive. Luko! Lead us forward. The xenos will be close behind.'

The Soul Drinkers advanced in a tight formation, Luko taking the far right of the line as it made its way between the first rows of tombs, the tech-guard following. Scamander, as was so often the case, was beside Tyrendian as they moved. His eyes were smouldering.

'Power spike,' voxed Voar.

'I don't like the sound of that,' said Luko's voice over the vox. 'Tighten up, Soul Drinkers! Mutual cover! Graevus, you're fast response!'

'Yes, commander,' replied Graevus, whose assault unit was just behind the main gun line. Half the Soul Drinkers squads advanced with the other half covering them, training their bolters down the long avenues between tombs.

'We'll need to get one of these open,' voxed Luko. 'They look solid enough.'

The tomb just in front of Luko, shaped like a chunk of battlement from an iron fortress, split open down the middle. Freezing vapour poured out, clinging to the ground like liquid. Green light bled from the darkness inside.

'Damn,' said Luko.

Luko dived to the side just as a blast of emerald light tore out of the sarcophagus towards him.

'Close up and cover!' yelled Sarpedon, watching from the centre of the line.

Luko's squad leapt into cover as blasts of power shredded the walls of the tombs beside them.

Sarpedon heard the grinding of metal on stone. The tomb next to him was opening, slivers of ancient stone flaking away from a stylised face sculpted as if it was half-buried in the floor. The golden sphere of the face's single eye rolled out of the fractured socket and thunked to the floor. Light bled from the socket, stuttering as something moved inside.

The stone split open, and the necron inside unfolded with an ancient majesty.

Its skeleton was tarnished gold inlaid with deep blue. Its eyes flashed green and crimson, and its skull was set into a headdress like coiled snakes cascading down over its shoulders. A cape made of linked panels of gold and steel clanked around it. It carried a staff topped with a blade, inset with a fat green jewel.

Sarpedon reacted first. He ducked beneath the edge of the split sarcophagus and heard the hiss of a blade cutting through air. He came up, bolter blazing, hammering shots into the necron's torso.

The necron turned on him and lashed out with his staff again. Sarpedon turned it aside with his forearm, but the staff fired a shard of brilliant green energy that threw Sarpedon off his feet.

Sarpedon slammed into the tomb behind him, splintering abstract carvings. The breath was knocked out of him and his head swam. Instinct took over, and he fired at the blurry gold shape advancing on him, rolling to the side and springing up on his arachnid legs.

The necron wrenched the bolter out of Sarpedon's hand and crushed it in its powerful metal fingers, flinging it away. Sarpedon drew the Axe of Mercaeno from his back, and, for an instant, barely a passing of time at all, it showed hesitation when it saw the force weapon in Sarpedon's hand.

It had no face to express emotions with, just a leering skull, but its body language suggested an apprehension that was beyond the scope of a machine's emotions.

The necron struck again and again. Sarpedon caught the blows on the haft of his axe, and flicked the butt of the weapon up into the necron's face, snapping its head back and sending it reeling. It was taller than him, perhaps twice as tall as a necron warrior, and it was stronger and more resilient by far, but it had a weakness that they did not.

'You were alive,' snarled Sarpedon. 'You used to have a soul.'

The necron might even have understood him. It didn't matter. It would get the message sure enough.

Sarpedon let the force well up inside him, spiralling around the aegis circuit built into his armour. It burst up into his mind like a volcano, and flowed out of him, hot and violent.

For the first time, the necrons bore witness to the Hell.

Sarpedon did not even remember when he had first discovered the Hell.

It might have been when he was a child, before the Chaplains of the Soul Drinkers ever found him. Or, more likely, it was a refinement of raw, formless powers he had demonstrated back then, and had first come to be in the Librarium of the Soul Drinkers flagship, the *Glory*, as Sarpedon was being tested and trained by the Chapter's librarians.

It was a form of telepathy, but a brutal, uncontrolled one, a raw mental bludgeon. It was rare indeed among psykers, but as a weapon it was formidable. Tyrendian's lightning and Scamander's fire were weapons in the simplest sense, implements of destruction. The Hell attacked its enemy's minds just as other Librarians attacked their bodies.

The key was fear. The hardest lesson Sarpedon had learned was that fear did not make itself. He had to find it in the enemy, draw it out and give it form. It was a strange thing for a Space Marine to think so deeply about fear, which the Emperor had created him to control and ignore as an unwanted sensation, but Sarpedon had to understand it.

What did a necron fear?

The necron wrapped its arms around Sarpedon, and, unable to crush him through his power armour, threw him against the tomb behind him. Sarpedon struggled to his feet. He could hear gunfire everywhere, and glimpsed more of the ornate necrons battling the Soul Drinkers all along the line. More were emerging from their sarcophagi. Some were being battered back by bolter volleys, but some had emerged among the Soul Drinkers and tech-guard, and were throwing bodies aside as they killed.

Sarpedon kicked out with his front legs, but the necron held firm. Sarpedon ripped the Axe of Mercaeno up into its torso, and felt the blade bite into unnaturally hard metal, gouging a furrow up to its throat. The necron hauled him into the air, and slammed him down on the roof of the tomb.

A spike of dark steel was driven through Sarpedon's backpack, through the back of his armour and out through his chest. He was impaled there, stuck like a pinned insect with his legs kicking out in every direction. The pain hammered through him, and he felt one of his lungs deflate, bubbling blood out into his chest cavity.

Like fear, pain was something a Space Marine might feel, but never bow to. Pain was the Emperor's way of reminding him there was work to do. An Astartes' duty overrode pain. It even overrode death.

Death. The necrons were death, the death that had descended on Selaaca. That was how the Selaacans must have seen them: an army of oblivion marching through their cities to snatch them away.

There was only one thing that death might fear.

The Hell took form. It was life, infinite, seething life, an avalanche of fecundity. A steaming spectral jungle unfolded, thousands of predatory eyes glinting. Every surface was covered in ravenous life. Insects swarmed in dark masses in every corner. Vines split the ancient stone of the tombs. They wrapped around the legs of the ornate necron, bursting into flower or seed. Slimy limbs reached up from the swampy floor and tried to drag the necron down.

It had a soul. Or at least, it used to. It had once been alive, and it still remembered some of what that meant. It still retained some of the personality of whatever damned creatures had become the necrons. That was all the Hell needed to take a hold.

'What is the alien? It is more than merely a creature of non-Terran origin. Such a thing would hold no holy disgust for us. The alien is an idea, a concept, deadly by virtue of its mere existence. The very possibility of the alien becoming a dominant force among the stars is corrosive to the human soul.'

– Daenyathos, *A Thousand Foes*

CHAPTER FİFTEEN

North of the space port gates, the advancing Undying crossed rifle range. The snipers yelled a warning, and the officers of the Raevenian army gave the order to fire.

Raevenian guns opened up in such numbers that the view from the walls was blurred, as if through heavy rain. The sound was appalling, like an earthquake, an endless exploding din.

Undying fell. Some were shredded beyond self-repair, smashed into shards of metal that phased out before they hit the ground. One of the lords, the tall, regal Undying with ornate carapaces, held up an onyx sphere that pulsed with black light, and the fallen Undying around him clambered to their feet, even scattered shreds of metal flowing back together like quicksilver to re-form into warriors.

One of the flying warriors crashed into the trees, a neat hole punched through its skull by a sniper's bullet. A rocket battery opened up on the walls, and a chain of explosions ripped through the front ranks of the Undying, throwing shattered warriors into the air.

There were so many of them. A man could not count them, and the destruction around them did not slow them down.

Death meant nothing to them, because they were death.

The Undying broke the cover of the trees to the south of the space port and met a similar curtain of fire from the southern walls, where the Raevenians had set up most of their heavy weapons: machine-gun nests, missile launchers and vicious mortar-like devices, which fired clouds of razor wire that turned the approaches into near-impossible terrain. The Undying warriors were slowed down by the wire that draped over them like silver spiders' webs, catching limbs and gun barrels. They tore their way through it with metallic hands, but they could only advance at a crawl, and the guns battered into them. The Undying nobles issued their silent commands, and the Undying broke formation, heading this way and that to make for less tempting targets. One noble was caught in a missile blast and was sheared in two, its lower half clattering to the ground, dead and useless. Its upper half was picked up and dragged along by the Undying around it.

Queen Dyrmida watched from the balcony of the space port's control tower, from where she could just see the tops of the monoliths approaching behind the main Undying line, and the shuddering of the trees to the south as they were battered by stray fire. It sounded like the air itself was tearing.

'You should take cover, your majesty,' said Kavins.

'I know,' said Dyrmida, 'but when they reach us, I will fight.'

'As shall we all. But your part in this battle has been played. Your plan has been put into motion, and you can do nothing now to change its course.'

'I can go to them and show them I am willing to earn my throne by fighting alongside them.'

'If we lose you,' said Kavins, 'more harm will be done than good.'

Dyrmida looked at Kavins, who had the face of a veteran that had been through plenty of wars and come out the other side with his zeal and aggression replaced with weary experience.

'I know all of this,' she said, 'but at least down there I would know I was doing something to aid my citizens.'

'Your majesty,' said Kavins, a note of urgency in his voice, 'I suggest you retire to the situation room. The Undying may have longer-range weapons than we expect, and you will be a prime target.'

Dyrmida followed the officer into the command centre. There were officers everywhere, coordinating the actions of the troops on the walls and on the landing pads. Raevenian soldiers stood guard to protect them, and Dyrmida knew how much they would rather be in the battle than waiting for the Undying to break through. The gunfire was loud, even here, making it impossible to concentrate on anything other than the approaching destruction.

'They're going through ammunition like it's water,' one officer was saying. 'We'll have to send runners.'

'Hold,' said another into a field telephone. 'Damn it, hold them at the west! I'm not having these things climb over undefended walls when our backs are turned!'

Officers saluted Dyrmida as she passed, and she returned their salutes almost unconsciously. The rear echelon detritus of war littered every surface: maps spread out on tables and floors or pinned to the walls, sidearms and ammunition crates, mess tins and furniture pushed out of the way to make room for impromptu conferences. Everything smelled of gun oil and sweat.

'Your majesty!' said a junior officer clutching the receiver of a field telephone. 'Another monolith spotted.'

'How many is that?' asked Dyrmida.

'Four. This one's to the south.'

'Then they will put up a fight there. Redeploy some of our anti-tank reserves. We must keep it from the walls if we can.'

'Yes, your majesty.' The officer began relaying her orders into the telephone in the abbreviated speech typical of her soldiers.

'Do we know yet what they do?' Dyrmida asked Kavins.

'The monoliths? Siege engines probably, but we won't know for sure until they get in range.'

'Keep me updated if any more emerge. Make their destruction a priority.'

'Already done.'

The queen and the officer reached the situation room. It was a flight control room hurriedly set up as a nerve centre, with a number of the control consoles removed and replaced with a map table. The map of the space port on it was covered in pins and annotations showing where the various units were stationed. A number of communications officers sat at the consoles relaying orders and reports.

'You,' she said to the officer watching the pict feed from the northern gates, 'what news from Iktinos?'

'None,' the officer replied. 'The Soul Drinkers have gone quiet.'

'Let us hope they find their voice when the gates fall,' said Dyrmida.

Situation reports were coming in on the size and composition of the Undying force. Dyrmida was soon overwhelmed by it all, the enemy seeming to get more numerous with every moment, even as their warriors were shot down.

In a corridor on a lower floor of the control tower, where an impromptu triage station had been set up to handle casualties from around the tower, a pair of medics looked up at the shouting nearby. Two soldiers approached, supporting a third. The wounded man was covered in blood, deep wounds in his chest and face.

'Over here!' shouted the medic.

The soldiers half-dragged their wounded comrade to the triage station and laid him down.

'What happened?'

'Looks like a mortar blew up or something,' said a soldier. 'Proper shredded him.'

The medic's partner opened a trauma kit, a bag packed with all the bandages, dressings and stimulants needed for a typical battle wound.

'He's messed up,' he said.

'Will he make it?' asked the soldier.

'Sure,' said the second medic without much conviction as he cut open the wounded man's fatigues.

'Damn it, that's a perforated bowel,' said the first medic, wrinkling his nose. 'You guys, get back to the walls. We'll deal with him.'

'Right.'

'What's his name?'

The soldier shrugged. 'Don't know. We found him wandering around outside. Must've come down off the wall.'

The soldiers left, wiping the blood off the fronts of their uniforms.

'Forget it,' said the first medic as the second took out a bundle of sutures and dressings. He was holding the wounded man's wrist. 'No pulse.'

'Then this is how it starts,' said the second. 'We decided where the bodies go?'

'Maintenance room, one floor down,' said the first. 'Lucky guy,' he said to the body. 'You get a body bag. They're gonna run out soon.'

The second medic headed to the other side of the corridor where a supply of black body bags was piled up against the wall.

Neither man noticed the green glow breaking through the dead man's eyelids.

The tomb-city gave the impression of having been silent for aeons. Now, it was filled with the din of gunfire, lasguns and bolters hammering, necron weapons hissing as they tore through stone, armour and flesh. The tech-guard were pinned down by the emergence of the necron lords, their advance cut into knots of soldiers and tech-priests, finding what cover they could before it dissolved around them.

Archmagos Voar noticed the masses of ghostly jungle spreading across the tombs, but he did not care much. He was concentrating on more immediate matters.

Another tech-guard died beside him, sliced in two. The men around Voar were yelling, running from cover to cover as they tried to out-flank the pair of necron lords that were sowing carnage through them. Lascannon fire from Magos Hepsebah streaked around them, but a shimmering energy field leapt up and dissipated the torrent of crimson energy.

'Device Gamma,' said Voar. One of the tech-guard behind him handed Voar a metal sphere, with a transparent section revealing twin hemispheres of metal wrapped in wire. Voar ran his hand over the activation panel and the device hummed to life.

He threw it like a grenade past the columns of the tomb behind which he was sheltering. It rolled along the ground between the two necron lords, and burst, throwing out a shower of white sparks: electromagnetic chaff, similar to the countermeasures used by the Mechanicus spacecraft, but crafted to interfere with the wavelengths that Voar had detected coming from the destroyed necron in his lab.

'Forward!' yelled Voar, his voice amplified to maximum.

Tech-guard charged forwards around him. Green flame danced around them, but it was wild and unfocused. Half-blinded and deafened, the necrons couldn't aim properly at the advancing tech-guard.

Fire poured into the two xenos. Plasma bursts crashed against their power fields, spitting globs of liquid flame everywhere. Two tech-guard hauled a multi-melta into place beside the tomb, one slamming a fuel bottle into its side as the other opened fire.

The power field around one of the necrons overloaded with a white flash. The lord was plated in pitted rose gold, its skull covered in deep scrollwork and its hands in silver blades. Each palm was fitted with a crystal from which it fired bolts of green fire, but, in its blinded state, it was shooting at random.

The multi-melta recharged and the tech-guard hammered fire at the shieldless lord again, the air rippling as pure heat radiation thrummed from the weapon. The necron's torso melted and shifted, revealing layers of circuitry beneath. The lord stumbled back, molten metal dribbling from its wounds.

Voar moved with rapid precision past the tomb and into range of the stricken necron. His manipulator units slithered from his shoulder, striking like snakes to implant their metal hooks in the necron's molten chest. Voar accessed his internal capacitor, and delivered a massive blast of power into the xenos machine, tailored to the exact frequency that would shatter its circuitry.

The necron lord's torso burst open, throwing chunks of metal ribs and spine. The remnants of the necron clattered to the floor. Its wounds covered over with quicksilver as it began to self-repair. Voar stood over it, snapping a manipulator into each of its eye sockets. He forced the remaining charge into it, and its skull exploded.

The second necron lord was similarly confused by the interference from device Gamma. Magos Vionel broke cover and stomped up behind it, grabbing the lord around the waist and hurling it against the closest tomb, splintering marble and bronze. Vionel's other arm fired three rivets into the lord, pinning it to the tomb through its neck and one arm.

The lord struggled. It was strong, but the fat rivets piercing its metallic frame held fast. Its senses were still scrambled, but it couldn't have missed Magos Vionel putting his enormous steel shoulder down and charging towards it.

Vionel impacted so hard that the tomb collapsed, and the lord was crushed down into a mass of broken stone. Vionel reared up and crashed down again, slamming his shoulder into the lord. He beat enormous metal fists against it, throwing out clouds of dust and shards.

The lord tried to drag itself to its feet, but there was nothing left of its motive systems. Its arms and legs were smashed and its torso split open. One eye had popped out, a flickering green lens dangling from a wire. It looked like a crushed insect, fluttering with the last sparks of life.

Vionel reached down and twisted the lord's head off. A couple of sparks flew from the stump of its broken spine, and then it died. Vionel dropped the battered metal skull and stomped it flat under an ironclad foot.

'It works, then,' voxed Magos Hepsebah.

'Forward!' ordered Voar again. The tech-guard advanced through the tombs, pausing to glance at the wrecked remains of the necron enemy.

Sarpedon pulled the Axe of Mercaeno from the necron's ribs and threw the thing aside. The Hell had worked. It had given him the opening he had needed to kill the alien machine.

'Here!' voxed Techmarine Lygris. Sarpedon saw that Lygris was clambering through the remains of the wrecked tomb. 'It was connected.'

Lygris had found an interface into the rest of the necron network, in the remains of the lord's tomb. It was a cluster of black crystals on the sarcophagus floor, like an obsidian flower, that would have fitted into the back of the necron lord's skull.

Sarpedon looked up to take stock of the situation. The nearest necrons had been destroyed or disabled by the Soul Drinkers and Voar's tech-guard, but more were waking, and their honour guard – the larger, less humanoid warriors the Mechanicus had codenamed the Immortals – were marching into the tomb city from outside.

The Soul Drinkers had to move quickly. If they were pinned down in the tombs, they would be swamped by necrons. Lygris had recovered much of his lucidity since the harvester, but he was still not the Astartes Sarpedon knew. Lygris would be risking his soul as well as his life if the necrons assaulted his mind once more. If Lygris gave the Soul Drinkers a chance to turn the battle, however, Sarpedon had to take it.

'Go,' said Sarpedon. 'Shield your soul, my brother.'

A dataprobe extended from Lygris's finger and spun like a drill bit. He bored into the crystal with it, slumping down as his consciousness slipped into the information landscape inside.

'Perimeter!' shouted Sarpedon. The Soul Drinkers moved up to form a cordon around Sarpedon's position, loosing bolter volleys at the necrons just visible advancing between the tombs.

Captain Luko slid into cover beside Sarpedon.

'I hope he gets out intact this time,' he said.

If there had been a soul in there, a mind that could think and comprehend, then it was so utterly alien that a human mind could not encompass its nature.

Lygris could feel nothing, see nothing. His mind would not let him. It was shielding him, closing like a pupil in a bright light, to protect him from being overloaded.

Lygris did not remember what he had seen when he bored into the crystal that had controlled the necron harvester. His memory, like his consciousness, had closed ranks to keep him safe from it. He had only the vaguest of impressions: of immense age, beyond human imaginings; of things born before mankind had crawled from whatever primal ocean had spawned it on ancient Terra; of power, and of hate.

Pure, mechanical, soul-crushing hate, as powerful as a supernova and as cold as the dead star that remained, that was what could kill him. That was what could take everything human in him and flay it away until there was nothing left of Lygris.

He could hide from it forever. He could shut himself off and save himself from that fate, but an Astartes had a duty that demanded everything from him, even unto death. Lygris had made that oath every time he had walked into battle for his Chapter and his Emperor. He would not back down from it now.

Lygris opened his mind, and let the hatred in.

Lygris was thrown clear of the shattered tomb in a shower of green sparks. Sarpedon caught him and dragged him into cover.

Necron fire was coming from every direction. The tech-guard had linked up with the Soul Drinkers, and together they formed an entrenched position among the tombs. They were holding well, but more necrons were arriving at the far end of the tomb-city, and emerald fire was stripping away the cover of the remaining tombs.

'We've got more coming in behind us!' voxed Luko, who was directing his squad's fire nearby.

'Keep them busy!' replied Sarpedon. He looked down at Lygris. He was unconscious, but alive.

Pallas arrived beside Sarpedon.

'He's out,' said Sarpedon. 'We need him.'

Pallas extended an injector from his medicae gauntlet, and stabbed it into a port in the neck joint of Lygris's armour. Lygris's system flooded with stimulants. He bolted awake, coughing up a clot of blood.

'Are you with us, brother?' asked Sarpedon.

'I am, commander.' Lygris's speech was slurred, and his movements were uncoordinated.

'Where do we go now?' asked Sarpedon.

Lygris struggled to his feet.

'Nowhere,' he said.

The ground shook. In the centre of the city, necron tombs sank into the ground, and an enormous square pit was revealed, taking up a good third of the city's area. Chunks of masonry and steel fell as titanic engines ground away beneath the city with a sound like an earthquake. The whole chamber shifted to accommodate it, the ground sloping towards it, the ceiling rising.

'Hold position!' blared Archmagos Voar's vox-unit. 'Steel yourselves! The Omnissiah wills the human soul to prevail! Before no xenos trickery shall we falter!'

The pit deepened and became a shaft of blackness. The dim light glinted on the tip of a structure emerging from its depths.

'Sweet spires of Mars,' whispered a tech-guard nearby.

Level by level, with a slow and alien majesty, a pyramid emerged from beneath the tomb-city.

'Death holds no fear only for the fool. An Astartes' duty is to control that fear and to turn it into a blind hatred of the end of his life, for it brings with it the inability to fulfil his duty to the universe.'

– Daenyathos, *Tome of Universal Truths*

CHAPTER SIXTEEN

The pile of bodies had started out as a single bagged corpse thrown into the command centre's storeroom. The room had been chosen because it was equipped with air-sealable doors, and no one wanted the stink of the dead filling the command centre.

There were about a dozen bodies there. Most of the dead from the unfolding battle lay where they had fallen, or in heaps below the walls. The bodies in the store room represented those who had made it to the tower for treatment and had succumbed to their wounds, or who had died closer to the command centre as weapons exploded or chunks of shrapnel flew from fire on the walls.

The pile settled again, a rattle of air escaping dead lungs. One of the corpses wriggled, like a shiny black worm, out from underneath the other bodies. It was the first body that had been thrown in there. Unlike most of them it had been zipped up in a body bag before being dumped in the room.

The seal on the bag split open. A bloody hand reached out and pulled the bag apart. The body inside, a Raevenian soldier caked in blood, clambered to its feet. It was half-bent over in a position that a human spine could not maintain for long, its head thrust forward like an animal's. Its wounds were so disfiguring it was impossible that it was still alive. Its eyes flickered green.

The corpse opened the door with the hiss of a breaking air seal. No one had thought to bar the door from the outside, since the idea of a corpse walking out was ridiculous.

The dead Raevenian shambled down the corridor, passing store-rooms full of abandoned equipment. Its gait became surer as it went, as if it was rapidly relearning how to walk. The corpse room was in the command centre's basement, and was not being used by any of the commanders and support staff of Queen Dyrmida's army. The muffled thunder of gunfire was the only sound aside from the clicking of metallic heels on the floor.

Footsteps came from up ahead. A soldier emerged from a bend in the corridor. He was wearing the uniform of a medic, and was dragging a body bag along behind him. His uniform was smeared with blood, and his hands were red with it.

The soldier saw the corpse and stopped.

'Hey,' he said. 'Hey, you're a live one, right? Stay there, don't move. I'll get you help.' He dropped the bag and hurried up to the corpse. 'Listen, sit down, and I'll get someone from upstairs. Got it? Speak to me, pal. Come on.'

The corpse grabbed the back of the soldier's neck and slammed him against the wall. Its other hand punched into the soldier's back and closed around his spine. It ripped out a handful of vertebrae.

The soldier gasped, and flopped to the floor, his legs useless. Before he could scream, the corpse reached down and slit his throat with razor-sharp fingertips. A whisper of breath gasped out of the wound, followed by a spray of blood.

The corpse stepped over the body bag as it left the soldier to die. It found the maintenance door it had been searching for. It was locked, but it rammed the palm of its hand into the door just below the lock and it burst open. A chunk of bloody palm was torn off and slipped to the floor. The corpse did not seem to notice. Blood-slicked metal glinted through the wound.

The room contained shelves of tools, lubricants, paints and other maintenance supplies. Set into the floor was a large metal hatch with a wheel lock.

The corpse knelt down and hauled on the wheel lock. Flakes of rust broke off, and the lock squealed as the corpse forced it open. With a boom, the lock snapped open and the corpse hauled the hatch up.

Burning green eyes looked up from the darkness of the maintenance space below.

The Undying climbed up through the hatch. They were skinnier than the warriors, lacking the broad carapaces over their shoulders, and they didn't carry any weapons. Instead, long silver claws folded out from their forearms, fitting over the ends of their fingers.

The corpse led them out of the room. One of them knelt down beside the dead soldier and slit his back open with its blades, removing bones and organs with inhuman speed and accuracy. Another opened the body bag and began doing the same to the dead soldier inside. A neat pile of organs and bones was piled up beside the bodies, arranged as precisely as the pieces of a machine. In less than two minutes, the soldier the corpse had killed was hollowed out, and the Undying pulled its still-clothed hide into it, fitting its limbs and torso inside. It pulled the dead man's face over its skull. The third Undying finished its dissection and did the same. The soldier it wore had been killed by a blast that tore away one side of his chest, its bloody metal ribs visible through the wound.

More Undying were coming up from the maintenance space where they had been waiting patiently for the infiltrator to let them through. They followed the corpse towards the stairwell leading up into the command centre. The three wearing the skins of the dead took the lead. The others went naked and undisguised, but it did not matter. Soon there would be enough bodies to go around.

The pyramid was immense. Its pinnacle tore into the ceiling, and its base had dislodged almost half of the tomb-city. Chunks of rubble tumbled down its sides like rain. The pyramid was made from glossy black stone, deeply inscribed with glyphs and patterns that echoed circuitry.

The pyramid was stepped, and on each level stood black menhirs, like the standing stones erected all over Selaaca, channelling information across the planet's surface. Somewhere in its vastness and majesty was a very recognisable arrogance, the proportions designed to awe, the triumphal pictograms of stylised necrons marching across wasted planets. The necron warriors were soulless, but the intelligence that had caused the pyramid to be constructed had enough of a personality left to want to proclaim its superiority.

A wide staircase hundreds of steps high led to the upper levels. The top quarter of the pyramid was a columned temple, its entrance flanked by obsidian statues of necron Immortals permanently at guard. Patterns of gold spiralled around the columns, pulsing with energy.

The rumbling stopped. The pyramid had forced its way fully into the tomb-city.

Techmarine Lygris, being helped along by Apothecary Pallas, looked up at the pyramid.

'It's another tomb,' he said.

'The intelligence?' asked Sarpedon. 'It's in there?'

'I can taste its thoughts,' said Lygris.

If Lygris had still been able to speak with his own tongue, thought Sarpedon, would he have detected a note of fear in the Techmarine's voice?

'Archmagos,' voxed Sarpedon, 'we need you to hold the base of the pyramid. Keep the necrons off our backs.'

'Very well, commander,' replied Voar. The tech-guard were just behind the Soul Drinkers, moving to take up positions among the tombs. Necrons were already emerging from the tunnel that led back up to the surface, the vanguard of the force that had pursued them through the ruins above. 'The time you have shall be bought with the blood of the Omnissiah's faithful. Do not waste it.'

'All squads!' ordered Sarpedon. 'Assault units to the fore! Soul Drinkers, advance!'

The Soul Drinkers broke cover and made for the base of the pyramid. The necrons that had survived the pyramid's emergence opened fire, but they were in disarray. The Soul Drinkers were as fast and ruthless as any Astartes, Graevus leading the assault units up front that leapt obstacles on their jump packs and brought down the necrons in their way with chainswords and bolt pistols. The tech-guard engaged the necrons on their flank, swapping fire with the aliens to tie them down and keep them from blunting the advance. Sarpedon glimpsed the fat bursts of laser from Magos Hepsebah, and even spotted a broken Undying being hurled aside by the industrial strength of Magos Vionel.

Lygris was on his feet, and snapped shots off at the necrons between the tombs. The Soul Drinkers had almost reached the pyramid.

'Heavy resistance,' voxed Graevus from up ahead. 'They're throwing warriors at us.'

'Open us up a path,' replied Sarpedon. 'Luko! Salk! With me! Up the steps!'

Sarpedon ran forwards at full tilt, Lygris struggling to keep up as Sarpedon scrambled over the ruined tombs in front. Pallas and Tyrendian were there, too, Tyrendian scorching the shadows between the tombs with a bolt of lightning that blew an Immortal to burning pieces.

The assault units were battling with the necrons up ahead. Sarpedon ran past them, leading the rest of the Soul Drinkers onto the steps.

'Support fire!' shouted Luko as his squad made it onto the steps. His Soul Drinkers turned and aimed down into the tombs, where dozens of necrons were massing to march on Graevus's embattled assault troops. 'Fire!'

Squad Luko raked the tombs with explosive fire. Necrons fell, clambered back up self-repaired, and fell again with massive wounds blasted through their metal carapaces. Squad Salk joined in, and a unit of tech-guard made it onto the bottom level of the pyramid to lend the weight of their las-fire to the battle.

Tyrendian and Scamander joined Sarpedon and Lygris at the front.

'How do we kill it?' asked Tyrendian. 'Assuming we even know what it is?'

'I don't know,' said Lygris. 'But we have to do it now.'

'Heads up!' shouted Scamander, looking towards the pinnacle of the pyramid. Hundreds of black motes were swarming from inside the temple entrance.

'Scarabs,' spat Lygris.

'Guns up! The xenos are upon us!' ordered Sarpedon. More and more Soul Drinkers were making it onto the pyramid steps, forming a firing line of bolters that was sweeping the ruined tombs of necron defenders. Many of them turned to see the new threat from above.

'Unless we are to shoot them all, one by one,' said Scamander, 'I suggest you all get down.'

Tyrendian looked at the young Librarian. 'Can you do it?'

'I can.'

'Then commander,' said Tyrendian, 'I suggest we all do as he says.'

'Everyone,' ordered Sarpedon, 'down!'

The Soul Drinkers threw themselves onto the steps. Scamander stood and walked forwards. The swarm descended: scarabs, hundreds of them, buzzing down on steel wings, their jaws glowing molten red as they prepared to bore through power armour.

Scamander raised his arms. His hands glowed orange. Ice formed around his feet, crackling across the black stone.

Scarabs flowed around him in a black cloud, eager to force their way through the joints of his armour and eat him alive.

Scamander yelled, and a wave of fire exploded from around his hands. Billows of flame radiated out from him, like a red storm with Scamander at its eye. Scarabs flew haywire, circuits burned out and wings on fire. The fire rippled over the heads of the Soul Drinkers, scorching the backpacks of their armour as it licked up the stairway and across the ornate slabs of the pyramid.

The roar of the fire died down. Burning scarabs were everywhere, pinging against the sides of the pyramid as they flew blinded and out of control. A metallic hail of dead scarabs fell, trailing smoke.

Scamander fell back onto the steps. His arms and shoulder pads smouldered. The rest of him was caked with ice, hissing where it touched the heated armour. Scamander began to roll down the steps, unconscious. Tyrendian hurried forward and supported him, hauling him into a seated position, and propping him up against a terrace of the pyramid.

'Apothecary!' called Tyrendian, but Pallas was already there. Scamander's mouth lolled open, and his eyes were rolled back.

'Keep moving!' ordered Sarpedon. The Soul Drinkers advanced up the pyramid, the tech-guard reaching the lower levels below them. Sarpedon could see Hepsebah's cannon raking the ruins below.

Only the temple remained before Sarpedon: the temple making up the top of the pyramid. Between the black stone columns of its entrance there was a darkness so profound that his enhanced eyesight couldn't penetrate it.

'I can feel it,' said Lygris. 'It's watching us.'

'Not for long,' said Sarpedon, and scuttled into the temple.

Unnatural dimensions assailed him. Space did not fold up correctly in the temple. Even in the darkness, the angles of the walls did not add up correctly, and even up and down seemed skewed, as if reality was being distorted through a lens. Sarpedon struggled to keep his footing as his equilibrium told him that left was right.

He was in a chamber of brushed steel, that much he could tell. But it was not a chamber, it was an intersection of a larger structure, one that could not possibly fit into the temple at the top of the pyramid. The necrons had folded this place to fit inside the structure, blaspheming against the basics of physical reality.

Above was a sky composed of information: half-formed chains of numbers and commands, flickering images of blueprints, chains of data streaming off into infinity. It hurt Sarpedon's eyes just to look at it. It didn't want to fit into his mind. He looked down at a floor, inlaid with the skulls and carapaces of necron warriors, beaten flat, perhaps damaged warriors recycled into building materials or some grand sacrifice of the alien machines to their leader.

Sarpedon clambered up the wall of the chamber, and reached the top to give himself a better view. A labyrinth of machinery led off as far as he could see: enormous engines, half-formed as if in the process of melting into slag; forges churning out necron warriors and scarabs; forests of captives, nothing more than skeletons wrapped in tendrils of bleeding muscle; grand tombs, their sarcophagi lying open, waiting to receive lords yet to be built; an immense spire of glowing steel with warships suckling power from it; oceans of inky black information, infested with hunter-programs that writhed and darted like translucent sharks; ziggurats of pure carbon, and monoliths of obsidian.

Sarpedon's mind whirled with the impossibility of it all. It could not be real, this patchwork of tech-heresies.

Lygris pulled himself up onto the top of the wall. Sarpedon could see that the Techmarine was exhausted. Some of the datavaults built into his armour had melted.

'It's information,' said Lygris, looking out across the hellforged labyrinth. 'This is what they want, what they plan to build. This is what they will do with the galaxy if they get their way. The wall between information and reality is thin here. Their designs and their plans, they... they break through.'

'Where is their ruler?'

'In the labyrinth, at its heart. I can take you to him. I can feel him watching me in every interface I have.'

'We must hurry,' said Sarpedon. 'This place could kill us as surely as the necrons.'

'Agreed,' replied Lygris. 'Follow me.'

The Soul Drinkers advanced into the temple behind Sarpedon, through the shadowy gateway that marked the temple threshold. They were thrown into disarray by the sudden shift in reality, but their officers ordered them forwards. Tyrendian supported Scamander, who looked semi-conscious and drained, his hands still smouldering, and his feet leaving icy prints on the mosaic of dismembered necrons on the floor.

'This just gets better and better,' snarled Captain Luko. 'Where's the thing we're supposed to kill?'

'Near,' replied Lygris.

'Good,' said Luko. 'Dismantling these machines has left me thirsty for a proper fight.'

Ghosts drifted through the walls of the labyrinth. They had the faces of necrons, emotionless skulls with burning eyes, but they drifted above the ground, trailing long whipping tails of cables and probes. Their hands were bundles of syringes and glowing blades. They were broader and far quicker than a necron warrior, and, most disturbingly of all, they were only half-there, transparent and shimmering as they flickered in and out of reality. A dozen of them emerged from the walls, moving swiftly to surround the Soul Drinkers. More of them were diving down from the information sky like spectral comets, a whole host of them, almost matching the hundred or so Soul Drinkers in numbers.

'Then drink your fill, captain,' said Sarpedon.

When the Undying had come to Raevenia, and even before, when the worlds of the Selaacan empire were winking out, one by one, tall tales of the aliens' capabilities had been swapped between the fearful citizens of Astelok. Among them were stories that echoed gruesome fairy tales of skeletal creatures that came invisible in the night and wore the skins of those they killed. No one really believed them, of course, for who could be left alive to pass them on? But still they spread, and became embellished with stories of glowing green eyes and blades for fingers, and a death that crept from the shadows unnoticed.

The officers and troops manning the command centre's situation room learned, in that moment, that the stories were true.

'Sentries to the situation room!' yelled General Damask, who was overseeing the command centre. 'Now! Gods, now!'

The door burst open, revealing the bloodstained machine beyond it. The room beyond the machine was in ruins, the communications officers inside cut to ribbons, lying in foul gory shreds on the floor, or draped over their switchboards.

Damask drew his sidearm and snapped shots into the Flayed One.

Shots hammered into its torso, and it fell backwards. Two more took its place, darting into the room.

Raevenian troops burst in through the far door. One of them swore and raised his gun immediately, spraying fire at the Flayed One. Bullet holes stitched across the doorway. The Flayed One hurtled through the fire and slammed into Damask.

It was heavy, all metal and blades. Bright slashes of pain opened up in the general's arms and hands as he fended off the blades that snickered down at him.

'Kill it! For the crown's sake get this thing off me!'

There was more gunfire as more troops burst in. A Flayed One fell, skull blown open. Another clawed its way along the ceiling like a huge metal spider, and dropped down on top of the first soldier, carving through his throat with its finger blades.

A metal hand closed around Damask's throat. It sliced shut, and his head came away, his neck cut to ribbons. His gun clattered to the floor, and the last sound he made was the long gurgling breath escaping from his severed windpipe.

'Infiltrators!' someone shouted. 'Undying! Seal them off!'

The soldiers in the room turned as the door behind them was hauled shut, a loud booming indicating that map tables and document cabinets were being piled up behind it. They yelled and swore and hammered on the door, but it stayed shut. They tried to kick it in and shoot the hinges off, but the half-dozen men in the situation room were trapped.

A Flayed One skewered a soldier through his ribcage from behind, lifted him up, and dashed his brains out against the edge of the map table in the centre of the room. Markers indicating the Raevenian positions around the space port scattered onto the floor, and blood spattered across the diagram of the space port's walls and landing pads. Another soldier backed against the door, and yelled as he fired on full-auto, emptying his gun's magazine at the Flayed Ones entering the room. The gun's movement clicked on an empty chamber, and bladed hands reached for him. He fought them off, screaming, even as his fellow soldiers were dragged down and butchered. Finally, his abdomen was slit open, and the scream caught in his throat, drowned in the blood gurgling up from a wound in his lung.

The Flayed Ones seemed barely to notice the barricaded doors. One of them, still wearing the tatters of the medic's skin, reached up and pulled down a ceiling tile, revealing a cavity between the ceiling and the floor of the level above. With inhuman ease, it slid into the space, followed rapidly by half the other Flayed Ones. The others turned to the metal shutters on the situation room's windows and began to tear them from the walls.

* * *

'Your majesty, they're here,' said Kavins.

Queen Dyrmida looked up from the field radio with which she had been trying to get an explanation for the din coming from the lower floors. She had set up her quarters on an upper floor, where she could have a good view of the unfolding battle, near the landing control room with its banks of communications consoles and monitors. 'They?'

'The Undying. Flayed Ones.'

Dyrmida stood up. 'How?'

'We don't know.'

Dyrmida drew her sidearm. She was well-practiced with it, as good a shot as any of her soldiers, but skill at arms had not saved the men undoubtedly dying beneath her feet. 'Can we get out through the lower floors?'

'No,' said Kavins. 'We're sealing all the ways up. A cargo lifter I had detailed to ferry ammunition to the walls is landing on the control tower roof.'

'Can we contain the Undying in this building?'

'Please, my queen, do not let that concern you. We must get you out of here.'

Kavins led her towards the exit leading to the stairwell. The other troops in the control room, mostly communications officers, were hurriedly disengaging their comm systems and checking their guns.

The sound of tearing metal came from the floor. One of the officers screamed and disappeared through a hole in the floor. Dyrmida caught a glimpse of bloody silver through the flesh of the soldier's legs before he was gone.

'Move!' shouted Kavins, spraying fire from his sub-machine gun at the hole.

Bullets flew in every direction. One soldier was caught by a stray round. A Flayed One dragged itself out of the hole and was shot to pieces. Another hole opened up, and another man died, blades slicing up into his abdomen and through his spine.

Dyrmida ran for the door, the officer close behind her. He slammed the door behind him and hauled its lock shut. The stairwell was white-painted and narrow, made to serve as a maintenance access to the roof of the tower. The door boomed with the stray gunshots hitting it, and Dyrmida heard the men trapped in there screaming.

Kavins had shut them in there to die so that there was more chance of the queen escaping. She knew that she should be ashamed of that fact, but the feeling was drowned out by her heart hammering in her chest.

She ignored the thought and pushed upwards. Gunfire echoed from below, mingling with the sounds of the guns on the walls. She hauled on the wheel lock on the door in front of her, and the door swung open to the roof. It was scattered with antennae and receiver dishes.

The smell of gun-smoke hit her. It was thick in the air, drifting in a pall from the soldiers on the walls. Across the landing pads, she could see her soldiers manning the defences, keeping up a hail of fire against the two columns of Undying approaching from the north and south. The massive black pyramidal vehicles, the monoliths, were drifting towards the main gates, apparently immune to fire, thousands of Undying teeming around them. The Soul Drinkers knelt on the other side of the gate, waiting. Hundreds of soldiers had flocked to hold the walls to the south, and heavy weapons thumped as they sent anti-tank shells and missiles into the Undying advancing through the smouldering remains of the forest's edge.

Kavins slammed the door shut and readied his gun.

'Hold here, your majesty,' he said. 'We'll get you off here soon.'

'Do not risk your life for me, Kavins,' said Dyrmida. 'Too many have died that way already.'

'It will not come to that.'

Kavins pointed as the lifter rose above the edge of the command centre roof. It was a stubby box-like craft with short stabiliser wings, and it rose on a pair of vertical jet engines on a column of rippling hot air. It was a small craft, big enough for perhaps half a dozen passengers. Through the cockpit windshield, Dyrmida could see the pilot, brow furrowed as he held the craft steady.

The rear access ramp of the lander opened, and the craft swivelled to bring the ramp over the roof. Metre by metre, the craft descended, until Kavins was able to run over and grab the lip of the ramp. He held his hand out.

'Your majesty,' he said.

Dyrmida put her foot on Kavins's hand and pushed herself up onto the ramp. Her upper body was on the ramp, and her legs were kicking out over the roof. She pulled herself towards the safety of the crew compartment.

Dyrmida heard gunfire over the roaring engines, and looked back to see Kavins firing at something on the edge of the roof.

It was an Undying, one of the Flayed Ones, still wearing the scraps of skin it had worn as a disguise. Bullets sparked against its skull, and it fell, but more followed it, clambering onto the roof.

Kavins paused for a moment to wave at the pilot, indicating that the lander should take off without him.

'No!' shouted Dyrmida. 'We can save you! Turn back!'

One of the Flayed Ones was scaling an antenna. Dyrmida, still clinging to the ramp, aimed her sidearm at the Flayed One and fired, but the shots snapped wide. She knew what it was going to do, and she couldn't do a thing to stop it.

The Flayed One leapt from the antenna onto the front of the lander.

Dyrmida could just hear, over the roar of the engines, the sound of the lander's front windshield shattering.

The lander lurched suddenly, almost throwing Dyrmida out. The cockpit door burst open, and the pilot flew back into the crew compartment in two pieces, his body carved apart from one shoulder to the opposite hip. The sundered corpse tumbled past Dyrmida as the lander pitched backwards. The blood-slicked Undying looked at Dyrmida through the open cockpit door, the gore from the pilot's death running thickly down its grinning skull.

Kavins looked up as the lander's shadow passed over him. He dived out of the way as its bulk flopped down onto the roof of the command centre. Half the roof collapsed into the control room below. Debris shattered up into one engine, and it exploded in a storm of fire and metal, throwing torn Flayed Ones off the roof. Flame billowed across the roof, and torn fuel lines sprayed through the fire.

Queen Dyrmida didn't know where she was or what was happening to her. All she knew was that one half of her world was agonisingly hot and the other was not. She rolled away from the flames, too confused and shocked to register the pain from broken bones in her leg.

She was still holding her gun, for her hand had closed around it in a lucky reflex. She wiped her other hand across her face, getting some of the blood out her eyes. Behind her was the wrecked lander, explosions shaking it as fuel cells cooked off inside. The spatters of blood on the lander's nose were blackening in the heat.

She saw Kavins in front of her. He was lying on his back, and a Flayed One stood over him. It squatted over his chest and punched its blades into his eyes. Kavins spasmed, and then he wasn't Kavins any more, but just another body laid low by the Undying.

Dyrmida tried to get to her feet, but her leg collapsed under her. The pain threw her into a white place of agony, and she nearly blacked out, forcing herself to stay conscious for a few moments more.

Flayed Ones were clambering over the edge of the roof and walking towards her. There was little hurry in their movements. They didn't need their speed now.

Their blades were so sharp that their edges glowed orange with the light of the flames, like slivers of fire. Dyrmida imagined them cutting through her, slicing her apart into bloody chunks.

She would not go through that. They would not carve her up while she was alive.

Queen Dyrmida of Astelok, Regent of Raevenia, put the muzzle of her pistol to the underside of her jaw.

The Flayed Ones advanced on her, fixing her with their burning green eyes. Their faces didn't change from the impassive rictus of metal. Somehow, it would have been better to see their hate.

Blades touched her skin.

Dyrmida pulled the trigger.

'How many have died? None but the Emperor knows. How many of their stories are remembered? Barely a drop in that ocean. Strive to overcome not only the standards of your heroes, but of everyone who has died forgotten.'

– Daenyathos, *The Bullet and the Skull*

CHAPTER SEVENTEEN

The blast ripped right through the ruins of the tomb, and sheared through Archmagos Voar's legs. Voar hit the ground, tech-guards running to his aid. One of them was shredded to atoms by another fat eruption of green fire, but two more grabbed Voar by his shoulders and dragged him clear, spraying las-fire at the necron destroyer that had fired on them.

Voar's auto-senses rapidly took stock. His legs, simple but sturdy motivator units, had been completely destroyed, one flayed off at the knee, the other fused and useless. They held no vital systems, and he could function at almost full capacity, save for the ability to move under his own power.

'You,' he said to the tech-guard kneeling beside him, firing rapid las-fire at the destroyer, 'Carry me.'

'Yes, archmagos,' said one of the tech-guard, and pulled Voar's arm over his shoulder so he could half-carry, half-drag Voar around.

The vox-net opened up. It was barely possible to make out voices among the distortion. Voar engaged his logic circuits and rearranged the static-filled snippets of sound into recognisable words.

'This is Sarpedon!' said the voice over the vox. 'We're under attack from some necron machines that can phase in and out. Bullets pass right through the damn things. Advise!'

'I had anticipated this application of their phasing technology,' said Voar. He amplified his vox-unit to address the tech-guard around him. 'Device Epsilon! Now!'

One of the tech-guard ran forwards carrying a second weapon similar to the device Gamma: a metal sphere wrapped in circuitry and wires. This one contained a power source that turned the metal translucent as it pulsed.

'Crystavayne,' voxed Voar. 'I am inconvenienced. Deliver device Epsilon to Commander Sarpedon.'

'Yes, archmagos.' Crystavayne ran through the ruined tombs and knelt beside Voar. The inferno pistol that Voar had given him was still in his hand, its muzzle glowing a dull red with the constant fighting.

'Archmagos, be still. I can fix the–'

'I am in no danger,' snapped Voar. 'The same is not true of Sarpedon. Deliver the device Epsilon. That is an order.'

'Very well,' said Crystavayne, taking the weapon from the tech-guard.

'And be quick,' said Voar. 'Ancient they may be, but the patience of the necrons has run out.'

The labyrinth was twisting again, warping space to throw the ghost-like necrons in greater number into the Soul Drinkers' position.

Sarpedon slammed the Axe of Mercaeno into the chest of one of the machines, and the power field split deep into its torso. The machine shifted out of phase with reality again, turning transparent, and the axe slipped through the apparition harmlessly. One of its limbs solidified, and stabbed a bundle of knives and injectors at Sarpedon. He was a fraction of a second quicker than the machine anticipated, and grabbed the limb with his free hand. He drew back his arm and hurled the necron at the wall, but, just in time, it shifted again and passed right through it.

'Give me a whole company of Traitor Marines to fight,' spat Luko, who was fighting back to back with Sarpedon, lightning claws blazing. 'At least when you hit them they stay hit.'

Soul Drinkers were dying to the necron ghosts. One lay, throat opened up, his helmet wrenched back off his head. Another was dragging himself along, trying to hold in his entrails as they spilled through the triangular hole slashed open in his armour.

One of the ghosts had been destroyed, phasing out a moment too late to avoid the volley of bolter fire that slammed into it. It lay half-shifted, flickering like an image on a faulty pict screen, back blown open and spilling ghostly circuitry across the floor. Another had been skewered through the head by a chainblade, and had fallen like a metal puppet with its strings cut. The others were faster, materialising to strike, and then becoming ghosts again faster than the Soul Drinkers could target them.

They functioned naturally in the abnormal dimensions, too, shifting in and out of folds in space, warping from one place to another. This was their home ground. The Soul Drinkers were the intruders, and the necrons had them trapped in their labyrinth.

One of Voar's tech-priests stumbled over the threshold into the midst of the Soul Drinkers. He looked mostly human, with only a medicae gauntlet on one hand and cranial interfaces in his scalp to suggest his augmentations. In one hand he held an inferno pistol and in the crook of his other arm was a device like an oversized grenade. Sarpedon remembered him as Magos Crystavayne, one of the officers of Voar's fleet.

'Commander!' shouted Crystavayne.

It was the only word he got out before the necron ghost behind him shimmered into reality and speared him through the back with both sets of blades. Injectors pumped to fill him with acids that would eat him away from the inside, and blades vibrated to slice easily through his bones and organs.

Magos Crystavayne slumped to his knees, still impaled on the ghost's blades. The ghost shifted back into spectral form, as twin fountains of blood sprayed from the magos's back.

With his last moment of life, Crystavayne thumbed an activation catch on the device he held. His inferno pistol dropped from his hand, and he slumped down onto his back.

The device split open. A glowing orange-white core was revealed, and it pulsed, flaring up to fill the labyrinth intersection with painful light.

The light died down, Sarpedon's auto-senses fighting to adjust. A necron above him shuddered as if its image was obscured by static, and suddenly it was real. Its skull split apart as its jaws opened, wrenching a tear across its face like a ragged grin, and it screamed.

'They're real!' yelled Sarpedon. 'Kill them!'

Most of the Soul Drinkers dropped to one knee and fired, blazing full-auto at the ghosts suddenly locked into their physical forms above them. Sarpedon saw one Wraith materialise halfway through the wall, writhing as its innards fused with the wall, sparks bleeding from its eyes.

Luko killed another, leaping over Sarpedon to grab the necron's tail of cabling and spine, dragging it down and slamming it into the floor. He leapt on it, and slashed its skull into three slices with a sweep of his claws.

Sarpedon saw something like panic in the movements of the necron ghosts. They were darting around at random, throwing themselves out of the way of angles of fire. It didn't work. Forced to stay in physical form by the Mechanicus device, they were little more than target practice for the Soul Drinkers.

'They're fleeing from us, commander!' voxed Sergeant Salk, who was kneeling, directing his squad's fire. One of the necrons clattered to the ground behind him, its head and one limb missing. With its capacity to phase out gone, the wreck stayed there, smouldering.

'More will follow,' said Sarpedon. 'Lygris? Can you lead us on?'

Lygris stumbled up to Sarpedon and leaned against the wall, breathing heavily enough to distort the vox-unit that Pallas had fitted him with.

'I can,' he said. 'It is far through the labyrinth, but I can lead us through… through the broken space. It will not be long before we reach it. It is talking to me.'

'What does it say?'

'That we will all die.'

Sarpedon pulled the Axe of Mercaeno from the body of the necron he had killed.

'For a creature of such intelligence,' he said, 'it has little imagination.'

'Follow me,' said Lygris.

It was surprisingly quiet by the main gates in the northern walls of the space port where Chaplain Iktinos and his flock waited for the real battle to begin. The gunfire from above was muffled by the walls and the gatehouses, and the Undying made little sound save for the grinding of their feet in the dirt and the occasional falling tree, knocked down by the advancing monoliths.

A few soldiers were running, here and there, to collect ammunition or carry wounded comrades to triage stations. Reserves waited nervously in a maintenance hangar, wishing, at the same time, that the Undying would not breach the walls, and that the aliens would hurry up and force their way in so they could get the fight over and done with.

The command centre was burning. Flame-shadowed smoke billowed from its tower, and the fire was spreading through the building. Communications from the centre had ceased.

A soldier ran from the direction of the reserve. He was wounded, one of his hands half blown off and the stump of his wrist wrapped in a bloodstained bandage. He had evidently been pressed into service as a messenger because he could no longer hold a gun. He was young, his face and short blond hair smeared with gun residue and blood.

'Chaplain!' he shouted as he ran. 'Chaplain! The centre has fallen. Queen Dyrmida is lost.'

Chaplain Iktinos knelt before the gates. The thirty or so Soul Drinkers with him knelt too, their heads bent in contemplation. Iktinos looked around at the messenger's approach.

'I see,' he said. 'Thank you.'

'We… we don't have anyone in command. Her generals are gone too.'

'That will be all,' said Iktinos, and turned away again.

The messenger stood for a moment, unsure what to say. Then he backed off, turned, and ran towards where the reserved were stationed, perhaps to see if there was anything else he could do.

'Soon,' voxed Iktinos quietly to his flock. 'Remember, my brothers. It matters not who survives, so long as there is one of us.'

The drone of a monolith's engines reached Iktinos's ears. It was on the other side of the gate.

'Nothing matters,' continued Iktinos, 'but the Salvation.'

Enormous energy weapons tore at the gate with a sound like industrial saws grinding through plascrete. The gates shuddered, and cracked lines appeared, describing a massive rectangular shape like another doorway set into the surface of the gates. The ground shook, too, thrumming with the scale of the power being unleashed.

There was panic on the walls. Men were running, some away along the top of the walls, others into the cramped stairways leading down. Some were standing clear of the defences, heedless of the danger, because on Raevenia a good death was as meaningful as a good life, and there were good deaths to be won defying the aliens, even now. Green fire rippled along the walls. Men fell, half their bodies flayed away. Some stood and defied for a few seconds more, yelling their anger and firing their weapons even as their bodies were flayed away into gnawed skeletons.

The cracks in the gate deepened into molten-edged furrows. A huge section of the gates fell inwards, slamming into the ground with a sound that deafened men. The Space Marines' auto-senses protected them.

The monolith, the size of a building, loomed over them, suspended a metre above the ground on a shimmering field of energy. Two more glided behind it. Undying warriors marched alongside it, hundreds of them in strict formation. Many of them had patches of bright silver where they had been shot down, self-repaired, and rejoined the advance. Closest to the moliths were the Immortals, the larger warriors with twin-barrelled weapons, their carapaces inscribed with ornate patterns as if to acknowledge the majesty of the moliths.

'Charge!' yelled Iktinos. The Soul Drinkers leapt to their feet and ran forwards, chainblades whirring, bolters stuttering fire into the Undying.

Some of the flock died there, immolated in the green flare that raked through them from the guns mounted at the pinnacle of the monolith, but it did not matter.

Only the Salvation mattered.

Lygris had been right. The short sprint through the labyrinth had been an unholy few moments of mutilated space and obscene dimensions, the soul-pollution of reality deformed by an alien will. Nevertheless, Lygris led them to the labyrinth's heart, and to what lay there.

Sarpedon saw the tomb of the necron overlord and wondered if there was anything in the galaxy that could truly be holy if such a thing could exist at the same time.

It was an enormous beating heart of grey flesh the size of a tank, a biomechanical mass surrounded by a tangled nest of cabling and wires, power conduits that dripped pure energy and chunks of alien machinery in glossy black slabs.

A conveyor system sent mechanical arms rattling overhead on tracks. They carried human bodies, captive Raevenians, and dropped them into vats of black metal from which ran thin cables glowing bright with their life force. The cables ran into the heart, and every time it took a revolting, fleshy beat the cables shone brighter and another body fell.

The Soul Drinkers ran into position behind Sarpedon and Lygris. They were too fine a cadre of soldiers to fall dumbfounded at the sight, but their shock was still obvious, engendering muttered oaths at its size and foulness, and growls of anger that such a thing should exist. Quite apart from its appearance, the heart emanated such a profound sense of wrongness that it made the labyrinth around it seem mundane.

'The necrons are advancing towards your position,' said Archmagos Voar over the vox. 'They are reinforced in greater numbers. We cannot hold and are falling back. We are slowing their advance, but they will be upon you soon.'

'Acknowledged,' replied Sarpedon. 'We've found it.'

'The intelligence?'

'Its tomb.'

'Then Emperor's speed, commander,' voxed Voar, 'and let the word of the Omnissiah speak of your wrath.'

'Graevus,' said Sarpedon, 'cut that thing open.'

Graevus led his squad towards the heart. Freezing vapour coiled around their feet as Graevus took his axe in his mutated hand.

'Steel your souls,' he said.

The Soul Drinkers behind him levelled their bolters at the heart.

The heart split open, and a gale of ice and chemicals roared out. Graevus was thrown off his feet along with most of his squad. The billow of white vapour was blinding.

Sarpedon drew breath, but his throat felt as if it was closing, so cold was the air. His ears were full of noise.

By his feet, Graevus was rolling onto his back and drawing his bolt pistol.

'Report!' shouted Sarpedon.

'Got nothing,' voxed Luko from behind.

'Sounds from behind,' said Salk. 'Covering.'

'Hold position!' ordered Sarpedon. 'Graevus, did you see it?'

'No,' said Graevus. 'Squad! Advance!'

Visibility was zero. Sarpedon could barely make out his own lower limbs reaching out before him. The faint glow of Graevus's power axe through the icy gloom was the only sight he had of his brother Astartes, and then it was gone. Sarpedon scuttled a few paces forwards, the Axe of Mercaeno heavy in his hands.

Green fire glimmered ahead: two eyes, burning.

'Contact!' shouted Graevus over the vox. 'Get down! Squad, down! Covering fire! Now!'

Sarpedon hit the ground, ready for the volley of bolter fire to tear over his head from the Soul Drinkers behind him. A few fingers squeezed down on triggers. Most did not have the chance.

The gale came again, a hundred times stronger. Graevus flew backwards and slammed into Sarpedon, almost throwing Sarpedon along with him. Sarpedon's talons dug in to the metal of the floor and he held on. Graevus bounced past, and two of his squad followed.

The vapour was whipped into a whirl, like a white-streaked tornado. Sarpedon could see Soul Drinkers being caught up in it, picked up off their feet or slammed into walls. Several tumbled away down the corridor through which the Soul Drinkers had advanced, their armoured forms clattering away through the labyrinth. Some were thrown right over the labyrinth walls.

Sarpedon gritted his teeth and dug in harder. Chunks of metal were swirling, smacking against him like shrapnel. Through the vapour, he could see the heart had split open, but it was still beating, slabs of torn muscle like immense petals of dead flesh pulsing obscenely.

The necron overlord that emerged from the storm was three times Sarpedon's height. Its skull hung low in its chest, its shoulders huge slabs of curved steel. Its torso was a sarcophagus, an ornate casket shaped like a scarab, inset with a fat black gem of datacrystal. Its arms were long enough to touch the ground, but its hands were, in spite of their great size, somehow elegant, the fingers like articulated knives.

Instead of legs, it had a hovering motivator unit like one of the floating necrons. Unlike them, its abdomen was equipped with dozens of limbs, like the legs of a centipede, wriggling underneath it as if searching for something to grab.

It held a scythe, wrought in twisted gold, as ornate as the average necron warrior was plain. Green flame rippled up the blade, matching the flame in the overlord's eye sockets.

Its skull was so long and gaunt that it lost any similarity to a human form. It had no mouth, as if the horizontal slit in a necron skull had been judged surplus to requirements. It was just a long, teardrop-shaped mask of metal, its eyes the only hint of the human form about it.

Its metal was dull red, flecked with gold, and it was gleaming. It had not slept under the earth of Selaaca, stained with age. It had been kept pristine in its obscene heart, perfectly preserved, waiting to wake.

Cables glowing with life force snapped off sockets in its thick spine, whipping around in the wind. Its fuel was the life force of the Selaacan captives being drained away in the vats.

Its burning eyes focused on Sarpedon, narrowing to emerald slits.

'*Die*,' it said.

'Brothers! For the future!'

Iktinos bellowed at the top of his voice, and perhaps some of his battle-brothers could hear him over the chaos erupting before the space port's ruined gates. The Chaplain's crozius carved down again, shattering through the metal torso of the Undying immortal in front of him, its head smashing through the glowing barrels of its weapon, spilling liquid power over the collapsing remains.

The monolith loomed over him. Iktinos's flock was setting about it with bolters and chainswords, the metal rents in its surface rippling and closing up as if the metal was alive.

They were surrounded, and they were dying. Five of the flock lay dead already. It was magnificent, this sight, for it meant that those brothers had died for the Salvation. A time would come when Iktinos would enter their names in a roll of honour, and they would become legends.

The monolith turned, and a rectangular pool of shimmering blackness that drank the light dominated the side facing Iktinos.

'Brother Vozh!' called Iktinos. 'Melta-bombs!'

Vozh had been in an assault squad before joining the flock, and a pair of large cylindrical melta-bombs were clamped to the sides of his bulky jump pack, explosives that burned hot enough to bore through armoured vehicles. Vozh ran through the chaos to Iktinos, handing the Chaplain the melta-bombs.

Vozh was surrounded by bedlam, hundreds of Undying, crowding around the Soul Drinkers. Their remains lay thick on the floor, only to phase out, one by one, making the ground undulate like the surface of a metal sea. The gatehouses on either side were crumbling and aflame, raked by fire from the monoliths. Without the Soul Drinkers, the Undying would have swarmed into the space port, and the whole place would have fallen in short order. Only the sheer ferocity of the Soul Drinkers was plugging the gates, for every Undying who made it through had no choice but to turn and fight them to avoid a bolter shell through the back of the skull or a limb lost to a chainblade.

The monoliths had been brought forwards to grind through the Soul Drinkers, to simply roll over them and crush them. That was not a fate that Iktinos accepted.

Iktinos shouldered his way past one Undying, and ripped the arm off the Immortal between him and the side of the monolith. He tore the pins from the melta-bombs, and hurled them both into the vertical pool in the monolith's side. Undying were emerging from the pool, the shapes of their skulls and carapaces forcing through the film of blackness.

The melta-bombs detonated. The surface of black liquid disappeared, and with it any parts of the Undying that had come through. Neatly severed skull sections and limbs clattered to the ground. The space beyond, deeply inset into the monolith's interior, was spattered with white-hot bolts of superheated matter boring through the metal.

Iktinos threw himself to the ground. Something inside the Undying vehicle ruptured, throwing chunks of burning coils and knives of living metal. The monolith groaned like a wounded giant, and listed to one side as anti-grav units burned out. Purplish flames licked from its wounds.

The stricken monolith blocked the gates more effectively than any makeshift barricade could. The vehicles behind it were trapped outside, and turned their weapons on the gatehouses to bring them down and force a gap open.

'Take it to them!' yelled Iktinos. 'My brothers, to me! Give them not one foot inside!'

The flock closed ranks, dragging the wounded. They crammed back to back, a tiny island of purple armour in the mass of tarnished steel that surrounded them.

It was the kind of fight a Space Marine was created for: face-to-face, brutal and lethal, where strength and determination counted for everything. The Undying might be relentless, they might feel no pain, but that counted for nothing in the face of the sheer killing power of Astartes with orders to stand their ground.

Brother Vozh died, half his head and one shoulder flayed away, even as he spitted an Immortal through the torso with his chainblade. Another Soul Drinker followed him, his legs blown out from under him, disappearing beneath the clubbing gun butts of the Undying that crowded over him.

The circle of Soul Drinkers shrank. More Undying were torn apart.

The future that Iktinos imagined would be worth every drop of Astartes blood.

Sarpedon hit the wall hard.

His mind was divided in two. One half, the human side, was full of pain and shock, battered against the inside of his skull and barely sensible. The other half, the Astartes mind, stepped back from the pain and panic, and coolly took stock of the situation. One of his rear legs was shattered, twisted and useless underneath him. His skull was fractured, and slathering blood down his face. His bolter was gone, clattered away somewhere in the labyrinth where Sarpedon knew full well he would not find it.

He was alive, and he was still holding the Axe of Mercaeno. The overall assessment, then, was positive.

Sarpedon had come to rest a short distance from the overlord's heart. The overlord had hurled him there, picking him up with one outsized metal claw and flinging him into the winds it conjured around it. Broken power conduits hung, dripping life force. Chunks of biomechanical machinery rolled along the ground, picked up by the ice-cold wind.

Sarpedon looked up. The overlord was drifting over the wreckage of its heart towards him, its scythe in its hand. Sarpedon forced himself to his remaining legs, the ruined one dragging behind him, spraying ichor from a ruptured artery.

'One day...' snarled Sarpedon, 'One day we will scour this galaxy of everything like you.'

The wind sounded something like laughter.

The overlord darted forwards and reared up, insect legs wriggling. Sarpedon tried to roll out of the way, but his rear leg buckled, and he slumped to two knees. The overlord was on him, the weight of its body slamming into him.

The legs on the overlord's underside wrapped around Sarpedon, and held him tight, lifting him up off the ground as the overlord reared again. Pincer-tipped limbs dug into the chitin of Sarpedon's legs. A metal hand pulled his head back, and the scythe blade passed in front of his face as it was brought down to the level of Sarpedon's throat.

Sarpedon forced an arm out from the overlord's grasp. He grabbed the scythe blade a finger's breadth from the skin of his throat.

The blade cut through the ceramite of his gauntlet. A line of red pain opened up along his fingers, and he knew that, in a few moments, he would lose them to the blade. He closed his fist around the blade and wrenched it down, trying to force it from the overlord's grip.

The overlord's grip held firm, but Sarpedon continued to pull the blade down. Seeing his opening, he twisted it around and used it to cut through one of the insect arms that held him. The overlord's limb clattered to the floor, picked up by the howling winds and sent spinning away.

Sarpedon's other arm was free. He tore the Axe of Mercaeno out of the overlord's grip, and ripped it up into the side of the overlord's abdomen. The blade sliced through the living metal of its carapace, and Sarpedon twisted, feeling circuitry and power coils crunching.

Sarpedon threw himself free of the overlord. The gales hit him again, and he stabbed his talons into the floor to keep himself from being carried away on the wind.

He tried to find his fellow Soul Drinkers. Most of them were scattered, unable to come to Sarpedon's aid as they were battered against the walls or thrown helplessly along the corridors of the labyrinth. He could hear gunfire, and knew that others were fighting the necron warriors that had made it through the tech-guard and into the temple.

He was on his own, but he did not feel frustrated or betrayed by that fact. He could leave the defence to his battle-brothers. He had made the decision to come to Selaaca and face the overlord, and in a way it was right that he should face the alien alone.

The overlord's scythe came down. Sarpedon ducked to the side, still keeping his purchase on the ground. He sliced up with the axe, burying it in the lower lip of the overlord's chest, and ripping it up through layers of metal. The overlord reared up, its eyes flaring in anger, and slid backwards on its anti-grav.

Sarpedon and the overlord faced each other, both wounded, separated only by a few metres of freezing vapour. The rent in the overlord's chest silvered over, closing up as its self-repair systems kicked in. It lowered its skull like an animal preparing to charge.

Sarpedon set his remaining back leg, anchoring himself to the ground, and drew the Axe of Mercaeno up into a guard.

He knew the overlord would charge, and the overlord knew he would drive off the first few strikes of the scythe with speed and strength well beyond any human the necrons of Selaaca had ever encountered. Faster than an unaugmented eye could see, Sarpedon parried the great curved blade as it arced down at him, throwing it back in the hope of forcing an opening to the overlord's torso or skull. The overlord, however, was as fast as Sarpedon was, and opened up paths of its own: a strike with the butt of the scythe to the side of Sarpedon's head, a lash with a lower limb that threw Sarpedon onto three knees, and a backhand slap that slammed into Sarpedon's chest-plate and drove shards of rib further out of position.

Sarpedon was going to lose. He was going to die.

He saw a bundle of cables glowing with life force, spraying liquid green power like a severed artery. It was whipping down from its mountings above the remains of the biomechanical heart.

Sarpedon ducked down low and sprinted along the floor, forcing his way against the wind. He rolled under the overlord, barely registering the scythe whipping down and slicing off his broken back leg. He scrabbled upright again and ran for the heart, expecting, any second, for the scythe to fall point-first and impale him like an insect on a pin, transfixing him wriggling to the floor while the overlord set about murdering the rest of the Soul Drinkers.

It did not come. Sarpedon was a split second too fast.

He grabbed the cable in one hand. It burned with power. Drops of life force spattered onto his armour and burned like molten metal.

He turned to see the overlord above him, scythe raised to cut him in half.

Sarpedon turned every drop of strength inside, and unleashed the Hell.

Light and life filled the biomechanical chamber. A sun burned overhead, a thousands suns, their brilliant light in every colour of the spectrum. Life boiled like a churning sea underfoot, swarms of insects, coils of vines and soaring trees, an endless landscape of life rolling out on a seething carpet. The light was burning, the raw anger of the stars fuelling a terrible mass of relentless life that boiled over and rose in a flood of limbs and organs.

The overlord reeled. Everything the necrons despised, everything that still held some meaning in what was left of its soul, flooded its alien senses.

It would only last a second. It was all Sarpedon needed.

Sarpedon leapt, letting the howling wind catch him and throw him towards the overlord. He drew back his arm, and drove it forwards as he fell onto the overlord.

His fist, clutching the bundle of cables, punched into the overlord's chest. The scarab split down the middle, and Sarpedon's fist drove deep into the machinery inside.

The life force still flowing through the cables discharged in a tremendous blast of raw energy, directly into the overlord's body. Systems overloaded, and capacitors burst with the sudden flood of power. Sarpedon was thrown by the force of the shock, clattering along the ground, his senses full of light and noise.

The overlord's anti-grav units ruptured, spraying green fire, and it tipped onto one side as it fell. It dropped its scythe and clawed at its chest, metal coming away under its claws.

Sarpedon learned that even a face with no features, with just a pair of burning eyes and an expanse of blank silver, could still register panic.

The overlord's chest exploded. Green liquid fire sprayed from the ruptured stump of its spine. Chunks of carapace banged off the walls, trailing flame.

Sarpedon shook the static out of his head. The overlord's body flickered with flame. One hand, still attached by a bent length of metal, flopped to the floor.

The overlord's skull had come to rest nearby. Sarpedon hauled himself to his feet and stamped on it, slicing it in two with the talon of one foreleg.

The wind had died along with the overlord. The other Soul Drinkers were making it into the heart chamber, bolters trained on the overlord's remains.

'Is it dead?' asked Captain Luko, his lightning claws unsheathed just in case.

'Yes,' said Sarpedon.

'What's going on back there?' came a vox from Sergeant Salk. 'The Undying just broke formation. It's as if they're blind.'

'The intelligence is dead,' said Sarpedon. 'There's nothing guiding them.'

'In that case, advancing,' replied Salk.

The bolter fire became thicker as Salk and his men advanced through the labyrinth, shooting down the necrons whose resistance suddenly fell apart, their tactics reduced to individual random movements.

Sarpedon looked back at the ruptured heart. Tangles of flesh-ribbed cabling lay around the cradle in which the overlord had slept, shaped something like a number of metal hoops, slick with greyish gore, strung with the wires that had held the overlord curled up like the larva of some giant insect. The freezing winds had left the flesh dead and whitish, caked in flecks of ice.

A thousand tiny silvery spiders swarmed from the dead petals, scurrying like a carpet of blades. Sarpedon hurried back as they approached, their tiny pin-like legs clicking along the metal floor.

They flowed over the body of the overlord. A group of them broke off and picked up the skull, and, before Sarpedon could reach it, they had brought it over to the rest of the body.

'Flamers!' shouted Sarpedon. 'Flamers forward!'

The head was back on the body. Sarpedon tried to grab it and wrench it back off, but the overlord's hand shot up and gripped his wrist.

The flame of its eyes lit up again. Liquid metal flowed into tentacles that reached from the overlord's ruptured breastplate. Its ruined, lopsided skull seemed to grin as it self-repaired and yanked Sarpedon off his feet again.

'When the battle is won, your work is not done. Your duty is not a destination. It is a journey. Victory is merely a landmark on that road. You will never reach a time when your work is done and you can leave the fighting to another. You will die with the road still to be walked.'

– Daenyathos, *Examinations Upon Duty*

CHAPTER EIGHTEEN

Lygris ran across the chamber just as the gunfire started.

He had seen the ruined body of the necron overlord, and had known that it was not over. A creature like that would not place the future of its existence in the fallible hands of a single physical vessel. The overlord that Sarpedon had fought was just a weapon, a machine under the creature's control. Its mind was something else entirely.

The Soul Drinkers opened fire, but the overlord dripped with bright silver liquid metal, and every bullet scar healed instantly. Sarpedon was held in close, the overlord trying to crush him or twist his head off. The Soul Drinkers were good enough shots not to hit their Chapter Master, but the overlord was shielding its head and torso, just waiting for its weapons to solidify from the mass of shimmering quicksilver growing from its back.

They would keep it busy. That was all Lygris needed.

Lygris reached the overlord's open sarcophagus, his feet crunching through layers of frozen flesh. The dataprobe slid from his finger. Inside the sarcophagus, nestling between the torn petals of muscle, was a column of black metal that ended in a complex shape like an open hand with clawed fingers, each claw ending in a jack that fitted into the back of the overlord's skull.

Lygris glanced back at the battle behind him. The overlord was a mass of silver tentacles, the resources of the cradle waking up just in time to arm him with more weapons every second. Sarpedon would be dead soon.

Lygris inserted the probe and let his mind drop away from his body.

The harvesting machine had been a crude cage of simple orders. The tomb-city had been a towering ziggurat of unholy light. The overlord's mind, the intelligence that commanded the necrons of the Veiled Region, was something that could not even fit into a metaphor conjured by Lygris's mind. There was no way it could make sense.

It was a storm of knives; a sea of hate; an erupting star of time, spewing the future, cold and metallic, into aeons to come.

There was just enough left of Lygris's soul to scream out a last note of defiance. Then, he let it take him over, and he prepared to spend the last moments of his life causing as much damage as he could to the overlord's mind.

The grip on Sarpedon's throat tightened.

The silvery limb wrapped around his neck, choking the life out of him. Other limbs, like silver snakes, snared his waist and arms. He was about to die.

Then, suddenly, its strength was gone.

Sarpedon turned around and planted a foreleg in the overlord's chest. He pushed off it, ripping silver tentacles away, and landed free of its grasp on the floor.

The light in the overlord's eyes was going out. The fresh bullet holes in its carapace were not self-repairing. Silver spiders fell from between the joints of its body, shedding like scales that plinked onto the floor.

The anti-grav motors died down, and the overlord's body sank to the floor. The final lights went out in its eye sockets, and its limbs and skull hung limply. It toppled over, and clattered onto one side.

There was no sound, save the faint hiss of the overlord's capacitors cooling down. Even the cables and conduits carrying the Selaacans' life force were turning dull.

Sarpedon watched the overlord for a long moment. Soul Drinkers advanced to stand beside him, guns trained on the machine's corpse.

Out of the corner of his eye, Sarpedon noticed movement. It was Lygris, lying in the remains of the biomechanical sarcophagus. He was convulsing. Sarpedon ran to him, and pulled his dataprobe out of the interface the overlord had used to direct the necron armies.

'Lygris! Brother!'

Lygris did not reply. Sarpedon turned his head over. The Techmarine's eyes had rolled back and were blank.

'Lygris,' said Sarpedon, 'it is done. The foe is dead. Share in this victory. Speak, brother! Speak!'

Pallas was at Sarpedon's side. His medicae gauntlet snickered open and a needle emerged. He inserted it into the port in the neck of Lygris's armour.

'His heart has stopped,' said Pallas. The gauntlet hissed as it injected a hefty dose of adrenaline into Lygris's veins. 'Nothing.'

The other Soul Drinkers were gathering. They were all battered by the overlord's onslaught. Some had broken limbs, or were clutching bloody rents in their armour. They stood in a circle around Sarpedon and Lygris, and none of them spoke.

Pallas's gauntlet injected Lygris again. He pulled off Lygris's helmet and held one of the Techmarine's eyes open with his finger, but it had rolled back and was blank. Blood ran from the tear duct.

Sarpedon watched.

'Brother,' he said. 'Do the Emperor's work. Stay alive.'

Sometimes, an Astartes could stay dead for a long time without a heartbeat, far longer than a normal man, and survive, sitting bolt upright and sputtering back to life with a new reason to seek revenge. Lygris did not.

'The necrons have broken off their attack,' voxed Salk from the labyrinth. 'They're in disarray.'

'Hold position,' voxed Sarpedon. He looked from Lygris to Pallas.

'Our brother,' said Pallas, 'is gone.'

Sarpedon closed Lygris's eyes.

'Take his gene-seed,' he said to Pallas.

The Soul Drinkers were silent. They had lost brothers before, friends and fellow warriors, irreplaceable and much missed, but they had never known a loss like this. Lygris had been there from the start. He was part of the Chapter's soul.

Luko stepped forwards from the assembled Soul Drinkers.

'He will join the Emperor at the end of time,' he said, 'and fight on.'

'We will join him there,' echoed Tyrendian. 'No brother is ever lost. He fights on a different battlefield now.'

'We all will,' said Sarpedon. He closed Lygris's eyes. 'In death he has avenged himself on these aliens. There will be time to mourn our brother when we have left this world. I will carry him. We must make haste back to the *Antithesis*.' Sarpedon switched vox-channels. 'Sarpedon to Voar. What is your situation? The xenos leader is dead. Come in, Voar!'

He heard nothing in reply but static.

'The tech-guard may have been overrun. Luko, Graevus, take the point. The rest, stay close. We're breaking out.'

Sarpedon hefted Lygris's body onto his shoulder, and the Soul Drinkers advanced.

* * *

Chaplain Iktinos stood surrounded by the bodies of his flock. The Undying had kept coming, thousands of them, but the flock had held firm and sold their lives for a price the Undying could not pay. The Soul Drinkers that still lived at the gate breach were a tiny island in the sea of alien steel, but they had not taken one step back.

The aliens faltered. Their relentless advance stumbled, in many cases literally, the warriors losing all coordination and sprawling uncontrollably onto the bloodstained ground. The monoliths ground to a halt, and their guns lowered and fell silent.

Iktinos clambered on top of the bodies and looked through the gates. The whole Undying army was milling aimlessly, its individual warriors reverting to crude placeholder programs that had them patrolling at random, firing ill-coordinated blasts up at the walls.

One of the surviving flock clambered over to Iktinos. His name was Brother Sarkis, and he had lost most of his leg, flayed away to the thigh. He changed the magazine of his bolter as he paused to draw breath.

'Chaplain,' he said. 'What has happened?'

'Sarpedon has been victorious,' said Iktinos. He switched to the vox-net of the Raevenian army. 'Sons of Raevenia! The Undying have been broken. Their minds are addled and their wills broken. Strike now, for Raevenia! Strike for your queen!'

The reserves broke cover and ran forwards, the foremost shouting war cries to spur their fellow soldiers on. The men taking cover on the walls emerged from shelter and brought their guns to bear on the Undying again. The few survivors of the command tower, bloody and ragged officers forming a crowd of walking wounded at a triage station, decided, as one man, to join in the final routing of the Undying.

For the sons of Raevenia, it must have been a glorious moment, one they would speak of for generations, and that would adorn works of art and fanciful histories long into their future.

None of that mattered to Iktinos.

They swarmed past Iktinos and his surviving flock. Gunfire hammered relentlessly, and the Undying fell in their hundreds, like cattle penned in to be slaughtered by Raevenian fire.

Less than a dozen of Iktinos's flock lived. They gathered around him now, most of them wounded, some hauling themselves up from beneath the bodies of the dead. They had all once been battle-brothers of the Soul Drinkers, but now they were something else, their personalities subsumed to Iktinos's. They served him now, and, through him, his master.

'I have brought us here,' said Iktinos, 'and we live. Thus has our victory been won. On this dismal and distant soil, we have sown the seed of mankind's future. We may not live to see the future unfold, but have faith, my brothers, that it will come to pass! The words of the prophet will out! His will shall be the truth!'

Iktinos's flock bowed their heads and knelt among the dead, the ground beneath them consecrated by the blood of their fallen brothers.

Iktinos took his copy of the *Catechisms Martial*, the manual of war written by the Philosopher-Soldier Daenyathos, from where it hung by a link of chain from the belt of his armour. He held it up to his chest, over his primary heart, and bowed his head in prayer.

'We may not survive what is to come,' said Iktinos. 'Those we once called brothers, the hunting dogs of the corrupt Imperium, may not see fit to spare our lives. It matters not. For him, what we have sought here will be found. He who has directed us, who has written out the future history of the galaxy for us to read, his will shall prevail. We have served! And so we, too, shall prevail!'

The Soul Drinkers at the gate clutched their own copies of the *Catechisms Martial* as they chanted.

'We shall prevail!'

The Soul Drinkers advanced at a run through the tomb-city. Gun smoke was heavy in the air, tinted by the unnatural haze of burned alien metals.

The necrons had scattered. They fell before volleys of bolter fire and a few well-placed chainblade thrusts from Graevus's squad. They were roaming at random through the remains of the tomb-city, even the ornate necron lords stumbling blind. Like those in the labyrinth before them, they were unable to mount a defence against the Soul Drinkers.

There was no sign of Voar and his magi, save for the bodies of the fallen tech-guard, draped in pools of blood over the wrecked tombs.

'Where in the hells are the Mechanicus?' snarled Luko. His body language suggested he would rather the necrons mount a proper defence, so he could get his claws into some metal.

'They fled,' said Sarpedon, still carrying Techmarine Lygris's body on his shoulders. 'Or were captured.'

'No survivors?' asked Graevus up ahead. 'No communications?'

'Let us hope,' said Tyrendian bleakly, 'that they did not take the *Antithesis's* transport craft with them.'

The Soul Drinkers crossed the threshold of the tunnel leading up from the tomb-city. The tunnels were similarly devoid of decent resistance. Graevus's squad cut down the few necron warriors that came towards them out of the blackness, or shot isolated scarabs off the walls.

'Voar,' voxed Sarpedon. 'Come in! Where are you?'

There was still no reply. Even as the Soul Drinkers approached the surface, the tech-guard's vox-channels were empty.

Sarpedon watched the battle-brothers around him as they covered the tunnel ahead of them and behind them. Every Astartes was battered, and many were wounded. There was not one who did not have a chunk of his armour flayed or sliced away. A few could not move on their own, and were supported by their battle-brothers. The force that marched towards the opening that led to Selaaca's fallen capital numbered barely one hundred Soul Drinkers. Even if Iktinos's force had survived on Raevenia unscathed, Sarpedon commanded little more than one-tenth of the Chapter's original strength. A Chapter under the Imperial yoke could expect to be disbanded with such irrecoverable losses, and added to the long list of Chapters that had been destroyed in the long war since the Age of Imperium began.

Sarpedon would not let the enormity of that hit him, not yet. There would be time to consider the Chapter's future later. For now, they had to rendezvous with Voar, if he was still alive, and get off Selaaca.

The ruins of Selaaca's capital became visible at the end of the tunnel. A few bursts of bolter fire shattered the scarabs still clinging to the walls and ceiling. The deep wound in the earth and the pall of smoke from the crash-landing pointed towards the resting place of the *Antithesis*, which Voar had assured Sarpedon contained enough transport craft and fast fighters to get the Soul Drinkers off the planet.

Sarpedon directed the Soul Drinkers to a ridge overlooking the stricken spacecraft, several hundred metres away. The battle-brothers formed up along the ridge, watching the approaches to the spaceship warily.

'Voar, come in,' voxed Sarpedon again, tapping into the ship's vox-net. 'We're making our approach to you. Acknowledge.'

'Still nothing?' asked Luko.

'Nothing.'

'Then we go in?'

'Yes. All Soul Drinkers,' ordered Sarpedon, 'approach in line! Expect resistance!'

As if in reply to his words, a blue-white lance of energy tore down from Selaaca's sky, and speared the *Antithesis* amidships. The sound was appalling, a shriek of superheated air ripping through the city. The ground shuddered, and ruins tumbled, bringing down necron structures, and revealing the raw stone of the fallen city through the wounds that opened up.

'Down!' yelled Sarpedon. 'Take cover!' He threw himself down on the reverse slope of the ridge, rolling Lygris's body off his shoulder to the ground by his side.

Chain reactions ripped through the hull of the *Antithesis*. The ship was hundreds of metres long, and, though double that length lay between it and the Soul Drinkers, the ground beneath them shook like an earthquake. Fissures opened up in the ruins, sending the remnants of Selaacan buildings and necron structures alike falling into the networks of tombs and warrior forges below. A flare of plasma ripped up into the sky from the ship's engines, and another chain of explosions tore right through the heart of the ship, rippling up the side of the hull and bursting its sides. Broadside guns and chunks of deck flew trailing flames. Bolts of molten metal fell in a searing rain, sizzling against the ceramite armour of the Soul Drinkers. The sound was tremendous, like the roar of a stormy ocean amplified a thousand times.

The din died down, but the heat rolled over the ridge, hot enough to scald the lungs. Sarpedon pulled himself up to the edge of the ridge so that he could see.

Over the course of several minutes and hundreds of explosions, the *Antithesis* was utterly torn apart. The final chain of detonations blew off its prow, and molten metal flowed from its severed neck in a red-black torrent, like thick gore from a massive wound. The ground below it sagged with the heat billowing out of the wreck, and, as it dissolved away, the huge charred hull sections began to sink.

Sarpedon looked up at the sky. The afterglow of the attack still flickered in the thin atmosphere. Only one force could do that to the wreck of the *Antithesis*. It had been an orbital strike, from a spacecraft flying high above them.

Sarpedon didn't have to say anything. All the Soul Drinkers knew what the loss of the *Antithesis* meant. They were stranded on Selaaca.

Sarpedon clambered back onto the reverse slope, and slid down onto his back.

'The necrons?' voxed Captain Luko.

'I don't think so,' said Sarpedon. 'That was a lance strike. Imperium tech.'

The sound of engines broke Sarpedon's concentration. He looked up to see three Thunderhawk gunships circling around the mushroom of smoke pumping from the wrecked spaceship. They were not Soul Drinkers craft. They were painted a deep golden yellow, with the image of a clenched fist stencilled on their sides and tail fins.

'Blessed Throne,' hissed Luko. 'What are they doing here?'

'Draw back! Defensive positions!' ordered Sarpedon.

The Soul Drinkers moved rapidly, Sarpedon pausing only to heft Lygris's corpse back onto his shoulder. The ruins of a civic building rose from the bottom of the slope, half-buried in debris from the necron excavation of the tunnel. Statues of the planet's dignitaries, missing heads or limbs, stood guard outside an empty doorway that lead to a half-collapsed dome. Soul Drinkers took up positions in the doorway, and behind the drums of fallen columns half-buried in the earth.

The Thunderhawks' engines got louder as they came down to land, vanishing just out of sight of the Soul Drinkers' position.

Salk was beside Sarpedon, in cover behind a length of fallen wall.

'We are betrayed, commander,' he said.

Sarpedon looked at the sergeant.

'We are,' he said.

Yellow-armoured Astartes were advancing into sight. Each Thunderhawk had carried about thirty Space Marines, so, an almost company-strength force surrounded the Soul Drinkers' positions with their bolters levelled at the ruins.

'Fists,' snarled Luko.

The Imperial Fists had once been a brother Chapter of the Soul Drinkers, both having been created from the Imperial Fists Legion following the Horus Heresy. They had the same primarch, Rogal Dorn, and many times before the Soul Drinkers had broken from Imperial rule, the two Chapters had fought, feasted and planned campaigns together.

'Give the order,' voxed Luko.

'Hold your fire,' ordered Sarpedon. 'All Soul Drinkers! Hold your fire until my order!'

'They will surround us,' said Tyrendian. 'Strike at them, cold and fast, as Daenyathos wrote!'

'No!' snapped Sarpedon over the vox. 'I will not die down here, not after all we have achieved! An Astartes' bolter is not a fit weapon to take the life of a Soul Drinker! Do not give your lives so cheaply!'

'We can take them, commander,' said Luko.

'Hold your fire!' barked Sarpedon again over the vox. 'That is an order!'

The air split and crackled in front of the main force. With a sound like tearing silk, reality burst open for a moment, and, suddenly, twenty Astartes in golden-yellow Terminator armour were standing in front of them: First Company Astartes, elites, wearing the ancient suits of Terminator armour their Chapter had carefully maintained since the days of the Great Crusade.

Their leader was bare-headed, a giant brute of a man with a blunt, solid face, a shaven head and several metal studs in his forehead. His ornate armour was emblazoned with images of stylised fists and lightning bolts. In one hand was a thunder hammer too large for even most Soul Drinkers to wield, and on the other was a shield bearing the heraldry of the First Company.

'Damnation,' said Sarpedon as he caught sight of the officer.

'You know him?' asked Luko.

'By reputation.'

The officer strode forwards, covered by the bolters of more than a hundred Imperial Fists.

'I am First Captain Lysander of the Imperial Fists,' shouted the Terminator officer. 'I am here to take you and your men into custody. I have the entire Third Company and half the First at my disposal, and guns in orbit trained on your position. As a fellow Astartes, I am willing to give you death in battle if you so choose, but if you resist, you will die. Make your choice.'

Lysander was a legend among the Astartes, especially the Imperial Fists and their successor Chapters, of which the Soul Drinkers were one. He was relentless and stubborn. When the battle needed a man who would stand firm and never break, and force the same out of his men, the Imperium had few better than Lysander.

He was also a man of his word. If he said he would wipe out the Soul Drinkers, he would do it.

Sarpedon looked between the Soul Drinkers sheltering in the ruins. If he ordered them to fight, they would fight. They would all die if he did that, to a man, for the wrath of betrayed battle-brothers was too powerful a force to spare any of them. At least then it would be over, and they would all have the peace that Luko had spoken of.

'It will not end like this,' said Sarpedon, but he was speaking to himself.

'Sarpedon!' shouted Lysander. 'Traitor and mutant! Show yourself!'

Sarpedon strode out of the doorway, his mutant form plain to see for the Imperial Fists whose guns focused on him. He saw their sergeants and captains, the Astartes carrying heavy bolters and missile launchers among their ranks, the dozens of bolters trained on him, all of them ready to turn him into a cloud of burning ceramite at Lysander's order.

'You are a disgrace,' said Lysander, 'to your Imperium and to your primarch.'

'It is the Emperor and the primarchs who are disgraced,' replied Sarpedon, 'by the corruption of the Imperium that has come to be.'

'Still you blaspheme!' retorted Lysander. 'Still you defy! My orders are to take you and your renegades in alive, but there will be few angry words spoken should I bring you in dead. One final time, down arms and surrender, and you will live long enough to appreciate that your deaths will be quick.'

Sarpedon scanned the troops behind Lysander once more. Among them, he spotted a figure dwarfed by the terminators, flanking the Imperial Fists captain, a normal-sized human, wearing the red robes of the Mechanicus.

'Voar!' shouted Sarpedon. 'You have betrayed us!'

'Did you expect anything less?' replied Voar calmly. He stepped forwards from between two of Lysander's Terminators, and pulled his hood back to reveal his almost-human face. 'Our alliance was a matter of expediency for both of us. As soon as I learned that we faced the Soul Drinkers, I contacted their fleet, which helped secure our journey to the Veiled Region. The path we forged through the Veiled Region was theirs to follow. Did you truly believe that a servant of the Omnissiah would not have seen the consequences of our alliance, and prepared accordingly? Do you think a servant of the Imperium and a scion of Mars could ally with renegades and mutants on your terms?'

'I expected nothing less,' replied Sarpedon, 'but my hatred of the xenos overcame that. What galaxy is this where I and my brothers are despised even more than the alien?'

'Enough words!' roared Lysander. 'Make your choice, Sarpedon!'

Sarpedon switched to the vox. Lysander would not hear him.

'Luko,' he voxed. 'If I fall, down weapons and surrender.'

'Surrender?' replied Luko. 'Commander, what are you...'

'Captain,' said Sarpedon, 'I trust you with what may be my last order. As an Astartes, as my battle-brother, execute it as I command.'

Sarpedon unfastened the seals on his helmet and took it off his head, casting it into the rubble and dust at his feet, so that he was face to face with Lysander. He took the Axe of Mercaeno off his back.

'If you want my Chapter,' he said, 'you will have to come and take it.'

Lysander smiled.

'There is some shadow of honour in you yet, mutant,' he said.

Lysander strode forwards, and Sarpedon advanced to meet him. The toxic atmosphere of Selaaca was raw in Sarpedon's throat, his augmented lungs fighting to make it breathable. It was worth it to look into Lysander's eyes.

'Hold your fire,' voxed Lysander to the Imperial Fists. He closed off the vox-link. 'What possessed you?' he said. 'What could make an Astartes forsake the Imperium he is sworn to defend?'

'I saw it for what it truly was,' replied Sarpedon.

'Duty to the Imperium,' said Lysander, 'must blind a man to its ills.'

'If you believe that,' said Sarpedon, 'then you will always be my enemy.'

Lysander hefted his hammer over his head, and roared as he slammed it down. Sarpedon jinked back, smacking the haft of the hammer aside with his axe. The impact of the hammer hitting the ground and discharging its power field threw Sarpedon onto his back talons, and he stumbled back as he tried to bear his weight on the leg he had lost to the necron overlord.

Lysander saw the opening. He swept the hammer in a massive arc, and slammed the head into Sarpedon's chest. Sarpedon was lifted off his feet and thrown back, tumbling end over end in the dust. Lysander darted forwards to finish him off, and the hammer arced down again.

Sarpedon rolled to one side, and the hammer pounded the ground beside him. Lysander rammed his shield into Sarpedon, and threw him back again. Sarpedon rolled to his feet, and the two Astartes faced one another again.

The breastplate of Sarpedon's armour was dented and smouldering. He had fought his way into the tomb and out again, and the mauling from the necron overlord had left him slower and weaker than before. His limbs felt heavy, and every movement hurt. Lysander was fresh to battle, and had come ready for a fight. Sarpedon could tell from the look in the Imperial Fist's eyes that he was enjoying this.

The two Astartes circled, sizing one another up for the next strike.

'Half the Second Company is arriving at Raevenia as we speak,' said Lysander with relish. 'If your Chaplain lives, we will have him in custody within the hour, your space hulk, too. It is over, Sarpedon. Your Chapter ceases to exist on this day.'

'Then you will have the Soulspear, too,' replied Sarpedon. 'It is in a void-safe in the armoury of the *Brokenback*. I trust you will take better care of it than the Mechanicus.'

'Blasphemer!' yelled Lysander.

Sarpedon ducked under the arcing blow of Lysander's hammer, and drove the axe up into Lysander's chest. The head of the axe tore through the ceramite of Lysander's armour, throwing sparks of power.

For a second, the two were locked together, Sarpedon fighting to wrench the axe from Lysander's armour. Lysander forced Sarpedon closer with his shield, and headbutted Sarpedon on the bridge of the nose.

Sarpedon reeled. He fell, leaving the Axe of Mercaeno embedded in Lysander's breastplate. He tried to get to his feet, but the hammer knocked his many legs from under him, and he sprawled to the ground again.

Lysander planted an armoured foot on the backpack of Sarpedon's armour, forcing him down into the dust. The lower edge of Lysander's shield pressed down on the back of Sarpedon's neck. Sarpedon could not move, pinned to the ground.

'If you expected an execution here and now, Sarpedon,' said Lysander, 'then I am pleased to disappoint you. Your death will serve as an example to the Imperium of the wages of betrayal. My Chapter's executioners will extract their debt in full view of Rogal Dorn, when we take you to the *Phalanx* and proclaim your crimes to the galaxy.'

Sarpedon could not reply. There were no words left. He looked up at the ruins where the Soul Drinkers were sheltering, and he prayed silently that Luko would do the right thing.

Lysander raised his shield, and slammed it down on the back of Sarpedon's skull. Blackness fell over his eyes and consciousness left him.

The last thought Sarpedon had was of his Chapter in chains, and of the sentence of death that would fall on them when the Imperium found them guilty.

PHALANX

CHAPTER ONE

Its like had never been built before, and would never be built again. The secrets of its construction dated from before the foundation of the Imperium of Man, its immense golden form crafted by engineers dead long before the Emperor first united Holy Terra.

The hull of the ship was many kilometres long, its upper surface bristling with weapons and sensorium domes, trailing directional vanes like long gilded feathers. Every surface was clad in solid armour plating and every angle was covered by more torpedo tubes and lance batteries than any Imperial battleship could muster. Countless smaller craft, repair craft and unmanned scouts, orbited like supplicants jostling for attention, and the wake of the titanic engines seemed to churn the void itself with the force of its plasma fire.

The fist symbol emblazoned on the prow was taller than the length of most Imperial spacecraft, proudly claiming that the ship belonged to the Imperial Fists Chapter, one of the most storied Space Marine Chapters in the history of the Imperium. The pale light of the star Kravamesh, and the lesser glow of the Veiled Region's boiling nebulae, played across thousands of battle-honours and campaign markings all over the beak-like prow. The ship had carried the Imperial Fists since the Horus Heresy, and its eagle-shaped shadow had fallen across a hundred worlds that had later shuddered under the weight of a massed Fists assault.

This was the *Phalanx*. Bigger than any ship in the Imperial Navy, it was a mobile battle station the size of a city, that dwarfed any Space Marine

Chapter's mightiest battle-barge. It might have been the most powerful engine of destruction in the Imperium. It was a symbol of mankind's very right to live in the stars. Its most potent weapon was the sheer awe that the golden eagle inspired when it appeared in the night sky over a rebellious world.

The *Phalanx* at that moment was not at war, but it was there for a conflict just as bitter. It was to be the seat of a trial at which the soul of a Chapter would be weighed, a stain on the Imperial Fists' honour would be cleansed and retribution would fall as sternly as if it had rained down from the *Phalanx*'s guns.

There was no doubt among the Imperial Fists that their mission was as vital to the Imperium as any crusade. For it was on the *Phalanx* that the Soul Drinkers would surely die.

'You will wish,' said the castellan of the Imperial Fists, 'that you still called us brother.'

The castellan seemed to fill the cell, even though it had been built to accommodate a Space Marine's dimensions. Its walls were plated in gold, studded with diamonds and rubies in the shape of the constellations across which the *Phalanx* had carried its Chapter in countless crusades. The channels cut into the floor formed intricate scrollwork. Even the drain for bodily fluids was in the shape of an open hand, echoing the fist symbol that was everywhere on board.

The castellan nodded to one of the Chapter functionaries through the small slit window. The functionary, a shaven-headed, drab man in a dark yellow uniform, activated a few controls on his side of the wall and the Pain Glove apparatus shuddered as power flowed into it.

Brother Kaiyon hung in the Pain Glove. He had been stripped of his armour, and the input ports set into the black carapace beneath the skin of his chest were hooked up to bundles of cables hanging from the ceiling. The Pain Glove itself resembled some strange mollusc, a lumpy, phlegmy membrane that covered Kaiyon from neck to ankle. It writhed against his skin, as if trying to ascertain the shape of its captive by touch.

'This one,' he said, 'was one of the flock.' The castellan's words were no longer directed at Brother Kaiyon. 'He was broken-minded even before we brought them here. I think, my lord, that he will either tell all, or be broken to gibberish.'

'You take eagerly to your task, noble castellan,' came a voice in reply from the room's vox-caster. It was an old and experienced voice, almost wearied with knowledge. 'So ready a hand at the tormentor's tools would be a sin in any but one of your responsibilities.'

The castellan smiled. 'That, my lord Chapter Master, is as high a compliment as I could hope to hear.'

The castellan's armour was crenellated like the battlements of a castle around its collar and the edges of its shoulder pads, and the vents around his torso echoed tall, pointed windows or arrow slits. He looked like a walking fortress, even the greaves around his shins resembling the buttresses of two towers on which he walked. His face was branded with a grid pattern – a portcullis, a forbidding entrance to the fortification he represented.

Kaiyon's face was scarred, too. The Space Marine seemed unconscious, but he proclaimed all his allegiances in the chalice symbols he had carved into himself. His scalp was red with raised channels of scar tissue. Though the rest of his body was hidden in the Pain Glove, the castellan knew that the rest of Kaiyon told the same story. Kaiyon was a Soul Drinker. He had written that fact into his flesh.

'I know,' said the castellan to Kaiyon, 'that you are awake. You can hear me, Kaiyon. Know, then, that nothing you do here, no token effort of resistance, will gain you anything whatsoever. Not even the satisfaction of delaying me, or frustrating my intentions to break you. These things mean nothing to me. The mightiest of fortresses will fall, though we can chip away but a grain of sand at a time. The end result is the same. Your Chapter has secrets. The flock of Iktinos has secrets. I will have those secrets. This is a truth as inevitable as your own mortality.'

Kaiyon did not speak. The castellan walked right up to Kaiyon, face to face.

The Soul Drinker's eye was slitted. He was watching the castellan, and even in that tiny sliver of an eye, the castellan could see his hate.

'What,' said the Chapter Master over the vox, 'if this one does not talk?'

'There are others,' replied the castellan. 'More than twenty of the surviving Soul Drinkers are members of this flock. I'll wager you'll have your answers with twenty renegades to break.'

'So long as Chaplain Iktinos himself is not reduced thus,' replied the Chapter Master. 'I wish him in possession of all his faculties for the trial. Justice is a mockery when it is administered on one already forsaken by sanity.'

'Of course, my lord,' said the castellan. 'It will not come to that.'

'Good,' said the Chapter Master. 'Then proceed, brother castellan.'

The vox-link went dead. The Chapter Master, as was traditional, need not witness this least delicate of the castellan's duties. The castellan gestured to the crewman at the controls, and a metal panel slid shut over the slit window.

'You have,' said the castellan, circling Kaiyon, 'one final chance.'

Kaiyon's hate did not falter.

'You understand, I must make this offer. I know as well as you do, between us two Space Marines, that it has no meaning. There are traditional forms that must be followed.'

The castellan flicked a few switches on the control console mounted on the wall, one from which snaked the wired now hooked up to the interfaces in Kaiyon's body. The Pain Glove slithered over him as if agitated.

The Pain Glove was a complex device. Controlling its many variables was akin to directing an orchestra, with great skill required in keeping every variable in harmony. Just a taste of the Pain Glove was enough to break normal men. A Space Marine required far more finesse – the Pain Glove was even used as a conditioning tool for the Chapter's novices in its less intense configurations.

The castellan was a maestro with the device. The membrane excreted chemicals that laid open every nerve ending on every millimetre of skin. The pulses of power humming through the cables stimulated every one of them into extremity.

Brother Kaiyon, in that moment, discovered just how much it took to make a Space Marine scream.

What will the universe remember of us? wrote Sarpedon.

What does it matter our deeds, the principles of our character, if it is the memory of the human race that matters? The future for us, when we are gone, is surely determined not by our deeds but by what is remembered of our deeds, by the lies told about us as much as by the truths of our actions.

Sarpedon put the quill down. The Imperial Fists had taken his armour and his weapons, and even the bionic which had replaced one of his eight arachnid legs. But they had left him with the means to write. It was a matter of principle that this cell, even though it was windowless and cramped, and allowed him no communication with his fellow Soul Drinkers, had a quill, a desk and a pot of ink. He was to defend himself before a court of his peers. He was at least entitled to the means to prepare his defence. They had left him his copy of the *Catechisms Martial*, too, the manual of the Soul Drinkers' principles and tactics authored by the legendary Philosopher-Soldier Daenyathos.

Sarpedon thought for a few long minutes. The pages of parchment in front of him were supposed to hold every argument he might make to justify his actions. Instead, he had poured out every thought into them in the hope that at least he would understand what he thought.

The galaxy will not think well of us, he wrote. *We are traitors and heretics. We are mutants. Should truth have any value in itself then it will do us no good, for these things are true. My own mutations are so grotesque that I wonder if there will be anything thought of me at all, for there is little room in any man's recollection for anything but this monstrous form.*

What does it matter what the galaxy thinks of us when we are gone? It is the only thing that matters at all. For we will surely die here. There is only one sentence that our brethren can lay upon us, and that is death. I must take what solace I can from what we will leave behind, yet there can be no solace in the story the Imperium will tell of the Soul Drinkers. Those who can will forget us. Those who cannot will hate us. Though I seek some victory for myself and my battle-brothers even in this, I can find none.

Perhaps one of my brethren can draw something other than defeat from our situation. I cannot. I look deeper into my heart than I have ever done, and I find nothing but failure and desolation.

Sarpedon looked over what he had written. It disgusted him. He screwed up the parchment and threw it into a corner of the cell. A Space Marine did not succumb to self-pity, no matter how true his failure seemed to him. He would lie to himself if that was what it took.

A gauntleted hand boomed against the cell door. Sarpedon looked round to see a window being drawn back to reveal a face he had last seen on the surface of Selaaca, looming over him as he lost consciousness. It was the face of Captain Darnath Lysander of the Imperial Fists First Company, a legend of the Fists and the man who had bested Sarpedon to take the Soul Drinkers into custody.

'I trust,' said Sarpedon, 'your captive is a wretched as you hoped.'

'Bitterness becomes not a Space Marine,' replied Lysander. 'I take no joy in the fall of another Space Marine. I have come not to gloat, if that is how low you think of me. I have come to give you the chance to confess.'

'Confess?' said Sarpedon. 'With no thumbscrews? With my skin still on my frame?'

'Do not play games,' snapped Lysander. 'We took those you call the flock; those who follow your Chaplain Iktinos. Their minds were broken before we ever took them in. Whatever influence your Chaplain had on them, it changed them. One of them has broken in the Pain Glove, and told us everything. Brother Kaiyon is his name. He thought the Lord castellan was Rogal Dorn himself, and spoke your Chapter's secrets to him as if the primarch had demanded it.'

'I have heard of your Pain Glove,' said Sarpedon.

'Then you know it is a part of the initiations every Imperial Fist has undergone. I myself have been subject to it. It served no more than to shake Brother Kaiyon out of the state the flock have fallen into since their incarceration here. He is insane, Sarpedon. He spoke through madness, not pain, and that madness was not our doing.'

'Then he could have spoken lies in his madness,' retorted Sarpedon.

'He could,' replied Lysander. 'My Chapter is even now ascertaining the truth of his words. This is why I have come here. If you confess, and that confession matches what Kaiyon had told us and can be proven true, then there may be some leniency won for your compliance.'

'Leniency?' Sarpedon rose up on his haunches. He had originally had eight legs, arranged like those of an arachnid, spreading from his waist.

He had lost one on an unnamed world, ripped off by a champion of the Dark Gods. Another had been lost on Selaaca, mangled in his fight with the necron overlord of that dead world. He still had six, and when he rose to his full height he towered over even Lysander. 'You talk to me of leniency? There is not one Imperial Fist who will abide anything but our execution! Our death sentence was decided the moment we surrendered!'

'Ours is a Chapter with honour!' shouted Lysander. 'Your trial is more than a mere formality. It is our intention to see every correct procedure and tradition adhered to, so that no man dare say we did not give you every chance to redeem yourselves. You will die, yes; I cannot lie to you about that. But there are many ways to die, and many matters of honour that can accompany your death. If you deserve a good death then you and your battle-brothers shall receive it. You can win a better death if you tell us now what we shall soon discover. Deceit, however, will win you nothing but suffering.'

Sarpedon sank back down to his haunches. He could not think what Kaiyon might have told the Imperial Fists interrogators. The Fists knew the Soul Drinkers were mutants – one glance at Sarpedon was enough to tell them that. The Fists had collected evidence of the Soul Drinkers' deeds, including many that had pitted them against the forces of the Imperium from which the Soul Drinkers had rebelled. He could think of nothing more damaging than any of that.

But what had happened to the flock? They were the Soul Drinkers whose officers had died in the gradual erosion of the Chapter's strength, and who had turned to Chaplain Iktinos for leadership. They had become intense and inspired under Iktinos, but insane? Sarpedon did not know what to make of it.

'I don't know what Kaiyon told you,' he said to Lysander. 'Good luck with confirming his words. I doubt whatever you find can make our fate any worse.'

'So be it, Sarpedon,' said Lysander. 'The trials will begin soon. The fate of your Chapter rests in no little part on what you will have to say to yourself. I suggest you think on it, if you believe your brothers deserve more than a common heretic's death.'

'I have nothing to say,' said Sarpedon. 'Certainly nothing that will change any fate you have in mind for me.'

'I could have executed you on Selaaca,' said Lysander. 'Remember that the next time you bemoan your fate.'

The window slammed shut. Lysander was correct. He had defeated Sarpedon face to face on Selaaca and few servants of the Imperium would have had any compunction about killing him out of hand.

Sarpedon turned back to the desk and took up the quill again.

I have seen, he wrote, *that our present and future, the mark we will leave*

on the galaxy, depends on the insistence of one misguidedly honourable man
to execute us in accordance with the word of law.

Is this a mockery by the galaxy, to condemn us by the virtues of another? I
could decide it is so. I could curse the universe and rail against our lot. But
I choose to see the Emperor has given us this – a stay of execution, a few
moments to have our say before our peers – as a gift to those who served Him
instead of the Imperium.

What can we make of this? What victory can we mine from such a thin
seam? It is the way of the Space Marines to see victory in the smallest hope. I
shall seek it now. My brothers, I wish I could speak with you and bid you do
the same, but I am isolated from you. I hope you, too, can see something other
than despair, even if it is only a thought turned to hope and duty when the
end comes.

Seek victory, my brethren. I pray that in your souls, at least, the Soul Drinkers cannot be defeated.

'Throne alive,' hissed Scout Orfos. 'Such death. Such foul xenos work.'

The surface of Selaaca rolled by beneath the Thunderhawk gunship.
Through the open rear ramp, the grey landscape rippled through ruined
cities and expanses of tarnished metal, obsidian pillars rising from deep
valleys choked with pollution and the shores of black, dead seas lapping
against shores scattered with collapsed buildings.

The human presence on Selaaca was now no more than scars, the
ruined crust of a long-dead organ. The necrons had built over it, vast
sheets of metal, pyramids, tomb complexes and patterns of obelisks
which had no discernible purpose other than to mark Selaaca as a
planet that belonged to them.

'Dwell not on the xenos,' said Scout-Sergeant Borakis. He was old and
grizzled where the scouts were young, his voice gravelly thanks to the
old wound on his throat, his armour festooned with kill-marks and trophies while the scouts under his command were not yet permitted to
mark their armour. Borakis leaned towards the open ramp, gripping the
handhold mounted overhead. 'It is not your place to seek to understand
the enemy. It is enough to know only that he must be killed!'

'Of course, scout-sergeant,' said Orfos, backing away from the ramp.

The Thunderhawk flew down low over a range of hills studded with
obelisks and pylons, as if metallic tendrils had forced their way out of
the ground to escape the bleak gravity of Selaaca. Patterns of silver like
metal roads spiralled around the peaks and valleys, and sparks of power
still spat between a few of the pylons.

'We're closing in on mark one,' came the pilot's voice from the cockpit
of the Thunderhawk. The crew were two of the thousands of Chapter
staff and crew who inhabited the *Phalanx*, a vast support network for the
Imperial Fists' campaigns. Using star maps developed by the Adeptus

Mechanicus, the strike cruiser *Mantle of Wrath* had penetrated further into the Veiled Region than any Space Marine craft before it, to follow up the information extracted by the castellan during his interrogation of a captive Soul Drinker.

The ground rippled as the Thunderhawk hovered down low to land. The landing gear touched the blasted earth and Borakis led his squad out. Borakis and his four scouts deployed with the speed and fluidity that years of training had given them, spreading out to cover all angles with bolt pistols. Borakis carried a shotgun as old and scarred as he was, and in his other hand checked the auspex scanner loaded with the coordinates the castellan had given him.

'Laokan! Take the point! Orfos, you're watching our backs. Kalliax, Caius, with me.' Borakis pointed in the direction the auspex indicated, over the dead earth.

Once, these hills had been forested. Stumps and exposed roots remained, shorn down to ground level. Up close the pylons looked like spinal columns worked in steel, blackened by the haze of pollution that hung overhead. The obelisks were fingers of a substance so black it seemed to drink the light. A faint hum ran up through the ground, the echo of machinery far below.

'The xenos have not departed this place,' said Orfos quietly. 'This world is dead, but these xenos never lived.'

'It is an ill-omened world,' agreed Scout Caius. 'I hope our work here is quick.'

'Hope,' said Borakis sternly, 'is a poisoned gift, given by our weaknesses. Do not follow hope. Follow your duty. If your duty is to fight on this world for a thousand years, scout-novice, then you will give thanks to the Emperor for it. Move on.'

The squad moved down the hillside into a narrow valley where mist coiled around their ankles and the valley sides rose like walls of torn earth. The auspex blinked a path towards a formation of rocks that would have been completely uninteresting if it had not corresponded to the location given by Brother Kaiyon under interrogation. On closer inspection the rocks formed two pillars and a lintel, a doorway in the valley wall blocked by a tangle of fallen stone.

'Charges,' said Borakis.

Brother Kalliax crouched by the rocks, setting up a bundle of explosive charges. The cog symbol on his right pauldron signified his acceptance as an apprentice to the Techmarines of the Imperial Fists.

'What do you see, Orfos?' said Borakis.

'No movement, sergeant,' replied Orfos, scanning the crests of the valley ridges for signs of hostiles.

The intelligence on Selaaca's hostiles was sketchy. The Imperial Fists had fought the necrons before, but their inhuman intelligence made the xenos impossible to interrogate and their goals could only be guessed at. Selaaca's necrons were, according to the interrogated Soul Drinkers, a broken and leaderless force, but there were certainly necrons still on the planet and no telling how they might have organised themselves since the Imperial Fists had captured the Soul Drinkers there.

'Ready,' said Kalliax.

The scout squad backed away from the entrance and Kalliax detonated the charge, blowing the blockage apart in a shower of dirt and stone. The blast echoed across the valley, shuddering the valley walls and starting a dozen tiny rockfalls.

'Move in,' said Borakis.

Laokan moved through the falling earth, his bolt pistol trained on the darkness revealed between the lintels. The darkness gave way to dressed stone and carvings inside.

The walls of the passageway were carved with repeating chalices, intertwined with eagles and skulls. The squad shadowed Laokan's movement as he crossed the threshold into the passageway.

The floor shifted under his feet. Laokan dropped instinctively to one knee. A line of green light shimmered over him and a camera lens winked in the ceiling as it focussed on him.

'Bleed,' said an artificial voice.

Laokan backed away slowly. The lens stayed focused on him.

'Bleed,' repeated the voice.

'Stand down, scout,' said Borakis. He walked past Laokan and drew his combat knife. The blade was as long as the sergeant's forearm, serrated and etched with lines of Imperial scripture. Borakis's scout armour, much less bulky than a full suit of power armour, had an armoured wrist guard that Borakis unbuckled from his left arm. He drew the knife along his left wrist and a bright scarlet trail ran down his hand.

Borakis flicked the blood off his hand into the passageway. It spattered across the walls and floor.

'Adeptus Astartes haemotypes detected,' said the voice again, the lens this time roving over the sergeant.

Light flickered on along the passage way, lighting the way deep into the hillside.

'We're in the right place,' said Borakis. 'Follow me.'

Borakis and the scouts entered the hillside, pistols trained on every shadow.

The *Mantle of Wrath* had two missions over Selaaca. The first was to deliver the scout squad to follow up the castellan's intelligence. The other was to begin the destruction of the Soul Drinkers.

The *Mantle* was one of the better-armed ships in the Imperial Fists fleet, but for this mission its torpedo bays had been stripped out and replaced with high-yield charges normally used for orbital demolitions. The *Mantle* did not have long to wait in orbit over Selaaca before its target drifted into view, its massive bulk darkening the glare of Selaaca's sun.

Few Imperial Fists would ever need more proof of the Soul Drinkers' corruption than the *Brokenback*. Many a Fist had fought on a space hulk, one of the cursed ships lost in the warp and regurgitated back into realspace teeming with xenos or worse. The *Brokenback* was as huge and ugly a space hulk as any had seen: hundreds of smaller ships welded into a single lumbering mass by the tides of the warp. Imperial warships ten thousand years old jostled with xenos ships, vast cargo freighters and masses of twisted metal that bore no resemblance to anything that had ever crossed the void.

Thousands of crew on the *Mantle* prepared the torpedo arrays as the strike cruiser manoeuvred into position. Damage control crews were called to battle stations, for while the *Brokenback* was unmanned no one could be sure of what automated defences the hulk might have. As the *Mantle* approached firing position, the Imperial Fists' officers and the unaugmented crewmen waited for the space hulk to leap into life and rain destruction from a dozen warships onto the *Mantle of Wrath*.

The hulk's weapons stayed silent. A spread of torpedoes glittered against the void as they launched from the *Mantle*, leaving ripples of silvery fire in their wake. Defensive turrets, which would normally have shot down every one of the torpedoes, stayed silent as the first spread impacted into the space hulk amidships.

Bright explosions blossomed against the void; flashes of energy robbed of power an instant later by the vacuum. Shattered chunks of hulls floated outwards in clouds of debris, leaving open wounds of torn metal in the side of the *Brokenback*.

The space hulk was too big to be destroyed with a single volley, even of the high-yield demolition charges. The *Mantle of Wrath* pumped out wave after wave of torpedoes. One volley blew an Imperial warship free of the space hulk's mass and the ship span away from its parent, trailing coils of burning plasma and revealing the twisted steel honeycomb inside. Ruined orbital yachts and xenos fighter craft tumbled out of the rents opened up in the hull.

Moment by moment, the whole *Brokenback* came apart. Selaaca's gravity drew the fragments down and the whole hulk rotated. The volley had opened up a weak point in the depths of the hulk's mass and an enormous section of the stern bent away from it, dragged down towards the greyish disc of Selaaca.

The *Brokenback* could not resist orbital decay any longer. Its idling engines, which did the bare minimum of work to keep it in orbit, failed as plasma reactors collapsed and power systems were severed. Over the course of the next few hours the stern of the hulk was scoured by the upper atmosphere and broke away entirely, followed by millions of chunks of debris raining down onto the planet. Like a dying whale the rest of the *Brokenback* lolled over and fell into the gravity well of Selaaca, gathering speed as it fell, its lower edges glowing cherry-red, then white, with friction.

The *Brokenback* disappeared into Selaaca's cloudy sky. Most of it, the *Mantle*'s augurs divined, would come down in one of Selaaca's stagnant oceans, the rest scattered over a coastline.

The *Mantle of Wrath* had fulfilled one of its duties. The space hulk *Brokenback* was gone, and no renegade would ever use it to resurrect the Soul Drinkers' heresies.

The only duty keeping the ship over Selaaca was the scout squad currently deployed on their service. Soon they would return, and the *Mantle* would leave this forsaken place behind forever.

Brother Caius died first.

The walls folded in on themselves, revealing rows of teeth lining the inside of a vast bristling throat. Caius had been the slowest to react. The rest of the squad threw themselves into the alcoves along the tunnel, which each contained statues of Space Marines with their armour covered in the ornate chalice of the Soul Drinkers. Caius's leg had snagged on the spikes and he had been dragged down the throat as it rippled and constricted; the sound of grinding stone competing with the tearing muscle and bone.

Caius did not scream. Perhaps he did not want to show weakness in his final moments. Perhaps he did not have time. When the corridor reformed, Caius's vermilion blood ran down the carvings and no other trace of his body remained.

Borakis hissed with frustration as Caius's lifesigns winked out on his retinal display.

'Caius!' shouted Orfos. 'Brother! Speak to us!'

'He is gone, scout,' said Borakis.

Kalliax held his bolt pistol close to his face, his lips almost touching the top of the weapon's housing. He crouched in the alcove opposite Borakis. 'Repaid in blood shall every drop be,' he said, face set.

'First, your duty,' said Borakis. 'Then let your thoughts turn to revenge.'

'This place was a trap!' replied Kalliax. 'I should have seen it. By the hands of Dorn, why did I not see it? Some mechanism, something that should not be here, it should have been obvious to me!'

'If you think you killed our brother,' said Borakis sternly, 'then take that pistol and administer your vengeance to yourself. If not, focus on your duty. This place was a trap, but it was not placed here in isolaaon. It protects something. That is what we have come here to find.'

The sound of breaking stone came from the alcove in which Brother Laokan had taken cover. The remnants of the alcove's statue toppled into the tunnel and smashed on the floor.

'Speak, novice!' ordered Borakis.

'Through here,' said Laokan. 'This is a false tunnel. Behind this wall is another way.'

Borakis braced his arms against the alcove walls and kicked hard against the statue. The wall behind gave way and the statue fell into the void beyond, revealing a long, low space lit by yellowish muted glowglobes set into the walls.

'Follow, brothers!' said Borakis.

Kalliax and Orfos kicked their way through the false wall and followed the sergeant into the hidden space. They had not yet completed their transition into full Space Marines but their strength was already far beyond that of normal men.

Up ahead of Borakis was a chapel with an altar, at the far end of the long room. The ceiling loomed down low, hung with stalactites that had formed from water dripping down. The altar was a solid block of grey stone topped with a gilded triptych depicting Rogal Dorn standing in the centre of a battle scene.

Borakis took the point himself this time. Now he knew there was danger here, he had a duty to place himself in its way, for part of his duty was to see his young charges safely back to the Chapter.

On the altar stood a chalice cut from black stone, studded with emeralds. Borakis kept his shotgun levelled on the altar as he approached it. The scouts spread out behind him.

The altarpiece's rendition of Rogal Dorn was in gold with diamond eyes. Dorn was twice as tall as the gilded warrior battling alongside him. The enemy were aliens, or perhaps mutants, humanoid but with gills and talons. Dorn was crushing them beneath his feet. It was a passable work. Dozens of higher quality could be found in the chapels and shrines of the *Phalanx*.

'Sergeant?' said Orfos. 'Anything?'

Borakis leant closer to the altar. The chalice was not empty. Something shimmered darkly inside it. In the dim light it was impossible to tell, but it looked like blood.

Blood could not remain liquid down here for the length of time the chapel had evidently been sealed. Borakis knew the smell of blood well enough. He put his face close to the chalice and sniffed, knowing his genhanced senses would confirm what the liquid was.

Borakis's breath misted against the polished stone. He noticed for the first time the thin silvery wires covering the chalice in a network of circuitry.

The warmth and moistness of a human breath made the filaments move. Expanding, they completed a circuit, wired through the base of the chalice to the mechanism behind the triptych.

Rogal Dorn's diamond eyes flashed red. A pencil-thin beam glittered across the chamber.

Sergeant Borakis fell, twin holes bored through his skull by the pulse of laser.

'Back!' shouted Laokan. 'Fall back!'

Kalliax darted forwards to grab Borakis's body by the collar of his armour and drag him away from the altar. The panels of the triptych slid aside, each revealing the veiny flesh of a gun-servitor supporting double-barrelled autoguns. Green and red lights flashed over Kalliax as he tried to scramble away, hauling Borakis's corpse with him.

The autoguns opened up, the gunfire filling the chamber to bursting. Kalliax almost made it to the hole leading to the tunnel. His armour almost held for the extra second he needed. Bursts of torn ceramite, then blood and meat, spattered from his back as bullets hit home. Kalliax fell to the floor as a shot blew his thigh open, revealing a wet red mess tangled around his shattered femur. Kalliax dropped Borakis's body and returned fire with his bolt pistol. His face and upper chest disappeared in a cloud of red.

Laokan and Orfos broke back into the tunnel, its walls still wet with Caius's blood. Orfos saw Kalliax die, and he felt that same instinct that must have seized Kalliax – grab the body of his fallen battle-brother, carry him back to the Chapter, see him interred with honour alongside the rest of the Chapter's venerated dead. But Orfos choked down the thought. That was what had killed Kalliax. Orfos would leave him to be entombed in this place. That was the way it had to be.

The back wall was falling in, showering the altar with rubble. The gun-servitors, one with a gun arm hanging limp thanks to Kalliax's bolter fire, lumbered out of their hiding place towards the surviving scouts.

'Don't look back!' shouted Laokan above the gunfire, and pushed Orfos into the carved corridor.

The walls shifted again. Orfos made a decision with the quickness of mind that years of hypno-doctrination and battle training had given him. He could go for the entrance of the tunnel, to escape back into the valley. But Caius had died in that stretch of tunnel – Orfos knew that way was certainly trapped. That certainty did not exist for the other direction, deeper into the structure built into the hillside. It was not particularly compelling logic, but it was all he had.

Orfos broke into a sprint towards the darkness at the far end of the tunnel. Laokan was on his heels, and the racket of the gunfire was joined by the grinding of stone on stone. The tunnel was closing up again, the ripple of shifting panels accelerating towards them from the tunnel entrance. Chunks of Caius's body were revealed, tumbling around the vortex of stone. A severed hand, a battered and featureless head, Caius's bolt pistol warped out of shape.

Orfos was fast. In the tests after each surgical procedure, he had always been. The sergeants of the Tenth Company had suggested his aptitude was for the Doctrines of Assault due to his speed and decisiveness of action.

Laokan was not so fast. He was a marksman. A trailing arm was caught between spiked panels and Laokan was yanked back off his feet. Orfos heard Laokan yell in shock and pain, and turned long enough to grab Laokan's boot, pulling his fellow scout free of the chewing throat.

Laokan's arm came off, bone and sinew chewed through. Laokan collapsed onto Orfos and tried to propel himself forwards, buying time for them both. Orfos grabbed Laokan's remaining arm and dragged him behind him as he carried on running.

Laokan snagged on something. Orfos hauled harder and dragged Laokan along with him, every nerve straining to keep his battle-brother free of the fate that had claimed Caius.

There was no light now. Even the scout's augmented vision, almost the equal of a full Space Marine's, could make out nothing but dense shadow.

The floor gave way beneath Orfos's feet. The lip of a stone pit slammed into the side of his head as he fell, and teeth cracked in his jaw. He was aware, on the edge of consciousness, of his body battering against the carved sides of the pit as he and Laokan fell.

Orfos woke, and realised that he had been knocked out. He cursed himself. Even if only for a moment, he should fight for awareness at all times. He had no bolt pistol in his hand, either. He had dropped his weapon. Borakis would assign him field punishment for such a failing. But Borakis, recalled Orfos with a lurch, was dead.

Orfos could still see nothing. He fumbled with the tactical light mounted on the shoulder of his breastplate. The light winked on and fell on the face of another stone Space Marine, far larger than in the alcoves above – twice life-size. Orfos read the inscription on the storm shield carried in the statue's left hand, a counterpart to the chainsword in its right. It read APOLLONIOS. Orfos recognised the trappings of a Chaplain among the weapons and armour of an assault-captain. Beside the statue was another of a Chaplain, this one inscribed with the name ACIAR.

'Brother,' said Orfos. 'Brother, what of this place? What have we found?'

Laokan did not reply. Orfos looked for his brother, who must have also been knocked out in the fall.

Laokan lay a short distance from Orfos, next to Orfos's bolt pistol.

Laokan's body was gone from the mid-torso down, and trails of organs lay behind him in bloody loops. Laokan was face down, nose in the dust.

Orfos knelt beside Laokan's corpse. 'Forgive me, brother,' he said, but the words seemed meaningless as they fell dead against the chamber walls. 'I can pray for you later. I will, brother. I promise I will.'

Orfos picked up his bolt pistol and let the light play around the chamber. A third statue was mounted high up, above the lintel of a doorway framing a pair of steel blast doors. This statue, again of a Space Marine Chaplain, bore the name THEMISKON. Orfos recognised the chalice symbol on the statue's shoulder pad, echoing the statues in the alcoves above. It was the symbol of the Soul Drinkers.

Another crime laid at the feet of the Soul Drinkers – this death trap, laid out to claim the lives of good Imperial Fists. Orfos spat on the floor. Whatever holiness this place might have had for the Soul Drinkers, Orfos wanted to defile it. Whatever it meant to them, he wanted it made meaningless.

Orfos looked up. The walls of a shaft rose above him. The carvings were probably deep enough to climb, but it would not be easy, and another fall might break a leg or an arm and render him unable to escape that way. He turned his attention to the door.

The metal was cold, drinking the warmth from Orfos's hands and face from a good distance away. A control panel was set into the stone. Orfos was not in enough of a hurry to press any of the buttons. He put a hand to the metal – it was freezing, and this close Orfos's breath misted in the air.

The doors slid open. Orfos jumped back, bolt pistol held level. Beyond the doors was darkness – the light on Orfos's armour glinted off ice and played through freezing mist that rolled from between the doors.

Orfos stepped slowly away from the doors. 'Whoever you may be,' he called, 'whatsoever fate you may have decided for me, know that I will fight it! I am an Imperial Fist! Die here I may, but it is as a Fist I shall die!'

The doors were open. The lump of ice inside, hooked up to the walls by thick cables hung with icicles, shuddered. An inner heat sent cracks blinking through its mass. Chunks of ice fell away. Orfos glimpsed ceramite within, painted dark purple under the frost.

The ice crumbled to reveal a shape familiar to Orfos. A massive square body on a bipedal chassis, squat cylindrical legs supported by spayed feet of articulated metal. The blocky shoulder mounts each carried a weapon – one a missile launcher, the other a barrel-shaped power fist ringed with flat steel fingers.

It was a Dreadnought – a walking war machine. All the Dreadnoughts of the Imperial Fists were piloted by Space Marines who had been crippled in battle, who were kept alive by the Dreadnought's life-support systems and permitted to carry on their duties as soldiers of the Emperor even after their bodies were ruined and useless. The Dreadnought's sarcophagus was covered in purity seals and the symbol of a gilded chalice was emblazoned across the front.

Orfos's bolt pistol would do nothing to the Dreadnought's armoured body. The power fist could crush Orfos with such ease that the pilot, if there was one, would barely register the resistance provided by Orfos's body before his armour and skeleton gave way.

It would be quick. A Space Marine did not fear pain, but Orfos did not see the need to pursue it as some Imperial Fists did. He had made his stand. He had not run; he had done his best to keep his battle-brothers alive. His conscience was clear. He told himself he could die. He tried to force himself to believe it.

The Dreadnought shifted on its powerful legs and the fingers of the power fist flexed. Flakes of ice fell off it. The cables unhooked and fell loose, showering the chamber floor with more chunks of ice. Lights flickered as the Dreadnought's power plant turned over and the chamber was filled with the rhythmic thrum of it.

'All this talk of death,' came the Dreadnought's voice, a synthesised bass rumble issuing from the vox-units mounted on the hull. 'Such morbidity. I have no wish to disappoint you, novice, but you will not die here.'

Orfos swallowed. 'What are you?' he said. 'Why lie you here, in a place designed to kill?'

'Your obtuseness has not yet been trained out of you,' said the voice again. Orfos looked for some vision slit so he might glimpse the pilot inside, but he could find none. 'My tomb was built to ensure that none but a Space Marine could make it this far. So sad the Imperial Fists chose to send scouts to do the work of a full battle-brother. But you have made it, and I have no intention to see you go the way of that unfortunate brother who lies behind you.'

'That is an answer to only one question,' said Orfos. 'I asked you two.'

'Then I shall introduce myself,' said the Dreadnought. 'I am Daen-yathos of the Soul Drinkers.'

CHAPTER TWO

'Greetings, great one,' said the lead pilgrim, his head bowed. Behind him snaked a chain of fellow pilgrims, decked out in sackcloth and, symbolic restraints around their wrists.

'I am Lord Castellan Leucrontas of the *Phalanx*,' replied the castellan. The cavernous docking bays of the *Phalanx* were Leucrontas's domain, just as the brig decks and Pain Glove chambers were his, and in spite of the high ceilings and enormous expanse of the docking chamber his stature still seemed to fill the place. 'Wherefore have you come to this place? You have not been asked, nor has your arrival been announced beforehand. I must warn you that accommodating your ship was a courtesy extended only in the light of it not being armed, and such a courtesy is mine to withdraw.'

The pilgrim's head seemed to bow even lower, as if his spine were permanently bent in an attitude of prayer. 'I would ask forgiveness, great one,' he said, in a rasping voice shredded by years of thunderous sermons, 'but it is not mine to offer apologies in the Emperor's name. For it is to do His work that we have come to this place.'

Castellan Leucrontas regarded the pilgrims emerging from the airlocks. Their ship, a converted merchantman, was a sturdy and ancient vessel, essential qualities for a craft that had evidently made it to the *Phalanx*'s isolated location at short notice. Nevertheless, there had been great risk in taking them so close to the Veiled Region, with its pirates and xenos, in an unarmed ship. The pilgrims had clearly been willing to court death to make this journey, and still more to risk the chance that the Imperial Fists would refuse them a berth and leave them to drift.

'Then you represent the Church of the Imperial Creed?' said Leucrontas. 'That august congregation has no authority here. This ship is sovereign to the Imperial Fists Chapter.'

The lead pilgrim pulled back his hood. The face inside was barely recognisable as a face – not because it was inhuman or mutilated, but because the familiarity of its features was almost entirely hidden by the tattooed image of a pair of scales that covered it. The image was an electoo, edged in lines of light, and the two pans of the scales flickered with intricately rendered flames.

'We come not to usurp your rule, good lord castellan,' said the pilgrim. 'Rather, we are here to observe. The standards, my brothers, if you please.'

Several other pilgrims jangled to the front of the crowd. Altogether there must have been three hundred of them, all hooded and chained like penitents. Several of them unfurled banners and held them aloft. They bore symbols of justice – the scales, the blinded eye, the image of a man holding a sword by the blade in a trial by ordeal. Other pilgrims were bent almost double by the loads of books strapped to their backs, each one a walking library. Still others had spools of parchment encased in units on their chests so they could pay out a constant strip of parchment on which to write. Some were writing down the exchange between their leader and the castellan, nimble fingers scribbling in an arcane shorthand with scratching quills.

'Our purpose,' said the pilgrims' leader, 'is to follow the course of justice. The Emperor Himself created the institutions that see justice called down upon His subjects and His enemies. We are the Blind Retribution, and whenever the process of justice is enacted, we are there to observe. It has come to the notice of the Blind that a Chapter of the Adeptus Astartes is to be tried here for several charges of rebellion and heresy. And so we are here to watch over this process and record all the matters of justice therein. This is the will of the Emperor, for His justice is the most perfect of all and it is to His perfection that we aspire.'

The castellan gave this some thought. 'It is true,' he said, 'that the *Phalanx* is to see these renegades put to trial. Your presence here, however, must be at the sufferance of the Chapter Master. I permit you entrance, but only he can permit you to stay, and should he withdraw my decision of welcome then you will be ejected.'

'We understand,' said the leader of the Blind Retribution. 'And we will obey. Might we beg of your crew some place to stay?'

'I shall have the crew find you lodgings,' replied the castellan. 'You can expect no more than an unused cargo bay. The *Phalanx* is large but it has no shortage of population.'

'We would ask nothing more,' said the leader. 'Ours is a way of poverty and denial. Indulgence dulls the sharp edge of justice, and luxury dims the focus. Now we take our leave, lord castellan. There are prayers and devotions to be made before our souls are fit to look upon the business of the Emperor's justice.'

Leucrontas watched as the pilgrims finished filing into the docking bay. They took loops of prayer beads from their robes and spoke droning prayers of thanks and humility.

The pilgrims were a small matter. The crew officers, who maintained the day-to-day workings of the *Phalanx* while the Imperial Fists attended the matters of war, could deal with them. Leucrontas had many more duties he had to see to before he could give the Blind Retribution another thought. Soon the Soul Drinkers would be in the dock, and many more powerful observers than the Blind Retribution would be watching the results closely.

The first sight Sarpedon had of this place was of the hands over his face, clamping the mask down.

Even then, barely conscious, the soldier's part of his mind demanded to know how he had been taken. Nerve gas, pumped into his cell? A rapid, merciless assault? Some drug administered by a sly needle or dart? He was angry. He wanted to know. His memory of the last few hours was a dark fog.

He thrashed. The hands clamping the mask to his face snapped away. They were not the gauntlets of Space Marines – Sarpedon was in the custody of Imperial Fists functionaries, unaugmented men and women who served the Fists as spaceship crew and support staff. The *Phalanx* was full of them. Somehow it was a greater insult that it did not take Space Marines to hold Sarpedon down.

Sarpedon struggled. He was held so fast he would have snapped his limbs before he loosened them. Incoherent voices shouted; medical code words barked between the staff of the *Phalanx's* apothecarion. Cold rivers wound through his body as sedatives were pumped into his veins.

Sarpedon was being wheeled on his back through a corridor with a ceiling that looked like the negative cast of a giant spinal column. The walls were webs of bone.

The sedatives took hold. Sarpedon couldn't even flex the muscles that had forced uselessly against his bonds. His eyes still moved – he looked down at his body and saw metal clamps around each of his limbs, holding them fast to the metal slab on which he lay. The *Phalanx's* crew must have had to make the restraints specially to fit his six remaining legs.

Sarpedon was also aware of a constriction around the sides of his head. No doubt it was an inhibiting device to dull his psychic powers. His cell had been fitted out to hold a psyker – the wards and anti-psychic materials built into its construction had rendered him completely blunt, unable to even taste the psychic resonance of his surroundings. The hood holding back his head made him similarly useless psychically. Not that he would have needed his psychic prowess to kill every one of the crewmen dragging him through the apothecarion, if only he could get free.

But they were just ordinary men and women, Sarpedon told himself. They believed as much as he did that their work was the work of the Emperor. Perhaps they were right.

Sarpedon passed through into a hall where the gnarled walls were lined with ceiling-high nutrient tanks, each with cultured organs suspended in viscous fluid. Gilded autosurgeons were mounted on the ceiling.

The next face that loomed over him was that of a Space Marine – close-cropped hair, hollow cheeks and a sharp chin and nose, with a bionic like a miniature microscope mounted over one eye. An eyebrow arched up.

'Behold the enemy,' said the Space Marine. It was an Imperial Fist by the symbol on his shoulder pad, and an Apothecary by the white panels of his armour. 'What manner of creature has the galaxy placed this time upon my slab? Many foul things have I seen, and some of them once human in form. But this! Ah, this shall be a challenge and a privilege. The imager!'

An ornate piece of machinery, like an arch of inscribed panels, was slid over Sarpedon. Sarpedon wanted to speak, if only to tell the Apothecary that he was no enemy, but a Space Marine as the Apothecary himself was. But his tongue was as paralysed as the rest of him. He had only his senses.

Speckles of light played against Sarpedon's retinas as lasers measured every aspect of him. A screen unfolded from one wall, in glowing green lines displaying Sarpedon's skeleton and the complex pattern of a Space Marine's organs.

'The weapons carried by a Space Marine begin with those augmentations within him,' said the Apothecary. 'All are present. Evidence here of extensive wounding and healing internally, as typical of a veteran. Most recent are extensive fractures to the skull and ribs. Note the abnormal shape of the omophagea, typical of this Chapter's gene-seed.'

The crewmen, the orderlies of the *Phalanx's* apothecarion, were scribbling down the Apothecary's pronouncements with autoquills.

'And he is awake,' continued the Apothecary, noticing the movement of Sarpedon's eyes. 'We have an audience! What think you, Lord Sarpedon, of the hospitality aboard the *Phalanx*?'

The imager moved down over Sarpedon's body. The orderlies had to manoeuvre it past Sarpedon's restrained legs.

'The mutations,' said the Apothecary, 'are implicit throughout. The subject's musculo-skeletal strength is at the top end. I doubt there is any man-mountain of a Space Wolf who can match him. Material mutations begin with the thickened lumbar spine and the pelvis.' Again the Apothecary addressed Sarpedon. 'And what a pelvis! All the scholars of Mars could not machine such a hunk of bone! I have no doubt the strengthening properties of its shape shall make it a classic of its kind. I shall have it preserved and gilded, I think, and keep it here among my most prized samples. Perhaps the Mechanicus shipwrights can use it to develop some new form of docking clamp? Certainly I shall not permit it to be incinerated with the rest of you.'

The imager moved lower. Now on the screen were the muscle-packed exoskeletal segments of Sarpedon's legs.

'The subject's legs number six,' said the Apothecary. 'These are the most significant material mutations. Originally they numbered eight; note the remnants of the bionic joint around the centre left and the recent partially healed damage to the rear right socket. The structure of the legs is roughly arachnoid but has no direct analogue. The uncleanliness of such deformities is profound. I have no interest in these. They can burn after the execution.'

The imager was withdrawn. Now Sarpedon found points of pain all over his body as the orderlies worked over him. They were looping wires and thin tubes around him, fixing them with needles in the gaps around his black carapace and in the muscles of his abdomen. One was slid into a vein in his neck, another on the underside of one wrist.

'Begin,' said the Apothecary.

Sarpedon was bathed in pain. It was a pure, unalloyed pain. It was not like a blade in his skin, or scalding-hot liquid, or any other pain he had suffered. It was completely pure.

Sarpedon's mind shut down. Nothing in his consciousness found purchase in the endless, white landscape of pain. Time meant nothing. He no longer felt his restraints, or his anger at the arrogance of the Apothecary in dissecting him like any other specimen. He no longer felt anything. He was made of pain.

The sensation of tearing ligaments loomed through the pain. It was subsiding, being replaced with the normal input from his senses. His legs had forced against the restraints. His neck muscles had almost torn against the psychic inhibitor holding his head in place and his lungs burned against the breastplate of fused ribs in his chest. He gasped, unable to control his body's reactions to the onslaught.

'Note the reaction to pain,' the Apothecary's voice continued. 'It is within normal tolerances. So we see the core of a Space Marine is present, but much embellished by corruption. I have no doubt that this subject can be considered a Space Marine by most definitions and can be tried as one.'

One of Sarpedon's legs hurt more than the others. It hurt more because it had some freedom of movement in the hip joint. The restraint holding it just above the talon was coming loose.

And he could move. Just a little, but he could do it. The sedatives were wearing off. The dose was too low. He had greater body mass than a normal Space Marine thanks to his mutated legs, and the less obvious mutations inside him had changed his metabolism. He was getting movement back.

Sarpedon fought against it. The Apothecary was describing the results of some blood and tissue sample tests to the orderlies. Sarpedon ignored them. The restraint was working loose. With the greater range of movement afforded to his other limbs, he could gain more leverage against their restraints and they, too, were giving way.

Sarpedon took in a breath. He forced his chest upwards and dug his talons into the slab, trying to level himself off it.

The ping of snapping metal alerted the Apothecary, who broke off his talk mid-word.

Bolts sheared. Metal bands fractured. Sarpedon's lower body ripped itself free. He thrashed one arm free in a matter of seconds – the orderlies starting back at the sight of their captive's lower limbs slashing around him.

Sarpedon reached up to the head restraint and tore it off its moorings. He rolled off the slab and sprawled on the floor. The drugs in his system were still powerful enough to rob him of his coordination and he could not get all his legs moving him in the same direction at once. He yanked the remaining arm free just as the Apothecary drew his plasma pistol.

'What are you?' slurred Sarpedon. He clawed at the inhibitor device still clamped around his temples. 'What can you claim to be that you judge me? I am not some xenos thing on a slide! I am of the Adeptus Astartes!'

'You are a traitor,' said the Apothecary. He had his plasma pistol levelled at Sarpedon's head. 'The dignity we give you in trying you before true and loyal Space Marines is more than you deserve.'

'But try me for what?' demanded Sarpedon. He lost his footing and crashed into one of the specimen tanks. The glass broke and the thick, cold nutrient fluid washed out over him, lapping around the feet of the orderlies who cowered against the far wall. 'How many enemies of man have fallen to the Soul Drinkers? How many catastrophes have we averted?'

'And how many Space Marines have fallen to you?' retorted the Apothecary. 'Our brethren in the Crimson Fists and the Howling Griffons could attest to that. If you had lost as many of your own to an enemy as mankind has to you, you would not hesitate to seek that enemy's death!'

Sarpedon tried to get to his feet, leaning against the wall behind him to force himself up. He tried to find a weapon among the debris around him, a shard of glass or a medical implement, but his head was swimming and he couldn't focus.

'If you had seen,' he said, 'what we had seen, then you would cross the galaxy to join us, though a legion of your own stand in your way.'

'Had I my mind, traitor,' said the Apothecary, 'I would have had you executed as soon as Lysander had brought you in, as a mercy to the human race so that you would be excised like the cancer you are. But the Chapter Master has said you must stand trial. He has more mercy in him than I, or any battle-brother I know. You should be sobbing your gratitude to us. Enough of this.'

The Apothecary operated a control on a unit attached to the waist of his armour. A white, dull sensation throbbed through Sarpedon's head, conducted from temple to temple by the inhibitor. Then Sarpedon was falling, his mind ripped free of his body. His sight failed and everything went white as he fell, and he did not stop falling until he could feel nothing at all.

The first to arrive to take their part among a jury of the Soul Drinkers' peers were the Howling Griffons. On their strike cruiser *Vengeance Incandescent*, the whole second Company attended their representative to the *Phalanx*. The Howling Griffons claimed a special place in the forthcoming trial, for they had suffered more than most at the hands of the renegades.

Chapter Master Vladimir Pugh had left his usual place among the tactical treatises and fortification maps of the Librarium Dorn to welcome Captain Borganor as he boarded the *Phalanx*. Attended by the second Company's honour guard, Borganor descended the embarkation ramp of his shuttle with a slight limp given him by the bionic with which his right leg had been replaced. His crimson and yellow armour was swathed in a deep blue cloak embroidered with his personal heraldry, an image in gold and black thread of a burning standard and a Howling Griffon with his head bowed in shame and his hands at prayer. Borganor was as blunt and crude as his gnarled features suggested, and with a clap of his hand against his gilded breastplate he acknowledged Pugh's salute.

'Chapter Master, it is an honour,' said Borganor. 'Would that I stand in your presence on a happier occasion, and without the stain of failure that still lies upon me.'

Vladimir Pugh of the Imperial Fists nodded sagely. He was, above all other things, a master tactician, a man of a solemn and slow manner, with a habit of dissecting a situation as cold-bloodedly as he weighed up potential recruits. The golden yellow of his artificer armour was polished to a mirror finish, and the red closed-fist symbols on his shoulder pads and breastplate shone as if they were cut from rubies. The intelligent face beneath his close-shorn hair suggested something more than a mere soldier. 'Long have I lamented the losses you suffered to the renegades,' he said to Borganor. 'It is an ill that will surely be repaid when justice is pronounced upon the renegades.'

Discomfort broke through Borganor's features for a moment.

'No doubt,' said Borganor. 'I wish to request one favour from you, however, before proceeding on.'

'Name it, brother-captain,' said the Chapter Master.

'That before Sarpedon is executed, I am first given liberty to remove his limbs, and leave him with a single leg, as he left me.' Borganor's eyes flitted to his bionic leg. 'My crippling was Sarpedon's doing, and I would repay him for it as a personal debt.'

'We are not here to execute your petty vengeance, captain,' replied Pugh. 'A far greater vengeance must be satisfied. If it is decided that the traitor Sarpedon is to suffer greatly before death, perhaps you can have a part in deciding the exact manner in which that suffering is to be inflicted. Until that decision is made, make justice your only goal.'

Borganor bowed before Pugh. 'Forgive me,' he said. 'Such hatred burns in my heart for all those that would befoul the name of Rogal Dorn.'

'That such hatred should have its voice,' said Pugh, 'is the reason you have your place at this trial.'

Borganor led the seventy Space Marines of the Howling Griffons onto the *Phalanx*'s docking bay. Their numbers were still recovering from their losses at the hands of Sarpedon and the aliens with which he had allied. Three companies of Imperial Fists, numbering more than three hundred Space Marines, were already stationed on the *Phalanx* – the Howling Griffons would be the next biggest contingent on board. But they would not be the only visitors to the *Phalanx* for the trial. Sarpedon and the Soul Drinkers had tangled with many Imperial servants, and every one wanted his voice to be heard.

In a golden orbital yacht launched from the Inquisitorial escort ship *Traitorsgrave*, Lord Inquisitor Kolgo made his entrance into the *Phalanx*. Ahead of him danced a troupe of acrobats and musicians, enacting in elaborate mimes and song the greatest achievements of their master's long career hunting the enemies of the Emperor. Kolgo himself, in jet-black Terminator armour bearing the 'I' of the Inquisition proudly on his chest, was flanked by several Battle-Sisters of the Adepta Sororitas. They were led by Sister Superior Aescarion, who had requested the duty of accompanying Kolgo so that she, too, could witness at first hand the trial of the renegades whose deeds she had personally witnessed. She had previously been assigned to Inquisitor Thaddeus, and she had no doubt that the Soul Drinkers were responsible for his death since he had disappeared hunting down evidence of their activities.

The Adeptus Mechanicus, who had more cause than most to despise the Soul Drinkers, were present in the form of Archmagos Voar. Voar had been instrumental in the capture of the Soul Drinkers, in doing so helping to set right an age-old debt owed to the Mechanicus by Sarpedon and his renegades. Alongside Voar was a ceremonial guard of gun-servitors, marching precisely in time. Voar's legs had been lost on Selaaca and so he moved towards the engine sections of the *Phalanx*, where he had been given quarters, on a set of simple tracks he had fashioned to use until more suitable replacements could be found. There was none of the hatred in him that the other attendees flaunted, for Voar was an analytical creature for whom emotion was an inconvenience.

The word had spread beyond those who had personally encountered the Soul Drinkers after they had turned renegade. The *Killing Shadow* of the Doom Eagles Chapter and the *Judgement Upon Garadan* of the Iron Knights dropped out of warp near Kravamesh and demanded that they, as loyal Space Marine Chapters, also take part in the trial. Shortly after this they were joined by contingents of Angels Sanguine and Silver Skulls, both Chapters who had heard of the Soul Drinkers' capture and found they had officers stationed close enough to Kravamesh to have a presence at the trial.

Chapter Master Pugh listened to their petitions. It was down to his judgement whether or not these Space Marines would be welcome. He accepted that the existence of renegade Space Marines was an affront to the whole Adeptus Astartes, and that the crime of any one renegade Chapter was a crime against them all, for it blackened the name of Space Marines, their primarchs and even the Emperor Himself. So Pugh gave the order for the Chapter representatives to be welcomed on board the *Phalanx*, and quartered among the monastic cells usually used by Imperial Fists who were on operations elsewhere in the galaxy.

Amid the pageantry of so many Chapters all announcing their presence and bringing their own officers and honour guards on board, the existence of a band of ragged pilgrims in the forward cargo sections was all but forgotten.

In the dusty, long-empty cargo hall, Father Gyranar knelt and prayed. Decades before, this place had been crammed with supplies of ammunition, food and spare parts long since used up, and it remained only in the memories of a few crewmen who recalled it when asked if there was somewhere the pilgrims of the Blind Retribution could be quartered. Those pilgrims now knelt on bedrolls or attended to their holy books, preparing their souls for the solemn duty of overseeing the great trial to come. No one had thought to tell them when the trial was expected to begin, but the pilgrims did not care. They would always be ready.

Father Gyranar, who had spoken with Castellan Leucrontas, was the oldest among them, and few of them were young. His own prayers were so familiar to him that he had to stop and think about the words, to stop them slipping through the well-worn channels of his mind. When he murmured that the Emperor's will was his will, he forced himself to pause and consider what that actually meant. That he had no will of his own, that he was the vessel for a higher power, that his own wishes and desires had long since withered away to be replaced with what the Emperor wanted for this particular instrument.

Gyranar carried a prayer book, but he had not opened it in thirty-seven years. He knew it by heart.

His evening prayers complete, Gyranar stood. 'Advance the standards,' he said.

The other pilgrims did not expect this. It was not a part of their normal routine. After a few moments of confusion the standards of the Blind Retribution were unfurled and held aloft.

'This place is now holy ground,' said Gyranar. His voice was brittle and frail, but the other pilgrims listened so attentively that he could have been no clearer with a vox-caster. 'The time for confession has come.'

'Confession, father?' said Brother Akulsan. He was the Blind Retribution's deacon, who oversaw the few permanent places of worship they had established on the worlds where they had settled for a while. On a pilgrimage such as this he became a second leader, a check to Gyranar's authority.

'Indeed,' said Gyranar. 'A confession most vital. There is in us all a sin. The task we undertake here is of such import that I would have it spoken aloud by all of us.'

'Many times have I made confession,' said Akulsan. 'Indeed, the very pride of confessing has itself become as a sin, and required yet more confession. I feel there is little in me that is still dangerous and unspoken, prideful though that thought may be.'

'Sister Solace?' said Gyranar.

'Every night I beg forgiveness for my failures,' replied Sister Solace, in a voice hoarse with endless prayers. Those not familiar with the Blind Retribution sometimes expressed surprise that Solace was a woman, for she had the dusty voice of an old man and it was impossible to tell gender through her robes. Most people never suspected there were women in the Blind Retribution at all. 'I yearn to be free of them. What confession can I make now that I have not in every moment before?'

'You know,' said Gyranar, 'of what I speak.' He had been kneeling but he now stood. He had never been a big man and now he was bent and drained, but still the pilgrims looked down or shied away a little as if he had the presence of a Space Marine. 'Though the greater part of your soul may deny it. Though you beg the Emperor that it not be true. Though you have forced yourselves to forget all but its shadow, yet all of you know of what I speak.'

The pilgrims were silent. The only sound was the distant hum of the *Phalanx*'s engines and the pulsing of the air recyclers overhead.

'Then I shall begin,' said Gyranar. 'O Emperor, I speak unto you the darkness of my deeds, and the poverty of this spirit so unworthy to serve you. My confession is of a time long ago, when first I wore the habit of the Blind. In the night as I lay in cloisters, a shadow came to me, clad in darkness. I am sure he was another brother of this order, though I know not his name. Perhaps it was that same father who counselled me in your ways. He said nothing, and did no more than place a chalice beside the slab on which I slept. Tell me, brethren, is there some confession in you that begs to be released, that has some of the same character as mine? Is there some echo of recognition that tugs at you, though it be gone from your memory?'

The pilgrims said nothing. So rapt were they by Gyranar's words that the Imperial saints could have descended in that moment and not broken their concentration on what the old man had to say.

'Then I shall continue,' he said. 'In this chalice was a liquid dark and cold. The shadow bid me drink with a gesture, and I did so, for I was afraid. And then into my mind there flooded a terrible waterfall of knowledge. I saw destruction and suffering! But I saw also the good that would come of it, the sinners that would be purged and the dead flesh of this bloated Imperium burned away. And I saw this time, when the Angels of Death, the Emperor's own warriors, shall be brought to trial before their peers, and I saw the part we were to play therein. The sin I confess is that I have known since that night that this time would come, and that the Blind Retribution must be there not only to observe that justice be done, but to enact a most crucial and terrible act that is the Emperor's will. I have kept it secret, locked up in my soul. Knowing that the day would come when everything I saw will come true. That is my confession. Who will follow mine with the excision of their own sin? Who?'

For a few moments, there was silence. Then one of the pilgrims raised a hand – Brother Sennon, one of the younger brethren who had been with the Blind Retribution only a few years. 'I drank of the chalice,' he said, his voice wavering. 'I saw... I saw the *Phalanx*. I thought it was a gilded eagle, a symbol of the Emperor's presence but... but when I looked upon this ship, I understood that whatever is to befall us must happen here. And it will be most dreadful. I saw flame, and blood, and torn bodies. Space Marines battling one another. There was a terrible injustice, I am sure, which by this violence might be averted. And... Father Gyranar, I am sure that I must die.'

'Brother Sennon,' said Gyranar, 'your courage is that of one far beyond your years and wisdom. To have made this confession here, before your brothers, is an act of great bravery. Who else here can show such valour? For he is not the only one with something to confess.'

'I, too,' said Sister Solace, 'have seen what I must do. It is indeed a terrible thing. But it was brought to me while at prayer. There was a searing pain about my temples and when my senses returned my mind was full of visions. I saw the *Phalanx*, and all that you have spoken of. I have hidden this for so long because I was afraid. I thought I was the only one. I thought that if I spoke of it I would be accused of corruption, and so I pushed it down to the depths of my soul. Only now am I able to acknowledge it within myself.'

More voices spoke out. Many had drunk of the chalice offered to them. Others had been struck by sudden visions while ill with a fever or at prayer. Some had been granted prophetic dreams. All of them had hidden what they had seen, and all of them had seen the same thing. The *Phalanx*. Fire and warfare. Destruction. And all had the same absolute certainty that what they saw was the Emperor's will. Every pilgrim cried out his own confession, finally unburdening himself of the dark thoughts that had been inside him since the days of his novicehood in the Blind Retribution.

Gyranar held up a hand to silence them. 'Now our confession is finished,' he said, 'is any one of you in doubt as to what he must do? Does any fail to understand his task in this, our final act of devotion?'

This time, there was silence again.

'Good,' said Gyranar. 'Then the Emperor's will must be done, dreadful though it is. And true, many of you will die, though the fear of death has no hold on you, I see.'

'Rather death,' said Brother Akulsan, 'than to live on with this task undone.'

'Good,' said Gyranar. 'Then we are all of the same mind. And now, let us pray.'

If Archmagos Voar could have truly admired anything, he would have admired the Forge of Ages. The complex angles of its construction, wrought in iron and bronze to form a great segmented dome, were lit from beneath by the molten metal running in channels between the four great forges in which blades and armour segments were being heated by crewmen in heavy protective suits. The sound of steel on steel rang like the falling of metallic rain. The work was overseen by the Techmarines of the Fourth, Seventh and Eighth Companies of the Imperial Fists: those companies present on the *Phalanx* for the trial. The

Techmarines checked each piece for flaws after its cooling in the huge vat of water in the centre of the dome, throwing those pieces that failed back into the streams of molten metal.

Voar did not really like anything in the traditional human sense, since he had lost much of his emotional centre over the course of his various augmentations. But as much as he could, he liked this place. It was a place of both industry and wisdom. The exacting standards of the Techmarines were something to admire, as was the devotion the crewmen had to the orders of their Imperial Fists masters. The Forge of Ages could have been lifted straight out of an Adeptus Mechanicus forge world, which was as high a compliment as a magos of the Mechanicus could pay.

Archmagos Voar had been summoned here. Ordinarily one did not summon an archmagos, but he was a guest here on the *Phalanx* and his datamedia still contained enough matters of etiquette to suggest he should accept the request to come to the Forge.

In the centre stood a Space Marine who was not a Techmarine. He wore Terminator armour, its yellow ceramite panels lit red and orange by the molten streams. He was testing the weight and balance of several hammers recently forged and left by the cooling pool. Each hammer was as long as a man was tall, but the Imperial Fist swung them as if they weighed nothing. He swung each in turn a few times, running through a simple weapons drill, then scowled and placed each one back in the pile. None of them seemed to please him very much. None of them, presumably, was the equal of the thunder hammer he carried strapped to the back of his armour.

'Demenos!' shouted the Imperial Fist over the din.

One of the Techmarines turned to him. 'Captain Lysander?'

'What grade of material are you using for your hammer heads? These things feel like they would splinter against a child's hand! And the shafts are about as sturdy as straw!'

Techmarine Demenos bowed his head. 'Many of my forgemen are new, captain,' he said. 'They have yet to understand the artificer's art. These weapons are exemplars of their competence thus far. They shall be used as training weapons, I would imagine.'

'If you wish to train our novices to fear the failing of their wargear, then they will do perfectly,' retorted Lysander. He picked up a sword this time and made a few thrusts and chops with it. 'This is better,' he said. 'This would go through a few skulls.'

'My own work,' said Demenos.

'Then you need to learn how to balance a hilt. Good work, though.' Lysander spotted Voar trundling between the forges towards him. 'Archmagos! I am glad you could come. I think perhaps this place is more suited to your tastes than the rest of the *Phalanx*.'

'I have no tastes,' replied Voar. 'A magos metallurgicus could gain no little pleasure from the specifications of your forges, no doubt, but my specialities lie in the fields of reverse engineering and theoretical mechanics.'

'Well, be that as it may,' said Lysander, 'the Forge of Ages itself is not why I requested your presence. This is.' Lysander took from a compartment in his armour a tube of black metal, as long as a normal man's forearm. Its surface was knurled into a grip and on one end it had a small control surface with indented sensors. 'Perhaps you recognise it?'

Voar walked up to Lysander and took the cylinder. Voar's bionic hand did not fit the grip well – it was sized for a Space Marine's hand.

'This is the Soulspear,' said Voar flatly.

'As seized at the Lakonia Star Fort,' said Lysander. 'The seed of the conflict between the Priesthood of Mars and the Soul Drinkers. We recovered it from the *Brokenback* before it was scuttled. I understand that it is to be considered your property. It was taken from you by the Soul Drinkers, and as heretics they have no right to it. Therefore its possession defaults to the Adeptus Mechanicus. Specifically, you.'

Voar turned the weapon over in his artificial hand. 'I confess that my dealings with emotive matters are long behind me,' he said, 'but still I have the impression, a remnant of some human sense if you will, that you are not happy about this situation.'

'The Soulspear is a relic of our primarch,' replied Lysander. 'Rogal Dorn himself found and re-engineered it. By rights it should belong to one of the successors of Dorn's Legion, the Imperial Fists or one of our brother Chapters. I have no shame in that belief. Any son of Dorn would say the same. But my Chapter Master has no wish to see another rift between the Adeptus Astartes and the Mechanicus, and I must bow to his decision. Here.'

Lysander touched a finger to one of the control surfaces and a tiny laser pulse punched a microscopic hole through the ceramite of his gauntlet's finger joint. Twin blades of pure blackness shot out of each end of the cylinder. The air sighed as it was cut apart by the voids of the blades.

'Vortex blades,' said Lysander. 'A vortex field bound by Throne knows what technology from before the Age of Imperium. Activated by a gene-lock keyed to the genetic signature of Rogal Dorn. This was wielded by Dorn's own hand, archmagos. A man of whom no Fabricator General can claim to be the equal. The saviour of the Emperor Himself at the height of the Heresy. The greatest soldier this galaxy has ever seen, and I say the greatest man, too. Remember that, whatever you choose to do with this relic. Fail to show Dorn's own handiwork the proper respect and the Imperial Fists just might choose to risk a new rift after all.'

'I see,' said Voar. 'Your information has been logged and will be made available to all those given the honour of examining this device.'

'In return for this,' said Lysander with obvious disdain for Voar's manner, 'the Chapter Master expects the Adeptus Mechanicus to conduct their part in the trial with all the honour that your status as a guest here demands. This is no place to settle a feud between the Soul Drinkers and the Mechanicus. No place for vengeance.'

'Your battle-brothers are not all of the same mind,' said Voar. 'Nor, logic suggests, will many of the visiting Chapters agree with such a stance. There is a great deal of vengeance sought on the *Phalanx*, and the better part of it stems not from the Mechanicus.'

'Chapter Master Vladimir Pugh has pronounced on the subject,' said Lysander. 'He has tasked me, among others, with seeing his word made law.'

'Then it shall be abided by,' said Voar with a nod of his head. It seemed the archmagos was not capable of any gesture of greater deference. 'Our interest is in justice.'

'If you cared about justice, archmagos, you would give the Soulspear to us.'

'And if you cared about justice, brother-captain, then Sarpedon would have died on Selaaca.' Archmagos Voar wheeled around and left the forge, the Soulspear clutched in his bionic hand.

CHAPTER THREE

The cell block had been built for the use of the Imperial Fists' own penitents. When battle-brothers believed themselves guilty of some failure, they came here, to the Atoning Halls. They knelt in the dank, cold cells lining the narrow stone-clad corridors and prayed for their sins to be expunged. They begged for suffering with which to cleanse themselves, a suffering regularly gifted to them by the various implements of self-torture built into the ceilings and floors of each intersection. Nerve-gloves and flensing-racks stood silent there, most of them designed to be operated by the victim, so that through pain he might drive out the weaknesses that had led to some perceived failing.

The cells had not been built with locks, for all those who had spent their time there had done so voluntarily. But the Atoning Halls had locks now. Its current penitents were not there by choice.

'Salk!' hissed Captain Luko. Luko was chained to the wall of his cell, with just enough freedom in his bonds to stand up or sit down. Like the rest of the Soul Drinkers imprisoned in the Atoning Halls, he had been stripped of his armour, with his wargear kept somewhere else on the *Phalanx* to be used as evidence in the trial.

'Captain?' came Sergeant Salk's voice in reply. The Soul Drinkers officers had mostly been locked in cells far apart from one another, but the Atoning Halls had not been built to contain a hundred prisoners and so it was inevitable two would end up in earshot.

'I hear something,' said Luko. 'They are bringing someone else in.'

'There is no one else,' replied Salk. 'They took us all on Selaaca.' Though Luko could not see Salk's face, the despondency, tinged with anger, was obvious in his voice. 'They must be coming to interrogate us. I had wondered how long it would take for them to get to you and me.'

'I think not, brother,' said Luko. 'Listen.'

The sound of footsteps broke through the ever-present grinding of the *Phalanx's* engines. Several Space Marines, and... something else. A vehicle? A servitor? It was large and heavy, with a tread that crunched the flagstones of the corridor.

Luko strained forwards against the chains that held him, to see as much as possible of the corridor beyond the bars of his cell. Two Imperial Fists came into view, walking backwards with their bolters trained on something taller than they were.

'Throne of Terra,' whispered Luko as he got the first sight of what they were guarding.

It was a Dreadnought. It wore the deep purple and bone of the Soul Drinkers, but to Luko's knowledge no Dreadnought had served with the Chapter since he had been a novice. He had thought the Chapter had not possessed any Dreadnought hulls at all.

The Dreadnought's armour plating was pitted with age. Its weapons had been removed, revealing the complex workings of the mountings and ammo feeds in its shoulders. Even so the half-dozen Imperial Fists escorting it kept their guns on it, and one of them carried a missile launcher ready to blast the Dreadnought at close range.

As it stomped in front of Luko's cell, the Dreadnought turned its torso so it could look in. Luko saw that its sarcophagus had been opened partially, and he glimpsed the pallid flesh of the body inside. Large, filmy eyes shone from the shadows inside the war machine, and Luko's own eyes met them for a moment.

'Brother,' said the Soul Drinker inside the Dreadnought, his voice a wet whisper. 'Spread the word. I have returned.'

'Silence!' shouted one of the Imperial Fists in front of the Dreadnought. 'Hold your tongue!' The Space Marine turned to Luko. 'And you! Avert your eyes!'

'If you wish me blinded,' retorted Luko, 'then you will have to put out my eyes.'

Luko had a talent for eliciting a rough soldier's respect from other fighting men. The Imperial Fist scowled, but didn't aim his gun at Luko. 'Maybe later,' he said.

'Daenyathos has returned!' said the Dreadnought.

Luko jumped forwards against his chains. 'Daenyathos!' he echoed. 'Is it true?'

'Daenyathos!' came another voice, then another. Every Soul Drinker's voice was raised in a matter of seconds. The Imperial Fists yelled for silence but their voices were drowned out. Even the bolter shots they fired into the ceiling did not quiet the din.

Luko did not know what to call the emotions searing through him. Joy? There could be no joy here, when they were facing execution and disgrace. It was a raw exultation, a release of emotion. It had been pent up in the Soul Drinkers since they had seen Sarpedon fall in his duel with Lysander, and now it had an excuse to flood out.

Daenyathos was alive! In truth, in the depths of his soul, Luko had always known he was not truly dead. The promise of his return seemed written into everything the legendary Philosopher-Soldier had passed down to his Chapter, as if the *Catechisms Martial* had woven into it a prophecy that he would walk among them once more. Amazingly, impossibly, it seemed the most natural thing in the galaxy that Daenyathos should be there when the Chapter faced its extinction.

Only one voice was not raised in celebration. It was that of Pallas, the Apothecary.

'What did you do?' shouted Pallas, and Luko just caught his words. They gave him pause, even as his twin hearts hammered with the force of the emotion.

'What did you do, Daenyathos?' shouted Pallas again, and a few of the Soul Drinkers fell silent as they considered his words. 'How have you fallen into their hands, the same as us? Have you come here to face justice? Daenyathos, warrior-philosopher, tell us the truth!'

'Tell us!' shouted another. Those words soon clashed with Daenyathos's name in the din, half the Soul Drinkers demanding answers, the other half proclaiming their hero's return.

Daenyathos did not reply. Perhaps, if he had, he would not have been heard. The Imperial Fists hauled open a set of blast doors leading to a side chamber that had once been used to store the volatile chemicals required by some of the torture devices. Its ceramite-lined walls were strong enough to contain the weaponless Dreadnought. The Imperial Fists marshalled the Dreadnought inside and shut the doors, slamming the thing that called itself Daenyathos into the quiet and darkness.

Outside it took a long time for the chants of Daenyathos's name to die down in the Atoning Halls.

More than three hundred Space Marines gathered in the Observatory of Dornian Majesty. Most Imperial battlezones never saw such a concentration of might, but these were not there to fight. They were there to see justice done.

The Observatory was one of the *Phalanx*'s many follies, a viewing dome built as a throne room for past Chapter Masters, where the transparent dome might afford a dramatic enough view of space to intimidate the Chapter's guests who came there to petition the lords of the Imperial Fists. Pugh had little need for such shows of intimidation and had closed off the Observatory for years.

It was one of the few places large enough to serve as the courtroom for the Soul Drinkers' trial. The ship's crew had built the seating galleries and the dock in the centre of the floor, an armoured pulpit into which restraints had been built strong enough to hold an accused Space Marine. The Justice Lord's position was on a throne the same height as the dock, facing it from the part of the gallery reserved for the Imperial Fists themselves.

The whole court was bathed in the light from the transparent dome. The Veiled Region was a mass of nebulae that boiled in the space outside the ship, nestling stars in its glowing clouds and swamping a vast swathe of space in the currents of half-formed star matter. Kravamesh hung, violet and hot, edging the courtroom in hard starlight.

The first in had been Lord Inquisitor Kolgo's retinue of Battle Sisters, ten Sororitas led by Sister Aescarion. They knelt and prayed to consecrate the place, Aescarion calling upon the Emperor to turn His eyes upon the *Phalanx* and see that His justice was done.

The Imperial Fists Fourth Company took up their positions, a hundred Imperial Fists gathering to serve as honour guard to their Chapter Master. Next the Howling Griffons filed in, Borganor scowling at the Observatory as if its tenuous connection with the Soul Drinkers made it hateful.

The other captains were next. Commander Gethsemar of the Angels Sanguine was accompanied by a dozen Sanguinary Guards, their jump packs framed by stabiliser fins shaped like white angels' wings and their helmets fronted with golden masks fashioned to echo the death mask of their primarch, Sanguinius. Gethsemar himself wore several more masks hanging from the waist of his armour, each sculpted into a different expression. The one he wore had the mouth turned down in grim sorrow, teardrop-shaped emeralds fixed beneath one eye. Siege-Captain Daviks of the Silver Skulls wore the reinforced armour of a Devastator, built to accommodate the extra weight and heft of a heavy weapon, and his retinue counted among them his Company Champion carrying an obsidian sword and a shield faced with a mirror to deflect laser fire in combat.

The Iron Knights were represented by Captain N'Kalo, an assault captain who wore a proud panoply of honours, from a crown of laurels to the many honoriae hanging from the brocade across his chest and the Crux Terminatus on one shoulder pad. He led three squads, his Iron Knights resplendent in the personal heraldry each wore on his breastplate and the crests on their helms. The Doom Eagles came in at the same time, represented by a single squad of Space Marines and Librarian Varnica. Where Varnica stepped, the stone beneath his feet bubbled and warped, his psychic abilities so pronounced that the real world strained to reject him, even with his power contained and channelled through the high collar of his Aegis armour.

Finally, Captain Lysander led in Chapter Master Vladimir Pugh. Pugh took his place on the throne – as the Justice Lord of this court he was the highest authority, and it was at his sufferance that any defendants, witnesses or petitioners might speak. Lysander did not stand in the gallery, for he was to serve as the Hand of the Court, the bailiff who enforced his Chapter Master's decisions among those present. Lysander looked quite at home patrolling the floor of the dome around the dock, and his fearsome reputation both as a disciplinarian and a warrior made for a powerful deterrent. A Space Marine's temper might move him to leave the gallery and attempt to disrupt the court's proceedings, even with violence – Lysander was one of the few men who could make such a warrior think twice.

The tension was obvious. When Lord Inquisitor Kolgo arrived to join his Battle Sisters, the sideways glances and murmured comments only grew. Space Marines were all soldiers of the Emperor but many Chapters did not have regular contacts with others and some had developed fierce rivalries over the millennia. The Imperial Fists had both retained the livery of their parent Legion and been feted above almost all other Chapters for the service to the Imperium – no little jealousy existed between them and other Chapters who coveted the honours they had been granted, and no one could say that such jealousy was absent from the court.

Fortunately, nothing papered over such schisms like a common enemy.

Sarpedon was led in, restraints binding his mutant legs, by a gang of crewmen marshalled by Apothecary Asclephin. Asclephin had conducted the investigations into Sarpedon's mutations – indeed, his findings were part of the evidence that would be presented to the court.

Sarpedon was herded into the dock, and his restraints fixed to the mountings inside the pulpit. Sarpedon still had the physical presence to demand a hush from the court in the first moments they saw him. He was bent by his restraints and he lacked the armour that was the badge of a Space Marine, but even without his mutations he would have demanded a form of respect with the scars and bearing of a veteran and the defiance that refused to leave his face. The inhibitor hood clamped to his skull just made him look more dangerous. One of Lysander's primary duties was to watch Sarpedon carefully and subdue or even execute him at the first suggestion that the Soul Drinkers Chapter Master was using his psychic powers.

Sarpedon's eyes passed across the faces of the assembled Space Marines. He recognised Borganor and Lysander, and Pugh he knew by reputation. Kolgo he had never met, but the trappings of an inquisitor sparked their own kind of recognition. Several times the Soul Drinkers had crossed paths, and swords, with the Inquisition. The Holy Ordos had sent their representative here to take their pound of flesh.

Then Sarpedon's eyes met Reinez's.

Brother Reinez of the Crimson Fists was alone. He had no retinue with him. His armour was pitted and stained, the dark blue of the Crimson Fists and their red hand symbol tarnished with ill maintenance. Reinez wore a hood of sackcloth and his face was filthy, smeared with ash. Strips of parchment covered in prayers fluttered from every piece of his armour.

There was silence for a moment. Their eyes had all been on Sarpedon, and none had seen Reinez enter.

'You,' said Reinez, pointing at Sarpedon. His voice was a ruined growl. 'You took my standard.'

Reinez had been the captain of the Crimson Fists Second Company during the battles with the xenos eldar on Entymion IV. The Soul Drinkers had taken the company standard in combat. Reinez was not a captain any more, and his trappings were those of a penitent, one who wandered seeking redemption outside his Chapter.

'The court,' said Pugh, 'recognises the presence of the Crimson Fists. Let the scribes enter it in the archives that–'

'You,' said Reinez, pointing at Sarpedon. 'You took my standard. You allied with the xenos. You left my brothers dead in the streets of Gravenhold.'

'I fought the xenos,' replied Sarpedon levelly. 'My conflict with you was sparked by your own hatred, not my brothers' wish to kill yours.'

'You lie!' bellowed Reinez. 'The life of the xenos leader was taken by my hand! But it was not enough. None of it was enough. The standard of the Second was taken by heretics. I travelled the galaxy looking for an enemy worthy of killing me, so I could die for my failings on Entymion IV. I could not find it. I turned my back on my Chapter and sought death for my sins, but the galaxy would not give it to me. And then I heard that the Soul Drinkers had been captured, and were to be tried on the *Phalanx*. And I realised that I did not have to die. I could have revenge.'

'Brother Reinez,' said Pugh, 'has been appointed the prosecuting counsel for the trial of the Soul Drinkers. The role of the Imperial Fists is to observe and administer justice, not to condemn. That task belongs to Brother Reinez.'

Sarpedon could only look at Reinez. He could scarcely imagine that any human being in the Imperium had ever hated another as much as Reinez obviously hated Sarpedon in that moment. Reinez had been shattered by the events on Entymion IV, Sarpedon could see that. He had been defeated and humiliated by warriors the Crimson Fists believed to be heretics. But now this broken man had been given a chance at a revenge he thought was impossible, and if there was anything that could bring a Space Marine back from the brink, it was the promise of revenge.

'The charges I bring,' said Reinez, 'are the treacherous slaying of the servants of the Emperor, rebellion from the Emperor's light, and heresy by aiding the enemies of the Imperium of Man.' The Crimson Fist was forcing down harsher words to conform to the mores of the court. 'The punishment I demand is death, and for the accused to know that they are dying. By the Emperor and Dorn, I swear that the charges I bring are true and deserving of vengeance.'

'This court,' replied Pugh formally, 'accepts the validity of these charges and this court's right to try the accused upon them.'

'Chapter Master,' said Sarpedon. 'This man is motivated by hate and revenge. There can be no justice when–'

'You will be silent!' yelled Reinez. 'Your heretic's words will not pollute this place!' He drew the power hammer he wore on his back and every Space Marine in the court tensed as the power field crackled around it.

'The accused will have his turn to speak,' said Pugh sternly.

'I see no accused!' retorted Reinez. He jumped over the row of seating in front of him, heading towards the courtroom floor and Sarpedon's pulpit. 'I see vermin! I see a foul stain on the honour of every Space Marine! I would take the head of this subhuman thing! I would spill its blood and let the Emperor not wait upon His justice!'

Lysander stepped between Reinez and the courtroom floor, his own hammer in his hands. 'Will you spill this one's blood too, brother?' said Lysander.

Reinez and Lysander were face to face, Reinez's breath heavy between his teeth. 'The day I saw a son of Dorn stand between a Crimson Fist and the enemy,' he growled, 'is a day I am ashamed to have seen.'

'Brother Reinez!' shouted Pugh, rising to his feet. 'Your role is to accuse, not to execute. It is to prosecute alone that you have been permitted to board the *Phalanx*, in spite of the deep shame in with which your own Chapter beholds you. Petitions will be heard and a verdict will be reached. This shall be the form your vengeance shall take. Blood will not be shed in my court save by my own order. Captain Lysander is the instrument of my will. Defy it and you defy him, and few will mourn your loss if that is the manner of death you choose.'

The moment for which Reinez was eye to eye with Lysander was far too long for the liking of anyone in the court. Reinez took the first step back and holstered his hammer.

'The Emperor's word shall be the last,' he said. 'He will speak for my dead brothers.'

'Then now the court will hear petitioners from those present,' said Pugh. 'In the Emperor's name, let justice be done.'

The archivists of the *Phalanx* were a curious breed even by the standards of the voidborn. Most had been born on the ship – the few who had not had been purchased in childhood to serve as apprentices to the aged Chapter functionaries. An archivist's purpose was to maintain the enormous parchment rolls on which the deeds and histories of the Imperial Fists were recorded. Those massive rolls, three times the height of a man and twice as broad, hung on their rollers from the walls of the cylindrical archive shaft, giving it the appearance of the inside of an insect hive bulging with pale cells.

An archivist therefore lived to record the deeds of those greater than him. An archivist was not really a person at all, but a human-shaped shadow tolerated to exist only as far as his duties required. They did not have names, being referred to by function. They were essentially interchangeable. They schooled their apprentices in the art of abandoning one's own personality.

Several of these archivists were writing on the fresh surfaces of recently installed parchment rolls, their nimble fingers noting down the transmissions from the courtroom in delicate longhand. Others were illuminating the borders and capital letters. Gyranar cast his eye over these strange, dusty, dried-out people, their eyes preserved by goggles and their fingers thin, bony spindles. Every breath he took in there hurt, but to a pilgrim of the Blinded Eye pain was just more proof that the Emperor still had tests for them to endure.

'Follow,' said the archivist who had been detailed to lead Gyranar through the cavernous rooms. This creature represented the dried husk of a human. It creaked when it walked and its goggles, the lenses filled with fluid, magnified its eyes to fat, whitish blobs. Gyranar could not tell if the archivist was male or female, and doubted the difference meant anything to the archivist itself.

The archivist led Gyranar through an archway into another section of the archives. Here, on armour stands, were displayed a hundred suits of power armour, each lit by a spotlight lancing from high overhead. The armour was painted purple and bone, with a few suits trimmed with an officer's gold. Each was displayed with its other wargear: boltguns and chainswords, a pair of lightning claws, a magnificent force axe with a blade inlaid with the delicate patterns of its psychic circuitry. The armour was still stained and scored from battle, and the smell of oil and gunsmoke mixed with the atmosphere of decaying parchment.

'This is the evidence chamber,' said the archivist. 'Here are kept the items to be presented to the court.'

'The arms of the Soul Drinkers,' said Gyranar. He pulled his hood back, and the electoo on his face reflected the pale light. The scales tipped a little, as if they represented the processes of Gyranar's mind, first weighing down on one side then the other.

'Quite so. Those who wish to inspect them can claim leave to do so from the Justice Lord. Our task is to make them available for scrutiny.'

'And afterwards?'

The archivist tilted its head, a faint curiosity coming over its sunken features. 'They will be disposed of,' it said. 'Ejected into space or used as raw material for the forges. The decision has yet to be made.'

'If the Soul Drinkers are found innocent,' said Gyranar, 'presumably these arms and armour will be returned to them.'

'Innocent?' replied the archivist. The faint mixture of mystification and baffled amusement was perhaps the most extreme emotion it had ever displayed. 'What do you mean, innocent?'

'Forgive me,' said Gyranar, bowing his head. 'A wayward thought. Might I be given leave to inspect this evidence for myself?'

'Leave is granted,' said the archivist. It turned away and left to take up its regular duties again.

Father Gyranar ran a finger along the blade of the force axe. This was the Axe of Mercaeno, the weapon of the Howling Griffons Librarian killed by Sarpedon. Sarpedon had taken the axe to replace his own force weapon lost in the battle. Such had been the information given by the Howling Griffons' deposition to the court. Its use suggested a certain admiration held by Sarpedon for Mercaeno. It was probable that a replacement weapon could have been found in the Soul Drinkers' own armouries on the *Brokenback*, but Sarpedon had chosen to bear the weapon so closely associated with the Space Marine he had killed.

It was a good weapon. It had killed the daemon prince, Periclitor. Gyranar withdrew his thumb and regarded the thin red line on its tip. The Axe of Mercaeno was also very sharp.

Across the hall from the axe was a pair of oversized weapons, too big to be wielded by any Space Marine, and with mountings to fix them onto the side of a vehicle. Gyranar knew they were the weapons of a Space Marine Dreadnought – a missile launcher and a power fist. They, too, were in the livery of the Soul Drinkers. Their presence told Gyranar that everything the Blinded Eye had foretold was coming to pass. He was a cog in a machine that had been in motion for thousands of years, and that its function was about to be completed was an honour beyond any deserving.

Gyranar knelt in prayer. His words, well-worn in his mind, called for the fiery and bloodstained justice of the Emperor to be visited on sinners and traitors. But his thoughts as they raced were very different.

The archives. The dome being used as the courtroom. The Atoning Halls. The map being drawn in the pilgrim's mind was beginning to join up. Soon, he would hold his final sermon, and the contents of that pronouncement were finally taking shape.

'Everything,' said Lord Inquisitor Kolgo, 'is about power.'

The inquisitor lord paced as he spoke, making a half-circuit around the gallery seating, watched by the Battle Sisters who accompanied him. His Terminator armour was bulky, but it was ancient, the secrets of its construction giving him enough freedom of movement to point and slam one fist into the other palm, stride and gesticulate as well as any orator. And he was good. He had done this before.

'Think upon it,' he said. 'In this room are several hundred warriors of the Adeptus Astartes. Though I am a capable fighter for an unaugmented human, yet still the majority of you would have a very good chance of besting me. And I am unarmed. My weapons lie back on my shuttle, while many of you here carry the bolters or chainswords that you use so well in battle. I see you, the brothers of the Angels Sanguine, carrying the power glaives that mark you out as your Chapter's elite. And you, Librarian Varnica, that force claw about your fist is more than a mere ornamentation. It is an implement of killing. So if you wished to kill me, there would be little I could do to stop it.'

Kolgo paused. The Space Marines he had mentioned looked like they did not appreciate being singled out. Kolgo spread out his arms to take in the whole courtroom. 'And how many would like to kill me? Many of you have experienced unpleasant episodes at the hands of the Holy Ordos. I am a symbol of the Inquisition, and casting me down would be to strike a blow against every inquisitor who ever claimed his jurisdiction included the Adeptus Astartes. I have, personally, gained something of a reputation for meddling in your affairs, and am no doubt the subject of more than a few blood oaths. Perhaps one of you here has knelt before the image of your primarch and sworn to see me dead. You would not be the first.' Kolgo held up a finger, as if to silence anyone who might think to interrupt. 'And yet, I live.'

Kolgo looked around the courtroom. The expression of Chapter Master Pugh was impossible to read. Other Space Marines looked angry or uncomfortable, not knowing what Kolgo was trying to say but certain that they would not like it.

'And why?' said Kolgo. 'Why am I not dead? I am satisfied that it is not through fear that you refrain from killing me. A Space Marine knows no fear, and in any case, the fulfilling of a blood oath takes far higher priority than the possibility of being lynched or prosecuted by your fellows. And as I have said, I myself am scarcely capable of defending myself against any one of you. So what is it that keeps me alive? What strange gravity stays your hands? The answer is power. I have power, and it is a force so irresistible, so immovable, that even Space Marines must make way for it sometimes. I say this not to tempt you into action, I hasten to say, but to show you that it is matters of power that determine so much of the decisions we make whether we understand that or not.

'This trial is about power. It is about who holds it, to which power one bows, and the natural order of the Imperium as it is created by the power its members wield. I say to you that the principal crime of the Soul Drinkers is the flouting of that natural order of power. You have refrained from violence against me because of the place I hold in that order. Sarpedon and his brothers would not. They act outside that order. Their actions denigrate and damage it. But it is this order that holds the Imperium together, that maintains the existence of the Imperium and the species of man. Without it, all is Chaos. This is the crime for which I condemn the Soul Drinkers, and thus do I demand to fall upon them a punishment that not only removes them from this universe, but proclaims the horror of their deaths as the consequence for railing against the order the Emperor Himself put in place.'

Kolgo punctuated his final words by banging his armoured fist on the backs of the seats in front of him. He turned, faced the Justice Lord, and inclined his head in as much of a bow as an Inquisitor Lord would give.

'Are you finished?' asked Pugh.

'This statement is concluded,' said Kolgo.

'Pah,' came a voice from the galleries. 'One of a thousand he would give if he had leave. The lord inquisitor's desire to hear his own voice borders on the scandalous!' The speaker was Siege-Captain Daviks of the Silver Skulls. The Silver Skulls beside him nodded and murmured their assent.

'You wish to make a counter-statement, siege-captain?' said Pugh.

'I wish for the statements to end!' snapped Daviks. 'This creature in the dock before us is not deserving of a trial. This thing is a mutant! In what Imperium of Man is a mutant afforded the right to be bedded down in this nest of pointless words? Reinez was right. I have never known a trial granted to such a thing. I have known only execution!'

Several warriors shouted agreements. Pugh held up a hand for silence but the din only grew.

'Kill this thing, kill all the creatures you hold in your brigs, and let this be done with!' shouted Daviks.

'I will have order!' bellowed Pugh. He was not a man who raised his voice often, and as he rose to his feet the calls for violence died. 'Apothecary Asclephin has borne witness that Sarpedon is to be tried as a Space Marine. There the matter ends. You will get your execution, Captain Daviks, but in return you must have patience. I will see justice done here.'

'A better illustration of power I could not have created myself,' added Kolgo.

'Your statement is concluded,' said Pugh. 'Who will speak?'

'We have not yet heard from the accused in the dock,' replied Captain N'Kalo of the Iron Knights. 'If we are to have a trial, the accused must speak in his defence.'

Pugh's recent interjections kept the retorts to N'Kalo's words to a minimum.

'I would speak in my defence,' said Sarpedon. 'I would have you all hear me. I did not turn from the authority of the Imperium at some perverse whim. For everything I have done, I have had a reason. Lord Kolgo's words have done nothing but to convince me further that my every action was justified.'

'You will speak,' said Pugh, 'whether those observing like it or not. But you cannot speak as yet, for further charges are to be levelled against you.'

'Name them,' said Sarpedon.

'That by the machinations of your authority,' said Reinez, 'four Imperial Fists died on the planet of Selaaca, three scouts and one sergeant of the Tenth Company. To the Emperor's protection have their souls been commended, and to the example of Dorn have they measured themselves with honour. Their deaths have been added to the list of crimes of which you are accused.' Reinez spoke as if reading from a statement, and the real anger behind his words was far more eloquent. He enjoyed pouring further accusations on Sarpedon, especially one that hit so home to the Imperial Fists on whose forced neutrality Sarpedon depended.

The Imperial Fists around Pugh made gestures of prayer. The other Space Marines gathered had evidently not heard of these charges, and a few quiet questions passed between them.

'I know nothing of this!' retorted Sarpedon. 'No Imperial Fist died by a Soul Drinker's hand on Selaaca. My battle-brothers surrendered to Lysander without a fight. The captain himself can attest to this!'

'These crimes were not committed during your capture,' said Pugh. 'Scout Orfos?'

The Imperial Fists parted to allow a scout through their ranks. In most Chapters, the Imperial Fists among them, a recruit served a term as a scout before his training and augmentation was completed. Since he was not yet a Space Marine, and since power armour was ill-suited to anything requiring stealth, these recruits served as infiltrators and reconnaissance troops. Scout Orfos still wore the carapace armour, light by the standards of the Adeptus Astartes, and cameleoline cloak of a scout. He was relatively youthful and unscarred compared to the Imperial Fists around him, but he had a sharp face with observant eyes and he moved with the assurance of a confident soldier.

'Scout,' said Pugh, 'describe to the court what you witnessed on Selaaca.'

'My squad under Sergeant Borakis was deployed to investigate a location that the castellan's command had provided to us,' began Orfos. 'In a tomb beneath the ground we found a place that the Soul Drinkers had built there.'

Sarpedon listened, but his mind wanted to rebel. He had never heard of any Soul Drinker travelling to Selaaca before he had gone there to face the necrons. The planet was not mentioned in the Chapter archives. It could not be a coincidence that of all the millions of planets in the Imperium, he should stumble upon one where some forgotten brothers had built a tomb thousands of years ago. A tomb which, as Orfos's evidence continued, had been built to keep all but the most determined infiltrator out.

Sarpedon felt a wrenching inside him as Orfos described the deaths of the other scouts. Orfos was well-disciplined and little emotion showed in his words, but his face and intonation suggested the effort he was making in bottling it up. Orfos had been trained to hate, hypno-doctrination and battlefield experience teaching him the value of despising his enemy. That hate was turned on Sarpedon now. Sarpedon felt, for the first time in that courtroom, truly accused. He felt guilt at the Imperial Fists' deaths, though this, of all his supposed crimes, was the only one that he had not committed.

'It was a Dreadnought,' Orfos was saying. 'The tomb had been built to house it. It had been kept frozen to preserve its occupant...'

'Justice Lord,' said Sarpedon. 'My Chapter has no Dreadnoughts. The last was lost with the destruction of the *Scintillating Death* six thousand years ago. It is made clear in the archives of–'

'The accused will be silent!' snapped Pugh. 'Or he will be made silent.' A glance from Pugh towards Lysander suggested how Pugh would go about shutting Sarpedon up. 'Scout Orfos. Continue.'

'The Dreadnought awoke,' said Orfos, 'and I voxed for reinforcements. A team of servitors and Techmarines made the tomb safe and disarmed the Dreadnought.'

'Did it speak to you?' asked Pugh.

'It did,' said Orfos. 'It placed itself in my custody, and told me its name.'

'Which was?'

'Daenyathos.'

Sarpedon slumped against the pulpit.

Daenyathos was dead. The heretic Croivas Ascenian had killed him six thousand years ago.

His mind raced. The impossibility of it stunned him.

Of all the names he might have heard listed as a traitor, Daenyathos was the last he would have expected. Daenyathos had written down the Soul Drinkers' way of war, and even after casting aside the

ways of the old Chapter, Sarpedon had still found infinite wisdom
in Daenyathos's works. Every Soul Drinker had read the *Catechisms
Martial*. Sarpedon had fought his wars by its words. It had given him
strength. Daenyathos was a symbol of what the Imperium could be –
wise and strong, tempered with discipline but beloved of knowledge.
Now the Philosopher-Soldier's name had been dragged into this sor-
did business.

And if he was alive... if Daenyathos truly lived still, as only a Space
Marine in a Dreadnought could...

'I swear...' said Sarpedon. 'If he lives... I swear I did not know...'

'And by what do you swear?' snarled Captain Borganor from the gallery. 'On your traitor's honour? On the tombs of my brothers you have
slain? I say this proves the Soul Drinkers are not mere renegades! I say
they have been corrupt for millennia, under the guidance of Daenyathos, sworn to the powers of the Enemy and primed to bring about some
plot of the warp's foul making!'

Voices rose in agreement. Sarpedon's mind whirled too quickly for
him to pay attention to them. If Daenyathos was alive, then what did
that mean? The Soul Drinkers had gone to Selaaca to stave off the necron
invasion of an innocent world, and yet Daenyathos had been there all
along. Sarpedon traced back the events of the last weeks, his capture, the
assault on the necron overlord's tomb, the battles on Raevenia and the
clash with the Mechanicus fleet, and before that...

Iktinos. It had been Iktinos who had suggested the *Brokenback* flee
into the Veiled Region. The Chaplain's arguments had made sense – the
Veiled Region was a good place to hide. And yet he had led the Soul
Drinkers straight to the tomb of Daenyathos. Iktinos must have known
Daenyathos was there. And yet Iktinos had been one of Sarpedon's most
trusted friends, the spiritual heart of the Chapter...

'Is he here?' said Sarpedon, hoping to be heard over the shouting.
'Daenyathos. Is he here, on the *Phalanx*?'

'He shall be brought to the dock in time,' replied Pugh.

'I must speak with him!'

'You shall do no such thing.' retorted Pugh. 'There will be no provision
made for you to plot further! When your trial is complete, Daenyathos's
shall begin. That is all you shall know!' Pugh banged a gauntlet. 'I will
have order under the eyes of Dorn! Lysander, bring me order!'

'Silence!' yelled Lysander, striding across the courtroom. 'The Justice
Lord will have silence! There is no Space Marine here too lofty of station
to be spared the face of my shield! Silence!'

'This farce must end!' shouted Borganor. 'So deep the corruption lies!
So foul a thing the Soul Drinkers are, and now we see, they have always
been! Burn them, crush them, hurl them into space, and excise this
infection!'

Lysander vaulted the gallery rail and powered his way up to Borganor. The Howling Griffons were not quick enough to hold him back, and it was by no means certain they could have done so at all. Lysander bore down on Borganor, face to face, storm shield pressing against Borganor's chest and pinning him in place. Lysander had his hammer in his other hand, held out as a signal for the other Howling Griffons to stay back.

'I said silence,' growled Lysander.

'My thanks, captain,' said Pugh. 'You may stand down.'

Lysander backed away from Borganor. The two Space Marines held each other's gaze as Lysander returned to the courtroom floor.

'There will be no further need for calls to order,' said Pugh. 'You are here at my sufferance. When my patience runs out with you, you return to your ships and leave. Captain Lysander is authorised to escort you. Scout Orfos, you are dismissed.'

Orfos saluted and left the gallery, the Imperial Fists bowing their heads in respect to him and his lost brothers as he went.

Reinez had watched the tumult with a smile on his face. Nothing could have pleased him more than seeing Sarpedon's distress, except perhaps Sarpedon's severed head.

'Who will speak next?' said Pugh. 'Who can bring further illumination to the crimes of the accused?'

Varnica of the Doom Eagles stood. 'I would speak,' he said. 'The court must hear what I have to say, for it bears directly on the nature of the Soul Drinkers' crimes. I bring not rhetoric or bile. I bring the truth, as witnessed by my own eyes.'

'Then speak, Librarian,' said Pugh.

The courtroom hushed, and Varnica began.

CHAPTER FOUR

The beauty of Berenika Altis was a strange thing, like a work of art not understood. It had been built in the shape of an enormous star, two of its five points extending out to sea on spurs of artificial land. Each point of the star was devoted to a different trade, the five legendary guilds that had built and financed this city. The shape was a reminder of its original purpose as an exclusive retreat for those who deserved better than the other bleak, stagnant cities of the planet Tethlan's Holt. At the centre of the star was the Sanctum Nova Pecuniae, once a palace existing purely for the beautification of Berenika Altis, and one that now served as the seat of government of Tethlan's Holt.

Fifteen days ago all communication had ceased with Berenika Altis. Eight million people had vanished. The planetary authorities, those who had not disappeared with the rest of the government, reacted as any good Imperial citizen would when confronted with the unknown. They had sealed off the city, quarantined it, and resolved to pretend that it had never existed.

The Doom Eagles were not satisfied with such solutions.

'A brittle beauty,' said Librarian Varnica as the Thunderhawk droned in low over the north seaward spur of Berenika Altis. The rear ramp was down and Varnica had disengaged his grav-couch restraints, holding onto the rail overhead to lean forwards and get a better look at his target from the air.

'I see only stupidity,' replied Sergeant Novas. His voice did not sound over the gunship's engines, but the vox-link carried it straight into Varnica's inner ear. 'A shift in the sea floor and two-fifths of that city would sink into the ocean.'

'Perhaps,' said Varnica, 'that's the point. Nothing speaks of wealth like spending a great deal of it on something that might be gone any moment.'

'Looks like they got their wish,' said Novas. 'Eventually. It wasn't the sea that got them, but something did,'

'Quite the conundrum,' said Varnica. 'What a puzzle box they built for us.'

As the Thunderhawk swooped lower, the streets were revealed. Each spur of the city had been dedicated to a different guild and though centuries of rebuilding and repurposing had followed, the original imprint remained. The Embalmers' Quarter was arranged in neat rows, the buildings resembling elegant tombs. The Jewelcutters' Quarter was all angular patterns, triangular sections of streets and many-sided intersections echoing the complex facings of a cut diamond. The Victuallers' District was a gloomy, sheer-sided area of warehouses and long, low halls. The industrial feel of the Steelwrights' Cordon was entirely an affectation, with rust-streaked metal chimneys and crumbling brickwork concealing the salons and feasting halls where the great and good of Berenika Altis had celebrated their superiority. The Flagellants' Quarter, founded with the money taken from those who paid to have their sins scourged from them, echoed the flagellants' frenzy with twisted, winding streets and asymmetrical buildings that seemed poised to topple over or slide into rubble. The Sanctum Nova Pecuniae held the disparate regions together, as if it pinned them to the surface of Tethlan's Holt to keep them from crawling off to their own devices.

The streets were visible now, the buildings separating into distinct blocks. The streets seemed paved with a haphazard mosaic of blacks and reds, the same pattern covering every avenue and alley.

It was a mosaic of corpses.

The smell of it confirmed the few reports that had reached the Doom Eagles. The smell of rotting bodies. It was familiar to every Space Marine, to every Emperor's servant whose business was death.

Varnica looked on, fascinated. He had seen many disasters. When not called upon to attend some critical battlezone, it was disasters that attracted the Doom Eagles. Some Chapters sought out ancient secrets, others lost comrades, others the most dangerous sectors of the galaxy to test their martial prowess. The Doom Eagles sought out catastrophe. It was less a policy of the Chapter's command, and more a compulsion, a dark fascination as powerful as the pronouncements of the Chapter Master.

This was a true disaster. Not the side effect of a war, or a revolt that had turned bloody. It was a catastrophe from outside, beyond the context of anything that had happened on Tethlan's Holt. The scale of death was appalling. Millions lay decomposing in the streets. And yet a part of Varnica's mind relished it. Here was not only a mystery, but a scale of horror that made it worth solving.

The Thunderhawk approached its landing zone, a circular plaza in the Embalmers' Quarter. Like every other possible landing site, it was strewn with bodies. Fat flies whipped around the Thunderhawk's passenger compartment as it passed through a cloud of them, spattering against Varnica's armour and the eyepieces of his power armour's helmet. He took it off as the Thunderhawk came down to land.

The grisly cracking sound Varnica heard was the cracking of bones beneath the Thunderhawk's landing gear. More crunched below the lower lip of the embarkation ramp as it opened up all the way. Varnica walked off the gunship onto the ground of Berenika Altis, pushing aside the bodies with his feet so he did not have to stand on them.

'Perimeter!' shouted Sergeant Novas. His squad jumped down after him and spread out around the plaza. Within moments the foul blackish flesh of the bodies was clinging to the armour of their feet and shins, shining wetly in the afternoon sun. The filters built into Varnica's lungs took care of the toxins and diseases in the air, but anyone without those augmentations would have vomited or choked on the stench

Techmarine Hamilca was last out, accompanied by the quartet of servitors that followed him everywhere like loyal pets.

'What do you think, Techmarine?' asked Varnica.

Hamilca looked around him. The tombs of the Embalmers' Quarter showed no sign of gunfire or destruction, and the sun was shining down from a blue sky. If one cast his gaze up far enough, there was nothing to see but a handsome city and fine weather. The bodies seemed incongruous, as if they did not belong here, even though they were undoubtedly the remains of this city's population.

'It is a beautiful day,' said Hamilca, and turned to adjust the sensors of his servitors.

'One day,' said Novas, 'they'll put your brain back in, tin man.'

Hamilca did not answer that. Varnica knelt to examine the bodies at his feet.

What remained of their clothing ranged from the boiler suits of menials to the silks and furs of the city's old money elite. The wounds were from fingers and teeth, or from whatever had been at hand. Tools and wrenches. Walking canes. A few kitchen knives, chunks of masonry, hatpins. One burly man's throat had a woman's silken scarf tied around it as a garrotte. Its previous owner might well have been the slender woman whose corpse lay, broken-necked, beside him. They had killed

582   *Ben Counter*

with anything at hand, which meant the time between normality and killing had been measured in minutes.

'It was the Red Night,' said Varnica.

'Can you be sure?' asked Hamilca.

'I admire your desire to gather evidence,' said Varnica, 'but I need see no more than this. It is my soul that tells me. So many places like this we have seen, and I hear their echo off the walls of this city. The Red Night came here. I know it.'

'Then why are we here?' said Novas. His squad was by now in a loose perimeter formation, bolters trained down the avenues of tombs radiating out from the plaza. Novas's Space Marines were well drilled, and Novas himself possessed a desire to be seen doing his duty, combined with a blessed lack of imagination. These qualities made his squad Varnica's escort of choice. They could be trusted to do their job and leave the thinking to the Librarian. 'The last time we came to a place touched by the Red Night, there was nought to find though we turned that place inside out. Why will Berenika Altis be any different?'

'Just smell,' said Varnica.

Novas snarled with a lack of amusement.

'Do not scorn such advice, sergeant!' Varnica breathed in deeply, theatrically. 'Ah, what a bouquet! Ruptured entrails! Liquefying muscle! They are fresh! Compared to the last places we visited, these bodies are ripe! We have got here earlier than before, Novas. These bodies still have flesh on them. We are not picking over a skeletonised heap but sloshing through the very swamp of their decay. Whatever brought the Red Night here, there is a good chance it still remains in Berenika Altis.'

'We shall not find it here,' said Hamilca. He was consulting readings from the screen built into the chest of one servitor. Another was taking pict-grabs using the lens that replaced both its eyes, roving across the corpse-choked streets. 'Not in these streets.'

Varnica held up the burly man's corpse. It was sagging and foul, the joints giving way so the limbs hung unnaturally loose. The head lolled on its fractured neck. 'He will not tell us anything more, that is for certain.' He looked towards the skyline at the centre of Berenika Altis. The Sanctum Nova Pecuniae rose above the necropoli of the Embalmers' Quarter, its spires scything towards the sky in golden arcs. 'Let's ask the people who count.'

The Red Night.

It was a wave of madness. Or, it was a disease that caused violent hallucinations. Or, it was a mental attack perpetrated by cunning xenos. Or, it was the natural consequence of Imperial society's repression of human nature. Or, it was the influence of the warp seeping into real space.

The Red Night caused everyone in the afflicted city to tear one another apart. The urge to do so came over them instantly. Most such disturbances led to an exodus of refugees fleeing the carnage, as the madness spread along some social vector. The Red Night, however, worked instantly. No word escaped the city, and so no one could intervene until the lack of communication forced an investigation and the first horrified reports came back of the scale of the death.

It had happened five times that the Doom Eagles knew of. Four times Doom Eagles Space Marines had reached the afflicted city to find nothing but a multitude of well-rotted bodies, their flesh turned to black slurry caking the gutters, and bones already starting to bleach. The fourth time, Varnica perceived a spiralling route that connected the instances of the Red Night and, more through intuition than calculation, plotted a route for his taskforce that took it within two weeks' travel of Tethlan's Holt. When the whispers of the Red Night had been intercepted by the astropath on the *Killing Shadow*, the strike cruiser commanded by Varnica, the ship had dropped out of the warp long enough to point its prow towards Tethlan's Holt.

In time, the Red Night would evolve completely into legend. Every voidborn shiphand would know someone who knew someone who had lost a friend to it. Collected tales of the Red Night would fill half-throne chapbooks. Melodramas and tragedies would be written about it. Street-corner madmen would rave about the Red Night coming the next day, or the next week, or the next year, to take up all the sinners in its bloody embrace.

Varnica would not let that happen. The truth about the Red Night would be uncovered before all hope of its discovery disappeared among the legends. Too often the Imperium caused the truth to atrophy, replaced by fear and madness. It was Varnica's duty, among the many a Space Marine had to the Emperor, to scrape back as much of the truth as he could from the hungry maw of history. Each time the Red Night had struck, he had got a little closer to that truth, something he felt rather than understood, as if the screams of the dying got more intense in his imagination each time he saw those dreadful dead streets from the sky.

The truth was in Berenika Altis. Varnica knew this as only a Librarian could. Only a psyker's inner eye could perceive something so absolutely. Varnica would discover the truth behind the Red Night, or he would not leave this city. He had never been so certain of anything.

The bodies suited the Sanctum Nova Pecuniae. It resembled a scene from a tragic play, painted by a master who placed it on a fanciful stage of soaring columns and marble, the dead contorted, their faces anguished, every clutching hand and sunken eye socket the telling of another story amid the drama.

The ground floor of the palace was a single vast space, punctuated with columns and shrines. It was possible to walk, and indeed see, from one side of the palace to the other from outside through the vast archways, without encountering a wall. To a new visitor the place would at first seem hollow, as if forming some metaphor for transparency or absence of government. The complex architecture of the roof, however, formed of overlapping vaults and petals, hid the spaces where the government actually met and did business. This was a metaphor, too, thought Varnica as he cast his senses around him, half as a soldier and half as an appreciator of the palace's art. The really important people in Berenika Altis existed on a higher plane, like a heaven sealed off among the friezes and inscriptions of the shadowy ceiling.

The Doom Eagles had entered through an archway, above which were carved words in High Gothic proclaiming that portion of the Sanctum Nova Pecuniae to have been built by the Guild of Steelwrights. Notable past masters of that guild were remembered in the statues that stood in alcoves, forming shrines to the exemplars of the guild's values. They held formidable-looking tools, multiwrenches and pneumohammers, and had faces that looked like they had been beaten out of steel themselves.

'These dead were not mere citizens,' said Hamilca, whose medical servitor was playing its sensors over a knot of corpses at the base of the nearest pillar. 'They wear the marks of nobility. Here, the badge of the Flagellants' Guild. This one wears cloth of gold and ermine.'

'The government must have been in session,' said Varnica. 'Perhaps the timing was deliberate?'

Novas spat on the floor. He was a superstitious type, and the horror of this place was more spiritual than the mundanity of the bodies outside. Showing his contempt with a wad of phlegm scared away the dark things mustering on the other side of the Veil, so the superstitions went.

A pillar a short distance away had a particularly dense heap of bodies around it. They were three deep, as if they had been clambering over one another to get at the pillar. Bloody smudges from fingers and hands painted the flutes of the pillar. Varnica walked over to them, picking his way past the master artisans and councillors who lay in his way. 'Here,' he said. 'There is a way up.' He hauled on one of the blade-like stone flutes and it swung open, to reveal a tight spiral staircase corkscrewing up through the pillar.

A body fell out. Its face had been torn so much it was impossible to tell the back of the head from the front. Two severed arms tumbled behind it, neither of them belonging to the first body. Varnica looked up the staircase and saw bodies wedged into the pillar, clogging it up before the first twist.

The leaders of Berenika Altis had thought the day-to-day business of government vulgar enough to hide it in the grand architecture of the

Sanctum. Men and women had died trying to get at the concealed working of government, even as they were rending each other apart. Was it some bestial remnant of memory that caused them to flee to the only place a nobleman might feel safe? Or had there been something in the madness itself that compelled them to seek something above?

Varnica said nothing. He simple forced his armoured form into the tight space of the staircase and began dragging down the bodies that stood in his way.

Hamilca's servitors aided the removal of corpses greatly. Thirty more of them lay beside the pillar, all horribly mauled as if chewed up and spat out, before Varnica reached the top. Novas's battle-brothers followed him up, crouch-walking in the cramped space.

Varnica emerged in a chamber of maps and portraits, a sort of antechamber before the government debating chambers and offices. The lower portraits, more stern steelwright masters along with well-heeled embalmers and jewelcutters in their leather aprons, were spattered with blood. Framed maps depicted early layouts of Berenika Altis and the changing political divisions of Tethlan's Holt. Various landmasses were drawn in differing sizes from map to map, reflecting their relative importance. Varnica remembered that every planet in the Imperium had a history like this, shifting, waxing and waning for thousands of years, while the Imperium beyond did not care unless something happened to end that history entirely.

The bodies here were clustered around one door. Hamilca moved to examine them while Novas's squad covered all the entrances.

Varnica took a better look at one portrait, mounted just high enough to have avoided the worst of the spraying blood. It was of a member of the Flagellants' Guild. It was a large woman, well-fed rather than naturally bulky, whose ample bosom was encased ridiculously in an embroidered version of a penitent's sackcloth robe. Spots of red makeup simulated self-inflicted wounds and her hair was piled up in a magnificent structure held in place by the kinds of serrated needles more properly used for extracting confessions. In one hand she held, like a royal sceptre, a scourge with three spiked chains, the implement of her guild's craft.

In the lower corner was a handprint in blood. It was made too surely and deliberately to have been accidental, from a flailing fist. Someone had used this wall to steady themselves. Someone wounded.

Varnica followed the tracks through the gory mess of the floor. 'They were following someone,' he said as he paced carefully towards the body-choked door. 'He was wounded and limping but he wasn't scrabbling along like an animal, as the rest of the souls were. They were after him. The Red Night sent them after one man in particular.'

The tracks led to the door where Hamilca's servitors were making a survey of the various wounds. 'They dashed themselves to death against the door,' said Hamilca. 'Few wounds from hands or teeth. They broke themselves here trying to get through.'

The door had been panelled with wood to make it in keeping with the rest of the government office, but that façade had splintered with the assault to reveal the solid metal beneath. It was a security door to keep out just the kind of frenzied assault that had broken against it.

Varnica sighed. He did not like having to use the full range of his talents. He had always felt that a psyker should properly be something subtle, an intelligence weapon, reading or remaking minds, perhaps astrally projecting to make the perfect spy. His own talents had taken a form that he found ugly in the extreme. Still, duties were duties, and he had the best way of getting through the door that would not risk destroying evidence beyond.

He clenched his right fist and thought of anger. The lines of the room seemed to warp around his fist, as if it were encased in a lens that distorted anything seen through it. Reality did not like it when he did this, and he had to fight it.

Black and purple rippled around the gauntlet. Sparks crackled across the segments of armour around his fingers. The region of deviant gravity Varnica willed into being bowed and seethed as he drew back the fist that now disobeyed the laws of force and energy.

Varnica punched the door clean off its mountings. The whole room seemed to shudder, its dimensions flickering slightly out of balance as Varnica's psychic power discharged in a thrust of force. The metal door clanged into the room beyond.

The Librarium of the Doom Eagles liked to classify its members' psychic powers according to categories and strength. Varnica's was referred to as the Hammerhand, a crude but effective power that typically augmented the Librarian's capacity for hand-to-hand combat. Varnica disliked the Librarium's testing of its intensity, but he conceded that it was powerful, and that it would get more powerful the more he exercised the mental muscles that powered it.

Varnica shook out his hand as the power around it dissipated.

Novas smiled. 'No door is locked when one wields the Emperor's key,' he said.

'Quite,' replied Varnica. *The Emperor's key.* It sounded rather more elegant than 'Hammerhand'.

The room he had opened was an archive. Ceiling-high banks of index cards, yellowing ledger books and scroll racks exuded a smell of old paper that almost overpowered the stink of decay.

On a reading table was sprawled the single body this room contained. It wore grand robes that suggested high office in the planet's government. The dead man still had a dagger in his hand, probably worn more for ceremony than self-defence. The point of the dagger pinned a handful of papers to the tabletop. Several opened drawers and scattered papers suggested he had rooted around and found them in a hurry, and in his last moments made sure that whoever found him would also find those specific documents.

The man had torn his own throat out with his other hand. He lay in the black stain of his blood. His body sagged with decay beneath the robes now filthy with old blood and the seepage of rot.

Varnica pulled out the dagger and looked at the documents this man had fought to call attention to, even while the Red Night was taking control of him.

They were receipts and blueprints for work done on the sewers beneath the Jewelcutters' Quarter, between seventy and forty years before. Varnica leafed through them rapidly. They were nothing more than the detritus of a civil service that loved to remember its own deeds.

'What was he trying to tell us?' asked Hamilca.

'He was telling us,' said Varnica, 'to look down.'

The first of them had a face like a knot of knuckles, deep red flesh that oozed hissing molten metal, sinewy arms that wielded a smouldering blade of black steel. It congealed up from the black mass of old blood pooling in the sewer; that drizzle of gore from the bloodshed above. Its face split open, tearing skin, and it screamed. A whip-like tongue lashed out.

More of them were emerging. Dozens of them.

The sewers. Berenika Altis's greatest achievement, some said. Hidden from the world above, each section of sewer was like a cathedral nave, a monument to glory for its own sake, lit by faded glow-globes and faced with marble and plaster murals. Most cities of the Imperium would have gathered here to worship. On Berenika Altis the combined efforts of the flagellants and the jewelcutters had created instead such a place to accommodate the filth of the city.

It was here the blood had flowed. It was here the Doom Eagles had come, following the signs left them by that unnamed nobleman who had died in the Sanctum. It was here they realised they were getting close to the secret of the Red Night.

'Daemons!' yelled Novas. 'Close formation. Rapid fire!'

More daemons were congealing from the blood that slaked the floor of the sewer section. They rushed at the Doom Eagles, hate in their eyes and their swords held high.

Novas's squad drew in close around Varnica and Hamilca. The ten Adeptus Astartes hammered out a volley of bolter fire. Three or four daemons were shredded at once, gobbets of their molten metal blood hissing against the marble walls. But Varnica counted more than twenty more daemons now charging to attack. Bolter fire would thin them out, but this was a task that had to be finished by hand.

Varnica thrust his right hand into the complex holster he wore on one hip. The sections of his force claw closed around his hand. When he withdrew it, it was encased in a pair of sharp blades in a pincer, each blade swirling with psychoactive circuitry.

Varnica let his psychic power fill his fists. Distasteful as it was, it was for encounters like this that he had trained his mental muscles. The air warped around his hands and the force claw glowed blue-white with its power.

The daemons rushed closer. Novas shot another down, blowing its yowling head from its shoulders. Varnica pushed his way between the two Doom Eagles in front of him and dived into the fray.

His force claw closed on one and sheared it in two. A fountain of red-hot blood sprayed over his armour, hissing where it touched the ceramite. His other fist slammed down, just missing the next daemon in his way and ripping a crater out of the flagstone floor. He span, driving his right elbow into the daemon and backhanding another hard enough to rip its whole jaw off.

He imagined his fists were meteors, smouldering masses of rock, attached to him by chains, and wherever he swung them anything in the way would be destroyed. That was the secret of many a psychic weapon – imagination, the ability to mould them in a psyker's mind's eye into whatever he needed them to be. Varnica needed them to be wrecking balls smashing through the hideous things that reared up around him. Their bodies were walls to be battered down. They were doorways to be opened with the Emperor's Key.

Rapid gunfire sprayed around him. Hamilca's servitors were not just scientific instruments – one had opened up, its torso becoming an archway of metal and skin within which were mounted a pair of rotator cannon. They blazed away at Hamilca's direction, even as Hamilca himself took aim with his plasma pistol and blew the arm off another daemon before it could fully congeal into existence.

Varnica's shoulder guard turned away one daemon's blade and he ducked under another. He rose, claw first, lifting a daemon above his head and letting the pincers snap open so the daemon was sheared in two. He stamped down on the blade of the first daemon and, as it fought to wrench its weapon up to strike again, Varnica drove an elbow into its face and punched it in the chest as it reeled. Purple-black light shimmered around the gravity well of his fist as it ripped through the thing's ribs and burst out through its back.

Hands grabbed Varnica by the collar and backpack of his armour, wrenching him down. He fought to straighten up but the strength and suddenness of the attack had caught him off-guard.

He saw the face of Novas, whose hands were pulling him down. Another Doom Eagle fired past Varnica, bolter shells blasting ragged holes in the daemon who had been about to decapitate Varnica with its blade.

'Must I nursemaid you through every fight?' growled Novas.

The Doom Eagles now formed an execution line to bring their bolters to bear on the remaining daemons. Varnica had scattered their charge and now they were trying to regroup, or to attack in ones and twos easily shot down. A final few volleys of bolter fire brought down the remaining daemons, blasting off limbs and shredding torsos. The remnants dissolved into the mass of blood and filth that covered the sewer floor.

Novas helped Varnica to his feet.

Varnica clapped the sergeant on the shoulder. 'You see, brother?' he said. 'We are close. Blessed is the enemy that announces himself to us so!'

'Blessed is your brother that keeps you alive,' said Novas.

'We know,' said Hamilca, adjusting the programming of his gun-servitor, 'that the enemy fears our   closing in on him. Therefore, we approach some place of significance to him. The documents from the Sanctum suggested the importance of a major intersection three hundred metres to our west.'

'It's the blood,' said Varnica. 'The bloodshed in the city finds its way down here, to the sewers. The enemy places himself some place where the blood gathers, and then... uses it? Fuels something with it?'

'Bathes in it, for all we know,' said Novas.

Varnica checked his wargear. The daemons' blood had burned pockmarks into his armour. Nothing important was damaged. One of Novas's squad had suffered a deep sword wound to one arm, and the helmet of another's power armour had been smashed. Varnica recognised the pugnacious features of Brother Solicus, a veteran of Novas's command. Solicus would make a point of ignoring the minor wound on the forehead and the blood that trickled down his face.

No great harm done, thought Varnica.

'Move on,' he said, and led the way westwards.

When he looked back on the Red Night of Berenika Altis, it would always be the face of Gunther Kephilaes that Varnica would remember first. That look of surprise when he saw the Doom Eagles entering his realm, to be replaced with an awful smile, as if they were guests he had been waiting for all this time.

The second memory would be of the writing on the walls. Kephilaes, later identified as an arch-heretic who had escaped repeated attempts to execute him on a dozen worlds, had chosen for his base of operations a cistern in the sewers of Berenika Altis. This place, an enormous tank built to accommodate overflow from the sewers, had been drained of water so that when the Red Night occurred, it had filled up with blood. The roof was an enormous dome carved with images of jewelcutters on one side, flaunting their elaborate arrays of jewellery and gems, and on the other a parade of flagellants lashing supplicants with their scourges. This dome, and every visible surface of wall and pillar, was covered in writing. At first it appeared black, but it was in fact a dark reddish brown. Every word had been written in blood.

Varnica, like every Space Marine, had been taught that speed of decision was essential in the opening seconds of battle. Even before Gunther Kephilaes's face had broken into that mad grin, Varnica had decided that Novas would pin the heretic down with gunfire while Varnica himself would close across the duckboards and jerry-built rafts that had been lashed together over the surface of the blood. Kephilaes sat on an island made of toppled pillars in the centre of the blood, hundreds of books and tattered papers lying on the broken stone or floating on the surface around his makeshift pulpit. Varnica could reach him, scale the drums of the broken pillars and get to grips with this heretic in a handful of seconds. He just needed those seconds, and the job would be done.

A few hand signals passed the orders on to Novas's squad, who immediately began to fan out around the ledge running around the cistern to get multiple angles of fire on the enemy.

Varnica knew by now why Kephilaes was happy to see them. These intruders meant fresh blood in which to dip the quill he held in one gnarled hand, the white feather stained with old blood. As Varnica ran forwards he noted the scholarly robes Kephilaes wore, the straggly white hair and hooked axe-like face, the way the substance of his large white eyes seemed to liquefy and run in greyish tears down his cheeks.

Kephilaes raised his quill and sketched a symbol in the air. The same symbol appeared scored into the chest of Brother Kouras of Novas's squad, the channel cut deep down through the armour in the flesh of the Adeptus Astartes's chest and abdomen. Kouras slumped to one knee and toppled forwards into the blood. Another of the squad ran to grab him and haul him onto the ledge. With a flourish, Kephilaes drew another symbol into the second Adeptus Astartes's face, the faceplate of his helmet sliced into pieces and revealing the red wetness of the scored meat inside. The second Space Marine was dead before he fell into the blood behind the first.

The gunfire began. Bolter shells erupted against the fallen pillars. Kephilaes drew a letter that hung in the air in lines of burning red, a complex sigil that formed a shield against which the bolter fire burst harmlessly.

Varnica leapt from one platform to another. This one nearly gave way beneath him. He jumped the last few metres, scrabbling for a handhold on the pillar drum he hit chest-first. A few more seconds. He needed a few more seconds, and then it would be over, and he would know what the Red Night meant at last.

He made his own handholds, the stone warping against his fingers as the psychic field around them leapt into life.

Kephilaes laughed and whooped as he scrawled in the air with abandon. Squad Novas dived for what little cover they could find as deep burning letters appeared sunk into the blood-spattered stone behind them. The letters were in an unfamiliar alphabet but somehow they made an appalling sense as Varnica glanced behind him. They were exultations, celebrations of some vast power that had reached down from the warp and torn out what little sanity this heretic had possessed. The white-haired lunatic above Varnica had done all this to extol the virtues of heresy.

Novas fell just as Varnica closed on the heretic. A message in that profane alphabet appeared across his face, chest and left shoulder. It said that this vile thing was no longer an enemy, but was a gift to the Dark Gods, with a message of thanks scrawled upon it, to serve as an offering. Varnica could see the wet masses of Novas's lungs pumping and the glistening loops of his entrails.

Varnica roared. The hate turned white around his hands and the fire blazing around them was almost too much for him to control. He scrambled up the last of the pillars and was face to face with the madman.

The man Varnica would later identify as Gunther Kephilaes seemed happy to see him. He held out his arms, and Varnica saw the letters he had carved into his own chest beneath his scholar's robes.

'Welcome,' he said.

Varnica punched the heretic in the face with enough force to topple a wall. Kephilaes did not come apart under the blow as honest human flesh would. Dozens of sigils burned pain fully bright around him, channelling the power away from him. Enough force got through to knock Kephilaes to his knees. He held up a hand to beg.

'No,' the heretic gasped. 'You do not understand. Look around you! You do not understand.'

Varnica bent down and wrapped his arms around a section of pillar. The psychic warp around his hands made it light. He hauled it up over its head, and felt a thrill of satisfaction as its shadow passed over the heretic.

Varnica slammed the stone down. The heretic was completely crushed, the last of his witchcraft protection bled away by Varnica's first assault.

Varnica felt the crunching of bones and the wet slurp of the flesh torn flat. Just to be sure, he lifted the stone again and hammered it down once more.

Something about the deadness suddenly in the air told him this heretic had breathed his last.

Their gods always abandon them, thought Varnica. In the end.

The Red Night had been created by Gunther Kephilaes to provide the vast amounts of angrily-shed blood he needed to write down what his gods dictated to him. This was the conclusion made by the Doom Eagles' Librarium after all the evidence, including the script transcribed from the walls by Hamilca's servitors, was presented to the Chapter.

Varnica had buried Sergeant Novas that morning. Novas and the three Doom Eagles who had died at Kephilaes's hands were laid on stone slabs, anointed with medical incense to seal up the wounds where their gene-seeds had been removed, and lowered into the funerary pits where the Chapter interred their dead. Novas was buried with his bolter, his copy of *Principles of Squad-Level Purgation of the Emperor's Foes*, and the shell of a bullet that had wounded him early in his career and which he had saved as a memento mori. Varnica had prayed at the graveside, and wondered how it was that an Adeptus Astartes, with his soul steeled against the worst the galaxy could throw at him, could still feel such a human thing as grief.

Now Varnica sat among the archives of the Chapter Librarium, surrounded by freshly inked tomes filled with the profane writings of Gunther Kephilaes. Some Chapters would have destroyed the writing on the walls, and compelled any Space Marine who had seen them to cleanse himself with fire or denial until their corruption was gone. But the Doom Eagles were not like those other Chapters. They wanted to *understand*.

The Librarium's scribe-servitors were still transcribing the complex code-language into High Gothic, and filling ledger after ledger with the ramblings that resulted. Varnica had one such book in front of him, leafing through the parade of obscenity. Kephilaes had been a prophet, in part at least, and the endless train of prodigies and omens filled Varnica's mind with images of stars boiling away and the galaxy burning from core to rim.

'Librarian,' came a familiar voice.

Varnica looked up to see Techmarine Hamilca walking among the small forest of servitors that chittered away as they wrote. 'I had heard tell I would find you here.'

'Where else would one find a Librarian,' replied Varnica, 'but in a library?'

Hamilca smiled. 'Your levity need be a shield no longer, Librarian. Not while you and I are the only ones to see it. The loss of Novas has affected you more deeply than an Adeptus Astartes is apt to admit.'

'One more trial on the path, brother. One more trial.'

'What did Kephilaes have to say for himself?'

Varnica closed the tome he had finished scanning through. 'At the last count, Techmarine, seventeen million people died so he could tell us that a great feathered serpent was going to swallow the sun. And that a plague of cockroaches would devour a great empire. No details on which sun or which empire.'

'Perhaps,' said Hamilca, 'this is a task that could be shared?'

'One mind, I fear, is better than two when it comes to such things. I consider reading Kephilaes's drivel a penance for losing good Doom Eagles under my command.'

'So be it, Librarian. I and my servitors shall be ready to assist you.' Hamilca finished making a few adjustments to the scribe-servitors, and the hum of their scribbling autoquills changed pitch slightly. 'And so, brother I leave you.'

'Wait,' said Varnica. Hamilca stopped just as he was turning away. Varnica had opened another volume of the heretic's writings. 'Here. And here. The same name. A daemon prince. This is a record of its deeds.'

'Kephilaes's patron?' asked Hamilca.

'Perhaps. It was one of the most powerful of its kind, one of the brood of the Change God. Throne alive, I fear I shall need the services of the Flagellants' Guild to purify myself after reading this. It was... it was a plotter without compare. A manipulator. "There was not one living soul without a flaw that he could not widen to a chasm into which that soul would fall. A saint would be prey to this great cunning."'

'This daemon prince,' said Hamilca, sitting opposite Varnica and taking a book for himself. 'It is active now? The Red Night was some form of sacrifice to it?'

'It is possible. There is more. Here – a record of its deeds. It polluted the gene pool of a triad of worlds, so they became barbarians and warred with one another. An obscene tale about Saint Voynara, who before she died gave in to despair and called upon this prince to deliver her. And its masterpiece, the crowning glory... by Terra, what foulness I see before my eyes!'

Hamilca leaned forwards. 'Librarian? What is it? What have you seen?'

'It took a Chapter of Adeptus Astartes,' read Varnica, 'and it found in them a fatal flaw. It was their pride. That same sin we all commit, brother. Our pride, our weakness. And it turned this Chapter into an instrument of its will, through trickery compelling them to do its bidding while they thought they were doing the Emperor's work.'

'What Chapter was this?' asked Hamilca. 'Many have fallen from grace or disappeared. Is this the truth behind the fall of the Brazen Claws or the Thunder Barons?'

'No,' replied Varnica. 'This daemon prince, when its name was spoken, was called Abraxes. The Chapter it commanded was the Soul Drinkers.'

CHAPTER FIVE

'It will not hurt, brother,' said Sister Solace to Brother Sennon. In the cramped cell, once the living space of an engineer among the cavernous workings of the *Phalanx*, a few candles guttered, giving a struggling yellowish light. In Solace's hands was a wide-gauge needle hooked up to a pump and an intravenous bag.

'I do not fear pain,' replied Sennon, who lay bare-chested on a mattress. Sweat beaded on his face in spite of his words, and his voice came from a dry throat. He had never looked younger. In the shadows he seemed a child, defying the cowardice that his youth should have brought him.

'We need not make ourselves suffer now,' replied Solace. 'The time for such things is over. Let the Emperor's kindness soothe you, and I shall make you as comfortable as possible.'

Sennon swallowed, and winced as the tip of the needle touched the vein Solace had located on the inside of his elbow. The needle slid under his skin, the pump began to work and the intravenous bag filled up. Solace hooked up a second bag, this one filled with a clear bluish liquid.

'Speak to me, my brother,' she said as Sennon's eyes drifted out of focus. 'What can you see?'

'I see you, my sister,' said Sennon. His throat constricted and he grimaced as he fought to breathe. Solace took his hand and squeezed. 'I see… this place is gone. There are no walls. The *Phalanx* is gone.'

'What is it? What do you see?'

'I see... a battlefield.' Sennon's body relaxed and his eyes seemed to focus on a point far off, past the ceiling of the cell with its rag-tag collection of mementos from a life among the engines of the *Phalanx*. Cogs and valves were piled up on a shelf beneath a metal icon painted with the symbol of the Imperial Fists. A few ragged sets of protective clothing were hung up above an alcove containing three pairs of battered steel-toed boots. A paltry collection of religious verses and children's stories filled a small cupboard beside the mattress on which Sennon lay, and on the ceiling a previous occupier had drawn images of stars and crescent moons. Sennon saw none of it. Solace thought for a moment that she could see an endless landscape of rolling plains and mountains reflected in the youth's eyes as his pupils expanded to black pools.

'It goes on forever,' said Sennon, his breath hushed. 'They are all there, all those who have died in the Emperor's name. They are there to join him in the battle at the end of time.'

'Tell me,' said Sister Solace. She adjusted the pump, which hummed louder as the liquid coursed faster through Sennon's veins. Gauges on the side of the pump read various pressures and she tried to keep them aligned. Too fast or too slow and the youth would die.

'I see billions of them, the uniforms of the Imperial Guard,' said Sennon. A million regiments, bayonets fixed, stretching across a world. And others too, ordinary men and women in a great throng. All the pious souls that have ever died. And at the forefront are the Adeptus Astartes, the Angels of Death!'

Solace looked up. A trickle of blood ran from Sennon's nose. 'As Gyranar told us?' she asked.

'Yes! Oh, sister, they are beautiful! Their armour gleams, and they have wings of gold on which to fly!' Sennon's face spread into a rapturous smile, even as blood collected in the corner of his mouth. 'Their eyes are aflame! Mighty blades shine in their hands. But... but the Enemy is here also. The Adversary. All the foul tongues of the warp have spoken into existence an army even greater!'

Sennon's body began to shudder. Solace took the youth's pulse from his wrist: his heart was hammering, his face now showing an awestruck fear.

'Speak to me of them, brother,' said Solace. 'There is nothing to fear in them. They cannot harm you. Speak to me.'

'Monsters without form. Flesh turned liquid, bathed in fire. Legions of the hateful warp-spawned, like regiments on the parade ground. Things of living corruption, smothered under a blanket of flies, seething masses of filth! Mountains of rot that vomit torrents of their progeny onto the field! And worse... sister, worse things, so sinful and lascivious in form that I cannot look away! Tear my eyes from them, sister, before they infect my soul!'

'Do not fear, brother. I am with you. The Emperor is with you. No harm can befall you, for you are under His protection. Believe in Him, believe, brother!'

'And still more,' continued Sennon, his voice speeding up into a near-gabble. 'The generals and the overlords of the Adversary. They tower! Their shadows cast whole continents into darkness! Mighty horned things, wielding blades wreathed in flame! I see a beast with a hundred heads, crowned with laurels of entwined bodies. I see... I see a creature red-skinned and immense, its wings blocking out the sun, the axe in its hand oozing blood! I can see all the galaxy's hatred in its twisted face. But it cannot harm me. Though its eyes fall on me, it cannot harm me!'

'No,' said Solace. 'It cannot.' She lacked the equipment to read Sennon's vital signs properly, so she had to do it by eye, reading the youth's pulse and the dilation of his pupils, the spasming of his fingers and toes, the alternating rigidity and weakness of his limbs. The *Phalanx* had some of the finest medicae facilities in the Imperium within its apothecarion and the sickbays used by the crew, but Solace had to do this work away from the eyes of the Imperial Fists and the *Phalanx*'s crewmen. It had to be done this way.

And if Sennon died, there were others. She would go through the whole Blinded Eye if she had to. If it came to it, she would do this to herself.

'I see the gods of the warp!' gasped Sennon. 'Saints take my eyes! Faithful hands strip me of my senses! I see such things that creation cannot contain! Talon and hateful eye, wing and feather, an ocean of rotting flesh and the awful knotted limbs of the eternal dancer! And yet... and yet they are in shadow, cast by a far greater light...'

Solace checked the gauges. Most of Sennon's blood was gone. The fluid that replaced it was pumping through him, but it might not be fast enough. This was the most dangerous point, where the body hovered between bleeding to death and being suffused with its replacement blood.

'The primarchs stand ready to command the host. Sanguinius the Angel paints his face with a million tears, one for every blood-brother who stands by his side. Russ and the Lion are side by side, their hatred for one another gone, the Wolves of Fenris and the Dark Angels standing proud. Guilliman and his host, vaster than any other army ever assembled. The Khan, the Iron-Handed One, and Vulkan, all gathered, exhorting their brothers to war! And Dorn, holy Dorn, sacred Dorn, the greatest of them, I see the banner in his hands spun from the starlight of every sun within the Emperor's domain! He is the Champion of the Emperor, the first to fight, the tip of His spear and the lightning that shall be cast down among the enemy! He shines like gold, such a blaze of fire that the enemy are blinded and they howl in anguish at the presence of such holiness!'

Sennon gasped and his eyes rolled back. Solace grabbed his hand and squeezed it tighter. 'Brother! Keep talking, brother! Tell me what you see! Sennon, tell me what you see!'

Sennon just gasped in response, spraying flecks of blood down his chin.

Solace scrabbled in the meagre selection of medical gear that lay on the floor around her. She found a syringe and tore its wrapping open. The syringe was pre-loaded with a fat needle as long as a finger and a steel cylinder of a body. Solace held the syringe point-down over Sennon's chest, muttered a prayer, and stabbed down.

The needle punched between Sennon's ribs. The liquid inside flooded into his heart and his whole body juddered as if hit with an electric shock. Solace had to lean over him and put her body weight on him to keep the needle from breaking off or tearing too big a hole in the youth's heart. Sennon gasped, sputtering more blood. A mist of it spattered against the side of Solace's face. His body tensed and arched, joints creaking.

Sennon slumped down again. He let out a long rattling breath from a painfully dry throat.

'I see the Emperor,' he murmured. 'He tells me not to be afraid. He tells me to fight.'

Solace looked down at the gauges and readouts again. They had stabilised. The exchange was complete.

She withdrew the needle from Sennon's arm and placed a dressing on the wound. She wiped the blood from his face with a wet cloth.

'You will fight, my brother,' she whispered. 'I promise.'

In the tumult following Librarian Varnica's evidence, Chapter Master Pugh had called an adjournment to the trial. Sarpedon had been led back to his cell, the Imperial Fists refusing any answer to his requests to speak with Daenyathos. The alleged presence of the Philosopher-Soldier still had his mind in a whirl. The dismay that he had felt to have Abraxes's existence revealed to the trial was a new counterpart to that confusion. Piece by piece, everything he had been sure of was falling apart.

He was grateful for the cell, though he had never thought he could think so. Its cramped walls and deadening psychic wards, smothering though they were, were preferable to the hatred that surrounded him in the courtroom. He crouched against one wall, and stared for a few minutes at the heap of crumpled papers, all that remained of his attempts to pen final words to his battle-brothers.

What could he say? What would make any difference? He had thought he would face this trial with dignity and courage, perhaps even to make his execution, when it came, a reluctant act on the part of the executioners. Now even that small victory felt very far away.

'I will not kneel,' he said to himself. 'I will not despair. I am Adeptus Astartes. I will not despair.'

'I fear for your sake, Chapter Master, that whether to despair is not your decision to make.'

Sarpedon's eyes snapped to the opening in the cell door. It was not the voice of a Space Marine – it was a woman. This one had a note of familiarity to it, though.

Sarpedon scuttled up to the door. Beyond it, flanked by a pair of Imperial Fists with bolters at the ready, was Sister Aescarion of the Adepta Sororitas. She, like the Space Marines, wore her full armour to the trial and still had it on now, a suit of polished black ceramite emblazoned with the iconography of the Imperial Church. Her own weapon was the power axe but it was strapped to the jump pack of her armour now and she did not have it to hand. She was a full head shorter than a Space Marine for she was not augmented like them, and had a stern, angular yet handsome face with red-brown hair tied back in a ponytail.

'I recall you from Stratix Luminae,' said Sarpedon.

'An encounter I would sooner forget,' replied Aescarion.

'None of us wish to remember the sight of an adversary who departs the battlefield alive.'

'And you are still my adversary,' said the Battle Sister. 'Nothing has changed on that score. You are a traitor.'

'And yet,' said Sarpedon, 'you willingly exchange words with me. It seems women are as a strange a breed of creature as men say.'

'Not as strange as a condemned prisoner who makes light of his situation,' said Aescarion with a withering look that had no doubt been the scourge of the Sororitas novices she had trained.

'I trust you have not come here to swap insults, Sister,' said Sarpedon.

Aescarion glanced at the Imperial Fists flanking her. 'If you please,' she said to them. 'A few minutes are all I ask.'

'Stay in sight,' replied one of the Imperial Fists. The two Adeptus Astartes parted and walked several paces down the corridor outside Sarpedon's cell, out of earshot.

'They run a tight ship, these sons of Dorn,' said Sarpedon. 'As strait-laced as they come. It must be a comfort to be in the presence of Space Marines who jump when Terra demands it.'

'I find no comfort while enemies yet live,' replied Aescarion sharply. 'But I have nothing but admiration for the Imperial Fists, it is true. I find a little of my faith in humanity restored.'

'I have faith in humanity as well, Sister. It is not the people of the Imperium I have ever had a problem with. It is the structures by which the Imperium maintains itself, clinging to existence through blood and cruelty. I have seen them over and over. And you have too, Sister Aescarion. Worlds condemned to misery or death. Freedom and rebellion given the same names and crushed beneath the mass of the shiploads of captives sent to Terra to–'

'Enough! Do not speak of such things.'

'And pretend, instead, that they never existed?' Sarpedon reared up and put his face close to the window in the cell door.

'No! Accept them as necessary for the survival of the human race, and turn our minds instead to the glory of our survival! That is how the Sororitas are taught.'

'You think this is survival?' Sarpedon held his arms wide, indicating not just his cell but everything beyond. 'The human race is in its death throes! It inflicts miseries upon its people to protect them from its enemies, and yet it is those miseries that bring such enemies into being! Why do so many desperate people turn from the Emperor's light and make pacts with the Dark Powers? Why do they cry out to be delivered and so walk right into xenos hands? The Imperium inflicts these wounds upon itself. It is nothing more than the slow death of mankind.'

'You will need to find a far better orator than yourself, Sarpedon, to sway the mind of a Sister of Battle,' retorted Aescarion sourly. 'I did not come here to let you practise your closing arguments on me. I am here about my late master, Inquisitor Thaddeus. You know of him?'

Sarpedon sat back down on his haunches. 'Yes. I knew him.'

'Personally?'

'A little.'

'Thaddeus had the chance to take you down on Stratix Luminae. Perhaps kill you. But he did not take that chance. I was with him at the time and I did not understand his decision. I still do not. I want to know why Inquisitor Thaddeus, a servant of the Emperor and sworn enemy of all that hates mankind, chose to let you go.'

Sarpedon's memories of Inquisitor Thaddeus were of a man who, at first sight, was completely out of his depth. He had looked like a functionary of the Administratum, some middle-ranking nobody. Some inquisitors proclaimed their office with the most obvious and terrifying battlegear they could find, huge retinues of warriors and experts, even fleets and armies of their own. But Thaddeus walked softly in his duties.

'After Stratix Luminae he tried to keep track of us, even after the Inquisition ordered us deleted from Imperial history,' said Sarpedon. 'When he found us on Vanqualis he had been hunting down every rumour of us. He had found… there were legends of us in places I was sure the Chapter had never been. One was of the Black Chalice. Another was the Ashen Grail. I did not give much thought to them at the time but now I fear there is some web that has been spun out there, in which the Soul Drinkers have their part but of which they are ignorant. Thaddeus was trying to unravel it.'

'But he did not succeed,' said Aescarion.

'No. I imagine he is dead. The Howling Griffons crossed our path there, perhaps Captain Borganor can tell you more after he stops complaining about me cutting off his leg.'

'But Thaddeus knew none of this on Stratix Luminae. Why not kill you then when he could?' insisted Aescarion.

'Perhaps,' replied Sarpedon, 'he knew we were right?'

Aescarion lost her cool for a second. She slammed the palm of her hand into the cell door. 'You dare!' she hissed. 'He would never have thrown in his lot with your kind. Thaddeus was a good man. The best of men.'

'But you want me to tell you that he was not corrupted. That hardly suggests you have great confidence in the man.'

'You are just toying with me, Sarpedon. I will not provide you with any more amusement. You don't know Thaddeus's motives and I will content myself with that.' Aescarion turned, about to rejoin her Imperial Fists minders and leave.

'He tried to warn us,' Sarpedon said. 'The Ashen Grail and the Black Chalice, and everything else he found, it all pointed to something he was trying to warn us about. I don't think even he knew what he had found, but his misgivings were deep enough for him to defy the deletion order and seek us out.'

'Then he was leading you into a trap,' said Aescarion.

'And you have misgivings too. Otherwise you would not have sought me out here. How many lashes would a Sororitas receive for conversing with a known heretic? And yet you come to my cell looking for answers. You see it too, just like Thaddeus did. Something about this trial is wrong and you know it. Daenyathos's return, here of all places, is no coincidence.'

'There is no coincidence. You came to the Veiled Region to seek him out. You and he both are puppets of that thing Abraxes that Varnica spoke of.'

'Well, Sister, if you have made up your mind about everything already there hardly seems a need to question me at all.'

Aescarion shook her head. 'Part of me wishes to know what must have to happen to an Adeptus Astartes before he can turn from the Emperor's light. But I fear that such knowledge itself has the power to corrupt. I should have let you keep your silence, traitor. I hope this trial ends before you can do any more damage.'

'Then I doubt you and I have anything more to say to one another.'

Aescarion didn't bother to reply. She turned smartly on an armoured heel and walked out of sight down the brig corridor. One of the Imperial Fists slammed the window shut, and Sarpedon was alone again.

* * *

When visitors sought an audience with Chapter Master Pugh on the *Phalanx*, he often chose to receive them in the Sigismarch Forest. This artificial woodland occupied an area amidships on one of the uppermost decks, its greenery illuminated by an artificial sun that made a circuit once every twenty-four hours. A river ran though it, fresh water diverted from the crew's drinking supply to create the illusion that the forest was just part of a far greater lush and peaceful land where, even on board a vast weapon of war, a place of contemplation might be found.

'So,' said Pugh, taking his place sat on a tree stump by the river bank where he was accustomed to receive his petitioners. 'Speak.'

In the clearing before Pugh stood Reinez. Behind him were the officers of the Adeptus Astartes who had come to the *Phalanx* for the trial. They included Varnica, whose evidence had prompted this re-evaluation of the whole trial. None of the captains and Librarians had brought their retinues with them, for this was not the place for a competitive show of arms.

'I put it to the Justice Lord,' began Reinez, 'that the accused Sarpedon must be considered a moral threat. Librarian Varnica's evidence proves the accused's complicity with powers of the warp. This trial must cease and the executions be administered immediately.' Reinez spoke with a snarling bluntness that made it clear he had thought this from the very start.

'I see,' said Pugh. 'Indeed, Varnica's statements have changed the complexion of this trial. And yet I must see to it that justice is not only done, but that no man can find any reason to suggest that the course of justice has not been followed. For evidence of warpcraft, I have but the evidence of one Adeptus Astartes. As high as the esteem in which I hold you, Librarian Varnica, you are but one.'

'That I cannot deny, my lord,' replied Varnica. 'But I know what I saw. The stink of the warp hangs over this whole affair.'

'And when was suspicion ever insufficient evidence in matters of a moral threat?' added Reinez.

'I know that you long to see Sarpedon dead, Reinez,' replied Pugh, pointedly omitting any rank when he addressed the Crimson Fist, for since Reinez had become a penitent he had abandoned all rank within his own Chapter. 'But this trial is not held to give you your vengeance. If you are to remain in the position of prosecutor you must be patient.'

'Patient? Must I have the patience to endure that heretic speaking in his own defence? And from whence shall I gather the patience, Justice Lord, to sit unmoved through all the lies of the Soul Drinkers? Is Daenyathos to speak, too? Luko, and Salk, and all the Soul Drinkers, are they to have their chance to utter corruption as well?'

'If that is what it takes for me to be satisfied that justice is done,' said Pugh, 'then yes.'

'The Soul Drinkers are not the only ones who will have their time to speak,' said another voice, one who had not joined in the discussion as yet. It was that of Captain N'Kalo of the Iron Knights. The Iron Knights were, like the Soul Drinkers, a successor Chapter of the Imperial Fists, and the stain on Dorn's honour had seemed enough to bring a delegation from the Iron Knights to the *Phalanx*. Suddenly, the other Adeptus Astartes present were not so sure that N'Kalo was here just as a matter of course.

'You have seen the Soul Drinkers for a moral threat?' asked Reinez.

'No,' replied N'Kalo levelly. 'I will speak in their defence.' N'Kalo's expression was impossible to guess at since his face was covered. He wore, even in the presence of the Chapter Master, a helm with an eye slit reminiscent of plate armour from some feudal world. Everywhere on him were hung campaign medallions, laurels and purity seals, the steel of his armour only just showing through the brocade of his many honours.

'Their defence?' snarled Reinez.

'N'Kalo, brother, what are you saying?' demanded Siege-Captain Daviks.

'I say just what I say,' replied N'Kalo. 'I wish to speak in defence of Sarpedon and the Soul Drinkers. Will you deny me that right?'

'I shall!' barked Reinez. 'As the prosecutor in the Emperor's name I deny you any right to interfere in the punishment of that heretic!' Reinez jabbed a finger in N'Kalo's face, but the Iron Knight did not flinch.

'Reinez!' shouted Pugh. 'This is not your decision to make.'

'By the Throne, I say it is! Upon my honour as an Adeptus Astartes, you will have to go through me before you utter one word that does not condemn the traitors!'

'If I may,' interjected Commander Gethsemar of the Angels Sanguine, 'I believe that the precedent exists for him to do just that.' Gethsemar, like N'Kalo, had spoken little, and his voice was a smooth, honeyed sound quite at odds with the warrior heritage of his Chapter.

'Is that what you desire, Reinez?' said Pugh. 'An honour-duel with Captain N'Kalo?'

'If that is what it takes,' replied Reinez, still face to face with N'Kalo. 'If the Emperor lends strength to my arm, N'Kalo stays silent and the Soul Drinkers are condemned no matter what he wishes.'

'And if I best you,' said N'Kalo, 'I say my piece.'

'It does not matter what you will do,' said Reinez. 'I have torn the throats from warp-beasts a million miles from any battle-brother. I stood on worlds as they died and fought through armies of the damned to survive. You are a child compared to me. You cannot win. Drop to one knee now, acknowledge me your superior, and there need be no duel. I will accept your surrender without your having to suffer at my hand.'

'I would not deny you the pleasure of breaking my bones,' said N'Kalo, voice still calm.

'Where is this duel to be held?' said Gethesemar.

'Here,' replied Reinez. 'This is the place where Sigismund, the first Templar, came to contemplate his duty, is it not?'

'It is,' replied Pugh.

'Then perhaps Captain N'Kalo will have the chance to contemplate his own duties as he lies on this ground beneath my boot.'

'Enough talk, Reinez!' said Pugh. 'Gethsemar, since you proposed it, you shall oversee the duel. Brothers, gather your Adeptus Astartes so that all will witness the result. N'Kalo, Reinez, select your weapons and make yourselves ready. Then we shall have no more discussion of this matter. The honour-duel shall be final. This is the Emperor's justice, and all aboard will hold to it as His word.'

'Amen,' said Reinez with a smile.

Gethsemar revelled in his role as master of ceremonies. He changed his mask for one with a stern brown and downturned mouth, ruby eyes and a stylised scar on one cheek. His Sanguinary Guard stood watch alongside him, glaives drawn, framed by the wing-like stabilising fins on their jump packs. Their gilded armour gleamed almost painfully bright as the forest's artificial sun came overhead and bathed the riverside glade in light. Lysander waited behind them, knowing that although he was here to enforce Pugh's will just as much as the Angels Sanguine, there was no need to impede Gethsemar's sense of showmanship.

Around the edge of the clearing were stood the Space Marines attending the trial. There had not been enough room for all the Howling Griffons so Borganor looked on flanked only by his honour guard. A single squad of Imperial Fists attended Pugh. Kolgo was there too, with his Sisters of Battle in attendance. The Iron Knights who had accompanied N'Kalo stood a little apart, perhaps aware that if their commander lost this duel they would be leaving the *Phalanx* very quickly.

Reinez had chosen his thunder hammer to fight with. It was a well-used weapon, its adamantium head well-scored in hundreds of battles. Reinez made a few warm-up swings, loosening his arms and shoulders, and the weapon thrummed through the air as if it were purring with pleasure at the impending combat.

N'Kalo had chosen a double-handed sword from the armoury of the *Phalanx*, a weapon normally wielded by the Imperial Fist chosen to serve as the Emperor's Champion while on campaign. As an Iron Knight who called Rogal Dorn his primarch like the Imperial Fists, N'Kalo had the right to wield such a weapon. It was a compromise – his own power sword, now held by one of his Iron Knights, was one-handed, and might have been shattered or knocked from his hand trying to parry Reinez's thunder hammer. The champion's blade would not break, but it would be slower.

'In the sight of Rogal Dorn,' intoned Gethsemar, 'beneath the aegis of blessed Sanguinius and of the Emperor of Mankind, our battle-brothers here seek justice through the clash of holy arms. May the Emperor lend strength to the arm of the righteous! Begin!'

For a long moment, neither Space Marine moved as they gauged each other's stance, deciding which way to go. Reinez crouched low, hammer held behind him ready to strike. N'Kalo's sword was up in a guard, the point hovering level with Reinez's eyeline.

Reinez moved first. N'Kalo barely reacted in time, bringing the blade down to block the blow that Reinez aimed at his legs. N'Kalo pivoted and caught Reinez with an elbow, but it clanged harmlessly into the Crimson Fist's breastplate. Reinez hooked N'Kalo's leg with his hammer and threw him head over heels backwards, to sprawl on the grass.

Reinez's hammer arced down. N'Kalo rolled aside as it slammed into the ground, throwing up a great shower of earth and leaving a crater in the dark soil. N'Kalo swung wildly, a vast steel crescent that Reinez sidestepped with ease before landing a kick so hard in N'Kalo's side that the Iron Knight was thrown to the ground again.

'I'll hear your surrender any time,' gasped Reinez. 'There is no shame in it. Any time.'

N'Kalo responded with a reverse strike from the ground, the sword's point arrowing up behind him towards Reinez's throat. Reinez batted it aside with the haft of his hammer and cracked the butt of the weapon into the side of N'Kalo's head. N'Kalo reeled and Reinez closed, driving his shoulder into N'Kalo's midriff and hauling the Space Marine off the ground.

Reinez hefted N'Kalo into the air and threw him. N'Kalo tumbled over the bank of the river and into the water, the powerful stream foaming around him. Reinez jumped in after him, dragging N'Kalo to his feet. The water came up to each Space Marine's chest. Reinez slammed a headbutt into the face of N'Kalo's helm, denting the ceramite faceplate.

N'Kalo drove a knee into the inside of Reinez's thigh. Reinez stumbled back a step, feet slipping on the stones and mud of the artificial riverbed. N'Kalo crunched an elbow into the back of Reinez's head and pulled his sword from the water again, slicing left and right. Reinez deflected each blow with his hammer or they glanced off his shoulder pads.

N'Kalo paused, having created the space he needed between the two combatants. He shifted his footing to plant himself more firmly on the bed of mud and rocks. Behind him, rapids rushed around several large boulders, plunging down a low waterfall. The branches of overhanging willows almost brushed the river's surface. If it were not for the two Adeptus Astartes struggling to shed one another's blood, it would have been a tranquil and beautiful place.

N'Kalo's breath was heaving. Reinez looked like he had barely broken a sweat. N'Kalo had not yet managed to draw blood from the Crimson Fist.

'Do you think this will be over?' said Reinez as he forged through the waters, trying to force N'Kalo back towards the rapids. 'If the galaxy turns upside-down and you beat me, how long do you think your victory will last? You think you will have any brothers here? They will turn their backs on you.'

'They are not so consumed with bitterness as you, Reinez,' replied N'Kalo. 'They have not let failure make them less of an Adeptus Astartes.'

Reinez's face darkened. He spat a wordless syllable of anger and charged – not at N'Kalo, but at the closest tree that clung to the riverbank. Reinez wrenched the tree free of its roots, showering dirt and loose stones across the water.

Reinez's anger gave him strength. N'Kalo had barely the time to get his sword up before Reinez slammed the shattered tree trunk into him, throwing him backwards into the water. The impact was enough to knock him senseless and his heavy armoured body thudded onto the riverbed, waters rushing around him.

Reinez pounced from the bank into the water, one knee pounding square into N'Kalo's solar plexus. Reinez hauled the Iron Knight over his head, out of the water, and slammed him down into one of the massive boulders making up the rapids. The boulder shattered under the impact and N'Kalo sprawled against it, water foaming white around him, unable to move.

Reinez planted a foot on N'Kalo's midriff. Both hands free now, his hammer holstered, he grabbed the lower edge of N'Kalo's helmet and wrenched it halfway around, forcing it off N'Kalo's head.

The helmet came free with a shower of sparks. Reinez was looking into a face severely burned, every blister and scour looking like it had just been inflicted, red and weeping. N'Kalo's lips were pale streaks in the blackened skin, his eyes kept open only by artificial surfaces of milky glass that made them look blind. His jaw and back teeth showed through the tears in his cheeks, and segments of cranium glinted as if polished between the stringy remnants of his scalp.

'When I am finished with you,' spat Reinez, 'you will look back and remember how handsome you were.'

Reinez shouldered N'Kalo over the rapids down the falls. The Iron Knight was barely sensible as he plunged into the pool formed by the waterfall. Reinez stood on the rapids, hauling another rock up from the riverbed. He hurled it down at N'Kalo, who got an arm up to ward off the worst of the impact but who was crushed down into the pool, trapped by its weight.

Reinez jumped down onto the rock that pinned N'Kalo in place. N'Kalo was not quite beneath the surface but little more than his ruined face could be seen above the water. Reinez stood and took his hammer off his back, holding it with both hands, the well-worn head of the weapon aiming down at N'Kalo's face.

Reinez drove the hammer down at N'Kalo. N'Kalo forced his sword out from below the rock and slashed the hammer aside. Expecting an impact and off balance, Reinez fell forwards, landing face to face with N'Kalo.

The other Adeptus Astartes had by now gathered on the bank of the river and they watched as the two Space Marine wrestled in the water, Reinez trying to force N'Kalo's head below the surface, N'Kalo trying to wriggle from under the rock and bring his sword to bear. The thunder hammer lay in the water, abandoned, as Reinez went at N'Kalo with his bare hands.

The watching Space Marines parted as Pugh joined them. He stood on one of the flat rocks that made up the rapids, no expression on his face.

N'Kalo hurled the rock away. Reinez had to jump back to keep his own legs from being trapped under it. N'Kalo slammed the pommel of his sword into Reinez's side and kicked out at him, trying to drive him against the stone wall carved by the waterfall. Reinez spun, locked N'Kalo's sword arm in the crook of his elbow and ripped the sword from N'Kalo's hand. Reinez threw the sword aside and it disappeared under the foaming water.

Both Space Marines were bleeding now. N'Kalo's armour was dented from the impacts, to the extent that it was as much a hindrance to his movement as protection. Reinez's nose might have been broken, judging by the blood spilling down his chest, black against the dark blue of his breastplate.

When the two closed in and locked up in a wrestler's clinch, every Space Marine watching knew it was for the last time. N'Kalo was a fine combatant, but his wounds, more severe on the inside than the outside, drained the strength from his limbs. Reinez had been fighting for the last few years without any battle-brothers at his side, learning to survive by his wits alone, with fists and teeth if need be. Reinez pushed N'Kalo down onto one knee, wrenched one of the Iron Knight's shoulders out of its socket, and dropped into a shoulder charge that smashed N'Kalo into the riverbank.

N'Kalo could not raise his free arm into a guard. Reinez slammed his fist into N'Kalo's face.

'They will cast you out!' roared Reinez, his fist hitting home again. 'They will banish you! You will know my pain!'

Reinez punched over and over. Ultra-dense Adeptus Astartes bone
fractured. N'Kalo's cheekbone caved in, then his jaw. One eye socket
was stove inwards, half-shutting his eye. Bloody skin clung to Reinez's
knuckles.

'Outcast! Pariah! You shall be no man's brother!'

'Stop,' said Pugh.

Reinez did not stop. Another half-dozen blows rained down. Broken
teeth clotted the blood that oozed from N'Kalo's shattered mouth.

The boot that cracked into Reinez's face belonged to Captain Lysander,
who had stepped out of the watching crowd at a signal from Pugh.
The blow caught Reinez by surprise and he fell backwards off N'Kalo,
sprawling in the water.

'I said stop,' said Pugh.

Reinez scrabbled to his feet, wiping the back of one gauntlet across his
face to remove the worst of N'Kalo's blood. 'You see?' he gasped. 'The
Emperor lent me strength. Dorn has spoken. The duel is over.'

'It is,' said Pugh. 'My brothers, the apothecaries among you attend to
Captain N'Kalo while the *Phalanx*'s own medicae staff are summoned. I
must have him conscious to present his evidence.'

'Lord Pugh!' protested Reinez. 'He was defeated! The duel was won! I
demand N'Kalo's silence as is my right by victory!'

'The duel is won, Reinez,' replied Pugh, 'but you may claim no victory.
We are not at war, and Captain N'Kalo is not your enemy. In showing
such brutality to him, even at the moment you became the victor, you
abandon all semblance of honour. In an honour-duel, that is as good
as a physical defeat. You have forfeited the duel, and Captain N'Kalo is
the winner.'

Reinez stood speechless in the rushing river as the Space Marines on
the bank picked up the winner and carried him off to the apothecarion.

The first thing Sarpedon noticed as he was led to the dock again was the
Iron Knight without his helm. He had encountered the Chapter once
before but there had been no way of telling, beneath the feudal helm,
if the Iron Knights' commander was the same Adeptus Astartes he had
spoken with on Molikor. Now, there could be no mistake. It was the
same man.

Half of N'Kalo's face was still hidden, this time by medical dressings
covering fresh wounds. The rest, however, was that familiar mask of
burn tissue, and the one visible eye was the same glassy prosthetic.

Sarpedon tried to hold N'Kalo's gaze, but he was shoved into the
accused's pulpit by the Imperial Fists who had escorted him from his
cell, and found himself looking at Lord Pugh.

'Justice Lord,' said Sarpedon before anyone else could speak. 'I would
know of my brothers.'

'They are safe and well,' said Pugh.

'And Daenyathos?'

'He is captive, like them. And like them, he has not been harmed.'

'I know that I am to die here, Lord Pugh. I wish to speak with my battle-brothers before that happens. And I must have leave to speak with Daenyathos, even if only to ascertain that the Dreadnought you hold indeed contains him. My Chapter thought him dead for thousands of years. I must at least see for myself that he lives.'

'What you ask is a luxury that cannot be afforded to the condemned,' replied Pugh. 'The nature of your crimes means that you cannot be given the chance to conspire further with your fellow accused. Such requests are denied.'

Sarpedon did not argue. It was a motion he had to go through. He had to show that he had not given up, not completely. It was a feeble gesture among so many warriors, but it was made.

'Brethren,' began Pugh. 'During the last adjournment the matter of the Soul Drinkers' defence was decided. Commander N'Kalo?'

Sarpedon realised that among the assembled Space Marines, he could not see Reinez.

N'Kalo stepped forwards. 'Brothers,' he said, and Sarpedon recognised the grating voice of an improvised vox-unit. It was hooked up to N'Kalo's dented breastplate, amplifying the voice that struggled to get past his shattered jaw. 'I must speak to you of a world called Molikor.'

CHAPTER SIX

Molikor's endless expanses of broken delta, islands of swampy grasses and gorse separated by the sludgy children of the planet's great rivers, were a good place to hide. An entire nation hid there among the rotten trees and root cages, the odd chunk of rock eroded clean by the passage of the shifting waters. They had their strongholds among the mangrove swamps closer to the shore, where the biting insects swarmed so thick they could pick a man up off the ground, and the waters were infested with a thousand different forms of sharp-toothed creature. That nation, which called itself the Eshkeen, was as much a part of the landscape as the dour grey-streaked clouds overhead and the way the soft ground threatened to swallow up a power-armoured foot. That nation had risen up in defiance. That nation had to die.

Commander N'Kalo took the magnoculars from the eyeslit of his armour. His augmented vision was enough to tell him that the foe had no intention of making itself seen, and a closer look had confirmed it. Behind him the strikeforce of nearly forty Iron Knights Space Marines was forming a perimeter lest the enemy close in from an unexpected angle, the bolters of Squads Salik, K'Jinn and Tchwayo scanning the indistinct horizon for targets. Sergeant Borasi's Devastator Squad had left its anti-tank weapons behind and sported a complement of heavy bolters, perfect for chewing through forested cover and ill-armoured enemies. Though the delta could have been deserted for all the Iron Knights could see, the Devastators were still ready to deploy, weapons loaded and shouldered.

'They give us good sport,' said Sergeant Borasi, standing just behind N'Kalo. 'It disappoints me so when the enemy show themselves too early.'

'Would that this were mere sport,' replied N'Kalo. 'The Eshkeen revolt against the rule of the Imperium. Books of atrocities have already been written about their campaigns of violence against the Imperial cities of this world, and if Molikor falls the whole of this frontier could follow.'

'Nevertheless, captain, I am reminded of the best hunting grounds of Seheris. Below the equator, where the great rivers of the Zambenar meet the oceans. I lose count of how many reapermaw tusks my bolter has won for me down there.'

'Then the hunting will be good, brother,' said N'Kalo, stowing the magnoculars in a belt pouch. 'If it is a hunt you see unfolding here.'

On Seheris, the home world of the Iron Knights Chapter, the unforgiving deserts and plains bred a thousand hardy peoples divided into tribes that treated the land as an adversary to be conquered. The Iron Knights were drawn from such people, and their wish to test themselves against an environment, as much as against a foe, never left them. They took pride in the fact that they fought in warzones which would have been deadly whether any enemy waited there or not – radioactive rock deserts, carnivorous jungles, archipelagos scattered across an ocean that seethed with sea monsters, and every other Emperor-forsaken place that a man could imagine. When the Parliaments of Molikor had requested help against a foe bent on exterminating the Emperor's presence on their world, the Iron Knights had seen not only a task to be achieved to keep the Ghoul Stars frontier intact, but the chance to test themselves against Molikor's own dangers.

Too often, thought N'Kalo, his brother Space Marines treated war as a sport. The fact that he could see beyond that had marked him out as commander material. That was why he had been sent here to Molikor, to oversee his eager battle-brothers as they killed every Eshkeen on the planet.

Mile after mile, the Eshkeen drew the Iron Knights in.

It was clearly their tactic. Even as he walked the paths laid out for him through the winding delta paths, N'Kalo knew that the enemy had laid on Molikor a trap to cut off, surround and butcher anyone the Imperium sent to fight them. He read the landscape like a book, like any Iron Knight would, and he saw the thinking behind every dammed stream and felled copse.

The easiest path into the delta forests and swamps, where the Eshkeen surely waited, passed through two towering forests separated by a stretch of swamp where the shallow waters rushed over the sodden grassland. The soft-edged shadows, cast by a sun hidden behind the overcast sky, rendered this gap dark and its footing uncertain. The ways on either side were deep and difficult to traverse, and N'Kalo's magnoculars had picked out the log dams on the distant highlands that had helped flood those regions to force any attackers to take the path between the forests.

N'Kalo's strikeforce reached the first shadows cast by the tallest trees. The forest was dense and tangled, an unmanaged mass of broken branches and diseased trunks, clustered around rocky hills that broke the surface of the marshes and trapped enough soil for the trees to grow. N'Kalo could see no sign of the Eshkeen, but he knew they were there as surely as if they were standing there in front of him.

'You cannot trap a Space Marine,' said Sergeant Borasi over the strike-force's vox-net. 'You can shut yourself in a room with him, but it is not he who is trapped.'

N'Kalo halted the strikeforce at the head of the forest gap. On the other side was a stretch of open marsh, tempting for any force making for the coastal strongholds with nowhere for the enemy to use as an ambush. N'Kalo imagined the Parliamentarian commanders who had fallen for such a trick, before Molikor had requested the assistance of Imperial forces, and how they must have decided that it was acceptable to risk this one ambush spot to ensure they had a clear run at the enemy. How many of them had the Eshkeen killed, moulding the landscape into their ally? How many cavalry forces had wheeled in panic on just such a path, stuck with thousands of arrows and, later, riddled with bullets from captured guns, fired from an enemy so well hidden it seemed the forest itself wanted them dead?

'Salik, Tchwayo, take the fore,' voxed N'Kalo. 'K'Jinn, cover the rear. Borasi, up front with me.'

The strikeforce took up position in the mouth of the trap. Borasi's Devastators knelt, heavy bolters covering their front arc.

To an observer unfamiliar with the Space Marines, it would seem the Iron Knights were pausing in trepidation, making up their minds whether to continue down the narrow path laid out for them.

'Open fire!' ordered N'Kalo.

The heavy bolters hammered out a dreadful cacophony as their fire shredded the edge of the right-hand forest, splintering tree trunks and sending clouds of spinning shards through the air.

'Advance!' shouted N'Kalo, his voice just audible over the din. 'Advance and engage!'

As the Devastators reloaded, the three Tactical squads ran for the forest, bolters spitting fire as they headed onwards. N'Kalo had his power sword in one hand and his plasma pistol in the other, and as the last splinters of tree trunk fell he caught the first sight of the enemy.

The Eshkeen were heavily scarified, and wore strips of coloured cloth and leather wrapped tight around them to ward off the spines and stingers of the forests. The ridges of scar tissue that ran across their faces and bodies were high enough to be pierced with bones and thorns, and spikes were implanted under the shorn skin of their scalps. They resembled the figures from some primitive world's visions of Hell. Perhaps they modelled themselves after Molikor's own myths, delving into their images of damnation to put fear into Parliamentarian hearts.

The Eshkeen returned fire as best they could as they dragged the wounded and dead from what remained of the treeline. Autogun and lasgun fire spattered down at the Iron Knights, hissing in the damp ground or ringing off ceramite. The Space Marines did not slow and headed straight for the enemy.

The ambush plan relied on the Space Marines staying in the open, thinking themselves unable to make any headway through the forest. Unfortunately for the Eshkeen, that plan, which would work horrendously well against the armies of the Parliamentarians, fell apart when confronted with an armoured Space Marine whose weight and strength could force him through the forest as fast as he moved in the open. Squad Salik reached the trees first and they did not slow down, shouldering their way between the tree trunks, rotten wood crumbling under their weight. The Eshkeen screamed war-cries as the Iron Knights were among them, streams of bolter fire criss-crossing through the forest and slicing Eshkeen in half.

N'Kalo felt, in spite of himself, a faint disappointment. None of the Eshkeen would get close enough for him to use his power sword. Already Squad Tchwayo were into the rapidly thinning forest. Men were dying among the twisted roots and falling tree trunks. N'Kalo would not take any heads today.

N'Kalo himself had reached the trees. Bodies lay twisted and broken among the fallen branches. One was still alive, moaning as he tried to force himself to his feet, apparently ignorant of the fact he had lost one of his arms at the elbow. Others had huge ragged holes in their torsos, cut down by bolter fire aimed at the central mass. Another had the side of his head crushed by a bolter stock. N'Kalo stepped over them, glancing around for targets as Borasi and K'Jinn advanced behind him.

Suddenly, N'Kalo could not hear the heavy footsteps and bolter fire of the battle-brothers behind him. He looked back, not wanting to slow his own advance, but he could not see them.

'Squads report!' said N'Kalo into the vox. Blank static was the only reply. 'Report!' he repeated, but got nothing.

The forest was seething. It was alive. The Eshkeen were barely recognisable as humans now, slipping in and out of tree trunks, their flesh merging with the mossy wood. They slithered along the ground like snakes, limbs as flexible as liquid, and slid into the ground before N'Kalo could take aim. They flitted overhead, birds on the wing.

'What witchcraft is this?' demanded N'Kalo. His power sword hummed into life and he slashed about him, felling the trees on either side as he pushed on. 'A Space Marine fears not such devilry! He knows no fear!'

The forest warped around him. Trees bowed in and hands reached out of the earth to snare his ankles. N'Kalo fired at movement, his plasma pistol boring a glowing orange channel through the foliage, but he could not tell if he had hit anything. Everywhere he cut left and right, forging on through the path he hacked. He called for his battle-brothers, but there was no reply. Faces were leering from the trees now, blood welling up from the ground. The sky, where he glimpsed it through the writhing branches overhead, seemed blistered and burned, as if some malignant energy was forcing its way down towards him.

N'Kalo slammed into an obstacle that did not give way to his weight. He stumbled back a pace and saw another horror. A Space Marine from the waist up, a mutated monstrosity below, insectoid legs tipped with vicious talons, reared up to spear N'Kalo's torso. The Space Marine was no Iron Knight – his armour was painted purple, with a gilded chalice on one shoulder pad, and the high aegis collar of a Librarian.

N'Kalo slashed at the apparition with his sword. The mutant brought up the haft of an ornate axe to turn the blow aside. Without seeming to move the mutant was upon N'Kalo, its weight bearing down on him, legs forcing him back onto one knee. One insect leg snared his sword arm and the other batted his plasma pistol aside.

The forest was shifting again, this time back to normal. N'Kalo could hear his battle-brothers' voices filling the vox-net.

'Fall back!' came K'Jinn's voice. 'Regroup at the far side!'

'I have brothers down!' shouted Salik. 'Forming defensive!' Bolter fire hammered away over the vox-net, volley and counter-volley shearing through the trees.

The mutant kicked N'Kalo's sword aside.

'What are you?' gasped N'Kalo. He struggled to get free, but the mutant was stronger even than a Space Marine.

'I am the truth,' replied Sarpedon.

The fortresses of the Eshkeen were cunningly wrought so as to be invisible from the air. The finest siege-wrights of the Imperium could not have strung out fortifications of wooden stakes and pit traps with such subtlety, seeding the approaches to the dense coastal forests so that attackers on foot would find their numbers thinned out well before they came within bowshot of the fortress walls. The fortresses themselves were built on two levels, the first hidden trenches and murder-holes on the ground, the second walkways and battlements in the trees overhead. The canopy was thick enough to hide them, and the short distances between them were made deadly with tangles of cured razorvine, layers of dried earth concealing stretches of sucking mud, and even nests of forest predators herded into position by the Eshkeen. Two Parliamentarian forces had driven this far into Eshkeen territory and none of them had been seen again, save for a couple of messengers permitted to live so they could explain that the Eshkeen were not impressed by the glittering cavalry regiments and sumptuous banners of the Parliamentarian armies.

The fortresses backed against the sea, although it was difficult to tell where the sea began. Mangroves formed layers of root canopy over the murky waters, infested with Eshkeen fishermen who found their harpoons were as adept at picking off soldiers wading out of landing boats as they were at spearing fish. The shallow waters and hidden reefs were enough to dissuade all but the most glory-hungry admiral from attempting a landing there. Unfortunately for the Parliamentarians they had once possessed such an admiral, whose ships now lay a few hundred metres from the shore where they had foundered, their men trapped there for months before starvation and Eshkeen snipers had seen to the last of them.

These defences, as formidable as they were, would not have stopped a force of Space Marines determined to enact justice on the Eshkeen. The Iron Knights, however, had not been given that chance.

The first N'Kalo saw of the Eshkeen stronghold was a ceiling of wooden planks and plaited vines. He struggled to move and found that he was not bound. He was high up in the air, the structure around him built into the thick, gnarled trunks of the mangroves. The humid air had a faint tang of decay, the smell of fallen plant matter turning to watery sludge, mixed in with the salt breeze off the sea. Eshkeen were everywhere at watch, eerily still as they scanned the approaches with their bows or guns to hand. N'Kalo saw, for the first time, their women and children. Some of the sentries were women, and a gaggle of children crouched in a doorway watching N'Kalo with a mix of fascination and fear. They were scrawny in a way that only growing up outside civilisation could explain, tough and sinewy, with painted skin echoing the scarring of their elders.

N'Kalo sat up. The children squealed and scattered. He was in a barracks or communal living space, full of empty beds. He could not see his weapons, but his armour had been left on.

He touched a gauntlet to his face as he realised his helmet had been removed. No wonder the children had fled. The burns he had suffered long ago, which he had chosen to hide under the knightly helm of his Chapter's commanders, must have made him look even more of a monster than any other Space Marine.

'Commander N'Kalo,' said a too-familiar voice. N'Kalo jumped to his feet as the mutant from the forest entered.

'Where am I? What of my brothers?' demanded N'Kalo.

'They are safe. I cannot permit them their liberty yet. They will go free soon, as will you.'

The mutant Space Marine was armed with his power axe and a bolt pistol, and N'Kalo had not been a match for him when he had his power sword. Unarmed, he did not fancy his chances against the mutant. Better to talk and wait for the right time than to throw his life away trying to fight here, when he was bound to fail. 'And you did not answer my question. What are you?'

The mutant shrugged. It was seemingly too human a gesture for such a grotesque creature. 'I am a Space Marine, like you. Well, not exactly like you.'

'You are a witch.'

'I am, if you prefer that term. I am Librarian and Chapter Master Sarpedon of the Soul Drinkers. And we are similar in more than just bearing the arms of the Adeptus Astartes. We are both, Commander N'Kalo, students of justice as much as of war.'

'Justice? My brothers have fallen at your hand!'

'Fallen, but not dead. My Apothecary is seeing to them. Two have bolter wounds and another was felled by a chainsword. Though they will not fight for a while, the three will survive. They are being held at ground level, below us, watched over by my battle-brothers. Sergeant Borasi gave us a great deal of trouble. He should be commended for his spirit, misplaced though it is. He owes us several broken bones.'

N'Kalo had heard of the Soul Drinkers. Like the Iron Knights, they were successors to the Imperial Fists, with Rogal Dorn as their primarch. N'Kalo had never met any of the Soul Drinkers but he recalled they were famed for their prowess in boarding actions and that they had won laurels during the battle for the Ecclesiarchal Palace during the Wars of Apostasy. N'Kalo and Sarpedon should have been brothers, not just as Space Marines but as sons of Dorn.

'Why do you oppose us?' said N'Kalo. 'We are here doing the Emperor's will!'

'The Imperium's will,' replied Sarpedon. 'Not the Emperor's.'

'And I suppose you, a mutant, one who has raised arms against my brethren, is the one doing the Emperor's will?'

'Looking at it that way,' said Sarpedon, 'I can understand your doubts. I do not believe, however, that you know the full story of what is happening on Molikor.'

'And you are going to tell me?' spat N'Kalo.

'No. I am going to show you.'

N'Kalo saw his brothers guarded by a ring of Soul Drinkers. The Iron Knights had been disarmed but, as Sarpedon had said, few of them were hurt. A Soul Drinkers Apothecary was operating on the wounded leg of one sedated Iron Knight – all the rest were conscious and, led by Borasi, started up a chorus of plaudits for their commander and insults hurled at Sarpedon as soon as they saw N'Kalo. A couple of the other Soul Drinkers were mutants, although not as dramatically malformed as Sarpedon. One had an enormous mutated hand, and N'Kalo wondered what other mutations were hidden beneath their armour.

It was a strange feeling to be led, not quite a captive and not quite an equal, through the Eshkeen forest by Sarpedon. N'Kalo's soldierly mind sized up every chance to attack Sarpedon, drag him down to the ground or stab him in the back with a fortuitous weapon snatched from a nearby Eshkeen, but Sarpedon had his own warrior instinct and every opportunity was gone before it began. If he had a weapon, N'Kalo thought, he could kill Sarpedon and, if not complete his mission, at least rid the Imperium of this enemy – but even with a bolter or a power sword in his hands, could he beat Sarpedon when he had been defeated before?

The Eshkeen watched curiously as N'Kalo moved through their domain. They walked paths almost hidden in the forest, avoiding traps and dead ends sown liberally throughout the forest. In places N'Kalo could see the waters of the ocean between the roots underfoot, and glimpse Eshkeen walking there, too, wading through the waters to fish or keep watch over the coastal approaches. In other places the ground underfoot was solid, with tunnels and bunkers dug into it. The Eshkeen themselves wore patchworks of body armour and scraps of captured uniform, the most colourful belonging to those who looked the most experienced and deadly. The right to sport the captured garb of the enemy was evidently a privilege that had to be earned.

In the heart of the stronghold was a fortification of stone instead of wood, concentric circles of jagged battlements forming a huge granite maw around a pit in the centre. Sarpedon followed a complex path through the fortifications, leading N'Kalo through them even though he could probably have scrambled over them with ease thanks to his arachnid limbs. The trees did not grow here, so an artificial canopy had been stretched out overhead, a lattice of vines and ropes woven with leaves to keep it hidden. There were no Eshkeen keeping watch among the fortifications, but many of them had gathered in the trees around the clearing to watch the two Space Marines descending to the pit.

'Like you,' said Sarpedon, 'we heeded the distress call from the Parliaments of Molikor. But we have learned to be circumspect. A little more suspicious, perhaps, of our own Emperor-fearing citizens. We arrived here without informing the Parliaments of our presence, and spoke instead to the Eshkeen. When we hear only one side of the story, I find we inevitably miss out on the more interesting half.'

The pit was a shaft lined with carved stones, forming a spiral frieze winding down into the darkness. The frieze depicted an endless tangle of human bodies, contorted and wounded, missing limbs or eyes, faces drawn in pain. The Eshkeen who had sculpted it, countless generations ago, had used a stylised technique that removed the subtleties of the human form and left only the pain. Winding wooden stairs provided a way down into the shaft.

'When Imperial settlers were brought to Molikor,' explained Sarpedon as he and N'Kalo descended the shaft, 'they sent out explorers to tame the marshland and forge a path to the ocean. They hoped to build a port on this coast and spread to the planet's other continents. They never managed it, mainly because the land was too marshy and the Eshkeen rather unfriendly. But one of them did find this.'

N'Kalo made note of Sarpedon's words with one half of his mind. The other half was trying to work out how he could turn on Sarpedon. They were alone now, and Sarpedon's fellow Soul Drinkers could not come to his aid. If N'Kalo got behind Sarpedon, and if he was quick enough, he could throw Sarpedon off the staircase down the shaft. But the fall would not be guaranteed to kill him – indeed, N'Kalo could now see the bottom of the shaft strewn with leaves and broken branches, and a Space Marine would barely be inconvenienced by the distance. He could grab Sarpedon's neck in a choke, but his aegis collar would make that difficult and besides, a Space Marine could go a long time before his three lungs gave out. By then Sarpedon could have climbed up the shaft and brought N'Kalo to the Soul Drinkers to face retribution.

And perhaps most importantly, N'Kalo felt a truth in Sarpedon's words. N'Kalo wanted to know what was hidden down here, what could cause a Space Marine, even a renegade one, to fight his brothers. So he held back and followed as Sarpedon reached the bottom of the shaft and headed down a tunnel that led away to one side.

This tunnel was also carved with images. Eyes and hands covered the walls, symbols of watching and warding. N'Kalo could hear, on the hot, damp breeze washing over him from the far end of the tunnel, the reedy strains of voices. They were screaming, hundreds of them, the sounds overlapping like the threads of a tapestry.

A cavern opened up ahead, wet stone lit from beneath by a blood-red glow. The screaming got louder. N'Kalo tensed, unsure of what was ahead, one part of his brain still watching for a drop in Sarpedon's guard.

'Molikor,' said Sarpedon, 'has a curious relationship with its dead.'

The tunnel reached the threshold of a sudden drop. Beyond it was a cavern, as vast as an ocean, filled almost to the level of the tunnel entrance by a sea of writhing bodies.

N'Kalo was all but stunned by his first sight of it. The awfulness of it, the impossibility, seemed intent on prying his mind from his senses.

The bodies were naked, men and women, all ages, the whole spectrum of shapes, sizes and skin tones. The glow was coming from their eyes, and from the wounds that wept bloody and fresh in their bodies. Many bore the scarring of the Eshkeen but there were countless others, from dozens of cultures.

'Who are they?' said N'Kalo.

'Everyone who has ever died on Molikor,' replied Sarpedon. 'No one knows how far down it goes. When you die on Molikor, your body decays and is absorbed by the earth. Then it reforms here, vomited back up by the planet. Here they are, everyone this world has claimed since the Age of Strife.'

'Why... why are you showing me this?' said N'Kalo.

Sarpedon unholstered his bolt pistol. For a moment N'Kalo thought the Soul Drinker would turn on him, but instead Sarpedon held it handle-first towards N'Kalo. 'Because I could not expect you to just take my word for it,' said Sarpedon. 'And besides, I haven't shown you anything yet.'

The bodies heaved up, like a breaking wave. N'Kalo barely had time to close his hand around the bolt pistol before they were surging around him, a terrible flood of gasping limbs. N'Kalo saw they were not corpses, nor alive, but something else, reborn as they had been at the moment of death and filled with the same emotions – fear, anger, abandonment. Their screams were wordless torrents of pain. One wrapped its arms around N'Kalo, trying to force his head down – N'Kalo blasted it apart with a shot to the upper chest and it flowed past him, reforming in a burst of blood-coloured light.

Sarpedon grabbed N'Kalo's free wrist. 'Follow,' he shouted above the screaming, and hauled N'Kalo off the edge of the drop and into the cavern.

It took a long time for the two Space Marines to forge their way through the dead of Molikor. Sarpedon's arachnid limbs proved adept at opening up a tunnel through the writhing bodies, and their path was lit by the red glow of whatever energy animated these echoes of the dead. The screaming was muffled now, like the crashing of a distant ocean, with the occasional shriek reaching through. N'Kalo followed as Sarpedon burrowed on, winding a path downwards. N'Kalo contemplated shooting him with his own bolt pistol, but then he would be trapped in this ocean of bodies and he did not know if he would be able to climb out of it. And besides, he wanted to know what Sarpedon had to show him. That curiosity was a human emotion, not that of a Space Marine, but nevertheless it gripped N'Kalo now.

Sarpedon pulled back a final veil of bodies and revealed an opening, like an abscess, in the mass. It had formed around a spike of stone, a stalagmite, to which was chained another body.

This body was that of a male Imperial citizen, N'Kalo could tell that at first glance. He had a glowing, raw hole over one eye where a bionic had once been implanted, and the Imperial aquila had been tattooed on one shoulder. He was the only one of Molikor's dead that N'Kalo had seen who was restrained in this way.

'This,' said Sarpedon, 'is Manter Thyll. He was sent by the Parliaments of Molikor to explore the delta marshlands. He found the Eshkeen and bargained his way into the pit, to see what they were so intent on protecting. They thought when he saw this place, he would treat its protection as a sacred undertaking just like they did. But they were wrong.'

Sarpedon took a data-slate from the belt of his armour. N'Kalo hadn't noticed it before, since his attention had been focussed on Sarpedon's abhorrent mutations to the exclusion of such a detail.

'This is the report he sent back to the Parliaments,' said Sarpedon.

The image was of poor quality, only just recognisable as the face of the man chained to the rock. In life, Manter Thyll had combined an explorer's ruggedness with a gentlemanly façade, his well-weathered face surmounted by a powdered periwig.

'–the Eshkeen had guarded it for generations, my lords. And though at first appearance it was a horrible sight, yet upon closer examination and the questioning of my Eshkeen hosts I came to understand it is the greatest treasure this world possesses. They are not living beings, you see, but they are not dead. They do not age, they do not tire. They simply exist. Think, my lords! Think what a resource they could be! An endless source of brute labour! If they can be trained then all is well, if not then a simple system of electronics and interfaces would suffice to make them useful. I believe that the dead of Molikor are the most potent natural resource on this entire–'*

Sarpedon paused the recording. N'Kalo stared dumbly for a few seconds at Thyll's image, then at the man's face.

'He came back to bargain with the Eshkeen for access to the pit,' said Sarpedon. 'They knew what he wanted by then. They killed him.'

'Did they chain his body here?' said N'Kalo.

'No. I did, so that I could show it to someone like you. What Thyll and the Parliamentarians did not realise, but what the Eshkeen have known for thousands of years, is that power like this cannot be tapped without consequences. The veil between realspace and the warp is thin here. The emotions of the dying find form in the warp and are cast back out into this pit. The ancestors of Molikor's tribes knew it, and they sent their best warriors to guard the pit. They grew to be the Eshkeen. When the Imperium settled Molikor, the Parliamentarians learned of the pit and they decided they wanted it for themselves, without having any idea what it truly was.'

Sarpedon began to tear at the mass again, opening a path back up towards the surface. N'Kalo could only follow, conflicting emotions coursing through him. The immensity of what Sarpedon was saying, the concept of a world that regurgitated its dead as these mindless things, the claim that the Parliamentarians were the aggressors and that the Eshkeen were the only thing standing between Molikor and damnation – it weighed on him, and would not sit straight in his mind. Everything N'Kalo had believed about Molikor, everything he had assumed, was wrong.

The First Parliament of Molikor, the Father of Power, the Imperial Seat, the Font of Majesty, towered over the assembled councillors like a second set of heavens. The dome of the First Parliament was painted to resemble a sky: dramatic clouds backlit by golden sunlight echoing fanciful images of Terra's own glories. The members of the First Parliament, drawn from the lesser parliaments of Molikor's cities, were resplendent in the uniforms of the planet's many militaries or the finery of their mercantile houses, wearing the symbol of the aquila to proclaim their loyalty to the Imperium.

Three thousand men and women were gathered beneath the First Parliament's dome, the centremost place taken by Lord Speaker Vannarian Wrann. Wrann, as the mouthpiece of the First Parliament, was recognised as Molikor's Imperial Governor. He was a sturdy and squat man, ermine-trimmed robes hanging off wide shoulders. He wore the massive gilded chain of his office around where his neck would have been had one existed between his barrel chest and shaven, glowering lump of a head. On the chain hung a silver aquila studded with diamonds and rubies, to match the fat gemstones on the rings he wore on his stubby fingers.

'Men and women of the First Parliament!' shouted Wrann. 'You sons and daughters of the Imperial Will! We hereby recognise Commander N'Kalo of the Iron Knights!'

N'Kalo made his way down the aisle towards the centre of the dome. Every eye followed him. Jaded as they were by every honour and beautification Molikor could place before them, the sight of a Space Marine was something new to them. Those closest shuddered in fear as N'Kalo walked past, for even in his knightly armour with its crests and laurels there was no mistaking that he was fundamentally a killing machine.

'Honoured councillors of Molikor,' began N'Kalo as he approached Wrann. 'Many thanks for receiving me to the heart of your government. The Iron Knights, as you do, claim the will of the Emperor as their warrant to arms, and in this we are brethren beneath His sight.'

'You are welcomed, Commander N'Kalo, and your brother Space Marines are granted all honours it is the First Parliament's right to bestow. Truly you stand before us as saviours of our people, as deliverers of our citizens from the threats that have so gravely beset us.'

Wrann's words were met with polite applause from the First Parliament's members. 'Do you come here to tell us that the rebellion has been quashed?' he continued. 'That the hateful Eshkeen will no longer plague our lands with their savagery, and that the Emperor's rule shall continue on Molikor?'

N'Kalo removed his helm. In spite of the need to keep up appearances, many councillors could not help grimacing or even turning away at the sight of N'Kalo's burned face, its skin here blackened, there deformed like wax that had melted and recooled, and elsewhere missing entirely.

'No, Lord Speaker,' he said. 'I have not.'

His words were met with silence. Those councillors who did not stare in grim fascination at N'Kalo's face glanced uneasily between their neighbours.

'Commander?' said Wrann. 'Pray, explain yourself.'

'I have seen the pit,' said N'Kalo. 'I have heard the words of Manter Thyll. When my Iron Knights answered the call for intervention from this Parliament, they did so without critical thought, without exploring first the history of this world and the true nature of its conflicts. Ours is the way of action, not contemplation. But we were forced into examining Molikor by allies of the Eshkeen, who also responded to your pleas for assistance, but to find out the truth, not merely destroy the Eshkeen as you desired.'

'Of what pit do you speak?' demanded Wrann. 'And this Manter Thyll? We know nothing of–'

'Do not lie to me!' shouted N'Kalo. The councillors sitting closest to him tried to scramble away, ending up on one another's laps to put some distance between them and the angry Space Marine. 'I sought to understand for myself. I went to the historical archives in Molik Tertiam. Yes, to that place you thought hidden from the eyes of outsiders! My battle-brothers stormed the estate of Horse Marshal Konigen, that hero of your history, and demanded of him the truth of why he first led his armies into the delta lands! We know the truth, my brothers and I. The war on Molikor is not about an uprising by the Eshkeen. It is about your desire to exploit Molikor's dead as labour for your mines and shipyards! It is about the wealth they can bring you! It is about your willingness to exploit the powers bleeding from the warp, and the Eshkeen's determination to prevent you from committing such a sin!'

'Then what would you have us do?' shouted Wrann. 'This frontier hangs by a thread! Without the war materiel that such labour could produce, we will never hold the Ghoul Stars! Humanity can barely survive out here as it is! Would you have us enslave our own? Would you have us grind our own hands to bone?'

'No,' replied N'Kalo calmly. 'I would have you leave.'

* * *

The *Judgement upon Garadan* made little concession to the embellishment and glorification that endowed many other Adeptus Astartes strike cruisers. It was every inch a warship, all riveted iron and hard, brutal lines, and as it hung in orbit over Molikor it seemed to glower down at the clouded planet. The lion-head crest, mounted above the prow like heraldry on a feudal knight's helm, was the sole concession to appearances.

Inside, the *Judgement* was much the same, with little to suggest the glorious history the Iron Knights brought with them. N'Kalo conducted most of his ship's business from the monastic cell in which he trained and meditated when his flag-captain did not require him on the bridge. The pict screen mounted on one wall showed a close-up of the space above Molikor's main spaceport. N'Kalo watched as a flock of merchant and cargo ships drifted up from the cloud cover, a shower of silvery sparks. On those ships was the Imperial population of Molikor, among them the Parliamentarian leaders. Those leaders had, less than three days ago, received an ivory scroll case containing orders to evacuate their planet on pain of destruction. Those orders were signed with a single 'I', which gave them an authority within the Imperium second only to the word of the God-Emperor Himself.

Inside the scroll case had also been a string of rosarius beads. It was a traditional message. If you defy these orders, they implied, then use these beads to pray, for prayer is your only hope of deliverance.

Events moved slowly in space, given the vast distances involved. The pict screen flicked between the views of the fleeing Parliamentarian ships, and the single vessel, its livery gold and black, that drifted in from its concealed observation position behind one of Molikor's moons. This ship, of which N'Kalo did not know the name, had arrived at Molikor so quickly it must have possessed archeotech or even xenos drives to have made so rapid a journey through the warp.

It was a vessel of the Inquisition. N'Kalo needed no communications with the craft to know that. His flag-captain had hailed it anyway and, as expected, there had been no reply. The Adeptus Astartes had done their job on Molikor. Now the Inquisition took over, and they answered to no one.

N'Kalo had seen quarantine orders enforced before. He hoped that everyone had got off Molikor safely. Though he had little love for the Parliamentarians, once the lead conspirators had been weeded out those who remained would be largely blameless Imperial citizens. The Inquisition would quarantine the world, destroy the spaceport and let it be known that it was forbidden thanks to the bizarre warp disturbance beneath its crust that caused it to spew its dead out as mindless facsimiles. The Parliamentarians who had sought to exploit the pit would be tried, questioned and probably executed for dabbling so willingly in matters of the warp. N'Kalo did not think much about their fates. Worse things happened to better people with every moment in the Imperium. He would not waste his thoughts on them. This was a grim business, but he had faith that this was the way it had to be.

The Soul Drinkers did not have faith, not in the Imperium. Perhaps that was understandable, thought N'Kalo. He had seen the same things they had, the same brutality and the spiteful randomness of how the fortunes of the Imperium were parcelled out. He had not strayed beyond the Imperial line – he had informed the Inquisition of the threat on Molikor, after all – but he was forced to wonder, considering the recent events there in his cell, whether he would have to have seen many more injustices to end up renegades like the Soul Drinkers.

'Commander N'Kalo,' came a vox from the flag-captain. 'We are receiving a communication, tagged for you by name.'

'Send it,' said N'Kalo.

'Greetings, commander,' said a voice that, until a short time ago, had been an unfamiliar one reaching N'Kalo's ears through the gunfire and crunching branches of the forest gap.

'Sarpedon,' said N'Kalo. 'I had not expected you to still be around. You should be warned that the Inquisition would dearly love to listen in.'

'My ship has communications even the Inquisition cannot intercept in a hurry,' replied Sarpedon. His voice was transmitted in real time, meaning the Soul Drinkers and their ship had to be close by. 'I wanted to thank you for doing the right thing by Molikor and the Eshkeen. You could have followed the Imperial line, but you did not. That takes something beyond mere bravery.'

'I did not turn in the Parliaments of Molikor to garner thanks,' replied N'Kalo. 'I did it because it had to be done. The moral threat on that world could not have been left unchecked. But I am glad that I was not the instrument of injustice and so I should pay thanks to you, for showing me all the paths I might take.'

'And yet I suspect that your gratitude will not prevent you from turning in a renegade and a mutant like myself,' said Sarpedon, 'and so I must leave here.'

'I concur, Sarpedon. That would be wise. I have one question before you go.'

'Speak it.'

'What happened to the Eshkeen?'

N'Kalo thought he heard a small chuckle. 'Do not fear for them,' said Sarpedon. 'My Chapter possesses the means to transport them somewhere they can start anew, and where the Imperium will not rediscover them for a very long time.'

'I see. For my sake it is best I leave it at that. Fare well, Sarpedon, and

I shall pray that our paths do not cross, for I feel if they do I must fight to bring you in.'

'I shall pray for that too, Commander N'Kalo. Emperor's speed to you.'

The comm-channel went dead.

In the hours to follow, the scanners of the *Judgement upon Garadan* detected the possible signature of a ship making a warp jump near the outlying worlds of the Molikor System. The signature suggested a ship far bigger than any Imperial craft, however, and one that seemed dark and shadowy as if cloaked by some stealth system beyond Imperial technology. N'Kalo did not challenge his flag-captain when the event was logged and dismissed as a sensor error, and the Soul Drinkers vanished from the Chapter history of the Iron Knights.

CHAPTER SEVEN

'And what,' said Captain Borganor of the Howling Griffons, 'does this excuse?'

The court was not as vocal as it had been after Varnica's evidence. Instead, it simmered. The Howling Griffons murmured oaths and spat on the ground. The Imperial Fists tried to stay impartial but they could not keep the disdain from their faces as N'Kalo's testimony had come to an end. Reinez had fought to remain silent, eyes closed, face down-turned and grim.

'How many of my battle-brothers does this return from their tombs?' continued Borganor. 'The Soul Drinkers intervened in some backwater spat. What does this say about them? They still fought the Imperial divine right. All they have achieved to tickle Commander N'Kalo's sense of righteousness is the deliverance of one band of savages to Throne knows what fate. Are we to absolve Sarpedon of my own brethren's fall? Will someone speak for the Howling Griffons?'

'Or for the Crimson Fists?' interjected Reinez. 'What have the Eshkeen done to earn a voice in this court? Every one of my fallen brothers is worth a thousand times the heathens the Soul Drinkers saved!'

'If I may,' interrupted Gethsemar of the Angels Sanguine, 'I feel I can shed a little more light on the matters pertinent to the fate of the Soul Drinkers.'

'What could you say, you gilded peacock?' spat Reinez.

'Reinez, you will yield the floor!' demanded Chapter Master Pugh.

'What has his kind suffered at Sarpedon's hand?' retorted Reinez. 'He comes here for nothing more than the spectacle of this mutant! This is entertainment for him! He treats the sacred ground of the *Phalanx* like a sideshow!'

'Your objections,' said Pugh coldly, 'are noted. Commander Gethsemar, say your piece.'

Gethsemar waited a moment, as if to ensure that all the attention of the court was on him. The mask he wore now had no tears, and the forehead and cheeks were inscribed with High Gothic text. 'Indeed, my piece is more relevant than any of the protestations Captain Reinez has yet made,' he said. 'And I feel that few will recall words more incandescent in this matter than those I have to say now.'

'Get on with it, you popinjay,' muttered Reinez.

'The Sanguinary Priests of my order,' continued Gethsemar, 'have long conducted studies into the link between the gene-seed every Space Marine carries within him and the blessed flesh of our primarchs, after whose characteristics the gene-seed of the original eighteen Legions was modelled. Indeed, much had been revealed to us of holy Sanguinius, the father of our own Chapter, and thus we gain revelations of him that steel our souls on the eve of battle. It so happened that the Angels Sanguine came into possession of a sample of gene-seed originating from the Soul Drinkers Chapter, delivered unto us in the hope that we could ascertain if their rebellion was founded in a corruption of such gene-seed.'

'Where did you get it from?' said Sarpedon. 'Which brother of mine supplied it?'

'No brother of yours, I fear,' said Gethsemar. 'It was given to us by the Soul Drinker to whom it belonged, one who had defied your usurping of the Chapter's command and sought, through Inquisitorial means, a way to exact his revenge.'

'Michairas,' said Sarpedon bleakly. 'I thought I had killed him. I did so at the second time of asking, on Stratix Luminae. I underestimated my old novice. He still tries for revenge, even after death.'

'And he has it,' continued Gethsemar. 'Space Marines of the court, Lord Justice, the Sanguinary Priests went about their research in the expectation that they would find the blueprint of Rogal Dorn's own flesh as the starting point for the Soul Drinkers' gene-seed. But they did not.'

'What are you saying?' asked Sarpedon.

'I am saying that Rogal Dorn is not your primarch,' said Gethsemar simply. 'I cannot say who is. The Sanguinary Priests have yet to complete their discourses on the matter. But Dorn's gene-seed is among the most stable and recognisable of all those among the Adeptus Astartes, and there can be no doubt that the Soul Drinkers do not possess it. This

is the news I came to the *Phalanx* to deliver. That is why the Angels Sanguine sought a place at this court.'

Sarpedon pushed against his restraints, half-clambering out of the
accused's pulpit. 'No!' he yelled. 'You have taken everything from us!
Our freedom! Our war! You will not take away Rogal Dorn!'

'The defendant will be silent!' yelled Pugh, above the sound of dozens
of bolt pistols being drawn. Every weapon in the dome was being aimed
then at Sarpedon, in case he burst through his restraints to do violence
to Gethsemar. Lysander stood between Sarpedon and Gethsemar, ready
to slam Sarpedon into the ground if he showed any signs of breaking
free.

Reinez did not move. He had seen all the damage done to Sarpedon
that could be done. For the first time since he had come to the *Phalanx*,
there was a smirk on his face.

Brother Sennon limped through the Atoning Halls, barely drawing a
glance from the Soul Drinkers who sat in its cells, chained to the walls
waiting for a decision to be made in the Observatory of Dornian Majesty. The news of Daenyathos's survival had left them as confused as
elated. The Philosopher-Soldier's presence there had been brief, a few
seconds, before the Dreadnought had been sealed away, and now none
of the Soul Drinkers could be completely sure they had seen him at
all. Their minds were occupied as the single pilgrim walked down the
corridor.

Two Imperial Fists walked behind him as guards, but Sennon looked
in more danger from his own health than from the Soul Drinkers. His
skin was bluish and sweating, his eyes rimmed with red, his shoulders
slumped as if he could barely hold up his own weight. His breath was
a painful wheeze.

He passed the cell where Sergeant Salk was held. The sergeant was
exhausted, his arms bruised from forcing against his restraints long past
the point where it was obvious he would not break free. Other Soul
Drinkers were at prayer or simply at rest, half their minds shut off while
the other half watched, a Space Marine's habit made possible by the
catalepsean node each had implanted between the hemispheres of his
brain. The Soul Drinkers had been fed by regular servitor rounds, but
that was the sole concession made to their comfort. Since Daenyathos
had been sealed away they had been silent, every one contemplating his
situation in his own way, eager for news of Sarpedon and the trial but
unwilling to beg their Imperial Fists captors for it.

One cell held Chaplain Iktinos. This cell had been sealed so no other
Soul Drinker could see or hear the Chaplain. Iktinos's rhetoric was considered one of the biggest threats to keeping the Soul Drinkers captive,
and so a steel plate had been welded over the bars of his cell. The Soul

Drinkers who had made up his flock, those who had lost their officers and gone to Iktinos for leadership, had been spread out through the Atoning Halls to minimise their ability to conspire. Sennon passed the sealed cell and touched it with two fingers, murmuring a prayer for Iktinos's soul.

Sennon halted at Captain Luko's cell, and knelt on the floor.

'Take care,' said Luko. 'You don't look like you could get up again.'

'I have come to pray for you,' said Sennon.

'Pray for yourself,' replied Luko. 'All the prayers that might help us were used up on Selaaca.'

'You are not beyond hope,' said Sennon, apparently unconcerned with the mix of pity and scorn with which Luko looked at him. Luko, compared to Sennon, was a chained giant, and the power held within every Space Marine was not lessened by the manacles that held him against the back wall of the cell or the bars that stood between the two of them. 'There is none so close to the precipice that the Emperor's grace cannot bring him back.'

'And what of those who have gone over the precipice? What about them? To pray for them is a sin, is it not?'

'I do not believe you are among them, Captain Luko.'

'You know my name,' said Luko.

'I have read of the Soul Drinkers,' said Sennon. 'The Imperial Fists made available much of their information so that my sect might better observe the process of justice. The Blinded Eye we may be, but we do not do our duty by remaining blind when knowledge is available.'

'The Inquisition passed a deletion order on us, you know,' said Luko. 'They could probably hang you for knowing we exist.'

'It is the Imperial Fists who hold sway here,' replied Sennon. 'The Inquisition may have its due from us once we leave the *Phalanx*, but that is an acceptable price to pay to see justice done in so grave a case as this.'

'It must be such a relief to see such a simple galaxy around you,' said Luko, but the scorn was drying out from his voice. 'Imagine knowing what is right and wrong. Imagine believing, completely believing, that one way was good and another was bad, and never having to think for yourself about it. I have such envy for you, pilgrim.'

'Then you doubt that you have taken the right path? Doubt is a sin, Captain Luko.'

Luko smiled without humour. 'Thanks. I'll add it to the list.'

'I shall pray for you.'

'No, you will not. I will not be prayed for.'

'You are in chains. You have no say in whether you are prayed for or not.'

That, at least, was something Luko had no stomach to argue. Sennon knelt before Luko's cell, eyes closed and head bowed. His breathing became quieter, and for all Luko knew the young pilgrim might have died there before his cell.

'I have such envy for you,' said Luko, too quiet for anyone but himself to hear.

Sarpedon barely registered the journey back to his cell as the Imperial Fists marched him out of the Observatory of Dornian Majesty once again. The first couple of times he had sized up his guards and the route they took for the best time to attempt escape. His hands were manacled but he still had the use of his legs – the six he had remaining, at least – and he was faster and stronger than any of the four Imperial Fists flanking him.

But he could not take them all down. They were armed and armoured; Sarpedon was not. The inhibitor collar prevented his use of the Hell, which might have sown enough confusion for him to flee. From what he had gathered about the layout of the *Phalanx*, it would be difficult to put any distance between himself and the dome, crammed with hostile Space Marines, before the alarm was raised. The idea of escape was now all but forgotten, filed away in that part of an Space Marine's mind where rejected battle plans lay waiting to be dusted off again.

Captain Borganor was ahead of Sarpedon and his Imperial Fist minders, at a junction of corridors where the science labs and map rooms surrounding the Observatory met the stone-lined corridors of the Atoning Halls.

'Halt, brethren,' said Borganor. 'I would speak with the prisoner.'

'On what authority?' said the lead Imperial Fist.

'On that of brotherhood,' said Borganor. 'I have no dispensation from Lord Pugh, if that is what you ask. I merely wish to put the question to the defendant that every Space Marine on this ship has longed to ask. I shall not hold you long. As a brother, I ask this of you.'

'We have all heard the outrages visited upon the Howling Griffons by the Soul Drinkers,' said the Imperial Fist. 'Ask if you will, but you shall not hold us long.'

'My thanks,' said Borganor.

The Imperial Fists backed away from Sarpedon a little to give Borganor a semblance of privacy as he approached Sarpedon.

Sarpedon thought again of escape. Or, at least, of fighting. He had beaten Borganor before, as evidenced by the bionic leg Borganor sported. But attacking the Howling Griffon would not get him free. More to the point, it would not achieve anything. Sarpedon had no particular hate for Borganor. The Howling Griffon was a victim of the viciousness of the Imperium, in his own way. Sarpedon backed down mentally, and decided that he would not fight here.

'What do you wish to know?' said Sarpedon.

Borganor was close to him now. He had been as bellicose as anyone in the courtroom, but Borganor seemed to have calmed down a little since then. Perhaps the certainty that the end was close, that Pugh and the other Space Marines were even now deciding how Sarpedon was to be executed, had cooled some of the fire in him.

'What do you think?' said Borganor. 'I want to know why.'

'Why?'

'Why you turned on the Imperium. In all the debating and argument, no one has yet understood why you turned the Soul Drinkers renegade. Was it Abraxes? Did your rebellion start with corruption? Speak the truth, Sarpedon, for there is no use for lies now.'

'We saw,' said Sarpedon, 'what the Imperium really was. I believe we had already known it, but that the weight of history and tradition muted that understanding in us. The Imperium is a wicked place, captain. How many citizens live free of fear and misery? I doubt you could name a single one. It is built on cruelty and malice. And in punishing its people and committing the evils it says are necessary, it gives a breeding ground to those enemies it claims to be fighting. The armies of Chaos do not materialise from thin air. They are made up of those who were once citizens of that same Imperium, but who were corrupted first by its horrors. That is what leaves them susceptible to the whispers of the Dark Gods. Were the Emperor able to walk among us still, He would look on what mankind has created in horror and seek to tear it down. The Imperium is not the last bastion against the enemy. It *is* the enemy.'

'Then you claim what Varnica said is untrue? That Abraxes never led you down his own path?'

'Abraxes used us, that is true,' replied Sarpedon. 'He took our anger at the Imperium and used it to manipulate us into destroying his enemies. But that anger was there before he got his claws into us, and we killed Abraxes for what he did. I am not proud of how blind he once made us. It was his touch that gave me these mutations, and I was ignorant of what they truly meant until Abraxes was gone. But he did not teach us to despise the Imperium. We managed that on our own.'

Borganor shook his head. 'So deep your delusions cut that you see them only as truth,' he said.

'I am minded to say the same about you, captain.'

'I begged of Pugh the right to kill you myself,' continued Borganor. 'To pay you back for all my battle-brothers you killed. For Librarian Mercaeno, a man far better than any of your brethren.'

'And did he grant you that right?'

'He did not.'

'You could do it now,' said Sarpedon calmly. 'These Imperial Fists would not turn their guns on you. You would finish me off before they could stop you, I have little doubt about that.'

'No, Sarpedon. I wanted to do it slowly.' Borganor was almost face to face with Sarpedon now. 'To pull your legs off like a child does to a fly.'

'Because I took your leg?'

'Because you took my leg. But I wanted to understand what could drive a Space Marine as far as you have gone, before I did it.'

'And do you understand?'

Borganor took a step back. 'I understand that Abraxes warped your minds and implanted in you the belief that your rebellion was your own idea. There must have been something dark and heretical in your souls to begin with, to let his influence in. You were the weakest of all your Chapter, which is why it chose you as its instrument. You are damned, and death is too merciful for you however it is administered. That is what I believe.'

'What a comfort it must be, Captain Borganor, to have the Dark Gods to blame for anything you are too afraid to understand.'

'Brothers!' came a cry from down the corridor. An Imperial Fists scout was running towards them. He paused to salute Borganor. 'Captain! Lord Pugh requests your return to the Observatory. A verdict has been reached.'

'Already?' said Sarpedon.

'There can have been little debate,' said Borganor with a grim smile. 'Good.'

'Then follow,' said the scout. 'The accused must be present. Any sentence will be carried out immediately.'

'Oh, I do not think anything will be immediate,' said Borganor. 'Remember, Sarpedon? As a child does to a fly?'

The Imperial Fists closed in around Sarpedon, shepherding him back towards the Observatory of Dornian Majesty. Sarpedon glanced back at Borganor, who followed. There was nothing in the Howling Griffon's demeanour to suggest he had any intention but to pull Sarpedon apart piece by piece, regardless of what Pugh decreed.

But he would decree execution, whatever form it was to take. There had been no doubt about that from the moment Sarpedon had squared up to Lysander on Selaaca. He had come to the *Phalanx* to die. He had taken comfort that his Chapter would be executed under the eye of Rogal Dorn, who at least would know that the Soul Drinkers were not the traitors the Imperium perceived them to be... But now, with Gethsemar's revelation, even that was in doubt.

Sarpedon would die alone. The galaxy was too cruel, he supposed, to have expected anything else.

'It is done,' said Brother Sennon. He clambered to his feet, unsteady, his knees having locked up during his long prayer.

'What did you ask Him for?' said Luko. There was sarcasm in his voice, but Sennon didn't seem to have picked it up.

'I asked Him for what He promises everyone. He grants us, if there is any piety in our hearts, a second chance. In our final moments we can be redeemed, if we are pure of heart when our souls come to be weighed against His example.'

'We must leave,' said one of the Imperial Fists escorting Sennon. 'Time in the heretics' presence is rationed. They are a moral threat.'

'My soul is steeled against such things,' replied Sennon. 'I am frail on the outside, but there is none stronger within than a follower of the Blinded Eye.'

'Be that as it may,' said the Imperial Fist, 'we all have our orders.'

'Of course.' Brother Sennon looked up and down the corridor of the Atoning Halls. At one end was a complicated rack, where Imperial Fists in the past had mortified their flesh to atone for some slight against the honour of their Chapter. At the other was a pair of blast doors, sealed. 'Is this where the Dreadnought is held?' asked Sennon, walking towards the doors.

'It is,' replied the Imperial Fist. 'We have no business there. Daenya-thos, if it truly is he, will be dealt with separately when the judgement has been pronounced.'

'To think of it,' said Sennon. 'He must be six thousand years old. He fought at Terra, you know, during the Wars of Apostasy. To us a time of legends, to him, living memory.'

'Past deeds mean nothing when corruption rules the present,' said the Imperial Fist. 'Brother Sennon, we must leave.'

Sennon was right in front of the blast doors now. He placed a hand against them, as if feeling for a heartbeat. 'Just a moment more,' he said. 'Just a moment.'

Sennon turned back towards the Imperial Fists, a smile on his face like that of a saint rendered in stained glass. He seemed about to speak again, and then Brother Sennon exploded.

The court was full, all the Space Marines in attendance to witness the condemnation of Sarpedon. After him the rest of the Soul Drinkers would be filed through here to receive their death sentences, but it was Sarpedon's that really counted. In the eyes of those who wanted venge-ance against them, Sarpedon *was* the Soul Drinkers, and his fate fell on them all.

Reinez stood, arms folded, waiting for the sentence as if he were in attendance as executioner. It was more likely that Captain Lysander would do the deed, standing as he was beside the pulpit with his ham-mer in his hand. Commander Gethsemar wore his weeping mask again, perhaps to remember the Space Marines who had died at Soul Drink-ers hands. N'Kalo wore his helmet again – presumably it had been hammered back into shape in the forges of the *Phalanx*, and N'Kalo's twice-ruined face was hidden once more. Chapter Master Pugh stood among the Imperial Fists, ready to pronounce his findings.

'The accused will take to the pulpit,' said Pugh.

Sarpedon did as he was told. If there had been a time to fight back, save for the ill-fated lashing out in the apothecarion, then it had long since passed. It would serve no purpose, either. He had no particular hate for the Space Marines who had gathered here to see him killed. He had been like them once, except perhaps a little more prideful, a little more arrogant. He did not even hate Reinez. A moment of pity, perhaps, but not hate.

'Sarpedon of the Soul Drinkers,' began Pugh. 'Words have been said for and against your conduct. The evidence gathered has been examined with criticism as well as zeal. I am confident that honour and tradition have been served in every action of this court, and that the conclusions we draw are true and just before the sight of Rogal Dorn and the Emperor Most High.'

'May I speak?' said Sarpedon.

'Speak if you will,' said Pugh, 'but our conclusions have been arrived at, and need only pronouncement. Your words will mean nothing.'

'My gratitude, Lord Justice,' said Sarpedon. 'Space Marines, I call you brothers, though I know you think yourselves no brothers of mine. When I turned on Chapter Master Gorgoleon and took command of my Chapter, I did it because I saw in us a terrible corruption. Not the corruption of the warp, nor some darkness of the xenos, but a very human corruption of the soul. We believed ourselves to be superior, to be the shepherds of the human race, for we were ordained within the priesthood of Terra with the role of watchdogs and executioners. Yet that priesthood, and the Imperium it ruled, were the true enemy. For every human killed or made to suffer by the predations of the warp or the alien, a billion more are dealt the same fate by the Imperium. The Emperor is just a hollow figurehead now, an excuse for the cruelty the Imperium inflicts, yet when He walked among us He strove for the safety and glory of every man and woman. Would you have me grovel and beg for forgiveness, for leading my Chapter to do the will of the Emperor when it conflicted with the malice of the Imperium? The death of every Space Marine weighs on me. The Howling Griffons and Crimson Fists who died in our conflicts I feel as sharply as the deaths of my own brothers. But I will not say that I am sorry. I have done nothing wrong. And if the story of the Soul Drinkers causes any one of you to doubt the right of the Imperium to oppress and murder the Emperor's faithful, then our deaths will not have been in vain.'

Reinez met Sarpedon's words with sarcastic applause, slow hand claps that echoed in the Observatory of Dornian Majesty. Everyone else was silent.

'Then I pronounce on you the sentence of death,' said Pugh, 'to be administered by the Imperial Fists swiftly, as befits the death of another Space Marine, and the striking of the name Sarpedon and those of all the Soul Drinkers from any bonds of oath or honour. To carry out this sentence I appoint Captain Lysander as executioner and Apothecary Asclephin as overseer. Sarpedon, you will be taken from this place to the Chapel of Martyrs where you will be killed, your body incinerated and any remains jettisoned into space. Your battle-brothers will follow. That is the pronouncement of this court.'

Sarpedon bowed his head. It was as good as he could have expected.

A stirring in the assembled Space Marines broke his train of thought. Several of them were looking upwards, through the dome. The smeared lights of the Veiled Region silhouetted a form approaching rapidly – a spaceship, smaller by magnitudes than the *Phalanx*, its engines burning full thrust as it hurtled right towards the dome.

Fire spat towards it. The automated turrets of the *Phalanx* had activated in time and the shape exploded in the brief burst of flame that was sucked away by the vacuum a split second later. But the ship was not vaporised, merely blown apart, and a chunk of its hull still spun on its original course towards the dome.

'The pilgrim ship,' said Lysander. 'Close the dome!'

The dome was protected by armour plates that began to close like the lids of a huge circular eye, but every Space Marine could see it would not close fast enough.

'Everyone out!' yelled Pugh. 'We are betrayed! Enemies abound! Brothers, flee this place!'

'The condemned seeks vengeance!' shouted Reinez over the growing commotion as the Space Marines left their seats and headed for the exits, the burning mass of the pilgrim ship's hull looming larger through the dome. 'His allies want to take us with him! I will not flee while this traitor yet lives!'

'Damnation, Reinez!' yelled Lysander. 'Get–'

The hull segment crashed into the dome. The armoured shutters were halfway closed when it hit. The dome shattered, shards of thick armoured glass falling like knives. The air boomed out and a terrible half-silence fell, the shrieking of metal and the howling of flame muffled as if coming from beneath the earth.

Sarpedon's augmented lungs closed his windpipes to preserve what air he had in his body. The disaster unfolded around him in slow motion. Space Marines were diving for cover from the chunks of burning metal raining down. In surreal slow motion, one Imperial Fist lost his leg at the knee, sheared off by a shard of the dome. Another, along with a Howling Griffon, disappeared under a torrent of twisted steel and fire. Space Marines were thrown aside as Pugh's honour guard fought to force him through the doors. Gethsemar's Angels Sanguine leapt from the seats out through the entrances on the exhaust plumes of their jump packs.

All was chaos. The bulk of the pilgrim ship's hull was wedged in the blinded eye socket of the dome, but it had split open along the lines of its hull plates and was spewing torrents of burning wreckage into the dome. Sarpedon couldn't see Reinez or Lysander, the two Space Marines who had been closest to him, and his body instinctively fought against his restraints.

One part of him was screaming that he had no air, and that even a Space Marine's three lungs could not hold out for long in hard vacuum. The other part fought to escape. Sarpedon had never tested his bonds in the pulpit properly, for there had never been any chance of him escaping beneath the sight of so many Space Marines. Now he pulled against the manacles and shackles with strength he was not sure he still had.

The structure of the pulpit gave way. Hardwood and steel broke under the force. Sarpedon ripped his manacles off and grabbed the struts of the shackles that held his six remaining legs in place. They broke away, too, and Sarpedon, though still dragging his restraints behind him, was free.

He ran for the nearest exit. A sheet of steel, a section of the pilgrim ship's deck, fell like a giant guillotine blade, and he skidded to a halt just before it sliced him in two. He scrambled up it, almost as nimble over a vertical surface as a horizontal one, and saw ahead of him the blast doors closing. A klaxon was blaring, the sound transmitted through the floor and his talons, explosions like dull thuds all around, the whole chamber vibrating as metal tore. He saw a dying Howling Griffon, one side of his torso opened up, organs trailing from his torn armour. His eyes were rolled back and he was convulsing. Sarpedon could not help him.

Sarpedon jumped and skidded through the blast doors. A tangle of wreckage was blocking them from closing completely. He hauled the twisted metal free and the doors boomed close, air howling around him and screaming in his ears as the corridor beyond repressurised.

Sarpedon took a breath. It felt like the first in a lifetime. His throat was raw as he gulped down air. His mind, tight and dull in his head, seemed to flow back to full capacity with the return of oxygen.

Sarpedon looked around him. He was in a tech lab, with benches heavy with verispex equipment and banks of datamedium racked on the walls. It was where Techmarines and their assistant crewmen would conduct experiments on captured tech, or craft the delicate mechanisms of bespoke weapons and armour. The walls were inlaid with bronze geometric designs and a cogitator stood against one wall like an altar, its brass case covered in candles that had half-burned away. The floor was scattered with broken equipment and the detritus of their work, thrown about by the gale of escaping air.

Sarpedon paused. He did not know the layout of the *Phalanx*. He remembered the way back to his cell well enough, but he doubted there was any point in returning there.

What point was there in doing anything? He could not escape the *Phalanx*, surely. The Imperial Fists would be hunting him down as soon as they had counted their own dead. He was free, but what did it matter?

It had to count for something. He fought the fatalism that had weighed him down since his capture. While he still lived, he could still fight, he could still make his life mean something...

'Sarpedon!' yelled a voice that he recognised with a lurch.

Reinez, his pilgrim's tatters even more ragged and his face scorched, limped from a doorway into the lab. He had been caught in the flames and the edges of his armour were singed, but he had not lost his grip on the thunder hammer that served him like an extension of his own body.

'Captain Reinez,' said Sarpedon. 'I see that neither of us is easy to kill.'

'You are not free, traitor!' barked Reinez. 'There is no freedom under my watch! I sought your execution, and it will happen this day!'

Sarpedon was unarmed and unarmoured. He had not fought for what was, by his standards, a long time, and his lungs and muscles still burned. But he was still a Space Marine, and the moment did not exist when a Space Marine was unprepared to fight.

Reinez charged, yelling as he held his hammer high. It was a move of pure anger, reckless, unthinking. Wrong. Sarpedon scuttled up one wall, talons finding purchase in the raised designs, and Reinez's hammer slammed into the wall behind him. The hammer ripped a deep dent in the wall, wires and coolant pipes spilling out as he wrenched it free.

Sarpedon clung to the web of lumen-strips and wires that covered the ceiling. Reinez yelled in frustration and swung up at Sarpedon, but he dropped down onto a lab bench in front of him and kicked a complex microscope array into Reinez's unprotected face. Dozens of lenses and sharp brass struts shattered and Reinez stumbled back, blinded for a moment.

Sarpedon pounced on him, front limbs striking down, back limbs wrapping around. Reinez fell back with Sarpedon on top of him, fighting for the hammer which was the only weapon between them. Sarpedon tore it from Reinez's hands and threw it aside, the power field discharging like caged lightning as the weapon tumbled across the room.

Reinez punched up at Sarpedon. Sarpedon batted Reinez's fist aside and followed up with a punch of his own, his knuckles cracking against Reinez's jaw. With his armour on, a gauntleted fist would have broken the jaw – as it was Reinez was merely stunned for a moment, long enough for Sarpedon to roll him over, lift him up off the floor and drive him head-first into the cogitator against the room's back wall.

Power flashed. Components pinged out of the ruined machine, valves popping, cogs firing out like bullets. Reinez pulled himself free, blood running down his face and the pitted surface of his tarnished breastplate.

'You are no executioner!' yelled Sarpedon. 'You failed! You have become this unthinking, hating creature, because you cannot accept that you failed! If you killed me your failure would still stand and your life would mean nothing! You should be grateful I never gave you the chance!'

Reinez coughed up a gobbet of blood. He was still standing, but he wavered as if his legs wanted to give way. 'Heretic,' he slurred. 'Vermin. You were never any brother of mine. The warp took you long ago. Your whole Chapter. Stained... tainted... down to your gene-seed... Even Dorn's blood rejects you!'

Reinez's hand flashed down to his waist and a bolt pistol was in his palm. He raised it in a flash.

Reinez was a fast draw, but Sarpedon moved faster. He crouched down onto his haunches, behind one of the lab benches. The bolt pistol barked and hit the lab bench, blasting sprays of hardwood and bronze shrapnel. Another few shots and it would come apart.

Sarpedon dropped his shoulder and barged into the bench. It came off its moorings and he powered it towards Reinez. The bench crunched into Reinez, pinning him against the wall and trapping the wrist of his gun arm.

Sarpedon reached over the bench and tore the pistol out of Reinez's hand. As quickly as Reinez had drawn it, Sarpedon had it against Reinez's temple.

'I let you live,' said Sarpedon. 'Remember that, brother.'

Sarpedon smacked the butt of the pistol into the bridge of Reinez's nose, crunching through cartilage and stunning Reinez again. The Crimson Fist's head lolled, insensible. Sarpedon let go of the bench and Reinez clattered to the floor. Sarpedon left him there, scuttling from the tech lab into whatever paths the *Phalanx* had laid out for him next.

The liquid explosive with which Brother Sennon had replaced his blood ignited, and incinerated him in an instant. The door to Daenyathos's cell was ripped off its mountings. The Imperial Fists accompanying Sennon were blown off their feet and hurled down the corridor of the Atoning Halls, their armoured weight crushing the rack that stood at the intersection.

Luko was knocked senseless by the shockwave. When his senses returned, his vision shuddered and his ears were full of white noise. He did not hear the footsteps of the Dreadnought emerging from the smouldering hole, but he saw the rubble-strewn ground shaking. Soul Drinkers stumbled from their cells, for the walls of the Atoning Halls had been forced out of shape and cell doors had sprung open. One or two of them had used shrapnel to lever their restraints open, and helped their fellows in neighbouring cells do the same. Two of them were on the Imperial Fists, who were still stunned and could not fight back as the Soul Drinkers grabbed their boltguns, combat knives and grenades.

Luko kicked against his own cell door. It was still held fast. A shadow fell over him, and silhouetted in the hazy light was Daenyathos. The Dreadnought body, even disarmed, was a powerful and terrible thing. Luko, still deafened, did not speak. The Dreadnought looked at him, the dead eyes of its mechanical head focussing, and then it walked on, disappearing into the swirl of dust and smoke.

Sergeant Salk appeared in the Dreadnought's wake. He had a pair of shears for cutting through chain or bone, likely taken from one of the cases of torture implements with which past generations of Imperial Fists had purified themselves. Salk shouted something that Luko could not make out, then worked on the hinges of the cell door until Salk could wrench it free.

Salk then cut the manacles holding Luko to the back wall, and helped him to his feet. Salk's words were getting through to him now, dulled by the ringing inside Luko's head.

'… have to go now! The Fists will be here in moments!'

'Who… who is dead?' said Luko. His own voice sounded like it was coming from somewhere else.

'Four or five of us, I think. Maybe dead, maybe hurt. There is no time to be sure. There is a way out through the far end, towards the archives.'

Luko saw Apothecary Pallas emerging from the dust and rubble, together with several other Soul Drinkers. Two more were forcing the door off another cell and Luko saw it contained Librarian Tyrendian, the inhibitor collar still clamped around his neck to quell his psychic powers.

'What of Daenyathos?' said Luko.

'He is not in his cell.'

'I saw that. Where did he go?'

'I do not know, brother. I have not seen Chaplain Iktinos, either. We must gather and find somewhere we can defend, brother. We are free, but not for long if we cannot make a stand.'

'Yes. Yes, brother, I agree. We must move.'

'What of justice?' said Pallas. The Apothecary was standing just outside the cell, Soul Drinkers gathering around him. His hands were slick with blood – he must have tried to save Soul Drinkers who had been wounded in the blast.

'Justice?' said Luko.

'We are renegades. We were brought here to face justice. Is it right to flee from it? And what will we do after we have fled? Fight all the Space

Marines on the *Phalanx*? We have less than a company's worth. There are three companies of Imperial Fists on this spaceship, and Throne knows how many from other Chapters. What does one more battle mean to us when the outcome will be the same? None of us is getting off this ship, captain. You know that.'

'Then stay, Apothecary,' said Luko. 'While there is freedom left for us, I for one will grasp it. There may not be much left for us, but to die free is worth a fight, I think. Come, brothers! We need to leave this place. Follow!'

Luko and Salk left the cell. Luko saw what remained of the Soul Drinkers Chapter – unarmed, bloodied, they were still marked by the manacles and shackles. But they were his brothers, and for one final time they would fight side by side. The Emperor only knew why Sennon had killed himself to buy this freedom for them – this was not the time to ask such questions. It was enough that they had the chance.

Luko was a man who seized his chances. He took the bolter offered to him by one of the other Soul Drinkers, and led the way through the Atoning Halls towards his final moments of freedom.

CHAPTER EIGHT

Luko kicked in the door of the archive. Musty air swept out, mixing with the cordite and rubble dust that rolled off the Soul Drinkers. The archive was a high-ceilinged, dim and age-sodden room with rolls of parchment mounted on the walls for several storeys up, and huge wooden reading tables over which bent the archivists, who looked up in surprise as almost sixty Space Marines stormed into their domain.

'Not too bad to defend,' said Salk, taking in the sight of the archives. 'Lots of cover, not many entrances.'

'At least we'll have something to read while we're waiting,' replied Luko.

The archivists fled. None of the Soul Drinkers had any heart to pursue them. They would tell the Imperial Fists where the escapees had holed up, but the Imperial Fists would learn that anyway, and too many people had died already.

'Spread out!' ordered Luko to the other Soul Drinkers. With Sarpedon and Iktinos elsewhere, it had seemed a natural fit for him to take command. 'Find something we can use! Weapons, transport! It's too much to hope to find a shuttle that can get us off this can, but that doesn't mean we shouldn't look.'

'And get me something to take this damned thing off!' Librarian Tyrendian was still wrestling with the inhibitor collar around his neck. 'Until then I have to think down to your level.'

Luko caught sight of movement and his eyes flickered to the dim interior of the archive. From the shadows shuffled an old, bent figure, wearing the same robes and symbols as the youth who had blown himself up to free the Soul Drinkers from the Atoning Halls. The archivists had all fled, but this man, who seemed more decrepit than any of them, showed no fear.

'Hail!' said the old man. Luko saw the rosarius beads and aquila icons of a pilgrim, and the symbol of the blinded eye embroidered on his robes. 'Brethren of the Chalice! How my heart grows to see you at liberty!'

'Who are you?' demanded Luko. 'One of your pilgrims died to free us, though we didn't ask for it. What does your kind want from us?'

'I want only for the path of fate to be walked true,' replied the pilgrim. 'Time has sought fit to grant me the title Father Gyranar. My brothers and I are the Blind Retribution, the seekers of justice, the instruments of fate, the Blinded Eye. For longer than I have been alive, fate has taught us of the part we are to play in the fulfilment of the Soul Drinkers' destiny.' Gyranar limped forwards and took Luko's huge paw in his tiny, dry hands. 'I rejoice that I have lived to see that time! When I drank from the grail, I dared not to beg of the fates that I witness the day the chalice shall overflow!'

'Explain yourself,' said Luko.

'We are a long line of those who have been tasked with making this day happen,' continued Gyranar. 'The Black Chalice, the Silver Grail, and countless others, have all followed the same path, one that would ensure they crossed paths with the Soul Drinkers so they could help destiny become reality. You must go free, Captain Luko, you and all your battle-brothers! You must fight here, and see that which must be, shall be! I have broken your shackles, but only you can strike the blows!'

'What fate?' demanded Luko. 'If we are here to do something, then it is news to me. We were brought to the *Phalanx* against our will, and at the risk of sounding ungrateful, our freedom was something equally unsought.'

'But now you fight one last battle!' said Gyranar. The old man's eyes were alight, as if he was looking beyond Luko to some religious revelation. 'Instead of a dismal execution, you die fighting, and in doing so your sacrifice will change the Imperium for the better! All human history hinges on this point, captain!'

Luko pulled Gyranar close. The old man barely came up to Luko's solar plexus. 'He who longs for one last battle,' Luko said darkly, 'has never truly fought a battle at all.'

'Fate cares not that its instruments are ignorant of their importance,' said Gyranar. 'I have been given the blessing of knowing what is to come. You, captain, are no less blessed for having it revealed to you at the moment of your glory.'

Luko let Gyranar go. The pilgrim had no fear. A Space Marine knew no fear because he mastered it, broke it down and discarded it as irrelevant. Gyranar had no fear to begin with, as if even an angry Space Marine bearing down on him was a scene from a play which he had seen many times.

'You remind me of someone I once knew,' said Luko. 'He was Yser, and much like you, a believer. He was the pawn of a power greater and darker than he could have imagined, and it killed him. You will find few friends among the Soul Drinkers, Father Gyranar.'

'As I said,' replied Gyranar, 'there were others. I am merely the most fortunate.'

'Captain!' yelled Tyrendian from deeper within the archive, among the shadows that clung around the many archways leading out from the main chamber. 'I've found something. You want to see it.'

Luko followed Tyrendian's voice. The Librarian stood in an archway leading into another chamber, this one lit sparingly by a few spotglobes that shone their shafts of light onto hundreds of exhibits, like the inside of a museum.

Almost a hundred suits of power armour stood there, on racks that made it look as if their owners were standing there in ranks. The armour of the Soul Drinkers, still spattered with the mud and ash of Selaaca, still with the scars of necron weapons and the claws of the wraiths that had nearly killed so many of them. Sarpedon's armour was there, battered by his struggle with the necron overlord. Luko's own armour, too, with the haphazard heraldry of his career as a renegade painted over the dark purple of the Chapter's livery.

Beside the armour were the weapons. Boltguns racked up as if in an armoury. The Axe of Mercaeno, Sarpedon's own weapon. Sergeant Graevus's power axe and Luko's lightning claws, the huge armoured gloves with their paint scorched and peeling by the constant discharging of the claws' power fields.

'The evidence chamber,' said Tyrendian with a smile.

'Arm up!' yelled Luko. 'Tyrendian, check around and find ammunition and power packs.'

'Perhaps we can make a stand after all,' said Salk as he saw the arms displayed before him. Several Soul Drinkers were already going for their armour, while Sergeant Graevus had gone straight for his power axe. With the axe in the sergeant's mutated hand he suddenly looked more like a Soul Drinker, more like a warrior, and less like anyone who could have been held captive.

Luko slid a hand into one of his lightning claw gauntlets. Its weight felt tremendous, and not just because Luko hadn't yet donned the power armour that would help compensate for its size.

'I used to dream,' he said to Salk, 'of all this ending peacefully. At least, I told myself, an execution is not a battle. But there is one last battle now. You would have thought I'd have learned by now that there is always one last battle.'

'Captain?' said Salk.

'I hate it,' said Luko. 'Fighting. Bloodshed. I have come to hate it. I have lied about this for a long time, Sergeant Salk, but there hardly seems much point now.'

'I can barely believe you are saying these things, captain.'

'I know. I disgust myself too, sometimes.'

'No, captain,' said Salk. 'You don't understand. You hate war, but you fight it because you know you must. There is nothing to disgust in that. Sometimes I take pride, or even pleasure, in it, and I take that and carry it with me to bring me through the worst of it. But without that, I do not know how I could fight. You are braver than I, Captain Luko.'

'Well,' said Luko, 'that's one way of looking at it.'

'Let's make our execution a little more interesting, brother,' said Salk.

Luko clamped one of his greaves around his left leg. 'Amen to that, brother.'

The commanders gathered in the Forge of Ages, safe from the decompression zones around the Observatory. In the ruddy glow of the forges they first counted off their surviving battle-brothers, appointed officers to take note of the dead, and then turned to the task of recapturing the Soul Drinkers.

There was no doubt that the Soul Drinkers had engineered their escape, with the use of accomplices among the pilgrims who had been allowed onto the *Phalanx* to observe the trial. Castellan Leucrontas had been silent as the commanders discussed their losses and the state of the *Phalanx*, for it was only a matter of time before his decision to allow the pilgrims onto the ship was examined.

No Angels Sanguine had been lost, added to which Commander Gethsemar and his Sanguinary Guard seemed completely unblemished by the carnage. Howling Griffons had died. Imperial Fists, present in the greatest numbers, had lost correspondingly the most. One Silver Skull and two Doom Eagles were missing, presumed dead and cast into the void by the explosive decompression. Crewmen in void suits were already taking their first steps into the Observatory dome, to hunt for the fallen among the torrents of scorched wreckage, but hopes were not high that survivors would be found.

'Brothers!' came a shout from the entrance to the Forge of Ages. Reinez, severely battered and bloodied, walked in, dragging an unarmoured Space Marine behind him. Reinez's armour, which had been in poor repair when he had arrived on the *Phalanx*, was now so filthy with blood and scorch marks that the colours of the Crimson Fists were barely discernible. 'Are you looking for answers? Perhaps a few explanations? I have done what you cannot do by bickering among yourselves, and found you some!'

Reinez shoved the Space Marine into the centre of the Forge. The captive showed no resistance, and fell to his knees.

'It is good that you are alive, Reinez,' said Chapter Master Pugh. Siege-Captain Daviks stepped forwards and lifted the bowed head of the Space Marine.

'He's a Soul Drinker,' said Daviks, pointing to the chalice symbol that marked the centre of the surgical scars on the Space Marine's chest. 'What is your name?'

'Apothecary Pallas,' said the Soul Drinker.

'One of the accused,' said Pugh. 'You were to be executed. Why did you not flee with the rest of the condemned?'

'Because we are not free,' said Pallas. 'I do not know why we were released, or who is responsible, but we did not seek it. I have been manipulated before, by Abraxes when our Chapter first turned from the Imperium, and I will not be used like that again. If I am to be executed here then so be it. I do not care about that any more. But I will not be a pawn in the scheme of another.'

'Then who?' demanded Daviks. 'Who committed this outrage? My battle-brothers died because someone set the Soul Drinkers loose. Answer me!'

'I don't know!' retorted Pallas. 'Someone who benefits from a battle on the *Phalanx*. Someone who wants a last laugh from the Soul Drinkers before we are gone. Your guesses are as good as mine.'

'They have left this one behind to sow confusion,' said Daviks to the other Space Marines. 'Recall the strategies of cowardice, as recounted in the *Codex Astartes*!'

'There has been dissent in the ranks of the Soul Drinkers before,' said Pugh. 'They turned on one another at Nevermourn. That this Apothecary chose not to follow his brothers in evading justice is not impossible.'

'Dissenter or not,' said Reinez, 'we should get everything he knows out of him.' Reinez took a tool from the closest forge – its metal prongs glowed from the heat. 'I suggest we not delay.'

'There will be no need for that,' said Pugh. 'If he is here to misinform us then he will be prepared to spread lies under duress. If he is not, then there is no need for the infliction of suffering.'

'Then what are we to do with him?' sneered Reinez. 'Give him a commission?'

'He is an Apothecary. He can help tend to the wounded,' replied Pugh. 'Apothecary Asclephin, you will oversee his work once he has answered one question.'

'Name it,' said Pallas.

'Where is Sarpedon?'

Pallas looked up at Pugh. 'The last I knew of it, he was in the court-room. You are in a better position to know his whereabouts than I.'

'Space Marines died in his escape' said Pugh. 'You understand that justice will fall on him sooner or later, and that your own manner of death will depend on how satisfied we are with your part in that justice.'

'I barely care for life or death any more, Chapter Master,' said Pallas. 'I do not know where he is. Decide among yourselves if I speak the truth, but I know that I do.'

'Another question, with which our Soul Drinker friend may not be able to help us,' said Gethsemar smoothly, 'is the location of Captain N'Kalo.'

Instinctively, the Space Marine officers looked around. They were all there save for N'Kalo. His Iron Knights were present, but not their commander.

'He made it out of the dome,' said Daviks. 'I saw him.'

'But he did not make it here,' answered Gethsemar.

'Then locating him is a priority,' said Pugh, 'but not one as high as locating Sarpedon and the Soul Drinkers who broke out of the cell block. If they have a plan then it most likely involves them staying together. If we are to break them with a minimum of losses, we must do so quickly, before they dig in. Lysander!'

'Chapter Master?' said Lysander with a salute.

'You will lead the hunt. You have our three companies at your disposal. Officers, I ask that you cede command to Lysander in my name, and that he send your battle-brothers as he sees fit. I need no reminding of the protocols it breaks to request you place yourselves under the command of another Chapter, but this is not the time to dally over such things.'

'I will kill Sarpedon,' said Reinez.

'You will not put the lives of my battle-brothers at risk,' said Pugh. 'If it is expedient, another will eliminate Sarpedon, not wait for your permission.'

'My oath of revenge is more important than life.' Reinez shoved Pallas aside as he took a few steps closer to Pugh. 'Even the life of a brother.'

'And delivering Dorn's justice upon the Soul Drinker is more important than either,' said Lysander, putting a hand on Reinez's shoulder pad. Reinez shrugged it off angrily.

'For one who despises time wasted in talking,' said Gethsemar, 'Brother Reinez does enjoy his little speeches.'

Reinez gave Gethsemar a look that could have killed a star, as the officers rallied their Space Marines for the hunt.

* * *

Captain N'Kalo forced off the slab of wreckage that pinned him down. His ears rang and the world was painted in blotchy blacks and reds. He was somewhere in one of the *Phalanx*'s tribute galleries, the deck divided into displays of art, standards and captured arms evoking the history of the Imperial Fists.

The ceiling had collapsed on him as he fled the dome. The galleries had sealed behind him before they were decompressed, but the shock-waves of the pilgrim ship's suicide attack had caused enough damage of their own. N'Kalo saw he had been trapped beneath a spiderlike cara-pace, complete and preserved in a transparent layer of resin, which had been mounted on the ceiling to give the impression it was about to ambush visitors to the galleries from above. The carapace was that of a creature with ten legs and a span of four or five metres across, and still bore the charred bolter scars that had felled it. It was the relic of a battle millions of miles and probably thousands of years distant.

On one side of N'Kalo was a mural of Imperial Fists dragging the enemy dead from sucking tar pits on a primeval world of volcanoes and jungle. The enemy had the blue-grey skins and flat features of the tau, xenos who had tried to expand into Imperial space and been fought to a stalemate at the Damocles Gulf. On the other side were armour plates torn from a greenskin vehicle, a strange, brutal majesty in the sav-age simplicity of their skull and bullet designs and the blood that still stained the lower edges of a tank's dozer blade.

N'Kalo tried to get his bearings. He did not know if he was alone. He looked and listened around him, trying to find crewmen or Space Marines through the displays and sculptures.

The hiss of a nerve-fibre bundle reached his ears. The clicking of one ceramite plate on another.

'Brother?' called N'Kalo. 'Are you hurt? Speak to me!'

There was no reply.

N'Kalo tensed. Perhaps Sarpedon had survived the attack, and was free. Perhaps the other captive Soul Drinkers were free, too. He could not afford to think of the *Phalanx* as safe ground any more. For all he knew, this was enemy territory.

N'Kalo drew his bolt pistol. He wished he had his power sword with him, but he had stowed it in his squad's cell-quarters when he had exchanged it for the executioner's blade in the duel.

On the wall next to the vehicle armour plates hung a bladed weapon shaped like a massively oversized meat cleaver, with teeth and jagged shards soldered to its cutting edge. A greenskin weapon. N'Kalo felt dis-taste as he lifted it from its mountings and tested its weight. A xenos weapon, and one that no Iron Knight should ever use, but circum-stances were extreme.

A shadow upon a shadow, through arches between the trophies

and memorials, coalesced into the shape of a power-armoured figure. N'Kalo ducked out of sight, behind the mural of the Imperial Fists' victory over the tau.

'I spoke for you,' said N'Kalo. 'No one else would. I spoke up for your Chapter! Do what the court did not and listen to me.'

Something metal clattered to the floor. Ceramite boots sounded on the tiles.

'Give yourself up, brother,' continued N'Kalo. 'If you will not, if you fight us here, your fate will only be worse.'

'It is not my fate,' came the reply, 'with which you should concern yourself.'

N'Kalo did not recognise the voice. It had an edge of learning and confidence, a calmness quite at odds with its potential for violence.

'Name yourself,' said N'Kalo.

'You will know my name soon enough,' came the reply.

N'Kalo risked a glance past the mural. The muzzle of a bolt pistol met him. He ducked back as the gun fired, blasting a shower of wooden shards from the edge of the wall.

N'Kalo dived past the other side of the mural, head down, barrelling forwards. He crashed through a display of captured standards, leaping the plinth to close with his enemy.

The bolt pistol fired again. N'Kalo took the shot on his chest, feeling blades of ceramite driven into his ribs. Not too deep. Not too bad. He would make it face to face.

N'Kalo led with his shoulder and slammed into his assailant. He saw not the purple armour of a Soul Drinker, but the skull-encrusted black of a Chaplain. The chalice on one shoulder pad confirmed the Chapter, however.

Iktinos. The Chaplain of the Soul Drinkers, and the man considered the most likely moral threat among the captives until Daenyathos had been dug up. The second man slated for execution after Sarpedon. Armed and armoured, and free.

N'Kalo drove the greenskin blade up under Iktinos's arm. Iktinos wrenched his own weapon around quickly enough to lever the blade away from him, throwing N'Kalo onto the back foot. N'Kalo realised with a lurch that Iktinos carried the crozius arcanum, the mace-like power weapon that served as a Chaplain's badge of office.

Iktinos smacked his bolt pistol against the side of N'Kalo's head. N'Kalo reeled, one side of his battered helmet caved in again along the cracks opened up by Reinez.

'Kneel,' said Iktinos, bolt pistol levelled at N'Kalo's face. 'Kneel and it will be quick. Is that not what the Soul Drinkers were offered? Submission for a quick death? Then that is what I offer you, Captain N'Kalo of the Iron Knights.'

N'Kalo dropped to one knee and grabbed one of the standards he had knocked onto the floor. It was an iron spear with a ragged banner hanging from it, the standard of some rebellious Imperial Guard regiment.

Another shot caught N'Kalo in the head. His helmet was torn open and one eye went black. N'Kalo thrust the standard pole forwards with everything he had, catching Iktinos in the hand and throwing the bolt pistol off into the shadows.

N'Kalo fell back onto one knee. He wrenched the ruined helmet off his head. He felt hot blood flowing down his face and his fingers brushed wet, pulpy mass where one eye had been. His head rang, and it felt like his skull was suddenly a few sizes too small.

A fractured skull, then. He had suffered that before. Not the worst. He could fight on.

Iktinos strode forwards, crozius in his good hand. He swung it down at N'Kalo, who deflected it away with the greenskin blade he had snatched off the floor at the last second. The blade shattered like glass and N'Kalo was driven onto his back by the force of the blow. He reeled, his good eye unable to focus, Iktinos just a black blur over him.

'Iktinos!' yelled Sarpedon. For a moment Iktinos thought that Sarpedon was the man attacking him, that he was back in the Eshkeen forests with his battle-brothers. Everything since then had been a dream and he had never left that stretch of marshland.

But no. Iktinos was the enemy. Sarpedon was somewhere nearby. Iktinos dragged N'Kalo to his feet and wrapped an arm around his throat, hauled him into a corner and grabbed his bolt pistol off the floor. The muzzle of the pistol was against the side of N'Kalo's head.

Sarpedon stood in the middle of the gallery, unarmoured as he had been in the courtroom.

'Iktinos!' yelled Sarpedon. He could barely believe that the first Soul Drinker he had come across since his escape was engaged in fighting the one Space Marine who had stood up for the Chapter at the trial. Still stranger was that it was Iktinos, and that he had already found his armour and weapons.

N'Kalo looked nearly dead. His face was barely recognisable as belonging to a human. One eye socket was a gory ruin. Iktinos had disarmed him, and now had him up as a human shield with a gun to his head.

'Chaplain,' called Sarpedon. 'What are you doing?'

'I am surviving,' said Iktinos.

'N'Kalo is my friend. Let him go.'

'The Soul Drinkers have no friends. N'Kalo is coming with me.'

'Hostages will do us no good, Iktinos! You know that!'

'Then it is for the best that I have him, not you. Do not seek to follow,

Sarpedon. There is only sorrow this way. Go to your brothers. They are re-arming in the archives.'

'What are you speaking of, Chaplain? Whatever fate waits for us here, are you not a part of it?'

Iktinos dragged N'Kalo towards a pair of double doors at the far end of the hall. 'Fight, Sarpedon! Fight on! That is what fate demands of you. Stand by your brothers and die a good death!'

'I know that someone has guided us here without my realising. Someone has used me just as surely as Abraxes did. Is it you, Iktinos?'

'Goodbye, Sarpedon. A good death to you, my brother!'

'Is it Daenyathos?'

Iktinos hauled N'Kalo through the doors. They boomed shut behind him. Sarpedon rushed forwards, trying to cover the ground to the doors before Iktinos could turn a corner and get out of sight.

Sarpedon heard the tiny sound of the grenade hitting the floor. He threw his arms up in front of him, supernatural reflexes giving him the warning a split second before the grenade went off in his face. The doors were ripped off their mountings and slammed into him, throwing him back across the display room, crashing through captured arms and victory monuments.

Sarpedon skidded along the floor on his back. When he came to a halt he brushed the debris from his eyes and saw the doorway was full of smoke and rubble. Sarpedon had no way of following Iktinos.

Daenyathos. Rogal Dorn. The pilgrim ship's suicide attack. Now Iktinos, with an agenda of his own. Everything Sarpedon had believed about the galaxy was falling apart, and he did not know how it could end but with his death and the deaths of every one of his battle-brothers.

One thing that Iktinos had said made sense. Sarpedon had to fight. He had to win a good death, and help his brothers do the same. He owed himself that much. It was not much to fight for, but at that moment it was all he had.

Sarpedon snatched up a sword from a fallen display behind him, and struck out for the archives.

Sometimes a cold wind blew through the *Phalanx*. It was a trick of the ship's atmospheric systems, or perhaps a random current created by the coolant pipes and superheated reactor cores of the engine sectors. It howled now through the science labs and triumphant galleries around the Observatory dome, strewn with wreckage. It picked up shards of debris and flapped the Imperial Fist banners that lined the way Chapter Master Pugh had used to enter the now-ruined Observatory of Dornian Majesty.

It stirred the dust in the Atoning Halls, whistling between the frames of the wrecked torture racks and the bars of the empty cells. A few Space

Marines lay there: Soul Drinkers who had been caught in the worst of the explosion and killed. Their battle-brothers had taken a few bodies with them but some still lay where they had fallen, their torn bodies still chained in their cells.

It turned the pages that lay on the reading tables in the archives. The reading hall was held by only a handful of Soul Drinkers, among them Librarian Scamander, the pyrokine who had not so long ago served as a scout. He crouched in the shadows cast by the dim light and the enormous parchment rolls, waiting with the Soul Drinkers chosen to stand watch with him. When the enemy came – for they had to be called the enemy now, no matter what they had once been – they would come through here, and in force.

The enemy was now gathering in the crew mess hall, which Captain Lysander had designated as the staging post for the assault on the Soul Drinkers. The Imperial Fists and Howling Griffons made up the bulk of the force and Lysander had already had to deal with the competing demands to be the first in against the Soul Drinkers. The *Phalanx* was Imperial Fists ground and they had the say on who should have the moments of greatest honour in the fight to come, but Captain Borganor had demanded that his Howling Griffons be given the task of charging into the archives and letting the first Soul Drinkers blood. Lysander had agreed, for the Soul Drinkers were enemy enough and he did not need vengeful Howling Griffons facing up to him as well.

Commander Gethsemar picked up a handful of rubble dust from a collapsed wall, felled by the shockwave from the Atoning Halls' explosion. He let the dust drift on the wind, as if it were a form of divination and from the eddies of the wind he could read the pattern of bloodshed unfolding into the immediate future. His war-mask was a death mask of Sanguinius, cast from the features of the divine primarch as he lay dying, felled by the Arch-Traitor Horus ten thousand years before. Sanguinius was unspeakably beautiful, and even stylised in gold and gemstones the death mask cast an aura of supernatural majesty that the Sanguinary Guard used as one of their deadliest weapons.

'What do you see?' asked Librarian Varnica of the Doom Eagles.

Gethsemar turned to Varnica but his eyes were hidden behind ruby panes set into the mask's eye sockets and his expression could not be read. 'Such fates that intertwine here, my brother, are beyond any of us,' replied Gethsemar. 'Long have our sages tried to unravel them. Long have they failed. They strive even now, knowing that the future will be forever hidden from them, but that to endeavour in such an impossible task is its own reward. Our immediate task here is far from impossible, but I fear a greater undertaking is revealed that will never end.'

'Explain,' said Varnica. 'As you would to a layman.'

'Think upon it, brother,' said Gethsemar. 'Here Space Marine fights

Space Marine. There is nothing new about that. But will it be the final time?'

'I think not,' replied Varnica.

'Then you begin to see our point. What is a Space Marine? He is a man, yes, but he is something far more. He is told that he is far more from the moment he is accepted into his Chapter, when he is little more than a child. His earlier memories may not even survive his training. He may conceive in his own mind of no time but one where he was superior to any human being. What might result from a mind so forged?'

'He has no doubt and no fear,' replied Varnica. 'Such alteration of a man's mind is necessary to create the warriors the Imperium needs. I see it as a sacrifice we make. We give up the men we might have become to instead serve as Adeptus Astartes. If you believe this is a mistake, commander, then I would be compelled to differ with you.'

'Ah, but there it is! Do you see, Librarian Varnica? It is true that what we do to our minds to make us Space Marines is as necessary as teaching us to shoot. But what sin is locked into us through such treatment?'

'Brutality?' said Varnica. 'Many times Space Marines have gone too far in punishing the Emperor's enemies, and ordinary men and woman have suffered as a result.'

'Brutality is a necessity,' said Gethsemar. 'A few thousand dead here and there mean nothing compared to the millions spared through the intimidation of our foes that our potential for brutality allows. No, it is a far deeper sin of which I speak, something not so far removed from corruption.'

'Corruption is a strong word,' said Varnica, folding his arms and straightening up. The threat was clear. 'Then what is it?'

'It is pride,' replied Gethsemar. 'A Space Marine does not just think he is superior to the ordinary citizens of the Imperium. He thinks, whether his conscious mind accepts it or not, that he is superior to other Space Marines, too. We all have our way of doing things, do we not? Would we all resist any attempt to change us, though violence may be the only route doing so can take? So prideful we are that Space Marines will never stop killing Space Marines. For every Horus Heresy or Badab War, there are a thousand blood duels and trials of honour brought about by our inability to back down. That is the real enemy we face here. The Soul Drinkers were turned from the Imperium by pride. It is pride that motivates us in destroying them, for all we talk of justice. Pride is the enemy. Pride will kill us.'

Varnica thought about this. 'Throne knows we all have our moments,' he said. 'But the mind of a Space Marine is a complicated thing. Can such a simple thing as pride really be its key? And from the way you speak, commander, I would imagine you have a solution?'

'Oh, no,' protested Gethsemar. 'The Sons of Sanguinius all accept that we are doomed. A Space Marine's destructive pride is the only thing keeping us all fighting, and we are the only thing keeping the Imperium from the brink. No, it is our way to observe our in-fighting for the death throes they are, to understand what we truly are before the end comes.'

Varnica smiled grimly. 'For all your gilt and finery, Angel Sanguine, you are a pessimist. The Doom Eagles seek out the worst atrocities the galaxy commits because we want to put things right. It will not happen in any of our lifetimes, but it will happen, and it is the Space Marines who will do it whether we are too prideful for our own good or not. Why fight, if you believe all is lost no matter what you do?'

Gethsemar shook out his hand, and the dust drifted away on the thin wind. 'Because it is our duty,' he replied.

Lysander stomped past, hammer in hand. 'Daviks and the castellan are in position,' he said. 'Make ready. Two minutes.'

Gethsemar and Varnica broke away to join their own squads. The main assault force, gathered in the mess halls, consisted of the Ninth and Seventh Imperial Fist companies and the Howling Griffons' Seconnd. Varnica and Gethsemar's squads were to follow the Griffons in and, if Borganor was to be believed, clean up the mangled remnants of the Soul Drinkers the Howling Griffons were sure to leave in their wake. Lysander was walking the lines, inspecting the Imperial Fists ranked up along the width of the crew mess hall. The rooms had been built for the normally proportioned crew of the *Phalanx* and the Space Marines could barely stand upright in it.

Whole planets had been broken by fewer than the two hundred Space Marines that the Imperial Fists fielded for this battle. The Howling Griffons were impatient, broken up by squads to be spoken to in turn by Borganor. Lord Inquisitor Kolgo was there, too, at the back of the hall with his Battle Sisters bodyguard, looking more like a battle observer than a combatant in spite of his Terminator armour.

Varnica returned to his squad. Sergeant Beyrengar, who had been elevated to squad command after Novas's death, had gone through the pre-battle wargear rites and prayers already. There was little for Varnica left to do.

'This is where the solution to that puzzle box lies,' he said. 'We have pursued the Soul Drinkers, though we did not know it, from the moment the heretic Kephilaes made the mistake of drawing our attention. What we began then, we finish here. We know what the Soul Drinkers are, and more importantly, we know what they are not. They are not our brothers. When you face one of them through a haze of gunsmoke, do not see a brother. See one more symptom of corruption, and excise him as you would any cancer of the human race.'

'Borganor!' came Lysander's yell from the Imperial Fists' lines. 'The honour is yours!'

'Gladly taken!' cried out Borganor in reply. 'Howling Griffons! Roboute Guilliman looks on! Let us show him a fight he will not forget!'

The deck of the *Phalanx* shuddered as the Howling Griffons advanced.

Scamander almost raised the alarm, but he realised that the silhouette entering the reading room was multi-legged. He stood and saluted. 'Commander!' he said. 'We did not know if you were still alive.'

'I had plenty of opportunities to die,' replied Sarpedon. 'I failed to grasp any of them.' He shook Scamander's hand. 'How long do we have?'

'Not long,' said Scamander. 'The Imperial Fists are gathering to attack us even now. They know we are here.'

'And the plan?'

'Hold the library stacks. Don't die. Circumstances demand our tactics be simple.'

'I see.'

'We have your armour, and the Axe of Mercaeno.'

'Then at least I will not die here unclothed! That would be too humiliating a way to go.'

Scamander smiled. For all the battles he had fought and the dangers his psychic powers posed, he was still a youth. By the standards of the Soul Drinkers, he was just a boy.

Sarpedon headed through the reading room to the archway Scamander had indicated. It led to a maze of bookcases and tables, shelves of volumes stacked high to the ceiling, a thin layer of dust covering everything disturbed by the armoured footprints of the Soul Drinkers. Sarpedon glanced at the books – histories of Imperial Fists actions, battle-philosophy, stories of individual Imperial Fists and their deeds. Sarpedon was reminded of the chansons the Soul Drinkers had once written, epic poems to glorify themselves. Sarpedon had abandoned his own chanson when he had thrown Michairas, his chronicler, out of an airlock during the First Chapter War. The thought gave him an unpleasant taste in his mouth.

Soul Drinkers saluted as he passed. He saw battle-brothers he had fought alongside for years. Some had argued against him, some had sided with him in everything, but they had all followed him into the Veiled Region. They had all accepted capture by Captain Lysander and the Imperial Fists without a fight, because he had ordered it. And they would die here ultimately, because he had ordered it.

'Commander,' said Sergeant Graevus as Sarpedon walked past. Sarpedon returned his salute and noted the Assault Squad that Graevus had assembled from the Chapter's survivors. He had picked veterans: bloody-minded Space Marines who could be trusted to give each centimetre of the stacks in return for buckets of blood shed by their chainblades. Sergeant Salk was instructing his squad, and paused to nod his own salute to Sarpedon. Sarpedon scuttled over makeshift barricades of upturned tables, and squeezed through the bottlenecks formed by the chaotic layout of the stacks. In the centre of the book-lined labyrinth, he found Captain Luko standing at a reading table.

Luko grabbed Sarpedon around the shoulders. 'Good to see you, brother,' he said. 'I thought the festivities would begin without you.'

'I would not miss it for the galaxy,' replied Sarpedon. 'How many of our brothers do we have here for the celebration?'

'A little under sixty,' said Luko. 'A few were lost in the escape. Pallas stayed behind. And others have gone missing. It is to be expected, I suppose, but it is strange…'

'Iktinos's flock,' said Sarpedon.

Luko took a step back. 'How did you know?'

'Iktinos is not with us,' said Sarpedon. 'His flock must have joined him.'

'Not with us? What do you mean?'

'Iktinos brought us here. He has been doing it for years now, manipulating us towards this place and time. Why, I do not know. Probably it is at the behest of Daenyathos. Whatever the reason, he has his goals and we have ours, and they do not coincide.'

'The Chaplain has betrayed us.'

'Yes,' said Sarpedon. 'He has.'

Luko's customary joviality was gone. 'I will kill him.'

'There will be a queue,' said Sarpedon. 'Focus for now on your survival. You have picked a good place to make our stand, brother. I would think twice before attacking such a place.'

'We have your armour, and your axe,' said Luko. 'They are stored behind that bookcase. We could not find the Soulspear among the evidence, though.'

'Then I shall do without. The Axe of Mercaeno is weapon enough for me.'

'You know, the Howling Griffons would want that back.'

'Then Borganor can take it from my dead hand,' replied Sarpedon. 'I have no doubt he will be seeking just that chance. Many stories will end here, captain. Borganor and I is just one of them. If we can give those stories endings worthy of these histories, then we will have won our victory.'

Scamander's voice reached them over Luko's vox. 'Captain! The Howling Griffons are advancing! I'm falling back towards Graevus's position!' The deep spatter of gunfire sounded over his words, and Sarpedon could hear the thuds of bolter impacts through the walls of the library.

'Then it is done,' said Sarpedon. 'I shall arm. To the end, Captain Luko.'

'To the end, Chapter Master,' replied Luko. 'Cold and fast.'

Sarpedon saluted. 'Cold and fast, Soul Drinker.'

CHAPTER NINE

The days following the Horus Heresy formed the forgotten apocalypse of the Imperium. The Heresy itself was the subject of legends known throughout the realm of mankind – the traitor Horus, waxing great in his jealousy of the Emperor, his treason against the human race and his death at the hand of the Emperor himself. The Scouring, the period of reformation that followed Horus's death and the Emperor's ascension to the Golden Throne, was an afterthought, a footnote in the approved histories preached by the Imperial Church. But the truth, appreciated only by a few historians who skirted with heresy in their studies, was that the Imperium was born in the Scouring, and it was born in a terrible tide of blood.

It was a time of vengeance. All those tainted by the deeds of Horus and the many who had sided with them, even worlds who had bowed to Horus under threat of destruction, were destined to suffer. The remaining loyal primarchs led a campaign of bloody reconquest in which collaborators were hanged in their billions. Planets full of refugees were purged lest their number contain the wrong type of war criminals. A thousand civil wars sprang up in the Heresy's wake, the combatants left by the Imperial Army to fight among themselves until the survivors were weak enough to be conquered, subjugated and re-educated.

It was a time of reform. The Space Marine Legions were split up into Chapters, a process which sparked its own share of shadow wars and near-catastrophes as Space Marines fought in all but open warfare for the right to the heraldries of their parent Legions. The Imperial Army broke up into millions of fragments, miniature fiefdoms with no central command. The Imperial Creed was born among the religious catastrophes that tore at humanity in the wake of the Emperor's ascension and the Adepta of the Imperium were formed to hold the shattered mass of humanity together. Born in desperation, the Priesthood of Terra and its component Adepta founded the principles of fear and suspicion that would determine their every action in the ten millennia that followed. Whatever image the Emperor had cherished for the future of humanity, its broken remnants were formed by the Scouring into something flawed, something half-born, something fearful when the Emperor had sought to form it from hope.

It was a time of Chaos. The powers of the warp had made their play for power over the human race and though the Emperor's sacrifice had thwarted them, they had sunk a thousand tendrils of influence into realspace and clung on jealously. The daemonic legions unleashed in the Battle of Terra took decades to hunt down and exterminate; the Blood Angels and their newly-formed successor Chapters seeking them out to exact vengeance for Sanguinius's death. Horus's acolytes had opened portals to the warp in the Heresy's dying days, seeking to seed the fledgling Imperium with secrets waiting to be uncovered and suffered by generations to come.

No one knew how many such portals had been built by the sorcerers and madmen under Horus's command. Some were vast gateways on forgotten worlds, ready for explorers or refugees to speak the wrong words or cross the wrong threshold. Some were built into the foundations of cities rebuilt in the Heresy's wake, runes worked into the streets or dread temples far beneath the sewers and catacombs. Others took stranger forms – prophecies woven into a tainted bloodline, the words of a story that opened the way a little more with every telling, a song sung by desert spirits which would become a gateway to the warp as soon as it was written down.

One gateway was an eye, ripped from some titanic predator that glided through the warp. Acolytes of the Dark Powers, gathered on a spacecraft in orbit around a star, brought the eye into realspace. Like another – living – planet, it settled into its own orbit. It looked out upon the void and wherever its gaze fell, daemons danced. The acolytes who had summoned it were shredded by the daemons that sprung up around them, their last thoughts of thanks towards the Dark Gods who had permitted them to be a part of such a glorious endeavour.

The Predator's Eye was seen in divinations and séances across the Imperium. It was Rogal Dorn who stood up and swore to close it. The Chapters that venerated him all sent their own champions to assist, and in orbit around the blighted star were fought many of the most terrible and costly battles of the Scouring. Rogal Dorn himself set foot on the Predator's Eye, evading the biological horrors that budded out of its gelatinous surface as well as the daemons that scrabbled to intercept him. But even as battle-brothers fell around him, Rogal Dorn did not falter. He was a primarch, and in him flowed the blood of the Emperor. He plunged a fist into the pupil of the Predator's Eye, and the eye, blinded, closed in agony.

Rogal Dorn's surviving battle-brothers included a number of Space Marine Librarians, and for three days without rest they enacted a ritual to seal the eye shut. Dorn led their chanting and finally a sigil of power, born of his own valorous spirit, was branded against the shut eye to keep it closed.

Dorn did not possess enough battle-brothers to destroy the Predator's Eye permanently. His Librarians were exhausted and many had not survived the ritual. He knew that one day he would have to return to finish the job. The Predator's Eye would have to be opened before it was destroyed, and so Dorn placed a condition on the ward that sealed it so that only his own blood could open it. He buried the Eye's location in myths and legends, such that no single Chapter would know the full story of its location and purpose, and swore that one day, when the countless other threats had subsided and he had found another corps of Librarians and champions to face down the terrible gaze of the Predator's Eye, the warp portal would finally be destroyed.

But the Imperium was beset on all sides by threats that did not let up. For every daemonic foe that was despatched, rebellion or the predations of the xenos would spring up, every new danger threatening a new form of oblivion for the Imperium. For centuries the Predator's Eye lay hidden just below the level of mortal sight, blinded yet possessing a bestial sense of anger and frustration born of the warp's own hatred. And eventually, Rogal Dorn died, to join the Emperor at the battle at the end of time.

The Predator's Eye remained orbiting its star, forgotten.

The name of that star was Kravamesh.

Scamander braved the first volley of bolter fire that streaked across the archive. The walls exploded in torrents of burned and shredded parchment around him as bolter rounds from the Howling Griffons flew wide. One caught Scamander in the chest and blew him back a pace. Another tore through the reading table in front of him and exploded against his thigh. A storm of shrapnel crackled against him.

'You will never see us kneel!' yelled Scamander and he looked up to the ceiling, his bared throat glowing scarlet. Flames licked up from his hands, over his shoulder guards and face. Ice crusted around the table and the floor around him as the heat energy bled into him to be concentrated and forced out by the psychic reactor that churned in his mind.

Scamander looked down at the Howling Griffons, face wreathed in flame. They were charging heedless towards him, competing for the honour of first blood. Captain Borganor was among them, ripping out volleys of bolter fire.

Scamander breathed out a tremendous gout of flame that washed over and through the first Howling Griffons. Some were thrown off their feet by the wall of superheated air that slammed into them. Others were caught in the blast, ceramite melting in the supernaturally intense heat, armour plates exploding. Three or four fell as the nerve-fibre bundles in their armour were incinerated, robbing them of movement as the joints melted and fused.

Borganor leapt through the fire, crashing through a reading table already collapsing to ash under the force of Scamander's assault. He took aim without breaking stride and put a bolter round square into Scamander's abdomen, throwing the Soul Drinker back onto one knee.

Other Soul Drinkers returned fire in the wake of Scamander's attack, and the Howling Griffons struggled through the flame to get into cover and drive them out. Borganor ignored the rest of the fight and dived under the table Scamander was using for cover, his bionic leg powering him forwards.

Borganor came up face to face with Scamander. Scamander's bolt pistol was in his hand and the two wrestled over their guns. Scamander was half-glowing with heat, half-slippery with ice, but Borganor kept the muzzle of Scamander's pistol away from him. His own bolter was too unwieldy for this close-quarters murder – he let it drop from his hand and took his combat knife from its sheath.

Scamander immolated himself in a cocoon of fire. Borganor yelled and fell away. Scamander got to his feet and blasted at Borganor as he stumbled away, holding the wound in his abdomen with his free hand.

Borganor rolled through the flames, bolter fire impacting on his shoulder guards and backpack. Chains of bolter fire hammered across the archive room and shredded parchment fell in a burning rain, filaments of ash rising on the hot air and flames licking up the walls. The huge rolls of parchment were ablaze, falling in spooling masses like waterfalls of fire and silhouetting the shapes of the Howling Griffons as they ran from cover to cover, firing all the time.

Scamander raised his free hand, black with charred blood from his wound. Flame sprayed from his fingers and Borganor grabbed hold of a table leg to keep the burst of fire from carrying him off his feet. He trusted in his ceramite, in the rites with which he had blessed his wargear and the spirit of Roboute Guilliman he had beseeched to enter his heart and make him more than a man, more than a Space Marine.

He trusted in the force of his vengeance, the shield of contempt which could spread out from his iron soul and keep him alive long enough to execute the traitor he faced.

Borganor forced himself forwards a pace, knife held out in front. Scamander raised his pistol again but Borganor swatted it away.

'Traitor,' hissed Borganor. 'Witch.'

Scamander replied with a breath of fire, a narrow tongue of flame as concentrated as a las-cutter's beam. Borganor ducked it and rammed the knife up into Scamander's face. The blade passed up into Scamander's jaw, ripping through teeth and tongue. The flame sputtered as a clot of blood sprayed from Scamander's mouth.

Borganor leapt forwards, a knee on Scamander's wounded stomach. Scamander fell against the back wall of the archive room, where he was bathed in the burning remnants of centuries of parchment records. Borganor grabbed the back of Scamander's head and wrenched it up, exposing the Soul Drinker's throat.

Scamander's eyes were full of hate. Borganor grinned as he saw the tiniest glimmer of fear there, a twitch at the corner of the eye.

'Everything you die for is a lie,' said Borganor, and slit Scamander's throat.

The Howling Griffon had to push the Soul Drinker's body up against the wall so the gout of fire that ripped from his torn throat shot upwards instead of into his face. The fountain hit the ceiling and spread, flame like liquid pooling outwards. Then it sputtered as if whatever fuelled it was running out and Scamander fell limp. Fire licked from the corners of his eyes, his mouth, his ears, and smoke coiled from the joints in his armour.

Borganor threw the body aside. He looked around him. The burning room was in chaos, half held by the Howling Griffons, half by the Soul Drinkers. Many Howling Griffons had died to the Soul Drinkers Librarian, but now Soul Drinkers were dying to the numbers and firepower of the Howling Griffons.

Borganor's fight with Scamander had brought him out of cover. Only smoke and flames concealed him from Soul Drinkers guns.

'Brothers! The trickster is dead! Let bolter fire be your truth!' Borganor yelled over the gunfire, standing proud of the fight even as bolter shots fell around him. He snatched his bolter up off the floor and got into the battle proper, hammering volley after volley into the hazy purple-armoured shaped that loomed through the smoke.

'Onwards! Onwards! This is but a welcome, my brothers! The celebration is yet to come!'

Sarpedon heard the gunfire, and smelled the smoke rolling in from the reading room. In the heart of the library labyrinth, alongside

Captain Luko, he waited for the wave to break against the Soul Drinkers defences.

'Scamander is lost,' said Luko.

'Then we have something to avenge,' replied Sarpedon calmly.

'I promised myself that no more Space Marines would die by my hand,' said Luko. 'I have made many such promises to myself, but I have a problem keeping them.'

'You promised yourself peace, captain,' said Sarpedon. 'You will have it. But not just yet. Hold on for a few more moments, for your battle-brothers.'

The first volleys of bolter fire, sharp and crisp, cackled from the interior of the library. The Howling Griffons were in, past Scamander's forlorn hope and into the death-trap the Soul Drinkers had created for them.

'At last it will end,' said Luko. 'I don't have to lie any more. Thank the Emperor it ends here.'

'And we decide how it ends,' added Sarpedon. 'How many men can ever say that?'

Luko did not reply. The power field around his lightning claws flared into life, and loose papers on the shelves scattered in the electric charge.

The gunfire rose towards a crescendo as the vox channels filled with bedlam.

'Side by side with me, brothers!' yelled Graevus, charging shoulder-first down the narrow corridors of the library. Burning books rained down around him, thousands of words flitting by as pages turned to ash.

Graevus crashed around a corner straight into a Howling Griffon wielding a two-handed chainsword like an executioner's axe. The blade screeched down and Graevus turned it aside with his power axe, his mutated strength redirecting the blow into one of the bookcases beside him. The chainsword tore into the ancient wood and the Howling Griffon paused for a moment to wrench it free. That was all the time Graevus needed to bring his axe up into the Howling Griffon's chest, carving through ceramite, ribs and organs as his opponent's chest was cleaved in two. The Howling Griffon was still alive as he fell but his death was held off only by his fury. His lungs were laid open, a well of blood flooding his bisected ribcage and pouring like an overflowing fountain across the dusty floor.

More charged in behind him. This was the position of honour for the Howling Griffons – the head of the charge, the first men in, who suffered the greatest chance of death but would bring out of the battle the greatest acclaim whether they fell or survived.

Graevus was supposed to have Scamander alongside him. Scamander was dead. Graevus would have to do the killing for both of them.

More Howling Griffons were forcing their way through the narrow library corridors. A burning, armoured form crashed through the bookcase ahead of Graevus – a Howling Griffon, blazing from head to toe, the shape of a flamer-wielding Soul Drinker just visible through the curtain of smoke and flame that surrounded him. Graevus hacked off the Howling Griffon's head with one slice of his power axe, whirled with the force of the blow and followed up with a lateral strike that shattered the chainblade in the hand of the Howling Griffon who charged around the bend just ahead of him.

Soul Drinkers behind Graevus vaulted over the body of the dead Howling Griffons to get to grips with the enemy. In the confines of the library there was no room for numbers to tell. The battle was a series of duels, vicious face-to-face struggles without enough room even to feint or manoeuvre. It was war without skill: strength and fury the sole factors in victory. Graevus had plenty of both.

A Soul Drinker fell beside him, a plasma pistol wound bored right through him in a charred tunnel. Graevus dived into his killer, slamming him against the bookcase and smashing the butt of his hammer into his face. The stunned Howling Griffon fell to one knee and Graevus cut off one of his arms, the backswing shearing the top half of his head off.

Another Soul Drinker died, shattered body riddled with bolter fire. A long corridor up ahead was swept with volleys of fire from a Howling Griffon with a heavy bolter at the far end. The bookcases were disintegrating and Graevus could see the tally the Howling Griffon had already reaped through rents in the wall. Burning books gathered in drifts around his feet, gutted spines falling while their pages flitted up towards the ceiling on a scalding breath of hot air.

Graevus charged on through the bookcase. It splintered underneath him. Heavy bolter shots erupted around him, filling their air with a thousand explosions. Graevus relied on his momentum to take him through the weight of fire and he slammed into the Howling Griffons warrior, hacking and wrestling as the two fell into the flames.

Graevus let the battle-lust in him take over. It was a rare that he permitted himself to completely let go, to abandon everything that made a Space Marine a disciplined weapon of war and allow the born warrior, the celebrant of carnage, to take control.

Graevus's mutated hand clamped around the Howling Griffon's head and dropped his axe among the burning debris. He twisted the Howling Griffon's head around until a seal gave on his helmet, and the helmet came away.

The Howling Griffon was the image of Graevus himself, a gnarled and relentless veteran, the kind of man that could be trusted to hold any line and execute any order when the fire came down.

These are our brothers, thought Graevus.

They are the same as us.

The thought broke through Graevus's battle-lust. He tried to force it down but it would not be quieted.

Graevus took a step back from the Howling Griffon. The Griffon, disarmed with his heavy bolter lying down in the wreckage, scrabbled away from Graevus. Graevus picked up his axe, not taking his eyes from his opponent.

'Fall back!' shouted Graevus. 'Fall back! To your lines! Fall back!'

An instant after Graevus gave the order, the library in front of him erupted in flame and ash. Heavy weapons hammered through the bedlam. The Howling Griffons had brought their big guns up.

Their first attack was to drag the Soul Drinkers into the fight, to bog them down in melee. The second was to shatter the cover of the library and fill the Soul Drinkers positions with burning ruin, to open up enough space for the Howling Griffons to use their numbers to their fullest.

Ordinary soldiers could not have done it. The men of the first line would have been at fatal risk from the heavy guns of the men behind them. But the Howling Griffons were not ordinary soldiers; the first Space Marines in trusted in the aim of their battle-brothers.

The library was torn apart. Graevus forged through the flames, kicking shattered wooden bookcases out of his way and shielding his face from the thousands of burning books falling as thick as a blizzard. Lascannon blasts lanced through the Chaos, glittering crimson and shearing through everything they touched. Fat white-hot bursts of plasma fire ripped out of the smoke.

Graevus saw the form of a fallen Soul Drinker at his feet. He grabbed the downed brother by the shoulder guard and dragged him after himself as he ran. The Soul Drinkers had fortified choke points and firebases further in and Graevus saw one of them up ahead, guarding a wide corridor with toppled bookcases and heaps of broken furniture as a barricade. The Soul Drinkers behind it – Graevus recognised Sergeant Salk among them – waved Graevus over and he vaulted the barricade.

The battle-brother he had brought with him had been shot in the thigh, hit by a lascannon blast. The leg was hanging on solely through the tangled strips of torn ceramite that remained of his leg armour. Graevus could not tell if the Soul Drinker was alive. Other Space Marines dragged him down out of danger.

'They're burning us out!' shouted Graevus to Salk. 'Big guns and flamers!'

'Then we are the gun line!' shouted Salk. 'We're ready!' He handed Graevus a bolter, no doubt taken from a wounded or dead Soul Drinker who had no more need for it. Graevus nodded, checked the movement of the bolter, and took his position kneeling at the barricade. His left hand was his trigger hand, because his mutated right was too large to fit a finger into the trigger guard.

Howling Griffons stalked through the smoke. It was impossible, with the smoke rolling thick and dense, to tell now where the remnants of the library stood, where they burned, and where they had been completely shattered. The air was too thick and toxic for a man to breathe; only the lung augmentations of the Space Marines kept both sides from choking. Visibility was well below bolter range.

Graevus could see the red and yellow livery of the Griffons, smudged and filthy through the haze and soot, reduced to a contrast between light and dark forming the quartered design the Griffons wore on their armour. Half a dozen approached down the fire point's field of view.

'Fire!' yelled Salk. The Soul Drinkers at the barricade, six or seven of them, including Graevus, opened fire. They rattled through half a magazine of bolter rounds each, pumping shells into the armoured shapes advancing on them.

Some fell, cut down. Others stumbled, alive but wounded. All who still lived returned fire and the barricade shuddered as the thick wooden slabs were chewed through, a layer of cover getting thinner with each half-second. Explosive shells threw handfuls of splinters into the haze and Graevus gritted his teeth against the stinging rain that fell against his face.

Salk swapped out a magazine. A Soul Drinker had slipped down to the floor beside him.

'It's not bad,' said the Soul Drinker. Salk clapped a hand to the wounded Space Marine's shoulder, then turned to fire another volley.

Graevus strained to see through the smoke. The wounded were being dragged away. A bookcase had been toppled for cover and the Howling Griffons were regrouping. Soul Drinkers up and down the line were sniping at movement but the Howling Griffons would not attack in ones and twos. They would advance again, coordinated to move as one.

'This is no battle,' said Graevus. 'This is not warfare. This is just…'

'Attrition,' said Salk. 'We killed Mercaeno. They all made an oath to avenge him. They're willing to spend a few of their lives if that means they are the ones who get to kill us. They have more bodies than we do. That's what it comes down to.'

'It's no way for a Space Marine to fight,' snarled Graevus. 'By the Throne, they could starve us out if they wanted. They don't have to die.'

Salk looked at Graevus, uncertain.

'They don't have to die!' repeated Graevus. 'Our Chapters are brothers! On Nevermourn it was different, but here there is no need to fight!

What does it matter to them how we are killed? None of us are leaving the *Phalanx* alive, this battle is needless murder!'

'They made an oath,' said Salk. 'Mere logic cannot compete with that.'

'Let none mourn the losses,' said Gethsemar. 'Let no sorrow cloud the celebrations of our victory. Bring joy, my brothers, as you bring death.'

In the shadowy confines of choristry chamber, the Angels Sanguine had gathered to pray. The chamber was lined with servitor choirs, the corpses of gifted singers transformed into machines that could sing for days on end without need for maintenance. On the *Phalanx* they were used in rituals of contemplation, when the deeds of Rogal Dorn were matched against every Imperial Fist's qualities and achievements. Now they were silent, their hairless heads bowed on their metal shoulders, the lungs stilled.

Gethsemar's war-mask glanced between his Sanguinary Guard, as if he were speaking a silent prayer that only each of his brothers could hear. Then Gethsemar drew his glaive, a two-handed power weapon with a blade of polished blue stone.

'We are ready,' he said.

'Thank Guilliman for that,' said Siege-Captain Daviks.

Daviks's Silver Skulls and the Angels Sanguine had gathered in the choristry chamber because it adjoined the library. Daviks's warriors, skilled siege engineers, had already set up the demolition charges on one wall. The sound of gunfire came from beyond it as the Howling Griffons alternately advanced through the burning ruin of the library and swept the chaos with heavy weapons fire.

'You see no art in war,' said Gethsemar. 'And if a Space Marine's life must consist of nothing but war and the preparations for it, that means there is no place in your lives for art at all. So sad, my brother. So sad.'

'We live with it,' replied Daviks.

'This is Borganor!' came a voice over the vox-channel. 'We have them engaged! Now is the time!'

'Very well,' replied Daviks. 'We're going in.'

Daviks gave a hand signal to the Silver Skull holding the detonator. The Space Marines backed off and knelt, turning away from the wall, and the charges went off. They were shaped to direct the full force into the wall and it disintegrated, leaving a huge black hole from floor to ceiling. The shockwave and debris toppled many of the servitor choir, once-human components spilling out.

Gethsemar's Angels Sanguine charged in before the debris had finished pattering onto the floor. Smoke boiled out past them and the gunfire was louder, the yells of orders overlapping with the cries of pain as Space Marines fell.

Daviks followed Gethsemar. His squad was a siege engineer unit, armed with bolters and demolition charges, while Gethsemar's was an all-out assault unit. Gethsemar soared forwards, his jump pack hurling him horizontally down the narrow alley of bookcases that confronted him. His Sanguinary Guard were equally nimble with their jump packs, jinking around the tight corners with bursts of exhaust, their feet barely touching the ground. A Soul Drinker watching the rear of the library was cut down as Gethsemar roared past him, his power glaive slicing the sentry's arm off before another Sanguinary Guard finished the job with a downward cut that nearly bisected him.

The first Soul Drinkers were reacting to the sudden second front opening up in the library. Daviks swapped bolter fire with Soul Drinkers who ran around the corner in front of him, scattering books in the volley of bolter fire his squad kicked out in reply. Two Soul Drinkers fell and Daviks paused in his advance for long enough to put a bolter round through the head of each. A Silver Skull did not take death for granted. It was his way to be sure.

Gethsemar fell back past a corner up ahead. His golden armoured body crashed against the bookcase behind him.

'Gethsemar!' yelled Daviks into the vox. 'What is it?'

The thing that lumbered around the corner after Gethsemar was an abhorrence that Daviks's senses could barely contain. Composed of screaming heads gathered in a roughly humanoid shape, its lumpen shoulders brushed the ceiling of the library. The terrible cacophony that keened from it was enough to all but stun Daviks, filling his mind with the awful sound of pain and grief distilled. The thing's hands were bunches of withered and broken human arms, arranged like fingers, and its head was a yawning maw ringed with bleeding jawbones. In its throat, thousands of eyes clustered. The thing stamped a pace closer to Gethsemar, trailing masses of entrails and tangled limbs in its wake.

Daviks's squad opened fire, covering Gethsemar as he scrambled out of the beast's way. Bolter fire thudded into its hundreds of heads but it did not falter. It turned to Daviks, mouth yawning wide as it roared, and a gale of utter foulness shrieked around the Silver Skulls.

Bloodied hands reached from the bookcases. Mouths filled with gnashing teeth opened up in the floor to snare their feet. The Angels Sanguine were stumbling through the confusion, laying about them with their glaives at every shape that loomed through the smoky gloom.

'Stand fast!' yelled Daviks. 'Onwards, brethren, for the honour is ours! Though the Griffons reap the tally, it is we who shall take the head of the arch-traitor! Sarpedon is here! Onwards and take his head!'

Daviks felt a flare of pride. It was unbecoming for him to lust after an

honour in battle, but it came unbidden, and he let it push him forwards
through the horrors unfolding around him.

He knew that Sarpedon was here.

He knew it, because he had walked right into hell.

'Do you know where you are?' said the grating metallic voice of
Daenyathos.

N'Kalo struggled. He was chained. His consciousness barely surfaced
over the thudding of pain, but the feeling of his restraints sang clearly.
He forced against them, but they held.

He had been battered senseless. He remembered Iktinos, the skull-
helm of the Soul Drinkers Chaplain emotionless as the crozius
hammered again and again into the side of his head. Where and how
still escaped him. He was a captive, he was sure, and over him stood
a purple-armoured Dreadnought that could only be the legendary
Daenyathos.

N'Kalo did not answer.

'You are somewhere you will never leave,' said Daenyathos.

N'Kalo was aware of a room of immense size. His vision swam back
beyond the Dreadnought and he saw that he was in a cargo hold, a
vast space that could hold legions of tanks and Rhino APCs. It was
empty now save for the area set up in the centre, at the heart of which
N'Kalo was chained. He was surrounded by a complicated circular pattern scorched into the deck, scattered with bones and flower petals,
gemstones and bundles of herbs, pages torn from books, human teeth,
bullets and chunks of rock torn from alien worlds. Around this sigil
knelt the pilgrims who had arrived on the *Phalanx*, they had claimed,
to oversee the trial of the Soul Drinkers, and they held their standards
of the Blinded Eye aloft. They were hooded and robed and issued a low
chant, dark syllables repeated in a terrible drone.

N'Kalo was aware that he still wore his armour and his battered helm
was back on his head. It made no sense for his captor to leave him
armoured. He might not have a weapon in his hand, but a Space Marine
in armour was still more dangerous than one without. It could help him
when he broke out, and there was no doubt in his mind that he would.
Whatever agenda Daenyathos had, and whether the Soul Drinkers were
heretics or blameless, Daenyathos and Iktinos had revealed themselves
to constitute a moral threat and N'Kalo had a duty to escape and bring
them to justice.

'You wear your thoughts on you as if they were written on your
armour,' said Daenyathos. 'You desire escape. That is natural. A Space
Marine is not created to be caged. And you desire revenge. You would
call it duty or justice, but it is ultimately death you wish on me for
orchestrating your defeat and capture. This, again, is natural. A Space

Marine is a vengeful creature. But do you see now, helpless as you are, what a pitiful animal you truly are? Freedom and vengeance – what do these things mean, when compared to the matters that shape the galaxy? How much does your existence mean?'

N'Kalo struggled again. His chains were set into the deck of the cargo hold. They were probably chains built into the deck to keep tanks from sliding around when the *Phalanx* was in flight. One Space Marine could not break them.

'My duty is within myself,' said N'Kalo. He knew he should have stayed silent, but something in Daenyathos's words, in the way he seemed genuinely passionate in spite of the artificiality of his voice, compelled him to reply. 'Though the galaxy may burn and humanity collapse, I must fulfil my duty regardless. And so I call myself a Space Marine.'

'That is the response of a weak mind,' said Daenyathos. The Dreadnought's body turned away to something off to the side, outside N'Kalo's frame of vision. 'You choose to ignore the matters that affect the galaxy, and shrink your mind down to one battle after another, one petty victory over some xenos or renegade, and tell yourself that such is the totality of your potential. I chose instead to abandon the duties that restrict me, and rise to become one of those very factors that mould the galaxy at their whim. It is a choice I made. Yours is a mind too small to make it. The Soul Drinkers were like you, and I had to make that choice for them. Were they wise enough to understand, they would have thanked me.'

Daenyathos's massive tank-like torso swivelled back to face N'Kalo. One of his arms was a missile launcher, while the other ended in a huge power fist. That fist was now encased in a gauntlet from which protruded several smaller implements – manipulator limbs, blades, needles, an assortment of attachments for finer control than the Dreadnought's power fist afforded.

'What is this?' said N'Kalo. 'Why have you brought me here?'

'That is a question I am willing to answer,' said Daenyathos. 'But not through words.'

A circular saw emerged from among the implements. N'Kalo tensed, forcing against his bonds with every muscle he had. He felt joints parting and bones cracking, shots of pain running through him as his muscular power pushed beyond the limits of his skeleton.

The chains did not move. Perhaps N'Kalo could break and twist his limbs until they could be slipped out of their bonds. Perhaps he could crawl away, steal a weapon from one of the cultists.

The circular blade cut through N'Kalo's breastplate. Sparks flew, and bright reflections glinted in the lenses set into Daenyathos's armoured head.

Daenyathos worked quickly, and with great precision. Soon the breastplate was lifted off in sections, smaller manipulator limbs picking apart the layers of ceramite until N'Kalo felt the recycled air of the *Phalanx* cold on his chest.

The chanting changed to a terrible falling cadence, a piece of music about to end. N'Kalo felt the power charging in the air and saw a glow overhead, as if from a great heat against the ceiling of the cargo hold. Crackles of energy ran down the walls, earthing off the massive feet of Daenyathos's Dreadnought body.

N'Kalo felt pain. He gasped in spite of himself, the impossibly cold touch of the saw blade running in a red line along his sternum.

The ceiling of the cargo hold was lifting off, metallic sections peeling apart and fluttering into the void like dead leaves on the wind. The hull parted and the air gushed out. The pilgrims looked up at the rent in the side of the *Phalanx*, calm and joy on their faces even as the sudden pressure change made their eye sockets well up red with burst vessels. Hoods were blown back by the swirling gale and, in spite of the pain, N'Kalo's mind registered the face of a woman ecstatic as foaming blood ran from her lips. Another one of the pilgrims was their leader, impossibly ancient, and his dry and dusty body seemed to wither away as he raised his wizened head to the origin of the light that fell on him.

The light was coming from Kravamesh, the star around which the *Phalanx* orbited. A burning orange glow filtered down through the debris swirling around the hull breach. The hull parted further, like an opening eye, and the last tides of air boomed out.

The pilgrims were dying, each moment robbing another of consciousness. N'Kalo realised his armour had been left on so that he could still breathe while the cargo hold fell apart.

The saw was withdrawn. Without air, the only sound was now vibrations through the floor. The faint whir of servos as a manipulator arm unfolded. The rattling breath N'Kalo drew through the systems of his armour as the cold hit the open wound in his chest.

'Do you know,' said Daenyathos, the sound of his voice transmitted as vibrations through his feet, 'what you are to become?'

N'Kalo gritted his teeth. He could see Kravamesh above him, its boiling fires, and though its fires looked down on him its light was appallingly cold.

'The key,' continued Daenyathos. The manipulators extended and hooked around N'Kalo's ribs. N'Kalo yelled, the cry not making it past the insides of his own armour. 'Dorn's own blood is the only key that will fit the lock he built around Kravamesh. The Soul Drinkers do not have it, though it suited me for them to continue believing they did. You have it, Iron Knight. The blood of Dorn flows in your veins.'

The manipulators forced at the edges of N'Kalo's fused rib breastplate.

The bones creaked. N'Kalo strained every muscle in his body, forcing against the pain as well as his restraints.

He saw Rogal Dorn, his golden-armoured body kneeling at the Emperor's fallen form. He saw the Eye of Terror open, and the battlements of Earth burning. Some ancient memory, written into the genetic material on which his augmentations were based, bled in the final moments into his mind.

N'Kalo felt the impossible pride and fury of Rogal Dorn. They filled him to bursting, too much emotion for a man, even a Space Marine, to contain. The primarch was an impossible creature, in every aspect superior to a man, in every dimension vaster by far.

N'Kalo could see Rogal Dorn at the Iron Cage, the vast fortifications manned by the soldiers of Chaos, the shadow of the entire Imperial Fists Chapter falling on it as Dorn orchestrated the assault.

The last images were ghosted over the monstrous eye of Kravamesh opening wide, vast and unholy shapes emerging from its fires.

Daenyathos punched the mass of his power fist into N'Kalo's chest, splintering through the ribs. Daenyathos ripped the fist free and N'Kalo's organs were sprayed across the cargo bay deck in the shape of bloody wings. The gore iced over in the cold of the void.

Daenyathos's massive form leaned back from N'Kalo. The pattern scorched into the deck glowed red as if it were drinking N'Kalo's spilled blood. The glow was met by the burning orange light from above. The head of Daenyathos's chassis looked up towards the tear in the hull as the fires of Kravamesh billowed suddenly close.

From space it looked as if a bridge of fire were being built, reaching from the mass of Kravamesh towards the speck of the *Phalanx*. Shapes rippled along the bridge, tortured faces and twisted limbs, howling ghosts that split and reformed like liquid fire.

The observation crews on the *Phalanx* saw it right away. Every sensor on the Imperial Fists fortress-ship screamed in response. But the *Phalanx* was embroiled in open warfare, its crew managing the Chaos unfolding from its archives, and without the whole crew at their stations the huge and complex ship could not react in time.

The tendril of fire touched the hull of the *Phalanx*. Daenyathos stood in the swirling mass of flame that incinerated the remains of N'Kalo and the pilgrims. From the flame emerged shapes – leaping, gibbering things, limbs and eyes that turned in on one another in an endless mockery of evolution. They danced madly around Daenyathos as if he were the master of their revel. Reality shuddered and tore as the insanity formed a huge circular gate in the centre of the cargo bay, the fire rippling around a glassy black pit that plunged through the substance of the universe and into a place far darker.

Daenyathos stood before the warp portal. The fires of the warp washed around the feet of his Dreadnought chassis, and the daemons slavered as they slunk through the flame. But Daenyathos did not falter. He had seen this moment a million times before. He had dreamed it over thousands of years in half-sleep under Selaaca.

Vast mountains of filth and hatred shifted in the darkness beyond the portal. Tendrils of their sheer malice rippled through the substance of the cargo hold, blistering up the metal of the deck with spiny tentacled limbs. Blood-weeping eyes opened up in the walls. The daemon cavalcade shrieked higher and higher as one of the forms in the portal detached itself and drifted, half-formed, towards the opening.

It coalesced as it approached, taking the shape of something at once beautiful and appalling. A vast and idealised human figure, glistening pale skin clad in flowing white silk, surrounded by a halo of raw magic. Torn minds flowed in its wake, ruptured spirits shredded into madness by the warp. A taloned hand grasped the flaming edge of the portal, hauling its vastness towards reality.

The perfect, maddening shape of the head emerged. Its features looked like they were carved from pure marble, its eyes orbs of jade. The music of the warp accompanied it, a thousand choirs shorn of their bodies.

'It is time,' said Daenyathos. 'The threads of the destiny meet here.'

'Free!' bellowed the daemon prince in its thousand voices. 'Banishment, agony, all over! A vengeance… vengeance flows like blood from a wound! The wound I shall leave in the universe… the hatred that shall rise in a flood. Oh unriven souls, oh undreaming minds, you shall be laid to waste! Abraxes has returned!'

CHAPTER TEN

Archmagos Voar was surrounded by a cordon of servitors as he hurried through the guest quarters towards the saviour pod array. Beyond the lavish guest rooms, he knew a shuttle could be found, normally used for diplomatic purposes but perfectly suitable for taking him off the *Phalanx* and onto one of the nearby ships – the *Traitorsgrave*, perhaps, on which Lord Inquisitor Kolgo had arrived, or a Space Marine ship like the *Judgement upon Garadan*.

Voar had betrayed the Soul Drinkers on Selaaca. None of his logic circuits entertained the concept that it might have been the wrong thing to do, either logically or morally. But that did not change the fact that the Soul Drinkers were loose and they might well want Voar, in particular, dead. The *Phalanx* was not safe for him.

Voar's motivator units, damaged on Selaaca, had been repaired well enough for him to make good speed through the nests of anterooms and state suites, winding around antique furnishings and artworks whose uselessness accentuated their sense of the lavish. The Imperial Fists were pragmatic in their dealings with the wider Imperium, willing to receive diplomats from the various Adepta in a fashion acceptable to the Imperium's social elite. The servitors Voar had taken from the *Phalanx*'s stores wound around the resulting tables, chairs and light sculptures with rather more difficulty than Voar himself.

Voar paused at the infra-red signature that flared against his vision. His sight, like most of the rest of him, had been significantly augmented to bring him away from corruptible flesh and closer to the machine-ideal. He had seen a heat trace, just past one of the archways leading into an audience chamber. Reclining couches and tables with gilt decorations, imported from some far-off world of craftsmen, stood before an ornate throne painted with enamelled scenes of plenty and wealth. Beneath the room's chandeliers and incense-servitor perches, something had moved, something interested in keeping itself hidden for as long as possible.

Voar drew the inferno pistol, another item liberated from the *Phalanx*'s armouries. The servitors, responding to the mind-impulse unit built into Voar's cranium, formed a tighter cordon around him. Their weapons, autoguns linked to the targeting units that filled their eye sockets, tracked as Voar's vision switched through spectrums. He saw warm traces of footprints on the floor, residual electrical energy dissipating.

Chaplain Iktinos knew he had been seen. There was no use in trying to stay hidden when he was over two-and-a-half metres tall and in full armour. He walked out from behind the dignitary's throne, crozius arcanum in hand.

'You have failed, Soul Drinker,' said Voar. There was no trace of fear in his voice, and not just because of its artificial nature. His emotional repressive surgery had chased such petty concerns like fear from his biological brain. 'Your escape from the *Phalanx* is a logical impossibility. You gain nothing from exacting revenge against me.'

'Logic is a lie,' came the reply. 'A prison for small minds. I am here for a purpose beyond revenge.'

Voar waited no longer. Negotiations would not suffice. He dropped back behind an enormous four-poster bed of black hardwood as he gave the impulse for the servitors to open fire.

Eight autoguns hammered out a curtain of fire. Iktinos ran into the storm, faceplate of his helmet tucked behind one shoulder guard as he charged. The armour was chewed away as if by accelerated decay, the skull-faced shoulder guard stripped down through ceramite layers, then down to the bundles of cables and nerve fibres that controlled it.

Iktinos slammed into the servitors. One was crushed under his weight, its reinforced spine snapping and its gun wrenched out of position to spray bullets uselessly into the frescoed ceiling. The crozius slashed through another two, their unarmoured forms coming apart under the shock of the power field, mechanical and once-human parts showering against the walls in a wet steel rain.

Voar ducked out of cover as Iktinos beheaded the last servitor with his free hand. Voar took aim and fired, a lance of superheated energy lashing out and slicing a chunk out of the Chaplain's crozius arm.

Voar's mind slowed down, logic circuits engaging to examine the tactical possibilities faster than unaugmented thought. He had to keep his distance since, up close, Iktinos was lethal, while Voar's inferno pistol was the only weapon he had that could hope to fell a Space Marine. The targeting systems built into his eyes would make sure that his second shot would not miss. As long as he saw Iktinos before the fallen Chaplain could kill him, Voar would get one good shot off. The plan fell into place, paths and vectors illuminating in blue-white lines layered over his vision.

Voar jumped out of cover, his motivator units sending him drifting rapidly backwards towards an archway leading into an elaborate stone-lined bath house, with a deep caldarium, a cold-plunge pool and a Space Marine-scaled massage table. Mosaics of Imperial heroes lined the walls and valet-servitors stood ready. Voar's inferno pistol was out in front of him, ready to fire.

Iktinos was not within his frame of vision. The archmagos's logic circuits fought to create new tactical scenarios. He should have been feeling panic, but instead his altered mind was generating a burst of useless information, a confused tangle of targeting solutions for a target that suddenly wasn't there.

Iktinos's armoured mass slid out from under the enormous massage table, crashing into the lower half of Voar's body. Voar was thrown against the archway. He fired, but Iktinos was moving too rapidly and the shot grazed him again, carving a molten channel along the side of his helmet. Iktinos slashed at Voar with his heavy powered mace. The archmagos cut his motivator units and dropped to the floor, and the crozius sliced through the stonework of the arch.

Iktinos's other arm grabbed Voar's gun wrist, spun the archmagos around and slammed him against the wall, his forearm pinning Voar's back.

'I am not here to kill you,' said Iktinos. 'Your life means nothing to me. Give me the Soulspear.'

'Take it,' said Voar. A small manipulator limb emerged from the collar of his hood. It carried the haft of the Soulspear, a cylinder of metal with a knurled handgrip.

Iktinos took the Soulspear and turned it over in his hand, keeping Voar up against the wall.

'To think,' he said. 'Such a small thing. Even now I wonder if it was this that set us on our path. Many of your tech-priests died over this, archmagos. Many of my brothers, too. It is right that it be delivered into the hands of Daenyathos.'

'You have what you came for,' said Voar. 'Let me go.'

'I made no promises that you would live,' said Iktinos.

Emotions that had not been felt for decades clouded Voar's face. 'Omnissiah take your soul!' he snapped. 'May it burn in His forges! May it be hammered on His anvil!'

Iktinos lifted Voar into the air and slammed the tech-priest down over his knee. Metal vertebrae shattered and components rained out of Voar's robes. Iktinos plunged the crozius arcanum into Voar's chest, the power field ripping through layers of metal and bone.

Senior tech-priests could be extremely difficult to kill. Many of them could survive anything up to and including decapitation, trusting in their augmentations to keep their semi-organic brains alive until their remains could be recovered. A few of the most senior, the archmagi ultima who might rule whole clusters of forge worlds, even had archeo-tech backup brains where their personalities and memories could be recorded in case of physical destruction. Voar did not have that level of augmentation, but Iktinos had to be thorough nevertheless.

Iktinos tore open Voar's torso completely and scattered the contents, smashing each organ and component in case Voar's brain was located there. He finished destroying the spine and finally turned to Voar's head. He crushed the cranium under his boot, grinding logic circuits and ocular bionics into the floor with his heel. Quite probably, Voar died in that moment, the last sensory inputs gone dark, the final thoughts flashing through sundered circuitry.

Iktinos finished destroying Voar's body, then took up the Soulspear. It was a relic of the Great Crusade, found by Rogal Dorn himself during the Emperor's reconquest of the galaxy in the name of humanity. He had given it to the Soul Drinkers at their founding, to symbolise that they were sons of Dorn as surely as the Imperial Fists themselves.

That was the story, of course. In truth, the origin of the Soulspear, like the rest of the Soul Drinkers history, was as murky as anything else in Imperial annals. The Soulspear was gene-activated and would only respond to someone with a Soul Drinker's genetic code, so whoever had created or found the artefact, it had not been Rogal Dorn. The Soulspear, like the rest of the universe, was a lie.

That did not mean it did not have its uses. Daenyathos understood that. Just like the Imperium, the Soulspear might be founded on lies, but it could still become a part of the plan.

Daenyathos's transformation of the Imperium would not be a pleasant process. Nothing worth doing ever was. But in spite of the blood, in spite of the suffering and the death, the universe would thank Daenyathos when it was done.

Iktinos left Voar's remains scattered on the floor of the diplomatic quarters, and headed towards the Predator's Eye to witness the Imperium's future unfold.

Gethsemar and Daviks charged into the heart of the library labyrinth at the same time, charging in from two directions to catch Sarpedon off-guard.

Sarpedon was never off-guard. Silhouetted in the flames that ran across the bookcases behind him, he turned to face the Angels Sanguine and Silver Skulls warriors as if he had been expecting them.

Daviks opened fire. Sarpedon's reactions were so fast that the bolter shots burst against the blade of the Axe of Mercaeno as the mutant flicked it up to defend himself.

Gethsemar erupted towards Sarpedon on a column of fire from his jump pack. Sarpedon's left-side legs flipped the reading table behind him into Gethsemar's path and the heavy hardwood slammed into Gethsemar, throwing the Angel Sanguine into a bookcase, which buried him in a drift of burning books.

In the middle of the fire and slaughter, it was almost poetry that unfolded as the fight continued. Daviks parried the Axe of Mercaeno with the body of his bolter, only to be thrown to the floor by Sarpedon's lashing legs. Gethsemar jumped to his feet and lunged with his glaive, Sarpedon ducking the blow with impossible grace and barging the butt of the axe into Gethsemar's abdomen to throw him off-balance.

Captain Luko vaulted through the flame to crash into Daviks before the siege-captain could join the assault again. The two warriors of the Adeptus Astartes traded blows as fast as a man could see, Luko's lightning claws lashing in great arcs of blue-white power, batting aside Daviks's bolter before Daviks could get a shot.

Gethsemar launched himself into the air and dived down out of the flames overhead. Sarpedon reached up and grabbed Gethsemar, hauling him in close where the Angel Sanguine's blade could not be brought to bear. Gethsemar and Sarpedon wrestled, Sarpedon using his mutated physiology to grapple from unexpected angles and drag Gethsemar to the floor. He forced the Axe of Mercaeno down, the edge of the blade pressing against Gethsemar's throat. Gethsemar fired his jump pack but Sarpedon was stronger, and his taloned legs dug into the floor to keep himself upright.

'Fall back!' came an order over the Imperial Fists vox-channel. It was Lysander's voice, transmitted to the Howling Griffons, Silver Skulls and Angels Sanguine. 'All troops, fall back to rally points! Disengage immediately!'

The moment's confusion this caused was enough for Sarpedon to drive a fist into Gethsemar's faceplate. The death mask of Sanguinius dented and blood spurted from the carved mouth. Gemstones pinged out of the gilded surface and Gethsemar juddered as the impact ran through his whole body.

Daviks saw that Gethsemar was going to die. He ducked Luko's swinging claw swipe and charged into the Soul Drinker's legs, hauling Luko off his feet and ramming him right through the bookcase behind. He threw Luko and, using the moment of distance he had opened up,

brought his bolter around and sprayed a volley in Luko's direction. The
Soul Drinker rolled out of the way, putting hardwood shelving and millions of burning pages between him and Daviks's gunfire, but that was
what Daviks needed.

Daviks sprinted to where Gethsemar lay, the shadow of Sarpedon's
axe cast over him by the light of the flames. Daviks grabbed Gethsemar's
wrist and dragged him out of the way as Sarpedon's axe came down, ripping a deep gash in the deck.

'We leave, brother!' gasped Daviks. 'Lysander has ordered us back!'

'The fight is not done,' replied Gethsemar, his voice thick with blood.
'The enemy still stands.'

'Lysander has command! We fall back! Muster your brothers and get
back to the choristers' chamber! We will cover you!'

The two Space Marines dropped back through the smoke and wreckage. Sarpedon watched them go, not eager to pursue them when their
battle-brothers must surely be just behind them.

Luko emerged smouldering from the wreck of the bookcase he had
been thrown through. 'Damnation, I will have your hide!' he yelled
after Daviks.

Sarpedon put a hand on Luko's shoulder. 'Stay, brother,' he said.
'Something is wrong.'

Graevus dared a glance over the barricade. The last volley of bolter fire
the Soul Drinkers had kicked out had not been replied. He saw the
shapes of the Howling Griffons receding through the smoke, a few
kneeling to fire while the majority fell back.

Graevus stood and took aim, firing off a few shots snapped into the
half-seen shapes through the smoke. Salk was beside him now, echoing
Graevus's own fire.

'They're retreating,' said Salk as he paused to swap magazines.

'We haven't hit them that hard,' said Graevus. 'I thought they would
be on us.'

'Then something else has happened,' said Salk.

'Don't be too thankful. They could be mustering for another push.'

'No,' replied Salk. 'Not when they had us pinned in place. Not the
Howling Griffons, not here. They would have pushed on until either
they or we were all dead. This… this is no plan of theirs.'

'Maybe logic prevailed,' said Graevus.

With the gunfire reduced to sporadic shots, the roar of the flames and
the clattering of armour became like another form of silence, as if the
library were in the eye of a storm that had just passed over and now
everything was still. Behind the barricade lay two fallen Soul Drinkers, brought down by bolter fire and shrapnel – one was dead, both
Graevus and Salk could see that, his torso split open and blood already

congealing in a crystalline mass around the enormous spine-deep wound. The other was still but the wound to his leg, severe though it was, should not kill him.

'We need Pallas,' said Graevus.

'We do not have him,' replied Salk. 'Soul Drinkers! Bring the fallen and retreat to Sarpedon's position! Brother Markis, Thessalon! Cover us!'

Other Soul Drinkers, the survivors of a dozen Howling Griffons assaults, were moving through the smoke. They looked like the ghosts of some long-distant battle hovering just on this side of reality, clinging on as they enacted the same bloodshed night after night. Most had survived with bearable wounds, but there had been no doubt that the numbers and fury of the Howling Griffons would have soon prevailed. But now the Griffons had fallen back, and in their place was surely an unknown enemy no more inclined to give the Soul Drinkers any respite.

'No,' said Graevus. 'On second thoughts, there is no reason here.'

'Bring me everything you know,' said Chapter Master Pugh.

'Of course,' replied Castellan Leucrontas. 'We know little, but I can confirm that the starboard dorsal cargo section has been lost.'

Leucrontas had been summoned to the Forge of Ages, which had become Pugh's command post. Pict-feeds from the battle site showed little more than screens full of smoke and the vox-channel was full of barked orders and the confusion that the sudden order to retreat had brought about. In spite of that, the Howling Griffons were falling back in good order and even now mustering around the crew mess. That was not the issue.

'Lost?' said Pugh. He leaned forwards on the steel throne from which the Imperial Fists Techmarines usually oversaw the work of the forge-crews.

'It is gone. Full breach and depressurisation. Any crew in the area are dead, no doubt.'

'Any Adeptus Astartes casualties?'

'I do not believe so.'

'What caused it?'

'The psychic wards built around the librarium contemplative chambers reacted,' replied Leucrontas. 'And the readings so far obtained are esoteric.'

'A psychic attack?' said Pugh.

'If so, my lord, it is a vast and destructive one, well beyond the capacity of an Adeptus Astartes psyker.'

'Then,' said Pugh, his chin on his fist, 'a moral threat? An assault from the warp?'

'Librarian Varnica's testimony did suggest the Soul Drinkers had daemonic allies,' said Leucrontas. 'And there is… something… happening to Kravamesh.'

'Kravamesh? The star? What has the star around which we orbit to do with the Soul Drinkers?' Pugh held up his hand before Leucrontas replied. 'No, castellan, I ask not for an answer. I merely muse upon it. We must see to the security of the *Phalanx* before we seek the origin of this new threat. Once the assault on the archives has been withdrawn, we must redeploy our strength around the dorsal cargo bays to keep them contained. A smaller force can maintain the cordon around the archives. Draw up the battle stations and see that Lysander has access to them. Nothing must get in or out of either area without running a gauntlet of bolter fire.'

'Yes, my lord. And the crew?'

'Order them to arms. Protect the critical areas of the ship. I had hoped that even after the escape this would be limited to Space Marine versus Space Marine. It seems events have compelled us to think beyond that.'

'It will be done.'

'Keep me apprised of everything, and…'

Pugh's voice was interrupted by the bleating of an alarm. From the armrest of the throne slid a pict-screen that shuddered into life.

'The tech-adepts must have got dorsal security back online,' said Leucrontas.

The screen showed a view of a corridor, bulkhead doors standing open along its length. Mist clung to the floor and rolled through the doorways.

Shapes were coalescing. Tentacles, eyes, mouths, malformed limbs, writhing masses of entrails that moved with an impossible impression of intelligence and malice. Teeth, blades of bone, tides of filth, all wrapped into dimensions that refused to fit into reality. Like a stain the madness was spreading out, a tide of filth and insanity that warped the fabric of the *Phalanx* as it advanced.

'Daemons,' snarled Pugh. He looked up at Leucrontas. 'Bring me the Fangs of Dorn.'

In the smouldering ruins of the archive, Sarpedon and his officers convened. The smoke that still clung to everything made it look as if they were wanderers in dense mist who had come across one another by accident. They gathered around one of the few intact reading tables, where the ground was knee-deep in charred pages and gutted spines.

Graevus and Salk joined Luko, Tyrendian and Sarpedon where they waited. 'The dead have been counted,' said Graevus.

'What is the tally?' said Sarpedon.

Salk stepped forwards. 'Fifteen,' he said. 'Those who remain number forty-seven.'

'Was it ever true that there were once a thousand of us?' said Sarpedon.

'No,' replied Tyrendian. 'The old Chapter boasted a thousand warriors. We are not that Chapter.'

'Then they died,' said Sarpedon, 'as we surely shall. Now is not the time to bar that truth from our souls. Many times a Space Marine facing death refuses to allow it into his mind, for by defying the inevitable we can sometimes rob it of victory. But not here. I think I accepted our deaths here when the Imperial Fists first faced us on Selaaca, but if any of you still rage against our fate then I ask you to abandon it. Take the certainty of death into yourselves, welcome it, and make peace with it. It is not an easy task, but now, it is the right path to take.'

'If we fight not to survive,' said Luko, 'then why? Why not simply present ourselves to the Howling Griffons so they might put a bullet in the back of our heads and be done with it?'

'Because there are matters unfinished amongst us that our enemy's retreat has permitted to us to address,' replied Sarpedon.

'You mean Daenyathos,' said Salk, 'and Iktinos.'

'We still have no understanding of what they intend here,' said Tyrendian. Somehow he, as always seemed the case, had come through the battle in the archive with barely any scar or blemish on him. Perhaps his psychic talent was not limited to throwing lightning bolts in battle, but also gave him some kind of inviolability, some ward against the ugliness of war. 'Presuming it was Iktinos, under Daenyathos's direction, who brought us to this juncture, there is no indication of what he actually wants to achieve here.'

'Then we shall find out,' said Sarpedon. 'The Howling Griffons will attack again soon, or a cordon will be set up to contain us. Either way, if any of us are to begin the hunt for Iktinos and Daenyathos then we must do so soon. I do not believe our whole force can move through the *Phalanx* quickly enough. The whole of the Imperial Fists and Howling Griffons will mobilise to stand in our way. But if a smaller force does so while the main force must also be dealt with, we will have a greater chance of breaking through any opposition and finding Daenyathos.'

'Then who will go?' said Tyrendian.

'Sergeant Salk,' said Sarpedon. 'I ask that you select a squad and accompany me. I cannot do this alone. Captain Luko, you shall take command of the rest of the Chapter.'

'You are our Chapter Master,' replied Luko. 'It is to your leadership that our battle-brothers look. Would you deny them that in their final battle? Let one of us go.'

'No, captain,' retorted Sarpedon. 'I am faster than any Space Marine. Foul as they are, my mutations serve me well in that regard. Not to mention, I would send no man to face Iktinos or Daenyathos save myself. And I may be their leader by right, but ask any Soul Drinker what man he would prefer to fight alongside and those who are honest will name Captain Luko.'

Luko did not reply for a long moment. 'If I was asked that question,' said Luko levelly, 'then I would say Chapter Master Sarpedon. Is it my fate that I will be denied that in these, our last moments?'

'It is,' said Sarpedon. 'I promised you peace, captain. It will come soon. I did not promise I would be there when it arrived. Forgive me, but these are my orders.'

Luko said nothing, but saluted by way of reply.

'Our objectives?' asked Tyrendian.

'Draw in our enemies, keep them busy. The fiercer the fight here, the shorter odds you buy for Salk and myself.'

'I shall round up a squad,' said Salk. 'I know who to choose. It will not take long.'

'Then we must part,' said Sarpedon. 'Remember, regardless of whose blood flows in us, we are still sons of Dorn. If there was ever a man who did not know when to give up, it was Rogal Dorn. We are blessed with a battle in which we cannot fail. Think on Dorn, and forget how to lose.'

The assembled Soul Drinkers saluted their commander. Then, to a man, they bowed their heads to pray.

Like a poisoned barb in flesh, like an infection, the warp portal had caused to grow around it a corrupted cyst that ran with blood and pain. From the steel of the *Phalanx* it had chewed out a great cathedral of gore, its arching ceiling ribbed with clotted veins of filth and its walls of vivid, oozing torn flesh. Blood washed in tides born of Kravamesh's gravity, like wine swirled in a bowl, and through it slithered all the foul things of the warp.

Every power of the warp wanted its hand played on the *Phalanx*. So many of their servants had been banished or destroyed by the Imperial Fists and the other Chapters represented there that even their aeons-old hatreds could not stop them from sending their minions to join Abraxes's own. Brass-skinned soldiers of the Blood God marched from the blood onto the shore of torn metal, their black iron swords at attention and their muscular bodies moving in time as if they were on a parade ground. Flitting snakelike things with long lashing tongues darted here and there, quick as hovering insects, snapping at the morsels of flesh that scudded on the surface of the blood. And a horde of decaying forms hauled on rusted chains as they dragged an enormous thing of rotting flesh out of the mire, a contented smile on its bloated face as it plucked a tiny squealing daemon from the rents in its skin and swallowed it down. It seemed that every shape of the warp's hatred was emerging from the blood-gate, beyond which vast intelligences gathered to watch this invasion of the Imperial Fists sanctum.

On an island of corroded metal, all that remained of the docking bay deck, stood Daenyathos. He seemed the only solid thing in an arena of flesh that mutated at the whim of the Dark Gods, as if the Dreadnought's chassis anchored the whole scene in realspace and without him it would all collapse into the warp under the weight of its own madness.

'I brought you here,' he yelled, voice amplified to maximum. 'It is at my sufferance that you walk again in the realms of the real. Abraxes the Fair, Abraxes the Magnificent, I call upon you to hear me.'

Abraxes rose from his throne of bodies, twisted and fused together from crewmen whose minds had shattered under the psychic assault of the gate's opening. The daemon prince's beauty was not marred by the blood that soaked his garments and ran down his perfect alabaster skin. 'Abraxes is not summoned,' he said in a voice like song. 'He arrives not at the whim of another.'

'And yet,' replied Daenyathos, 'you are here. For who else would I bring forth to have his revenge on Sarpedon of the Soul Drinkers?'

Abraxes leaned forward. 'Sarpedon? And yet here I thought that Imperial Fists, as delicious as they would be, were the sole morsels I might find here to soothe my hunger. Yet Sarpedon is here... where is he? The gate is opened fully and the daemon army is ready to march. I would march upon him first, and destroy what remains in celebration of my revenge!'

'I imagine,' said Daenyathos, 'that he will come to you. But mere slaughter is too small an objective for one such as Abraxes, is it not? To butcher a starship full of Space Marines is a worthy endeavour for any petty prince or aspiring daemon, but for Abraxes? Surely your dreams are grander than that?'

'Explain yourself!' demanded Abraxes. 'I grow impatient. See! The horrors of Tzeentch march to my tune. A thousand of them emerge from the warp at my whim! I shall lead them forth without delay unless your words are profound indeed.'

'This is a spaceship,' said Daenyathos. 'A spaceship as huge and deadly as any the Imperium has ever fielded. And now it is a spaceship with a warp portal. I have stolen the Predator's Eye from the star Kravamesh and embedded it in the *Phalanx*. What could the great Abraxes desire more than a doorway into the warp from which spills all the legions under his command, and that he can take between the stars as he wishes?'

Abraxes clenched a fist, and his thoughts could almost be read on his face. They were not human thoughts – they would not fit in a human mind. 'I shall extinguish stars,' he said. 'I shall weave a pattern across the galaxy, even unto Terra!'

'I can lead you there,' continued Daenyathos. 'For a lifetime I studied the path that will take you beyond the reach of the Imperium's cumbersome armies and into the orbits of its most populous worlds. It is a path that leads to Terra, I assure you. But it leads also through the very soul of humanity! Imagine world after world falling, drowned in madness, their last sane vision that of the *Phalanx* appearing like a dread star above them! A thousand times a thousand worlds shall share this fate, so that by the time you reach Terra it shall be to deal the death blow to a species cringing on its knees before you!'

'And for what reason would a Space Marine lead me on such a dance?' said Abraxes. 'You who were born of the Emperor's will. You who have sworn so many oaths to destroy all such as me. Why do you wish your species to undergo such a tortuous death?'

'I need no reason,' said Daenyathos. 'Hatred is its own justification.'

'Ah, hatred!' said Abraxes, jumping to his cloven feet. The blood washed around his ankles, mindless predators slithering from the foam. 'The human gift to the universe. The greatest work of man. Even your Emperor himself was in thrall to it. There has been no creation to rival it. It builds worlds and brings them down. Aloud it is war, and in silence it is peace. The human race is nothing but a trillion manifestations of hatred! When humanity is gone, I think I shall preserve alone its hatred. From it I shall mould whatever I see fit to succeed them. Hatred alone shall rule among the stars.'

'And so it shall be,' said Daenyathos. 'But first, the *Phalanx* must become your own.'

'That,' replied Abraxes with scorn, 'is a task worthy of my notice only because Sarpedon's death shall be a part of it. Sarpedon is the last of the universe I once knew, one in which Abraxes could fail. When he is gone, only victory shall be left. I can see the fates twining out towards destruction. There is no thread that humanity can follow to safety. Sarpedon dies. They all die. Then your universe shall follow!'

With the atonal braying of a hundred pipes, Abraxes's army gathered on the blood shore. Greater daemons, hateful lumps of the warp's own will given form, were the generals of a thousands-strong army. Bloodletters of Khorne chanted in their own dark tongue, bodies smouldering as their lust for slaughter grew. Abraxes's own horrors were a shuddering tide of formless flesh, shifting in and out of solid forms at the speed of thought. Plaguebearers, emissaries of the plague god Nurgle who had once been Abraxes's sworn enemy, fawned around the enormous drooling avatar of rot that was their leader.

Abraxes strode to the head of his army. In response, the walls of the cyst opened into vast orifices, leading towards the interior of the *Phalanx*. Lesser daemons scrambled forwards, shrieking and gibbering with the joy of approaching battle. The lords of the daemonic host howled a terrible cacophony of bellowed orders and the army advanced, horrors of Tzeentch following Abraxes like the wake of a battleship.

Daenyathos could see in the army's advance another thread of fate winding its way towards a conclusion. Even Chaos had to observe the inevitability of fate. Abraxes, a being that had perfected its use of unwitting pawns such as the Soul Drinkers, had been drawn by that same fate to serve Daenyathos's design. Through Abraxes, Daenyathos's own will would be done.

It had taken so long and so much to reach this point, but that was merely a prelude. The bloodshed on the *Phalanx* was the true beginning of Daenyathos's remaking of the galaxy.

Sarpedon had nothing but raw instinct to go on. He knew a little of Daenyathos and rather more of Iktinos's ways, but even so it was barely more than guesswork that took him through the cordon of Imperial Fists and into the vast training section of the *Phalanx*, where sparring circles and shooting galleries were equipped with hundreds of target-servitors and racks of exotic weapons from cultures across the galaxy.

The industrialised sections of the *Phalanx*, the cargo bays and engineering sections towards the rear of the ship, were the best place for a single Space Marine to hide. Even a Dreadnought would find places to hole up there. That was where Sarpedon resolved to look, but first he would have to cross the training sections.

'We should take the mock battlefield,' said Sergeant Salk. His squad, picked from the survivors of the battle in the archive, was advancing in a wide formation to give them the widest angles of vision. Ahead, a jumble of deck sections formed a series of slopes, hills and valleys, each section on hydraulics which could move them into a new topography to create a constantly changing battlefield. It was here that Imperial Fists recruits were put through days-long battle simulations, waves of target-servitors and the shifting landscape combining to create a test that was as much mental as it was physical.

'Agreed,' said Sarpedon. 'We must make good time.'

'If we find Iktinos, commander, what will we do?'

Sarpedon raised an eyebrow. 'Kill him,' he said. 'What do you think?'

The atmosphere of real battlefields clung thickly to the recreation. It was not just the bullet scars from live-fire exercises on the forests, ruined villages, jungles and alien environments wrought from flak-board and steel. It was the echo of all the imaginary wars that had been fought there, battles which had their own echo in the real bloodshed the Imperial Fists trained there later encountered. The skills they learned there served them well, or failed them, in the depths of war on Emperor-forsaken alien worlds, and the traces of those desperate times clung to the mock fortifications like a freezing mist.

'Contact!' came a vox from up ahead.

'Close in!' ordered Salk. 'Cover and report targets!'

688   *Ben Counter*

Ahead was the recreation of a village ruined by shellfire, craters moulded into the floor sections and the blank, broken walls featureless save for the empty eyes of windows and doorways. A building in the shape of a chapel, its walls devoid of sculpture, dominated the centre of the village with its bell tower tailor-made for snipers. Sarpedon scuttled into the shell of a mock house, crouching down on his haunches by a doorway. Sarpedon couldn't see most of Salk's squad, spread out and in cover as they were, but he knew they were there.

At the far end of the mock village, Reinez walked into plain view. The Crimson Fist's armour still had the filth and scorching of battle, and in the quiet he jangled with the many icons and seals hanging from him. He looked just as Sarpedon had left him in the lab, battered and bruised, but with none of his fires dimmed.

'Sarpedon!' called Reinez. 'I know you are here, you and your traitors. I think we left some business undone when last we met!'

'Orders, commander?' voxed Salk quietly.

'Hold,' replied Sarpedon.

'We could take him down.'

'You have my orders. Hold fire.'

Reinez walked forwards to the town square in the shadow of the church. 'Well?' he shouted. He had his hammer in his hand, and scowled at the ruins as he searched out the purple of Soul Drinkers armour. 'Do not tell me you care nothing for the fate of Reinez! You took my standard, you humiliated me, you cast me out from my own Chapter with your treachery! How can you do all this and yet let me live?'

Sarpedon stood up from his cover and walked into the open, his talons clicking on the hard deck sections. Reinez watched him coldly, wordlessly.

Sarpedon took the Axe of Mercaeno in one hand. 'This need not happen,' said Sarpedon. 'We are both Space Marines. For one to shed another's blood is heresy.'

'You speak of heresy?' barked Reinez. 'You, who have already slain so many of my brothers? There has not been enough Adeptus Astartes blood spilled yet for my liking. A few drops more and then it will be done.'

'Reinez, I have no quarrel with you here. I seek one of my own, the one who has orchestrated all that you have railed against. It is he who deserves all your hate, just as he deserves mine. If you truly want revenge for what happened to your brothers then let me pass or join me, but please, do not stand in my way.'

'You knew it would not end any way but the two of us to the death,' said Reinez. 'You knew that from the moment a Crimson Fist fell to a Soul Drinker's hand. Fate will not let us go and it will kill one of us before either walks away.'

Sarpedon let out a long breath. 'Then that is the way it must be,' he said. 'You have argued for a reckoning since you arrived on the *Phalanx*. You will have it, if that is what you truly want.'

Reinez crouched down into a guard, hammer haft held across his body. He flexed and bounced on his calves, judging distance and winding up for the strike.

Sarpedon knew that Salk's squad had all their guns trained on Reinez. They would not fire. Perhaps they would if Reinez killed Sarpedon, but by then it would not matter.

Reinez darted forwards, faster than Sarpedon remembered him moving. Sarpedon whirled and swung the Axe of Mercaeno around, slamming the head into Reinez's side. He discharged a blast of psychic power through the force blade and though Reinez caught the worst of the blow on the haft of his hammer, the explosive force was enough to throw him from his feet and into the flakboard side of the fake church. The wall buckled under his weight, but Reinez rolled to his feet and swung his hammer at ankle height as Sarpedon charged to follow up.

Sarpedon leapt up. He scuttled along the wall, talons clinging to the flakboard.

Reinez tried to get his bearings, unused to fighting an enemy who could climb walls like a spider.

'Now!' yelled Reinez. 'Now! Fire! Fire!'

From every direction, bolters hammered. Muzzle flashes betrayed hidden firing positions around the far side of the mock village. Bullet fire ripped into the flakboard around Sarpedon, and a flash of pain burst through one of his back legs. Sarpedon ran up the wall and onto the roof of the church, volleys of fire chewing through the church all around him. In the lee of the church tower he found a semblance of cover, the flakboard tearing apart and the tower sagging above him.

'Contacts everywhere,' voxed Salk. 'It was a trap. Engage!'

'Who are they?' demanded Sarpedon.

'It's us,' came Salk's shocked reply. 'It's Soul Drinkers!'

Sarpedon could glimpse purple armour among the debris and gunsmoke of the firefight erupting across the village. Iktinos's flock, the Soul Drinkers who were loyal to the Chaplain first and Sarpedon a distant second, whose allegiance Sarpedon had been too blind to question.

'You are too honourable, Soul Drinker!' yelled Reinez from somewhere below. 'Too quick to give a sworn enemy a fair fight! Now it will be the death of you all!'

Reinez clambered up the wall and vaulted onto the roof. Sarpedon lunged and the two fought, axe and hammer flashing, blows parried and driven aside as bolter fire shrieked around them. Sarpedon hacked a chunk out of Reinez's shoulder armour. In response, Reinez stamped down on Sarpedon's wounded leg to pin him in place and crunched the head of his hammer into Sarpedon's chest. Sarpedon was faster than Reinez but the Crimson Fist had prepared for this fight for many years and this time he had the advantage of numbers. Iktinos's flock comprised many more warriors than Salk's squad and among the flock were those with good enough aim to pick out Sarpedon from the melee. Bolter fire slammed into the tower behind Sarpedon or sparked from his armour, knocking him back a pace or throwing him off-balance.

Sarpedon powered forwards, a desperate move more suited to a rude brawl than a duel to the death. Forelegs and arms wrapped around Reinez, forcing him down under Sarpedon's greater weight.

'What have you done, Reinez?' growled Sarpedon.

'Iktinos promised me a chance to kill you,' replied Reinez, voice strained as he fought to burst Sarpedon's hold on him. 'There was nothing else anyone could offer me.'

'Iktinos is the enemy! He is the source of all this suffering.'

'Then I will kill him next,' snarled Reinez.

Sarpedon picked up Reinez and threw him down, putting all his strength into hurling the Crimson Fist off the roof. Reinez landed badly and Salk's return fire drove him into the cover of a ruined building adjoining the church.

The flock were moving across the village. More than twenty of them had survived the breakout from the Atoning Halls, double Salk's numbers. Sarpedon recognised Soul Drinkers he had called brothers, who had been stranded when their officers were killed. Iktinos had taken them in and Sarpedon had been grateful that the Chaplain was willing to give them spiritual leadership. But Iktinos had been warping them, finding their sense of loss and turning it into something else, a devotion to the Chaplain alone that meant they followed him instead of Sarpedon. The Chapter Master had been confronted with many results of his failures as a leader, but none of them had struck him as sharply as the sight of the flock did then, moving with murderous intent across the town square to batter Salk's squad into oblivion.

Salk's Soul Drinkers were falling. They were surrounded and outgunned. Salk himself leaned out from cover to fell one of the flock, and in response a cluster of shots knocked him out of sight in a shower of blood. Sarpedon's twin hearts felt like they were tightening in his chest, all the heat squeezed out of his body to be replaced with cold and dust.

Sarpedon leapt down from the church into the centre of the village. He landed in the heart of the advancing flock. Faces he had known for years, since before the First Chapter War, turned on him and saw nothing but an enemy. Sarpedon saw nothing in them any more, no brotherhood, no hope, none of the principles that had made them turn on the old Chapter's ways. He was their enemy, and they were his. Suddenly, it seemed simple.

Sarpedon knew the closest Soul Drinker to him was Brother Scarphinal, one of Givrillian's squad. Givrillian had been Sarpedon's closest confidant and best friend, and he had died on a nameless planet to the daemon prince Ve'Meth. There was nothing left of Givrillian's command in Scarphinal now. His eyes were blank and his bolter turned towards Sarpedon without hesitation.

Sarpedon struck Scarphinal's head from his shoulders with a single shining arc, the Axe of Mercaeno slicing through the Space Marine's neck so smoothly the blood had not yet begun to flow when Scarphinal's head hit the floor.

Something dark and prideful, a relic of the old Chapter, awakened in Sarpedon. The love of bloodshed, the exultation of battle. Sometimes, those places locked away in his mind could be useful, and it was with a strange sense of relief that he let the bloodlust take him.

Sarpedon roared with formless anger, and dived into the carnage.

CHAPTER ELEVEN

The *Phalanx* had been designed – whenever it had been designed, before the Age of Imperium – to survive. Any hostiles who boarded the immense ship might find themselves trapped in the tight, winding corridors of the engineering and maintenance areas just beneath the hull's skin, separated from the ship's more vulnerable areas by hundreds of automated bulkhead doors and whole sections of outer deck that could be vented into hard vacuum with the press of a control stud.

The hostiles currently on the *Phalanx* had bypassed every design feature intended to contain them. They had been disgorged directly into the ship's interior, spilling through cavernous shuttle bays and swarming into crew quarters, riding torrents of blood through automated cargo motivator systems. The *Phalanx* had no way to stop the daemonic invaders.

So it was up to the Adeptus Astartes instead.

Chapter Master Pugh stood at the threshold of the Sigismunda Tactica, and looked out across the battlefield. It spanned the barracks deck and was a kilometre and a half wide. This was the vulnerable heart of the *Phalanx*, the ground across which an invader could charge with impunity from the lost starboard docking bays towards the engines and reactors. The Forge of Ages anchored one end, beyond which was a tangle of engineering areas and power and coolant conduits. The other flank terminated in the Rynn's World memorial, an amphitheatre of granite inscribed with the names of the Crimson Fists lost in the infamous near-destruction of their fortress-monastery. Beyond this memorial were the steel catacombs, tight nests of cramped candlelit chambers where generations of crew members were laid to rest in niches scattered with bones. The conduit decks and catacombs would slow down the invaders' advance, funnelling them through the open areas of the barracks, chapels and hero-shrines rolling out in front of Pugh.

'I can smell them,' said Captain Lysander, emerging from the Sigismunda Tactica behind Pugh. 'The enemy are close.'

'Of course you can smell them,' said Pugh. 'I wonder if we will ever get the stink of the warp off my ship.'

'Borganor is in position at the Forge of Ages,' continued Lysander. 'Leucrontas and the Ninth will hold the memorial.'

'And everyone else will take the centre,' finished Pugh. 'Can it be held?'

'Our Third and Fifth are enough to hold anything,' said Lysander.

'You realise you will stake your life on that belief?'

'We all will, Chapter Master. If this line breaks, everyone on the *Phalanx* will die.'

'Tell me, captain. Is it wrong that I have dreamed of a day like this?' Pugh drew the Fangs of Dorn from the scabbards on either side of his waist – twin power swords, their blades broad for stabbing, their hilts semicircles of glinting black stone. 'That I have knelt at the altars of Dorn and prayed that one day I would face the enemy like this, in a battle that will decide whether my Chapter lives in glory or is banished to a penitents' crusade in disgrace? I have begged the Emperor to give me such a battle, toe to toe, no retreat, everything at stake. Is it wrong that I feel some joy in me that it is here?'

'We all see something else in battle,' replied Lysander. 'Perhaps it is a mirror in which we see a reflection of ourselves. I see a grim task to be completed, something ugly and crude, but an evil necessary for the survival of our species. You see something different.'

'Most Imperial Fists would simply have said "No", captain.'

'Well, that's why you made me a captain.'

Among the complexes of barracks cells and the shrines to long-dead heroes, the Third and Fifth Companies of the Imperial Fists were taking up their battle positions. Low buildings formed the anchoring points beneath the grey sky of the ceiling. Battle-brothers knelt to icons of past captains and Chapter Masters, their home suddenly transformed into a battleground.

The Tactica itself was one of the most defensible buildings on the deck. It was a circular building of black stone, its arched entrances leading to dozens of map tables on which famous past battles of the Imperial Fists had been recreated. The buildings over which Imperial

Fists had fought and died were scrimshawed from alien ivories and laid out on miniature battlegrounds of polished obsidian. In the Tactica, named after Sigismund, one of Dorn's greatest generals and the founder of the Black Templars Chapter, Imperial Fists officers could contemplate victories of the past, dissecting the battle plans the Chapter's leaders had enacted and the follies of the enemies who tried to stand against them. If the Imperial Fists and the other Adeptus Astartes on the *Phalanx* could prevail, perhaps the Tactica itself would be recreated on one of those ornate maps.

Lord Inquisitor Kolgo was walking among the map tables, casting his eye over the Imperial Fists history. He wore black Terminator armour embellished with silver symbols of the Inquisition, making him even bulkier than a Space Marine in power armour. His Battle Sisters retinue kept a respectful distance, Sister Aescarion waiting patiently with power axe in hand.

'I take it,' said Pugh, 'that you know rather more about the forces of the warp than can be entrusted to lesser minds like ours.'

Kolgo looked up, as if he had not expected to be interrupted, to see Pugh walking through one of the Tactica's lofty archways. 'It is a burden we inquisitors must carry, Chapter Master,' he said.

'If there is anything we could do with knowing, then now is the time to tell us.'

Kolgo took a set of Emperor's Tarot cards from a silver case set into his breastplate. On one of the map tables, one which represented a volcanic battlefield where the Imperial Fists had shattered an assault by the xenos tau, he laid out three of them in a row.

'"The Silver Ocean",' said Kolgo, pointing to the first card. 'One who cannot be grasped or comprehended, as subtle as quicksilver. An unknowable foe. The second is "The Altar", a symbol of majesty and glory. But it is inverted, and followed by "The Plague". The enemy is inscrutable and majestic, but that majesty is false and conceals an ocean of foulness beneath its beauty. It is a vessel of corruption in the form of something wonderful. I see the hand of the Lord of Change in the enemy we face, but the foe is its own creature, driven by its own desires.'

'You know what it is?' said Pugh.

'I have my suspicions, which I will not share until they become certainties, especially where the God of Lies is concerned.' Kolgo gathered up the cards and put them away. 'This is more than a battle over your vessel, Chapter Master. That is all I am willing to say.'

'Then keep your own counsel, lord inquisitor, as long as you fight alongside us.'

Kolgo smiled. 'Have no fear on that score.'

'Chapter Master,' came a voice over the vox-net. The rune signifying

Castellan Leucrontas pulsed against Pugh's retina. 'The enemy is sighted.'

'What is their strength, castellan?' demanded Pugh.

'Hundreds,' came Leucrontas's voice. 'They are advancing on two sides. Holding position.'

Pugh strode out of the Tactica. His own Imperial Fists were in position among the shrines and barracks, and he spotted the colours of the Silver Skulls and Angels Sanguine among them. 'Lysander,' he ordered. 'Be ready to counter-advance on the castellan's flank. Keep the memorial from being surrounded.'

'Yes, Chapter Master,' said Lysander. 'Other orders?'

Pugh did not reply. Instead, he was looking past the Imperial Fists positions ahead of him, towards the steel horizon broken by the spires of hero-shrines and the fluttering banners of the mustering grounds.

The daemon army was advancing. The horizon seethed, a mass of iridescence bleeding into view like a bank of incandescent gas. The sound of its music washed over the Imperial Fists lines, an awful cacophony of a thousand shrieking voices. Shapes towered over the lines, winged masses surrounded by mountains of daemonic followers tumbling over one another like insects swarming from a hive.

'The Emperor has granted you your battle,' said Lysander. 'Now is the time to give thanks.'

'There will be opportunity for that when the victory is won,' said Pugh. 'Kolgo! Get your Battle Sisters to the lines! We are attacked on all fronts!'

From the daemonic horde emerged another winged monster, this one bathed in light as if Kravamesh's light was falling in a bright shaft onto its pale haloed form. It was framed by feathered wings and its skin was so pale it seemed to burn, like ivory lit from within. Its perfect face projected its beauty and authority even as far as the Tactica. Even Pugh found it difficult to tear his eyes away from it, as if it was a vision that originated inside his head and burned its way outwards.

'Behold, your future!' the monster bellowed, its voice tearing across the battlefield like a razored wind. 'I am the end of empires! I am the woes of men! I am Abraxes!'

Sarpedon skidded across the blood-slicked surface, the Axe of Mercaeno smouldering in his hand.

Brother Nephael faced him. Nephael's bolter magazine was empty, his last few shots fired wildly through a storm of his own battle-brothers, and he had no time to change the magazine. He snatched Brother Kalchis's chainsword off the ground and swung it as Sarpedon came crashing towards him.

Sarpedon span on a front leg, out of the reach of the chainblade. He swung in low, axe hacking down at Nephael's leg. Nephael didn't have the speed of Sarpedon, and he didn't have the strength. The axe caught Nephael below the knee and flung him head over heels. Sarpedon charged into Nephael as he fell, slamming the flock member into the ground.

Sarpedon rolled Nephael over so he was face up, Sarpedon's weight on the Soul Drinker's chest. He ripped the chainsword from Nephael's hand and threw it aside.

Sarpedon tore Nephael's helmet off. The face revealed was more youthful than most Soul Drinkers, the hair cropped close and the eyes set into bruised slits.

'Where is Iktinos?' demanded Sarpedon.

'He is the future,' spat back Nephael.

'Where is Iktinos?' shouted Sarpedon, slamming the back of Nephael's head into the ground to punctuate each word.

'Go to Terra,' said Nephael, 'when our work is complete. You will find him kneeling at the foot of the Golden Throne.'

Nephael wrenched an arm free and drew his combat knife. Before he could drive it upwards Sarpedon had slithered off him and buried the Axe of Mercaeno in the Soul Drinker's head, cleaving it in half down to the floor.

Sarpedon got back to his feet. Around him, the mock village was strewn with bodies and blood. He had killed them all.

The members of Iktinos's flock who had ambushed him and Salk had fallen either to Squad Salk's guns or to Sarpedon himself. He had dived among them, these Space Marines who had once sworn to follow him to extinction, and he had cut them to pieces. Cracked skulls spilled red-black pools across the flakboard floor. Limbs torn off lay orphaned from their owners, who in turn lay where Sarpedon had speared them with talons or carved them open with the Axe of Mercaeno. Nephael had been the last of them alive but they had all been men that Sarpedon recognised.

That was not mere blood spattered up against the false chapel and ruins. It was the blood of Space Marine. It was the blood of brothers.

Sarpedon forced his pulse and breathing to slow. It had felt good, he was ashamed to realise, to finally come to grips with the enemy that had manipulated his Chapter towards execution. In the middle of the fight, he had felt a certainty that could only be born of the sure knowledge that the man facing you would kill you if you did not kill him first. Now, he was surrounded by dead brothers, and the doubts came back. He swallowed them down, demanded that he become calm.

Reinez had fled. The Crimson Fist could not be seen among the ruins. Sarpedon could not see any movement among Salk's positions, either. Sarpedon ran to the ruin in which Salk had taken shelter, its flakboard now chewed up and splintered by bolter fire.

Salk lay on his back in a ruin of torn flakboard. Bolter impacts had broken through the ceramite of his chest and abdomen. He turned his head weakly, and Sarpedon saw that one side of his face was a pulpy ruin, shattered bone poking through a mass of blood that had already coagulated to a crystalline rind.

'Brother,' said Sarpedon. 'Speak to me. Tell me that Salk has not fallen.'

'Forgive me,' sputtered Salk. 'Failure is my sin.'

'No, Salk. None has been more steadfast than you. There is no failure.'

'Then this is certainly not victory. I had not thought it would be so bleak. I thought there would be some… heroism.'

Sarpedon leaned down close to Salk, unsure if the sergeant's drifting eyes were able to focus on him at all. 'I will kill Iktinos.'

'I know you will. Not for me, commander. Do what has to be done. For everyone.'

Sarpedon tried to pick up Salk, thinking perhaps he could get the fallen sergeant back to the archives where the other Soul Drinkers could tend to him. But he felt Salk getting lighter in his arms, as if the life were evaporating from him and leaving an empty body behind. Sarpedon saw the light going out in Salk's eyes, something impossible to describe, changing with infinite subtlety as the Soul Drinker, his friend, turned into just another body.

Sarpedon held Salk for a long moment. Some primitive emotion in the back of his head begged the Emperor to breathe life back into Salk. Salk had been as solid a squad leader as Sarpedon had ever commanded, before or after the First Chapter War. He had earned his laurels on Stratix Luminae and thereafter proved an unsung and dependable lynchpin of the Soul Drinkers' most desperate moments.

Now, Salk was gone. That was the calibre of man Iktinos and Daenyathos were running down in their charge towards whatever mad future they had concocted.

Sarpedon placed Salk on the ground, and murmured an old prayer. It called upon the Emperor and anyone who served him to shepherd the fallen towards the End Times, to make sure his wargear was waiting for him when he lined up alongside the Emperor for the battle at the end of existence. The fake battleground was a poor burial place for anyone, let alone a Space Marine, but for Salk and the brethren of his squad it would have to do for now. Perhaps the Imperial Fists would give them a basic funeral, dying as they did fighting a mutual enemy.

Sarpedon looked behind him, to the bodies of the fallen flock. The fact that they had been sent to ambush the Soul Drinkers at all meant Sarpedon was getting close. The flock meant Iktinos, and Iktinos meant some measure of revenge.

Revenge. That was all Sarpedon had left now to fight for. But everything a Space Marine did was for revenge, and for Sarpedon, as he picked up the Axe of Mercaeno and headed towards the far side of the training deck, it was just enough.

Castellan Leucrontas jumped from cover and led the counter-charge.

It was an insane move against the insane enemy advancing on the Rynn's World memorial. A mad show of bravado, a hand played against an enemy where such crazed fury was the only way to shock them and drive them back.

Leucrontas was followed by more than fifty Imperial Fists of the Ninth Company. They vaulted over the carved stone tableaux of battle scenes from Rynn's World, ducking at a run past the slabs inscribed with the names of the lost. They were framed by the sweeping wings of the stone amphitheatre, as if the battle were a grand stage play and this was the climactic scene.

The daemons surged forwards. A titanic being of rotting flesh, its body a vast bloated sac bulging with torn veins and maggoty slabs of muscle, was hauled forwards by their front ranks. It chortled and moaned as if the whole thing were an enormous joke that only it could understand, a mix of the idiotic and cunning on its wide lolling face. Hundreds of daemons pushed it from behind and a hundred more pulled it forwards on rusted chains embedded in its flesh.

'I will not wait for the enemy to do as he will!' yelled Leucrontas as he ran, his storm bolter out ready to fire. 'If he is eager for our blood, let us drive onwards and drown him in it!'

Leucrontas opened fire. Fifty bolters echoed him, full-auto fire burning through magazines. The front rank of the daemons disappeared in a mass of foul torn flesh, torsos bursting like bags of blood and maggots, broken corpses trampled underfoot. A tide of black corrupted blood washed forwards around the Imperial Fists' feet and flies descended, a black haze of them swirling as if controlled by a single ravenous mind.

The daemons were all about Leucrontas now. His storm bolter rattled in his hand, twin barrels glowing blue-hot, until the hammer fell on an empty chamber. Leucrontas dived into the torn mass of flesh around him, combat knife in one hand, bolt pistol in another, laying about him with chop and thrust even as he picked out leering one-eyed heads and put a bolter round into each he saw.

A rusted chain fell to the ground, dropped by the daemons hit by Leucrontas's assault. The daemons fought to surround the castellan and he resembled nothing so much as a walking fortification standing against a sea of hungry foes, the crenellations of his armour holding off blades of corroded iron and lashing, filthy claws.

The Imperial Fists saved him. Charging on in his wake, they forced the daemons back. Some, with chainswords and combat shields, fought the ugliest sort of battle imaginable, hacking away at the daemonic mass and trusting in their wargear to protect them. Others formed a cordon to keep the daemons sweeping around and cutting off Leucrontas, kneeling to fire disciplined execution squad volleys into the press of enemies.

The greater daemon loomed overhead. Its bloated shadow fell over Leucrontas. The daemons were no longer hauling it forwards and its faces creased in frustration. It reached futilely towards the Imperial Fists, flabby claws flapping at nothing. It forced a stumpy leg forwards as it began to propel its own enormous bulk towards the enemy.

It thundered forwards a step. It smiled now, eager to get to grips with the yellow-armoured figures embedded in the melee below.

Among the steps of the amphitheatre and the monumental sculptures, the rest of the Ninth appeared. Armed with the company's heavy weapons, they picked out their targets under the orders of their sergeants who acted as spotters. They pointed out the slavering beasts being goaded towards the front line, the gibbering daemons bearing icons of the warp on their standards. But most of all they pointed out the greater daemon, the monster shambling one step at a time towards the castellan.

Lascannons and heavy bolters opened fire. The memorial's grey stone was painted crimson by the pulses of las-fire. Massive-calibre fire hammered into corrupted flesh, and liquefied muscle and entrails flowed so thickly they were a viscous tide flooding around the legs of the battling Adeptus Astartes.

The greater daemon was battered by the weight of the fire. Its skin tore and split, and loops of intestines slithered out in a crimson-black mass. Tiny gibbering creatures spilled from its wounds, gambolling through the battle lines in their new-found freedom. Its lips parted and it bellowed, face creasing in pain, tiny red eyes narrowing further. Its vast throat yawed open, a red wet pit lined with teeth and inhabited by a long, thick tongue that lashed as if it were its own ravenous creature.

'Now,' yelled Leucrontas. 'Onwards! Onwards!'

The greater daemon leaned forwards into the fire. Even as the flesh of its face was stripped away by heavy bolter blasts, it smiled at the yellow-armoured figure battling towards it. It reached down with a flabby arm, fingers spread to snatch up Leucrontas.

Leucrontas saw it coming. He rattled off half the magazine of his bolt pistol blasting off the greater daemon's thumb. The hand crashed down onto him and his combat knife sliced through tendons. Another finger, as long as a Space Marine was tall, fell useless.

The remnants of the hand closed around the castellan. Leucrontas fought to push the fingers apart, but the greater daemon was stronger, and it was hungry.

Leucrontas fought on as he was picked up off the ground. Imperial Fists dived in around the greater daemon's feet, hacking at its ankles to bring it down, or carving into its titanic belly to cripple it. The greater daemon seemed not to notice them at all.

'Hello, little one,' the daemon said as it raised Leucrontas to its face. Its voice was a terrible rumble, the gurgling of its corrupted lungs as deep as an earthquake. 'What a blessed day is this, my grandchildren! I have found a new plaything!'

Leucrontas's reply was lost in the hungry howl that roared from the greater daemon as its jaws opened wide. The daemon dropped Leucrontas down its throat and swallowed with an awful wet sucking sound, like something vast being yanked out of a pool of sucking mud. The daemon laughed, a deep, guttural sound that shook the stones of the Rynn's World memorial.

The Imperial Fists line bowed as the daemons surged forwards once more. Chainblades rose and fell, barely breaking the surface of the fleshy tide surrounding them, and the guns hammered an endless stream of shells and las-blasts into an equally unending mass of enemies. The greater daemon reached down and parted the daemonic sea in front of it, revealing a knot of Imperial Fists fighting back to back, covered in gore.

The greater daemon leered down at them, took in a great ragged breath, and regurgitated a torrent of bilious filth onto them. The crushed and dissolved remains of Leucrontas crashed over them, the acidic torrent flooding through the seals of their armour and digesting them even as they scrambled to get out of the foul sticky mass.

'Fall back,' came an order from one of the heavy weapons squads' sergeants, taking up command in the wake of Leucrontas's death. 'We cannot hold.'

In the face of the appalling sight of the greater daemon's assault, even Space Marines could do little but retreat and retain what order they could, forcing the daemon army to pay for the ground they took with volleys of bolter fire.

The message that reached Chapter Master Pugh was fragmented and rushed, but its meaning was clear. The Rynn's World memorial had been lost. The first victory in the Battle of the *Phalanx* had gone to the enemy.

The echoes of the battle reached through the *Phalanx*. It was not mere sound, although the explosions of heavy weapons fire and the thunder of the daemons' advance shuddered for many decks around. It was a psychic echo, a cacophony of screaming and cackling that wormed into the back of the skull and rattled around as if trying to find a way out.

Abraxes, it cried. *I am Abraxes.*

The echo shuddered through the mess halls near the archive, where a rearguard of Imperial Fists and the surviving Iron Knights formed a cordon to keep the Soul Drinkers penned into the ruined library. Sergeant

Prexus of the Imperial Fists had to keep the itch for battle in check, for among the Adeptus Astartes under his command he knew there burned the urge to get into the fight unfolding elsewhere.

'Sergeant,' came a vox from one of the battle-brothers keeping watch over the expanse of the mess hall. 'I hear movement, beyond the doors. I think they are advancing.'

'To arms, brothers,' ordered Prexus. In a moment the Imperial Fists and Iron Knights were behind barricades of upturned furniture or crouched in the cover of doorways, bolters trained towards the double doors, chained shut, through which the Howling Griffons had advanced into the library just an hour ago.

The doors banged on their hinges, chains shuddering. A second blow wrenched one door away completely and a single Soul Drinker stepped through. He went bare-headed, his hair shaved into a single black strip along his scalp, his hands encased in lightning claws. But the power fields of the claws were not activated and the Soul Drinker was alone.

Prexus held up a hand, belaying any order to open fire.

'I am Captain Luko of the Soul Drinkers,' said the newcomer.

'I know who you are,' replied Prexus. 'Are you here to surrender?'

'No,' said Luko. 'I am here to kill Abraxes.'

Imperial Fists trigger fingers tightened. 'Explain yourself,' said Prexus.

'Abraxes is the leader of the force that assails you. You know it and I know it. I have been in its unclean presence before, at the Battle of the *Brokenback* when Sarpedon banished it to the warp. Now it has returned when we are at our weakest to have its revenge, and kill as many Imperial Fists as it can into the bargain. We have heard your vox-traffic and seen the pict-feeds. We know that Abraxes has brought a daemonic legion onto the *Phalanx* and we want to fight it.'

'I have my orders,' replied Prexus. 'You will go nowhere.'

'Then we will go through you,' said Luko. 'I see you have perhaps forty Space Marines. I have a few more, but you are no doubt better equipped and you have no wounded among you. Do you think you can kill us all here? It would be little more than the cast of a die to decide between us, I think. And we are going to die here whether it be to Abraxes's legion or your bolters, so we have nothing to lose. Will you still stand against us, sergeant?'

'There will be no need for bloodshed here,' came a voice from behind Prexus. It was one of the Iron Knights, who walked out of cover into the open.

'Borasi!' said Luko, his face breaking into a smile.

'Captain.' The two Adeptus Astartes approached and shook hands. 'You will have to trust me that this time we meet, I shall break no bones of yours.'

'I shall hold you to that, sergeant,' said Luko.

'You know this warrior?' demanded Prexus.

'We met on Molikor,' said Borasi. 'We were compelled by circumstance to trade blows before we had our facts straightened out for us.'

'I knew you were a poor choice for the rearguard,' said Prexus. 'You could not be trusted to treat the enemy as an enemy.'

'I think there is another enemy on the *Phalanx* you should concern yourself with rather more,' said Luko.

'Let the Soul Drinkers fight Abraxes if they wish it,' said Borasi. 'I will take responsibility. Let them die facing its daemons. That is execution sure enough for anyone.'

'I am in command here!' barked Prexus. 'You are under my authority, sergeant! You are here only at the sufferance of...'

The sudden burst of chatter over the Imperial Fists vox was loud and rapid enough to grab Prexus's attention.

Chapter Master Pugh's voice cut through the chatter. 'All forces of the Ninth, fall back to the centre! All other forces, move up to the front! The Rynn's World memorial is lost and Castellan Leucrontas has fallen. Let them be avenged!'

'You heard, sergeant,' said Borasi. 'You have your orders.'

'The Imperial Fists will shoot you on sight,' said Prexus. 'It doesn't matter if you want to join the fight or not. They will kill you as soon as they see you have left the archives.'

'They can try,' said Luko. 'Although they may decide their ammunition is better spent elsewhere.'

'Fall back!' ordered Prexus. 'Squad Makos, take the fore! Iron Knights, take the centre! Move out, Borasi. Do not follow us, Luko, or we shall see just how that close fight you spoke of turns out.'

Borasi saluted Luko as he returned to join the other Iron Knights. The Imperial Fists kept their guns trained on Luko as Prexus's force withdrew from the mess hall, the chatter over their vox-channels continuing to illustrate the collapse of Leucrontas's force and the approach of the bulk of the daemon army.

When the way was clear, Librarian Tyrendian and Sergeant Graevus emerged from the archives to join Luko.

'It's bad,' said Tyrendian. 'I can feel it. Realspace is screaming in my mind. It is Abraxes, I have no doubt about that, and banishment has given him strength through hate.'

'What now, captain?' asked Graevus.

'We have to avoid the Imperial Fists lines,' replied Luko. 'And the Howling Griffons, for that matter. We head for the memorial.'

'I wondered,' said Iktinos, 'how long you would take. You disappoint me. I had thought a reckoning would have happened long before Selaaca, that you would have seen through what I and my fellow

Chaplains have been doing, and that some other thread of fate would be needed to bring you to Kravamesh. But it is as if you were an automaton, programmed to do as Daenyathos wrote six thousand years ago.' He turned to face his opponent, the scar on his skull-faced helmet still smouldering. 'As if you were following his instructions as precisely as I.'

Sarpedon had found Iktinos in the dorsal fighter bays, three decks up from the training decks. He had followed a Space Marine's instinct, the best escape routes, the avenues of flight that allowed for the most cover and the best firing angles, and he had emerged in this cavernous place with its ranks of deep space fighter craft, to see Iktinos making his way across the seemingly endless concourse.

There were fifty metres between the two Soul Drinkers as they faced one another down a row of fighter craft. Each craft was enormous, bigger than the Thunderhawk Gunships of the Space Marines, with blunt-nosed brutal shapes that made no concession to the aerodynamics irrelevant in the void. When the *Phalanx* went to war, these were the craft that swarmed around the vast ship like hornets, but with the enemy having invaded from within they were silent and ignored.

'I have asked myself many times how we have come to this point,' said Sarpedon. He fought to keep his voice level. 'Now I would like to ask you.'

'You presume that I know,' said Iktinos. 'Daenyathos knows. We follow. That was always enough for us.'

'For you? The Chaplains?'

'Indeed. Ever since Daenyathos fell on the *Talon of Mars*, we have followed the teachings he handed down to us in secret. The rest of the Chapter, meanwhile, has followed the commands he laid out in the *Catechisms Martial*, encoded in his words so that you acted by them and yet remained ignorant of them.'

'Tell me why we are here!' snapped Sarpedon. 'And I hear the name of Abraxes in my head. I hear his pride and his lust for revenge. What has brought him to the *Phalanx*? You?'

'Daenyathos knew that one would rise from the warp at his behest. That it happens to be Abraxes is a testament to fate. He must have been lurking beneath the surface of the warp, hungry for any taste of the Soul Drinkers who bested him. Abraxes is just another pawn, Sarpedon, like you, like me.'

'There are those who have tried to use my Chapter for their own ends before,' said Sarpedon. His grip tightened on the Axe of Mercaeno. 'Do you recall, Chaplain Iktinos, what happened to them?'

Iktinos drew the haft of the Soulspear from a holster at his waist. His thumb closed over an aperture in the alien metal, a micro-laser pulsed and drew blood through the ceramite of his gauntlet. The gene-lock activated and twin blades of purest liquid black extended from either end of the haft. 'I recall it very well, Sarpedon. I recall that they were amateurs. Daenyathos factored them in, as well. Nothing has occurred that he did not foresee and plan for in advance.'

'Including your death?' said Sarpedon. He crouched down a little on his haunches, the bundles of muscles in his legs bunching ready to pounce.

'If that is what occurs,' said Iktinos, no emotion in his voice, 'then yes.'

Sarpedon circled to one side, talons clicking on the deck. He passed under the shadow cast by the nose of the closest fighter craft. Iktinos followed suit, no doubt gauging Sarpedon's stance, weighing up everything he knew about the speed and fighting skills of his one-time Chapter Master.

The air hissed as molecules passed over the Soulspear's blades and were sliced in two. The sound of distant battle reached the fighter deck as a faint rumble, a shuddering as if the *Phalanx* itself were tensing up. The blank eyes of the fighter craft cockpits seemed to stare, watching for the first move.

Iktinos moved first.

The Chaplain sprinted forwards, Soulspear held back to strike. Sarpedon ducked to one side as Iktinos covered the ground in impossibly quick time, and swung out a spinning, dizzying strike with the Soulspear. The blades of blackness flickered around Sarpedon as he twisted and dropped to avoid them. A chunk of ceramite, sliced from his shoulder pad, thudded to the deck, and a fist-sized lump of chitin from his remaining back leg was cut away.

Sarpedon kicked out and caught Iktinos's shin, He hooked the Chaplain's leg with a talon and tripped him. Iktinos rolled and came up fighting, one end of the Soulspear arcing up and the other slashing from right to left. Sarpedon, poised to slash down with the Axe of Mercaeno, had to jump back to avoid them.

'What is left, Sarpedon?' said Iktinos, the Soulspear held out in front of him like a barrier. 'What is left when every effort you have made to be free has been at the behest of another? What remains of who you are?'

'I am not a traitor,' said Sarpedon. 'That is more than you can say.'

'Treachery is meaningless,' replied Iktinos. 'There are no sides to betray. There is survival and oblivion. Everything else is a lie.'

Sarpedon leapt up onto the side of the fighter craft behind him, and launched himself from above at Iktinos. Iktinos was not ready to be attacked from above and he fell to one knee, spinning the Soulspear in a figure-eight to ward Sarpedon off. Sarpedon landed heavily, let the momentum crouch him down to the deck, and cut beneath Iktinos's guard. The Axe of Mercaeno carved through one of Iktinos's knee guards, drawing blood, but the impact was not enough to discharge

Ben Counter

Sarpedon's psychic power through the blade. Iktinos rolled away and Sarpedon charged on, Iktinos slashing this way and that, Sarpedon too quick to be hit.

But the Axe of Mercaeno was too unwieldy to get through Iktinos's guard. The Soulspear's twin blades, each a vortex field caged by some technology long-lost in the days of the Great Crusade, would slice through the axe as surely as through flesh or bone. Disarmed, Sarpedon would be as good as dead. He feinted and struck, slashed and wheeled, but Iktinos was just beyond his blade's reach.

Iktinos had known this day would come. He knew how to fight with the Soulspear – he had gone over this fight Throne knew how many times in his head.

The two passed beneath the hull of the fighter craft. Sarpedon scuttled up the landing gear and clung to the craft's underside, trusting in the novel angle of attack to keep Iktinos off-guard. Iktinos paused in his counter-attacks, Soulspear wavering, waiting for a blow from Sarpedon to parry.

'Fate has a hold of you,' said Iktinos. His voice still betrayed little emotion, as if he were a machine controlled from far away. 'If you die, Daenyathos has planned for it. If you live, he has planned for that, too. If only you understood, Sarpedon, you would kneel down and accept a quick death for the blessing it is.'

'And if only you understood, Iktinos, what it means to be Adeptus Astartes.' Sarpedon hauled himself a couple of steps sideways, Iktinos mirroring his every movement. 'The Soul Drinkers are nobody's instrument. We are not here to be wielded and used as Daenyathos or anyone else pleases. He chose the wrong puppets for his plan.'

'And yet,' replied Iktinos cooly, 'here you are, at the time and place of his choosing.'

'What I shall do to him is not something that he would choose.'

Iktinos darted forward and slashed at the landing gear. The Soulspear sliced cleanly through the steel and hydraulic lines and the craft shifted downwards, all its front-half weight suddenly unsupported. Iktinos dived out of the way and Sarpedon did the same in the opposite direction, yelling with frustration as he scrambled to avoid being crushed by the fighter's hull. The fighter thudded to the deck and rolled in Sarpedeon's direction, forcing him to back up further. Iktinos was out of sight.

'What does he want?' shouted Sarpedon. 'If his plan is already fated to succeed, then at least tell me that. For what purpose has he enslaved us?'

'For the galaxy's good,' came the reply from above. Iktinos stepped into view atop the fallen fighter craft, standing just above the cockpit. 'What is it that you have railed against for so long? The galaxy's cruelty? The Imperium's tyranny? Daenyathos saw it six thousand years before it ever occurred to you. He is not just going to batter his Chapter to pieces fighting against it. He is going to cure it.'

Sarpedon began to climb towards Iktinos, up the near-vertical curve of the fighter's hull. 'And how?' he demanded.

'What other cure is there for all mankind's ills?' said Iktinos. 'Blood and death. Pain and fear. Only through this can the path of the human race be made straight.'

Sarpedon was level with Iktinos now, the two Soul Drinkers facing one another on top of the fallen fighter craft. From here Sarpedon could see the dozens of such craft ranged along the deck, the cylindrical fuel tanks and racks of missiles standing between them. 'There is too much suffering,' said Sarpedon. 'There will be no more.'

'Not for you,' said Iktinos.

This time Sarpedon struck first, the Axe of Mercaeno flickering out too quickly for Iktinos to parry. A good blow from the Soulspear would slice the axe in two and make it useless, but Sarpedon was a fraction of a heartbeat too fast. The axe carved not into the ceramite of Iktinos's armour, but into the hull of the fighter beneath his feet. The hull's outer skin came apart under the axe's blade and Iktinos's foot was trapped. The Chaplain fell backwards, unable to arrest his fall. Sarpedon ripped the axe out of the hull and brought it down, but Iktinos forced his head out of the way just before Sarpedon bisected it. The axe was buried again in the hull, the whole head embedded in the metal.

Sarpedon pinned Iktinos's arm with one of his legs before the Chaplain could raise the Soulspear. He bent down and grabbed Iktinos by both shoulder guards, hauled him up into the air, and hurled him down off the fighter's hull with every scrap of strength he could gather.

Iktinos slammed down into the fuel tank standing beside the fighter. His impact half-flattened the cylinder of the tank and ruptured it. Thick reddish fuel spurted onto the deck.

Sudden pain flared in the leg with which Sarpedon had pinned Iktinos's arm. He looked down to see the stump of the leg, sliced so cleanly through, a scalpel could have left no neater a wound. The leg itself was sliding slowly down the curve of the fighter's hull. Iktinos had got off one last strike as he fell.

'Close, my brother,' called down Sarpedon. 'But I can live without that leg. I still have five, and that's more than I need.'

Sarpedon sprang down from the hull to the deck, just as Iktinos was extricating himself from the wreckage of the fuel tank. Fuel glistened all over him. 'Your fate is decided,' he said. 'What happens here means nothing. Nothing.'

'You betrayed us and you will die for it,' replied Sarpedon. 'That means enough for me.'

Sarpedon raised the Axe of Mercaeno and ran its blade along one of the stubby control surfaces of the fighter. The razor-sharp metal drew sparks, which fell white-hot into the rivulets of fuel creeping towards him from the ruptured fuel tank. The fuel caught light and flame rushed towards Iktinos.

The fuel tank bloomed in a tremendous billowing of blue-white flame. Sarpedon ducked behind the fighter to shield himself from the blast of heat. He caught a glimpse of Iktinos disappearing in the flame, the Chaplain's form seeming to dissolve in the heart of the fire.

The sound was a terrible roar, and the fighter shifted on the deck, pushing against Sarpedon as he crouched. The wave of heat hit and Sarpedon felt the chitin of his remaining legs blistering in it, the paint of his armour bubbling, the side of his unprotected face scalding.

The noise died down, replaced with the guttering of flame. Haphazard shadows were cast against the walls and ceiling of the hangar deck by the fire as it continued to burn. Sarpedon limped out from behind the fighter, his balance uncertain as he adjusted to moving with one fewer leg.

Iktinos, on fire from head to toe, dived out of the flaming wreckage. He crashed into Sarpedon who was unprepared, and fell to the deck under Iktinos's weight. Flames licked at his face as he stared for a moment into the skull-mask of the Chaplain's helm, like the face of one of the Imperial Creed's many damned, leering up from a lake of fire.

CHAPTER TWELVE

The daemonic horde hit the Imperial Fists line in a tide of flesh.

It broke against barricades and makeshift bunkers, concentrated bolter fire chewing through the daemons as quickly as they could advance.

In other places it swept through in a flood, swamping Imperial Fists in a mass of limbs and bodies. Some defences were denuded by pink and azure flame, blasted from the orifices of misshapen creatures dragged along on the tide of Abraxes's own incandescent daemons. Others were outflanked by lightning-fast monsters with purplish skin and lashing tongues that swept around firepoints to strike from behind. A massive red-winged daemon, axe in one hand and lash in the other, strode at the head of its bloodletters and with vicious strike cleaved one of the tanks brought up from the *Phalanx*'s hangars in two, spilling flaming promethium around its feet.

The Imperial Fists line bent under the weight of the assault, Space Marines vaulting their barriers to take up new positions closer to the Tactica before they were overrun. Bolter fire competed with the shrieking of daemons in the din of the battle. The whole deck seemed to bow and buckle under the weight of it, as the monastic cells and chapels of the Imperial Fists disappeared under the flood of Abraxes's assault.

At the heart of the line, Chapter Master Pugh stood with the Fangs of Dorn in his hands. One of the Librarium novices stood before him, holding up a huge tome normally bound closed by chains and psychic seals. It contained prayers of purity and strength of mind, of which a commander had to be mindful when facing the corruptive forces of Chaos. Ahead of him, Lysander marshalled the strongest defences, a handful of tanks and several squads of Imperial Fists along with Kolgo's Battle Sisters, holding position as the daemon army grew closer with every moment.

'What manner of foe is Chaos?' mused Pugh. Beside him stood Lord Inquisitor Kolgo, ready for battle with a power fist encasing one hand and a rotator cannon on the other, each weapon engraved with prayers and wards of destruction.

'Better men than I have gone mad seeking the answer to that question,' replied Kolgo. 'The question of Chaos cannot be answered.'

'And yet we must seek an answer,' said Pugh. 'For we must fight it. In ignorance, we fight as if in the dark.'

'Better that than be corrupted by what we see,' said Kolgo. He flexed the mechanical fingers of his power fist, and they crackled as the power field sprung into life around them.

'I trust in the strength of my soul, inquisitor,' said Pugh. Ahead, Imperial Fists were scrambling into cover beside the second line as the daemons galloped and shambled closer, multicoloured flames dancing over the battlefield. The pale, lithe shape of Abraxes himself was just visible in the rear ranks, watching and controlling his battle, using up the lesser daemons under his command to buy his victory one death at a time. 'I shall not become one with the enemy by understanding it. The more I learn of Chaos, the more I hate it, and the fiercer I fight.'

'Overestimating one's resolve is a more dangerous form of ignorance than fighting in the dark.' Kolgo span the barrels of his rotator cannon, jewel-encrusted hammers clicking down on gilded chambers.

'Then let us put our theories into practice,' said Pugh.

'I concur,' said Kolgo. 'Shall we?'

'Brothers!' yelled Pugh over the vox. 'To the fore, my brothers, with me! Through hell and to victory, onwards!'

At Pugh's words, the Imperial Fists broke cover and charged. The reserve force holding the Tactica ran from behind its map tables and the shelter of its archways. The Space Marines crouched behind their defences, muttered their prayers and leapt over the defences, bolters blazing and chainblades whirring. Pugh led the counter-attack right into the face of the enemy.

The twin blades of the Fangs of Dorn were not made for an elegant battle. They were not weapons for duelling or weaving a dance of feint and deception. They were made for this brutal and ugly fight, the press of bodies and the triumph of strength and resolve over skill, where they could rise and fall with every stab piercing a belly or driving up into a throat.

Pugh slew a dozen daemons in those first few seconds, and Abraxes's horrors fell before him, opening up a gap in the daemonic lines. Imperial Fists charged in behind him and exploited the gap, forging in further.

Kolgo stood atop a rampart and hammered volley after volley from his rotator cannon into the host. The Battle Sisters formed up around him, Sister Aescarion directing their fire with a gesture of her power axe. A pair of Predator tanks rumbled up from either side of the Tactica, each roar of an autocannon echoed by an explosion of flame and torn daemonflesh deep within Abraxes's lines.

Without warning the horrors seemed to melt away, dissolving into the rear ranks at a mental command from Abraxes. In the few seconds of respite, the Imperial Fists saw ranks of bloodletters marching out to replace them. In their centre was a greater daemon of the Blood God, allied to Abraxes's cause by the raw slaughter that battle on the *Phalanx* promised. It stepped over the front rows of bloodletters and a massive cloven hoof slammed down among the Imperial Fists, crushing a battle-brother under its immense weight.

'Onwards! Onwards! The warp fears us so, to place such horrors in our way!' Pugh's voice, even amplified over the vox, was barely audible over the foul, shuddering gale of the greater daemon's roar. Pugh hacked through the first couple of bloodletters to reach him as he jumped up onto the half-fallen wall of a chapel, tumbled and scorched in the first assault, that brought him up above the level of the swirling combat around him.

The greater daemon turned its shaggy, bestial head towards Pugh. Imperial Fists were hacking their way through the advancing bloodletters to form up around their Chapter Master, but the greater daemon could simply step over the melee, and in moments its shadow passed over Pugh.

The Imperial Fist held the Fangs of Dorn out wide, presenting himself as a target to the greater daemon, taunting it with his refusal to flee from the monstrosity.

'You dare walk into my domain, and shed the blood of my brothers?' yelled Pugh. 'Who do you think you face here? What victory do you think you can win? All the fury of the warp will falter against the soul of one good Space Marine!'

The greater daemon bellowed and raised its axe, already slick with Adeptus Astartes blood. The axe arced down and Pugh jumped to the side, the blade cleaving down through the ruined chapel. Pugh stabbed both the Fangs of Dorn through the greater daemon's wrist and ripped them out again, snapping tendons and tearing muscle. The greater daemon pulled its arm back and howled in anger, following up its axe blow with a strike from its whip.

The whip moved too fast for even Pugh to avoid. Its barbs lashed around his leg and the daemon yanked him off his feet, into the air, and cast him down to the ground in the heart of the bloodletters.

The Soulspear was still in Iktinos's hand. Its glowing black blade was being forced up under Sarpedon's chin, towards his throat, to slice his head off. Sarpedon grabbed Iktinos's wrist and fought the Chaplain, but death had unlocked some new fortitude in Iktinos and in that moment the two were matched in strength.

Sarpedon could feel the skin on his face burning. Pain meant something different to a Space Marine compared to a normal man, but it was still pain and Sarpedon struggled as much to avoid blacking out as he did against Iktinos.

The Axe of Mercaeno was trapped under Iktinos. Sarpedon tried to wrench it free, but Iktinos would not relent. He tried to roll over so Iktinos would be trapped beneath, but the Chaplain would not budge, as if he was anchored to the deck.

'You obey,' hissed Sarpedon. 'Obedience only comes from one place.' He saw his own features reflected in the eyepieces of Iktinos's mask, the blistering wounds creeping up his face. 'It comes from fear.'

Sarpedon let go of the axe and reached up to place his hand on the back of Iktinos's head. He found a grip and tore the Chaplain's helmet away.

Iktinos's face was charred and twisted by the heat. The bubbling skin was stretched tight over the skull, the eyes buried in scorched pits, the scalp coming apart. There was no dimming in the hate on Iktinos's features. The pain made it stronger. There was almost no resemblance to the face that Sarpedon knew, none of the Chaplain's calm and resolve, just the intensity of his hatred.

'I know what you fear,' said Sarpedon. His hand clamped to the back of Iktinos's burning skull, and he unleashed the full force of the Hell into the traitor's mind.

The pain helped. Normally Sarpedon unleashed the Hell out wide, capturing as many of the enemy as possible in its hallucinations. This time he focused it until it was a white-hot psychic spear, thrust into Iktinos's mind like a hypodermic needle loaded with everything the Chaplain feared.

He feared Daenyathos. Fear, in some deep and unrecognisable form, was the only thing that could force a Space Marine to obey with such unthinking, unquestioning ferocity. Everything that Sarpedon knew about the Philosopher-Soldier was forced into the point of fire and turned into something appalling.

Like a god of the warp itself, the form of Daenyathos loomed in front of Iktinos's mind's eye. Daenyathos appeared as he had in illuminated manuscripts of his *Catechisms Martial*, but vast in size and infinitely more terrible. Around his legs rushed a torrent of broken bodies, all the Soul Drinkers whose lives he had spent following his monstrous plan. His armour was inscribed with exhortations to death and torture, words of the *Catechisms Martial* twisted and devolved. Thousands of innocents were crucified against the armour of his greaves. His chest and shoulder guards were covered with the forms of the betrayed, sunk into the armour as if half-digested. The heroes of the old Chapter – Captain Caeon, Chapter Master Gorgoleon and the victims of the First Chapter War, manipulated into conflict to satisfy Daenyathos's desire for a Chapter at odds with the Imperium. The dead of Sarpedon's Chapter, from Givrillian to Scamander, Captain Karraidin, Sarpedon's dearest friend Techmarine Lygris and all the others who had fallen.

Around the collar of Daneyathos's armour were clustered his allies in treachery. The cruellest of inquisitors who had forced the Soul Drinkers into the extremes of exile. Aliens despatched by Sarpedon and his brethren, as Daenyathos watched on, satisfied that they had played their part – the necron creature who had almost killed Sarpedon on Selaaca, the renegade eldar lord of Gravehnhold, the ork warlord of Nevermourn, all gathered in celebration.

Alongside them were the very worst of his allies. The followers of the Dark Gods – Abraxes, Ve'Meth, a host of Traitor Marines and daemons. The mutant Teturact and his legion of the dead. And Daenyathos himself, his face lit by the fires of wrath itself, laughing with the agents of betrayal of whose wickedness he had been the architect.

Daenyathos looked down at Iktinos, pinned squirming below him like something trapped in a microscope slide. The vastness of his displeasure, mixed with a terrible knowing mockery, hammered into Iktinos's mind as fiercely as any weapon that Sarpedon could have wielded.

Iktinos screamed. In his mind, the sound was lost among the laughter of Daenyathos, who revelled in seeing one of his most self-important pawns being forced to understand his own insignificance. In reality, the sound was so completely unlike anything a warrior of the Adeptus Astartes should ever utter that Iktinos ceased to be a Space Marine in that moment.

The Chaplain's grip relaxed. Sarpedon threw him off and rolled out of the flames. He stood over the prostrate Iktinos.

Iktinos's mind had utterly shattered. Sarpedon's psychic senses were not sharp, but even he could feel it, a growing void where once the Chaplain's soul had been, into which were tumbling the fragments of his broken personality.

'I own you now,' said Sarpedon. 'I am the one you obey. Tell me everything.'

* * *

The faces of the daemons crowded round, twisted and jeering, the solid mass of their features broken by the black iron blades that cut down to finish off Chapter Master Pugh.

The Fangs of Dorn were just suited to fighting this close, where they parried and stabbed as if moving in Pugh's hand by some will of their own. Perhaps Dorn himself wielded them in those moments, reaching from the Emperor's side to lend his own skill to Pugh's struggle to survive.

It would not be enough. There were too many of them, every one eager to be the one who carried the skull of a Chapter Master back to the warp, to throw it at the foot of the Blood God's throne.

Pugh stabbed up into a daemon's ribcage even as he turned another blade away from his hearts, and prepared to die.

A streak of orange flame burned across his vision, swathing the contorted face in fire. He was aware of glossy black armour embellished in red, and the blade of a power axe shimmering as it cut in every direction. Hands grabbed him and dragged him out of the mass. Pugh looked up and saw the unfamiliar face of a woman above him, streaked with blood and grime, teeth gritted.

'Not while we live,' she hissed through her teeth, 'shall they take such a prize.'

She hauled Pugh to his feet. He recognised Sister Aescarion, the Superior of Lord Inquisitor Kolgo's retinue. The jump pack she wore on her back smouldered, its exhaust vanes glowing a dull red, and the path she had carved through the daemons as she dived into the throng after Pugh was closing as the bloodletters fought to swamp him again.

'My thanks, Sister,' said Pugh as he found his footing.

'Through me, the Emperor works,' she replied.

The two stood back to back as the bloodletters closed. Now Pugh could let the Fangs of Dorn do their finest work, stabbing so rapidly up into the advancing daemon ranks that every moment another of them fell, ribcage split open or burning entrails spilling from a ruptured abdomen. Aescarion fought with her axe in one hand and a pistol in the other, quickly rattling off the pistol's magazine and then taking the axe in both hands.

A Sister of Battle could not match a Space Marine's sheer strength and skill. Few unaugmented humans could approach a veteran Superior's ability, but even so she was just that – human, without the extra organs and enhanced physiology of the Adeptus Astartes. But what she lacked in their physical superiority, she made up with in faith.

It was not a Space Marine's mental fortitude that Pugh witnessed in Aescarion. A Space Marine was a master of his fear, his mind so strong he could face even the daemons of the warp and remain sane. Aescarion was different. It was not conditioning and strength of duty, raw bloody-mindedness, that fuelled her. It was faith. She believed so com-pletely in the Emperor's hand guiding her, in the place she had in His plan, that it was as plain to her as the enemy closing in around her. She did not fear them, because in her mind she was not a human being with human frailties. She was a hollow vessel that existed to be filled up with the will of the Emperor and used as He willed it. There could be no fear, when whatever end befell not her, but the Emperor.

Pugh led the way back towards the Imperial Fists lines, opening up a path as the Fangs of Dorn flashed as quickly and deadly as the teeth of a giant chainblade. He had to force his legs out of the sucking mire of gore and entrails around his feet. Aescarion's axe gave her reach and she swung it in great arcs as she followed, smashing falling blades aside and keeping a good sword's length between her and the bloodletters.

The mass parted and Aescarion's Battle Sisters crowded forwards, flanking Pugh and battering the daemons back with bolter fire. The Chapter Master could see Lysander atop a barricade, swatting aside one of the horrors with his shield and pointing with his hammer to direct the heavy weapons set up around the Tactica. Everywhere he looked, there was carnage. Here, the Imperial Fists launched forwards in a coun-ter-attack; there, the line broke and leaping horrors or galloping fiends poured through the lines like air bursting from a hull breach.

Pugh made it over the altar of a shrine, used as the lynchpin of a bar-ricade of chapel pews and statues. Inquisitor Kolgo was standing in the chapel, its columns fallen and its nave strewn with the bodies of dae-mons and Space Marines. With a moment to breathe at last, he turned to help drag the Battle Sisters following him over the altar into shelter. Aescarion leapt over the barricade on the exhausts of her jump pack, the gauntlets of her power armour smoking with daemon blood up to the elbow. Battle Sisters and Imperial Fists manned the barricade, pouring bolter fire into the bloodletters trying to follow.

'Did it work?' said Pugh, catching his breath. 'Is it fallen?'

By way of answer, Kolgo simply pointed towards the ruin where Pugh had made his stand against the greater daemon.

The winged daemon was slumped against the wall, its wings in bloody tatters and its armour torn. Another volley of heavy fire slammed into it, punching through its corded red muscles. One of its wings was sheared through and fell broken, tattered skin fluttering like the canvas of a ruined sail. Pugh had brought the daemon into the open, forced it to stand proud of the daemonic host while it fought him. He had bought his heavy weapons the time they needed to draw a bead on the target and spear it on a lance of concentrated fire.

The greater daemon was taking its time to die. Heavy bolter fire rip-pled up and down it. The daemon dropped its lash and tried to force itself back to its feet, leaning on the ruined wall for support. A lascannon blast caught it in the chest and bored right through it, revealing its gory ribs and pulsing organs. The daemon roared, blood spattering from its lips, and toppled over into the horde.

The Imperial Fists cheered as the daemon died. Lysander led them, raising his hammer high as if taunting the daemons to respond.

The sound was drowned out by the laughter that rumbled through the *Phalanx*. It was the laughter of Abraxes, observing the slaughter from the rear ranks. The object of his amusement lumbered into view on the Imperial Fists flank – a greater daemon of the Plague God, the enormous bloated horror that had killed Leucrontas and broken the force holding the Rynn's World memorial. The daemon's laughter joined Abraxes's own as it was herded forwards by its attendant daemons, and it clapped its flabby hands in glee at the prospect of new playthings.

'Can we kill another one, Chapter Master?' voxed Kolgo.

'It is not a question of whether we can or not,' replied Pugh. 'We will do so or we will be lost.'

'Behold this icon of sin!' shouted Aescarion to her Battle Sisters. 'Witness the corruption it wears! In the face of this evil, let our bullets be our prayers!'

The expression on the greater daemon's face changed. Its enormous mouth downturned and it frowned, its eyes widening in surprise, a caricature of dismay and shock. Tiny explosions studded the rubbery surface of its flesh, not from the direction of the Imperial Fists centre, but from behind it.

Pugh jumped onto a fallen pillar to get a better view. He glimpsed the flash of a power weapon – power claws, slashing through the plague-bearers, illuminating the edges of purple armour.

'It's the Soul Drinkers!' came a vox from the nearest Imperial Fists unit.

Pugh recognised Captain Luko now, followed by what remained of the Soul Drinkers Chapter. A bolt of lightning arced from the ceiling, earthing through the daemon, burning away masses of charred flesh – Tyrendian, the Soul Drinkers Librarian, marshalled the lightning like a conductor with an orchestra as the other Soul Drinkers ran into the fight around him.

Pugh paused for a second. The Soul Drinkers were the enemies of the Imperial Fists, rebels and traitors. But the daemons they both fought were a fouler enemy even than the renegade. The legions of the warp were the worst of the worst.

'All units of the Fifth,' ordered Pugh. 'Join the Soul Drinkers and counter to our flank! Third and Ninth, hold the centre!'

The Predator tanks emerged from the barracks they were using for shelter and rumbled towards the growing battle on the flank. Imperial Fists units broke from their positions and followed them. Pugh watched

as the Fifth Company and the Soul Drinkers caught the plague daemon's force from both sides.

'Dorn forgive me,' said Pugh to himself.

Captain Luko looked into the eyes of the daemon, and he saw there
everything that mankind had learned to fear.

Something in those unholy eyes had tormented the sons of Earth ever
since creatures first crawled out from beneath the mud. Humans had
told tales of it, had seen it in their nightmares, before their species had
finished evolving. It was the force that inspired the weak flesh to corrupt
and rot away, the purest of fears, of death and pain and the unknown
wrapped up into one faceless, malevolent will.

Since there had been intelligent minds to contemplate it, the Plague
God had existed, turning vulnerable minds to corruption and evil
through the fear of what it could do to their flesh. But now there were
no vulnerable minds for it to exploit, no kernels of doubt that could
grow into desperation and surrender. A Space Marine did not have that
weakness. Now, this avatar of the Plague God had to fight.

The plaguebearers that attended the greater daemon were caught
by surprise by the Soul Drinkers, who charged from the warren of the
catacombs without warning. The daemons did not scatter or run as
mundane troops might, but they did not have enough numbers in the
right place and the Soul Drinkers had destroyed dozens of them in the
first seconds. Luko had taken a worthy toll with his claws and bolter
fire had done for the rest. Now Luko was face to face with the greater
daemon, its burning and blood-covered form quivering with rage and
pain, and everything they had earned in those moments would be lost
if he faltered now.

'I have killed your kind before!' yelled Luko, knowing the daemon
could hear him even through the battle's din. 'But you have never killed
anything like me!'

The daemon snatched up one of the chains its followers had used to
drag it. It raised the chain over its head and brought it down like a whip,
the links of the chain slamming into the deck. Luko threw himself out
of the way, the floor beneath him buckling under the impact.

Plaguebearers following the greater daemon shambled to its side. A
dozen of them carried between them an enormous sword of oozing
black steel, its pitted blade edged with bloody fangs that looked like
they had just been torn from some huge beast's jaw. The greater daemon
bent down and took up the sword in its other hand, and the pits in the
metal formed mouths that screamed and howled. Luko saw the souls
bound into the blade, pitiful souls who had pledged themselves to the
daemon in ignorance or desperation.

The daemon raised the blade over its head, point down aimed at

Luko. Luko got to his feet and slashed at the plaguebearers who tried to
hem him in, the shadow of the blade falling over him as he realised he
could not get out of its way.

A bolt of blue-white light hit the sword and the whole weapon lit
up, power coursing through it. The daemon bellowed as the flesh of its
hand burned off, falling in charred flakes. Its fingers, stripped to bloody
bone, let go of the sword and it fell to the deck with a tremendous clang.

Behind Luko, Librarian Tyrendian leapt from the Soul Drinkers ranks.
Lightning leapt from his fingers and played around Luko, burning away
the plaguebearers who tried to close with him. A bolt struck the greater
daemon, earthing in blue-white crackles of power through its skin and
leaving crazed burn patterns across its bulk.

Luko leapt over the fallen sword and punched forwards with a claw,
spearing through the back of the daemon's ruined hand. The daemon
yanked the hand away and lashed at Luko with the chain again, as if
it had been bitten by a troublesome insect and was trying to swat it
before it could bite again. The chain whipped into Luko at chest height
and threw him back into a pack of plaguebearers. Luko slashed in every
direction, hoping that each wild strike would catch one of the diseased
daemons closing on him.

'Brother!' yelled Tyrendian. 'Fall back! We cannot lose you!'

Luko flung the last plaguebearer off himself and rounded on the
greater daemon again. Too late, he saw the daemon had loped a massive stride closer, the mass of its belly like a solid wall of flesh bearing
down on him. Luko turned and tried to run but the daemon moved
faster than its bulk should have allowed, hauling its weight off the floor
on its stumpy back leg and stamping down next to Luko, bringing its
weight down onto the Soul Drinker.

Luko crashed to the deck, his lower half pinned under the weight of
the daemon. The foul, oozing mass of muscle and flab was crushing
down on him with so much weight, Luko could feel the ceramite of his
leg armour distorting under the pressure.

Luko twisted around as best he could, lightning claws held in front
of him in the best guard he could manage. The greater daemon's face
loomed past the curve of its belly, and it was smiling. Luko could feel
the deep rumble of its laughter as it saw its prey trapped beneath it.

'Here!' yelled Tyrendian. 'Here! You want to eat?' Tyrendian put his
hands together, as if in prayer, and thrust them forwards, a twisting
bolt of electricity lancing into the greater daemon's shoulder. It bored
through the flesh, charred layers flaking away to the bone.

Tyrendian was walking forwards, every step flinging lightning into the
greater daemon. He passed into its shadow, his face edged in hard white
and blue by the power playing around his hands.

'Tyrendian! No!' shouted Luko, but Tyrendian did not back off. As the daemon's gaze fell onto him he stood his ground, casting another lightning bolt up at the daemon's face.

The greater daemon dropped the chain, and reached a massive flabby hand over Tyrendian. Tyrendian did not move. Tyrendian had never picked up a scar in battle - never, it had always seemed, even been afflicted by the patina of grime and blood that covered every soldier. He always appeared perfect, less a soldier and more a sculpture, a painting, of what a Space Marine should be. Framed by the battling plaguebearers and borne down upon by the greater daemon, there could be no more powerful symbol of purity facing the very embodiment of corruption.

The daemon's hand closed on Tyrendian. Tyrendian gritted his teeth as the daemon lifted him off his feet, and the air thrummed with the power gathering around his hands. Crackles of it arced into the deck or into the daemon's hand, but it did not seem to feel them. It licked its lips and its mouth yawned wide, showing the multiple rows of teeth that led down to the churning acidic pit of its stomach.

'No!' yelled Luko, his words almost lost by the force with which he shouted them. 'Tyrendian, My brother. Do not do this, not for me. My brother, no!'

The greater daemon flung Tyrendian into the air, and the Soul Drinker disappeared into its mouth.

Luko screamed in anger, as if by doing so he could force the grief down and bury it.

The daemon laughed. So pleased was it by its kill, that it did not notice for a few seconds the blue glow growing in the centre of its belly.

Luko rolled back onto his front and covered himself with his lightning claws. He saw plaguebearers approaching to butcher him, or perhaps hack his legs off to free the rest of him so he could be fed to their lord. He had never seen anything so hateful as their one-eyed, horned faces split with rotten grins, gleeful at their master's kill and the prospect of feeding him another Soul Drinker.

The rising hum from inside the greater daemon told Luko he had only moments left. That was all the plaguebearers needed to get to him.

'Come closer,' he shouted at them. 'Let us become acquainted, my friends. Let me show you an Adeptus Astartes welcome.'

The hum turned to a whine. The greater daemon noticed it now. It groaned, and placed its hand to its belly, face turning sour and pained. It roared, and the terrible gale of it drowned out Luko's voice as he yelled obscenities at the plaguebearers.

The daemon's belly swelled suddenly, like a balloon inflating. The daemon's eyes widened in surprise. It was the last expression on its hateful face – surprise and dismay.

The daemon's belly exploded in the tremendous burst of blue-white power. Luko was slammed into the floor with the force of it. The plaguebearers were thrown backwards, battered by the wall of force that hit them. A great cloud of torn and burning entrails showered down, covering Soul Drinker and daemon alike. Lightning arced in every direction from the shattered body of the greater daemon, ripping into the plaguebearers surrounding it, lashing across the ceiling, boring through the floor.

In the old Chapter, some had speculated on just how much power Tyrendian could gather. If collateral damage and his own survival were no issue, it was guessed by the Librarium that their bioelectric weapon could detonate himself with massive force, as great a force of raw destruction as a whole artillery strike. They had never been sure, and never sought to find out, for Tyrendian was too valuable a weapon of war to risk him finding out how much power he could concentrate within himself.

Now, the question had been answered. Tyrendian could gather inside himself enough electric power to destroy a greater daemon of the warp. He had detonated inside the daemon's belly with such force that all that remained, tottering above Luko, was a thick and gristly spine on which was still mounted the ragged remnants of the greater daemon's skull. The shattered stumps of its ribs and a single shoulder blade, clinging by tattered tendons, alone suggested the bulk of its chest. Green-black brains spilled from the back of its ruptured skull, and across the front of it was stretched the daemon's face, still wearing that expression of surprise.

The daemon toppled backwards, the ruin of its upper body slapping to the deck. The weight on Luko relaxed and he dug a claw into the deck in front of him, dragging himself out from under the daemon. He looked back and saw that only the lower portion of its once-vast belly remained, its legs connected only by skin, the many layers of entrails and organs now just a charred crater.

The plaguebearers nearby had been blasted back off their feet. Many had been burst apart by the lightning unleashed by Tyrendian's detonation. The whole deck surrounding the daemon's corpse was buckled and burned. Luko's own armour was charred and bent out of shape, giving him only just enough free movement to walk away from the destruction towards the Soul Drinkers lines.

Luko's ears rang, and the sound of gunfire barely registered through the white noise filling his head. He looked around, dazed, trying to blink away the fog that seemed to smother his mind. There was no sign of Tyrendian. Quite probably he had been vaporised by the force of the power he had unleashed. There would be nothing to bury.

Sergeant Graevus ran forwards and grabbed Luko, dragging him away from the reforming plaguebearers and thrusting him behind a fallen pillar for cover.

· Yellow-armoured figures came into view, approaching from the direction of the Imperial Fists centre. Without the greater daemon to anchor them, the plaguebearers wheeled in confusion, running in ones and twos into the bolter fire of the Imperial Fists, cut down and shredded into masses of stringy gore.

Graevus held his power axe high and yelled an order that Luko couldn't quite make out through the ringing. The Soul Drinkers vaulted from cover and advanced, bolters firing, even as the Imperial Fists did the same. Caught in a crossfire, leaderless, the plaguebearers seemed to dissolve under the weight of fire, as if in a downpour of acid.

Luko's senses returned to him as the whole flank of the daemon army collapsed, the servants of the Plague God ripped to shreds by the combined fire of the Soul Drinkers and the Imperial Fists.

The two Adeptus Astartes forces met as the last of the plaguebearers were being picked off by bolter fire. Luko found himself looking into the face of Captain Lysander.

'At last, we meet as brothers,' said Lysander.

'Thank the Emperor for mutual foes,' replied Luko without humour.

'Pugh has requested that we fight now as one. Will you take your place in the line?'

'We will, captain,' said Luko. 'There are but few of us, and one of our best was lost killing that beast. But whatever fight we can offer, the enemies of the warp will have it.'

Lysander shouldered his power hammer, and held out a hand. Luko slid his own hand out of his lightning claw gauntlet, and shook it.

'They're falling back,' came Pugh's voice over Lysander's vox. 'But in order. All units, withdraw to the centre and the Forge and hold positions.'

'Abraxes would not abandon the fight,' said Lysander, 'even with their flank collapsed.'

Luko watched as the last few plaguebearers fled through the ruins of barracks and shrines, as if responding to a mental command to give up the fight. They were cut down by bolter fire, sharpshooters snapping bolts into them as they ran. 'He has a plan,' said Luko. 'His kind always do.'

'What are they doing?' asked Kolgo.

Sister Aescarion, crouched among the ruins of the front line's barricades, watched through her magnoculars a moment longer.

'They are building something,' she said.

The daemons had retreated a little under an hour before, but not all the way back to the cargo holds. Instead they had formed their own lines a kilometre away, almost the whole width of the deck. They had cut power to as many of the local systems as they could, resulting in the

overhead lights failing and casting darkness across the battlefield as if
night had fallen. Fires twinkled among the daemons' positions, illuminating hulking shapes of iron with designs that could only be guessed
at in the gloom.

'Building what?' said Kolgo.

Aescarion handed him the magnoculars. 'War machines,' said Aescarion. 'At a guess. It is impossible to tell.'

Kolgo focused the magnoculars for himself. Daemons danced around
their fires and tattered banners stood, fluttering in the updrafts, casting
flickering shadows on the engines they were building. 'Building them
from what?'

'Perhaps they are bringing parts through from the warp,' said
Aescarion.

The Imperial Fists had rebuilt what defences they could and were now
holding their makeshift line again, watchmen posted at intervals to
watch for any developments among the enemy. The Space Marine losses
had been tallied, and they were heavy. Leucrontas's command had
almost been wiped out; only a couple of dozen stragglers now joining
the centre. Most other Imperial Fists units were little over half-strength.
Borganor's Howling Griffons, in the Forge of Ages, had fended off skirmishing forces that tested their strength, and were mostly intact save
for a few felled by shrieking, flying things that swooped down among
them, decapitating and severing with their snapping jaws. The Imperial
Fists now holding the line in front of the Tactica were crouched, much
as Aescarion was, scanning the daemon lines for the first signs of an
assault. The sound of metal on metal drifted across, along with strains
of a grim atonal singing.

'Come,' said Kolgo. 'Pugh has called a council of war. We shall not
have to settle for sitting and watching for much longer.'

Aescarion followed the inquisitor through the darkness. On every side
were Space Marines who had suffered wounds in the battle but returned
to the fray. Many were missing hands or limbs, or had segments of their
armour removed to allow for a wound to be cast or splinted.

The most severely wounded were laid out in the Tactica itself, on
or around the map tables. Apothecaries worked on chest and head
wounds, with healthy brothers rotated in to serve as blood donors for
transfusions. As Aescarion and Kolgo entered, another Imperial Fist was
lifted off a map table by two of his battle-brothers and carried towards
the archways leading to the building's rear, where the dead were being
piled up. A lectern-servitor with a scratching autoquill was keeping a
tally of the dead in a ledger.

Officers were gathered around one of the central tables, which represented the canyon walls and xenos settlement of some ancient battle.
Pugh was there, along with Lysander, Borganor and Librarian Varnica of

the Doom Eagles. With them stood Captain Luko and Sergeant Graevus of the Soul Drinkers.

Aescarion stood apart as Kolgo joined them.

'Lord inquisitor,' said Pugh. 'Now we are all present. I shall dispense with any formalities as time is not on our side. We must decide our next course of action, and do it now.'

'Attack,' said Borganor. 'I cannot say why Abraxes withdrew his army, for it is unlike the daemons' manner of war, but it is certain that we shall not get any such respite from them again. We must lead a counter-offensive as soon as we can, before they finish whatever infernal contraptions they are building. Therein lies the only chance of defeating them.'

'I agree, Chapter Master,' said Lysander. 'We have borne the brunt of their assault with greater fortitude than Abraxes expected. They regroup and perhaps reinforce as we speak. Attack them and destroy them. It is the only way.'

'They outnumber us,' countered Librarian Varnica. 'A full assault will result in defeat for us, every tactical calculation points towards it.'

'Then what would you have us do?' said Borganor. 'Wait for Dorn's own return? For Roboute Guilliman to appear amongst us?'

'Attacking would make the most of what advantages we have,' said Luko. 'We are at our best up close, charging into the face of the enemy.'

'So are daemons,' said Graevus.

'True,' said Luko. 'Very true.'

'There must be other ways,' said Varnica. 'We fall back to a smaller, more defensible part of the *Phalanx* and force them to attack on a narrow frontage. Lure them in and kill them piece by piece.'

'That would give them the run of the *Phalanx*,' said Pugh. 'Abraxes would do with this craft as he wished. His daemons could surround us and perhaps render the whole section uninhabitable by introducing hard vacuum or radiation. With Abraxes in charge they certainly would.'

'The question is,' said Varnica, 'does such a scenario promise our deaths with more or less certainty than walking across the barracks deck and into their arms?'

'So,' said Pugh. 'We give Abraxes my army or we give him my ship. Any other suggestions?'

'There is one,' said a newcomer's voice. The officers turned to see Apothecary Pallas. He was attending to one of the wounded nearby, using a cautery iron to sear shut the stump of an Imperial Fist's severed left arm.

'Pallas,' said Luko. 'I had not realised you lived. I did not think I would speak with you again.'

'Chapter Master,' said Pallas, continuing to work on the wounded warrior. 'What was to be our manner of execution?'

'We have not the time to waste listening to this renegade,' said Borganor.

'Execution by gunshot,' said Pugh, ignoring Borganor. 'Then incineration.'

'On the Path of the Lost?'

Pugh folded his arms and stepped back a pace, as if some revelation was growing in his mind. 'Yes,' he replied. 'You were to walk the Path.'

'It is traditional,' continued Pallas, 'that the condemned among the sons of Dorn be forced to walk the Path of the Lost. It runs from the Pardoner's Court, just a few hundred metres from this very building, and across the width of the *Phalanx* along the ventral hull. It emerges near the cargo holds, where our incinerated remains could be ejected from the ship. Is this not correct?'

'It is,' replied Pugh. 'You know much of this tradition.'

'I read of the ways in which we would die after I refused to join my brothers in their breakout,' said Pallas. 'It seemed appropriate for me to do so, that I might counsel my brothers when the time for execution came.'

'And what,' said Borganor, 'is your point?'

'My point is that Abraxes has at his command more than a mere army,' said Pallas. The cautery iron had finished its work in closing the wound and Pallas now wrapped the wound in gauze as he spoke. 'He brought his army onto the *Phalanx* somehow, and he brings components for his war machines and no doubt reinforcements for his troops. He has a warp gate, a way into the immaterium, and it is stable and open. Only this explains his capacity to attack the *Phalanx* at all.'

'And the Path of the Lost,' said Luko, 'leads from here to the region of the warp gate.'

'Among the dorsal cargo holds,' said Pallas. 'A sizeable force could not make it through the Path, certainly not without alerting Abraxes to divert his forces to defending the portal. The majority of the force must stay here to face his army and keep it fighting. A smaller force, a handful strong, takes the Path of the Lost and strikes out for the warp gate's location. As long as Abraxes possesses a gate through the warp any attempt to defeat him here is futile, for he will just bring more legions through until we are exhausted.'

'Insanity,' said Borganor.

'Captain Borganor,' said Pugh. 'I have no doubt that your hatred for the Soul Drinkers is well deserved, for they have done your Chapter much wrong. But what Pallas says has merit. It does not matter if we shatter Abraxes's army, he still has a means to conjure a new one from the warp. Remove that, and we buy ourselves a thread that leads to victory.'

'You are not seriously considering this?' said Borganor.

'I will go,' said Luko. 'The Soul Drinkers have suffered at the hands of Abraxes before. If we are to die on the *Phalanx*, then let it be in seeking revenge against him.'

'And none but the Soul Drinkers have faced Abraxes before at all,' added Graevus.

'You will need a Librarian,' said Varnica. 'And since they are in such short supply, I had better go with you.'

'Varnica?' said Borganor. 'You were among the first to condemn the Soul Drinkers!'

'And if you are correct in your mistrust, I will be among the last to be betrayed by them,' said Varnica. 'But the Chapter Master is right. There is no other way. Thin as the thread is, unwholesome as the Soul Drinkers reputation might be, I must follow that thread for it is all we have.'

'And I,' said Sister Aescarion, stepping forwards. 'The Inquisition must have a presence. My lord inquisitor is most valuable here, leading the defence of the *Phalanx*. In his stead I offer myself to accompany the Apothecary's mission.'

'I shall appoint an Imperial Fists squad to accompany you,' said Pugh. 'I can spare no more. The rest of my warriors must remain to hold the line.'

'I wish Apothecary Pallas given leave to join us as well,' said Luko.

'You have it. Kolgo, Borganor, Lysander and myself shall continue to command the defence. These are the wishes of Chapter Master Pugh, and hence are the wishes of Rogal Dorn. Go now to fulfil your orders, brothers and sisters. Should I see you after the battle, then all shall be joyful. If not, I shall await you at the end of time, at the Emperor's side, when we shall have our revenge for everything the enemy has done to us.'

The officers departed to organise the defence of the Tactica and the Forge of Ages. Across the cavernous barracks deck, the war machines of the daemon army grew higher.

CHAPTER THIRTEEN

It was a dismal thing, killing Chaplain Iktinos.

Iktinos was, by then, a barely sensible wreck. The infliction of the Hell had broken his mind so thoroughly that there was nothing left of the Chaplain save for his physical shell. The man that had once been the paragon of the Chapter and the hidden traitor were gone.

Sarpedon had carried Iktinos to a cluster of saviour pods adjoining the fighter craft deck. In the event of the huge hangar doors failing or some disaster befalling the fighter deck, the crew could use the pods to escape the *Phalanx*. The entrances to the pods were circular shafts leading down from a slanting wall, like the open mouths of steel worms waiting to swallow the desperate crewmen as they fled. Oil stained the walls and ceiling, and the chill of the near-vacuum could not be completely kept out by the hull insulation. It was no place for a Space Marine to die, suited only to a shambolic, almost apologetic excuse for a death.

Should the saviour pods themselves be compromised, an emergency airlock was set into the outer skin of the hull beside the entrances to the pods. A crewman in a voidsuit who took that exit could conceivably survive an extra hour or two in space, and perhaps even be picked up by a rescue craft. Sarpedon placed Iktinos's limp form on the deck and turned the wheel-lock, opening the airlock's outer door.

'If you have anything you wish to add, Chaplain,' said Sarpedon, 'now is the time.'

Iktinos did not reply. Sarpedon looked down at him, at his burned face and scorched, dented armour, and regretted speaking. The Chaplain was barely drawing breath.

Sarpedon placed a hand against Iktinos's charred skull. Sarpedon had never possessed any great talent for diving into the mind of another. Some Librarians of the old Chapter had specialised in peeling apart another's consciousness, diving down and extracting secrets the subject himself did not know. Others read minds on a vast scale, divining troop movements from an opposing army as fast as their orders spread. Sarpedon had only been able to transmit, albeit at the tremendous telepathic volume that manifested as the Hell. Nevertheless he had sometimes caught echoes of the strongest emotions, an aspect of the sixth sense that all psykers possessed in some degree. He tried to read something from Iktinos then, to divine some final thought from the man he had once considered his closest ally in all the universe.

There was nothing. Complete deadness, as if Iktinos were an inert object with no mind at all.

Then Sarpedon caught something, faint and intermittent, like a signal from a dying transmitter light years away. It was the howling of a desolate wind, the sound of emptiness more profound than silence. It whistled through the ruined architecture of a mind as empty as a bombed-out city, as alone as a world where life had never evolved. It was as if there had never been a mind in there at all, scoured and scrubbed from the wind-blasted stones by a terrible extinction.

Sarpedon alone had not done this. The Hell was indiscriminate and crude, a force of destruction, certainly, but not accurate or thorough enough to erase the personality of another. Iktinos had done this to himself. The shattered fragments of his soul had gathered themselves into a whole coherent enough only to self-destruct. A logic bomb planted by Daenyathos's teachings, a way to destroy any compromising memories trapped in a fractured mind. An atrocity quite in keeping with the Philosopher-Soldier's conviction that everything he did, no matter how obscene, was for a good beyond the conception of lesser human beings.

Sarpedon knew now what Daenyathos planned. It was no less appalling than the betrayal of the Soul Drinkers had suggested. It was entirely appropriate that Abraxes, an icon of treachery and malice, should himself just be a cog in such a scheme. The annihilation of Iktinos's personality was similarly in keeping with Daenyathos's way of doing things.

Iktinos had not completed his mental suicide before the unconscious part of him, the one laid open by the Hell, had submitted to Sarpedon's request. Iktinos had, indeed, told Sarpedon everything.

Sarpedon hefted Iktinos's body into the airlock. He slammed the inner door shut and turned the wheel to lock it again. Through the thick portholes Sarpedon could see the multicoloured nebulae of the Veiled Region, unknowable and hungry. Sarpedon would give its ravenous young stars something to feed on.

He tried to think of something to say to Iktinos, some powerful parting statement that would both condemn the traitor and express regret that the Chaplain, his old friend, was gone. But there was no point. Iktinos could not have understood anything in his current state, even if the words did reach him through the heavy airlock door.

Sarpedon thumbed the control stud set into the wall beside the door. Pneumatic cables hissed as the airlock was depressurised. A warning light strobed, then the airlock's outer door opened and the remaining air whistled out. Silence followed and Iktinos's body, dislodged from its resting place by the final decompression, drifted out of the airlock and beyond the grasp of the *Phalanx*.

A craft the size of the *Phalanx* was typically surrounded by a halo of debris and thin gas out to a distance of several tens of metres. Sarpedon watched as Iktinos's body fell beyond the halo zone, into the pure void. At some point the Chaplain had finally died, but it hardly seemed much of a distinction with his mind already destroyed.

The outer door slid shut again, and Iktinos's body became lost through the condensation misting on the porthole as the airlock filled back up with air. Sarpedon turned away.

Iktinos was dead. Sarpedon had kept one of the promises he had made to himself. As tough as taking on Iktinos had been, the next promise would be harder to fulfil. Sarpedon knew where Daenyathos was and what he was trying to do, but the way he would stop the Philosopher-Soldier had yet to make itself clear.

It did not matter. The time for weighing up the risks and probabilities of battle had come and gone some time ago. Now, Sarpedon had something to fight for, and there was no deadlier weapon than that in a Space Marine's hands.

'Throne behold us,' whispered Pallas as he set eyes on the Path of the Lost for the first time. 'Watch over us, my Emperor. Watch over us.'

The Path of the Lost, as recorded in the archives of the Imperial Fists, was a dark place. Its floors were covered with grates to allow the blood to drain out, and a thousand rusting torture devices were piled up as detritus in its shadowy corners as the fashions of punishment changed. An Imperial Fist might have the honour of being interrogated in the Atoning Halls or perhaps brought in chains before the Chapter Master – but those who were outsiders, prisoners of war or condemned heretics would be banished to the Path of the Lost. There would be doled out their tortures or executions away from the eyes of the Chapter down in the *Phalanx*'s rusting, filthy underbelly.

That would have been bad enough.

The strike force advanced, fire teams covering one another, as they crossed the threshold and entered what the Path of the Lost had become. The horror of the warp's invasion had bled down inevitably into the Path, some unconscious malice dragging the warp's dark energies into the torture chambers and execution grounds.

Across the walls and floors shimmered the torn faces of the Path's dead. Delicate eldar features, each forced into a dying rictus, bulged from the warping metal. Like drowning swimmers struggling to the surface, humanoid shapes broke the surface to sink down again, an endless pulsating mass of bodies. The ghosts of mutant renegades, fouled with horns or sloughing skin, pushed against the fabric of reality, teeth gnashing.

'There must be a million dirty secrets down here,' said Luko, casting an eye across the constant parade of the executed and damned.

'Nothing of your concern,' said Sergeant Prexus. His squad had been charged with forming the bulk of the strike force, with nine more Imperial Fists under his command.

'I think it is, sergeant,' replied Luko. 'All those dark deeds the Imperial Fists thought hidden from the universe, they might well come back to bite us down here.'

'If you are finished,' said Sister Aescarion, walking between the Imperial Fist and the Soul Drinker, 'time is a factor.'

Prexus's squad advanced into the cluster of execution chambers that marked the entrance to the Path of the Lost. Pallas, Luko and Graevus followed the Imperial Fists in, Varnica and Sister Aescarion watching the angles behind them.

Several tiled rooms with drains built into the floor, walls crazed with old bullet holes, had seen hundreds of captives executed in the past decades and centuries. Now those walls bulged as if they held veins fed by a vast heart, faces and hands pressing against the surface. The floor quivered underfoot as grasping hands tried to snare the feet of the Imperial Fists.

'Steel your souls,' said Sergeant Prexus, his chain-sword held ready as he took point. 'Recall the parables of Rogal Dorn. He walked into the hell of the *Vengeful Spirit*, and though assailed on every side, he did not fall. Though the Angel fell, the strength of our primarch's soul did not let him follow. Though the Emperor was laid low, Rogal Dorn did not know despair. Let his strength be your strength, my brothers. Let his strength be yours.'

'We are watched,' said Varnica. He slid a hand into his force claw gauntlet, and it snickered shut around his wrist.

A shape flashed through the execution chambers, half-glimpsed through the gaping doorways and holes in the collapsed walls. The

Imperial Fists gathered into a battle formation, gathered around Prexus with bolters aimed out in all directions. Pallas was beside Prexus, his own bolter ready.

'They envy us,' said Varnica. 'No matter how grave our situation, it cannot compare to the unfinished business of the dead.'

More shimmering silver-grey forms rippled in and out of sight, flitting from electric chair to injection table to gallows. Quicker and closer they came, the howling of their voices growing, until they were like a tornado of torn souls with the strike force trapped in the storm's eye.

'Hold fast,' cried Prexus. 'The enemy shows its hand. Its foulness here is manifest.'

Reality bowed and flexed around Varnica's force claw as he channelled his psychic power into the Hammerhand. Aescarion dropped to one knee, power axe ready, and was taken aback to see Graevus take up the same posture beside her, his own power axe in his mutated hand.

One of the ghosts tore from the mass and arrowed towards them. Varnica leapt, drawing back his force claw. The spirit had the hollow face and alien eyes of the eldar, the inhuman geometry of its frame the very essence of the xenos. The ragged matter of its body echoed the curved shapes of its once-elegant armour, shredded into streamers of spirit-stuff by the ravages of its grim death.

Varnica's force claw closed on the spirit and sheared it in two. The wall of force generated by the eruption of his Hammerhand power ripped the xenos spirit apart, a sphere of energy bulging outwards from the impact.

Varnica skidded to the floor. With ear-splitting screams, more of the *Phalanx*'s dead were shrieking into the Imperial formation. Aescarion swatted at one, the blade of her power axe scything through a vaguely human mass of glowing energy. The discharging power field shredded the spirit into a cloud of falling sparks.

'Open fire!' yelled Prexus, and ten boltguns hammered in unison. Shapes rippled along the floor and grabbed at their feet, while ghostly hands reached from the floor. Prexus was snared by hands clutching at his ankles, and he cut them through at the wrist with a swipe of his chainblade. Apothecary Pallas speared an apparition through the throat with the needles of the narthecium he wore around one hand, the medical device doubling as a weapon up close.

From the maelstrom coiled a serpentine apparition, terminating in the gnashing face of some foul mutant, its features knotted into a mass of tentacles trailing behind it. Its long gnarled fingers were tipped with metal blades, and shards of bone stabbed from the echo of its form.

'The Vizier!' yelled Prexus.

The apparition grinned, its face almost splitting in two along a fissure lined with fangs. It dived, too fast for the Imperial Fist in its way to avoid it. The Vizier dived into the Space Marine, its whole length disappearing into the warrior's breastplate. The Imperial Fist was suffused with a blue-white glow bleeding from between the plates of his armour and shining through the eyepieces of his helmet, and he dropped his boltgun as he was wracked with sudden convulsions.

Varnica ripped one of the ghosts from the swirling mass, impaling it on his force claw, and slammed it into the ground where it dissipated. He turned to see the Imperial Fist in the throes of possession. Shards of bone were bursting from under the Space Marine's forearms and shoulder guards.

Prexus leaped onto his possessed battle-brother, wrestling him to the deck. Varnica pushed through the cordon of Imperial Fists to Prexus's side. He withdrew his hand from his force claw, attaching it back onto the holster at his side, and placed his hand against the possessed warrior's forehead.

Aescarion and Graevus joined the Imperial Fists cordon, slashing at the ghosts that swooped close. Luko was on his own, pivoting and slashing in every direction, his lightning claws perfectly suited to this fight where he was assailed from all sides. Scraps of spirit flesh floated down like shed leaves, faces breaking into ragged scraps of detritus as their distant screams died with them.

'In the name of the Emperor and His mighty soul that shields us all from the enemy,' yelled Varnica, 'I cast thee out. From this good brother's soul, where you shall find no purchase, I cast thee out!'

Power arced off the Imperial Fist's armour. The possessed form forced itself to its feet and threw off Prexus with strength beyond even a Space Marine. Prexus crashed into the tiled wall of an execution chamber, sliding down among the rubble and old bloodstains. Varnica kept hold of the possessed Space Marine, his hand still clamped against his forehead.

The faceplate of the Imperial Fist's helmet became like liquid, rippling and shifting into a face that was an animal mass of tentacles. A forked tongue flickered from its lipless mouth.

'This spirit tastes good,' it hissed.

'Out, daemon,' shouted Varnica. 'The Emperor's light burns you. The iron of this warrior's soul cages you. Out, out, wither and die!'

'Do you know how much is left of him?' slavered the Vizier. 'He has barely a name. The rest of him I consume. I shall leave him a shell with the mind of an infant.'

'I said out!' yelled Varnica. The shape of the Vizier rippled around the Imperial Fist, stretching and deforming as if it were being pulled from the body by invisible hands. Finally, with a shriek, it came away and the Space Marine clattered to the floor, insensible.

Aescarion and Graevus leapt on the Vizier as it writhed, confused for a moment. Aescarion's axe bisected its face, the power field burning through the spectral matter. The Vizier threw her to the floor with a lash of its long tail, but Graevus's axe was already descending towards where its neck should be. The axe cut through it and its head was sheared from its body. The serpentine form dissolved into the air, and the head had shimmered away to motes of light before it hit the ground.

The ghosts dissolved away, slinking back into the shadows. The Imperial Fists tracked their bolters through the darkness as Luko watched the rag-like slivers of ghostly flesh erode away from his gauntlets.

Silence fell again, broken only by the plinking of tiles falling from the bolter-scarred walls.

'What was it?' asked Pallas, cradling the fallen Imperial Fist's head and undoing the armour seals around his neck.

Prexus picked himself up from the deck. 'The Vizier,' he spat. 'A mutant warlord. A psyker. Centuries ago he was captured and brought to the *Phalanx*. He died down here. I do not recall the whole story.'

'I imagine it was far from unique,' said Luko.

Pallas removed the Imperial Fist's helmet. The faceplate was still twisted into a semblance of the Vizier's tentacled face. Underneath, the warrior's face was bloodied and battered, with growths of bloody bone poking through the cheekbones and scalp. He drew a shallow breath and winced.

'Brother Dolonis,' said Prexus, kneeling beside the wounded man. 'Can you fight?'

'No, my brother,' gasped Dolonis in reply. 'The pain… is everywhere. It has changed me. My body is not… not my own. I can still hear it laughing…'

Aescarion cast her eye over Dolonis's body. Shards of bone had penetrated through his armour all over. Knots of it were forcing his shoulder pads away from his body and knife-like growths jutted from his greaves. A pool of rapidly congealing blood was spreading beneath Dolonis.

'We must leave him,' said Aescarion.

'He is a battle-brother,' replied Prexus.

'He cannot fight and we cannot take him. And the enemy has been within his mind. He is a moral threat. If he lives, we will be back for him, but for now we must leave him.'

'I agree with the Sister,' said Varnica. 'You have not seen the ruin a possession can make of its victim. The possessor can plant a piece of itself that can continue even after the daemon is dead.'

Prexus stepped back from Dolonis. 'Brother. I cannot make this decision for you.'

'Leave me,' said Dolonis, the words causing him obvious pain. 'Just put my bolter in my hand.'

Prexus handed Dolonis his gun. Aescarion knelt beside him and took a loop of prayer beads from a pouch at her waist. She pressed them into Dolonis's free hand.

'Pray for us, brother,' she said. 'We will pray for you.'

Pallas gently lowered Dolonis to the deck.

'We need to move on,' said Luko, stepping over the rubble further into the tangle of execution chambers. The feeble light reached to the threshold of another warren, this time of cell blocks of tight winding tunnels lined with steel doors and stretches of manacle-hung walls. 'If Abraxes's influence has woken the old dead here, then he probably knows we have disturbed them. We must reach his portal before he sends his own forces down here.'

Prexus did not, or could not, say anything further. With a final glance at Dolonis, he led his squad out of formation towards the deeper regions of the Path.

'You fight well, Sister,' said Graevus as he and Aescarion took up their position in the middle of the marching order.

'You expected otherwise?' said Aescarion.

'I did not mean…'

'We are the daughters of the Emperor,' she said, 'just as you are his sons. I may not have two hearts or three lungs, but I have every bit the resolve of a Space Marine.'

'So I saw,' said Graevus. 'You were quick to leave Dolonis to his fate.'

'As I would with a sister of mine,' said Aescarion sharply. 'A sense of brotherhood has its benefits, but taken to extremes, I fear it can become a weakness as much as a strength. The history of the Imperium is a litany of failings caused by brotherhood misplaced.'

Graevus bit back any reply. The Path of the Lost closed around them, the cramped warrens of cells forcing the Space Marines to split up, and it felt for all the galaxy as if the *Phalanx* were swallowing them whole.

By the fires of the forges they had built, the daemons' war engines were taking shape. One of them was a huge horned thing, a battering ram with cylindrical cages for wheels in which some of the lumbering daemon-beasts would doubtless be herded to drive it forwards. Another was a catapult with a shield mantle reaching almost to the deck's high ceiling, piles of alien skulls being heaped up behind it as ammunition. A machine like a massive mechanical crab was being assembled with tanks of some caustic bilious substance on its back, hooked up to the cannon on its coiling tail. Impish daemon-wrights scrambled over the surfaces of the war machines, while legions of bloodletters stood guard and the shapeshifting horrors of Abraxes swarmed in an endless squirming dance. The remains of the greater plague daemon had been dragged behind the tumbledown fortifications and putrefied into a cauldron of bubbling rot, from which more plaguebearers were being birthed by the minute.

Lord Inquisitor Kolgo watched the flickering fires reflected off the

pitted metal of the half-finished daemon engines. His Battle Sisters retinue shadowed him at a respectful distance as he leaned against a fallen
wall behind which a couple of Imperial Fists had taken up their position
in the line. 'We will have to attack before they are finished,' he said.

'I know,' replied Chapter Master Pugh. 'That is why Abraxes is building them. He wants us to emerge from safety and march towards them,
to give them the defensive ground instead of us.'

'And we will attack,' said Kolgo. 'We cannot stand back and give them
the *Phalanx*. It is written in the fate that Abraxes loves to weave so much.'

'It seems that you have divined the future, lord inquisitor,' said Pugh.
Any bitterness in his voice was well hidden. 'Abraxes is not the only one
reading the runes.'

'Fate has us all in its snares, Chapter Master. It is an inquisitor's duty
to perceive it.'

'And what does fate say will happen to us?'

'Truly? If you so wish, Chapter Master. Fate has decided that Abraxes
shall bring his great cunning to bear and with it, defeat a force of brave
but bull-headed Space Marines, bringing a great tragedy to pass.'

'That is fate?'

'That is fate.'

'Then, lord inquisitor, I shall fight fate.' Pugh pointed to a knot of
rubble in the no-man's-land between the armies. It was the remains of
a hero-chapel that had been toppled by the daemons' advance. 'There
still stands the statue of Chaplain Pausanias,' he said. 'They could not
topple him. See? He lacks an arm, and the rest of him has seen better
days, but he stands.'

'Like us?' said Kolgo.

'You miss my point. Pausanias was a dark seed. He was brought
onto the *Phalanx* as a novice, recruited like thousands of others. Unlike
most of them, he was found worthy as an Imperial Fist. But there was
a darkness in him. A pride. He sought the greatest glory in battle, and
battle-brothers died for his failings.'

'A warrior's sin, rarely acknowledged,' said Kolgo.

Pugh ignored the inquisitor. 'We saw too late what he was,' he continued, 'and when his charge against a gunline, seeking to capture the
standard of the enemy, cost the life of his squad's sergeant, he was banished to the Atoning Halls for his paucity of spirit. Fate had decided that
Pausanias should be a lesson to us, lord inquisitor. He was destined to
be a parable of warning to future novices, a disgrace as a Space Marine to
be mourned and despised. But Pausanias was not resigned to accepting
that fate. He scourged away his pride in the Atoning Halls. He returned
lower than the novices, lower than our crew. He worked in the engines
of the *Phalanx*, until the Chapter welcomed him back into its ranks. He
died a Chaplain, a spiritual guardian of our battle-brothers, because he

had fought that fate which had bound him so tightly and fought to live beyond it. He defeated his fate and is remembered here for it. I shall emulate him, if the Emperor wills it, and confound the designs of this daemon prince.'

'It sounds to me, Chapter Master, that an Imperial Fist does not know when to give in.'

'We do not know, lord inquisitor, what giving in even means.'

From the shadows cast by the daemons' fires, a Space Marine scout crept towards the Imperial Fists lines. The yellow of his armour was smeared with ash, as was his face, to break up his outline in the gloom.

'Scout Orfos,' said Pugh as the scout got closer, 'if these old eyes fail me not.'

'You shame me, Chapter Master,' said Orfos as he took his place in the line. 'I should aspire to get within a knife thrust of you before you notice me.'

'Friend and foe have tried, brother. That I still stand suggests no foe, at least, has succeeded yet. What news do you bring of the enemy?'

'Within two hours, they will finish building their war engines,' replied Orfos. 'They are preparing rituals to possess them with daemons. Heaps of skulls and entrails piled up, and sigils wrought in blood, I have seen. They have brought supplicants through, still human, though barely, and they writhe and chant to gain the attention of their gods. Such rites of the flesh I hesitate to describe, but the beasts they build will have a cunning born of their possession as well as their own raw strength.'

'Can we survive them, if they are sent against us?' said Pugh.

'I do not know if the *Phalanx* itself will survive them,' said Orfos. 'We counted six of them. The scorpion beast, the battering ram and the catapult are clearest to us from here. A burrowing worm of steel lies coiled and slumbering out of our view, with a contraption of brass and skulls that I suspect will house the spirit of a greater daemon and a beast of flesh knitted together, as if predators of the warp had been butchered and their carcasses divided to be formed into one single monstrosity. All look as if they are nearing completion.'

'You and your brother scouts have done well,' said Pugh.

Orfos saluted and headed back through the lines to join the other scouts arriving in ones and twos from their mission.

'Then within two hours,' said Kolgo, 'we attack.'

'That is one fate I will not seek to avoid. My Fangs of Dorn have not seen enough blood yet, not quite.'

'If Luko's mission does not succeed, this will be the last the *Phalanx* sees of any of us.'

'Are you afraid, lord inquisitor?'

Kolgo replied with a smirk and turned back towards the centre of the

Imperial Fists position, where his Battle Sisters were waiting patiently for their master.

When Kolgo was out of earshot, Pugh looked again towards the daemon engines growing more complete by the moment. He took the Fangs of Dorn in his hands, their blades scarred with burning daemon blood and muttered to himself.

'Is it wrong that I have prayed for this?'

By the time the strike force of Imperial Fists and Soul Drinkers reached the Panpsychicon, two more of Prexus's squad had been lost. In the warren of cells and tunnels, where the Space Marines were forced to move through each junction and bottleneck in knots of two or three, unseen foes had snatched at them from the darkness.

Befanged faces had loomed, gnashing and spitting bile. The walls had fallen in, or pits had opened in the floor. Cackling creatures had flitted past junctions ahead, too quick to see or shoot. One Imperial Fist had been dragged into a cell by hands of shattered, bloody bone; by the time his battle-brothers had reached him, there was nothing left in the cell but torn scraps of ceramite and the blood slathered across the walls and ceiling.

The second had been killed by invisible hands as his brothers watched. Even as they tried to haul him down from the ceiling where he had been carried, his head was wrenched around almost backwards and his spine snapped. The forces holding him had dissipated instantly, dropping the corpse to the deck and leaving only silence behind.

So the strike force warily emerged into the wide space ahead of them, leaving the labyrinth behind, only to wonder where the next threat would come from.

'What is this place?' said Luko, the first to step out of the cell block tunnel.

'The Panpsychicon,' said Prexus behind him. 'An experiment.'

'Was it successful?' asked Luko.

'It had lain down here unused for two hundred years,' replied Prexus. 'Is that answer enough?'

The circular expanse of the Panpsychicon was bounded by smooth walls inlaid with mosaics. The names of a hundred great battles from Imperial Fists history were depicted there in patterns of brightly coloured stone shards, surrounded by complex heraldries that spiralled into an unbroken pattern. Even the name Terra was picked out among the heraldry, commemorating the part the Imperial Fists had played in the battle for the Emperor's Palace ten thousand years before.

In the centre of the Panpsychicon was a device of steel and crystal that reached the ceiling, something like a set of interlocking spider's webs in which were suspended cut slabs and chunks of crystal-like giant gemstones. A rainbow of colours reflected from every surface, creating a maddening nest of shapes and light that refused attempts to view it as a normal object in three dimensions.

Luko's foot disturbed a manacle set into the floor. It was one of dozens set in concentric circles around the central device.

'Some enemies resist traditional interrogation techniques,' said Prexus. 'Psykers amongst them. The Panpsychicon was built to rid them of their mental barriers.'

'It is a machine,' said Sister Aescarion, 'for grinding down men's souls? The Inquisition makes use of such things, but with varying success. And never have I seen one on such a scale.'

'These are matters of the past,' said Prexus. 'We must press on. We close on the cargo sections, but we must not allow ourselves to be slowed further.'

The whole room shuddered. Handfuls of dust spilled from cracks in the ceiling and the mosaiced walls shed their tesserae. The Panpsychicon's device shone and glimmered as its crystals shook and, with a grinding sound from beneath the floor, began to rotate.

'How many died down here?' asked Luko, crouching to keep his footing as the room shuddered with greater strength.

'That depends,' said Prexus, 'on what you mean by "die".'

Shapes of captives, manacled to the floor, flashed in the strange colours of light emitted by the spirit-grinder device. Crackles of light played across the walls.

'Go,' said Luko. 'Go, get through. Do not give it the chance to...'

Luko's sentence was cut off by the burst of energy that tore across the Panpsychicon. The Space Marines were picked off their feet and slammed into the wall, shattering the mosaics beneath them. Shackles of lightning held them there, struggling against the force. Graevus's mutated arm pushed free of his restraints but the rest of him was held fast.

Luko tried to shut his eyes, but the same force holding him in place was prising them open. He forced himself onto his side and pushed with an arm and a leg, feeling some give in his bonds.

'Resist!' he yelled over the growing sound, a rumble combined with a skull-shuddering whine, emitted by the spirit-grinder as it opened up into a mass of articulated arms dripping with shimmering crystals. 'Resist it. Fight back!'

Luko's bonds snapped. He slid to the floor, still pushed back by the wall of psychic power pulsing from the centre of the room. He could see Sister Aescarion screaming as her body, without the strengthening augmentations of a Space Marine, was battered against the wall like a plaything in the hand of a spiteful child.

Luko took a painful step towards the centre of the room. The apparitions manacled to the floor were writhing, contorted impossibly, as he stepped through them, forcing himself forwards.

All I want is peace, said a voice in the back of his head.

'No,' said Luko. 'No. Get out! Get out!' He pushed forwards another step.

He caught sight of his hands. The lightning claw gauntlets were gone. His hands were pitted and rotten, dead flesh peeling away from bone eroded by disease.

He forced himself to see the gauntlets and they crackled back into view, the illusion banished from his mind.

'Do not believe it!' he shouted, not knowing if anyone could hear him. 'We are Space Marines! We shall know no fear!'

The force was gone. Luko fell to the floor. But it was not the deck of a spaceship – it was mud, wet and deep. The hand he threw out to steady himself sunk into the mud up to his elbow and he felt it cold against his face.

Something whistled overhead. An artillery shell. Gunfire crackled from all directions.

Luko was surrounded by war. Mud and trenches, battalions charging to their deaths, armies locked face to face in dense jungles and shattered cities. Burning fighter craft fell like comets overhead. Battleships overturned, spilling thousands into an ocean covered with burning oil.

Luko had been in wars before. He had spent his life in them. But this was different. This was every war he had ever seen, every one he had ever heard of or imagined, all layered on top of one another in an awful mass of solid conflict and death.

He could see billions dying. He could see the face of every man and woman, no matter how distant or confused the slaughter, as they died. They struggled along the gore-filled trenches holding their guts in, laser burns all over their bodies, begging for the Emperor to deliver them death. A legion of them crawled on their bellies, blinded by clouds of corrosive gas, vomiting up a bloody torrent as their insides were eaten away. They screamed in silence, the sound robbed from their voices as they fought against the mudslides and building collapses that entombed them, their lungs crying out for breath they could not draw, limbs and organs crushed. They fell from the sky and were driven mad by the blind horror of a thousand battlefields hurtling up at them. They drowned. They burned alive.

The endless battlefield spread out as far as Luko could comprehend in every direction, and some monstrous trick of dimension told him that it went on forever. It was above him, where the embrace of the void snatched the breath and life from crewmen thrown from ruptured spacecraft. It was below him in the intense heat and pitch darkness where armies fought like rats, ignorant of friend or foe, reduced to terrified animals murdering one another with bare hands and teeth.

The weight of it, the certainty of its unending malice, slammed down on Luko and he could not get to his feet. He was in a filthy trench choked with bodies, a carnivorous jungle humming with disease and the bloating foulness of the dead, a ruined city where men died over a bullet-ridden room or a deathtrap crossroads, the hull of a dying space-craft where all was darkness and fire. He was at the heart of every war that had ever been fought or ever would, and before him was played out every violent death that the galaxy would ever see.

His body was rotting away because he was dead, and yet he could not die. Death itself was not an escape. He would be here, witness this, forever.

It was not real. Luko knew it was an illusion. But it was not something projected into his mind – it came from inside him.

'Captain!' yelled someone very far away, with the unfamiliar cadence of a woman's voice. 'Captain, focus! Drive it out! Hear me!'

A hundred layers of war were piled up on top of one another. Luko forced himself to look at the bloodshed and the suffering, to go through every incarnation until he found one that didn't fit. A single circular room, haunted and tortured, on a spaceship. He saw himself lying on the floor, convulsing at the mercy of the Panpsychicon's spirit-grinder. He pushed himself to his knees, and so did the Luko he saw. He looked around and saw the face of Sister Aescarion ghosted over the trench-works and burning fortresses.

Luko lunged drunkenly towards the spirit-grinder. His lightning claw sliced through the tangle of struts and wiring. Crystals rained down and shattered.

Sister Aescarion followed him in destruction. She buried her power axe deep in the machine's core, and grimaced as she tried to wrench it out. Luko was unable to judge distance or direction properly and slashed around him with abandon, scattering components of the psychic machine.

The thousand wars peeled away and fell apart. Fortresses turned to dust. The mud dried and blew away, leaving a desert devoid of battle. The Panpsychicon became the dominant reality, then the only one, and Luko was able to shake the confusion from his mind.

The Space Marines lay in various stages of consciousness. Varnica was on his feet, too. The Imperial Fists were scattered, groaning and shifting as their own realities returned to them.

One did not move. Pallas, holding his own head in pain, knelt beside the Imperial Fist and read his lifesigns off the fallen warrior's armour.

'He is gone,' said Pallas.

'What was his name?' asked Graevus, who forced the words out in between coughs as he knelt, bent double.

'Gorvan,' replied one of the other Imperial Fists.

'Prexus?' said Luko. 'Sergeant?'

Aescarion tapped Luko on the shoulder guard and pointed to the wall near the cell block warren. Prexus sat against the wall, his bolt pistol in his hand, his chainsword discarded on the floor. His head lolled, revealing the massive exit wound in the back of the skull. Prexus's brains were spread up the wall behind him, thrown across the mosaic in the characteristic pattern of a bolter wound.

No one said that Prexus had shot himself. They didn't need to.

'What must he have seen?' said Pallas.

'Think not on it,' said Varnica. 'Let us move. Sister, commend their souls.'

The strikeforce crossed the Panpsychicon, armoured feet crunching through the remains of the psychic machine. Aescarion, head bowed, followed the Space Marines towards the double doors at the far side of the room, murmuring a prayer for the departed.

Sarpedon braced his remaining talons against the floor and put all his strength into forcing the bridge doors open. The blast doors, automatically sealed in the event of boarders entering the *Phalanx*, creaked and gave way a little. Hydraulic lines split and the resistance lessened, and the doors slid open wide enough to admit the bulk of a Space Marine.

'Daenyathos!' shouted Sarpedon as he stepped onto the bridge of the *Phalanx*.

The bridge was a palace, built to glorify the captain who had once held court there – Rogal Dorn, primarch of the Imperial Fists Legion, the first master of the *Phalanx*. Under him, this ship had darkened the sky of Terra itself when Horus laid siege to the Emperor's Palace. A mighty throne, three storeys high, dominated the bridge, plated with gold. The flight of steps leading to the oversized pulpit-throne was flanked with displayed weapons captured from enemies or discovered during the Great Crusade.

The vast viewscreen facing the throne, taking up most of the curving wall of the bridge, showed a panorama of the Veiled Region, with the star Kravamesh glowing along one edge. Kravamesh had turned dark and smouldering, black swarms scudding across its burnt orange orb, as if the star were drained of power to fuel the gate across to the warp that had brought Abraxes into realspace. Below the screen were dozens of command helms, each controlling one of the *Phalanx*'s many vital systems, and even when stationary they should have been bustling with crewmen and Imperial Fists overseers. Now, only a few slumped dead crewmen remained, felled by bullet wounds where they had sat.

One body was piled on the floor beside his chair. In the chair, at the communications helm, sat a hunched elderly figure, bony fingers playing across the controls. The man turned at Sarpedon's voice, revealing an ancient, lined face broken by a smile.

'Lord Sarpedon,' said the old man. 'For so long I have waited for this. Of all the pieces of Master Daenyathos's future, you are the one that shines the brightest in his plan. I am Father Gyranar, honoured to lead my congregation.'

Sarpedon stalked warily through the bridge, casting his eyes over the monumental sculptures looming in the shadows around the edge of the bridge, the suits of ancient armour gleaming and polished around the foot of the throne-mount. 'Where is Daenyathos?' he said.

Gyranar stood up, his bent frame meaning he was barely taller than when he sat. A trembling finger pointed as the old man took a few steps towards Sarpedon. 'So blessed am I that I lived to see this. I dared not hope it might be during my lifetime that the threads would come together, that the one Daenyathos wrote of would lead his Chapter to the fulfilment of our dreams. But you stand before me, Lord Sarpedon. And we all stand at this confluence of fates.'

Sarpedon hefted the Axe of Mercaeno and scuttled within a lunge and a strike of Gyranar. 'I said, where is Daenyathos?'

'Threaten not those who are merely carried on the eddies of the fates we weave,' came an artificial voice, amplified from somewhere behind the throne-mount. 'Men like Father Gyranar are ignorant of their fate and impotent to change it. But you and I, Sarpedon, we are different. We are the authors of our fates. It takes men like you to forge the channels into which the future will flow. And men like me to decide what that future is.'

The shape of a Space Marine Dreadnought stomped from behind the throne-mount. The colours and heraldry of the Soul Drinkers were polished and gleaming now, as if it had just stepped from the forges of the old Chapter. A missile launcher and a power fist were mounted below its massive shoulders and purity seals fluttered from the blocky mass of the sarcophagus.

'Iktinos told me everything,' said Sarpedon. 'I know why you are here. You will take the *Phalanx* across the galaxy and disgorge Abraxes's armies everywhere you go.'

'That is true,' said Daenyathos. 'But did he tell you why?'

'He tried,' said Sarpedon. 'But I could not believe such a thing spoken from the lips of a Space Marine, even one as corrupted as Iktinos. So I would hear it from you first.'

'It is simple, Sarpedon,' said Daenyathos. The chassis pivoted so that the Dreadnought's head, shaped like an oversized Space Marine helm, looked up at the huge viewscreen and the stretch of void it showed. 'The galaxy is corrupt. Its people are damned and its rulers are cruel. This is the same conclusion as yours, is it not? The Imperium is a dark and savage place, a breeding ground for the desperation that gives the forces of the warp the chance to do their wickedness in our universe. It is through suffering that the Imperium will be remade. Great suffering, on a scale beyond the imaginings of lesser minds. Thanks to the plan crafted by me and executed by many, including you, Abraxes and the *Phalanx* will combine to spread such suffering that the Imperium will be remade stronger and more just.'

'And you will rule it?' said Sarpedon.

'Of course,' replied Daenyathos, the green-lensed eyes of the sarcophagus focusing on Sarpedon again. 'Who else could?'

'You understand,' said Sarpedon, 'that I must try to stop you. I may die, for no doubt you have included this very eventuality in your plan. Nevertheless, if there is the smallest chance that the people of the Imperium can be spared that fate, then I must take it.'

'Of course,' said Daenyathos. 'I would expect nothing less. You have been a loyal servant to me, Sarpedon, though you played your part unknowingly. It pains me not a little to have to kill you. But you will fight to the death to protect the same Imperium you profess to despise, and so I must ensure you hinder me no further.'

'It is the Imperium I hate. Not its people. Its people are innocent.'

'Innocence is a falsehood created by weak and fearful minds,' said Daenyathos.

'Well, then. I do not think there is anything more to say.'

'Indeed, Chapter Master Sarpedon. I would finish this without delay.'

'And I would oblige you.' Sarpedon crouched down on the five legs he had left, Axe of Mercano held low ready to charge.

Daenyathos's targeting auspex flickered as it registered Sarpedon, feeding information into the Dreadnought's internal cogitators.

Sarpedon yelled and sprang to one side as a volley of missiles shrieked from Daenyathos's launcher, and the bridge of the *Phalanx* was suddenly full of fury.

CHAPTER FOURTEEN

The scouts brought back word that the daemons were loading their war engines with ammunition, heaps of smouldering skulls and ballista bolts of ensorcelled brass. The scorpion machine was being filled with boiling venom, biomechanical poison sacs swelling in billows of steam, daemons scrambling across its lacquered carapace.

Word reached the Imperial Fists lines. Chapter Master Pugh made his decision instantly, for there was, in truth, no decision to be made.

Lord Inquisitor Kolgo stood proud of the defences, his Battle Sisters gathered around him, the fires of the daemons' forges flickering against his polished Terminator armour. He watched the daemon masses swarming into formation in response.

'Lackeys of the warp!' yelled Kolgo. 'This is what you begged for. This is why you were spewed from the guts of the immaterium. To face us, the Emperor's own, the shield of mankind! Well, now you have your wish. Rejoice as we cleave you apart. Give thanks as we shoot you down. This is what you wished for. Come, rush onto our blades!'

The daemons leapt over the barricades of wreckage, shrieking in response. The heralds of their gods bellowed and keened the songs of the warp, and darkness gathered around like the eclipse of a distant sun.

Into the darkness charged the Imperial Fists.

On the map tables of the Tactica Sigismundi were dozens of battle-fields rendered in stone miniature, some of them depicting meticulous surgical strikes with every element of an Imperial Fists force working in harmony, perfectly coordinated, each squad shielding the next while catching foes in a lethal crossfire. Others were battles of attrition, the Imperial Fists relying on their enhanced bodies and wargear to keep them fighting when the enemy were breaking down. But some of them, the fewest, were headlong charges, frontal assaults into hell which only a Space Marine could hope to survive. It was written in the *Codex Astartes* that a Space Marine should never be used in such a way, that his value to the Imperium was too great to be thrown away in a pell-mell slaughter in the teeth of an entrenched foe.

But the *Codex Astartes* could not cover every possible battle. It could not predict that one day the *Phalanx* itself would be invaded, and that between its survival and its destruction stood a last-ditch battle where the enemy could only be fought face to face in the open, with no strategy in the Chapter Master's arsenal to change it into anything other than a pitched battle, a duel to the death.

Pugh and Kolgo led the charge. The weapons already operating on the daemon engines opened up and flung burning comets into the midst of the Imperial Fists, throwing armoured bodies into the air. Daemons surged forwards, heedless of organisation or rank, overcome with a lust for the fight that spread like a fire.

This was the way it had to be. Pugh drew the Fangs of Dorn and dived into the mass of daemons. Kolgo followed him in, rotator cannon hammering, the barrels glowing hot.

The rest of the Imperial Fists crashed into the enemy. If they were to die, it would be in defence of their Chapter. Few of them gave any thought to the chance they might live.

Sarpedon skidded along the floor of the bridge as the missiles streaked over him, the sound of the air ripping behind him as scalding rocket exhaust billowed around him. The sound of the impacts behind him was so loud it wasn't even a sound, just a white wall of noise that blocked out all hearing except for the alien echo rippling around the *Phalanx*'s bridge.

Sarpedon was ready for the shockwave. He took the worst of it on his shoulder and let the impact throw him into the foot of the throne pedestal, front legs collapsing beneath him to absorb the impact.

Father Gyranar disappeared in the mass of smoke and flame. Shattered components from consoles rained down, chunks of burning metal and cabling. Cracks ran up the viewscreen, marring the view of the Veiled Region with black jagged fingers.

Sarpedon dragged himself into the dubious cover of the nearest statue, an Imperial Fists Apothecary plated in gold.

'Did you think,' said Daenyathos's artificial voice from the throne, 'that I had not thought I would face you one day? You, or someone like you. Why do you believe I selected a Dreadnought as my vessel?'

Sarpedon hauled himself up the nest few steps, crouching down behind a statue of an Emperor's Champion from some campaign of distant legend. His nervous system seemed struck out of kilter by the missile impacts, his legs uncoordinated, his head ringing.

'If you know the future,' said Sarpedon, forcing his mind to keep up with his surroundings, 'then you know how this ends.'

The response was another burst of missiles, triple contrails spiralling towards Sarpedon. The Space Marine flung him across the steps leading up to the throne. The Emperor's Champion disappeared in a burst of golden shrapnel, and the other two missiles howled past to impact against the viewscreen. Sarpedon dug in with claws and fingers, clinging to the side of the throne pedestal. Bursts of pain against the side of his face registered, in a detached, soldierly way, as shards of shrapnel embedded in his skull. One eye suddenly shut down, his vision cut in half, depth gone, the scene in front of him becoming ever more otherworldly.

Massive shards of the viewscreen fell away like black glass daggers, shattering against the floor. Chunks of the Veiled Region seemed to have fallen away with it, the galaxy turning dark piece by piece, a broken mosaic of decay.

Sarpedon's nervous system caught up and the wrenching pain from his hips told him he had been hit worse than he realised. He looked down at the pulpy mess of fibrous muscle and broken exoskeleton. He had three legs left, and chunks of mutated limb lay straggling down the steps behind him. No wonder he had felt out of control. He was trying to push himself forwards on legs he didn't have.

Sarpedon scrambled forwards a little further, to the shadow of the throne. Daenyathos was in silhouette, the light from the viewscreen having died, and looming over Sarpedon he looked less like a Dreadnought and more like the vision that Sarpedon had forced into Iktinos's mind – vast, monstrous, toweringly powerful, invulnerable to the efforts of a mere man.

'It could have been anyone,' continued Daenyathos, the missile ports on his arm closing. 'Caeon could have led the Chapter astray. Gorgoleon. Iktinos. It could have happened centuries earlier or later. Whoever it was, I always knew I would have to face one of you. For you, this is the end. For me, this is just another footnote.'

The storm bolter on Daenyathos's power fist arm clicked its action and Sarpedon was suddenly looking down its barrel. Daenyathos couldn't fire any more missiles – Sarpedon was too close, the shrapnel too dangerous. Daenyathos could not risk damaging his Dreadnought chassis now.

Sarpedon tried to take cover again but Daenyathos's aim was too good. The first volley of bolter fire shredded the step in front of him, gold plate and granite dissolving under his hands. The second slammed two shots into his torso, the bolter shells penetrating the ceramite and bursting against Sarpedon's breastplate of fused ribs.

He felt the bone breaking. The sensation was clear among the shock that hammered through him. Twin craters were blown open in his chest and the air touched the mass of his lungs, the pulsing surface of his heart. Sarpedon fell onto the steps and rolled onto his back, gasping as his body recoiled.

He was a Space Marine. He would survive this. He could survive anything. Before, he had doubted. But now, so close to death, his certainty was complete. He would survive this. He was Sarpedon, Chapter Master of the Soul Drinkers, a man the galaxy had sought to kill, yet who had survived long enough to breathe the same air as the only enemy he had ever really had.

Sarpedon planted a hand on the step in front of him and turned himself over. His remaining legs fought to push him up onto his talons. He looked up, blood running down his face, thick gobbets of it pumping from the wounds in his chest. The Axe of Mercaeno was still in his hand.

'There is no future,' he said through blood-spittled lips. 'There will be others like us. They will break out of this cage of a galaxy, they will bypass everything you have engineered to stop you. Human beings cannot be kept caged by fate. Not all of them. Someone will remember us, and someone will follow.'

Daenyathos took careful aim and blasted another storm bolter volley into Sarpedon. This one hit the wrist and elbow of his right hand, the one in which he was carrying the Axe of Mercaeno. The bones of Sarpedon's forearm shattered and his arm fell useless, the Axe of Mercaeno clattering down the steps.

The pain did not come. Sarpedon did not let it. He forged forwards a few steps more, so the massive armoured legs of Daenyathos's Dreadnought were just a couple of metres from his face.

Daenyathos's power fist reached down and snatched Sarpedon up off the floor, the articulated fingers closing around his shoulders and waist. Sarpedon's head lolled like that of a rag doll, his legs dangling uselessly under him, as he was held immobile up in front of Daenyathos.

Sarpedon could see, through the eyepieces of Daenyathos's armoured helm, the eyes of the man inside. They were full of amusement, as if Sarpedon were an animal or a child playing at being a soldier, something to be pitied and taught its place, something to be mocked.

'Did you truly think something like you,' mocked Daenyathos, 'could kill me?'

'I didn't have to kill you,' replied Sarpedon. 'I just had to get you close.'

Sarpedon's one good hand reached into the ammo pouch at his waist. Daenyathos registered what Sarpedon was doing and the servos in his power fist whined.

The massive fingers of the fist closed. Sarpedon could feel the ceramite around his torso tensing and buckling, massive pressure crushing down. The seconds stretched out and he imagined, in precise detail, how his organs would look being forced out of his chest under the pressure, hearts bursting, tatters of lungs oozing out, entrails following, the awful wrongness of his distorted body filling him in the moments before death.

It seemed an age before his fingers closed around the haft of the Soulspear.

The artefact's twin blades speared outwards, caged vortex fields consisting of anti-space where no material substance could exist.

The pressure forced Sarpedon's right arm out of place. His shoulder blade split and the joint crumbled. Each segment of the destruction registered like stages in a scientific experiment, observed with calmness and detachment in those moments before the pain receptors fired and reached Sarpedon's brain.

Sarpedon whipped the Soulspear up, one blade swinging up through the sarcophagus that made up the armoured centre of the Dreadnought. Sarpedon's wrist flicked and the other blade arced up to complete the cut, two slashes of blackness that between them formed a plane separating the front of the sarcophagus from the body of the dreadnought.

The pressure relented. The power fist fell inactive, the energy no longer focused through its servos to crush Sarpedon's torso.

The energy finally went out of Sarpedon. The weight of the Soulspear, negligible as it was compared to a boltgun or the Axe of Mercaeno, was too much. The weapon fell from his fingers. The blades disappeared and the short metal length of its haft tumbled down the steps before the throne.

The front of Daenyathos's sarcophagus followed. It clanged as it fell end over end down the steps, the sound echoing off the walls of the bridge, the final sound as it hit the floor like the tolling of a bell.

Sarpedon's breaths were shallow. The ruination of his shoulder hit him and the pain was like a sun burning where his shoulder had once been, a ball of fire surrounding the mass of ripped muscle and cracked bone.

He forced the pain down. He had suffered before. It meant nothing. His eyes focused, and he was looking into the face of Daenyathos.

The whole front of the sarcophagus was gone, and the life support cradle was revealed in which Daenyathos had spent the last six thousand years. It was a biomechanical tangle of cabling and artificial organs, pipes and valves hissing cold vapour, blinking readouts mottled with the patina of centuries.

The Philosopher-Soldier hung among the cabling, restrains locking him into the life support systems. He was pale and withered, his limbs atrophied, the skin shrunken around his skull and ribcage. Red welts had swollen up where pipes and wires pierced his skin, carrying the mental signals that moved the Dreadnought body around him. His eyes were squinting in the sudden light, pupils shrunk to nothing.

Sarpedon had never seen such a pathetic example of a Space Marine. The musculature was gone, the skin stretched around a body starved of movement for six millennia. Daenyathos gasped in shock, the feeling of outside air alien to him now.

The grip of the power fist relaxed. Sarpedon clattered onto the steps of the throne mount. Daenyathos was in shock, unable to function, and for a few seconds he would be unable to know where – or even what – Sarpedon was.

Sarpedon, one arm hanging limp and useless at his side, clambered up the front of the Dreadnought until he was level with Daenyathos. He tore out handfuls of cabling, wires slithering out of Daenyathos's stick-thin limbs. Dribbles of watery blood spattered onto the gilded steps. Sarpedon grasped Daenyathos around the neck – his hand easily encircling the scrawny throat – and pulled Daenyathos out of the sarcophagus.

The Philosopher-Soldier's body came away easily, Daenyathos unable to put up a fight. Sarpedon carried him down the steps to the deck of the bridge, his remaining talons kicking aside chunks of smouldering debris. The Dreadnought chassis remained standing before the bridge captain's throne, gutted of its occupant, silent and unmoving.

'Wait,' gasped Daenyathos in a voice that could barely struggle above a whisper. 'You are a part of this. You can be something great. Imagine the role you could play in a galaxy remade by me. Imagine it.'

'I have a better imagination than you realise,' said Sarpedon, grimacing as he dragged himself towards the blast doors at the back of the bridge. 'I have seen it, and it is no place for me.'

'Where are you taking me?' hissed Daenyathos, a desperation in his voice that had never been there before.

Sarpedon did not answer. Daenyathos's protests were lost in the sound of the flames licking up from the ruined bridge.

'Forge on,' cried Luko as he forced himself another pace through the sucking mire of gore. 'Just a few paces more. Onwards, there he stands, our prey. Onwards!'

The daemonic cyst had responded to the strike force like an organ threatened by infection. It had filled back up with blood, its fleshy walls erupting in tentacles to snare the intruders and drag them down into the gore. Attendant daemons had uncoiled from the filth and leapt to attack.

Abraxes stood up from his throne of twisted corpses, the spectral image of the battle on the barracks deck fading around him as the newcomers grabbed his attention.

'You are beneath my notice, and yet I must stoop to kill you,' he said, his voice like a bass choir. 'Your presence offends me.'

The remnants of Squad Prexus crashed into the horrors forging through the lake of blood. The Imperial Fists wrestled with things that grew new limbs and fanged mouths at will. One Space Marine was dragged down into the blood and half a dozen horrors leapt on top of him. Spiny hands ripped him apart. An armoured leg was thrown between them, a trophy of the hunt, and the warrior's head was pitched against the fleshy wall.

Sister Aescarion and Graevus fought like one individual, the axe of one parrying while the other struck. The two whirled in a dance that took them through the assaulting daemons, cutting mutating bodies open and shattering horned skulls. Luko followed in their wake, stabbing the surviving daemons with both lightning claws, lifting them proud of the blood and thrashing them into shreds.

Behind Abraxes burned the portal. It was a shimmering circle, edged in blue fire. Beyond it could be glimpsed something that resembled the void of space only in its darkness. The masses of power, like mountains of seething energy, loomed in that darkness, and carried with them a sense of appalling intelligence. They were watching, these powers of the warp, eager for the last obstacles to be removed so they could force the whole potential of their chaotic hatred through into realspace.

The sight of them could drive men mad. The Space Marines had to force their eyes away, for they could become lost in contemplation of that towering evil. Even this slight glimpse of the warp could corrode the mind. On the shore in front of the portal were still engraved, on the rotten remains of the cargo bay deck, the sigils that had called the portal into beings, and they burned blood-red with anticipation.

Abraxes strode into the gore. A blade appeared in his hand, a sword of frozen malice, and he cleaved it down into the battle around his feet.

Luko felt his gut tighten as he saw Apothecary Pallas in the blade's path. Pallas tried to yell something in defiance, but Abraxes was pitiless and did not grant him the chance. The blade carved down through Pallas's shoulder and came out through his abdomen on the other side, slicing him in two across the torso.

The two halves of the Apothecary's corpse flopped into the blood. Daemons pounced on them to tear the remains apart.

Luko realised he was yelling, a cry of horror and anguish. Pallas was his friend, in a galaxy where friends were rare.

Aescarion reached the shore where Abraxes's throne stood. Graevus was still waist-deep in the blood, fending off the daemons that sought to drag them both down.

'What means your strength?' shouted Aescarion over the cackling of daemons and the thrumming of the gate. 'That your arm can lay low a Space Marine? What does this mean laid against the might of the God-Emperor's children?'

Abraxes turned to look down at the Battle Sister. 'It means that you die, whelpling girl,' he replied, shaking Pallas's blood from his sword.

'Destroy my body if you will,' shouted back Aescarion. 'But you cannot break my spirit. A prince of daemons might claim the heads of every enemy he faces, but he will never count the soul of a Battle Sister as a trophy!'

Abraxes raised a hand, and purple-black fire flickered between his talons. 'You do not challenge the warp, child,' he sneered. 'I shall keep your mind as a pet, and you will worship me.'

Fire lashed down at Aescarion. The Sister of Battle was driven back by the force that hammered into her, and a halo of flame played around her head as Abraxes's magic tried to force open her mind.

The Battle Sister screamed, but she did not fall.

Luko realised what Sister Aescarion was trying to do. He threw aside the body of the daemon he had killed, and pushed on through the gore.

Librarian Varnica reached the metallic shore. The portal howled above him, the winds of the warp tearing at him as he tried to keep his footing. He clambered out of the blood, kicking free of the sucking limbs that tried to ensnare his ankles.

He had to force himself not to stare up through the portal. He could feel the vast intelligences beyond probing at his mind, pushing against the mental shield that every Librarian built up over years of psychic training. They were whispering to him, promising him power and lifetimes of pleasure, or threatening him with such horrors a human mind could not comprehend.

Varnica snapped himself free of their influence. He could not let them trick him, not now, not when he was so close, when the means for closing the portal were right in front of him.

He broke the fascination with the portal just in time to register the power hammer arcing towards him.

Varnica brought up his force claw to turn the hammer aside. The hammer's head slammed into the ground, throwing shards of metal everywhere. Varnica rolled back, shrapnel pinging off his armour.

Reinez stood over him. The Crimson Fist was a hideous sight – scorched and battered, his helmetless skull little more that burns and new scars. The deep blue and crimson of his armour was almost lost under the grime of battle. Reinez pointed his hammer at Varnica.

'You,' he said. 'You spoke against them. Now you fight alongside them. You fight to take the gate for yourselves! You are one with them in perdition!'

'Damn you, Reinez!' retorted Varnica. 'Have you become so blind? The warp has played us all; you, me, the Soul Drinkers, all of us, and we have to put it right!'

'Lies!' yelled Reinez.

Anger made him careless. The hammer blow was a haymaker and Varnica dodged back from it easily, raising his claw ready to snap it forwards. But Reinez had strength on his side, born of a desperate hatred. If Varnica was caught, he would die.

Varnica's muscles tensed for the strike. But it felt like he had hit a wall, as if something invisible was holding him fast.

His enemy was a Space Marine. Varnica had never raised arms against a brother of the Adeptus Astartes before. The wrongness of it stayed his hand. He could not shed a brother's blood. Even now, with all hell erupting around him, he could not do it.

Reinez jinked forwards and drove the butt of the hammer into Varnica's midriff. Varnica stumbled back, almost pitching into the blood. Varnica kicked out at Reinez's legs and the Crimson Fist was caught, stumbling a half-pace onto one knee. Varnica rolled out of his way and used the second he had bought to jump back to his feet.

'Think, Reinez!' said Varnica. 'The warp has used your anger. It has turned you against your brothers! Join us and help end all this!'

Reinez's reply was a wild swing that almost took Varnica's head off. Varnica forced his eyes away from the hellish vastness of the portal overhead, channelled a torrent of psychic power into his claw, and prepared to take a Space Marine's life for the first time.

Sister Aescarion felt her mind pried from her head and crushed in Abraxes's claw.

She fell to her knees. The screaming agony in her head blocked out everything save the shadowy image of Abraxes, edged in black fire, and the wicked bone-white slash of his grin.

She felt a million vicious hands reaching through her soul and clawing at the inside of her head. She heard a million voices cackling about what they would do to her when she was broken. Place her in the body of a monster, rampaging through the warp's enemies, fuelled by her pain. Rend her into a thousand pieces, each one imprisoned in some maze of torment. Send her shrieking through the immaterium, a formless ghost driven mad by the warp's malice. Turn her into one of them. Use her as their slave and visit a million indignities upon her.

The tiny sliver of Aescarion that remained scrabbled at the walls of her skull, trying to find some purchase to keep herself from falling into nothingness. Then, she found it.

A golden figure, his armour burning with the fire of faith, in his hand a blade that was justice. He was crowned with dominion over mankind. The Emperor, the protector of the human race. Though Aescarion might have nothing left save that which was in Abraxes's hand, she still had her faith. That was something the daemon prince could never have. That was what she had taunted him with – that core of her, the armoured and inviolate place that all the powers of the warp could never hope to breach.

Abraxes roared. He wanted it. He wanted to shatter that faith. But he could not. She denied him, and in his rage he forgot everything else unfolding around him.

Luko scrambled up the pinnacle on which Daenyathos had stood to watch the opening of the portal. The spire of corroded metal still stood proud of the gore, its pitted surface affording enough hand and foot-holds for Luko to reach the top. From here he could see the whole cyst, and the sheer futility his strike force faced.

Three Imperial Fists remained. Graevus fought off the daemons try-ing to rush Sister Aescarion. Aescarion was on her knees, screaming, linked to Abraxes by a torrent of black flame pouring from the daemon prince's hand. Varnica was wrestling at the threshold of the warp portal with Reinez, the Crimson Fist kneeling on Varnica's chest and pounding down at the Librarian with gauntleted fists.

Each Space Marine was an island in a sea of daemons. More of the things were emerging from the gore with every moment, and it would take seconds for them to overwhelm the warriors.

One part of Luko told him that they had done well to get this far, that to die facing Abraxes toe-to-toe was as good a death as any of them could have hoped to drag back from fate.

But the rest of him, the greater part, was driven only by rage. The Soul Drinkers had destroyed Abraxes once already, and lost many of their battle-brothers in doing so. Now he had returned as if he had a right to walk in the same universe as the Soul Drinkers, as if the lives lost to banish him had meant nothing.

Sarpedon had impaled Abraxes on the Soulspear, an image still burned into Luko's mind. It had been the moment that the warriors of the Chapter realised what they must truly be – slave to neither the Imper-ium nor the warp. Abraxes's return had undone that moment. That he had dared, that he had sought to make the Soul Drinkers very existence meaningless, sent anger pouring through Luko that he couldn't have stemmed if he had wanted to.

And he didn't want to. It felt good. This was what warriors spoke of when they talked of the glory, the rush, of battle. This was what Luko had never truly felt; now it was impossible to resist.

He crouched and drew back both claws, an animal ready to pounce. Abraxes's attention was focused on Sister Aescarion and the daemon prince had no idea Luko was even there.

It would be a difficult leap. There was nothing easy about what he would have to do if he made the jump. But the anger in him swallowed up those useless facts and bade him dive from the pinnacle towards the twisted grin on Abraxes's face.

Aescarion saw through her haze of pain as Luko dived towards Abraxes. The Soul Drinker thrust his twin lightning claws into the daemon's face.

The claws punched through Abraxes's skin around his left eye, sinking up to the knuckle. Luko braced his feet against the daemon's upper chest and yelled as he pulled, muscles of his neck standing out as sharp cords as he put all his considerable strength into it.

Abraxes had not seen it coming. He had been savouring peeling apart Aescarion's mind, and the shock of Luko's assault stunned him for a moment. That was all the time Luko need to wrench Abraxes's eye out of its socket, a flourish of his claws throwing the orb down to the bloody shore like a comet with a tail of ragged flesh.

Abraxes screamed. Wrapped up in his howl was a strangely human sound, a note of pain and shock. It was the first sign of weakness Abraxes had shown, an echo of some frailty that a human could recognise. He took a step backwards, scattering bodies from the foot of his throne as he stumbled towards the portal.

Luko hit the ground hard beside Aescarion. She still knelt, one hand on the floor, hair clinging to the sweat on her face. She was pale and blood ran from her nose and ears.

Luko looked away from her. The momentum he had bought would not last for long. Aescarion would have to fend for herself.

Luko ran forwards, rolled past Abraxes's cloven foot and slashed at the back of his ankle. His claws bit through daemonic flesh and severed tendons whipped from the gash. Abraxes fell back another half-pace, his screams turning to anger.

Graevus leapt from the gore to join Luko. His axe hacked down into Abraxes's knee and the leg buckled, Abraxes putting a hand down to steady himself.

Abraxes, falling back, had passed halfway through the warp portal behind him. His hand pushed down against a silvery island of power that gathered in the warp, the dark intelligences of the immaterium buoying him up. They would force him forwards again, expel him from the haven of the warp to finish the job of killing the Space Marine standing between the Dark Gods and an eternity of slaughter.

Graevus leapt up onto Abraxes's chest.

'We killed you once,' he snarled, swinging his axe up high. 'And this time, we've had practice.'

Graevus drove the axe down into the daemon prince's chest. The blade carved down through muscle and bone. From the cavernous wound burst a fountain of light, raw power unleashed like blood from an artery. It caught Graevus square in the chest and threw the Soul Drinker to the ground, armour smoking.

Abraxes got onto one knee and held his sword up, point first. Glowing blood poured from his ruined eye as he measured the blow and stabbed the sword down into Graevus's right hip, impaling the Space Marine through the meat of his leg and pinning him to the ground.

'Killed me?' hissed the daemon prince. 'Soul Drinker, you did nothing that day but bring your own death a moment closer!' Abraxes twisted the blade and Graevus's leg came apart, a welter of blood mixing with the gore spattered across the metallic ground in front of the portal. Graevus screamed and his axe fell from his mutant hand.

Luko charged at Abraxes, knocking the blade aside with a swipe of both claws. Abraxes's remaining eye narrowed as it focused on Luko.

Reinez kneed Varnica in the midriff hard enough to dent his armour. The Librarian fell to the ground and Reinez straddled his chest, bringing his hammer over Varnica's skull head-down, ready to piston it into the Doom Eagle's face.

Reinez's gaze fell on the lump of seething putrescence that a few moments a go had been Abraxes's eye. It lay in a whiteish mass, dissolving its way through the cargo bay floor, its pupil breaking up in its corrupt substance.

Beyond the eye, Luko was battling the daemon prince, fending off a swipe of the daemon's claws with his own gauntlets.

'We're trying to kill it,' said Varnica, following Reinez's gaze. 'It's the only real enemy here. No matter what you think of us, Reinez, killing Abraxes goes beyond it.'

Reinez said nothing. Varnica rolled out from under him, struggling to one knee. He was battered and broken, bones fractured all over his body, bruised organs bleeding inside. Reinez was a better warrior than Varnica. If he made the decision, the Crimson Fist would kill him.

Varnica saw, as Reinez did, that Abraxes was halfway through the portal, straddling the gap between reality and the warp.

'We have to close it,' said Varnica. He pointed to the sigils on the floor beneath the feet of the two warriors. 'The blood of Dorn opened it. The same blood will close it.'

'You spoke against them,' said Reinez, breath heavy. 'You... you wanted them dead.'

'No one is leaving this place alive, Reinez,' said Varnica. 'The Soul Drinkers will die. You have your wish. Now kill this blasphemy. Guilliman's blood runs in my veins, and Throne only knows what runs in the Soul Drinkers. Only Dorn's blood will seal the gate. Only yours.'

Varnica couldn't be sure if Reinez understood. He certainly couldn't be certain that the Crimson Fist, as he stepped back and dropped his guard, was inviting him to strike. Perhaps Reinez left himself undefended as he absorbed the realisation that Abraxes was the true force for destruction, that the Soul Drinkers, the *Phalanx*, the carnage around him were all parts of what the Daenyathos and the daemon prince had orchestrated. Or perhaps he really did understand that his blood alone would seal the gate, just like N'Kalo's had opened it.

Varnica did not wait for clarification.

He forced every drop of pain in him into the pit of his mind, and channelled it, ice-cold, into the psychic circuits built into his force claw. He lunged and punched the claw into Reinez's chest.

The Crimson Fist's mouth opened and a breath escaped him, the shock to his body too much for him to form words.

Varnica yelled and the psychic power discharged like a massive electrical surge through the claw, the Hammerhand snapping the blades open and tearing Reinez's chest almost in two. Organs glinted for a moment in red light bathing the cyst.

Reinez fell back and the wellspring of blood inside him burst up through his ruined chest. The blood of a Crimson Fist, spiced with the gene-seed taken from the genetic print of Rogal Dorn, washed over the glowing symbols on the floor.

Varnica placed a palm on the floor, Reinez's blood lapping around it. He had unleashed a great deal of his psychic reserves in killing Reinez – Reinez, as hard to kill as he was, had needed a massive burst of psychic power to ensure his death. Varnica would have to use everything he had left, drain himself past the limit of safety – and sanity.

Varnica wrapped his mind around the unreality of the portal above him, drawing on the power that surged through the sigils on the floor, and began to crush the warp portal closed with the force of his will.

Luko leaped over the stricken Graevus and slammed into Abraxes. He speared both claws into the sides of the daemon's jaw and headbutted Abraxes in the nose. Gristle split and blood sprayed. Abraxes shook his head and threw Luko off.

Luko skidded along the blood-slick ground. Graevus was trying to get to his feet nearby, one leg buckling under him, his thigh a bloody ruin of pulpy flesh and shattered bone.

'What matters this effort?' said Abraxes. 'Why must you fill what remains of your lives with such toil?'

'Think on what remains of your life, daemon,' spat Luko. 'My toil will go on. Yours ends here.'

'Pitiful,' sneered Abraxes. 'Which one of you can face me that will not pay for it with his life? What mere man stands my equal, to fence words with me?'

'I seem to remember,' said Luko, 'that it was a mere man who speared you through the chest and threw you back to the warp to begin with. It was men who brought you back. *You* should be kneeling to *us*.'

Abraxes bellowed in rage. He snatched up his fallen blade and charged. Luko met the charge with his own, shoulder down, sprinting at the daemon prince. Luko dropped to the ground and rolled, just as Abraxes's sword sliced towards him at chest height. The blade passed over him and Luko sprang up, driving both claws through Abraxes's foot.

Abraxes bellowed and wrenched his foot off the ground, Luko's claws sliding from the flesh. The daemon prince took another step back, and blinded for the moment by his anger, he did not see that once more his back foot passed beyond the boundary of the warp gate.

The circumference of the gate shrunk. Varnica was closing it, metre by metre. Luko ran forwards and speared down through Abraxes's other foot, pinning it to the ground. The power field discharged in a staccato of noise and light, energy arcing to the floor.

The warp gate's uppermost edge closed down on Abraxes, like a slow-motion guillotine. Abraxes saw, perhaps a second or two too late, what Luko was trying to do.

A single Space Marine could not kill Abraxes. Sarpedon had managed it, but he was a mutant beyond a human's strength and speed, and he had wielded the Soulspear. Luko couldn't do it on his own. But he didn't have to.

The edge of the shrinking gate bit down into Abraxes's shoulder. It sliced through tendons and bone, and daemonic blood dribbled glowing from the wound. Abraxes's face creased in agony and shock.

He tried to force himself out from the gate, but Luko kept him pinned in place. The gate bit down further into Abraxes's upper chest, and blood sprayed now from sundered arteries.

From beyond the portal, from the endless masses of hatred that boiled there, a terrible wave of scorn burst out. The warp's evils saw their servant trapped and dying, and saw all that he had promised withering away. The strands of fate he had woven, which would take him across the galaxy disgorging the warp's malice in the form of torrents of daemons, were snapping. The future galaxy where the *Phalanx* travelled the stars bringing Chaos everywhere it went, that dark tapestry Abraxes had concocted with the human Daenyathos, was unravelling.

They were disappointed. Whatever they truly were, whatever passed for emotions in their godlike souls, the powers of the warp were most disappointed in Abraxes's failure.

The daemon screamed, but the sound did not last long. His lungs and windpipe were severed. His body reformed around the damage, echoing the mutability of the horrors he commanded, but it was not enough. Tentacles slithered from his wounds and bony growths burst in every direction, but the force was too great.

Luko pulled his claws out and stumbled backwards. The portal was closing, and it was cutting the daemon prince in two. Abraxes was wedged in, the sides of the portal slicing into him – he didn't need Luko keeping him in place now.

Luko knelt beside Graevus. 'Come, brother,' he said.

'Where?' said Graevus, watching the portal slicing down through Abraxes's sternum into his abdomen. 'There is nowhere left for us.'

'There is one place,' said Luko. 'Let's go.'

Captain Borganor's Howling Griffons smashed into the daemonic host, joining the Imperial Fists in the wild melee seething around the daemon engines.

But the daemons were legion. Tens of thousands had gathered, and every one now dived into the slaughter. The scorpion-like daemon engine rumbled and raised its segmented body up on eight armoured legs, the tail coiling over its back.

On columns of fire, the Angels Sanguine leapt through the air onto the daemon engine. The engine shuddered and its tail swept them off its back. Commander Gethsemar was thrown to the ground and the engine's insectoid head loomed over him, bronze mandibles dribbling liquid metal.

'Not yet, brother!' shouted a voice, and Siege-Captain Daviks plunged out of the daemon throng to grab the Angel Sanguine by the gorget. He dragged Gethsemar out of the way of the engine, even as it vomited molten metal from its fanged mouth.

A hundred similar stories were playing out amid the butchery. Men were dying for their brothers, or killing all around them in revenge for seeing their friends fall. But there would be no one to remember them.

The daemonic army was too big. The war engines were being completed even as daemon blood swamped the deck, ankle-deep. The Imperial Fists and the Howling Griffons, and all the souls who had come to the *Phalanx* for the trial of the Soul Drinkers, were going to die there.

A terrible scream erupted from every direction at once. It was a strong as a gale, and it shuddered the fabric of the *Phalanx*. Space Marines stumbled, stunned by the force of the noise. But daemon hands and blades did not take advantage of the distraction to cut the Space Marines down.

The daemons were howling, but not with rage – they were struck with a terrible anguish, dropping to their knees or just standing and screaming. Iron swords fell from bloodletters' hands. Horrors turned in on themselves, liquid flesh imploding constantly as if trying to escape to some place inside.

Pugh shook the bedlam from his head. It was a sound of abandonment and death, the dying cry of something tremendously powerful, something that had not believed it could die.

'Abraxes has fallen!' yelled Pugh, barely even to hear himself over the echo in his ears. 'The head of the beast has been struck off! Brothers, sisters, sons and daughters of the Emperor! Call down death on what remains!'

The Fangs of Dorn seemed to flash of their own accord in his hands, stabbing through the crush of daemons around him. Gethsemar and Daviks got to their feet, pushing back the horrors that had closed in over them, and fought side by side as the warriors of their Chapters carved through the mass to reach them.

Lord Inquisitor Kolgo shouldered his way into the shadow of the daemon engine. His rotator cannon hammered volley after volley into the bronze skull of the engine, and the machine reeled as if in shock, the daemons possessing it unable to strike back. The Battle Sisters accompanying the inquisitor lent their own fire, and heavy weapons from Imperial Fists at the back of the battlefield sheared its legs off and bored bleeding holes in its carapace. A burst of lascannon fire severed its tail and the weapon toppled to the ground without firing a shot. Stricken, the daemon engine let out a metallic groan as it sunk to the ground, accompanied by the shrieks of the daemon spirits inhabiting it.

Lysander led the way. His thunder hammer was a beacon that the other Imperial Fists followed. It rose and fell, leaving mountains of torn bodies and lakes of daemon blood in its wake. The Imperial Fists rampaged over the barricades and stormed through the daemon forges, clambering over the unfinished war engines to batter back the warp spawn that tried to regroup to face them.

The daemons fought with no coordination or intelligence. Many collapsed, flesh discorporating as the warp-magic that sustained them in realspace failed. The Imperial Fists gathered in firing lines to shred their enemies with bolter fire, or launched massed assaults with chainblades and glaives. Siege-Captain Daviks and the surviving Silver Skulls directed the heavy weapons towards the largest daemons, the warpheralds, before they could organise a resistance.

It was grim, bloody work. There was no joy in this victory. It was a crude and brutal business, wading through the remains of the enemy, as the Imperial Fists passed through the forges and pushed on towards the cargo bays where the heart of the infestation had been planted.

* * *

Varnica picked up the semi-conscious Sister Aescarion and carried her clear of the collapsing portal. Abraxes was dead, his physical form split almost in two by the shrinking portal, and his spirit ripped out and thrown back into the cauldron of the warp to be punished. Luko and Graevus knelt by the portal and Varnica followed their gaze as they looked across the cyst to where the first of the Imperial Fists were entering.

Lysander was the first to wade towards the collapsing portal, through the blood which was choked with the bodies of daemons and the strike force's Imperial Fists. The captain cast an eye over the carnage, over the unnatural warping of the ship around him, at the sorry remains of Apothecary Pallas, Reinez, and the last of Prexus's squad.

'Brother Varnica,' said Lysander. 'Is it done?'

'It is done,' said Varnica. 'I and this Battle Sister, and these two Soul Drinkers, are the only survivors. But it is done.'

Lysander stepped up onto the ground that broke the blood surface around Abraxes's throne. The throne of corpses was withering and flaking into dust, as if years of decay were piling on them at once. 'Captain Luko. And Brother Graevus, if I am not mistaken.' He held out a hand. 'There is nothing left for you to fight for. I am sure that many will argue for leniency, but you are still in the custody of the Imperial Fists. Come with me.'

Luko stood up, and hauled Graevus unsteadily onto his feet. Beside him, the portal had shrunk to just over head height, and Abraxes's body was cut all the way down through his abdomen, leaving the half outside the portal completely severed.

'Captain Lysander,' said Luko, 'there is no place in this galaxy for the Soul Drinkers. Not in the cells of the *Phalanx*, or in the grip of whatever punishment is decided for us. Not even in freedom. The whole galaxy has been against us for so long that there is nowhere we could go and nothing we could do. So no, we will not hand ourselves over to your custody.'

'I'm ready,' said Graevus.

'As am I, brother,' said Luko. He looked back towards Lysander, and the other Imperial Fists making their way into the cyst. 'Wish us luck. You are our brothers, in spite of everything. I have one thing to ask of you. The Inquisition tried to delete us from history. Please, make sure that we are not forgotten.'

Luko helped Graevus limp towards the portal. Lysander watched them go, and with a wave of his hand stayed the guns of his Imperial Fists.

Luko and Graevus walked through the portal, into the warp, into whatever waited for them there.

The portal closed completely, cutting off the madness of the warp from realspace, and the cyst fell dark.

* * *

It was some time later, as the Imperial Fists and Howling Griffons were killing off the last of the daemons running loose around the cyst, that a blade of black energy sliced through the fleshy growths on the walls. Behind the growth was a doorway from one of the other cargo holds, in the direction of the *Phalanx*'s bridge. The blade was that of the Soulspear, and it was in the hand of Sarpedon.

The Chapter Master of the Soul Drinkers was near death. Torn stumps of legs dripped ichor. Half his face and one eye were a torn mess, shredded by shrapnel still poking from the pulpy flesh. Open bullet wounds, plugged by congealed blood, were livid against his chest, and one arm hung shattered from a twisted shoulder joint. Sarpedon seemed barely able to walk on the three legs that remained – but the Imperial Fists did not see a defeated man. Wounded, near death, but not defeated.

Sarpedon placed the Soulspear's haft back in an ammo pouch and picked up a pale, tangled shape at his feet – a body, atrophied with age, which had once been that of a Space Marine.

The Imperial Fists gathered without an order, their bolters levelled at Sarpedon. Chapter Master Pugh stood to their front, both Fangs of Dorn in hand.

Sarpedon limped to where half of Abraxes's corpse still lay, his blood drying on the sigils scorched into the floor. They were all that remained of the portal that had opened there. The Imperial Fists saw the wounds on Sarpedon, the torn stumps of severed legs, the twisted shoulder and dented armour. Sarpedon looked like he had gone through enough to kill any other warrior of the Adeptus Astartes twice over.

Sarpedon held up the body in his hand, carrying it by the scruff of the neck. It was alive, and it looked across the assembled Imperial Fists with fear on its face.

'This is Daenyathos,' said Sarpedon. 'This is the man who brought Abraxes forth from the warp. This is the man who manipulated my Chapter and yours, because he believed that mankind had to suffer to make it stronger.'

Imperial Fists took aim along their bolter sights at the mutant.

'Hold your fire, brothers,' said Pugh.

'But he was wrong.' Sarpedon dropped his arm and let Daenyathos hang down, dragging along the floor. 'He thought mankind did not suffer enough. But it suffers too much. Men like Daenyathos, like the powers of the warp themselves, are symptoms of humanity's misery. But we can put it right.'

'Just as you did, Sarpedon?' said Pugh. 'You are the only one of your Chapter remaining. Even if your path could redeem the Imperium, how can it be walked when you yourself could not walk it?'

'Because I was a fool,' replied Sarpedon. 'I did not see that Daenyathos was pulling the strings. I walked into the role he had prepared for me, and I almost played it to the end. But you have seen my failings. You know the pitfalls. And when you fail, those who follow you will learn from you, too. And we are the only ones who can begin it. We, the Space Marines, we have the closest thing this Imperium has to freedom.'

Lysander stepped forwards. 'And what is to say that one of us will take up this torch, Sarpedon?' he said.

'Nothing,' replied Sarpedon. 'If you can ignore your conscience. If you can see the Imperium in the new light the Soul Drinkers have shone on it, and yet still do nothing to stem its suffering, then I suppose there is nothing to say that. If you are content to continue witnessing the death throes of the human race, that is. If you can think your work complete when the Imperium devours itself day by day. If you can do all that, then the light will die out here, with me. But if the conscience of a single battle-brother here, or of any who even hear of us, is inflamed as ours was, then it will burn on.'

'You have said your piece, Sarpedon,' said Pugh. 'We must take you back in. Your case will be decided anew. Daenyathos must be punished. Cast down the Soulspear and let Lysander place you back in custody. It's over, all of it.'

Sarpedon looked down at the sigils branded on the floor around his feet.

'I understand,' he said, 'that only the blood of Rogal Dorn could open the Eye of Kravamesh. And whatever flows through me, it is not Dorn's blood. Correct?'

The floor beneath Sarpedon glowed and smouldered. The thrum of caged power reverberated through the cyst.

'Sarpedon,' croaked Daenyathos. 'What are you doing?'

Light gathered and crackled, sending haphazard shadows across the cyst.

'Stop!' shouted Pugh. 'We will open fire!'

'The blood of Dorn,' shouted Sarpedon over the growing sound, 'flows through those who fight his fight. When he marched in the Great Crusade, it was to save humanity in unity, not to unite it only to cast it back into the dark. This was the Emperor's goal. Though His road has not been travelled for ten thousand years, you can put the human race back on it. If you choose to. If you dare.'

Light crackled, flaring across the cyst like a tongue of flame from a star. A crack in reality re-opened, the impossible colours of the warp seething beyond.

'Sarpedon!' screamed Daenyathos. 'No! You do not know what lies beyond!'

'But you do,' replied Sarpedon. 'And I see how you fear it. Perhaps I should fear it too. But I can fight it, and you cannot.'

Daenyathos's last words devolved into a scream as Sarpedon carried him through the portal, dragging the Philosopher-Soldier over the threshold and out of reality.

The portal slammed shut behind them, its fires darkening again, leaving only an echo of its power.

Sister Aescarion blinked in the light, her eyes struggling to kill the glare. She had been asleep for a long time, and her head still pounded.

The last thing she remembered was Abraxes standing over her, his grin turning to a scowl of frustration just as Luko dived into him, ripping out the daemon's eye. Everything after that had been a blur of noise and fury.

She sat up and swung her legs over the edge of the bed in which she had awoken. She was in the apothecarion of the *Phalanx*. Dozens of Imperial Fists lay comatose in the beds around her, their armour piled up beside them, lifesign monitors blinking and beeping. A spindly medical servitor trundled between them, reading off vitals and administering doses.

Aescarion was a little unsteady on her feet. She was wearing the shapeless under-robes that Battle Sisters wore when not in armour. Her wargear was piled up beside her bed, and from the scars on her armour and the blade of her power axe she wondered that she could walk now at all.

She wandered through the apothecarion. All was cool and quiet, the wounded tended by servitors or lying in suspended animation induced by their catalepsean nodes. Aescarion felt the cold metal of the deck on her bare feet as she walked out of the apothecarion and into the great lofty passageway, one of many running most of the length of the *Phalanx*.

Scaffolding stood against the walls, servitors and crew members working at the dark stone that clad the passageway. Statues and inscriptions lined the passage and a great panel of plain stone could be seen between the scaffolds. The servitors and masons were working at one of the lower corners with chisels and granite saws, a drift of stone dust building up at the base of the wall.

Chapter Master Pugh approached. His armour was clean and repaired, but he still had the minor scars of the recent battles on his face. The crew saluted and bowed their heads as he approached.

'Sister!' he said. 'It is good that you are again among us. Varnica explained to me your actions at the portal.'

'They are not something I wish to revisit,' replied Aescarion. 'I shall meditate on them myself. Such things should be considered in private.'

'An Imperial Fist would be lauded as a hero,' said Pugh.

'I am not an Imperial Fist. A daughter of the Emperor cannot be prideful.'

'Perhaps the same can be said of a Space Marine,' said Pugh. 'Though even a Chapter Master must be careful to whom he says it. Our next journey is to the Segmentum Solar, Sister. Lord Inquisitor Kolgo suggested that we take the *Phalanx* to Saturn, where his colleagues from the Ordo Malleus can assist in cleansing the daemonic stench from this ship. It will take time, and no little negotiation with the daemonhunters, but the *Phalanx* will fly as holy ground again.'

'That we stand here now tells me that Abraxes was defeated,' said Aescarion. 'But what of our own? How many were lost?'

'More than half those who fought,' replied Pugh. 'A terrible blow. But we will recover. We have done so before.'

'And the Soul Drinkers?'

'None remain,' said Pugh.

'Then it is over.'

'In a manner of speaking,' said Pugh. He turned to continue up the corridor in the direction of the bridge. Aescarion watched him go, not sure what to make of his parting words.

She turned back to the wall, where the masons were starting to work again. She walked between them, running a hand over the surface, the still-rough letters awaiting detailing and polishing.

TYRENDIAN, read the letters that passed under her fingers.

LUKO.

GRAEVUS.

The next column bore the names of Imperial Fists – Sergeant Prexus, who had died in the Panpsychicon, Castellan Leucrontas, all the Imperial Fists who had died. And alongside them, listed as brothers in death, were the Soul Drinkers.

SARPEDON, read the last name to be inscribed.

In a manner of speaking, it was over. The Soul Drinkers were gone. Abraxes was destroyed. But the idea of them remained. Their names were listed among the fallen, and in the Tactica Sigismunda the battle in the cyst would be recreated. Generations to come would live in a galaxy where the idea of the Soul Drinkers existed, an idea that had so nearly died in the execution chambers of the *Phalanx* and the book furnaces of the Inquisition.

It would live on among the Sisters of Battle, too. It was not Aescarion's place to judge the right or wrong of what Sarpedon had stood for – but it would not die when she could keep it alive. Even if only as a warning, the cautionary tale of Daenyathos who pulled puppet strings that almost threw the Imperium into a new age of darkness, she would remember.

She turned away from the inscriptions and walked back towards the apothecarion, still unsteady. At Saturn, in the Inquisitorial dockyards of Iapetus, she could try to put her thoughts in order and decide how the story of Soul Drinkers should be passed on so it would remain intact among the currents of the future. But there were wounds that needed to heal first. She would decide that another day.

The masons continued their inscribing as Aescarion walked away, carving the story of the Soul Drinkers into the stone among the lists of the dead.

ABOUT THE AUTHOR

Ben Counter is the author of the Soul Drinkers and Grey Knights series, along with two Horus Heresy novels, and one of Black Library's most popular Warhammer 40,000 authors. He has written RPG supplements and comic books. He is a fanatical painter of miniatures, a pursuit which has won him his most prized possession: a prestigious Golden Demon award. He lives in Portsmouth, England.